# The Papers
of
# Solar Pons

*New Adventures
of the
Sherlock Holmes
of
Praed Street*

# The Adventures of Solar Pons

## *by August Derleth*

In Re: Sherlock Holmes (The Adventures of Solar Pons)
The Memoirs of Solar Pons
Three Problems for Solar Pons
The Return of Solar Pons
The Reminiscences of Solar Pons
The Casebook of Solar Pons
The Chronicles of Solar Pons
Mr. Fairlie's Final Journey
Praed Street Papers
A Praed Street Dossier
The Adventure of the Unique Dickensians
The Unpublished Solar Pons
The Final Cases of Solar Pons
The Dragnet Solar Pons
The Solar Pons Omnibus
The Original Text Solar Pons Omnibus

## *by Basil Copper*

The Dossier of Solar Pons
The Further Adventures of Solar Pons
The Secret Files of Solar Pons
The Uncollected Case of Solar Pons
The Exploits of Solar Pons
The Recollections of Solar Pons
Solar Pons versus The Devil's Claw
Solar Pons: The Final Cases
The Complete Solar Pons

## *by David Marcum*

The Papers of Sherlock Holmes, Volume II (*One story*)
The Papers of Solar Pons

# The Papers of Solar Pons

*New Adventures
of the
Sherlock Holmes
of Praed Street*

by
**DAVID MARCUM, PSI**

Based upon the works of August Derleth

Authorized and Published with the Permission
of the August Derleth Estate

*Belanger Books*
2017

The Papers of Solar Pons
New Adventures of the Sherlock Holmes of Praed Street
© 2017 by David Marcum

ISBN-13: 978-1978343023
ISBN-10: 1978343027

*Print and Digital Edition © 2017 by Belanger Books, LLC
All Rights Reserved. No part of this book may be used or
reproduced in any manner whatsoever without written
permission except in case of brief quotations embodied
in critical articles or reviews.*

*This book is a work of fiction. Names, characters, businesses,
organizations, places, events, and incidents either are the
product of the author's imagination or are used fictitiously. Any resemblance
to actual persons, living or dead,
events, or locales is entirely coincidental.*

Stories by David Marcum ©2017, All Rights Reserved
Foreword by August Derleth reprinted
by permission of the August Derleth Estate
Forewords by Roger Johnson, Peter Blau, Bob Byrne, Tracy Adam Heron,
and Derrick Belanger used by permission. ©2017, All Rights Reserved

For information contact:
**Belanger Books, LLC**
61 Theresa Ct.
Manchester, NH 03103

derrick@belangerbooks.com
www.belangerbooks.com

Based upon the works of August Derleth
Authorized and Published with the Permission
of the August Derleth Estate

Cover and Design by Brian Belanger
*www.belangerbooks.com* and *www.redbubble.com/people/zhahadun*

Author photo by Dan Marcum

David Marcum can be reached at:
*thepapersofsherlockholmes@gmail.com*

# CONTENTS

## *Forewords*

The Beginnings of Solar Pons    1
    by August Derleth

Re: Sherlock Holmes    7
    by David Marcum, *PSI*

The Sherlock Holmes of Praed Street    17
    by Roger Johnson, *PSI*

Remembering Luther Norris    20
    by Peter Blau, *PSI*

Solar Pons: Almost Holmes    22
    by Bob Byrne, *PSI*

Pons is Back    25
    by Tracy Adam Heron, *The August Derleth Society*

On the Return of Solar Pons    26
    by Derrick Belanger, *Publisher*

## *The Papers of Solar Pons*

    *A Word from Dr. Lyndon Parker*    33

I.    The Adventure of the Doctor's Box    37

II.    The Park Lane Solution    64

III.    The Poe Problem    78

IV.    The Singular Affair of the Blue Girl    100

V.    The Plight of the American Driver    132

*(Continued on the next page . . . .)*

| VI. | The Adventure of the Blood Doctor | 152 |
| VII. | The Additional Heirs | 175 |
| VIII. | The Horror of St. Anne's Row | 220 |
| IX. | The Adventure of the Failed Fellowship | 242 |
| X. | The Adventure of the Obrisset Snuffbox | 268 |
| XI. | The Folio Matter | 300 |
| XII. | The Affair of the Distasteful Society | 321 |

## *A Sherlock Holmes Adventure*
### *Re: Solar Pons's Origins*

| The Adventure of the Other Brother | 343 |

### *Appendices*

| Basil Rathbone's Solar Pons Films | 435 |
| Chronologicist's Notes | 438 |
| The Solar Pons Stories | 440 |
| About the Author | 445 |

# The Beginnings of Solar Pons
## by August Derleth

Originally published in
*A Praed Street Dossier*
(1968)

**Pons, Solar**, born ca. 1880, in Prague. Son of Asenath Pons, consular official at Prague, and Roberta McIvor Pons; younger brother of Bancroft Stoneham, in His Majesty's Service. Public school education; Oxford *summa cum laude*, 1899. Unmarried. Member: Savile, Diogenes, Athenaeum, Cliff Dwellers, Lambs. Est. private inquiry practice at 7B Praed Street, 1907. British Intelligence, World War I, II. Monographs: *An Inquiry into the Nan-Matal Ruins of Ponape* (1905); *A Logical Approach to the Science of Ratiocination* (1917); *The Chess Problem and the State of the Mind* (1919); *The Inductive Process* (1921); *On the Value of Circumstantial Evidence* (1925); *An Examination of the Cthulhu Cult and Others* (1931). Widely traveled. Residences: New York, Chicago, Paris, Vienna, Prague, Rome, 7B Praed Street, London, W.2. Telephone: Ambassador 10000.

This is what one reads of him today, but it was not always thus. As a matter of fact, even this much information was not known about Solar Pons until close to two decades ago [*from when Derleth wrote this in 1968 - Editor*] when Anthony Boucher pressed me for it, and I had to examine the chronicles to discover these facts.

Solar Pons came into being out of Sherlock Holmes, just as Holmes came out of C. Auguste Dupin, all chronicled date about Dr. Joseph Bell of Edinburgh University to the contrary. In a sense, Sherlock Holmes is C. Auguste Dupin. In the same sense, Solar Pons is Sherlock Holmes. But while Sir Arthur Conan Doyle considerably updated Sherlock Holmes, I made little attempt to do so with Solar Pons, save only for a couple of decades or so. He remains for Pons a retired contemporary to whom Pons always refers as "the Master".

At the outset, I wrote to Sir Arthur to ask whether he intended to write more adventures of Sherlock Holmes. I waited for at least a year after publication of *The Casebook of Sherlock Holmes*. Early in autumn of 1928, when I was in my junior year at the University of Wisconsin, and holed up in a solitary back room at 823 West Johnson

Street, Madison, Wisconsin (now the site of a rather impressive new dormitory), he replied – by means of a terse message scrawled upon my own letter – that he did not. He seemed, as I recall it now, unnecessarily emphatic about it, as if this decision, made once previously and set aside, were now irrevocable, and no amount of persuasion would this time cause him to change his mind. I wrote him that if he were not going to write further adventures, I would try my hand at it – but of course, this was impossible, for who was I to put upon paper new adventures of the illustrious Sherlock Holmes, of whom my maternal grandmother had always spoken as "the greatest detective who ever lived", since she, like so many other readers of The Canon, was firmly convinced that Sherlock Holmes lived, not in that sense of the continuing life given him by the Baker Street Irregulars, but as an actual man of flesh and blood, who might be appealed to in cases of dire necessity.

The form the stories must take was patent. Not that ridiculing imitation designed for laughter, the parody, but that fond and admiring one less widely-known as the pastiche. I needed first a name, syllabically similar to that of Sherlock Holmes. So Solar Pons was born because I thought of Solar in its suggestion of light, and Pons as the bridge – "bridge of light" seemed to the adolescent mind singularly brilliant, which, of course, it was not.

Any other setting but England seemed out of the question. But in point of fact I knew very little about England, and even less about London. The England I knew and loved – having been all my life a pronounced Anglophile, despite an ancestry originally French, now largely Bavarian – was the England of Thomas Hardy, George Eliot, John Galsworthy, Jane Austen, Richard Jefferies, Gilbert White, Joseph Conrad, Mary Webb, W. H. Hudson – and the London that was the highly romantic and colorful city of Charles Dickens, Sir Arthur, Sax Rohmer, R. Austin Freeman, and some other writers of detective and mystery fiction. This was admittedly neither much nor very accurate, insofar as even a tenuous reality for the Pontine tales was concerned.

Not long before beginning the first adventure of Solar Pons, I had read and enjoyed a novel by Cecil John Charles Street, under his pen-name of John Rhode, entitled *The Murders in Praed Street*, published in 1928, and when I cast around for the setting of the Pontine quarters, it was Praed Street that came instantly to mind. Perhaps my memory of the Dr. Priestley novel included some impressions of the milieu – that is, the naming of streets familiar to the Canonical works, but of this I can no longer be certain. When I consulted *Baedeker's London and Its Environs* – which I had found necessary to buy, the first book on an expanding shelf that must now number close to two-hundred books, ranging from street and provincial guides, to such comparatively recent works as A. J. P. Taylor's *English History: 1914-1945*, Eilert Ekwall's *The Concise Oxford Dictionary of English Place-Names*, Paul Ashbee's *The Bronze Age Round Barrow in Britain*, the Allen-Maxwell *The British Isles in Color*, and John Betjeman's *An American's Guide to English Parish Churches* – and learned that Praed Street was, for a hardy walker, actually within walking distance of 221b Baker Street, the Praed Street address seemed providential.

Thus Praed Street became the headquarters of Solar Pons, and specifically number 7 – for no reason but that this number came to mind and was set down, and number 7B, because Holmes was at 221b, though I then supposed that *B* indicated the second floor, when in fact, in London *B* designates the third floor – or what to American readers would be the third floor, since the first floor in London is that floor above the ground floor, which is the American first. I had no idea whatsoever about the actual and real Number 7, Praed Street, until late 1961, when Mr. Ian M. Law, who had visited Place of Hawks that summer, returned to England and considerately provided me with photographs of 7 Praed Street, which turned out to be next door to a cinema, and did have three floors, and could very readily have housed a private investigator and his amanuensis in their third floor quarters.

With the background fixed, however vaguely, in mind, I sat down and in one afternoon and evening wrote "The Adventure of the Black Narcissus" – my Baedeker's *London* at my elbow – which is precisely the kind of tale an amateur of nineteen would be likely to conjure up. Thereafter, this feat accomplished, the career of Solar Pons might have flatted and come to an unnoticed end, had it not been for a small circumstance. Harold Hersey, an indefatigable publisher, was at that time beginning a new string of pulp magazines in New York, and on impulse I sent the first Solar Pons story to him. Within a week came a check for $40.00, and – even more important, a letter saying that he would buy as many more Solar Pons stories as I cared to write for his magazine, *The Dragnet.*

With this promise of monetary reward added to what had already developed into a powerful compulsion, I went to work and in rapid succession, by dint of cutting classes here and there, I wrote "The Adventure of the Missing Tenants", "The Adventure of the Broken Chessman", and "The Adventure of the Late Mr.

Faversham". Harold Hersey bought them at once. In "The Adventure of the Black Narcissus" Solar Pons made his initial public appearance in the February, 1929 issue of *The Dragnet*. He appeared for the second time in the September issue of that year with "The Adventure of the Broken Chessman".

I was now committed. In one day I turned out three pastiches – "The Adventure of the Viennese Musician", "The Adventure of the Limping Man", "The Adventure of Gresham Old Place" – and before the week was out, I had added "The Adventure of the Muttering Man", "The Adventure of the Black Cardinal", and "The Adventure of the Sotheby Salesman". Two were immediately scheduled for publication, and the others accepted. And, counting my dollars to come in on publication, I went out to satisfy the most ardent of my desires – the acquisition of a library to supplement my shelves of Conan Doyle, Sax Rohmer, J. S. Fletcher, H. C. Bailey, Ernest Bramah, Lewis Carroll, Mark Twain, and half-a-dozen other favorite authors. In one heady afternoon of buying, I acquired – on a charge account – $400 worth of books – by Proust, Dostoievsky, Tolstoi, Thomas Hardy, Turgenev, Robert Frost, Edgar Lee Masters, Sherwood Anderson, Sinclair Lewis, Andre Gide, Oscar Wilde – everything, in fact, I had wanted most badly – $400 worth, which I counted on Solar Pons to pay for. But alas! – the month was October, 1929 – the market crash separated Harold Hersey and Solar Pons from *The Dragnet*, and, though Pons made three more appearances – in *Detective Trails* and *Gangster Stories*, in addition to *The Dragnet* in December, with "The Adventure of the Late Mr. Faversham" – his career had been effectively arrested.

I was left with $400 in debts and several returned manuscripts, as well as one new story of which I thought a trifle more favorably than I did its predecessors – "The Adventure of the Norcross Riddle". Though I had learned so early in my career a valuable lesson every writer must learn sooner or later – not to count my chickens before the eggs were hatched! – Solar Pons was put on the shelf, while I went to work to complete studying for my B.A. in 1930, and then after graduation took an editorial post with Fawcett's, at that time in Minneapolis – the result of Donald Wandrei's recommendation after his rejection of the offer of that post. It was not congenial work, for all that my associates were pleasant and co-operative; I could not stick it much longer than four months and came home to do or die at writing, having managed in my short time as associate editor of *Mystic Magazine* – a short-lived Fawcett venture, to pay off my indebtedness, not alone at my editorial salary, but with the addition of payments for fiction and non-fiction turned out in my spare time.

I settled in at home and began to chronicle the saga of Sac Prairie, turning my inclinations toward detection into a series of book-length stories featuring Judge Ephraim Peabody Peck, who appeared in ten books and no more - *Murder Stalks the Wakely Family, The Man on All Fours, Three Who Died, Sign of Fear, Sentence Deferred, The Narracong Riddle, The Seven Who Waited, Mischief in the Lane, No Future for Luana,* and *Fell Purpose*. My regional fiction and poetry began to find berths in a gratifying variety of magazines ranging from little reviews like *This Quarter, The Midland, and Pagany*, to established magazines like *The Atlantic Monthly, The New Republic, Scribner's, Household, The Commonweal*, and many others; mystery novels were being followed into print by serious works like *Place of Hawks, Still Is the Summer Night, Wind Over Wisconsin, et al.*, and I had been awarded a Guggenheim Fellowship to carry on the Sac Prairie Saga. As the years went by, Solar Pons was all but forgotten, but, truth to tell, Solar Pons had always had more reality in my thoughts than Judge Peck, for all that the estimable Judge operated in a milieu I knew very well indeed.

Yet Solar Pons might have been forgotten, had it not been for another fortuitous circumstance. Over a decade after the last - and I thought final appearance of Solar Pons (in *Gangster Stories* for March, 1930, in "The Adventure of the Black Cardinal") - Ellery Queen began to assemble stories for his anthology, *The Misadventures of Sherlock Holmes* (1944). I remembered "The Adventure of the Norcross Riddle" and wrote to Fred Dannay, asking whether he would like to see the pastiche. He welcomed it. So I undertook a retouching and retyping and sent it in. He accepted and published it; Irregulars read it with pleasure. Both Dannay and Vincent Starrett inquired about Solar Pons and, learning that there were enough tales for a group, urged that they be put out in book form.

Even so, I was far from convinced. I looked them all over; they seemed to me very amateurish indeed. None ranked with the single story published in the *Misadventures*, and I quietly resolved to let the idea of a Solar Pons collection die. Quite by chance, however, while discussing with Ray Palmer, then with Ziff-Davis in Chicago, the idea of a horror story anthology (later successfully published by Rinehart as *Sleep No More!*), I mentioned the possibility of a Solar Pons collection. Palmer urged me to put it together and, without committing Ziff-Davis to it, asked to see such a book with a view to publication.

With that added incentive and the promise from Vincent Starrett to write an introduction to the book, I went home and got to work to assemble a collection to be titled *"In Re: Sherlock Holmes": The Adventures of Solar Pons* – because, on the day I had decided to write a Holmesian pastiche, I had opened my desk calendar at 823 West Johnson at random and written "In re: Sherlock Holmes" to remind myself to write the story on that day, which I did. But when I re-examined those early stories – published and unpublished – there were then an even dozen – I found most of them simply too inept to be published. So I got to work and wrote new stories, while revising the old.

I kept "The Adventure of the Black Narcissus", "The Adventure of the Norcross Riddle", "The Adventure of the Sotheby Salesman", "The Adventure of the Limping Man", and "The Adventure of the Late Mr. Faversham". The new tales were "The Adventure of the Man with the Broken Face", "The Adventure of the Frightened Baronet", "The Adventure of the Purloined Periapt", "The Adventure of the Lost Holiday", "The Adventure of the Three Red Dwarfs", "The Adventure of the Retired Novelist", and "The Adventure of the Seven Passengers". These stories made up the first collection, which was duly submitted to Ziff-Davis, and presently rejected.

By this time, however, I was infected with the virus. I was no longer so willing to trust any publisher with Solar Pons and, since I already had a publishing venture of my own in Arkham House – begun in 1939, six years earlier – I took especial pleasure in establishing a new imprint – Mycroft & Moran, the directors of which were, of course, Mycroft Holmes and Colonel Sebastian Moran ("the second most dangerous man in London") – in fixing upon Baskerville type for the Pontine tales, and commissioning a deerstalker as a colophon from Ronald Clyne, who had lent his artistry to the improvement of jackets for Arkham House books – and in 1945 Solar Pons made his bow in book form in the first collection, a full-length pastiche of *The Adventures of Sherlock Holmes*.

August Derleth<br>1968

# In Re: Sherlock Holmes
## by David Marcum, *PSI*

I make no secret of the fact that I'm a Missionary for the Church of Sherlock Holmes, and have been since 1975, when I was ten years old and first discovered The Great Detective of Baker Street. Over the years, I've collected thousands of traditional stories beyond the pitifully few original sixty, and I've written some too, as well as editing books that encourage even more of them. But surprisingly, before I ever read my first Holmes tale, it turns out that I'd encountered Solar Pons, two years earlier when I was eight years old. I credit the enjoyment that I had from that first reading about Pons for familiarity that it provided to that kind of narrative style, and for making me so receptive when I discovered Holmes and Watson.

When I was eight years old in 1973, I first discovered the joy of reading, and what hooked me was a mystery story. One day in third grade, my class was in the library and the teacher told us that we had to check out a book. With no ideas about what to choose, and getting a little desperate, I looked around, and finally a title jumped out at me. I grabbed it and checked it out, little realizing that it would change my life.

No, it wasn't a book about Holmes or Pons. What I found was *The Mystery of the Green Ghost* (1965) by Robert Arthur (1909-1969), the fourth book in a relatively new – at that time – children's mystery series, *The Three Investigators*. It was the first mystery that I'd ever read, and there was no going back.

Reading that series led directly to Pons, and then indirectly to Holmes. Partially the nature of The Three Investigators books themselves prepared me to enjoy those kinds of stories. They had perfectly linear mysteries with real clues, and a main character who sleuthed in a Holmesian way. They were well-written, and I can – and do – still go back and enjoy them today.

When The Three Investigators books were first published in 1964, creator Robert Arthur had been an established author for many years, writing short stories and also scripts for radio and television. He was also a gifted editor. After creating The Three Investigators, Arthur edited a series of oversized hardback mystery anthologies for children with famed film director Alfred Hitchcock's name on them, as if Hitchcock had edited them himself. However, they had an acknowledgement on the copyright page stating: *The editor gratefully* acknowledges the invaluable assistance of Robert Arthur in the preparation of this volume. The assistance he provided was doing all the work.

One of these anthologies, *Alfred Hitchcock's Daring Detectives* (1969), included a Pons story, "The Adventure of the Grice-Paterson Curse" (De Waal 5624). Arthur, writing as Hitchcock, stated in the book's introduction:

> *"And last, but not least, as a special treat I am including a detective who may seem oddly familiar to you, though the name is strange. Who exactly is Solar Pons, of 'The Adventure of the Grice-Paterson Curse", and his companion, Dr. Parker? Surely they can't be – No, no, they are not the Great Detective and his medical friend in disguise."* Arthur goes on to state that *"[t]hey are instead two characters created . . . to carry on a tradition known and loved by every reader of detective stories."*

That story was truly my first introduction to the Holmes-Watson template, although I didn't realize it then. As anyone who has read it knows, "The Grice-Paterson Curse" is amazing. It's still my favorite Pons adventure to this day, and it made a deep impression on me.

I'm sure that memories of this tale were still resonating in my subconscious when I picked up my first real Holmes book two years later, in 1975. By that time, I had read and re-read The Three Investigators, and had moved on to The Hardy Boys – not as good, but there was the advantage that there were more of them. My desire to own the books I love, rather than take a chance on finding them at a library, happened early, and even then I was trying to track down every Hardy Boys book that I could. I had a friend who had some, and I wanted them, and he didn't. We worked out a trade, but I realized that, in my greed, I was letting him have an unfair advantage. Negotiations proceeded, and he threw in an abridged Whitman edition of *The Adventures of Sherlock Holmes*. Of course I recognized Holmes – who doesn't? – but I didn't really want that book. "He's a detective, too," cajoled my friend, and my aforementioned greed finally pushed me to accept the deal.

And I promptly forgot about the Holmes book until a few weeks later, when I happened upon *A Study in Terror* (1965), a Holmes film on television. I liked it, and went back and found that copy of *The Adventures*. There was no turning back.

I'd enjoyed everything about "The Grice-Paterson Curse" so much that when I started "The Red-Headed League", the first story in the Whitman edition, I already had a familiarity for the format in my head, and Holmes and Watson found ready acceptance there.

So it turns out that I discovered Pons first, which is *not* how most people find their way to Holmes and Watson and Baker Street.

I'd mostly forgotten about Pons until after that until, sometime in my early teens, I saw a set of Pinnacle paperbacks at the local bookstore featuring a Holmes-like figure in a deerstalker, but with that oddly familiar name of *Solar Pons*. I begged for them as a birthday present, and bless my wonderful parents - I received them.

Since then, I've read the Pons adventures many times over the years. For instance, I remember when I was thirteen, and being aware that my horrible algebra teacher - from the *first* time that I had to take algebra; She later won a teaching award, but I don't know how - was watching me read about Pons in one of those Pinnacle paperbacks in class, and *not* making me put it away and think about math like she should have. (Of course, as I've matured I realize that maybe I probably ought to take some of the blame, too.) Later, with my very first paycheck from my very first job, I telephoned The Mysterious Bookshop in New York - not to order something about Sherlock Holmes as might be expected, but rather a copy of the two-volume boxed set *The Solar Pons Omnibus*, edited by Basil Copper, which I had seen advertised several years earlier. This became my first grown-up Pons purchase. (Thank you, Otto Penzler!)

Pons has always been known and loved within the Sherlockian community, but awareness of him in the wider world waxes and wanes. In the 1920's, a few original stories appeared in pulp magazines. As chosen by editor Ellery Queen, a Pons tale appeared in the very rare *The Misadventures of Sherlock Holmes* (1944), and with subsequent encouragement by Ellery Queen and Vincent Starrett, Derleth published the first Pons short story collection, *In Re: Sherlock Holmes* the following year. Other collections followed, right up to Derleth's death in 1971. Each was met with great enthusiasm by that group acquainted with Mr. Solar Pons of Praed Street. But it was a small group.

In the 1970's, Pinnacle published the aforementioned set of paperbacks that initially caught my attention. I don't know, but I assume that these were successful enough that the Pinnacle people decided to publish new Pons stories after Derleth's death, written by British horror author Basil Copper. (A complete list of the Pons volumes and stories by Derleth and Copper are included in the Appendices.)

Copper had already been associated with the Pontine Canon when he edited *The Solar Pons Omnibus* (1982), billed as the first complete collection of Pons tales – although it wasn't quite complete. There was also some controversy involved when Copper took it upon himself to smooth a number of Derleth's Americanisms that crept in while he was writing as British Dr. Parker. These had long been accepted by Pons fans, as it was understood that Parker had lived for a period of time in the United States, and therefore the occasional American phrase or grammar would slip in and wasn't considered too shocking.

Copper's changes were the first steps in what became a somewhat contentious relationship between him and the Pons community. His own Pons stories were somewhat longer than Derleth's, and were also written in a markedly different style. However, they were also popular, and I was very glad to have them. He eventually published six volumes of original Pons tales, and in his later years, he also produced several editions in which he revised some of what was in those first volumes, rather cantankerously (and ironically) disliking the way that they had originally been edited. He wrote his own Pons novel, *Solar Pons versus The Devil's Claw* (2004), and in 2017, PS Publishing posthumously released a very handsome two-volume set of Copper's *The Complete Solar Pons*.

In 1995, after a number of years of re-reading the Pontine Canon and researching various questions as they occurred to me, I noticed that a Pons case was mislabeled in Ronald De Waal's incredible *The World Bibliography of Sherlock Holmes* (1974). This massive book has a whole section, pages 416-424, devoted to Pons and Parker. Item 5642 states that "The Obrisset Snuffbox" is one of the adventures contained in Derleth's posthumous collection *The Chronicles of Solar Pons* (1973). However, that statement isn't true, and it's one of the rare errors in De Waal's masterpiece. "The Obrisset Snuffbox" is actually an "untold case" that's mentioned in Pons story "The Adventure of the Seven Sisters".

Just to make sure, I checked both of my copies of the Pons stories, the Pinnacle paperbacks and the Copper Omnibus, and it wasn't there. Puzzled, I did some further research and learned that *The Praed Street Irregulars* (PSI), the Solar Pons society, was being maintained by George Vanderburgh of Canada. I wrote to him (by letter, pre-internet), asking if he had any information as to whether there actually had been a story called "The Obrisset Snuffbox" that might have been inadvertently left out of certain later editions of the books. He confirmed that it was a mistaken entry. Then – due to my curiosity and obvious devotion the Pontine Cause – he offered me an investiture in the PSI under the fitting *sobriquet* of "The Obrisset Snuffbox". I gladly accepted, and George and I began to irregularly correspond.

A few years later, George, who is the publisher of *The Battered Silicon Dispatch Box*, began to discover and release various "lost" Pons items, assembled from August Derleth papers. These included new stories and fragments, as well as an entire previously undiscovered Pons novel, *Terror Over London*. Additionally during that time, he assembled the massive two-volume *The Original Text Solar Pons Omnibus Edition* (2000). Of course, I purchased all of them. Amazingly, in many cases – before I even knew about their existence – George would send me the volumes, knowing that I was be immensely interested.

In the meantime, as I was able, I also purchased the original Mycroft and Moran editions of the Pons books, along with filling in all the other available editions of Pons books by both Derleth and Copper.

As I explain in the introduction to "The Adventure of the Other Brother", located at the end of this volume, I was able to start writing my own Holmes stories in 2008, during a period of time when I was laid off from a civil engineering job at the start of the big recession. When thinking about what to write, one thing that I most wanted to address was the question of who, actually, was Solar Pons, and what was his relationship with Sherlock Holmes? Holmes is often referred to in the original Pons stories, an off-screen presence and influence on Pons in so many ways. I had finally worked out the answer to my own satisfaction, and that story, "The Other Brother" – along with eight others – was published in 2011 in *The Papers of Sherlock Holmes*.

That came about after I had contacted George Vanderburgh, my Solar Pons friend, and he published the book through his Battered Silicon Dispatch Box. Later, it was republished in 2013 by MX Publishing, as I tried to both generate new interest in Pons, and also to spread my own theory as to his origins.

Several years ago – I'm not sure how many now! – I noticed that there was someone doing really excellent work on the internet to promote Pons. I got in touch with him, and we emailed a bit, stopped for a while, and then started again – a lot ever since. This person is an incredible Pons scholar and a knowledge database named Bob Byrne.

I was very happy when he asked me to write a couple of essays for his online *Solar Pons Gazette*, found at *www.solarpons.com* He had an idea about having a future issue consist of new Pons pastiches. Since I'd written some Holmes stories, I was interested, and sat down in mid-2014 and wrote my first Pons story, "The Adventure of the Doctor's Box", intersecting Pons and Parker with the world of Holmes and Watson. It was so much fun, I wrote another. And then another.

When I had three, I stopped for a while. But then I began to pester Bob: *What about,* I asked, *instead of putting these online, we see about making them into a real book, with the permission of the Derleth Estate?*

Time passed. Since 2013, I've been able to make three extensive Holmes Pilgrimages to London and other parts of Great Britain. And while these were almost entirely Holmes-related, I did work in a number of Pons sites, including multiple visits to No. 7 Praed Street – which doesn't look anything like it did in Pons and Parker's days. I've also eaten several times at the Fountains Abbey Pub in Praed Street, located between No. 7 and Paddington Station. (That's the traditionally accepted location where Pons and Parker first met in mid-1919.) And of course, so many Holmes-related sites, such as Scotland Yard, are also Pons sites too.

In recent years, I've been lucky enough to make a number of great friends within the Sherlockian community. In early 2015, I had the idea of assembling and editing a collection of new Holmes stories, and it ended up being the largest collection of new Holmes adventures ever as part of one ongoing series, *The MX Book of New Sherlock Holmes Stories*. The author royalties go to support the Stepping Stones School at Undershaw, one of Sir Arthur Conan Doyle's former homes. The project, as of this writing, has raised funds for the school in five figures, is now eight massive volumes with two more in the planning stages. There are over one-hundred contributing Sherlockian authors, and over two-hundred new stories have been written for these volumes about the *true* Sherlock Holmes, set in the correct time period.

Being involved in this project, and finding new contributors, has made me fearless. I'm not afraid to ask anyone to participate. Some big names have turned me down, but I've gotten so close. Others, such as bestselling authors Jonathan Kellerman and Lee Child, have very generously donated their time to write forewords for some of the books.

I've long since learned that if you don't ask, you'll never know. With that in mind, and with the boldness that I learned by being a federal investigator in a previous career, and also simply by managing the editing of the MX anthologies, I decided to ask and see if the time had finally come to have a new Pons collection, containing stories written by me.

Bob Byrne put me in touch with Tracy Heron of *The August Derleth Society*, and he in turn gave me the address of Danielle Hackett, August Derleth's granddaughter, and the co-owner and President of Derleth's original publishing company, Arkham House.

I emailed her and made my pitch. Questions were asked and answered. I introduced her (by email) to publisher Derrick Belanger. More questions were asked and answered. And then – a contract to produce a new volume of Solar Pons stories.

As this had progressed, I was writing more of them, confident that things would work out successfully. And they did.

News leaked out, and then an official press release appeared in April 2017: Arkham House, in association with Belanger Books, would be publishing *The Papers of Solar Pons.*

Since that time, I've received a great deal of support from Sherlockian friends and Solar Pons fans. And this in turn has generated the possibility that a Pons anthology by different authors might be in the works, and that the original Pons books, so long out of print, will finally be released in new editions to both the people that have wanted them for so long – they're very hard to find, and expensive when they are found! – and also a new generation that doesn't even know Pons yet but loves Holmes, and needs to be educated about the former.

I suspect that most of the readers of this book are already Pons fans. However, if you haven't found and read the originals before, I highly encourage you to do so. Those are the real deal! Copper took over for Derleth, and he wrote some great Pons stories too – *but he wasn't Derleth.* Likewise, the stories in this new book are *not* going to be quite the same as what was written by The Pontine Master. These will inevitably reflect my own style and agenda. For instance, I encourage the consideration of Pons in light of Holmes, and several of the stories in this book were written with that specifically in mind, as you'll see. You have been warned! But I assure you that every effort has been made to bring you authentic adventures of Solar Pons of Praed Street.

I want to thank many people. First and foremost, thank you with all my heart to my patient and wonderful wife of twenty-nine-plus years (as of this writing) Rebecca, and our son, Dan. I love you both, and you are everything to me!

Special *thank you*'s go to:

- *Danielle Hackett and Damon Derleth*: I can't tell you both how much I appreciate the opportunity to write this book, allowing me to help remind people about the importance of Solar Pons, and also what a great contribution your grandfather August Derleth made to the world of Sherlock Holmes. I hope this is just the start of a new Pons revival.
- *Derrick and Brian Belanger*: We've already worked together on some great Holmes projects, and when I came to you both with this idea, you recognized its potential and jumped in feet first. Thank you both for being such great co-conspirators in all of this. It's been really amazing, and I look forward to working with you both on future Pons and Holmes projects.
- *Bob Byrne*: You are a great friend, and I appreciate all the support you've provided to me. I also honor all the amazing hard work you've done to keep Pons's memory green. In terms of this book, you were the guy with the initial idea to have new Pons adventures. If you hadn't put that idea out there, I wouldn't have been motivated to write the first story. Thank you especially for that. I really look forward to future discussions as we see what new Pons vistas await.
- *Roger Johnson*: Back in 2011, when the first edition of *The Papers of Sherlock Holmes* was published, I sent you a copy, because it really mattered to me that you review it. I had no idea then that you were also a Ponsian. Since then, you've become a great friend, and I've been very fortunate to get to see you and your wife, Jean Upton, on all three of my Holmes Pilgrimages to London. You've helped me with a great many questions along the way, and supported every idea I've come up with, and I was really tickled when, as I planned for my first Holmes Pilgrimage in 2013, you hurriedly arranged for my membership in *The Solar Pons Society of London* (which you founded), quickly mailing my

membership card so that I would have it on my person as I explored London, visiting both Holmes and Pons sites. I had that card with me every time I visited No. 7 Praed Street. As always, thank you so much.

- *Marcia Wilson*: You are an amazing person and extremely talented writer of Sherlock Holmes stories – or I should say *Inspector Lestrade* stories, with some Holmes thrown in. You have truly found Scotland Yard's Tin Dispatch Box. The first fan letter I ever wrote was to you, and since then you've become a great friend. You're a Pons scholar too, and I very much appreciate your input on this book, as well as all the support on numerous other projects.

- *Tom Turley*: I'm very glad to have met you through the Wonderful World of Holmes, originally by email, and finally in person. You write very insightful Holmes stories, dealing with the niches that have been ignored for far too long. I appreciate your thoughts in general and for reading this manuscript and observing (and not just seeing) errors in it.

- *Tracy Heron*: Thank you so much for putting me in touch with the Derleth Estate, taking time to answer so many of my questions, and for writing a foreword. As a member of the August Derleth Society (ADS), you attempt to increase awareness of Derleth's works, and I hope that this book will add to that effort.

- *Peter Blau*: You are a Sherlockian legend and one of the original PSI's, and although we haven't (yet) met in person, I'm very proud that you're a part of this book. I always enjoy our emails and in-depth exchange of Holmesian information.

- *George Vanderburgh*: Thank you for taking time to answer my questions back in the 1990's, for sending me newly discovered Pons material before I even knew that it existed, for publishing my first book, and for investing me in *The Praed Street Irregulars* as "The Obrisset Snuffbox". I'm very proud to be in the exclusive PSI, and very appreciative for your help.

I also want to thank those people are always so supportive in many ways: Steve Emecz, Mark Mower, Denis Smith, and Dan Victor.

Additionally, much gratitude is given to Will Murray (the authorized continuer of the adventures of Tarzan and Doc Savage, along with many others), and William "Bill" Patrick Maynard (the authorized continuer of books about Pons's contemporaries, Fu Manchu, Denis Nayland Smith, Dr. Petrie, *et al.*) for their advice about continuing another author's characters. Special thanks to Bill Maynard for advising me regarding how to refer to *The Devil Doctor.*

My gratitude goes to both Rand Lee and Richard Dannay, of *Ellery Queen* lineage, for being my email friends and letting me run an idea past them.

Much appreciation to Nick Utechin for giving me the behind-the-scenes tour of Oxford on my Holmes Pilgrimage No. 2 in October 2015, which ended up being relevant to this volume in a small way. I especially enjoyed visiting *The Eagle and Child* pub, and noticing that, above the table where The Inklings gathered, was a shelf holding a red-bound copy of *The Hound of the Baskervilles.*

And last but certainly *not* least, **August Derleth**: Founder of the Pontine Feast. Present in spirit, and honored by all of us here.

This book has been a labor of love, with my admiration of Pons and Parker beginning in the early 1970's, and the writing of these stories stretching over the last several years. I hope that it's enjoyed by both long-time Pons fans and new recruits. The world of Solar Pons and Dr. Parker is a place that I never tire of visiting, and I hope that more and more people discover it.

Join me as we go to 7B Praed Street. *"The game is afoot!"*

David Marcum<br>
"The Obrisset Snuffbox", *PSI*<br>
August, 2017

*Questions or comments*<br>
*may be addressed to David Marcum at*<br>
thepapersofsherlockholmes@gmail.com

# The Sherlock Holmes of Praed Street
## by Roger Johnson, *PSI*

In 1928, while he was a freshman at the University of Wisconsin, August Derleth wrote to Sir Arthur Conan Doyle, saying that if there were to be no more Sherlock Holmes stories, he, Derleth, intended to try his hand at something similar. He was clear about his intentions: "*The form the stories must take was patent. Not that ridiculing imitation designed for laughter, the parody, but that fond and admiring one less widely-known as the pastiche.*" The only conceivable setting for his new detective Solar Pons and his amanuensis Dr. Parker was Holmes's own city, London. The young author knew London only from books, but he researched as thoroughly as he could, and of course he was intimately familiar with the chronicles of Sherlock Holmes.

The first Pons story, "The Adventure of the Black Narcissus", was good enough to be snapped up by *Dragnet* magazine, and others followed in quick succession. The game was afoot!

I was still at school in the early 1960's when I became aware of Solar Pons. As an admirer of the weird tales of H.P. Lovecraft, I'd been excited to learn that HPL's publisher - Arkham House, founded and run by August Derleth — had an agent in London, one G. Ken Chapman. Naturally, I started to buy Arkham House titles from him, having them delivered to my school, because I didn't want my parents to know how much I was spending. (And those were the days when a guinea - in today's terms £1.05 - would buy a $3.00 book.)

But it wasn't only Arkham House stock. There was also Derleth's other publishing house, Mycroft & Moran, which specialised in detective stories, notably the tales of Mr. Solar Pons of Praed Street. That was even more exciting: I was a devotee of Sherlock Holmes, and this literary tribute appealed to me. I ordered a copy of *The Memoirs of Solar Pons* (the first volume, rather pretentiously titled *"In Re: Sherlock Holmes" - The Adventures of Solar Pons*, was temporarily out of stock). Then, of course, I had to have the rest . . . .

And there was yet more. A society in honour of Solar Pons had recently been founded in California, and in emulation of America's senior Sherlockian fraternity it was called *The Praed Street Irregulars*.

The chances that I'd ever be considered for membership in the Baker Street Irregulars were negligible, but the *Praed* Street Irregulars might be a different matter. I wrote a letter of enquiry to the founder, Luther L. Norris, whose prompt and friendly reply was accompanied by a card testifying to the fact that I was now a member of the *PSI* with the titular investiture of "Geoffrey Thompson".

Luther encouraged four of his Sherlockian/Solarian friends to write to me, and they soon became my friends as well. John Bennett Shaw and Ted Schulz have, like Luther himself, passed beyond the Reichenbach, but Peter Blau and Jon Lellenberg remain as fixed points in a changing age.

Luther Norris also encouraged me to contribute to the *PSI*'s journal, *The Pontine Dossier*, and in time he asked me to found, or more accurately co-found, a British scion, to be called *The Solar Pons Society of London*. I agreed, on condition that it would require as little work from me as possible. Luther himself awarded membership in the new society to several people, but he never told me who or even how many, so I felt justified in not keeping a list of members. In fact, in nearly half-a-century of *The Solar Pons Society of London*, there have never been any meeting or any publications.

Before his death in 1971, August Derleth found time among his other work to write and publish five volumes of Pons stories, as well as a short novel, two novellas, and *A Praed Street Dossier*, which contains a good deal of interesting background information and some shorter exploits of the redoubtable Pons. *The Chronicles of Solar Pons* appeared posthumously in 1973. And that was that. There was no falling-off in quality; the later stories are, if anything, better than the early ones, because Derleth's writing matured and improved as he aged, and because he cared about Pons and Parker. Even though his regional novels were and are regarded as his finest contribution to letters, you would not have heard him complaining, as Conan Doyle did of Holmes, that Solar Pons "took his mind from better things".

After Derleth's death, the published stories were edited by Basil Copper (who rather controversially corrected many errors and adjusted many Americanisms) and published in 1982 in a handsome two-volume omnibus edition. Copper was also authorised to create more exploits for Pons. His preferred length was notably longer than that of the originals, but the style, flavour, and atmosphere are exactly right, while the protagonists are unmistakably the authentic Solar Pons and Dr. Parker. It was a rare case of an imitation imitated, and possibly unique at the time.

Unique no longer, as the present volume attests! In 2011, *The Papers of Sherlock Holmes* showed us that David Marcum writes well, that he knows and loves the Holmes Canon, and that his imagination is more than equal to creating new adventures for The Sage of Baker Street. His subsequent stories and novels have confirmed that impression; so, given his respect for August Derleth and his deep affection for the sleuth of Praed Street, Mr. Marcum is obviously the ideal person to take up Dr. Parker's pen and continue the saga of the redoubtable Solar Pons.

Roger Johnson<br>
"Geoffrey Thompson", *PSI*<br>
June, 2017

# Remembering Luther Norris
## by Peter E. Blau, *PSI*

It's grand to see August Derleth's *Solar Pons* back again and widely available to a new generation of readers, and it's nice indeed to be reminded of a good friend: Luther L. Norris, who did so much to "keep the memory green" for Solar Pons.

Luther was born in 1920 in Indiana and served in the U.S. Army during World War II in Alaska (where he met and befriended Dashiell Hammett), and stayed on in Alaska after the war, working as an editor and collaborating with Thomas Wiedemann Sr. on a collection of poems (published as *The Saga of Alaska* in 1946) and writing stories about the old Yukon prospectors (published as *Sourdough Tales* in 1947).

After he moved to Culver City, California, he helped manage the Doheny Plaza, corresponded with Stan Laurel, and was an early member of the *Sons of the Desert* (a society for fans of Laurel and Hardy), became active in the science-fiction community, and eventually found the worlds of Sherlock Holmes and Solar Pons.

Luther was a Sherlockian first, coming to the attention of readers of *The Baker Street Journal* when he offered copies of a statuette of Sherlock Holmes sculpted by Luques Whitmore in 1963. Luther quickly found kindred spirits in southern California, and received his thoroughly appropriate Investiture ("Monsieur Oscar Meunier, of Grenoble") from *The Baker Street Irregulars* in 1966. He privately published Roy Hunt's portfolio of Sherlockian prints *The Something Hunt* in 1967, James. C. Iraldi's pastiche *The Problem of the Purple Maculas* in 1968, and many other titles still treasured by Sherlockian collectors.

He also was a firm friend of August Derleth, and a dedicated champion of Solar Pons. Just as Solar Pons was created as a tribute to Sherlock Holmes, Luther founded *The Praed Street Irregulars* (PSI) in 1968 as a tribute to *The Baker Street Irregulars*, bestowing Investitures, membership certificates, and a Praed Penny as a membership token, and presiding over annual dinners.

Eventually he launched The Pontine Press with Mary and Irving Jaffee's collection of Sherlockian pastiches, *Beyond Baker Street* in 1973. Luther also edited nine issues of *The Pontine Dossier* from 1967 to 1970, and six more issues of a new series from 1970 to 1977, offering a delightful mix of Sherlockian and Pontine contributions.

He happily inspired others to follow the trail he blazed: His good friend Ted Schulz created *The Old Soldiers of Praed Street* as a tribute to Bill Rabe's *The Old Soldiers of Baker Street*, and Roger Johnson founded *The Solar Pons Society of London* as a tribute to *The Sherlock Holmes Society of London*. (Luther was a Colonel in the society's *Maiwand Outpost*). All of his friends and correspondents enjoyed his grand sense of humor, and he was widely mourned when he died on January 27$^{th}$, 1978.

Ted Schulz revived *The Praed Street Irregulars* in 1983, succeeding Luther as the "Lord Warden of the Pontine Marshes", and choosing the name "The Pontine Pines" for his home in Flagstaff, Arizona.

Luther's friend Irving L. Jaffee once described Luther as a "non-conforming individualist", and so he was. Not wanting to be bothered by mundane telephone calls, he happily maintained an unlisted number, until a visiting Sherlockian, unable to reach him by phone, finally tracked him down and explained there was no need to pay the phone company extra for an unlisted number. "Just list yourself under a different name," the visiting Sherlockian suggested, and that's exactly what Luther did – listing himself as Solar Pons. "People who know me will know how to find me," he explained.

Of course the listing had consequences: Luther wrote to a friend that he began to receive all sorts of mail for Solar Pons, "such as a chance to win a free trip to Paris, a low-cost rate at Forest Lawn, and a chance to get a set of cookware at half-price."

Luther was an avid and generous collector (many collectors are eager to add to their collections, but generous collectors are delighted to share with others), a welcome correspondent, a splendid friend. We are all in his debt for his devotion to Sherlock Holmes, and especially to Solar Pons.

Peter Blau<br>
"The Broken Chessmen", *PSI*<br>
August, 2017

# Solar Pons: Almost Holmes
## by Bob Byrne, *PSI*

Type "Sherlock Holmes" into the Search field on a certain well-known online bookseller's site and you get over 20,000 results. Since Sir Arthur Conan Doyle only wrote sixty Canonical tales about Holmes (you may discuss among yourselves the merits of including "How Watson Learned the Trick" and "The Field Bazaar"), that's quite a large number. The majority are original Holmes stories written by nearly as many authors.

As you can imagine, results vary, with only a relatively few authors managing to both emulate Doyle's style and also write a good Holmes story. I've attempted it myself with mixed outcomes (and that's probably being generous). But I believe that the best non-Doyle Sherlock Holmes we've seen was created over eighty years ago – and he's not even named Holmes!

Back in 1927, when Babe Ruth and his fellow "Murderers Row" were destroying the American League, a young student at the University of Wisconsin wrote to Doyle, asking if there would be more Holmes stories, *The Casebook* having been recently published. A year later, the student received his own letter back, with a "*terse message scrawled upon (it)*," indicating that the author was done with the world's first private consulting detective. By accounts it seemed rather "nothing to see here, move along" in tone.

So, August Derleth randomly picked a day in his desk calendar (remember those?) and scribbled, "*In re-Sherlock Holmes.*" And when that day, lost to time, arrived, Derleth sat down and wrote "The Adventure of the Black Narcissus", featuring Solar Pons. The doyen of Holmes scholars, Vincent Starrett, said of Pons, "*The best substitute for Sherlock Holmes known.*"

And it's Solar Pons who gets my vote for the best Holmes pastiche. I've written elsewhere why Pons is more than just a carbon copy of Holmes. But there's no denying that when one reads about Pons, Dr. Parker, Inspector Jamison, Mrs. Johnson, and the rest of the Praed Street cast, that it is all rooted in Holmes and Baker Street.

Derleth sold "The Black Narcissus" and quickly wrote nine (!) more stories, a few of which were published. However, the stock market crash wreaked havoc with fiction magazines, so Derleth put Pons on the shelf and continued on to receive a B.A. degree in 1930. He began his prolific writing career after graduation, but it would be Judge Peck, not Solar Pons, who scratched his mystery itch.

Derleth offered the unpublished "The Adventure of the Norcross Riddle" to Frederic Dannay (one-half of Ellery Queen) for the upcoming ill-fated anthology, *The Misadventures of Sherlock Holmes*. The tale was included, though Doyle's sons (Adrian and Denis) fought the project and legally ensured that it would never be reprinted.

But Dannay and Starrett encouraged Derleth to compile his Praed Street stories and to publish a Pons collection. Even with such high-powered support, no publisher would take on the project, fearing opposition from the Doyle Estate. Having already founded his own publishing company, Arkham House, Derleth established a new mystery imprint, Mycroft and Moran (a nice tip of the deerstalker to Holmes), for *In Re: Sherlock Holmes: The Adventure of Solar Pons*.

The Doyle brothers threatened legal action but nobody ever bullied August Derleth. The book was published and Derleth would continue writing about Pons right up to his death in 1971. The actual number of stories in the Pontine Canon was debated in print by yours truly and this book's author and can be found in Issue 7 of *The Solar Pons Gazette* at *www.SolarPons.com*, but we both agree it is more than seventy!

Anthony Boucher, a giant in the mystery and science fiction fields, summed it up well:

> "*Sherlock Holmes's decision to live alone in the bee-loud glade left an abhorrent vacuum in the life of London; but of all the Holmesian commentators, only August Derleth perceived the obvious truth – that the vacuum had to be filled. And how admirably Solar Pons fills it!*"

After Derleth's passing, the Estate authorized Basil Copper to write more Pons tales. Copper chose a longer form, less than a novella but more than a short story, and added to the history of Praed Street before parting ways with the Derleth Estate.

There have been a few pastiches, parodies, and entries from Dr. Parker's Notebooks in issues of The Solar Pons Gazette. But you now hold in your hands the FIRST collection of new Pons pastiches in over twenty years. With Derleth's originals out of print (at least in the U.S.) since 1973 as well, this is a momentous occasion in Pons history!

David Marcum, a fellow member of The Praed Street Irregulars, is well-known in the Holmes community for originating and editing (and of course, contributing to) *The MX Book of New Sherlock Holmes Stories* series, which is now at eight volumes and growing.

The books are characterized by their commitment to the original style of Sir Arthur Conan Doyle's stories. No time-travel, vampires, or gender-changed characters. David wants stories that make the reader feel like they are reading about Doyle's Holmes and Watson – not contemporary society's much-changed interpretation.

So, if anybody was going to officially continue the Pons saga, he got my vote. And early on in the very first story, "The Doctor's Box," we get Marcum's Parker sounding like Derleth's Parker. And *that's* what we want in a new book of Pons tales.

One of the joys of the Pons stories is that even though motor cars have replaced hansom cabs and the telephone is a valuable tool, rather than a novelty, they still feel quite Victorian, and that solidifies the link with Holmes. As David shows, one can read about Pons in a Holmes frame of mind. And there's a warmth in that – even in a chilly Victorian rain. Pons refers to Holmes as his "illustrious predecessor" in the original stories, acknowledging him as "The Master". As Starrett decreed, Pons is Holmes's successor and David emulates that feeling.

The sleuth of 221b Baker Street is retired but living on the Sussex Downs during Derleth's stories, and you'll find plenty of Holmes in this new collection. David loves to play The Game – a long-time hobby among Sherlockians in which Holmes and Watson are treated as if they really existed. (David may add an editorial comment regarding my inference that they didn't....) He does the same with Pons throughout the stories. For example, there's a reference to an unnamed Belgian detective in the first story. Derleth did the same, including said detective in "The Adventure of the Orient Express". You will also find traces of a very large New York City detective whose possible Holmes ancestry has been speculated upon. And of course, the stories are peppered with references to other unrecorded cases: Something Parker and Watson both did liberally, to readers' delight.

I am thrilled to see the much-neglected Pons featured in new adventures. The pen of Doctor Parker has been dormant for far too long. We can only hope that there will be more untold tales and that David Marcum will write them!

Bob Byrne
"The Extra-Terrestrial", *PSI*
August 2017
*www.solarpons.com*

# Pons is Back
## by Tracy Adam Heron

I never met August Derleth, having personally been placed into circulation when he was but six years from passing, but growing up in the same environs caused his writings to strike a deep chord. Echoing the words of the August Derleth Society (ADS) founder Richard Fawcett, *Walden West* is a book that "deeply affected my psyche."

Years served on the ADS board of directors heightened my awareness of Derleth's versatility as a writer and the intrigue of his broad appeal. Each board member had their own favorite genre and if you'll indulge me an understatement, the temperament of weird fiction devotees contrasted sharply with that of the *Sac Prairie Saga and Poetry* rabble.

My enjoyment of reading Derleth's books is sweetened by the quiet knowledge that so many more lie in front of me waiting to be read for the first time. Rue the day when that is no longer true; I will read slowly. A question posed itself often in my mind, *"Now that he's gone, who could possibly pick up where he left off . . . especially with those delectable Pons adventures?"*

The answer is elementary.

David Marcum is tracking fresh footprints in the dew-covered grass, in hot pursuit of Pons and Parker, just as Derleth himself pursued the legacy of Sir Arthur Conan Doyle's world famous detective. This decades-long relay is now handed securely to Marcum whose stories are as fresh as they are faithful. Pons fans have lamented for years that no more adventures are being offered. Now with the rare blessing of the Derleth estate, the wait is over and the game, again, is afoot.

Pons is back.

Tracy Adam Heron<br>
August Derleth Society<br>
*www.augustderleth.org*<br>
July, 2017

# On the Return of Solar Pons
## by Derrick Belanger

The first time I encountered a Solar Pons story was in a hardbound collection of mysteries from the 1940's and 1950's. Mixed in with the hardboiled detective stories of dames and hard drinking gum shoes was a traditional detective story, one that felt like an original Doyle story, yet did not involve Sherlock Holmes. More perplexing was the fact that the story was written by August Derleth, whose name I knew at the time solely as the savior of the Lovecraft mythos. How did a crafter of such weird fiction come to write such a traditional detective story? Were there more out there?

Fortunately, there were. Lots more. I did my research and learned that Derleth had penned at least sixty-seven original Pons stories (there's some debate on whether the count is higher), and that he had intended them to be pastiches. As a young man, he even wrote to Doyle asking if he could write new Sherlock Holmes stories, was denied by the Great One, and thus invented Solar Pons.

It is that denial by Sir Arthur which, I believe, led to the greatness of Solar Pons, the Sherlock Holmes of Praed Street. Here we have a pastiche which in many ways is not a pastiche. Pons is clearly based on Holmes, but he has his own unique cases and he solves them in his own unique way. Pons's biographer, Dr. Lyndon Parker, had spent time in the U.S., which helped explain why the Watsonian character would let slip with American terms and slang. We also have a bit of an expanded pastiche universe with a Fu Manchu character and a tribute to Christie's *Murder on the Orient Express*.

Sadly, while Doyle's Holmes has grown in popularity with hundreds of new stories published each year, Pons has largely been forgotten beyond his most diehard fans. With this new collection, Belanger Books and Arkham House hope to rectify this situation.

David Marcum has crafted this exceptional collection of twelve new tales of the Sherlock Holmes of Praed Street. The stories are pastiches in the Derleth tradition, and they solidify the Holmes/ Pons connection as the two detectives finally meet in one of Marcum's adventures.

If this collection is your first encounter with the Sherlock Homes of Praed Street, we hope you will seek out Derleth's original adventures and see for yourself their greatness. We also hope that this book is just the beginning of a Solar Pons revival and that more new Pons collections are forthcoming.

Thank you and the game is afoot!

Derrick Belanger
Publisher
July, 2017

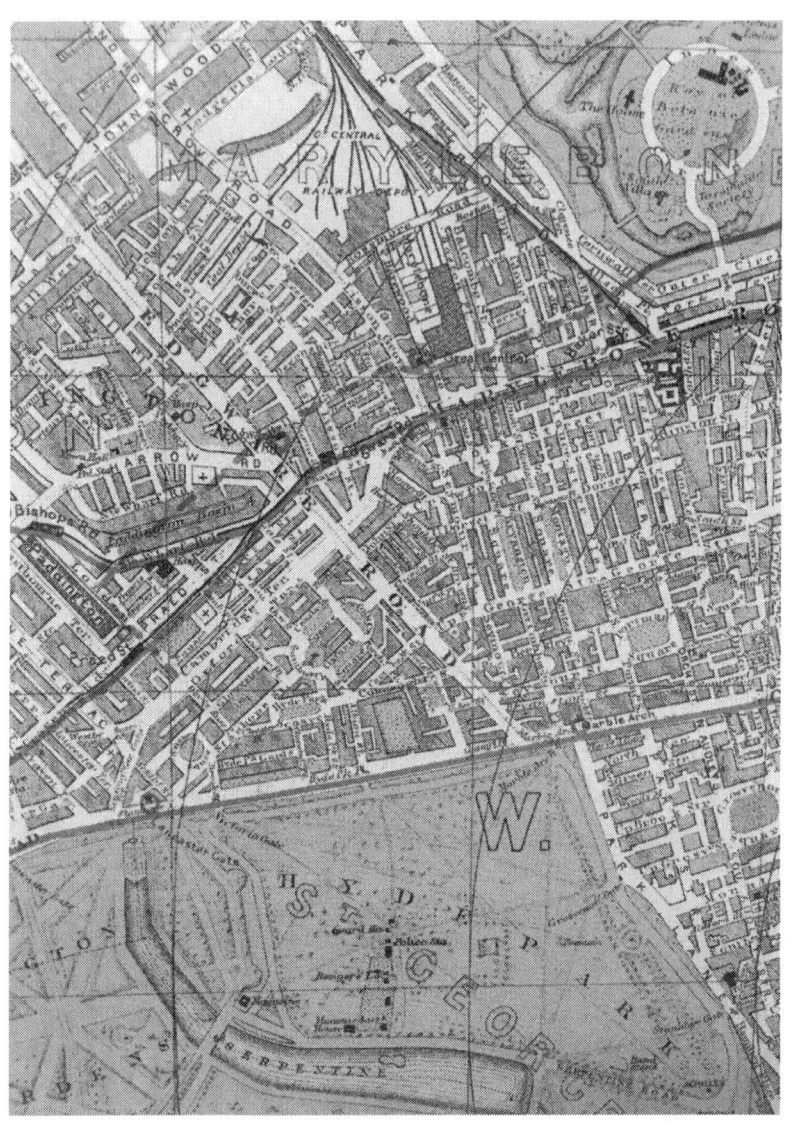

# The Papers of Solar Pons

**Pons, Solar**, born ca. 1880, in Prague. Son of Asenath Pons, consular official at Prague, and Roberta McIvor Pons; younger brother of Bancroft Stoneham, in His Majesty's Service. Public school education; Oxford *summa cum laude*, 1899. Unmarried. Member: Savile, Diogenes, Athanaeum, Cliff Dwellers, Lambs. Est. private inquiry practice at 7B Praed Street, 1907. British Intelligence, World War I, II. Monographs: *An Inquiry into the Nan-Matal Ruins of Ponape* (1905); *A Logical Approach to the Science of Ratiocination* (1917); *The Chess Problem and the State of the Mind* (1919); *The Inductive Process* (1921); *On the Value of Circumstantial Evidence* (1925); *An Examination of the Cthulhu Cult and Others* (1931). Widely traveled. Residences: New York, Chicago, Paris, Vienna, Prague, Rome, 7B Praed Street, London, W.2. Telephone: Ambassador 10000.

*From "The Beginnings of Solar Pons" by August Derleth,* A Praed Street Dossier *(1968).*

**Parker, Dr. (Cuthbert) Lyndon**, born ca. 1878, in Ramsgate, Kent, Third son of Charles Knightley Chetwode Parker, C.B., civil engineer, and Florence Mary Agatha Ramsden, eldest daughter of Rev. Dorance Simgrove Ramsden, D.D., M.A., Minor Canon of Rochester Cathedral and Perpetual Vicar of Shapcote Monachorum, Kent. Marriages: Louisa Parker *née* Skelton (1908-1912 – Louisa Parker died on the *S.S. Titanic*, 15 April 1912); Constance Parker *née* Dorrington (1933-    ). Education: Dover College; University College, London; Heidelberg University; Medical School, Columbia University, New York. M.R.C.P., London, 1897; M.R.C.S., London, 1898; B.Ch., London, 1899; M.D. Columbia, 1901. Employment: Principal Medical Officer, The Allegheny Sheet and Tube Corporation, 1901-03; Principal Resident Physician, Diseases of the Ear, Nose and Throat, Harrison's Hospital, Madison, Wisconsin, 1903-08; Medical Superintendent, Jefferson Institute for the Treatment of Paraplegia and Epilepsy, Auburn, New York, and Consulting Honorary Surgeon, Auburn Penitentiary, 1908-10; Principal Administrator, Mansura Royal Ophthalmic Hospital (1914-1915); Gazetted as $2^{nd}$ Lieutenant, Royal Army Medical Corps, January 1915. Served in various theatres of war, chiefly in the Middle East. Ended service as Brevet Colonel, R.A.M.C., 1919. Returned to London June 1919, resumed private medical practice. Honors: Order of St. Sava, $1^{st}$ Class (Serbia); Order of the Crown, $2^{nd}$ Class (Roumania); Order of Polonia Restituta, $3^{rd}$ Class, Order of the White Eagle, $4^{th}$ Class (Poland); Order of Liberation by Provisional Republic (Austria – Refused permission to accept by Inter-Allied War Commission). Publications: *Considerations of an Alternative Treatment for Ophthalia to the Recognized Treatment by Silver Nitrate* (*Journal of Ophthalmology*, November 1906-April 1907 and *The Lancet*, October 1908-March 1909); Investigative narratives in various journals (1929-    ). Residences: 7B Praed Street (1919-1933), South Norwood, London (1933-    ).

*Adapted from "(Cuthbert) Lyndon Parker" by Michael Harrison,* The Casebook of Solar Pons *(1965).*

# A Word From
# Dr. Lyndon Parker

"'Sherlock Holmes,'" the waiter said softly as he wiped the nearby tables. He had noticed my interest in the man who had just entered the pub. "That's who he is. 'The Sherlock Holmes of Praed Street' is what the papers call him. His real name's Solar Pons. Ain't much choice between the two, eh?

I had to agree, if only based upon the man's deerstalker hat and Inverness. The waiter moved on, but I continued to surreptitiously watch the fellow at the bar. He had entered just moments before and had taken time to speak to the barkeep before glancing idly around the room, relatively empty at this time of day. When I felt his gaze turning my way, I shifted my attention back to the envelope upon which I had been writing. However, something must have attracted his attention, for he stepped over and began to list out facts about me that were obvious to him, but would have been missed by everyone else. "Sherlock Holmes indeed," I thought. This, then, was my first meeting with Mr. Solar Pons.

We formed a tentative friendship that very afternoon. He recognized my dissatisfaction with the conditions I had found upon my recent return to England from Egypt, just two days before on the *Ishtar*. The things that I'd seen in the War had been terrible, and I'd returned to my homeland, hoping to find something, I suppose, of my lost youth - a *panacea* that might restore just a piece of my damaged innocence. What I had already seen of the capital, as I traipsed the streets looking for lodgings, had disappointed me, to put it mildly, and had nearly convinced me to make my way back to the docks and try somewhere else.

Pons recognized this in our first conversation, and I almost believe that he felt it his mission, at least initially, to show me that there was still some good in the world, and when evil was encountered, that it could be fought and defeated.

As I learned more about about him, and began to understand his work, I realized that he was the very man to do it.

He informed me that he was a private detective who embraced the methods of ratiocination and deduction. Over the next few months, as I got to know him better, I began to accompany him on his investigations, and then to take notes - first simple journal entries to record this or that statement of wisdom or philosophy upon some subject or other, and then narratives of greater length and depth for posterity and – I'll admit – also for publication, although that came years later.

Having very little to distract me in those early days, I was quite grateful for the opportunity to record his methods. He truly lived what he had described in terms of conducting investigations in the classic sense. In those days wherein scientific criminal detection was finally respected, based closely upon the work of Mr. Holmes of yesteryear, and where so many of those modern methods had begun to be adopted by the police, Pons understood that the close observation of trifles was still necessary, and often the best way to successfully solve a riddle – be it something that would simply eliminate a problem from someone's life, or perhaps it might be a more serious matter in which a criminal was revealed and punished.

Throughout those early days, and in fact through the years when Pons was in practice between the two great wars, I saw first-hand why he had initially been described to me as "The Sherlock Holmes of Praed Street". He consciously encouraged that association with the now-retired sleuth of Baker Street, both in his methods and dress, and his manners and his affectations. I could see that some clients came to him thinking that he *was* Sherlock Holmes. This often amused him, and he was quick to point out to them that Mr. Holmes, whom he referred to frequently as "The Master" or "My Illustrious Predecessor", was now rusticating as an apiarist in Sussex, but that he, Pons, would help as best he could. And the help he provided was of a most excellent quality indeed.

It was unavoidable that Pons's footsteps would occasionally cross paths with people and places that had been associated at some time in the past with Sherlock Holmes's cases. Pons had a long association with The Great Detective, and I knew that in each instance when he intersected with some aspect of Holmes's career, he was pleased to be able to touch a portion of this or that former investigation, much the same way that a modern pianist would thrill at being able to sit and play at one of Beethoven's own *pianofortes*.

I've occasionally referenced Sherlock Holmes in a few previously published narratives, but until this time, I've conscientiously avoided laying before the public some of those cases which had a more direct connection. However, in cleaning up my files, I've at last brought myself to select for this new volume several of those for public presentation, along with a few others that I've hoped to reveal for quite a while. I hope that readers will enjoy these chronicles, and that they will be appreciated as revealing a new facet to the character of my friend, "*The Sherlock Holmes of Praed Street*", Mr. Solar Pons.

Dr. Lyndon Parker, M.D.<br>London

# The Adventure of the Doctor's Box

I had seldom seen my friend, Mr. Solar Pons, rise to such great heights as he did in the spring of 1930. We had ranged far and wide in those months, and our many adventures included travel to Wales to investigate the terrible matter of the Aberystwith Prevention, and to Ripon in Yorkshire at the behest of an Earl whose eldest daughter was finally and tragically implicated, after many long years, in the seamy circumstances relating to the concealed death at the Abbey house of the son of a Turkish minister, back before the War. But I believe that what gave Pons the greatest satisfaction in the first half of that particular year was being able to retrieve the stolen property of an old and much missed friend.

On that particular morning, I paused in the entrance to the Edgware Road Station, pressed from behind by the early morning travelers anxious to exit and be about their business, while being dodged from the front by those in a hurry to reach their trains. I had spent the better part of the night called out on a confinement case. Now, returning home with the promise of one of Mrs. Johnson's hearty English breakfasts, I was momentarily stopped by my dread of stepping into the spring rain falling just outside the station. A heavy-set veteran stood in the entrance beside me, his empty sleeve pinned to his shoulder, and calling out "Brolly! Get your brolly!" in a hoarse voice. I must admit that I was sorely tempted. However, I did not have far to go, and I had no need of yet another spontaneously-purchased umbrella cluttering up an already cluttered sitting room. Finally, realizing that the only way to progress was to proceed, I dropped a few coins in the veteran's cup and accepted the necessity of walking the last few blocks to my familiar door. As I heard a murmured "Thanks, guv," I sighed, hunched my coat collar higher upon my neck, and made my way through the crowd and into the deluge. I immediately regretted not actually taking an umbrella a few moments before.

A few hurried steps down Chapel Road brought me to the Edgware Road corner, where I was luckily able to keep going forward, as traffic on either side was momentarily at a standstill. The wind was from the south, and the full spray pelted the left side of my face as I passed across the unprotected intersection. Then, reaching the Praed

Street side, I entered the shelter of the buildings, and the wind died around me almost immediately.

It was only a few more steps to No. 7, where I had shared lodgings with Mr. Solar Pons for over a decade, following my return to England after the War. I had joined my friend on a number of adventures over the years, and therefore it was no surprise for me to see a limousine parked in front of our door. At first I thought it had something to do with the recently-concluded matter of Mrs. Rowden, who, it will be recalled, was later hanged. Pons had worked closely on the matter with his friendly rival, the former Belgian policeman who had set himself up as a consulting detective following his immigration to England in 1916, and was now living in Whitehaven Mansions.

However, I soon realized that I was mistaken. The driver watched me carefully as I approached, and nodded as he recognized me, even as I recognized him as well. It was the regular chauffeur of Pons's brother, Bancroft, of His Majesty's Government.

Mrs. Johnson met me at the door, kindly helping me divest myself of my drenched overcoat. "Mr. Bancroft is upstairs," she said softly, not realizing that I had just seen his chariot outside. "And Inspector Jamison is with him as well."

I thanked her for the information, and then entreated her as to the possibility of obtaining some breakfast. Her smile changed to a scowl. "It was ready twenty minutes ago, but Mr. Pons told me to wait."

"I understand," I smiled with understanding. "Perhaps some coffee, then? To sustain me until our visitors depart?"

"There is already some upstairs," she replied, "but I'll see about warming up a fresh pot for you, Doctor. How was your case last night?"

"Successful," I replied. "Twins."

Mrs. Johnson made a joyous noise and said, "Oh, my," with a smile. Then, she turned toward the kitchen while I mounted the steps to our sitting room.

As I reached the upper landing, I heard Pons's voice from the other side of the closed door. "Come in, Parker, come in." Stepping inside, I found Pons in his usual armchair near the chemical table, while his much-heavier brother Bancroft sprawled upon the settee. Inspector Jamison, who had been seated in the basket chair centered in front of the fireplace, rose and turned to face me with a nod.

"Sit down, Parker, sit down by the fire," said Pons. "You look as if you are half frozen. One would never know that it is springtime in

London. However, the glass is going up, and I'm confident that the weather will be better as the day progresses."

"Coffee, Doctor?" asked Jamison, gesturing toward the pot on the dining table.

I shook my head. "Mrs. Johnson has indicated that she'll be bringing a fresh pot shortly."

"Excellent," said Pons, as Jamison returned to his seat, pushing his legs toward the fire. "Are the new mother and both babies doing well?"

I settled into my seat with a smile. "And how did you deduce that there were twins?"

"It was rather a long shot, I'll admit, but your air of weary satisfaction indicates that the delivery was successful. Although you did not mention the fact when you departed early this morning, I had observed that you loaded your medical bag with twice the normal supplies that you normally carry when delivering a baby. In addition, when you spoke on the telephone early this morning to the father, you commented on the fact that the due date was earlier than anticipated, but that this should have been expected when considered with the 'unusual circumstances,' as you phrased it, along with the mother's above-average weight gain. Finally, of course, there are the two cigars tucked into your coat pocket. A gift, no doubt, from the enthusiastic father. These facts, when taken together, tend to indicate a multiple birth, and a successful one at that."

I nodded. "To be savored at a later date," I said, tapping the cigars with a smile.

"If we might continue," said Bancroft, somewhat crossly. "Events in Ijmuiden are progressing rapidly, and I am needed elsewhere. I presume, brother, that you wish me to begin at the beginning for Dr. Parker's benefit?"

"If you do not mind," replied Pons. "You had barely begun your initial recitation of the facts before Parker's timely arrival, and hearing the problem presented a second time might suggest an additional line or two for our inquiry."

"Very well," said Bancroft. Turning his great brow in my direction, he stated, "Dr. Parker, the matter is a simple one, and yet it must be handled discreetly and quickly. It seems that the tin dispatch box which belonged to the late Dr. Watson has gone missing from its customary location in the Waterloo Place vaults of the old Cox and Company."

His mention of the box, as well as my dear friend Watson, instantly caught my attention. The old gentleman had passed away the previous July, nearly ten months earlier. Like everyone who knew him, we had somehow assumed that he would keep going forever.

"As you are no doubt aware," Bancroft continued, "the good doctor had kept his most incendiary remaining records in that box, which was a souvenir from his Afghan service. Following his injuries at Maiwand, fifty years ago this July, he returned to England with the box, a pension, shattered health, and not much else to his name.

"Over the last decade or so, following his service in the War, Watson had been in the habit of completing a number of manuscripts, expanding upon the notes he had made of hundreds of cases into more easily readable narratives. A number of these, related to the less sensitive matters, he gave away freely to the individuals that had been involved in the original investigations. Others have been stored in less secure locations. Lord knows just where all of Watson's notebooks will eventually turn up, or when, or how. But the original tin box he reserved for those matters which were deemed too sensitive, either by Sherlock Holmes or the government itself, to be given away or left untended.

"Last night, one of the watchmen in the bank building, James Burroughs, made his usual rounds through the public areas and down into the vaults. He is one of three men who are responsible for the building and its contents after hours. He left the main lobby to make his regular eleven p.m. pass through the vault area, checking in with the night supervisor, John Worth, before he left. When he did not return at the appointed time, the third watchman, Kevin Russell, was sent to see where he was."

Bancroft turned to Inspector Jamison, who had been sitting quietly in the basket chair, listening intently to the tale. "Inspector? Would you continue with Scotland Yard's subsequent participation?"

Jamison shifted in his seat. "A call came in by telephone at 11:25 p.m., explaining that there had been an assault and possible robbery at the Waterloo Place offices of Lloyd's, formerly Cox and Company. We - "

"Excuse me," said Pons. "I wondered about this earlier. You stated that the call indicated that the robbery was at the Waterloo Place offices. It was my understanding that the Doctor's tin dispatch box was always kept at the old Charing Cross offices of Cox and Company, at 16 Charing Cross Road."

"Really," I said. "I had always assumed that it was in the Cox and Company branch on the Strand, just east of Charing Cross Station. Was I mistaken?"

"Actually, neither of you is correct," replied Bancroft. "Initially the box was kept at the small branch tucked into Craig's Court, off Whitehall near Trafalgar Square. But the doctor indiscreetly mentioned the box's existence in one of his publications eight or nine years ago – "

"Eight, I believe," said Pons. "In 'The Problem of Thor Bridge' as I recall."

Bancroft nodded and continued. " – and it was decided to move the box and its contents to the larger and more secure offices in Waterloo Place, around the time of Cox and Company's absorption into Lloyds. Watson was in complete agreement with our decision at the time."

"Thank you," said Pons. "Pray continue, Inspector."

"Officers arrived on the scene soon after the initial telephone call and determined that the watchman, Burroughs, had been found unconscious on the floor, next to the iron door that led into the section of vaults where the Doctor's box is kept."

"Did he have any sort of wound to explain his unconsciousness?" I asked.

"There was a lump on the back of his head," said Jamison. "He recovered within a few moments of our arrival, slightly nauseated, but with no other signs of distress. Upon questioning, Burroughs indicated that he had no idea how he had been attacked. He recalls seeing a light coming from the gate leading to that particular vault. He has no memory of the attack, or what happened after that, until he awoke."

"Not uncommon with a head injury," I said. "Often the memory is completely blank for minutes or even hours prior to the incident. Sometimes, but not always, the lost memories will return at a later time."

Bancroft nodded and continued. "Officials of the bank were summoned, and a subsequent inventory of the vault contents revealed that nothing was missing – except for the tin dispatch box."

"Of the three watchmen working that night, who had keys to the vault?" asked Pons.

"None of them," replied Jamison. "Two of the three directors have keys that they keep with them, and the only available set kept on the premises is locked in a safe in the Head Teller's office, and he does not have the combination. Only the two directors with keys have it, and at least one of them must be present each day that the bank is open if that safe is required to be unlocked."

"Why only two directors?" asked Pons. "Why not the third?"

Jamison answered, "The oldest director, Sir Clive Damory, is somewhat enfeebled due to age, and no longer has keys or takes any active participation in the day-to-day activities at the bank. In fact, he is permanently bedridden, and even though we initially sent a message to his home, not knowing his condition, his staff refused to wake him, explaining that he was unable to provide any assistance."

"And his keys?" asked Pons. "What became of them? Were they returned to the bank?"

"They have been in the locked safe in the Head Teller's office since his illness began, along with other keys related to the bank's operation, including the vault keys. We have verified that they are still there."

"After the discovery of the assault and the open vault door," Bancroft continued, "messages were sent to the two active directors. They live within short distances of the bank, and both arrived in short order, within a few minutes of receiving their messages."

"And the other directors are – " asked Pons.

"Milton Gallagher and Sir Phillip Morton. Word reached Sir Phillip at his club, and Mr. Gallagher had just returned home from a banquet, where he had been all evening with his wife," Jamison responded.

"Gallagher's alibi?" asked Pons."

"Unimpeachable," replied Bancroft. "He was seen continuously by over three-hundred guests for periods of time both before and after the robbery was taking place."

"Milton Gallagher?" I interjected. "The industrialist?"

"Correct," replied Bancroft. "Following his return a few years ago to this country from South America, after a couple of decades abroad, he married a young heiress and began to make himself known in earnest. He now sits as director on several boards, but his primary interest is with the Cox and Company branch of Lloyds."

"When did he take that position?" asked Pons. "I seem to recall that Lloyds took over Cox and Company in 1923, when they were hemorrhaging millions."

"Actually, by the time Lloyds took over, Cox and Company was already Cox and King's, following Cox's acquisition of the Henry S. King firm the previous fall. By absorbing Cox's, Lloyds gained the branches in India, Burma, and Egypt that Cox's had earlier gained from King's.

"Sir Phillip was with Cox's at the time of the take-over, while Milton Gallagher has only recently hitched his wagon to Lloyds, in late 1928. Gallagher was given the ongoing task of righting the affairs of the former Cox branches."

At that moment, Mrs. Johnson came in with a fresh pot of coffee. She filled a cup for me, and offered refills to the other men. Pons and Bancroft refused, while Jamison accepted and settled back with a satisfied sigh.

Pons, who had been sitting with his long fingers templed before his face, leaned back in his seat, and tugged on his ear. "I take it, brother, that you have not been to the bank."

"Correct. My shoes?"

"Of course."

Jamison, who had heard this type of thing nearly as much as I, sat up. "Shoes? I don't understand."

Pons smiled. "Parker?" he said. "Care to have a go at it?"

I thought for a moment, glancing at Bancroft's footwear. Then, shifting my eyes to Jamison's feet, I understood. "The missing water stains?" I asked.

Pons laughed and clapped his hands. "Bravo, Parker. You really are coming along. Explain to the good Inspector."

Taking a sip of coffee, I arranged my thoughts, and then said, "Your shoes, Inspector, have several sets of recently dried watermarks from today's rain, at different levels and degrees of darkness upon the leather." I gestured toward his legs, with his feet stretched toward the fire. "There is a wetter, darker line near the sole, and then lighter marks higher up, which must have occurred at different times. My own shoes show these as well. Mr. Pons's shoes," I said, indicating Bancroft's highly-polished pumps, "only display the slightest indication of water stains, really only light spotting across the polish.

"The Cox and Company building in Waterloo Place has no awning or *porte cochere*, and the building is set back nearly twenty feet from the street. Crossing the wet pavement at the bank, and then again here in Praed Street, would have left several water patterns reflected on your shoes, while the few spots indicate only one stop out in the open, presumably here." I realized a fallacy in my argument, and added, "Of course, you should have had two sets of water stains on your shoes, receiving the first while climbing into your automobile to travel here. May I assume then that you came from your office in Whitehall where there is a *porte cochere*?"

"You may," replied Bancroft. "Well done. You have an apt pupil here, brother."

Pons nodded, and then sat silently for a moment, before asking, "What of my Illustrious Predecessor in Sussex? Has he been informed? Will he join us in the search for the box?"

Bancroft shook his head. "He is out of the country at present. State business. It is up to you."

Pons appeared to be on the verge of asking another question, when there was the sound of the front doorbell ringing. In a moment, the sound of a big man climbing the steps was heard. A knock was followed by the entry of a constable, who wordlessly handed a sheet of paper to Inspector Jamison.

Reading it quickly, he stood and looked at each of us. "The tin dispatch box has been found, where it was hidden in Gallagher's private office. Empty," he added, "of course."

Pons sprang to his feet, moving toward his bedroom, even as he shrugged out of his dressing gown. "Parker, will you be able to soldier on for a little longer without breakfast?" he asked, disappearing into the other room.

As Bancroft Pons struggled to his feet, I replied in the affirmative, although without enthusiasm. As Pons returned to the sitting room, Jamison and Bancroft began putting on their overcoats. I let Mrs. Johnson know that I would not be eating after all, and retrieved my own damp overcoat from its peg, drawing it on as well.

"I will not be joining you," Bancroft stated as Pons held open the door to the stairway landing. "I have other urgent matters requiring my attention, and I leave the affair entirely in your hands. Let me know of anything that I can provide for you."

"A list of the particular cases that were still in the tin dispatch box would be helpful," said Pons. "If such a thing exists."

"I will have a messenger bring it to the bank posthaste," replied Bancroft.

Then we departed, Bancroft Pons climbing into his limousine and stating to the driver to make for Whitehall, while Pons, Jamison, and myself joined the constable in a waiting police vehicle.

As we made our way across London, heading for Waterloo Place, I thought more about Watson's passing the previous summer.

In mid-July 1929, Pons and I had been asked to accompany Pons's mentor, Sherlock Holmes, whom Pons often referred to simply as "The Master," in something of a rescue mission to Zagreb, in the Balkans. While specific details of this matter which must remain secret until later in this century at the earliest, after the passing of the individuals involved, I can say that it involved Pons's cousin, who normally worked in New York as a private detective while living as an eccentric semi-recluse under an outrageous *nom-de-plume* akin to "The Black Wolf" – a name that he had assumed following his adventures in the War. (On a related note, in communications from his cousin, Pons was referred to inexplicably as "Hitchcock".)

At some point in the past, during his post-War Continental travels, Pons's cousin had adopted a young girl named Anna who had remained in Europe, and had subsequently gone missing. Pons's cousin had left his home in New York and traveled to Zabreb to search for the girl, and had quickly been jailed by the ruling family, who apparently had something of a grudge against him.

Somewhat against his better judgment, Holmes had allowed Watson to accompany us. Although he was in his late seventies at that time, Watson was still a hearty and hale fellow, and the trip itself had seemed to pose no threat to his health, in spite of the possible physical dangers that we faced. I believe that the prospect of accompanying his old friend on one more investigation had thrilled the old fellow.

Although the mission was a complete success, Watson became ill with pneumonia on the return journey. Upon our arrival in England, Watson traveled on to Holmes's Sussex farm near the cliff of Beachy Head, instead of returning to his own London home. Pons and I had accompanied them there, my self-appointed duty being to care for our old friend. Nevertheless, after we had settled in, Watson's condition worsened, and he died peacefully a few days later.

Holmes, like Pons, was never one to reveal many of his emotions, but one could easily see that the passing of his oldest friend hit the fellow hard. No doubt he blamed himself for allowing Watson to accompany us on the journey. However, we all knew that Watson had lived a long and full life, and his funeral was as much a celebration as it was a sorrowful event.

My thoughts were pulled back to the present as the automobile turned a corner rather quickly. We made our way down Edgware Road to Marble Arch, and then Oxford Street to Regent Street, and so on until we arrived at our destination. The bank, a great white edifice, was set back slightly from the street, the words "Cox & Co." still cut into the stone over the door.

As we climbed out of the automobile, Jamison said, "I've kept the watchmen here."

"All night?" asked Pons, pausing on the sidewalk. I noticed that the rains had stopped, and there was a significant break in the clouds to the south. A constable posted by the door did not so much as waste a glance our way. "And what of the directors?"

"Just the watchmen," replied Jamison. "Of course, Sir Clive wasn't here at all, and the other two directors went home an hour or so after they were summoned, returning here again later this morning."

"I hope," I said, "that the injured watchman, Burroughs, received medical attention."

"He did, Dr. Parker, I assure you. And we didn't start questioning him until we were certain that he could take it."

As a medical man, that sounded less than satisfactory to me, but I decided to hold my tongue until I could make an examination and ascertain Burroughs's condition for myself.

Pons turned and led us toward the door. Stepping inside, I found myself blind for a moment. Even the gloomy day outside was brighter than the inside of the venerable financial institution. It took a moment for my eyes to adjust, but I was aware that Pons, who had the uncanny ability to see in situations of low light, was already progressing across the floor.

Jamison, apparently as incapacitated as I was, paused beside me for a moment. Then, when shapes and objects became somewhat clearer, we both moved to follow Pons, who was walking briskly toward a door at the rear of the room, bracketed by two constables, obviously our destination.

He said a word or two before we arrived, and they parted to let him through. We followed and found ourselves in a long hallway extending toward the back of the building. Jamison moved to place himself beside Pons, who turned and said simply, "The vault?"

Jamison moved to the left, and turned this way and that until he reached a plain concrete staircase descending into the lower levels of the building. After several twists, we reached a long hallway, the low lighting reflecting dully off the concrete floors. Ahead, a constable stood next to our obvious destination, with its door standing slightly ajar, unlike the other secured chambers on either side.

Pons motioned for us to stay back, muttering something about how there had already been a stampede in the hallway before he was even able to make an examination. Bent low, and making his way around the stolid constable, he approached the vault door, holding his lens this way and that, and orating a series of low mutterings to himself as he did so. Reaching the vault itself, he took several long moments to examine the lock of the massive gated doorway.

Each vault along the hallway was in fact a cell, resembling something from a prison, rather than a sealed strong-room. In each of the closed chambers around us, we could see various crates, cartons, and files stacked well back from the bars lining the hall. I mentally questioned the security of such an arrangement, but kept my thoughts to myself.

I became aware that Pons had stepped into the actual open vault. Taking a chance and moving forward, I bent to look at the keyhole that he had recently examined. I was still doing so when he joined me.

"No hint of lubricating oil, and no scratches, eh, Parker?"

"None indeed," I replied softly. "One of the keys, then?"

"Most likely." Raising his voice somewhat, he spoke to Jamison, still by the foot of the steps. "May we speak to the watchmen now?"

With a nod, Jamison led us back upstairs, and on a roundabout path to a room in the back of the building. Stepping in, I noticed a number of lockers along the wall, and a small setup at the side of the room for making tea.

Seated around a scuffed table were three men, obviously from their uniforms the ill-fated night watchmen. Standing along the walls were two more constables.

One of them, which I assumed to be Burroughs, was seated on the far right, a bandage on his head. From the way that he leaned his head on his hand, he appeared to be dozing. I stepped around the table and awakened him, introducing myself as a doctor and offering to examine his injury. Without a word, he allowed me to unwind the bandage, which turned out to be completely unnecessary, as there was no blood. The skin over the contusion was unbroken, and even though I could tell that my examination was somewhat painful, there was no indication of any permanent injury. Leaving the bandage off, I squeezed Burroughs's shoulder and rejoined my companions. Pons was speaking.

"Mr. Worth, was there anything unusual about last night, up until the time Mr. Burroughs did not return from his rounds?"

"Not at all, sir. It was as routine a night as you could have wished for."

"Do you agree, Mr. Russell?"

"Completely, completely," he replied, with a slight Irish brogue. He was a small fellow in his twenties, younger than either Worth or Burroughs, who were both in their forties.

"Is it normally Mr. Burroughs's responsibility to check the vaults each night?"

Burroughs lifted his eyes, as if Pons were leading to some sort of implied accusation of guilt, but before he could interject, Russell stated, "No, not at all. We take turns. Keeps us fresh, you know.

Jimmy went on the eleven o'clock circuit, and I stayed in the main area with Mr. Worth."

"The entire time?" asked Pons.

"Yes," answered Worth. "We had all been talking in the few minutes leading up to eleven. Then, Jimmy - that is, Mr. Burroughs - rose and went on the rounds. Mr. Russell and I continued our discussion, until we realized that Mr. Burroughs was overdue. At that point, Mr. Russell offered to go see if he was all right. It was just a very few minutes later that he came running back, telling me to get help."

"And that is when you telephoned?"

"That is correct, sir."

"The police records show that you did not call until 11:25. Isn't that a rather long time for Mr. Burroughs to be gone on his rounds."

Worth seemed to hesitate for a moment, and Russell intervened. "That was my fault. We started talking about the Australians coming for the Test Match next month, and time got away from us. Jimmy should have been back by a quarter past, but it came and went before we realized that he hadn't returned."

Pons nodded for a moment, and pinched his lip. Then, he said, "Mr. Burroughs, what was your experience? Do you have any idea who attacked you?"

The injured man shook his head and then winced, having forgotten the knot on the back of his head. "Not a thing, sir. I made the usual rounds through the ground floor to the back of the building, checking a few doors, and then making my way to the vaults. At the bottom of the stairs, I remember seeing a light ahead of me that shouldn't have been there, but after that, it is all a blank. I don't remember anything else until Kevin was helping me to sit up at the vault door."

"Quite. I understand from Dr. Parker that it is not unusual for such memory loss to occur in relation to a head injury, although occasionally the memories do return. You will be sure to let us know if you remember anything else, won't you?"

Burroughs nodded carefully.

"Mr. Worth, is it normal that Mr. Burroughs only made his rounds throughout the ground floor and the vault, and that he didn't go upstairs to where I presume the offices are located?"

"Perfectly, sir," replied Worth. "We make a pass or two upstairs throughout the night, but not as often or as regular as we do downstairs, in the vaults."

Pons turned toward Jamison and myself and lowered his voice. "I believe that these men may be allowed to return to their homes. I assume that they have been searched?"

Jamison nodded. "And the rest of the building?" Pons continued. "Any signs of the missing papers from the tin box?"

"Not a thing," said Jamison softly. "The tin box itself was discovered during the routine search of Gallagher's office, but no papers whatsoever. We had initially spent our time searching the vaults and the ground floor. We had only gotten around to searching upstairs after nothing was found below. That's why word only came to us about the tin box being found while we were still in your rooms.

"And," Jamison added significantly, "there is no sign of any papers having been burned either. The char-women were in and out between six and eight p.m., and cleaned the office fireplaces then. There was nothing freshly burned in any of the grates after that time, and the building is heated with gas. Somehow, the papers have been removed from the building."

"May I see a log of when the bank employees departed?" asked Pons. "Is such a thing maintained?" He turned toward the three watchmen. "Mr. Worth? Is there a log of when the employees depart for the day?"

"Yes, sir. It will be at my desk."

"Excellent. Jamison?"

"Right away," said Jamison, whispering to a constable, who departed from the room.

"The three of you may leave," said Pons. "But please remain at home today in case we have any further questions for you."

As the watchmen left the room, the constable returned, slipping in between the departing Burroughs and Russell. He held out a leather-bound volume, similar to an accounting journal. Pons took it and flipped quickly to the last entry, showing the arrival of employees that morning. Turning back one page, he scanned the entries where each employee's arrival and departure times from the previous day were noted. Then, he looked back on a random sampling of older pages, before stating, "They are very meticulous indeed. There are no obvious instances of any employees signing into the building and then not signing out. Each name is accounted for." He handed the book to me. "Do you see the curious anomaly, Parker?"

I took the book, and looked at some of the pages, including that of the previous day. Jamison pressed beside me, glancing at the entries as well. As Pons had said, each employee that had arrived at work on a particular day was then shown to leave that day. There were no inconsistencies."

"Every employee who is listed as coming in is also listed as departing."

"Exactly, Parker. That is the curious anomaly."

Closing the book, I handed it back to Jamison. Our eyes met and shared a silent glint of amusement at our friend's mysterious ways.

"And now," said Pons, "I should like to speak to the directors. Is there any point in speaking to Sir Clive?"

"No, sir," replied Jamison, "I was being kind earlier when I stated that he is essentially bed-ridden. In fact, he really has no awareness of the world around him at all, and he has no significant connection with the bank any longer. I am informed that there will be a reshuffling of directors at some point in the future to replace him, although there has been no pressing necessity up to this time. As the bank is part of Lloyd's, the directors at this location are more like daily managers than full-fledged directors in the old sense."

As Jamison led us back through the building, we were met at a turning of one of the hallways by a solemn man whom I recognized as one of Bancroft Pons's agents. Reaching into his coat, he removed a folded sheet of heavy bond, which he handed to Pons. Reading through it quickly, Pons made a sound which might either indicate interest or dismissal, and handed the paper to me. I held it so that Jamison could read it as well, while Pons pulled his notebook from his pocket and began to write.

The document, in Bancroft Pons's neat and anonymous fist, was simply a short list of the cases which still remained in the tin dispatch box. Among those given were some I recognized, and others that I did not. "James Phillimore" and "Isadora Persano" were named, along with "Some Notes on the Ripper Affair", "Dreyfus", "The Other Brother", and "The Eye of Heka". There were ten or twelve others, concluding with "The Cutter *Alicia*" and "The Politician, the Lighthouse, and the Trained Cormorant".

Jamison jabbed a finger under the reference to the Ripper. "I'll bet it's that," he said softly, with a touch of awe in his voice. "I'd give a month's pay to read the truth about that one. What do you think, Mr. Pons?"

Pons finished his note, tore it loose and folded it, and handed it to the messenger. "Some additional questions for my brother, if you please, Wilbanks." The man gave a nod and departed. Then, without answering Jamison's question, he said, "Onward to the directors, if you please."

We went up an elaborate stairway, lit on one side by tall windows. I could see that the earlier rain clouds had completely dissipated, revealing a bright blue spring day. The thick carpet muffled our footsteps. At the top, a man in livery opened the door, allowing us entrance into a luxurious suite of offices.

Jamison gestured for us to precede him into a large well-appointed room. Seated behind the desk was a big man with a large head and a lion-like mane of steel-gray hair. This, I knew from seeing numerous photographs in newspapers and periodicals, was Milton Gallagher. Seated across from him was a smaller fellow, looking pale and somewhat ill. I deduced that he was Sir Phillip Morton, the third director. Across the room, watched by yet another constable, was a box, sitting on a table underneath a tall window.

I crossed the room toward the item in question, noticing that a cloth of some sort had been tossed across the table top to protect its beautifully unmarred finish from the box's rough metal. I touched the lid, almost reverently, reading on top:

## *John H. Watson, M. D.*
## *Late Indian Army*

As I raised the lid, noting that the contents were indeed missing, Pons joined me. Quietly, he said, "Notice the lock, Parker."

Lowering the lid, I bent to see what he meant. The small padlock was hanging from the metal loop, snapped shut. The hasp was not fastened behind it. Unless the lock was to be unlocked and removed, the hasp could not be replaced to completely close and secure the box.

Pons leaned down to sniff the lock's keyhole. "Nothing. The same as on the vault lock. No new oil. No scratches. Someone had a key for this lock as well," he whispered. "And the thief carefully snapped the lock closed, almost respectfully, when he had removed the contents of the box." Raising his voice, he called Jamison over.

"Who has keys for this lock?"

"Why, I understand that one is kept at your brother's office. And Mr. Holmes has Dr. Watson's old key."

"And there is one here at the bank, as well," said a strong voice from across the room. "In the Head Teller's safe." Looking up, I saw that Milton Gallagher was sitting upright in his tall leather chair, watching us intently like a hawk. Across from him, Sir Phillip was slumped, his head resting on his propped arm, darting glances at us and then looking away.

"Indeed," said Pons. "And the reason?"

"Why, I believe that it was at the request of your brother's department," replied Gallagher. "In case one of the other keys was lost, where better to secrete the spare than at a bank?"

Pons's eyes narrowed, but he did not immediately reply. Then, he turned to Jamison. "Has anyone checked to see if the key to the dispatch box lock is still on the premises?"

Jamison seemed chagrined. "Not yet. I'll see to it now." He stepped to the side of the room and spoke softly to a constable, who quickly departed.

As this was taking place, Pons stepped over to the desk where the two men sat. "Mr. Gallagher," he said, "do you have any theory as to how the tin dispatch box ended up in your office?"

"None whatsoever," replied the powerful man. There was something about him that was barely suppressed, like a great running machine that was disconnected from its work. "I only returned an hour or so ago, after being here late last night. In my absence, the building had been thoroughly searched, this floor apparently last, and the dispatch box was discovered behind that sofa over there." He gestured toward the shelves on the right, blocked by the conservative and rather uncomfortable looking brown couch.

"About last night," said Pons. "I understand that you were summoned to bank not long after you arrived home from a banquet."

"That is correct. My wife and I had been to a dinner honoring a German diplomat, one of those chaps doing some work to secure credit to rebuild their roads and bridges. My wife is quite involved in these foreign causes, you understand, and it was felt that our presence there would help add to the overall success of the evening.

"We had barely been home for fifteen minutes, just enough time to start my second tipple of brandy, when a policeman requested my presence at the bank. I said good night to my wife and rushed over here."

"With the policeman?" asked Pons.

"No, I had my man get the car back out. I did not see the necessity of riding in a police vehicle, no matter what the emergency."

"I see," said Pons, with an infinitesimal flash of amusement in his gray eyes. "And how long were you here last night?"

"Not more than an hour, I suppose. Long enough to answer questions about what was missing. Long enough to determine that all that the thief had wanted was the box."

"You keep a list of the contents of the vaults?"

"Yes, and particularly *that* vault. Government secrets, you know. Sir Phillip here maintains those lists."

Pons turned toward the man in the chair on the opposite side of the desk. Sir Phillip shifted slightly, sat upright, facing Pons. He cut his eyes toward Gallagher, as if the mere mention of his name by the man was some sort of betrayal.

"We have several items in the vault in question which, although under the protection and interest of the government, are also owned by private individuals that have a right to maintain access to them."

"And you are the director responsible for them?"

"We - that is, all three of us - are responsible for them," said Sir Phillip. "But of the current directors, not counting Sir Clive, who is no longer active in bank affairs, I have been here the longest. For over ten years, actually, well before Lloyds took over, so I am most familiar with the vault's contents."

"And has anything like this ever happened before? Specifically, have there ever been any other attempts to get at Doctor Watson's papers?"

"Possibly. In 1927, there was a break-in at the small office Craig's Court location, which provided services to ex-military men, and where the Doctor's box was originally kept. At the time, Mr. Holmes and the Doctor were satisfied that someone was trying to get at and destroy the papers, not realizing that they had long-since been moved here. After the doctor published a somewhat indiscreet reference to the box in one of his cases several years ago, we - that is, the government and the directors at the time, as you were not with us yet, Mr. Gallagher. Sir Terrill was still alive then - determined that the box should be placed in a more secure location."

Pons took a step back, so that he could face both directors. "I understand that you both live fairly close to the bank," he said, "so that you were able to be here quickly after you were summoned."

"That is correct," said Gallagher. "I live on Charles Street, near Berkeley Square, although my wife wishes for us to move away from London. And Sir Phillip, here, lives in St. James Street."

"Yes," agreed Sir Phillip. "My wife died a number of years ago, and we had no children. Eventually I chose to live in a suite of rooms at my club. It has been a satisfactory arrangement for me."

"I see. And was it any inconvenience to return last night when you received the summons?"

"None at all. I had stepped out for a breath of fresh air, and when I returned, I received a message that I was required at the bank. I made my way over here as quickly as possible."

At that moment, the door opened, and Bancroft's agent, Wilbanks, stepped in and murmured something to Pons, who nodded in reply. Turning back to the directors, he stated, "I appreciate your assistance in this matter, and I expect to have news for you shortly. In the meantime, may I assume that you will remain here at the bank?"

Gallagher nodded. "I had planned to take care of some things today, regardless of last night's events. And you, Sir Phillip?"

Sir Phillip nodded, and ran a hand over his hair, patting the thin strands into place. "Yes," he said. "Yes, I will be here as well."

Pons nodded and turned toward the door, followed by Jamison and myself. Stepping into the hall, we discovered Bancroft Pons standing with an expression of irritation on his face. As Jamison pulled the heavy door shut, Bancroft started to speak, but Jamison's constable returned at that moment. "The key to the box's lock is not in the safe," he rumbled.

Pons nodded. "As I expected." Turning to his brother, he said. "You are just in time."

Bancroft replied softly, "As requested, I have returned. Am I to assume that you have news?"

"Possibly," said Pons. "But first, do you have the answers to my questions?"

"Of course," said Bancroft, handing a couple of sheets of paper to my friend.

After a moment of study, Pons asked, "Have they been under observation since their departures this morning?"

"Of course," said Bancroft. "Both returned to their homes after leaving the bank, and did not leave again until returning later this morning. Each came directly here, where they have remained since that time."

"And no visitors?"

"No visitors," replied Bancroft.

"What about Sir Clive? Is he truly a non-factor in this affair?"

"If anything, I have since determined that his condition is even worse than we first believed. His family provides round-the-clock care for him, but he is bed-ridden, and not expected to survive until summer. His directorship at the bank has been allowed to continue simply because there has been no need to replace him, as the directors here are somewhat second-tier, if you catch my meaning.

This bank, which was taken over by Lloyds, has directors that have been allowed a certain amount of authority, but all important matters are ultimately decided by their masters at the main institution."

"Did you bring the warrants?"

Bancroft patted his coat. "For whichever you determine is needed."

"Quicker than I had dared to hope," said Pons.

"My *own* Illustrious Predecessor," said Bancroft with satisfaction, "managed to set a system in place that can function with amazing speed when required. We have a process for something like this. Shall we go?"

"By all means," said Pons, turning toward the stairs.

I glanced at Jamison, and could see that he looked as lost as I felt. However, years of assisting Pons in his investigations had given me the sure confidence to understand that a solution – and a successful one at that – was within sight.

Bancroft's limousine was waiting out front, and we quickly climbed in. I began to have a dim view of what was happening, and I waited anxiously to see our destination. I was only somewhat surprised when we made a sharp turn to the south, around the Crimean War Memorial, and then west into Pall Mall. Past the Athenaeum, the Army and Navy, and the Diogenes Club we sped, quickly turning into St. James Street. There, a number of police cars were waiting in front of a nondescript club. Some of the members crowded into the bow window, looking out with mixed disdain and alarm.

As we stopped, several constables moved to join our vehicle. Standing at a distance behind them, I saw and acknowledged our old acquaintance Inspector Japp, as well as my cousin, Chief Inspector Charles Parker. He greeted me with a nod. Pons and I stood waiting while Bancroft struggled out of the vehicle. My friend directed my attention to the bow window and the curious onlookers. "That's Langdale Pike's old dominion," he stated softly. "What he wouldn't have given to hear this story."

With everyone now assembled on the pavement, we quickly entered the building, and Bancroft Pons moved to the front of our group, placing a warrant in the hands of the speechless man attempting to block our way. Then, crowding into an ancient lift, we rode to the first floor. One of the constables led us around a corner and to a door, guarded by a second officer. "Open it up," said Bancroft. The constable by the door produced a key, and in moments we were inside.

The search was quickly accomplished. While Pons and his brother simply stood and watched, the policemen fanned out. I gave a desultory look on a few shelves and behind a settee, but it was Jamison who announced success.

On the desk, barely hidden under a pile of loose documents and newspapers, he had discovered a series of journals and other related ephemera, some quite yellow with age. He picked them up and shuffled through them, pulling out one in particular. "'The Ripper Affair' " he read aloud, looking as if he would dearly like to untie the red ribbon that bound the thick file.

Pons stepped to the desk and took the stack of papers out of Jamison's disappointed hands. He took out his list and flipped through the items, checking them off until he made a satisfied noise while pulling out a thin packet. "The notes relating to the Politician," he said, meeting Bancroft's gaze. Opening it, he quickly scanned the pages with satisfaction. "It all seems to be here."

"Excellent," said Bancroft, moving toward the telephone. After giving the operator a number, he waited for a moment, gave a few quiet and sibilant instructions, and turned away. "He is being arrested now," he said. "I'm having him brought to Praed Street. I thought that we could question him there just as easily as anywhere."

"A splendid idea!" said Pons. "And now perhaps Parker can convince Mrs. Johnson to make him some delayed but well-earned breakfast."

He turned back toward the desk, looking at it for a moment while tugging the lobe of his ear. Then, he moved his hand into the mound of papers there and plucked out a small shiny object. "The missing lock box key," he announced. "The man was either certain that he would not be suspected, or he simply isn't very good at this sort of thing."

"Both," said Jamison shortly.

Back in Praed Street, our automobile pulled to the curb immediately behind a police vehicle. As we climbed out, Milton Gallagher exited from the front next to the driver, looking around angrily until he spotted Inspector Jamison.

"I demand to know the meaning of this!" he cried, taking a step toward us. Emerging more slowly from the back of the car was Sir Phillip Morton, his hands hidden by a draped overcoat, apparently to cover the manacles linking his wrists.

"The fault is mine, I fear," said Bancroft Pons, taking a step to place himself between the wealthy director and the inspector. "I wished for your presence in order for you to listen to Sir Phillip's explanation, and perhaps I was not entirely clear when I gave the instructions to have you brought here. And I believe," he added, "that, while you are not complicit in this particular matter, there are some aspects of what has happened that might serve as something of a warning for you in the future."

"Why, I will not be – " he began, but Bancroft Pons had turned away from him and was crossing the pavement to the front door of No.7.

Inside, Pons pulled me back and asked softly with a smile, "Breakfast first, Parker?" but I simply shook my head and motioned for him to proceed ahead of me up the stairs.

In the sitting room, Pons and I found our usual seats, joined by Bancroft and Jamison, who sat where they had been an hour or so earlier. Sir Phillip was in a chair pulled over from the dining table, while Milton Gallagher made do on the settee with Bancroft, muttering to himself about being forced to ride in a police conveyance. A constable stood by the door, until Bancroft motioned him over, saying, "I think that we can dispense with these." He pointed at Sir Phillip's handcuffs, now revealed by the removal of the man's overcoat.

Mrs. Johnson brought fresh coffee, and I rose and made myself useful before settling back as Pons began to speak to Sir Phillip.

"By now," he said, "you realize that the papers have been found in your rooms. Your attempt to frame Mr. Gallagher by clumsily leaving the tin dispatch box in his office really accomplished nothing, save to serve as another indicator of your involvement in this affair."

Sir Phillip hung his head, offering no response, while Pons continued. "From the time that the crime was described to me, I suspected that it was an inside job, as they say. The fact that the watchman was attacked as he made his rounds, while nothing else out of the ordinary that night had occurred, led me to believe that someone connected with the bank knew specifically what was to be taken from the vault, and the best way to go about it.

"When we arrived downstairs, it was obvious that there was no sign of any forced entry upon the vault gate, and no damage whatsoever to the lock, suggesting that a key was used. Again, this reinforced my idea that the theft was carried out by an insider. Subsequently, we learned that the only keys to the vault were either in the safe, where that one remains, or those belonging to two of the directors.

"Of course, the ideal plan would have been for the documents in question to have been taken from the dispatch box, which would then have been relocked. The key to its lock would have been returned to the safe, and the dispatch box left in the vault. The vault door would have been relocked, and no one would have been the wiser about the theft until there was some reason to look in the box, perhaps months or even years from now. However, the fact that the guard, Burroughs, was struck and the box taken out of the vault suggested that the plan had somehow gone awry, and the thief had panicked.

"Sir Phillip, why were you surprised by the watchman on his rounds? Was the vault door more difficult to open than you had imagined? Did you have trouble finding the dispatch box amongst all the other items stacked inside? Or were you simply unaware of the watchman's scheduled rounds?"

Finally, Sir Phillip raised his eyes and looked at each of us, before locking his gaze with Milton Gallagher. Only then did his countenance break. With something like a sob, he turned his face back toward Pons.

"I couldn't find the box," he said. "I had always known of its existence, and the specific vault in which it was located. It had been described to me – *but I couldn't find it!* I lost track of time, and had just located it when I heard the scuff of the watchman's shoes on the stairs.

"Without grabbing my light, which I was afraid had already been seen, I dashed into one of the dark insets of one of the other vault doors in the hall. I had taken the precaution of bringing a life preserver with me, and as the man passed my position, I reached out and hit him.

"Even as he fell, I realized that he would soon be missed. I was afraid to stay in the basement any longer, fearful that I might meet one of the other watchmen as well. Rather than open the dispatch box then, I took it with me and hurriedly made my way upstairs, afraid at every turn that I would be discovered.

"In my office, I used the key to the box that we keep at the bank, which I previously obtained. Then, taking out the papers, I realized that I had to find a way to hide the box in order to avoid being incriminated, as I couldn't return it to the vault. I was wearing gloves, so I knew that I would not leave fingerprints. I was aware that my . . . employer in this matter had an interest in my co-director, Mr. Gallagher, who has some connection with the papers contained therein, so I thought that it would be useful to leave the box in his office as leverage. I placed it behind the sofa, and made my way back to my office, where I – "

Gallagher, who had been sitting quietly on the periphery of our little group, rose angrily to his feet. "You lie!" he cried. "I have nothing to do with anything that would have been investigated by Sherlock Holmes and Dr. Watson years ago while I was a child!"

"I believe that you have sadly miscalculated, Sir Phillip," said Pons. "While it is true that there *is* a connection between Mr. Gallagher and some of the papers contained in the dispatch box – "

Gallagher turned toward Pons, who held up a hand to still his protest. " – a connection which I believe is unknown to him," he added, "your employer, as you wish to refer to him, would have preferred the connection to have remained unknown, in order that pressure could be exerted on Mr. Gallagher in the coming months and years."

Gallagher sank back into his chair. "What – " he tried to say, and then again, a much less confident man than the fellow that we had initially met in his office a short time ago. "What do you mean, Mr. Pons? What sort of pressure could have been exerted over me? My life is blameless!"

"As I said, there is a connection between you and the papers in the dispatch box. Or more specifically, between your *wife* and the papers."

"My wife?" asked Gallagher, astonished.

"Yes. While we were at the bank, it occurred to me to ask Bancroft for a list of the documents that were still kept in the Doctor's box. His list suggested several possibilities, and based on that, I sent queries back to my brother about possible connections between the individuals involved in the matter at the bank and those who had initially been associated with the original investigations.

"Those cases in that box were my first primer and copybook. In my younger days I studied them intensely, and I recall all aspects of them. Over the years, as my practice has taken on some of the responsibilities originally incurred by that of The Master, I have made it my business to keep track of various individuals that were involved in those old investigations.

"Many of them have died, and in other instances the matters involved are not nearly as dangerous now as the government would have us believe." Bancroft started to interrupt, but Pons raised a hand and continued. "But one of the cases still has a great potential to be as explosive as the authorities fear. It is known popularly as 'The Politician, the Lighthouse, and the Trained Cormorant'. "

"By the time that I received the list of the box's contents, I was fairly certain that the theft was an inside job, and more specifically that it had either been carried out by you, Mr. Gallagher, or by Sir Phillip, since the vault door had been opened by one of your two keys.

"Bancroft, instantly perceiving the direction of my questions, quickly narrowed down the larger list and focused on the individuals in question, those related to the matter of the Politician. He determined that your wife, Mr. Gallagher, is the younger, and that is to say, the *very much younger*, sister of Lord D------, who was a politician in the fall of 1902, when his activities were discovered and stopped by Sherlock Holmes and Doctor Watson. His ingenious scheme to aid the Germans in a matter involving a lighthouse and a trained cormorant was narrowly defeated. Although his guilt was known in higher circles at that time, he was not arrested, and has spent the time since then apparently trying to rehabilitate himself."

Bancroft joined in, saying, "Lord D------ was closely watched during the War, to see if he participated in any attempts to aid the enemy, but we believed that he had learned his lesson. In 1927, there were some attempts to get at Watson's papers, but efforts were made through the press, and in Watson's own writings in *The Strand*, to warn off whoever was responsible. There was no evidence that Lord D------ was involved in those particular attempted thefts, but there was no evidence that he was *not*, either. We believed that the warnings all those years ago were entirely effective, and that Lord D------ was still behaving himself. That is, until a few months ago, when his pro-German proclivities began to reassert themselves.

"As you are aware, he has been hosting a series of events to supposedly foster British-German relations. And through his sister, your wife, you have been involved in these affairs as well."

"But . . . I did not know there was anything objectionable about this," said Gallagher. "The Germans have nothing but good feelings toward us now. It is in everyone's interest, especially in these trying financial times, to work together."

"Not so, Mr. Gallagher," replied Bancroft Pons. "Not at all. There are elements in Germany, even as we speak, that are taking advantage of the recent financial collapses in order to work toward a re-armed and re-fortified Germany. And I can tell you that if that were to happen, we would soon be involved in another war that would make the events of the last seem like a practice barrage."

Pons stated, "I have no doubts that your employer in this matter, Sir Phillip, was the man who tried to get those papers in 1927. Recently, he probably sensed that he needed more positive participation from Mr. Gallagher, and sought to bring pressure on him. He realized that Mr. Gallagher's wife was Lord D------'s sister. In spite of the fact that Lord D------ was his own creature, the employer decided to coerce the young lady, and through her, you as well, Mr. Gallagher. And having the original documents implicating Lord D------ from Doctor Watson's box would serve perfectly. Your wife would have no idea that the matter had been settled nearly thirty years ago. She would believe that, in order to save her brother from the old charges against him that were contained in the tin dispatch box, she would have to throw in her lot heart-and-soul with the pro-German forces. And you, Mr. Gallagher, would be pulled along with her."

"Pons," I said, "you have mentioned this 'employer' several times. Who is this person?"

"You have heard of him before, Parker. Only last January, in that matter you referred to in your notes as 'The Seven Passengers', we encountered him. Surely you recall our acquaintance with Baron Ennesfred Kroll?"

Suddenly it became clear to me. The sinister machinations. The pro-German leanings. The familiarity with Dr. Watson's notes.

Sir Phillip nodded. "You are correct," he mumbled. "That is the man."

"I assume that he has some sort of hold over you," stated Pons.

"Gambling debts. The old story. He approached me, and it was clear he knew exactly what he wanted out of the box. I was only supposed to take the file relating to Lord D------. Baron Kroll indicated that if things were managed correctly, the absence of the documents might never be noticed.

"Through the regular course of my duties, I was able to obtain the key to the dispatch box. I had planned to return it later in the same manner. Last night, I knew that Gallagher had a function to attend, and that there was no possibility that he would be staying late. I hid upstairs until after everyone had gone – "

"And that," interrupted Pons, "was the curious anomaly of which I spoke, Parker. Each employee was shown in the daily logs, where their entrances and exits were duly recorded. But nowhere was there an instance of the comings and goings of the directors."

"Of course," I cried. "That was what you meant. Every employee that entered was recorded as having departed, but since the directors were never recorded one way or the other, there was no arrival or subsequent departure time shown. The record was complete, and yet incomplete."

"Therefore," added Pons, "I knew that it was possible for one of them to have stayed in the building. Mr. Gallagher's alibi at the dinner was unimpeachable, thus pointing the finger even more firmly in the direction of Sir Phillip."

"I waited until quite late," continued Sir Phillip, as if he hadn't been interrupted at all. "I made my way down to the vault. I've told you how I was nearly discovered, and how I panicked. I made my way back upstairs to my office, opened the box, and retrieved the documents. Then, thinking that Baron Kroll's interest in them was somehow supposed to damage Mr. Gallagher, I thought that hiding the box, which I needed to be rid of anyway, would best be done by placing it in my fellow director's office." He lowered his head, and then glanced toward Gallagher. "I am so sorry."

Gallagher did not speak, and seemed to still be in some sort of mild shock after learning about his brother-in-law.

"And then," asked Pons, "did you simply hide until the police arrived?"

"Yes," said Sir Phillip. "I placed the documents in my case and waited in the shadows downstairs, in the stairs to the upper level, until I saw the police enter the building. In the confusion as they rushed to the vaults, I managed to slip out, whereupon I quickly walked away and down to Trafalgar Square for a while, attempting to calm my nerves. By the time I returned to my club, the summons back to the bank, which I should have realized would come soon, had arrived.

"I hid the papers in my room – not very well, apparently." He sighed. "I suppose that I won't be going back there."

"Have you notified Baron Kroll that you have the papers?" Pons asked.

Sir Phillip nodded. "I sent him a wire earlier this morning, after I went home. I am to await instructions."

Pons looked toward Bancroft. "Surely he has seen all of this activity and that his plan somehow went astray. Do you think anything useful can still come of it?"

Bancroft gave a satisfied smile. "We can prepare something rather quickly for him that looks like Watson's notes from 1902, but with substantially new and misleading contents," he said. "That is," with a more ominous tone, "with Sir Phillip's cooperation."

Sir Phillip looked up. "What? Oh, of course. Anything that I can do . . . ."

"But," interrupted Inspector Jamison, "surely the next step is to arrest this Baron Kroll?"

"It is not that easy, I'm afraid," said Bancroft Pons. "He has diplomatic immunity, you know, and we are all playing something of a waiting game right now."

"Do you mean to tell me that we have to sit down under this?" cried Jamison. "Are you saying that no one can ever get level with this German devil?"

"He will be stopped," said Pons. "I can assure you of that. He can be beat. But you must give me time – you must give me time!"

# The Park Lane Solution

As I climbed the steps to our shared sitting room, I heard the sound of an automobile pull up and stop just outside the front door. This was not an unusual occurrence in Praed Street, so near Paddington Station, and just because the vehicle rested outside the door of No. 7 did not mean that it was related to the concerns of my friend, Solar Pons. But by that time, having known and shared rooms with Pons for several years, it seemed more likely than not that something was soon to be afoot. I was correct, and while this turned out to be one of Pons's more simple investigations, I believe it was also one that gave him some of the greatest pleasure.

I found Pons standing by the mantel, a twinkle in his eye. "A successful consultation?" he asked.

"Indeed," I replied. "Have you already deduced that, or are you simply being polite?"

"Just polite. I trust that the patient will survive?"

"Sir Henry will live to fight another day."

"I am glad indeed. I observed that you left in rather a hurry last night, following our completion of the matter of the amateur philologist."

"That is correct." I set my bag down in its accustomed place behind the door. "I must admit that following Sir Henry's last attack, I expected the worst."

I started toward one of the tall windows overlooking the street. "I believe we are to have a visitor. I just heard a car stop at the door. Although," I said, moving past the table to the window for a look, "I would have expected them to have knocked us up before now."

"Ah, Parker, I must congratulate you on your willingness to share your conclusions, but I must also correct your tentative footsteps into the drawing of them. The car did stop here, but no one will be coming up. In truth, it is a previously arranged driver sent to carry me to the scene of a new investigation. I was reached by telephone not fifteen minutes ago. Your arrival is most timely. Would you care to accompany me?"

I thought of the coffee and hot breakfast that I had been anticipating only a few moments earlier. I believed that Mrs. Johnson was going to prepare something special, as she occasionally does when she knows that I have been out upon a difficult case. But interest in my friend's investigations trumped even hunger. "Give me five minutes," I said.

"Splendid!" replied Pons.

After only three of my allotted five, and with a quick word to Mrs. Johnson, Pons and I were in a plush auto, moving briskly along the mostly empty Edgware Road.

Although it was mid-May, the morning was still cool, and I pulled my coat a bit tighter.

"You mentioned that you received a telephone call?" I prompted.

"From Sir Albert James."

"One of the heroes of the Gallipoli landing in '15?"

"The same. He led a group of marines' charge against incredible odds."

"I believe it was for that action that he was knighted."

"That is my understanding as well. When he telephoned this morning, he seemed in something of a state."

"About?"

"Ah, Parker, that was not explained. He simply indicated that I should expect his car and driver, and that he would provide further details upon my arrival. Your entrance was fortuitously timed indeed."

The car made its way by the Marble Arch and around Speaker's Corner, and so into Park Lane. From my vantage, I could see dew-covered Hyde Park stretching into the distance, while on his side of the car, Pons was looking expectantly at the fine houses rolling by.

The car stopped smoothly in front of a lovely older home. The driver slid out to open the door, and Pons and I found ourselves standing in front of No. 427, the only people on that part of the street at this early hour.

The driver returned to his vehicle and slid away, likely to make his way into the mews that undoubtedly ran behind these houses, where he would await his next summons. As I watched the car depart, Pons stopped for a moment, staring inexplicably at the walk in front of the steps leading to the door, a small smile playing about his lips. Then the front door of 427 opened, and a man appeared in the doorway above us, like a great bear reared on its hind legs. He stated, more quietly than I could have imagined for someone of his size, "Mr. Pons! Thank you for coming! This way!"

His voice was reserved and hushed, as if to impart a feeling of stealth, but it still seemed unnaturally loud in that quiet morning, and it shocked me, but not so much as when I realized that the man who had opened the door was Sir Albert himself.

When we had mounted the steps and crossed the threshold, I saw that our host was not as large and overbearing as he had first seemed. In actuality, he was probably only five-seven or five-eight, but at least fifteen or sixteen stone. He had a large torso and a great head resting upon it. His hair was brushed straight back from his brow, and his beard consisted of a moustache and chin-whiskers stretching halfway down his chest, in the manner of some of the American Confederate Generals of old, while his cheeks were clean-shaven. Although I knew him to be in his mid-forties, his skin looked young and healthy, but there were dark circles under his eyes that caught my professional notice.

"Thank you for coming, Mr. Pons," he said quietly, almost as if we were being led into the house in secret. Then he glanced toward me.

"My associate, Dr. Lyndon Parker," indicated Pons.

"My thanks to you as well, Doctor," said Sir Albert. "Please excuse my opening the door. After my military experiences, I found it difficult to fall back into the expected and regimented order of things here at home. My servants are mostly former soldiers who were under my command, and even though they have no hesitation at following my orders, I feel that I should lead from the front, so to speak, and take care of matters myself when I can."

"Very enlightened of you," said Pons. "I believe that we will see more of this in these years following the upheaval of the War."

"Nice of you to say so, Mr. Pons. I still feel that I have to explain my actions, which I suppose I would not do if I were completely used to the idea myself. I wish my honored in-law was in agreement with my thoughts."

"Indeed?" said Pons diplomatically and enigmatically. After all, what else could he say?

Sir Albert nodded. "That is the root of my problem. There has been a theft, something negligible belonging to my father-in-law. He is staying with us for the month, and he insists that my valet, Drummond, was the culprit. I refuse to believe it, but my father-in-law demands Drummond's immediate dismissal."

Pons began to remove his Inverness, which Sir Albert took, along with Pons's deerstalker. I removed my overcoat as well, handing it and my hat to our host. I had served in Egypt during the War with men such as Sir Albert, who had no qualms at dirtying their hands along with their men. The respect these fellows earned was boundless – but I still felt odd handing my outerwear to the buoyant knight reaching for it.

"May we see the scene of the theft?" asked Pons.

"Certainly," replied our host, having disposed of the coats and hats. He led us to a magnificent staircase.

Pons paused for a moment at the foot of the stairs. "Have you owned this house for long?"

"My father bought it in late '94, when I was a boy," said Sir Albert. "It belonged to the Earl of Maynooth, but after his second son was killed here, they wanted no further part of it." We began to climb the steps. "Of course, we weren't exactly welcomed into the neighborhood then, you understand. My father had made his fortune in the manufacture and sales of carriages, and the people along Park Lane looked down upon that, as you might expect. But gradually they became used to us, if not friendly. It didn't hurt that our fortunes continued to grow while some of theirs declined. When I married my wife, it improved our pedigree considerably, and after the knighthood, none of them seemed to mind having a knight living in this part of the street."

He tossed off these facts as we climbed, but I could sense that underneath, there was still some resentment about the way his family had been treated while he was growing up, made to feel as if they were *nouveau riche*, and therefore not truly welcome.

"My mother had died years ago, and my brother and sister have long since moved away. My wife and I continued to live here with my father, who passed unexpectedly while I was in Italy. Since then, it's been my wife and children and myself. With," he added in a somewhat wry tone, "frequent visits from my wife's father."

"His wife does not make the journey?"

"She passed away years ago, when my wife was a child."

We had reached a closed room on the front of the second floor. Sir Albert opened the door and gestured for us to enter. "This is my father-in-law's room. The family is down at breakfast right now, so we shouldn't be disturbed."

Pons entered and glanced around and from side to side. There was a wide window overlooking Park Lane. We looked out, and I could see that the morning traffic twenty or thirty feet below us was increasing. Across the street, about a hundred yards away on the Hyde Park side, stood a cab stand, with drivers huddled together over steaming cups of coffee or tea.

"And this was where the theft occurred?" said Pons, turning back into the room.

Sir Albert affirmed as such, gesturing toward a bureau along the south wall. "A pair of diamond cuff links, removed the night before and left there by Drummond, who was assisting my father-in-law, as his own man had not made the trip."

"I believe your father-in-law is Lord Belliver, who made such a mark during the War by providing cloth from his mills for the manufacture of military uniforms."

"Correct," said Sir Albert. He seemed to hesitate for a moment, and then said, "And some would state that he not only made his mark, but his fortune as well. When I met and married his daughter before the War, his affairs had been in steep decline, but he certainly seized the opportunity that was presented by the conflict to reverse his situation."

"Yes," said Pons, rather tactlessly in my opinion, "The dailies have occasionally bandied the term *profiteering* about rather freely."

Sir Albert nodded. "It has been the subject of some rather heated discussions, as you might imagine. I have rather strong views on the subject, having grown up in a family with manufacturing interests, and then going to War and obtaining yet another perspective. But for the sake of my dear wife, whom I might add is in agreement with me on the matter, our discussions thankfully occur on a limited basis.

"However," he continued, "Lord Belliver's strong ideas about class divisions are another source of friction, and as he knows the high respect I have for my man Drummond, it seemed that he was almost too enthusiastic in his attempts to lay the blame for the missing items at Drummond's feet."

Pons nodded, and then spent a few minutes peering at the top of the bureau. I did not know what he expected to find. As Drummond had been serving as Lord Belliver's valet, any evidence of Drummond's presence in the room would be completely understandable.

"Is it known that I have been invited to make an investigation?"

"No. I thought that it would be best if you appeared as a *fait accompli*, so to speak. My father-in-law found the cuff links missing upon rising this morning, and he immediately started a row, accusing Drummond of the theft. I managed to calm him down and shepherd the family toward breakfast. Then I thought of you, having heard from my friend, Major Woburn, how you so ably disentangled him from the snares of the Ashford Phantom, as the newspapers called it. I'm thankful you were able to arrive so quickly."

Pons nodded, and then said, "I would ask that you both wait in the hallway for a few moments while I make my examination." We complied, and Pons then proceeded to work his way around the room, moving clock-wise from the door to the bureau, around to the wide window, and so on to the bed. He crawled and stood and crawled again, all the while making a series of low mutters to himself, punctuated by the occasional click of the tongue or a sharp whistle. He weaved behind chairs and standing lamps, looked under the bureau and the bed, and even worked his way into the large closet as well. I had observed all of this numerous times in the years since I had been accompanying Pons on his investigations, but Sir Albert was seeing it for the first time, with equal parts amazement and amusement. He glanced at me once or twice, when Pons contorted himself in an especially twisted fashion to look under this or that piece of furniture, but I simply smiled reassuringly.

Finally Pons stood, brushed himself off, and joined us at the door. "It was only the cuff links that were missing?"

"Yes. When my father-in-law arose, he noticed that they were gone from the top of the bureau. He says they were not especially valuable, but his immediate reaction was to accuse Drummond, who never lost his head throughout the entire affair. The bellows of my father-in-law woke the rest of the house, although I was already up. I came in a hurry to find out what was the matter, only to discover Drummond standing at attention in the doorway, while my father-in-law faced him, shaking a finger in his face."

"And you chose not to call the police?"

"It certainly seemed unnecessary to me, and even unwise. My father-in-law agreed, commenting on the avoidance of scandal, but that did not stop him from demanding some sort of immediate action against Drummond, who has already been tried and convicted in Lord Belliver's mind. He demanded immediate dismissal on the spot."

"Does Lord Belliver not realize that such an action would open you both up to legal recriminations, should the accusations prove to be false?"

Sir Albert smiled. "Lord Belliver has a more medieval attitude toward those he considers to be his lessers. He seems to feel that his simple declaration is enough, and that will be the end of the matter, as the accused will graciously tug his forelock and back away, considering himself fortunate."

Pons quickly walked up and down the hall, looking into the open doors. "Is your father-in-law staying alone on this floor?

"That is correct. The servants sleep above, and my family occupies the rooms below, on the first floor."

"Isn't it rather odd that Lord Belliver is on this floor all alone?"

"Not particularly. On the floor below, the rooms are either occupied by my family, or set up as playrooms or a sewing room.

Additionally, my father-in-law made it rather clear that when he visits, this room, larger than the others on this floor, suits him best."

"It is quite obvious that this large room takes up a sizeable portion of the square footage of this floor. I believe it was used as a sitting room at one time?"

Sir Albert nodded, looking slightly puzzled. "Indeed, although I'm not sure how you knew. It was that way when my father bought the house from the Earl of Maynooth, but he soon converted it into the master bedroom for himself and my mother. Later, when she died, my father moved down a floor to where the rest of us slept. But how did you know? It was completely redecorated years ago."

"I have some previous knowledge of this house," replied Pons. Then he stood in thought for a moment, tugging at the lobe of his left ear. Finally he seemed to reach a decision. He crossed his arms and looked around with twinkling eyes. "This has been an interesting study, but perhaps it is time to nudge things toward a speedy resolution. Parker, here, was out all last night on a difficult medical case, and he has not yet had his breakfast."

Sir Albert looked abashed. "Why, Dr. Parker, if I had but known, I would have made arrangements for you. It is not too late . . . ."

The initial idea sounded tempting, but then I decided to trust Pons's statement that the matter would be concluded soon, and that in all likelihood I would be back in Praed Street very shortly indeed.

"Forgive me if this is none of my business," said Pons, "but I have the sense that your father-in-law's visits are something of an unpleasantness."

Sir Albert nodded. "Nothing to forgive there. I put up with him because of my wife, but in truth she feels the same as I. It is truly a case of absence would make the heart grow fonder."

Pons nodded. "I have some memory that your father-in-law is a rather superstitious man."

Sir Albert gave a short laugh. "That he is. He has all sorts of things he will or won't do, and he's absolutely terrified of ghosts, although he won't admit it. I used to work little comments into conversations years ago, such as mentioning some spirit that was supposed to haunt a theatre where we were attending a play. My wife urged me to stop, as she said it was unworthy of me to bait him so."

"Nevertheless," said Pons cryptically. Then, he stated, "I would like to speak with Drummond, if I may."

"Certainly. If you'll just wait in that small sitting room across the hall, I'll have him come up immediately."

We entered the room, finding a settee and a number of comfortable chairs. The window looked out of the rear of the house, onto the rooftops and chimneys of Mayfair. Pons found a seat with his back to the window, while I placed myself to the side.

In a moment, the valet, Drummond, entered the room. He was about the same age as Sir Albert, but thinner, with almost a feral look about him. His dark hair fell as a comma across his right eye, and there were small scars across his forehead. I had seen those before, the result of unavoidable sparks associated with some types of artillery fire, forming powder burns and tattoos on the skin.

Pons gestured toward a chair. "Please close the door, Drummond. This will not take long at all." Drummond complied, and then sat patiently on the edge of his chair, each hand placed on its corresponding knee.

"Sir Albert has informed us of the accusation made this morning by Lord Belliver. Do you wish to make any comments?"

"Well," said Drummond, with an accent containing traces of our northern neighbors, "it's a load of codswallop, if you'll pardon me saying so. I helped take the cuff links off last night, and left them on top of the bureau. After that, I removed myself downstairs, and thought no more about it until the yelling started this morning. I came on the run, thinking there was a fire. As I topped the stairs, there was Lord Belliver, pointing his finger at me and calling me a thief." He shook his head and gave a bitter laugh. "I suppose that's it then. I'll be lucky to get out of here without being arrested."

"Not at all," said Pons. "Sir Albert believes you to be innocent, and more importantly, I *know* that you are."

Drummond glanced up sharply at my friend. "You do?"

"Yes. But can you offer any explanation as to why Lord Belliver would be so quick as to accuse you?"

"Not at all. Granted, he's never cared for me, after he found out that I knew him of old, but that has nothing to do with anything, I'm sure."

"Knew him? How so?"

"My father was one of his managers. I grew up in one of the villages where Lord Belliver's mills are located. My father was with him when times were good, and then bad, and then good again during the War."

"What about that connection would lead him to dislike you."

"Wa-al," Drummond replied slowly, with some reluctance. "After the War, when Sir Albert brought me with him back here, I was surprised to discover that my master's wife was Lord Belliver's daughter. The next time he came to visit, I took the liberty of introducing myself, and reminding him of my father's connections. I thought that he might have a friendly feeling toward me, but from that moment he's treated me with nothing but suspicion."

"Did you mention this to Sir Albert?"

"No, sir. It weren't my place to do so. Lord Belliver never brought his own man with him, as there isn't space here for that, so we both made do with each other. But I must say that his attitude toward me has grown worse in just the past few months, although mine never changed, in spite of the feelings of my old dad."

"Indeed? And what feelings would those be?"

"Hmm, I have to say that he don't think too highly of him anymore, and that's for sure. He respected him well enough before the War, but from what I've seen since I returned, my old dad, now retired, doesn't have much good to say. I gather that he saw some things during those years that he couldn't abide."

"I expect that you're right," said Pons. "No doubt the recent murmurings of investigations into war profiteering have given Lord Belliver a few sleepless nights. Possibly your presence, and your connection to your father, is a painful reminder of something that Lord Belliver would like to ignore or forget."

Pons stood then and offered his hand to Drummond. "I don't think that this matter will need to concern you anymore. Thank you for your time."

Drummond returned Pons's grip with a puzzled look. "My pleasure, sir. If there's nothing else then . . . ?"

Pons gestured towards the door, and Drummond departed. We heard him descend the stairs, and in a few moments, Sir Albert returned with a questioning look on his broad and bearded face.

"We progress, Sir Albert," said Pons. "If your father-in-law has finished with his breakfast, might we trouble him for a few moments?"

"Certainly, certainly. I'll go fetch him now." As the fellow went in search of Lord Belliver, Pons led me back across the hallway and into the father-in-law's bedroom. Again, he placed himself in a chair with his back to the window and sat. I chose to remain standing, awaiting the arrival of the two other men.

In a moment the sound of their return was apparent by the thumping on the stairs. Sir Albert was led into the room by a small man in is sixties, leaning forward as he walked as if charging toward a battle.

"This is Mr. Solar Pons," said Sir James, "and his associate, Dr. Lyndon Parker. May I present – "

"There is no need for your presence, sir!" the small man interrupted with a thundering voice as Pons rose. "My son-in-law was instructed not to call the police."

"But I am not of the police, Lord Belliver," replied Pons smoothly. He gestured toward a chair opposite his own. "Won't you have a seat? This will not take but a moment."

After a couple of deep breaths, followed by a puff that very much resembled the sound made by a vexed animal, Lord Belliver lurched toward the chair. He glanced toward Pons, and then turned his angry gaze on our client. "Albert, there was no need for this. Your man is a thief. Why prolong things? You should have listened to me and sacked him first thing."

"Forgive me, sir," said Sir Albert tightly, "but I don't agree with your assessment of Drummond's character."

"Nor do I," said Pons, pulling Lord Belliver's gaze back to him. "Would you mind shutting the door?" he asked Sir Albert.

When Sir Albert had done so, and had resumed his standing position at the foot of the bed, Pons reached into his pocket and pulled out a dark object, holding it where Lord Belliver could see it. "Would you mind explaining this?" he said.

Sir Albert and I both stepped forward. Pons appeared to be holding a knotted black cloth of some sort, only an inch or two across. Upon closer examination, I realized that it was a black sock, tied in the middle and wadded into a ball. Something appeared to be contained within the closed toe of the garment.

"I found this in your closet," said Pons, "pushed into a pocket of one of the pieces of your luggage, and underneath a rolled newspaper." He tossed it, and then caught it is his palm, where he bounced it a couple of times. It made a faint metallic sound, much like that made by coins in one's pocket. Pons began to untie the knot. "Shall we see what's inside?"

Lord Belliver lowered his gaze and rested his head on a hand, propped on the arm of the chair, covering his eyes. He didn't look up as Pons shook a pair of cuff links from the sock and into the palm of his other hand.

"Why, it's the stolen cuff links. Any ideas, Lord Belliver, why Drummond might hide them so curiously in your luggage?"

The silence extended awkwardly, until finally, with a shuddering deep breath, the old man spoke. "He did not steal them. I . . . I hid them there."

"To achieve his dismissal," said Pons.

Lord Belliver nodded, but did not speak.

"But why?" asked Sir Albert, his voice tight. He was obviously struggling to avoid saying something to his father-in-law that might be later regretted.

Lord Belliver didn't answer, and Pons filled the silence. "Drummond's presence is a reminder of things that your father-in-law did during the War that he would like to forget. Drummond informed us that his father was one of Lord Belliver's managers during the War, when fortunes were being made. Perhaps, Lord Belliver, you are now somewhat ashamed of the manner in which you spent *your* War?"

At this, the man looked up with a grimace. "You have no idea what it's been like. Since the War. People who were friends before, even when times were hard, shun me now, whisper behind my back. Even the men who did the same as I. There is talk of investigations. And I cannot even tarry here at my daughter's home without seeing the accusations in the eyes of my son-in-law's valet. Last night, it seemed even worse. I've recently had news – news that more questions are going to be asked. When your man Drummond was assisting me, his very presence seemed to aggravate my unease. I know now that he did or said nothing to warrant my actions, but at the time, I decided to have him removed from my presence, so that my visits here might be of an easier nature.

"I conceived the idea of accusing him of a theft. It would be over and done with, and it wouldn't involve the police. I didn't realize . . . I did not realize that my own son-in-law would stand in my way and defy my wishes." His tone, which had started in an embarrassed and rather penitent manner, grew sour as his gaze lifted toward Sir Albert.

"Drummond was at my side at Gallipoli," said our host, his voice tight and his eyes mere slits. "I would not dismiss him simply upon your say-so."

Into this tension, Pons said, "Perhaps it was not your father-in-law's fault."

Both men turned toward my friend with no little surprise.

"Not his fault?" said Sir Albert. "How could that be?"

"I simply mean that his unease may have been amplified by the emanations within the house, and particularly from this room."

Lord Belliver's gaze widened in surprise. "*Emanations?*"

"That is correct. I would not be surprised if the very idea of framing Drummond were not somehow whispered into your ear by the presence that occupies this very space."

Sir Albert glanced at me in puzzlement, but wisely did not speak. Pons continued, "No doubt your recent worries have made you susceptible to being influenced in your actions by *the other side.*"

Lord Belliver swallowed. "What do you mean, Mr. Pons?"

Pons glanced to the right and left and waved his hand. "This room, Lord Belliver. It was the location of a most terrible murder, in a most strange and unexpected form, between the hours of ten and eleven-twenty on the night of the thirtieth of March, 1894."

Lord Belliver hitched himself forward on his chair, as if fearful of touching it. "Murder? Of whom do you speak?"

"Ronald Adair, the second son of the Earl of Maynooth," replied Pons. "The Earl was, at that time, governor of one of the Australian colonies. Adair's mother had returned from Australia to undergo the operation for cataract, and she, her son Ronald, and her daughter Hilda were living together in this house.

"Following an evening of card-play with some of his associates at the Bagatelle, Adair returned to this room, which was a sitting room then, and locked the door. At eleven-twenty that night, his mother, who had been out, returned and, desiring to say good night, attempted to enter. When she received no response, the door was forced, and Adair was found on the floor – " Pons paused, and pointed to an area near Lord Belliver, " – probably right about there, in line with the front window. His head had been horribly mutilated by an expanding revolver bullet, but no weapon of any sort was to be found in the room. Clearly, the young man had been murdered."

"I recall something of the case," said Lord Belliver softly. "As I remember it, a military man, a Colonel back from India, had been cheating at cards, and young Adair had caught him out. Faced with exposure, the Colonel found a spot across the road in the park and shot him through the window with an air rifle. The police inspector received a lot of attention in the press for piecing it all together."

"It was actually a matter handled by my Illustrious Predecessor. As was usually his practice, he allowed the police to take the credit." Pons looked at different corners of the room. "As far as I know, he was never actually a visitor here in the house, although he did look around outside. In fact, it was in front of the house that he bumped into an old friend. I've always wanted to visit here myself, and considered myself fortunate when I received Sir Albert's telephone call this morning, allowing me to do so."

Pons turned toward me. "What do you think, Parker? Would Doyle be interested in having a look here?"

"I believe so," I replied, catching Pons's drift. "This type of thing is just his cup of tea."

"Doyle?" said Lord Belliver. "Why, do you mean Sir Arthur? I heard him speak about the spirits last year. Why would he be interested in this matter?"

"This would fascinate him to no end," said Pons, an innocent expression on his face. "A violent murder from nearly thirty years before, resulting in a restive spirit that can influence the thoughts and control the actions of a weak-minded man, even to the point of convincing that same man to commit a crime by framing an innocent. With the facts discovered from this one investigation, Sir Arthur could no doubt absolutely cement his arguments toward the presence of spirits, and their influence in our world. Of course, it goes without saying that you will be famous, Lord Belliver. May I ask, are you aware of any other instances in which the ghost of young Ronald Adair has taken possession of you against your will?"

I glanced again at Sir Albert, who was clearly onto Pons's game, and was wisely letting it unfold without any hindrance. Perhaps a smile twitched about his bearded lips as Lord Belliver stood abruptly. "No, no, I haven't been possessed, as you say. At least, not before last night. Or so I believe. I really cannot recall any other time when that might have happened. Of course, I did not know it was happening last night, either, so if it *did* happen before, I was unaware of it . . . ." He looked right and left, and then towards his closet. He seemed to make a decision.

Turning toward his son-in-law, he said, "Albert, I cannot apologize enough, and I hope that you will convey those sentiments to your man as well. I . . . I was not in control of my own actions. I can see that now. I think it would be best if I leave. This morning. Now. I'll just pack up – no, no need to send up your man. I'll take care of myself. If you can let Lydia know . . . ."

Within fifteen minutes, Lord Belliver and his hastily-packed bags were placed in a cab. As Sir Albert's wife and children waved in puzzlement from the front door, I stood with Pons and our client by the foot of the stairs.

"That was . . . amazing, Mr. Pons," said Sir Albert when his wife and children had vanished within the house. "I've heard of killing two birds with one stone, but it's going to take a little thinking to see just how many birds fell with this effort."

"I must apologize," said Pons, "if I overstepped my place and exorcised this house of your father-in-law. It is perhaps unfair to prevent him from further visits with his daughter and grandchildren."

Sir Albert smiled. "I assure you that his presence was always a much greater disruption to all of us than a pleasure. In any case, we also visit his home a couple of times each year, and that is enough to be going on with."

"Excellent."

"However," added Sir Albert, "I do not believe that I'll share the ghost story that was part of your ultimate solution with the family. There is no need to reveal that part to my wife and children, and my wife will be satisfied to know that her father left in embarrassment following the exposure of his plot against Drummond."

"No ghosts need apply," said Pons.

"Exactly. I myself will do my best to forget that the crime which you described ever took place in that upper room. And I think that I will have it remodeled into a fine study. A good cigar and the occasional glass of brandy are the only spirits that I'll allow."

And so it proved. Following that affair, I became friends with Sir Albert, and visited him on numerous occasions in his remodeled study. He turned out to be an excellent companion indeed, and I'm happy to report that he was never again haunted by the living presence of his troublesome father-in-law.

# The Poe Problem

"It simply isn't *seemly*, Mr. Pons," said our guest, sitting primly forward on the basket chair between Solar Pons and myself on that cold December morning, his knees pressed together and his hands balled into fists.

I had dropped by to visit my friend, having seen much less of him since my marriage the previous summer to the former Miss Constance Dorrington. Mrs. Johnson had been absent when I let myself in, using my old key. 7B Praed Street had been my home for so long that, when I remarried, Pons urged that I keep it - a gesture which I greatly appreciated.

That morning, I was passing nearby when I decided to check in and see what latest mischief had been occurring in my absence. As I reached the top of the landing, Pons, recognizing my step, bade me to enter, whereupon I discovered that he already had a visitor. I made as if to withdraw, but I was waved toward the cheery fireplace and my old chair.

"Mr. Ned Pohl, this is Dr. Parker," said Pons while I leaned toward the fellow to shake hands. I could see, as he partially stood and extended his toward me, that he was a curious sort, his hand cool and limp. He was only halfway over five feet, dressed in an ill-fitting suit, and seemingly quite pale, even for a winter's day. He reseated himself with a grimace of distaste, as if forcing himself to occupy that chair once had been a pesterment, and to do so twice was nearly unacceptable.

"Mr. Pohl was only beginning to relate his tale," explained Pons. "You're just in time."

"I can only afford to fund one . . . *operative*, Mr. Pons," said the little man.

My friend's eyes twinkled. "My rates never vary, whether I handle the matter alone, or if I involve others. Isn't that correct, Operative Parker?"

"Quite." I stretched my legs toward the fire and tried not to smile.

"Now, Mr. Pohl, please begin again with your story."

The fellow made his comment about the unseemly nature of the business, and then elaborated. "I am the Corresponding Secretary of the 'Edgar Allan Poe Society - United Kingdom Division'." He said this with a great deal of pride, and looked from one to the other of us, gauging which one was more impressed. I'm afraid that we both disappointed him.

"Indeed," drawled Pons. "And is there an equivalent organization in North America, then?"

"Well, not that I'm aware of."

I asked, "Is there that much interest on this side of the ocean regarding the late American author?"

"Sir!" Our visitor was shocked. "Of course there is! Why, I . . . I - " At this point, he seemed to find himself at a loss for words.

Pons glanced my way, as if to assure himself that I was paying attention. "You intimated," he said, "that you are related to the famed writer."

Pohl collected himself and intertwined his fingers. "Not closely, no," he said. "I have traced my lineage back a number of generations, and can find a tenuous lateral connection between my family and that of 'Cousin Edgar', as I jokingly call him. However, I am not, in fact, that closely related, much to my dismay. However, seeing Poe's name on a book of tales when I was a child, but for a few letters so nearly the same name that I proudly carry, did spark my interest in reading them, much to my everlasting joy."

A flash of amusement crossed Pons's eyes. "And did you found this society?"

"I did not. It was already in existence when I learned of it."

"Yet you are now the secretary to this organization devoted to Poe's works?"

"Corresponding Secretary. And yes. As I said, the group had already been in existence for a number of years when I was old enough to join. I found, to my dismay, that they were indifferent stewards of their responsibility. They didn't devote the proper serious attention that such matters deserve. Very lackadaisical, you understand. Irregular meetings, irregular scholarship, and irregular methods of limiting their membership to only the true admirers of The Master. Why, they were willing to simply let anyone in!"

I glanced at Pons. He frequently used "The Master" in conversation as a euphemism when referring to his own mentor. If he noticed my look, he ignored it.

"I have even," added Pohl darkly, as if this were the final telling fact, "assembled an irregular newsletter."

"Really," said Pons with a twitch of his lips, crossing one leg over the other. "Fascinating." He steepled his fingers before his eyes and observed the client with deeper interest. I knew that he was cataloging any number of items about the fellow, and I attempted to do the same, as I felt that I might be asked later what I had seen.

Closer examination revealed that Mr. Pohl had no wedding ring, and that his left sleeve was shiny, indicating that he favored that arm, and that he did a lot of writing. In truth, his left shoulder was somewhat higher, indicating that he routinely sat for hours every day and week in a position with that arm propped on a too-high desk. His clothing was rather worn, and his necktie was at least five years out of date. Additionally, he needed a haircut.

After a silence had stretched awkwardly, Pons finally asked, "And how may we be of service?"

Pohl, who had fallen into a reverie after mentioning his newsletter, no doubt lost in memories of past triumphs, looked up with a start. "Eh? Oh, yes, yes. I need your protection, Mr. Pons. I feel that my very life may be in danger."

"You have been threatened physically?"

"I have."

"Come, come, Mr. Pohl. I am not a bodyguard, and do not sell my services as such. I can give you a list of half-a-dozen individuals, both professional and otherwise, who can take on that role."

"But, sir, you were recommended to me by no less than Mr. Ebenezer Snawley!"

"What? Is he still among the living? I haven't seen him since – how long has it been, Parker?"

"Assuming that you haven't seen him on some other occasion since that singular Christmas dinner, it has been over a dozen years, at least."

"I agree. Tell me, Mr. Pohl – How does an interest such as yours, in the famed American author of the macabre, overlap that of a particularly unique Dickensian?"

"More than you might expect, sir. We sometimes run across one another at book auctions. Only yesterday afternoon I encountered him – we were both at Rathham's, where they were selling a *Tamerlane* first – and during the course of our conversation, I explained my problem and he gave me your name."

"And did you bid?"

"No sir, I did not. I cannot afford a treasure such as that. But I wanted to see who *did* buy it, to ascertain if that person might be considered worthy of being approached to join the Society, or perhaps even 'The Gold Bugs'."

"Pardon me?" I said, suddenly wondering if it was time to make my way to the sideboard for a substantial restorative.

"'The Gold Bugs'. It is a sub-group, a steering committee, made up those who are most dedicated amongst us to the study of Mr. Poe's works."

I had to glance toward the tall windows looking onto Praed Street. I could not meet Pons's eyes for fear that I would burst into gales of laughter. My dilemma worsened when Pons stated – likely with a straight face, although I could dare not look at it – "Really. I would have thought something more along the lines of 'The Casks of Amontillado'. Possibly, 'The Masques of the Red Death'. Or more prosaically, 'The Poe Patrol'."

I could not resist. "Perhaps 'The Poe Folk Upon the Moors'"

Quoth Pons, "Nevermore," and I could resist no longer. The laughter that I had been holding back for so long now rolled forth, and Pons, I was pleased to see, joined me, raising a hand to cover his eyes. Our guest, however, was not amused.

As I was wiping away tears, Pohl stood, his hands now balled at his side, and two livid spots of color on his otherwise white cheeks. "Good day, sir!" he cried. He turned, looking this way and that, and I realized that he was searching for where he had left his coat and hat. Spotting them on the pole beside the door, hanging with Pons's Inverness and deerstalker, along with my rather ordinary overcoat, he took a step, and then another, before Pons leapt to his feet, and before I knew it, he had turned Pohl back to the fire and his chair, murmuring soothing apologies and offering him refreshment.

Mollified, the little man accepted a brandy, and I nodded at Pons to include me as well. Soon, we were sipping quietly, waiting for that moment after any tension when everyone tacitly agrees to put it behind them and move forward with the conversation, previous disagreements provisionally tabled by an unspoken social treaty.

"Please tell me more of this threat, Mr. Pohl," said Pons with genuine interest.

"I believe that someone is trying to kill me!" the little man cried.

Suddenly, in spite of the comic aspect brought to the affair by the wee fellow before us, the matter became much more serious. As they say, even the paranoid can have real enemies, and who could deny that someone as innocuous as the man before us couldn't have accumulated one or two as well.

"Tell us the specifics," said Pons simply, putting his brandy on the side table, re-steepling his fingers. and closing his eyes in concentration. Pohl looked confused and glanced my way, but I nodded at him reassuringly, and he continued.

"By day, I am a bookkeeper with a minor firm near the City. But, as you will have gathered, my true passion is concerned with all aspects of Edgar Allan Poe. I have had this interest since I was a boy, and by good fortune, I stumbled upon the Society three years ago. After proving myself worthy, I joined in fellowship with this like-minded group of individuals. Later, I was able to found 'The Gold Bugs'.

"Our society, of which I have risen to be the *de facto* leader, is an exclusive one. We study the works of the great Poe with solemn gravity – *all* of the works, you understand. Fiction and non-fiction. Poetry, short stories, novels, essays, and even *Politan*, his unfinished script from nearly a hundred years ago. For quite a while now, we have raised the scholarship of Poe's works to a previously unequalled level.

"You may have noticed over the last few decades how the works of Shakespeare have been steadily elevated by scholars so that they are now perceived to be masterpieces, when for quite a while they were considered to be . . . less so. It is our goal to do the same for Poe's works."

"Is everyone," interrupted Pons, "in your society in agreement with this pursuit?"

"Oh, yes. While the organization may have originally been founded as something of a social club, a number of us have helped to weed out the chaff and purify the bloodlines, so to speak, so that only those with the purest of motives, according to our strict lights, are now members."

"I take it that you relate all of this because you consider it important – because someone is in disagreement with your interpretation."

"Yes." He grimaced at the memory, and then took a sip of the brandy. "Yes," he repeated. "Allen Blount. The Interloper!"

He spoke as if it were a character in a melodrama: *The Damsel! The Hero! The Interloper!* I almost felt the urge to laugh again, but that would have accomplished nothing, and I could see how serious this was for Pohl. Pons's eyes were still closed, and I nodded for the client to continue.

"A couple of years ago, I received an inquiry about my newsletter, asking if earlier issues were available for purchase. Of course, the letter was from Blount. Curse the day that I ever responded! But he was polite, and more importantly, he offered to pay, so I gathered some spare copies and sent them along. We began to correspond, friendly at first, but as things progressed, his tone began to change."

"Was he threatening even then?"

"No, no. Nothing like that. But I could tell that he didn't appreciate Poe in the correct way."

"The *correct* way?"

"Yes. He seemed to have a fascination for just certain aspects of The Master's works, without appreciating the greater *corpus*, as it were. Specifically, he seemed fixated upon those three stories featuring Poe's detective, C. Auguste Dupin."

Pons opened his eyes. "A worthy object of study," he said. "I believe that Poe is credited with creating the detective story, is he not?"

"True, true. Just one of many reasons that the man is so worthy of admiration."

"Then what is so wrong with Mr. Blount's interests? Surely anything that helps to shore up support in your literary hero cannot be a bad thing."

"You don't understand, Mr. Pons. Edgar Allan Poe is not Blount's literary hero. His hero is *Dupin*, the fictional *creation*, whereas our society is interested in the *creator*."

"Fictional?" said Pons. "Are you so sure? I have it on good authority that, in this case, Poe was simply the Literary Agent, so to speak, of the unnamed chronicler of the three Dupin adventures."

Ned Pohl looked aghast, as if someone had just foully cursed in church. Pons, obviously anxious to avoid a repeat performance of the angry attempted exit of a few moments ago, quickly paddled backwards from these turbulent waters. "What has Mr. Blount done specifically to cause such concern?"

Pohl seemed to be willing to be guided back toward his story. "I first knew that Blount's interests lay in the wrong direction when he began to write letters regarding different articles in our newsletter, not just to me, but to other members as well."

"What sort of letters?"

"Simply as I've explained. He seemed to focus on those few details, and not upon the greater tapestry. He refused to acknowledge Poe's other works as having the same level of importance as the Dupin stories. He repeatedly submitted articles about the character, written in such a way as to focus attention away from Poe."

"And you refused to publish these articles."

"Certainly. I refuse to give a platform for someone who refuses to espouse the correct way to study The Master. After that, he had the gall to publish some of his own articles independently, in . . . in *competition* with my own works. The unbelievable impertinence of

83

the man!" His small hand curled into a fist. "Some of these articles . . . I can barely speak it."

"Yes?"

"He dared to write his own new stories using the Dupin character! As if anything more than The Master's works would ever be necessary! Or tolerated."

"And the letters? To you and the others? What form did they take?"

"They followed the same path. All he wanted to discuss was the detective." He actually sniffed at this point. "I found it offensive."

"What was the response from the other members of the group?"

"Mixed. Some appeared to tolerate his misplaced enthusiasm, and wrote back to him. I understand that several have entered into a regular correspondence with him."

"And has he been to any meetings of the Society?"

"He most definitely has not. Attendance is by invitation only."

Pons raised his eyebrows, and I said, "That's rather curious, is it not, Mr. Pohl? To maintain an organization with the purpose of promoting an author's work – "

" – And the study of his life as well," interrupted Pohl.

"As you say. And yet, in doing so, you limit the effectiveness of what you're doing by the organization's very exclusivity."

"That is what Blount said when he threatened me."

"Ah, we come to it, then. What exactly *did* he say?" asked Pons.

"Why, that reexamining the works of Poe in the same ways, year after, was no different than those bygone church members who wasted so much time and intellectual energy arguing theoretically about how many angels could dance on the head of a pin. He was trying to convince people that there were alternative ways to study The Master."

"No, Mr. Pohl. I meant, what did he say in terms of threatening you? Or was there perhaps a note?"

"No, Mr. Pons, he accosted me in person, two nights ago."

"Had you met before?"

"We had not. Our only contact had been through our correspondence."

"How did you know it was him?"

"He identified himself."

"How would you describe him?"

"I . . . I cannot. It was at dusk, in the street. And he was wearing a heavy coat and hat. But he told me his name."

"How did the encounter occur?"

"I was intending to try a restaurant in Belgravia, a little place that I had heard about."

"Which restaurant?"

"Why, The Brass Lamp."

"I know of it. Go on."

"I was approaching the door when a man walked out of the shadows. I didn't know him at all, and frankly ignored him, until he called my name. I looked up, and saw him glaring at me with a fierce scowl.

"'Ned Pohl!' he rumbled, too low for anyone around us to hear. 'Long have I looked forward to this day!'

"'You have the advantage of me, sir,' I told him, looking nervously from side to side. We were alone in the street, and I could look for help from no one else.

"He crowded in closer, holding out a hand as if in greeting. But he kept approaching, taking hold of my arm, quite roughly. 'My name is Allen Blount,' he said. 'I believe you know who *I* am.'

"'Indeed,' I replied, my discomfort growing by leaps and bounds with his sudden approach. 'How may I help you, sir?'

"'It's too late for that!' he hissed. 'I simply asked for your fellowship in those areas where we share a mutual enjoyment, but you rejected me with your arrogant exclusionary ways.'

"I started to deny it, to pretend that I had no knowledge of what he spoke, but I knew that he possibly did have some grounds to be upset. His letters had been friendly enough, I suppose, for all of their heretical and distasteful beliefs regarding The Master's works. Several of the other members of the Society had even suggested that he be invited to attend a meeting, if not as a member, then at least to have an exchange of ideas. Yet I had discouraged this, and in the end had won over a majority to my side. No invitation was given, and I informed him so by letter – with great pleasure – that his *infra dig* opinions would not be tolerated or welcomed."

"I believe earlier that you mentioned the whole situation wasn't 'seemly'. Do you mean just his opinions, or was there something more?"

Pohl sniffed. "Truth be told, I question his origins. I understand his people are from Nottinghamshire." He made this statement as if it were completely self-explanatory, and thus no other facts were necessary. I certainly didn't understand what objection this could hold, and I doubted from his expression that Pons did either, but he didn't pursue it.

"And what of the actual threat? Does what you've told us constitute the entire nature of it?" asked Pons.

"Not at all. Blount continued to keep a tight hold on my arm, while leaning closer. Never blinking, never raising his voice, he proceeded to list for me what I might expect for blocking his ambitions and 'degrading' him, as he put it – destruction of all that I hold dear. My property burned, my employment eliminated! Finally, if he chose to do so, he said that he could end my very life as well!"

"Good heavens," I muttered. "All of that passion and anger over the works of a dead author?"

"Yes, Doctor, all of that!" snapped the little man.

"Any man can end another's life or burn his property," I said, "but does he have the resources to 'eliminate' your employment, as he threatened?"

"I cannot honestly say. I wouldn't think so. He has a job as a common civil servant, and I'm unaware of his having any extensive financial resources. Perhaps, if he were better off, I would have considered him for membership in the Society, in spite of his offensive views. As it is . . . ."

Pons glanced my way before asking, "What happened next? Did you call for help? Did you inform the police?"

"No, nothing of that sort. He simply released my arm and then walked past me, vanishing into the night. The pavement was crowded with any number of Christmas merrymakers, but the encounter had been so quiet, so subtle, that no one seemed to have noticed anything out of the ordinary. Certainly no one was watching us, or offered to come to my aid. I had rather lost my appetite at that point, as you might expect, and returned home without knowing whether the restaurant was actually any good or not. Yesterday, I took advantage of a half-day from work to attend the auction, and was given your name by my acquaintance, Snawley."

"How did that happen?"

"We were discussing our passions, and – with this event fresh in my mind – I explained how such enthusiasm could take a dark path. It was then that he suggested your services."

"As I said earlier, Mr. Pohl, I am not a bodyguard. What exactly would you like for me to do?"

"Ideally, to save me. But should something happen, I wanted my story told, so that the guilty party's involvement would be known to one honest, independent agent."

"Let us hope that matters don't progress to that finality," said Pons. "However, in the meantime, is there nothing that you could do to make amends with this man? Can you not admit Mr. Blount into your fraternity?"

"What? An amateur dilettante such as he? Absolutely not. His interests in the The Master are entirely perverted and low class. I know for a fact that he is interested in attending our special gathering next month, but there is no way that he shall be allowed!"

"What is special about this gathering?" I asked.

"We always have a noteworthy meeting in January, it being the anniversary of The Master's birth, but this will be a unique event. The one-hundred-and-twenty-fifth birthday, on the nineteenth. How can I let in someone who would cheapen it so?"

"How indeed?" queried Pons, uncrossing his legs, signaling that the interview was coming to a close. "Then, if there is nothing else that I can do, I will keep an eye on the newspapers, Mr. Pohl, and avenge you, should you become newsworthy."

The man's eyes narrowed, and he tried to discern if he was being ridiculed. I, who knew Pons so well, understood that he was, but in so buried a manner that the client would not recognize it for certain. However, I also saw something in Pons's expression that informed me he had perceived something about the matter that contributed to a deeper interest.

"In the meantime," added my friend, "let me provide you with the names of a couple of bodyguards, should you feel the need." He jotted a few lines onto a pad, tore the sheet free, and handed it to the little man, who took and shoved it into his waistcoat pocket without reading it.

Tipping up his brandy glass, and holding it patiently to get the very last drop – for it was very good brandy – Pohl stood, nodded to both of us without offering his hand, and walked to the door. Quickly donning his coat and carrying his hat, he let himself out without comment. In a moment, we heard the street door close with a bang.

Only then did we both release the newly accumulated laughter that had threatened to make itself known throughout much of Pohl's narrative. I was afraid that he might hear it from the street. When it had died away and our eyes were wiped, we settled back in our chairs, new tots of brandy beside us.

"Do you take his story seriously?" I asked.

"It has some points of interest."

"Interest, yes. But validity? It's difficult to believe that something like this can be carried to such a level of seriousness."

"And yet, we have seen it before, have we not? Did he not just refer to our old acquaintance, Ebenezer Snawley?"

I nodded in agreement. Like Pons had been earlier, I was surprised to hear that Snawley was still among the living. He had seemed ancient when we met on that long-ago Christmas of 1920. I had only been living at 7B for a little over a year, even then still trying to adjust to life in London after the events of the War, along with the completely different lifestyle from that I had adopted in Egypt. Meeting Snawley, who came to Praed Street in a hansom cab drawn by an ancient horse, had been very much like an earlier pre-War London. The old man was as fanatical about Charles Dickens as Ned Pohl seemed to be about his distant "cousin", and my amazement had only grown when, during the course of the investigation, it was revealed that there was someone else as urgent and strident about "Boz" as old Ebenezer Snawley. Therefore, I shouldn't have been too surprised that there were other literary fanatics moving about in the world.

"What did you make of our new client?" asked Pons, interrupting my musing. I explained what I had seen about Pohl, and he nodded. "I don't fancy that you've missed too much. You did pick up on the fact that his attendance at the auctions at Rathham's seems a bit above his means, as indicated by his wardrobe."

"What do you think of his tale?"

"Curious. But I hear two or three a week that are more similar than different, as you may recall. It is the price that I pay by throwing open my door and selling my services. Most of these *contretemps* come to nothing."

"But you're not going to wait until he's killed, are you?" I asked, only half-facetiously.

"I don't believe things need progress to that point. I'll put out the word here and there and see what I can turn up. In the meantime, how is Mrs. Parker?" asked my friend, effectively turning the course of the conversation into a completely different direction.

And so Christmas came and went, and I spent it enjoying my newly married life. We passed into 1934 and, although I saw Pons on several occasions throughout those weeks, I confess that I neglected to ask if he'd had any news about his odd visitor. I gave no more thought to the jarring complaints of Ned Pohl until one morning, nearly a week past the Ides of January, when I saw that same unique name written before me in my morning newspaper. I noticed the date, the twentieth day of the month, and realized that the gathering memorializing the American literary figure had been held just the night before. I read through the article twice, the second time with greater attention, explained a bit of the affair to my wife, and then arranged for my neighbor to take care of my practice for the day – a reciprocal arrangement that I must confess led to my being in his debt far more often than he in mine. Thus, having made my arrangements and carrying the newspaper, I set off for Praed Street.

I found Pons distracted. He had obviously been up all night, carrying out one of those abstruse chemical experiments that threatened to suffocate all those within a breathing radius. Making my way across the room's toxic fog, I threw open a window, letting the fumes spill into the street, hoping that they would thin before someone called the fire brigade. Only then was I noticed, so great had been Pons's concentration.

"Ah, Parker, you arrive just as I've obtained my proof." He held up a piece of litmus paper, stained blue. "This will free an innocent man."

"And if you had died in here from these gases?" I coughed. "Who then would have been left to save him?"

"You make too much of it," he riposted. "Much of that smell is from simple Acetic Acid, following a reaction with Sodium Bicarbonate. I found that the reaction from combining the two makes an excellent cleanser to make the etching on this little brass plate more readable." He vaguely gestured at something on the deal tabletop.

I did not follow up on that. "With all of that complicated chemical equipment, and your years of accumulated knowledge and experience, the best that you can do is to mix vinegar and baking soda?" I asked.

He smiled. "I *did* carry out a few other, more complex, experiments as well. And besides," he said, tossing aside the litmus paper and standing up, "mixing those two compounds is always fun to watch, don't you think?"

"You're no better than a schoolboy," I muttered, holding forth the newspaper. "Have you seen today's news?"

"Not yet. I was knocked up early this morning in relation to this other matter. Let me just dash off a pair of telegrams, and then you shall have my full attention."

It was not so simple as that. After writing the telegrams and passing them to the page boy, he went into his room, ostensibly to wash up and change his clothing. By the time he returned a quarter-of-an-hour later, Mrs. Johnson had delivered a pot of coffee and a quick reply to one of Pons's wires. He poured a cup, read the telegram, dashed off a response, took a sip of coffee, seemed to burn his lip, sat down in his chair opposite mine, and said, "Is this about Mr. Pohl?"

I nodded and said, "You indicated that you hadn't read the news."

"And I have not. But I know today's date, just one day after the gathering of the clans, so to speak. Last night was the meeting of the Poe Society – " here he stopped to close his eyes for a moment as he digested that thought, " – and as I've been expecting the matter to approach a crisis around this time, I'm not surprised. Additionally, while you have visited since then, our last 'professional' collaboration, if it may be called that, was on that day just before Christmas, when Mr. Pohl related his troubles. It seemed likely that your news would be in relation to him. I take it, then, that he's been reported dead."

"Nothing is confirmed, although it's assumed to be so. He didn't show up at the meeting last night, but in the middle of it, a messenger arrived, carrying a hastily scrawled note from him, saying that he was in fear for his life, and expected an attack at any moment from Allen Blount, identified specifically. The other members then summoned a constable, who in turn communicated with an inspector. They obtained entry to Pohl's flat, where there were signs of a struggle, and even a small amount of blood."

I referred back to the newspaper. "Nothing seemed to be missing. His clothing was there, as was his only piece of luggage. This was confirmed, to the best of her knowledge, by his landlady. Additionally, his wallet, with something over twenty pounds in it, was lying on his desk. The landlady, who is somewhat deaf, hadn't heard anything of the struggle, but that is considered insignificant, considering her condition.

"It is believed that Pohl, having been given some indication of an imminent attack, notified the meeting, since he believed the members there were his only friends. (This was confirmed by statements that Pohl had made to the members themselves, already tracked down by some dogged reporter.) Sometime after sending the warning, he was attacked in his room, which is on the ground floor back of the building, with its own door. His lodgings are on Fetter Lane, not far from the Temple, and with last night's fog, it's believed that his body could have been taken by night and thrown into the river. They are dragging it now."

Pons narrowed his eyes. "Why would he go to the trouble of notifying the meeting? Why not simply find a constable on his own? Or tell his landlady when he arrived home that he expected some danger? Or most of all, why not send a message to me? He had, after all, gone to the trouble of consulting me to avenge his death, should it happen. Surely it might have occurred to him that I could also prevent it."

"Possibly our subtle ridicule of him at the time rankled him as he later recalled it. It could have festered and grown in the intervening weeks. Have you had any further communications with him?"

"No, but that doesn't mean that the matter has entirely left my thoughts." He pulled on his earlobe. "What of Allen Blount? Has he been arrested?"

"Not as of the time this article was written, although he was being sought for questioning."

"Am I to assume that your presence here at this time of morning, without your medical bag, indicates that you are prepared to spend the day seeking out the truth of this matter?"

"It's every man's duty to bring a murderer to justice!" I declared righteously, and then realized how pompous that I sounded.

Pons smiled in acknowledgement while he stood. "I believe this problem can be easily wound up, but there are a few details to verify, just to be certain that I'm on the right track. There's always a chance . . . ." His eyes narrowed. "I learned painfully, a long time ago, to cross all the *t*'s before absolutely committing to an explanation." He glanced at the mantel clock. "I shall be ready in five minutes." And he entered his bedroom, closing the door behind him.

I finished my coffee and read through the article once again, but with no new insights. When Pons rejoined me, I joined him in heading downstairs. Before exiting the house, he gave a note to Mrs. Johnson, with instructions to "set this in motion, please." Then, without further explanation, we exited and found a cab, settling in on the way to our first stop at Scotland Yard, and the office of our old friend, Inspector Jamison.

He was as stout and solid as ever, and after exchanging pleasantries and best wishes for the New Year, now well under way, we heard what he knew about Mr. Pohl's disappearance. It didn't substantially vary from the newspaper reports, although it seemed the Yard wasn't too worried yet.

"As you say, Mr. Pons, it seemed a bit odd that he would send his plea to the meeting, when there were other, better ways of getting help."

"And Allen Blount? Has he been detained?"

"He was only interviewed. And that's a curious circumstance. He was found at home with his wife, hosting a small dinner party for a few friends. He hadn't been out all evening, as verified by a number of witnesses. However, he showed us a note that he himself had received earlier that night, requesting that he be at the Trafalgar Square Fountain if he wanted to learn something – unspecified – that would be to his benefit. He told us that he ignored it and stayed home, carrying on with his previous plans."

Jamison pushed papers around on his desk until he found the mysterious missive. It was about four inches square, folded once, on cheap paper and written in blue ink. The message was exactly as he described, and offered no clue in terms of awkward phrasing or unusual handwriting. "The envelope?" asked Pons.

"Gone. This was sent to Blount's place of work. He oversees some of the sanitary piping offices near the river. A secretary opened it early in the morning, as she does all the correspondence, and had thrown away the envelope before passing the message on to Blount."

"No matter," said Pons with distraction. He pulled at his earlobe, and then returning to the present, he called out an address on Bartholomew Lane in the City. "That is where Pohl worked. You might find something of interest if you head that way."

Jamison was puzzled, but having known Pons for quite a while, he thanked him and said he'd make his way there directly, asking us if we'd be joining him. "Not quite yet," was the cryptic reply, and then we departed. "Perhaps in an hour or so," he added as he walked away.

Outside, Pons gave an address in Mayfair, we settled into our waiting cab for the quick trip while I hoped for some explanation. As usual, none was forthcoming. Pons's unhesitating direction to the cabbie as to where to go next confirmed that he had already done some additional research and investigation into this matter since Pohl's visit in late December.

Soon we stopped before an impressive home in Bruton Place. Pons's name quickly gained us admittance, and we were almost immediately led into the presence of Lady Sylvia Hayes, a bright-eyed woman in her early sixties, whom I learned was a prominent and founding member of the Society, and also a 'Gold Bug'.

"Yes, that's right. Last night was the yearly meeting when we celebrate Poe's birthday. It was rather special, you know, as it was the one-hundred-and-twenty-fifth."

"And the meeting was held here?"

"It was. Initially, we rotated amongst the other member's homes, but since my husband died a few years ago, it's been agreed that the affair would take place here."

"And in the midst of it, a messenger arrived with Mr. Pohl's note."

"He did. Of course, we had remarked upon Ned's absence, as he sometimes takes this so much more seriously than the rest of us, and it was a surprise that he would miss it for no apparent reason. After we read the note, we looked for the messenger, but he was already gone."

"You say that Mr. Pohl takes this much more seriously. In what way?"

"Oh, his insistence that the Society only accept members that conform to his ways of thinking. He runs his little newsletter – we never had one until he started it, you see – like a martinet, only approving essays that satisfy his strict interpretation of the ways to admire Edgar Allan Poe. He's managed to convert a number of members to his way of thinking – a dangerous path, in my mind. This is turning into something very different from what was intended when a few of us started having gatherings years ago. I believe that if things continue along these lines, there will be a day when I will no longer participate."

"From what you have heard, was Mr. Pohl's dislike toward Mr. Blount exceptional when compared to some of his other beliefs?"

"It was. Mr. Blount's particular doorway into the enjoyment of Poe was through the Dupin stories. He had written and submitted some essays encouraging this viewpoint, but their very existence would sometimes make Ned Pohl nearly apoplectic with rage. It became even worse when he saw that some of the other members, myself included, enjoyed this new viewpoint, and had even entered into regular correspondence with Mr. Blount. Often our meetings were becoming almost single-minded diatribes, as directed by Ned, about maintaining the alleged purity of our cause, and against Mr. Blount personally. I almost felt as if I were being subjected to the political speeches of those Brown Shirts in Germany. This is part of why I was considering dropping out altogether."

While she never came out and said it, she skated toward a near relief if it turned out that Ned Pohl were truly gone – although she was always quick to indicate that she hoped that he would be found all right, and that she was certain that Allen Blount had nothing whatsoever to do with what had occurred the previous night. We thanked her for her time and returned to our cab. Pons gave an address near the Thames, from which I rightly assumed that we were going to speak next to Allen Blount.

The man himself turned out to be in his early fifties, congenial and happy to see us. He gestured around us – "Bazalgette's old offices," – as he led us back to his own room, cluttered with reports and incomprehensible plans sheets, the likes of which I had seen as a boy on the desk of my father, a civil engineer. We settled into chairs before Blount's desk in his pleasant office, and Pons explained our mission. Blount seemed to be puzzled as to his own involvement in the matter, having first learned of it from the police visit that morning. "I knew that Ned Pohl had conceived a profound dislike for me," he said, "but why he would send a note with my name on it, telling that he expected me to attack him, makes no sense at all."

"You are probably not aware," said Pons, "that he visited my rooms in Praed Street a few weeks ago, indicating that he feared for his life, based on a threat you made against him outside a restaurant."

"What?" Blount half stood, before returning to his chair. "That's absurd. I've never threatened him! I've never even met him! Our only contact has been through the mail. I wrote and asked to purchase copies of his Poe newsletter, looking to see if there were any essays regarding Dupin. He and I sent a series of letters, but I quickly discerned that my interest in only one aspect of Edgar Allan Poe's writings was offensive to him. I disengaged at that point, and began to correspond with other members of the Poe Society. It has simply been a pleasant diversion for me. I only learned this morning from the police just how truly upset he was by the whole business."

"Enough to say that you threatened him?"

Blount shook his head. "Again, I've never met him. I can't imagine why he's trying to pull me into this maelstrom."

"And last night's note? An invitation to a rendezvous in Trafalgar Square?"

"That is something that didn't tempt me at all. I don't go out after hours if I can help it, and certainly not to something that sounds as dodgy as that! In any case, we were having guests. I certainly wouldn't have missed that for some anonymous appointment. Do you think that Pohl sent the message?"

"Possibly."

Blount had nothing else of relevance to add, and the talk pivoted to the more easy-going topic of Dupin. Pons had some unique "inside" information on the subject, much to Blount's amazement and delight, and we left with firm handshakes and the agreement to continue the discussion at some point in the near future, in more convivial surroundings.

Our next stop was Bartholomew Lane, in The City. We were now heading toward Pohl's place of work, although Pons was singularly uncommunicative during the drive. I wanted to ask what else he had discovered in the weeks since Pohl's visit, in addition to what had already been revealed – namely, how he had known the location of Lady Sylvia's home and where to find Allen Blount. However, I knew that he would reveal all in his own good time.

We arrived to find several police vehicles parked in front of the imposing structure. Pons led us inside, and through doors marked Burton and Hale. There seemed to be a great deal of confusion, with policemen interviewing various employees singly or in small groups all around us. We made our way toward the back of the great room, where Inspector Jamison stood with a tall, elderly man, hunched forward and wringing his arthritic fingers.

Jamison saw us and said, "You were right, Pons."

"Pons?" said the old man. "I received your wire an hour or so ago. You were correct, sir. It's all been taken, and if you hadn't notified us, the loss might not have been discovered for weeks. Months, perhaps!"

My confusion was only growing by leaps and bounds. After nearly a decade-and-a-half as Pons's friend, I knew that he liked to keep all aspects of an investigation to himself, until he was certain of every fact and had every thread in hand. Additionally, there was something of the showman in him, waiting for the moment when, like a magician, he could pull aside the curtain and reveal that the beautiful woman had been changed into a rabbit. However, there was a limit to what I would put up with, and I think that Pons knew that I was approaching it. He began to explain.

"It brings me no satisfaction to be correct, Mr. Hale, but I am glad to have been able to provide some assistance in the matter. My suspicions were aroused by a patently odd story related to Dr. Parker and myself some weeks ago by Mr. Pohl, when he explained that he had been threatened by a man named Allen Blount who, like himself, was an *aficionado* of American author Edgar Allan Poe."

Mr. Hale, as the elderly man had been identified, nodded. "He keeps a small bust of that Poe fellow on his desk. It's always been a harmless eccentricity, or so I thought – a man named Pohl who fancies himself distantly related to an author named Poe."

"Your Mr. Pohl, in trying to come up with a clever real-life plot, clumsily attempted a distraction to cover his intended crime. He set the scene by telling us of the threat toward him, played out against the background of a British Edgar Allan Poe Society." He went on to explain what Pohl had told us in Pons's sitting room, and also some about the literary group. "His story sounded fishy at best, and I have been approached too many times in the past by people seeking my help as an alibi for their own crimes. I've come to recognize the signs."

"So he falsely accused Allen Blount of threatening him, and then of likely killing him," said Jamison.

"And more importantly," added Hale, "he has absconded with a fortune in bearer securities that had been under his management, leaving the theft so cleverly hidden that, without your wire earlier this morning, Mr. Pons, the loss might have gone unreported."

Pons nodded. "I believe that you would have found them sooner than that. After all, following Pohl's attempt to fake his own death last night, you would have had to reassign his accounts to someone else. The loss would have been noticed."

"Not necessarily. He hadn't just stolen the securities. He had altered the books, and arranged things so the loss wouldn't have been immediately obvious. Without your information this morning, we wouldn't have known where to look, and to look so soon."

"Apparently, you've known about this since soon after Pohl's visit," I said. "What other actions have you taken?"

"Oh, simply a bit of digging here and there into this life. His background, his activities."

"It's a pity," said Hale, "that you couldn't have prevented the theft entirely."

"At the point he first brought himself to our attention, he had committed no crime, unless his alterations of your records at that point had already crossed the line. And there was no reasonable evidence then to make such an accusation that would result in your verifying it one way or the other. He was simply an angry little eccentric with a fixation on a manically strict interpretation of Edgar Allan Poe.

"He had to have enough rope to hang himself, and while he set about doing so, I intended to keep an eye on him, and be ready when he did. I was fairly certain that the meeting of the Poe Society last night would be of significance in his plan, as it turned out to be."

"Nevertheless," said Hale, "while I appreciate your intervention, and how it has shown us the problem, I do wish that you could have warned us ahead of time, so that the securities wouldn't have actually been stolen."

"I wanted him to commit himself. Having done so, I expect that now we should go and arrest him and, incidentally, retrieve your property."

"Oh ho! You know where he is, then?" asked Jamison.

"Of course. I've had him followed almost since the beginning, and certainly during the last few days, when I believed that he would make his move."

Pons, Jamison, Mr. Hale, and I made our way outside where a police car was waiting. Pons gave an address in Little Coram Street, and we slid smoothly on our way. "I believe," explained Pons, "that Pohl's initial idea to involve me was to give credence to his framing of Allen Blount in his supposed murder. However, after meeting with Parker and myself, he realized that doing so might be a mistake, and he revised his plans, instead sending a note to the Society meeting, hoping that when he disappeared, I would not be involved.

"As I said, I had investigated him and already formulated an idea as to his intentions. I checked with the staff at The Brass Lantern, questioning them about the night he said he was threatened by Blount. They informed me that, not only did he eat there that night, contradicting his claim that he had not, but that he is in truth a regular patron, when he told us that he was trying it for the first time.

"I communicated with the individuals whom I listed as possible bodyguards, and neither had been approached by Pohl. While this is in itself not conclusive, as he may have simply not wanted to associate with their likes, it was – when taken with other facts – indicative.

"I also sought out old Ebenezer Snawley, whom Pohl said had recommended me. That part was true, but Snawley elaborated, indicating that Pohl's questioning was much more direct, reflecting a concerted desire to know details about me. Apparently Snawley tells the tale of my assistance to him many years ago to whomever will listen, and Pohl already knew about me when approaching Snawley, instead of being recommended by Snawley first.

"Mr. Snawley also confirmed that Ned Pohl *did* bid on and win several expensive Edgar Allan Poe-related items at the auction that day at Rathham's, in contrast to his usual watch-only policy, indicating that he had already begun to convert some of the securities to cash.

"During the past few weeks, Mr. Pohl was observed visiting the Capital and Counties Bank in Oxford Street. By calling in a few favors, I learned that he was known there under the name 'Roderick Usher', the main character in 'The Fall of the House of Usher'. He had recently set up a new account, reflecting a few recent and rather large deposits. The account documents showed a residence in Little Coram Street, the same one where we're headed now. Mr. Pohl's intentions were becoming more and more clear, and when I learned this morning that he had pulled the lanyard, so to speak, and fired his opening volley, I was not surprised."

The car pulled to a stop in a rather rough street, and we climbed out. Pons waved his hand twice, and a lad shambled out of the nearby shadows. I recognized him as Aidan Quill, one of the Praed Street

Irregulars, as Pons likes to call them. He touched his cap and said, "He's been up there all morning. Wilson told me that he got in last night and didn't go back out."

"Thank you, Aidan," said Pons, putting some coins in the lad's hand. Then, gesturing for us to proceed him, we went inside.

It was a dark little building in a row of the same. Pons moved past us and led the way up several flights of stairs to the third and top floor. At the back, he paused before a heavy door. "There is no way out but through this door," he whispered. Then, he knocked three times.

After a moment, a voice that I recognized said, "Who is it?"

"Gasfitter, sir," said Pons in a nasal tone. "Report of a leak in the building."

A pause, and then, "Oh, all right." We heard the sound of what was mostly likely a chair being pulled back from its position against the doorknob. Then, a bolt was drawn, a lock turned, and the door opened.

Jamison stepped forward, pushing the door back as he went. "Police!" he cried, reaching a hand toward the little man who had been knocked backwards.

The inspector's hand closed on empty air. Pohl had dodged with surprising nimbleness from his grasp. Pons and I crowded in behind the policeman, closely followed by Mr. Hale. Pohl, already shocked by the intrusion of a strange policeman, was literally stunned for just a moment as he recognized both Pons and me, and then his former employer.

"Pohl!" roared Mr. Hale. "You thief! Where are the securities?"

Pohl's eyes darted to the right, and I saw that there was an open case upon a battered table. Folded clothing was piled beside it, and within was a thick sheaf of papers. Pohl was obviously calculating his various chances of getting by us and out the door, and whether or not he could retrieve the case before doing so. Hale saw the direction of Pohl's glance, and he took a step toward the case, passing in front of Jamison.

That seemed to decide the matter for our captive. He bolted, but not toward the door as expected. Rather, he trod backward toward a window, overlooking the court behind the building. In two steps, he was throwing it open and pushing a leg through. With a cry, Pons moved toward him, with me only a foot or two behind. Pohl was already leaning out, reaching for what we would later see was a drain pipe leading from the roof to the ground, far below.

He seemed to get a grip upon it, but he hadn't counted on the accumulated January ice. His fingers slipped, and he only had the one chance. Before Pons's fingers could close upon his clothing, he was gone, tumbling backwards with a terrible cry. Physics tells us that a falling object only takes a second or two to cover the distance from that window to the ground, but it seemed to stretch much longer than that before we heard a terrible thump on the wet paving stones below.

Pons looked out the window for a moment, and then pulled himself back in, shaking his head sadly. The rest of us were speechless. I eventually looked outside as well, confirming that the terribly broken little man would not arise and escape.

Later, as we were returning to Praed Street, Pons spoke. "I blame myself. I had all of the pieces lined up. Perhaps if I'd managed things a little better, he wouldn't have ended this way."

I disagreed. "He brought it upon himself. His own actions set this in motion, and without your intervention, perhaps he could have ruined the life of Allen Blount."

"Not likely. No one would have taken that amateur invention of his too seriously."

"Possibly. But in any case, you are not responsible for the choices he made. He had obviously scouted out that drain pipe, thinking he could slide down if capture was imminent. He didn't count on the unseasonal cold. His unfortunate death is no different than if he'd bolted from us on the street and had been hit by an omnibus."

Pons sighed. "I suppose so."

"A neat piece of work from start to finish," I continued. "Despite the outcome, you managed it very well. And it certainly was an eye-opener to me, to see the obsessive interest that these people will show in relation to authors."

"True. An eye-opener indeed. Poor Ned Pohl. How could he have been so wrong? I wish that I could have told him the truth about Dupin, who was infinitely more interesting than his chronicler."

And then Pons proceeded to relate many amazing and fascinating things about the topic that I cannot repeat here, all through our journey back to Praed Street, and on into the afternoon as well.

# The Singular Affair of the Blue Girl

"If you cannot rid me of this torment, I fear that I shall be dead within a month!" cried the shaken old man, rolling forward to greet us from the shadows of the musty library. "The Blue Girl is warning me, and I don't know what to do!"

Just a moment before, we had been led to this room by the butler, Breverton, where my friend, Solar Pons, and I were introduced to Sir Milton Frieze, hero of the second Boer War, and a man self-described in his telegram as "plagued".

"You must calm yourself, sir," I answered, wishing that I had retained my coat against the October chill permeating this room and looking forward to the promised tea, which the butler had been instructed to request from the kitchen.

"Indeed," said Pons, calm in the face of the man's terror. "You must not succumb to the local atmosphere. It has been quite a while since my last visit to this part of the world, and personally I always find it quite rewarding in terms of interesting experiences."

His matter-of-fact tone seemed to settle Sir Milton. I understood the reasons behind Pons's statement, but I was not sure that I could completely agree with it. Dartmoor might be fascinating or intimidating, and possibly quiet and brooding – yet I believe that any rewards to be found there might be classified as being in the eye of the beholder.

I glanced back toward Sir Milton, now in his late sixties, who had finally reached us in his wheelchair. Certainly he'd had years of practice getting around in it, or so I understood from the short *précis* of the man's life that Pons had provided on the train. Yet, as he fought to propel himself, he seemed awkward and uncertain, as if he were still just learning to use it. He moved with frustration and suppressed anger, even after all these years, at the situation in which he found himself.

He must have seen something akin to pity in my expression for, as he struggled to settle his nerves, he waved us to nearby seats, saying, "It wasn't always like this, you know. My wound didn't cause my paralysis – at least not immediately." Talking about the past appeared to settle him. "I was near an explosion at Heilbron in 1900 – during one of the attacks on the convoys. That was in late May, and I was back here a month later. I healed up just fine, married, had my sons." He grimaced. "The early years went well. But then it all soured. First my wife sickened and died, while the boys were still but lads, ten and twelve. Then, the shrapnel that was still in me worked its way around as it sometimes does, closer and closer to my spine, until I ended up as you see me now. And now . . . ."

"Yes?" queried Pons.

Sir Milton, who had started to seem upset again, was saved from providing what would seemingly be an unpleasant answer by the arrival of a stout and smiling woman, nearly the same age as Sir Milton, with a tray holding the much anticipated warm beverage. "Thank you, Mrs. Dodd," said our host. As cups were poured, Sir Milton abruptly apologized, stating that perhaps we would have welcomed something stronger. However, both Pons and I assured him that the tea suited us perfectly.

After the woman left, Sir Milton sighed. "That is the cook," he explained. "We keep a very small household now, just a few servants who have been with me for years."

His voice dropped off as he became lost in his own thoughts, and after a few quiet moments, Pons spoke. "You were saying?"

Clearly, Pons thought that Sir Milton was ready to discuss the reason that we had been requested to travel here. However, the knight placed his tea, nearly untouched, on a nearby table, and continued on a safer tack. "My two sons, Hilary and William, each entered the military. Both eventually rose to the rank of major. Following in my footsteps, I suppose. My old regiment, you know. Went out to India, the pair of them, not long after they each finished university. While there, Hilary - he was the oldest - met a native girl." He dropped his eyes. "Married her, you see. Without telling me. And then he brought her home."

He fell silent again, and I wondered what this had to do with the reason that he had summoned us here. His wire had included some vague reference to the Blue Girl of the manor becoming restive after many years of absence, and that if he continued to be plagued, he was in danger of losing his sanity. Pons's index had contained just a hint of relevant information, really no more than a passing reference, handwritten in the margin at some long distant time, explaining that the Blue Girl was the legendary resident ghost of Ivyfell, the ancient manor of the Frieze family. Understanding that our visit was related to his worries over a ghost, the old man's detour into tales of family tensions was puzzling. Soon I was to understand.

"And how long ago was this?" I prompted.

Sir Milton raised his eyes, and for just a moment, I saw a hint of anguish peeking from the depths. "Somewhat over two years. Spring of '28. We argued, Hilary and I. Bitterly. I told him that he'd been a fool. I . . . I said many things that I now regret. He left in the night without saying goodbye, taking the girl with him. Back to India." He shook his head. Then, much quieter: "Not long after, I received word that he'd been killed in a railway accident. The girl as well."

He stopped to clear his throat, gazing toward his fingers, intertwined in his lap. After a moment, Pons prompted him. "I am sorry for your loss, Sir Milton, as is Dr. Parker, I'm sure. But how does this relate to the unusual message in your request for our presence? You wrote of some phantom that has apparently revived after a long absence. I must warn you that I'm here out of curiosity, and also due to the favor that was called in by our mutual friend, Major Elliott Thursby, but I am not a believer in ghosts."

A grim smile crossed his face as Sir Milton said, "Ah, Mr. Pons, if you'd lived here as long as I have, you wouldn't say that. The Blue Girl appeared with great regularity when I was a boy, as she had for our family for hundreds of years, although she began to let longer and longer periods pass without showing herself. Eventually, I thought that she had used herself up, if that's possible. But she's back . . . and I think it's because I . . . because of how I treated my son." He raised his eyes, and the anguish was palpable.

Pons settled back in his chair and steepled his fingers before his face. "Indeed. And why would she choose to make her presence known now, after remaining quiet for so many years?"

Sir Milton lowered his voice and, looking from one to the other of us, said, "It is related to her own pain, I suppose."

"How so?" I asked quietly.

"The story has been told here for centuries, you understand, but so much is simply calcified legend by this point that it's hard to know the actual truth. The tale dates from the mid-sixteenth century, and the dissolution of the monasteries. The remains of one such building, never very important, is the foundation for this house. As the story goes, a serving girl from nearby Coombe Tracey had fallen into an illicit romance with one of the monks that lived here in the monastery. It remained a secret, but when the King's cronies - including one of my own ancestors - came to take the land and buildings, there was understandable resistance. The girl, whose name is sadly lost to history, hearing that her beloved was in danger, came rushing as fast as she could to find him. It was a foolish act, for she quickly fell into the hands of the surrounding soldiers. They paraded her outside, hoping to provoke a reaction – and they did. The monk – her lover – raced outside to save her, thereby leaving the monastery doors wide open for the marauders to take it.

"The monk didn't care, however, as he was willing at that point to betray his vows and his brothers just to save the girl. He reached the spot outside where she was being held, supposedly upon the hill that you passed on the curve up to the house, and threw himself at the soldiers, in spite of being hopelessly outnumbered. He was slaughtered there in front of the girl, with as little thought as if he had been a sheep. She, being ignored for the moment, leapt back from them with a dirk liberated from one of her persecutors. They laughed, thinking that she too meant to attack them, but instead she gave a cry and fell upon her dead love's body as she pierced herself through the heart."

He stopped for a moment, while I continued to envision the brutality of that long-gone age. Gradually I pulled my focus back to the dark room, with its cold stone walls, ineffective fire, and mullioned windows looking out on the rolling fog, giving the impression that we floated in the clouds.

"It is said that ever since, she cannot rest due to her act of self-murder while on holy consecrated ground. And so she has been seen over the centuries, a figure of sadness in the house and grounds, never at peace, and appearing to members of my family during times of our own sadness and impending tragedy. She was regularly seen, for instance, during the months before my wife's death, by all of us – the staff as well."

"And yet," said Pons, "you indicated that she seemed to appear less and less as the years of your own life passed, until she no longer appeared at all."

"That is so. Perhaps it is because spirits lose their essence after such a long period of time. Or possibly she *has* made other appearances, and I have simply ceased to notice her, as one would a forest creature that appears at the edge of one's vision so often that it is no longer worth remarking upon."

"Something," I countered, "has apparently brought her once again to your attention."

Sir Milton nodded. "It was the return of my younger son, William, from India, for the first time since he joined the Regiment five years ago."

"He didn't come home when your other son died?"

"No. There was no funeral, as there was no body, you see. Only a simple memorial service. The train accident occurred on a trestle bridge that collapsed into a gorge somewhere near Bhusawal. Hilary and the girl were never found."

"Your daughter-in-law, you mean," pressed Pons.

A look of sadness crossed the old man's face. "Yes." He cleared his throat. "I was a fool, gentlemen. I came to fatherhood late in life, after letting myself settle into incorrect and backwards beliefs. I had decided early on just who my sons should be, based on some ridiculous adherence to tradition and family history, and I did not take into account that they had become grown men with their own plans. I would like to think that I would have seen sense at some point about Hilary's choice of a bride – but the opportunity was taken from me, even as my son's life and . . . and that of my daughter-in-law were taken from them." He held a shaking hand to his brow.

"But what about the return of your younger son could have prompted the reappearance of the Blue Girl?" I asked.

"William came home nearly a month ago, in the latter part of September. I had very much looked forward to his return, but our happy reunion was not to be. As soon as he arrived, I could see that he blamed me – not for Hilary's death, you understand, but because of the unpleasantness between us at the end that had driven him . . . *them* away. He said that he had seen Hilary and the girl – that is, to say, Prisha – after their return to India following our arguments here, and had heard from Hilary some, if not all, of the terrible things that I said. After his return home, William related to me – quite angrily, I might add – how hurt Hilary had been by my rejection, and his worry, right up to the day of his death, that I would somehow find a way, from here, to undo the marriage."

"Impossible?" I said. Then, " Would you have tried?"

"No! Of course not, even if I could have. As soon as they had left England, I realized my idiocy, but pride kept me from making the first move to apologize. And then . . . and then it was too late."

"So William returned home and reopened the old wounds," summed up Pons.

"More than that," replied Sir Martin. "My situation with Hilary will never be resolved. But now William hates me as well, and he makes no secret of it. We barely speak. My only comfort is that he shows no indication of leaving now that he is here, and somehow I may yet be able to make amends to him, if I have the chance."

"But you've had no luck so far."

"No. I must admit that, with the coolness that lies between us, I've been unable to satisfactorily approach the subject. And now . . . the Blue Girl is warning me. Warning me that I'm the next to die!"

He realized that his voice had climbed in an unbecoming manner. "I hope that I'm wrong," he indicated in a calmer tone "I hope that there will still be time for us to repair our relationship."

"Have a care, Sir Martin," warned Pons. "You thought that there would be time to repair the breech with your older son, and Fate intervened. Do not make that mistake again. Do not wait."

The man in the wheelchair nodded. "I'm sure that the Blue Girl is trying to give me the same message – hence her reappearance. But I don't know how to begin."

"You have not heeded this warning that you believe her to be offering," said Pons succinctly.

"It is not that easy."

Pons looked exasperated, but chose to change the subject. "Tell us of the Blue Girl's recent appearances."

Sir Martin nodded, as if now we were getting somewhere. "The first occurrence was not long after William's return. We had quarreled, on the very day of his arrival, and it had continued each day thereafter. He had taken to avoiding me – sadly, that has continued to the present. I was in my bedroom for the night. I sleep on the ground floor now, you see. After losing the use of my legs, I've been unable to venture upstairs.

"I was in my bed, which lies near the window overlooking the south grounds – "

" – And the drive by which we arrived today as well."

"Precisely. As you will recall, the weather in late September had been unnaturally cool, especially here on the edges of Dartmoor, but that day had been clear and pleasantly warmer than earlier in the month. I had my window slightly open. The moon was rising in the east. It was nearly full, and as it topped the trees, the hilltop that I described, where the Blue Girl was killed, came into sharp relief. There she stood, on top of the rise, highlighted by moonlight and gazing toward my room with great sadness."

Pons shook his head. "How can you know her expression?" he asked impatiently. "If she was facing you with the moon low in the sky and to her side, her face would have been in shadow. And that hill is nearly three-hundred feet from the front of the house."

"All I can tell you is that I perceived sadness. Perhaps it was in the way that she stood."

"Hmm."

"Why do they call her the Blue Girl?" I asked. "Is it a manifestation of this sadness that accompanies her, or does she actually radiate a bluish color?"

"There has always been an actual blue tint to her," said Sir Martin. "It was certainly the case when I was younger, and it was still so when I saw her on the hillside. Her dress was blue, and seemed to have a glow about it."

"And how often have you seen her since?"

"In the four weeks or so since William's return, I would guess eight or ten times."

"You do not know for sure?"

Sir Martin thought. "Eight."

"Always in the same location?"

"No, I saw her on the hillside only the once, although I've looked each night since from my window before falling asleep. But I've seen her at twilight a few times from that window, moving along the edge of the trees visible from this room, where I spend the greatest part of my time here. Also she appeared once in the entry hall as I went through from here on my way to dinner. She seemed to glide across the first-floor balcony at the top of the stairs, running between the two wings."

"Have you pointed her out to anyone else, or sought confirmation? From your butler, perhaps?"

"No, Mr. Pons. I've kept it to myself – I suppose to hide my shame at how she is chastising me."

"Are the places that she had recently appeared the same locations where you observed her in your youth?" I interjected, imagining how it would be to look from my own window, perhaps at bedtime, or while moving from one room to another, and seeing a troubled spirit from the corner of my eye.

"Why, no," said Sir Martin, a little surprised that the thought had only just occurred to him. "She always appeared at the rear of the house, even when my wife was dying. That part of the building is the oldest part of the house, the section that was the original monastery, and likely built as early as a millennia ago. The rest of the house – this room for instance, the entrance and stairs, the room in which I sleep, and some of the upstairs bedrooms – while dating from the late sixteenth and seventeenth centuries, were added sometime after my ancestor, one of Henry VIII's supporters, was given the property."

"Interesting," muttered Pons, who had been thinking quietly for the last moment or so, his hand wandering idly to tug at his ear lobe before dropping to tap upon his lower lip. "So in addition to the Blue Girl's reappearance after so long of an absence," he continued, "she has also shifted her base of operations, so to speak."

"Perhaps," countered Sir Martin, a little defensively, "she has had to move to where I can now be found so that she can deliver her message."

"A message that, you believe, is purposed to exacerbate the guilt related to the circumstances connected with the loss of your son and daughter-in-law."

"More than that, Mr. Pons. To warn me of my impending death. I'm certain of it. William's return, and possibly his anger at me in connection with Hilary's death, have served to re-energize and revive the Blue Girl. After all, her own story was connected with tragic love and loss, and no doubt she responds to such pain in others."

"*When you have eliminated the impossible....*" muttered Pons.

"What did you say?" asked Sir Martin, but Pons didn't reply.

At that moment, the wind, which had been blowing the fog fitfully since our arrival, seemed to increase, rattling the mullioned windows locked against it, and moaning slightly down the chimney to whip the feeble flames of the nearby fire. I gave an involuntary shudder, a fact which did not go unnoticed to my discreetly amused friend. Without thought, I rose and walked to the window. The fog, in spite of the wind, had thickened, and instead of being dispersed, it only swirled, obscuring the surrounding trees and hillside for a moment before they became visible again. It had been a damp and heavy fog, reminiscent of the worst of London – no light mist, this! – and I wished again for my coat as I returned to my chair and poured myself another cup of tea, now sadly grown cold.

Sir Milton declined my offer to refill his cup, and Pons ignored me, leaning forward in his chair, as if preparing to rise. "Thank you for inviting us down, Sir Milton. There do seem to be some points of interest about the matter. Would it be possible to speak with your son?"

"Certainly, certainly." Then his eyes took on a worried look. "But please, Mr. Pons, don't tell William why you are here."

"Surely he suspects?" said my friend. "I've rarely found a house that had any secrets for very long. A servant learns something, makes a connection, and shares with someone else another shard of relevant fact. Soon the whole story is pieced together. It would surprise me greatly if your son hasn't been included in that web of information by now."

"Not possible," said our host. "As I said, I've told no one that I've seen the Blue Girl, and I never spoke as to why you were invited. I even had myself taken into Coombe Tracey to send the wire, lest anyone read what I'd written."

"Then why do they think we are here?" I asked, unable to avoid the obvious question, and setting down my cup. The tea was too cold to warm me.

"I've mentioned to Breverton that I'm thinking of selling some of the paintings upstairs, and that I've asked for your help to assist in vetting a dealer or two that have questionable reputations. It will allow you to look around the house, ostensibly examining the paintings, while instead looking for clues as regards the reappearance of the Blue Girl."

"And if I find these clues?" asked Pons. "What would you have me do then, Sir Milton? Clearly you have gone over to the side of the spiritualists, and I am *not* an exorcist."

The old man squeezed his eyes shut. "I do not know, Mr. Pons," he whispered. "I do not know. I suppose that I'm hoping that, in spite of my lifetime of belief, you will disprove this phantom. If her recent reappearances are not in truth a ghost at all, then it means there is some human agency at work. And if there is a human agency, then perhaps knowing the explanation will in itself provide comfort – and to know that I haven't in truth been condemned in some way by the Blue Girl, come back to rebuke me for losing my son and his wife."

As he spoke, his tone continuously thickened, and he barely uttered the word *wife* before he gave a single short sob, raising a shaking hand to his eyes. The fellow was clearly in a bad way, and Pons and I looked away for a moment, uncomfortable at seeing the raw emotion of the man exposed. Then, after he had regained himself, Pons spoke again. "We will try to find an answer, if possible, but I can make no promises." He stood. "And now, might you have your man Breverton show us into your son's presence?"

Sir Martin wheeled awkwardly to a nearby desk and stabbed at a button. I heard nothing, but within moments the butler had entered the room, whereupon he was asked where William was located.

"The upstairs drawing room, sir," came the reply.

"Please show our guests to him." I noticed that Sir Martin didn't have Breverton check first to make sure our intrusion would be welcome.

"This way, gentlemen."

I looked back as we entered the hall to see the knight sigh while he wrestled his chair around, starting to roll toward the window which looked out onto the eastern grounds.

Breverton pulled the door shut and turned to lead us to the stairs. Pons spoke his name, and the old man stopped and turned with a curious expression upon his face. "Have you been with Sir Martin for very long?" he asked.

Breverton's eyes narrowed, almost imperceptibly, as he considered the balance between his distaste at answering questions regarding his master and being courteous to a guest. "I have, sir. I was hired in 1901, the year that Master Hilary was born."

"So you knew both boys well, then."

He said nothing for an instant that was just long enough to be noticeable, and replied simply, "Yes." Then, "Sir." Then his expression softened, and he added, "All of the staff has been here that long, or longer. Mrs. Dodd, the cook. Hayes, the gardener. The understaff as well, what little there are of them now." He swallowed, his brittle façade cracking for a moment. "We all watched the young masters grow up."

"Do you think that Major Frieze, Sir Martin's younger son, will have any objections to the sale of some of the paintings?"

Breverton's relaxation at hearing the question was unmistakable. I was uncertain as to what he thought that Pons was seeking to learn, but clearly this topic was considered acceptable. The man's lined face became almost friendly.

"Not at all, sir. I don't believe that he feels any sentimentality toward them whatsoever. But of course, you will need to question him about that yourself."

"Certainly." And we resumed our passage across the hall.

There were two symmetrical stairways at the back, framed by doorways opening deeper into the ground floor. Each led up to a landing that stretched across the first floor level. The hall was dark, although the cold damp of the room where Sir Martin spent so much of his time was not so apparent here. I wondered why the old knight chose to stay in his study under such unpleasant conditions – penance, perhaps? Possibly the rest of the house was no better.

We climbed the closer rise of stairs on the right, and as we moved across the first floor landing, I recalled that Sir Martin had seen the Blue Girl here once during her recent return. Although I knew better, I glanced at the floor and walls, hoping to see some sign of her passing – perhaps a cunning preparation of phosphorous, possibly brushed against a railing or the carpet – that might betray a human agency as the cause of the manifestations. There was nothing.

I fleetingly thought that Pons might ask Breverton about the ghost, before I remembered that our purpose here was supposedly related to the sale of artworks. Any undue curiosity might raise unwanted questions – although I wondered how Pons could get at the meat of the investigation without giving anything away.

We turned through a doorway and wound down a long hallway whose walls were covered with paintings, dark with age and only barely visible in the poor light. With many of the doorways in the hallway closed, it was impossible to see much, if anything, about the artworks that we passed, but I thought that I recognized some of the clothing and styles that would suggest the Dutch school, so prevalent in the days when ownership of the Ivyfell property was first assumed from the monks who had died defending it.

The house had been growing warmer as we walked through it, causing me again to question why Sir Martin shut himself up in his cold study. Our progress down the hallway continued until Breverton stopped before an open doorway on our left which led into a small anteroom, thence opening in a different direction into a larger, well-lit chamber.

The intermediary passage had prevented a great deal of the room's light from escaping into the hallway, and our eyes had little time to adjust before being shocked by the bright conditions. Even as he was coming into focus, revealing a much more pleasant place in which to spend one's time, and I could tell that the room's sole occupant, a man in his late twenties, was rising from a plush chair to greet us, laying a book down onto a nearby table.

"Mr. Solar Pons, and Dr. Lyndon Parker," intoned the butler. "Gentlemen – Major William Frieze." Back to the man now facing us, Breverton continued, "Your father asked that you speak with them, sir." He added nothing further, nodded his head deeply, and then departed, pulling the previously open door shut behind him.

The young man's friendly countenance had transformed instantly into a look of suspicion as he heard mention of his father. "About the paintings, no doubt," he said.

Pons gave a slight smile in my direction, his eyes twinkling as his notion of a house with no secrets was verified. I wondered just how much they did know of Sir Milton's sightings of the Blue girl, despite his secrecy.

"That's right," said Pons. "So you are aware, then, that your father is considering selling some of them?"

"There has been some talk. Might I ask which ones?"

"Oh, I am sure that I couldn't say. My brief is more to determine the honesty of the prospective buyers." He lowered his voice. "There have been incidents where some other old families considering similar sales have had unpleasant . . . *incidents.*"

"Incidents?" The man thawed a bit as he became intrigued. "What kind of incidents?"

"Thefts. Before the paintings could be sold, the houses were burgled and the paintings taken. On three separate occasions, after preliminary inquiries were made about offering the items for sale, they vanished within a fortnight. One particular dealer had been in communication with the sellers in all three instances."

I recognized the vague details being mentioned by Pons from a case that had occurred a year or so before. However, he had been actually hired by the suspected auction house, Rathham's, to prove their innocence, instead of the other way around, subsequently establishing that they were being framed by an American who had recently arrived upon these shores.

"I've heard nothing of this," said Major Frieze.

"It is unlikely that you would have. It is in the interest of both the police and the insurance companies to keep matters like this quiet as a way of managing the investigation and also the flow of information. If the criminals are puzzled as to what the authorities do or do not know, they may get careless and make a mistake."

"There is some truth in that, I suppose," the young man nodded.

"In any case," added Pons, "I understood from your father that you've only been back from India for a little over a month."

His eyebrows rose. "That's correct."

"Then it's unlikely that you would have heard of the thefts. Tell me, Major," Pons continued, "have you seen anything unusual since you've been home? Around the house, I mean."

"Such as?"

"Oh, strangers on the grounds, or in the nearby villages."

"No, nothing of that sort. Anyway, I've tended to stay close by the house. In spite of growing up here, returning after having spent five years in India is still something of a shock."

"I see." Pons frowned as if thinking of something, and then looked up with something of a sheepish smile. "I'm afraid that I have to ask . . . ." he began.

"Yes?"

"Well, Dr. Parker and I were having a discussion on the train from London, and I happened to recall the story of the Blue Girl of Ivyfell."

"Really?" asked the young man, who then turned to look at me, as if wondering what I had to say about it. "Our ghost is known in London?"

Clearing my throat at the sudden and surprising turn in the conversation, I responded, "Yes. I've heard some mention of it. Dashed interesting, isn't it?"

"Parker," added Pons with a smile, "is quite the collector of tales of the occult. Hauntings, to be more specific. Isn't that so, Doctor?"

Inwardly I frowned, but uncertain as to Pons's game, and unwilling to take a chance on spoiling it, I concurred – while taking a dig back at my friend in the process. "Yes. Pons's practice frequently puts him into locations with ghostly reputations – old houses, graveyards, the odd crossroads at midnight, and even buildings such as this with grim pasts."

"A former monastery," said William Frieze, thawing a bit.

"Yes," said Pons. Then, with a bit of a hurry in his voice, as if getting it out before he lost his nerve, he said, "Have you seen her? The Blue Girl?"

Without pause, the Major replied in a matter-of-fact tone, "Of course. We all have, at one time or another."

"Really? Tell us more."

"About what you'd expect, I suppose. When I was younger, we – my brother and I – would sometimes see a glowing shape pass in the distance, at the end of a hallway, or on the far side of a room."

"Always in the house, then?"

"Yes."

"Ah. I had thought that I read something about her death occurring outside."

"It did. On the hill by the drive." He smiled at some memory. "But we never saw her there, and there was never anything frightening about that spot. She only appeared in the house."

"Fascinating. And have you seen her since returning from India?"

"Why, no. We – that is, I'm unaware that anyone has seen her in a very long while." He appeared to be considering it for a moment, as if the idea that someone could have seen the ghost recently was something that had not occurred to him.

"Unfortunate," said Pons. "We had hoped that her appearances might be a regular thing."

"You mean that you hoped to see her while we are here," I corrected.

Major Frieze's expression hardened. "Ivyfell is not a music hall, gentlemen, providing scheduled performances twice a day of low entertainment for paying customers."

Pons was quick to apologize. "We never meant to imply anything along those lines," he said. "Forgive me if I've implied otherwise." He took a breath, changing the subject. "Would it be possible to see some of the paintings? Just to have some idea what might be coveted, and where they are kept, should you unfortunately come to the attention of the thieves?"

The man seemed to regain his native good humor, and within a few minutes, he was walking with us down the hallway, deeper into the rear of the house, holding up an old-fashioned lantern, apologizing for the lack of electricity, and giving us a knowledgeable rundown of the various artworks hanging on the walls. The farther we progressed, the older became the walls and appurtenances of the building around us, and the brooding weight of the place was a nearly physical sensation. "Are we now entering the remains of the original monastery?" asked Pons, pointing at the ancient wooden beams exposed through the worn plaster.

"We are. Although the dissolution took place nearly four centuries ago, the monastery itself is much older, having likely been built around in the 1100's, or even earlier.

Holmes nodded, and Major Frieze resumed his narration. Pons seemed much more interested in the paintings in this part of the house than before, leaning in and taking long looks at both the pictures and the frames. At one point he gave some indication of satisfaction, although I could not see why. He seemed to be looking at a portrait that seemed much more insignificant than its neighbors, and there was nothing that made it seem any better than what we had seen before. His reaction was a small thing, and would have only been noticed by someone well acquainted with him for a number of years – and certainly not by the young man who continued to relate knowledgeable anecdote after anecdote concerning the artwork, his earlier hostility springing from our connection to his father now forgotten – at least for the moment.

At the end of the hallway, Pons looked around one last time and said, "This has been a great help to us, Major. The Doctor and I must be getting back to London, but your time and knowledge has been much greatly appreciated."

I thanked our guide as well, and he led us back toward the middle of the house. Returning to the well-lit drawing room, he shook our hands warmly and rang for Breverton, who arrived momentarily to escort us downstairs.

On the ground floor, we were deposited again in the presence of Sir Martin, who once more offered us something from the decanters tabled along one wall. We declined, and Pons stated, after glancing toward the window, "I believe that the weather might hold, at least for a while longer. Might we borrow a trap and pony to assist in our return to the station?"

"Certainly." The old man, who had improved a bit since our arrival, looked newly stricken. "But . . . but surely you don't intend to leave so soon? Can't you help me? What can you find in London that relates to matters here?"

"That is where the seat of government lies," replied Pons vaguely. "It was the government, after all, that first took the monastery from the monks, and it was the King's soldiers who killed the girl. Perhaps we will find something about her in the old records that will answer some questions."

"I see . . . ." said Sir Martin, unconvinced and clearly at a loss at our abrupt cessation of the on-the-scene investigation.

"If you don't mind," continued Pons, "I'd like to use your trap to make a few stops before we depart. It's so very rare that I'm able to journey to Dartmoor, and there are a few sites, as well as an acquaintance or two, that I would revisit while we're here. Would it be all right to leave the trap at the station?"

Sir Martin appeared puzzled. "Of course. It isn't unusual for visitors returning to London to do that very thing, and there is a standing arrangement to have it brought back. But please tell me, before you go – do you see any light, Mr. Pons? Was William able to give you any information?"

"I was intentionally vague with him," came the reply. "But he is certainly quite knowledgeable about the paintings. Tell me, Sir Martin," he continued, abruptly changing the subject. "Were your sons happy here while they were growing up? I ask because, after his initial reluctance at speaking to us at your request, he seemed quite even-tempered, even pleasant – as if he is glad to be back. Almost carefree, as a matter of fact – and also as if he is quite proud of his home."

"Indeed, both of my sons were quite happy throughout their youth, even after the terrible illness that took their mother. They had a fine childhood, I believe, exploring the moor, having their little adventures. I'm certain that William has fond memories of the place. I suppose that's why he returned here after leaving the military, in spite of his anger with me."

Pons nodded and stood. "That will be all for now, then. Dr. Parker and I will make our visits to our local friend, and then return to London. We shall be in touch soon."

Breverton was again summoned, and he soon had the wheels in motion to have a nice little two-wheeled trap a fine strong horse brought around. While we waited under the butler's silent gaze, Pons and I retrieved our coats and hats, Pons talking lightly the whole time about how long it had been since we have been able to sit down with our friend, the minister of the Grimpen church.

Taking up our bags – as we had each brought a small grip on the assumption that we would be staying the night – we climbed into our conveyance, and as I was about to gig the horse into motion, Pons held up a hand. Motioning Breverton closer from where he had been watching in the doorway, he lowered his voice and said, "It became apparent during our conversation with Sir Martin that the death of his older son still causes him grief."

The butler, puzzled at the statement and clearly wishing to avoid any indiscretions, nodded warily, especially as he was probably uncertain as to our status with his master.

"Do you see any hope for a reconciliation with his younger son?" Pons continued.

"I . . . believe . . . I *hope* . . . that in time, something of the sort might occur."

Pons nodded and thanked him. Then I set the horse in motion, and we headed down the drive. As we passed the hillside on our left, rising thirty treeless feet above us, I couldn't help but look that way, attempting to see some sign of the presence that had so unnerved the old knight.

"'*No ghosts need apply*'," said Pons, reading my thoughts.

"That," I countered, "is not even your dictum."

"Simply because I didn't say it first does not mean that I can't adopt it," he replied. "Was the first to proclaim '*Do unto others as you would have them do unto you*' the only one allowed to say that?"

I laughed. Pivoting the subject, I noted, "I take it that we are not actually returning to London."

"My statement was accurate. We will visit our friend in Grimpen, and *then* return to London. But we have one or two other chores to accomplish between the two."

"And of course it suited your purpose to let them think that we were leaving sooner rather than later."

"Yes. I hope that it wasn't too clumsy when I tried to divert their attention. By driving ourselves and mentioning vague visits to a friend, we won't be expected directly at the station, and hopefully no one will feel the need to personally observe us climbing onto the Exeter train.

Doing so would only force us to disembark there and find another train to come back."

"But you truly *do* intend to visit our friend, I presume?"

"Of course. I hope to make use of his curious and wonderful library."

"Did you not learn enough on the way down here? You spent enough time reading it on the train." I nodded towards his bag, where an old black leather volume, pulled from his shelves in Praed Street that morning, had rested since our arrival in Devonshire.

"I suspect that our friend will be able to focus our lens on more precise information than was included in the general survey summarized in Dr. Mortimer's fine book."

As the fog piled and then retreated around us, we continued to talk, our conversation drifting from Sir Milton's problem to other past associations with the wild land around us. We soon left Haytor Vale behind us, and passed by the turn to Hound Tor, with Baskerville Hall off in the same direction. I still remembered that night half-a-decade before when that fool Leighton Forbes, scrambling along the tall rocks of the Tor, dropped his pistol when he thought he saw the ghost of his wife, when in fact it was the indifferent wife of a shepherd, taking an evening meal across the moor to her husband. Still, the resulting accidental gunshot was enough to spook Colonel Throckmorton out of his hiding place in the nearby stone circle – and Pons later admitted to the sheepish Forbes that if the gun hadn't fired, we never would have caught the man later described in the press reports as "The Scoundrel of Chudleigh Knighton".

We topped a hill, and I couldn't resist stopping the horse for just a moment to gaze out upon the drop toward Grimpen, and the vast moor stretching all around it. It was late afternoon by then, and the sun was descending in the west, mostly hidden by dark building clouds. It was still clear in the direction we faced, and behind us the layer of fog that had chased us along the way had been left behind for the moment, although it was building once again around the rock outcroppings, pouring down here and there across the road. The effect of the October wind down in the lowland, much stronger than here on the high ground, was evident as the gorse bushes flexed and bent with the regularity of ocean waves. Overhead, there were sharply defined bars of light radiating up from the hidden sun, the rays stretching like a fan through the clouds, spread in all directions. When I was a child, my mother had called these "God Lights", and as always, the phrase reminded me of her whenever and wherever I saw them.

Closer to us, the blue and darker blues of the uneven patchwork of fields and occasional treacherous bogs, separated by the meandering ancient rock walls, spread to our right and left so on out of sight. And closer still, a wild moorland pony and her colt noisily tugged at grass by the road, not twenty feet away, tails twitching and eyes covertly watching us, but all the while making no move to flee. Our own horse ignored them, feeling imperious, I suppose.

With a sigh, I set him into motion once again and we started down the hill, quickly losing sight of the incredibly beautiful, and yet powerfully lonely, vista as the trees and rock walls rose around us. I recalled reading once that a Devonshire man always swears by his country, and I could understand why - specifically if he were from Dartmoor. Although the moor was a cruel and forbidding place, there was something ancient and beautiful about it as well that, once seen and experienced, could never be forgotten. I had only been given the opportunity to visit here on a limited handful of occasions, and I questioned myself, as I had before, why I didn't come back more often.

Throughout my pondering, my friend sat quietly beside me, deep in his own thoughts. Had he also been considering that stark beauty, or did his mind run instead to past investigations, both his and those of his Illustrious Predecessor, that had taken place in and around this forsaken spot? I knew that he had been raised on tales of Dartmoor happenings, and that in his own time he'd had quite a few adventures here as well.

Our ruminations were fittingly interrupted by the distant baying of a hound. I felt a chill run over me, and not from the raw and rising wind.

The tall tower of the fourteenth century church that marked the village, one-hundred-and-twenty feet high I had once been told, had been in sight for quite a while, and it was there that I finally stopped the horse and we descended from our conveyance, tying him to a nearby post. All around us, in both the street and the grassy area before the church, were nearly a dozen cows, some grazing, others turning to face the stiffening wind. Two people in the distance, standing before the post office beyond the church, both made from the local stone, gave us a glance while they continued their conversation, but then they turned away. I knew that to them *we* were the unusual creatures that they had turned to observe, and not the cattle.

I glanced toward the ancient graveyard beside the church and recalled our visit to this place several years before, when summoned by Reverend Basil Collins regarding the silver hoard found in one of the aged crypts. At the time, we had become friends with the man, and he had related the famous story of the 1600's lightning strike on the church's tower, about a century after Ivyfell had been stolen from the monks, when it was claimed the Devil himself had been responsible for the damage to the church while visiting to collect souls – or so the story went. That was our first meeting with Reverend Basil, as the locals called him, and we had found him to be a lively thinker and excellent amateur historian. I knew that Pons hoped to find our friend inside the church, as did I.

And fortunately he was there.

He was pondering a curious rectangular stone propped against one wall, rather like a martial-looking gravestone with a carved shield at the bottom and some lizard-like hand gripping a battle-axe near the top. He looked up as we entered, and it took seconds only for him to recognize us, hurrying forward to warmly shake our hands, all the while good-naturedly chastising us for not letting him know of our visit.

After a moment of small talk, I asked about the unusual carving. "It's the Tucker Stone," replied Reverend Basil. "Not as old as it might appear. Several decades ago, one of the parishioners, a Mr. Tucker, contributed greatly toward repair of some stonework here in the church, and this carving was a part of that. Some felt that this stone – that's the Tucker crest – was constructed to Tucker's glory, rather than to God's, and it was conveniently 'lost'. It has only been recently rediscovered at the nearby vicarage, when a garden wall collapsed. During the repairs, the stone was uncovered, buried in leaves and earth where it had been hidden long ago. Now I'm trying to decide just what to do with it. Replacing it here is liable to reopen old arguments, even after these long years. It may be for the best to send it away for safekeeping with a lady from the congregation who is moving to Newton Abbot." He laughed and shook his head. "But enough about the high dramas of Grimpen. To what do I owe the pleasure?"

I was uncertain as to how much Pons would choose to reveal, but he apparently felt that the minister was trustworthy – and rightly so. He told of our summons to Dartmoor, the circumstances related to Sir Martin's sons, and the younger's recent return, now supposedly causing the unnerving restlessness of the Blue Girl.

Reverend Basil nodded. "Of course, none of what you've described with Sir Martin's sons is much of a secret around here, but I have to confess that the reappearance of the Blue Girl after all these years is disappointing. I had hoped that, at long last, she had found peace."

"You believe in her, then?" asked Pons, but without any surprise in his voice.

"Why not? I believe that we all have souls, and in the infinite complexity of God's Universe, with infinite variations and circumstances and combinations of events and causes and effects, it's entirely possible that the path taken by some of the departed can be especially convoluted and troubled, full of detours and unfinished business and dead ends, if you'll pardon the expression, and an extra need to be healed of life's pain. Besides being a man of God, I'm a Dartmoor man, and here we understand the more fundamental aspects of nature. We see things to which the city folk have long since become numb."

"You'll understand," countered Pons wryly, "that I seek a more earthly explanation. To concede the involvement of the other world takes things beyond my purview."

"Certainly, certainly. And I expect that you wish to make use of my library, as you did in the matter of the crypt treasure."

"Yes. I did some research while coming down on the train, but the volume that I brought with me was clearly based on older works, and specific mention is made of several that are kept here."

"In the vicarage, you mean," said Reverend Basil, gesturing around us. "Better there than in this cold church. I inherited them, you know, and I confess that they have become a great fascination to me." He nodded his head. "Let's go next door."

He led us out the front and along a short walk to the adjacent stone building. The fog that had finally followed us down the hillside from the east began to drift around the church and over the wall separating us from the ancient cemetery, swirling around the crooked gravestones and crypts. The damp air suddenly seemed ten degrees colder, and the dying light of the day took on a strange silvery glow. I was glad to get inside, where Reverend Basil's venerable housekeeper, Mrs. Wallace, remembered us from our previous visit and offered tea. Before I could agree, Pons declined, somewhat to my dismay, and she bustled out, smiling and pulling the door shut behind her.

Pons wasted no time, setting down his bag and withdrawing the old heavy book that had been the object of his studies during the journey. Reverend Basil smiled.

"Ah, I thought it might be Mortimer's," he said. "You're right that he referenced a goodly number of materials from this very library. He wrote it a good forty years ago, with the help of my predecessor."

The minister turned to me and elaborated. "One of our more famous moor residents, Dr. James Mortimer. He had a fascination with local history. *Has*, I should say, since I don't suppose it has abated."

"You haven't seen him recently?"

"Alas, no. After the death of his wife last year, he moved down toward Galmpton, where he now lives with his daughter and son-in-law. The young fellow is a gardener at Greenway." He smiled. "I'm sorry. I do rattle on so. But I often wish that the doctor was still around here, and he could answer your questions so much better than I. And he would have loved to meet you."

"Actually," replied Pons, "we have met. It was several years ago, when we were asked by Conan Doyle to join him on one of his spiritualism quests."

"Sad to hear of his passing."

"It was."

While Pons searched and flipped to relevant portions of Mortimer's book, I added, "Sir Arthur had arranged for us to join him while he participated in a séance with Doctor Mortimer's wife - as you know she fancied herself something of a medium - and we were supposed to function as independent witnesses."

"Really? I would have dearly loved to be there. And what was your testimony?"

"Let us just say that we remained unconvinced."

Pons gave a muttered, "Ha!" while the Reverend nodded, realizing there was more to the story, but that this was one tale that he wouldn't be hearing - at least not from us. Rubbing his hands together, he asked, "Well, then. What do you need to know?"

Pons tapped the black book with a long forefinger. "The doctor did well to leave out any supernatural clap-trap, instead keeping his book along the straight-and-narrow of historical fact. No Blue Girls or Hounds here. He sticks to what he set out to relate - the history of the various historical buildings on the moor. Baskerville Hall. The Prison, and the home of the Cabells in Buckfastleigh. Lewtrenchard Manor. This church. And of course, Ivyfell. His account of the former monastery is quite clear, but I had hoped that some of the original source materials might show something of the earlier buildings, in addition to the main structure that later metamorphosized into the manor house. Maps or drawings, perhaps. Or even just a few descriptions that Dr. Mortimer chose to leave out."

Reverend Basil nodded, with a knowing look in his eyes. "I believe I know exactly what you seek, Mr. Pons. And Dr. Mortimer did leave something out – intentionally, as a courtesy to the owners of Ivyfell, who wouldn't want just anyone knowing *all* of its secrets."

He turned and walked directly to a low bookshelf near a window filled with old and rippled glass. I could see that outside, the fog had now completely enveloped the building. I suddenly had a sense of guilt regarding our poor horse, carelessly tied to the post. I hoped to return to him soon, and if this took too long, I'd go anyway.

"Here we are," said the minister, turning and placing a flat folded parchment on a nearby table. It was browned and yellowed with age, and he opened it carefully. "I suppose," he said, "that this is the kind of thing they would like to have at Ivyfell, but somehow, with it already being a part of this collection, it just made sense to archive it here."

Pons, intent on looking over the document, said nothing, while I murmured, "I understand."

Looking past my friend, I could see that the heavy sheepskin was a map, badly faded, showing a number of squares and irregular rectangles that must have represented buildings, connected by both solid and dashed lines.

"Do you see it, Parker?" He pointed a finger, without touching it, toward the larger of the shapes. "That would be the original monastery, now the back part of the house where we examined the paintings." His hand hovered over and followed one of the dashed lines that ran toward the bottom of the map. "And this, I believe, is a tunnel."

Reverend Basil smiled and nodded. "Exactly, Mr. Pons. The whole property is honeycombed with them, left over from the ancient days. They ran to-and-from the monastery buildings, which themselves were built on much older structures, dating to prehistoric times. The tunnel that you are indicating – "

" – runs from the old remaining part of the main building in a southerly direction, under the newer front of the house, and so on to a termination point directly underneath the hill that we passed coming and going."

"That's right. The hill where the monk and the Blue Girl died. Dr. Mortimer chose to leave any mention of these tunnels out of his text, feeling that specifically identifying them would generate interest of the wrong sort, and might possibly provide a way for dishonest folk to enter the house."

"Rightly so," I said. "But what does that have to do with this matter, Pons? Is it related to what Sir Milton has seen? Is someone getting into the house through them?"

"That is what we are about to find out," said Pons. "I have an idea which can only be verified by direct investigation."

"I've seen all that you have seen," I said, "but no doubt my observation was lacking. I know that you seemed to notice something in the upstairs hallway, near that smaller painting. Did that give you a clue?"

"Excellent, Parker! That indeed was a confirmation. But I had already formed several theories, and the mostly likely was confirmed by the expression on Major William Frieze's face during our initial conversation in the drawing room."

As I cast my mind back to those moments, Reverend Basil interrupted. "What are your plans, gentlemen?"

"Why," answered Pons, "to return to the manor and gain entry into the tunnels. I suspect that the one on the hillside is now accessible."

Reverend Basil smiled. "I would be honored if I could accompany you."

"As you wish," said Pons, and within ten minutes, we were back outside, having gathered a few supplies. Now wrapped in blankets thoughtfully provided by Mrs. Wallace, we retrieved our patient but quite damp horse from the front of the church. With the good Reverend seated behind us on the rear of the trap, we turned back the way we had come, slowly in order to make certain that we stayed in the road.

The less said of that unpleasant journey, the better. Our valiant and patient beast pulled us back up to the high ground, and so on across the moor. Pons drove this time, with that assurance that he exhibited in all of his endeavors. Initially, Reverend Basil had twisted in his seat, attempting to chatter about this or that, but as we progressed, his excitement diminished and he fell silent. The only sounds were the steps of the horse along the road, and the faint and monotonous squeak of the turning wheels.

Eventually, I had some sense that the surroundings had changed, and realized that we were in that area around the manor that was protected by tall trees, no doubt planted hundreds of years ago as a wind break, either by Sir Milton's ancestors, or perhaps by the monks before them. Pulling to the side of the road, Pons directed the horse to one of the nearer trees. Pulling the reins, he leapt down and tied the fellow to a branch, pausing a moment to rub the beast's nose and whisper softly to him, no doubt apologizing for yet again leaving him tied outside on such an unpleasant night. Then, seeing that the

Reverend and I had climbed to the ground, he led us without a word back across the road and toward the high hill.

The grass here to the south of the manor was kept short, but the wetness still penetrated my boots. Soon the grade changed, and we began to ascend the hillside, a steeper climb than I would have expected from having seen it before at a distance. Still, it was just a moment before we were at the top, each trying to control our breathing so as to appear before the others as if it had been no great difficulty. I would have expected the Reverend, so used to walking about the moor on a daily basis, to recover first, but it was Pons who set himself into motion, working his way back and forth across the summit in a grid-like pattern, bent forward and eyes on the ground.

I didn't know what he expected to find, especially in the fading and oddly reflected light, but it was only a moment before he gave a soft cry of discovery. Disregarding the damp grass, he dropped to his knees and began to dig his fingers into the turf. While Reverend Basil watched with an enlightened smile, I stepped forward to help, but Pons already had a grip on something. He tugged twice, and with a sudden release, a segment of the earth began to raise in a smooth manner, revealing a dark rectangular opening, about the width of a man's shoulders.

I could see that it had been covered by a cunningly crafted hatch cover made of local stone, with a thin layer of soil and grass on top to disguise it. "The plants rooted on the lid are of a slightly different color," explained Pons, laying back the obviously heavy contrivance. "It has been opened recently, disturbing the roots.

"Brilliant," said Reverend Basil, leaning in. "Notice how it's shaped so that it will curve down over the rim of the tunnel entrance, preventing rain and melting snow from leaking in."

"Indeed. And now, the light, if you please?"

Reverend Basil pulled a pocket torch from his coat pocket, an item specifically requested before we had left the vicarage. Pons turned it on and aimed it into the opening. We immediately saw a wooden ladder, propped against the wall. "Fairly new," he said. "Certainly not left over from the days of the Dissolution. Shall we?" And without waiting to hear our agreement, he stepped onto the ladder and descended, his fore-and-aft cap disappearing into the hole, even as the light from his torch decreased with distance.

"It's only about eight feet deep," he called softly from the bottom. "I'll hold the light while you join me." The minister and I quickly traversed the ladder, which was quite solid and of modern construction. At the bottom, we found ourselves in an ancient arched stone chamber, opening immediately on one side into a steep stone stairwell that dropped into the hillside.

Without a word, Pons set off, moving slowly as we all found our footing. I wished that we had another torch, but Reverend Basil had apologetically explained that he only had the one. In spite of that fact, and the peril of slick stone steps and no hand rails, we quickly reached the bottom without incident, and found ourselves at the start of a long stone tunnel, arched in the same manner as the upper chamber, stretching in what I assumed was the same direction as shown on the map in the minister's library – north, to the manor house.

We made our way steadily, if awkwardly. Each of the stones in the tunnel's wall, ceiling, and floor were about a foot square, and mortared with whatever had passed for concrete in those long-ago days. The arch was low, only about five feet tall at its highest point, and we were forced to shuffle ahead in a bent-over manner. Pons, being the tallest, had the worst of it, and I could see him, a black shape ahead of both me and the minister, outlined by torch light, bobbing his head this way and that to avoid the dangling roots that threatened to drag his ear-flapped cap completely off his head.

The change in the tunnel was sudden. We had walked across uneven flooring and under caressing roots, with the ever-present idea in the back of my mind that a collapse was imminent, even after all of these years of stability. Then, the roots vanished, the floor seemed to even out, and there was even a perceptible lessening of dampness in the air – but make no mistake, it had not vanished.

"We are now under the house," I said in low tones.

"Precisely," whispered Pons. "Tread carefully."

I knew that he meant to go quietly, and our pace, already slow, reduced to a near crawl. It wasn't long before we reached the first of what turned out to be several side tunnels and chambers. Pons cast the light from the torch into each, allowing us to look at the empty darkness branching into different directions, but we made no move to explore any of them. The mustiness in the air manifested itself into a haze that hung before the light, obscuring any clarity when trying to see into the various passages and rooms.

Pons continued to lead us along the main path under the house. Then, he paused and bent over, before standing up and showing an object held delicately in his left hand, illuminated by torchlight. It was round, about two inches in diameter, and of some dark color. I leaned closer, uncertain as to what he'd discovered. Then, to my surprise, I realized what it was – a multi-colored gutta-percha ball, as might be found in any two-penny bin across the breadth of England.

Pons gave it a slight squeeze. "New," he said, before dropping it into his coat pocket. Then he led us on.

In just a moment, we reached a steep stone stairway, similar to the one inside the hill, but with much dryer steps. Pons turned to us and put a finger to his lips. Then we climbed twenty or thirty feet, each step slower and slower. I knew why Pons was decreasing the already snail-like pace – we could all hear the soft sound of voices ahead of us.

Finally we reached the top step. We moved onto a narrow landing, and Pons shut off the torch. A thin irregular strip of light was on the floor ahead of us. As my eyes adjusted, I could tell that it was at the bottom of a framed doorway, currently covered by some sort of hanging curtain. The voices that we had heard, no more than murmurs, were coming from beyond this veil. They were conversational in tone, with no indications of urgency or stress. Several were the deep tones of men, and once the lilting sound of a woman. Then, there was a loud and short hiccup of laughter, before someone abruptly shushed, causing it to cease. Soon, however, the conversation resumed.

Pons looked from one to the other of us, nodded, and stepped forward, pulling back the curtain.

"I believe," he said in full voice, holding up the ball that he had retrieved from his pocket, "that the child misplaced this in the tunnel."

The cozy family scene – and it can be described in no other way – that we found inside the brightly-lit stone room came to a halt, as if we were witnessing a tableaux constructed to represent a group suddenly hearing bad news. Only a small boy, about three years old and nestled in the woman's lap, continued to move, writing on a slate tablet with a piece of chalk. He glanced our way, but dismissed us as uninteresting.

"Major William Frieze," said Holmes to the young man that had given us a tour just a few hours ago. And then to the other man, "And Major Hilary Frieze, I presume. And this must be your lovely wife, Prisha. I confess that I had not anticipated the chance to meet your son."

The woman, having seemingly recovered first, wrapped her arms protectively tighter around the boy, who wiggled in resistance. Both men stood as one, facing us with the mien of soldiers suddenly encountering an unexpected threat.

"Who are you, sir?" said the taller man on the left, clearly showing the features of both his brother William and his father, Sir Milton.

William held up a hand. With a defeated tone, he said, "It is Solar Pons and Dr. Parker, Hilary. I told you about them - they came to look at the paintings this afternoon." Then he saw our companion behind us. "Reverend Basil?" He sounded puzzled, and almost like a child. "What are you doing here?"

"He has betrayed us!" hissed his brother Hilary. "He has obviously led them straight here through the tunnels."

"No, no," began Reverend Basil, raising his hands in a placating gesture.

"There was no betrayal, sir," interrupted Pons. "My theories as to your survival and subsequent return to your family home were already established, as well as the possibility of the existence of these secret passages and rooms, well before we approached Reverend Basil for assistance."

"How?" asked William, taking a step forward. "Why are you here? What business is this of yours? It has nothing to do with the paintings."

"It never did," replied my friend. "Your father asked us here because he is terrified. He believes that he has seen the return of the Blue Girl, and that it portends his own death."

"The Blue Girl?" said Hilary, frowning. "Nonsense."

"Nevertheless, it's true," I said. "He believes that it is related to his guilt at driving you and your wife away, sir, and the subsequent anger of his returning son."

"He has no guilt," muttered William. "He never said a thing."

"He didn't want you to know," I returned. "And I understand that from the time you arrived, there has been almost no communication with you."

"Am I right to assume," added Pons to Hilary Frieze, "that you, as well as your wife and child, returned to Ivyfell at the same time as your brother?"

"We did. William wanted to come home, and I felt the same - although I didn't want to see my father. We worked it out between us that we can stay here, in the secret parts of the house - at least some of the time."

"For how long?" I asked. "This environment is no place for a child."

"Oh, it isn't all the time," said the woman, speaking for the first time. "Hilary's father can no longer come upstairs, so we spend great parts of the day in the upstairs portions of the house, well away from where he might see or hear us."

"Then I take it," said Pons, "that the servants were all in on this deception?"

William winced. "I suppose that it is a deception, although I hate to think of it that way. But Hilary deserved to be able to return to his family home, and we couldn't bear the continued unpleasantness that would result when dealing with father."

"You misjudge him," I said. "He has regretted the argument that drove his older son and wife away from the time that they left. Then he believed you both dead, only adding to his pain. But he is an old soldier, and he apparently shared neither his grief nor his change of heart with anyone. When you returned home," I continued, speaking to William specifically, "you never discussed the matter with him, and thus never learned of his regret."

"And then he began to see the Blue Girl," added Reverend Basil.

"That would have been you, madam," said Pons to the young mother in the chair, wearing a dress of a peculiar electric blue color.

"I'm afraid so," she said, her grip now markedly relaxed around the child, who had set aside the slate and was sleepily leaning against her, a thumb tucked in his mouth. "I favor this shade of dress – it suits me, you see – and it may have inadvertently suggested a connection to this Blue Girl of whom I've been told."

"You were seen on several occasions by Sir Milton when you were careless, both on the landing in the front hallway, as well as walking in the grounds at night, and once on the hill at the tunnel entrance."

"I knew that going out front was a mistake," grumbled Hilary.

"I *did* become careless," she said. "I suppose that I believed too much in what I'd heard about how my father-in-law kept to himself, thinking that he surely wouldn't see me. We stay in these rooms here, behind the walls, during parts of the day, while venturing into the main house at others when we won't attract his attention. Still, I felt the need for fresh air, and would sometimes leave by the rear entrance. I should have stayed back there, where only the servants would see me, but I must have tread too far toward the front, where I was seen."

"And your appearance on the hill?" I said. "Did you climb it, or come through the tunnels?"

"The tunnel. I had gone exploring soon after we came here, and opened the tunnel one evening at dusk, climbing out to look around in daylight. When we first arrived in England, William came on ahead, and he told the servants what he intended. They were overjoyed to know that my husband was alive, and while some felt guilt about not telling his father that we would soon be here, they agreed to go along with the deception. Not long after our arrival, William then opened up the tunnel entrance, so that the underground passages might have some ventilation."

"So you did not enter the house that way when you first arrived?"

William looked shocked. "Of course not! Can you imagine carrying a child down those dangerous steps?" No, we simply waited until my father was asleep one night, and then everyone came in quietly by the front door." His gaze softened at the memory. "You can't imagine a more silent yet jubilant homecoming."

Pons smiled wryly. "If you have as much run of the place as you say, why bother with the tunnels at all?"

She smiled. "Because my husband and his brother William are like little boys, and they became enamored with this plan of the secret passages, as they had when they were young."

Hilary cleared his throat. "My wife is correct, of course." Then he smiled as well. "Will and I found the tunnels when we were lads. It was our secret. I don't believe that my father even knows of them. They became a part of our games while growing up. Most lead out into the grounds, towards various buildings that were associated with the monastery but have long since vanished. Those tunnels simply terminate at blank walls or cave-ins. The only way in and out of the tunnels now is the doorway into this secret room, which you just entered, and outside through the hill entrance."

Pons pointed toward the wall behind them. "And I would wager that this room opens into the hallway where we viewed the paintings this afternoon."

William nodded. "Correct. That was where Hil and I originally found the entrance as boys. But how did you know?"

"There is a slight vertical crack that runs up, along, and back down there, indicating the presence of a doorway. Additionally, there was the slightest indication of unusual wear upon the floor by that wall, as well as tell-tale dust patterns that revealed a source of ventilation from this location. Based upon my earlier research, the idea of a tunnel underneath the older part of the building wasn't out of bounds, and it was later confirmed by research at the Grimpen vicarage."

"That is what you saw," I interjected. "In the hallway. The outline on the wall. I believed that you found a clue in the painting."

"So my father *isn't* selling the paintings?" queried William.

"No. As I said, he asked us here because he believes that the Blue Girl is warning him of an upcoming tragedy."

"But . . . that is absurd," said Hilary.

"And yet, your father believes it. All resulting from the fact that he never told anyone of his regret at forcing you to leave, and more importantly, that you led him to believe in your death, as well as that of his wife."

The man lowered his eyes. Then, his voice quiet, he replied. "I am deeply ashamed of my actions. My wife and brother have chastised that decision from the beginning, but I was adamant, as my anger toward my father only grew, especially after the birth of our son, whom I knew would not be welcomed in his own family home."

"The railway accident at Bhusawal . . . ." I prompted.

Hilary Frieze nodded. "We were supposed to be on that train, but it left without us. After the wreck, I realized that I could divest myself of my connections to my father – if he didn't want my family, then he didn't want me either. However, no such reasons applied to us in India. Prisha's family obviously knew that we did not die. William knew. We only allowed my father, and the people of this village, to believe that we had perished."

"I suspected as much," said Pons. "If we hadn't been fortunate enough to find you here tonight, I would have instituted inquiries in London tomorrow to see if you were still listed as living on the rolls of your old regiment."

"But how did you suspect it?" I asked Pons. "You've explained how you determined the possible use of the tunnels, but what made you think that the supposedly dead man and his wife were living in them to begin with? Is it related to your earlier comment at the vicarage about the expression on William's face?"

Both brothers and the lady looked puzzled, and Reverend Basil added, "Yes, I heard that, too. What do you mean?"

"It is the simple truth. When William was showing us about this afternoon, he showed anger when discussing his father. But when he mentioned his brother, with whom he had been close, and who had supposedly died so tragically just a couple of years earlier, there was no distress at all. Not even a narrowing of the eyes or slight tightening of the throat, such as one might expect when considering the passing of one so close in such a terrible way."

"But," said William, "I might have simply become accustomed to the loss. Can you really have made these leaps of guesswork based on such thin threads?"

"Not guesses," replied Pons. "Logical conclusions, based upon years of cumulative experience."

"Speaking of cumulative," interrupted the minister, who had been watching all of this with varying expressions of puzzlement, wonder, and joy at seeing the young family, very much alive, "there is a tremendous amount of cumulative and unspoken misunderstanding tied around this house, and who knows how long it would have continued if Mr. Pons had not severed the knots. It is time, boys, to speak to your father."

The brothers looked at one another, and then Hilary toward his wife. She smiled and nodded, and the older brother visibly relaxed, as if a great burden had slid off his back and broken at his feet. Turning, as if to leave it where it lay, he said, "This way, gentlemen."

I glanced at my watch and was surprised to see that it was not nearly as late as I had supposed, only about five p.m. It seemed that we had spent much longer traveling to and from Reverend Basil's vicarage, and then gaining access to the long-abandoned tunnels, whose only visitors for years had been two inquisitive brothers that had come to know the forgotten secrets of their own home, only to put them to such a strange purpose decades later.

From the drawing room where we had first met William, Breverton was summoned. His amazement at seeing us all there – the Frieze family, Pons and myself, and the Reverend, nearly cracked his old façade, but he recovered quickly. Hilary asked, "Is my father in his library?"

Breverton nodded, a hint of a smile appearing across his face. Hilary then said, "William, I believe that you should break the news to him." His younger brother agreed, and went before us along the hallway, across the landing, and down the stairs to the library door. With a look back at all of us, he knocked and, being bade to enter, vanished from our site.

We all stood in the hallway, Hilary and Prisha both taking turns holding their now sleeping son, whom I learned from quiet whispers was named Milton, after his grandfather. This indicated to me how much Hilary had still secretly cared for his father, likely not even admitting it to himself. Pons leaned patiently against a heavy table, his arms folded, while Reverend Basil beamed and Breverton – possibly violating protocol to have done so – stood with the quickly summoned Mrs. Dobbs and the rest of the staff in one of the doorways leading to the rear of the house, the cook frequently wiping her eyes with her apron.

It wasn't long before the door to the library opened and William leaned out, smiling and with a hint of tears rimming his eyes. He gestured excitedly towards his family, who shook off any signs of nervousness and walked quickly to the open door. William let them pass and gave a smile to the rest of us as well before stepping back. As the door shut, we could hear the sound of Sir Milton breaking down into sobs of joy.

Later, the evening progressed very much as one would expect. We were invited to stay for dinner – actually, we were invited to stay the night – but Reverend Basil insisted that we put up with him at the vicarage. As we took our leave, I saw that the old manor would be the site of a most festive affair, with the old man speaking happily and looking ten years younger. He couldn't talk enough with his daughter-in-law, while frequently glancing at his newly-returned son, often reaching out and touching him, as if to reassure himself that the fellow was real. And he kept his grandson close, held securely upon his lap – a spot in which the boy seemed quite content to stay.

Of course, lest someone worry, the horse that had pulled us back and forth from Grimpen had been rescued from the fog hours earlier, and – after a good feed and grooming – he was put back to work to return us to the vicarage for the night. I again took the reins and, as we drove away from the manor, I paused and looked back, trying to see through the ever-thickening fog.

"You won't see her, Parker," said Pons. From my position, turned in my seat to see the house and grounds, I could see Reverend Basil nodding in agreement.

"Why, Pons? Because you don't believe in ghosts?"

"No," answered the minister for him. "Because the Blue Girl only appears to signify sorrow, and clearly, thanks to your visit, this is now a house of joy."

I looked back one last time, gigged the horse, and the fog closed around us.

# The Plight of the American Driver

"Mr. Pons?" said the man with the American accent. "My name is J. Taylor Leyton. I believe that we have an appointment."

I shook my head with a weary smile, for it had been a long day. "I am Dr. Lyndon Parker. I share lodgings here with Mr. Pons. Let me show you inside."

I unlocked the door to 7B and let him precede me. Pushing the heavy door shut behind me on the early morning Praed Street traffic, heading to and from nearby Paddington, I divested myself of my coat, and then helped Mr. Leyton hang his as well. Mrs. Johnson appeared from the kitchen, but nodded and retreated when I waved at her before gesturing to our guest that he should make his way up the steps ahead of me, where Pons no doubt waited in the sitting room.

He was in the corner by the window, hunched over one of his chemical experiments. Even as I cleared my throat to attract his attention, he turned with a smile. I was grateful that whatever he had been doing didn't involve one of those foul concoctions that could drive a man to his club and raise complaints from the neighbors and passers-by in the street. It was far too warm on that late June evening to find somewhere else to meet with Pons's client.

I introduced Leyton to Pons, and we found our seats, Leyton sitting perched at the front of the basket chair between us, facing the cold fireplace. Pons turned to me. "And is your patient well?"

I nodded. "He is." Three days earlier, I had also spent a long spell, assisting an old and recalcitrant patient work his way through a crisis of his own making. I had returned that evening to find that Pons was expecting a visit from a Mr. Hewitt Colvin of Lurgashall, Sussex. We had traveled down there early the next morning, spending our time interviewing various members and connections of the old Sussex Archers about a twenty-year-old death and a new one. The following night, last night in fact, Pons had set one his masterful traps, and had caught the killer. After everything was settled, it was too late to return to London, and we had stayed overnight in the home of our host. I had envisioned a leisurely return to London, but a telegram arrived, relating that my presence in London was needed urgently again for my patient, who had fallen into the same spiral as a few days before.

"Did you see the morning papers?" Pons asked before a puzzled Leyton.

I shook my head, and Pons handed one to me, folded to an inner page. "Ah," I said softly, seeing that one of the individuals involved in our Sussex case had cheated the hangman.

"And now, Mr. Leyton," said Pons, leaning back and steepling his long fingers before his lean face. "I believe your note mentioned something about you being 'railroaded', a uniquely American expression. You are familiar with it, Parker?"

I nodded, for I had lived for a number of years in the United States.

"And who," continued Pons to our foreign guest, "is responsible for this 'railroading'?"

"A man named Nicholas Welter."

"Pray, what are the circumstances?"

Our client pursed his lips and settled back more comfortably into the chair. While at first he had seemed rather highly strung, I saw now that he was simply angry. In his early forties, he was well dressed, somewhat expensively but in good taste. His clothing was quite American, and he hadn't adopted any British fashions, as many often do when traveling abroad. He had a wedding ring, and there were no signs that he smoked. With an inner smile, I realized that sharing rooms with Solar Pons for just over eight years had certainly started to influence me!

"I work for the Atlantic Telephone and Telegraph Company, specifically in making arrangements for increased development between our two countries in terms of more trans-Atlantic cables and the like. I've spent time here in England on a couple of occasions, this being my third trip. On the earlier visits, I was coddled by our local employees, being chauffeured from meeting to meeting, from my rooms at the Langham to meals, and so on, always protected and in a cocoon. On this trip, I decided to be a bit more independent. I arrived just a week ago Wednesday, and instead of letting my every move be coordinated, I leased an automobile and set about learning my way around.

"Last weekend, I drove north, first to Hampstead, and then circling east as far as Chelmsford! I must admit that I did a better job once I got out of town, and I almost started to feel comfortable. I had a refreshing journey, staying in a really fine little inn somewhere on the road east of London, and returned on Sunday night, had the Langham store the car wherever they do that sort of thing, and turned my mind back toward business.

"Monday morning, I was scheduled to have a meeting in an unlikely location in Rotherhithe, at the Queen Catherine Shipping Company. They were the low bidders to transport materials to and from our sea-going crews working on the new cables. I rounded up my coworkers who are involved in this phase of the project, and headed toward our rendezvous."

"A moment," interrupted Pons. "Who are these other men, and from where did you *round them up?*"

Leyton frowned. "Nicholas Welter, as I mentioned. He also works for Atlantic Telephone. He is an American, but has been living in London off and on for the last three years, in his own rooms in Bloomsbury. Then there's Amos Hastings, also American, who acts as something of a liaison when necessary between our company and locals. Finally, there is James MacDoig, from Scotland. He comes from a family of engineers, involved for generations in the building of lighthouses. His assistance is contracted as needed in these cable projects, and he has been invaluable. His family has a fine home in Hanover Square."

Pons nodded. "And your suspicion has obviously settled on Mr. Welter. What happened?"

Leyton leaned forward a bit. "We all met at the Langham, where we had a bit of breakfast and discussed our upcoming meeting. Then my car was brought around, and we set out. As we negotiated our way down the Commercial Road, the traffic became ever thicker and more complex, and I admit that I was becoming more nervous with every moment. This was easily the most complex situation in which I'd ever driven, and I was regretting my earlier impulse to take us to the meeting. I'd already made one wrong turn, and had to circle back to the main road, barely making it across traffic to the correct lane without nearly killing us. Finally we found the correct road, Broad Street. As we made our way east, I started to relax. At that point, a man standing near the corner of the Queen Catherine offices started waving for us to turn left into a street called 'Butcher Row'.

"Thinking that he was expecting us and was directing us where to park the automobile, I complied. Even as I turned into the street, remembering to stay to the left instead of the right as we do in the States, a battered automobile pulled out in front of me, where it had been closely parked by the side of the building. I quickly applied the brakes, while the vehicle in front strangely did the same. The front of my rented automobile did no more than touch the rear of the other before I came to a complete and jarring stop.

"To my amazement, the other vehicle then lurched into motion. But instead of continuing north along Butcher Row, he intentionally veered into the brick wall immediately adjacent to the pavement! There is no walkway there, and the old wall of the building is next to the road. With a metallic shrieking, the other automobile scraped along the building for ten or twenty feet before steering back toward the center of the road before stopping. Then, I could see the driver attempt to open his own door, but it had apparently been jammed or damaged by the encounter with the brickwork. He crawled across and exited on the passenger side, angrily pushing the door shut, and walking toward my vehicle.

"I climbed out, more amazed than upset. Looking back, I saw that the man who had waved me into making this turn was gone. Welter, who had been in the front seat with me, looked a bit ill, while Hastings and MacDoig were whispering to themselves.

"The other driver marched up to me, wishing to know why I had damaged his vehicle! I was at a loss for a few seconds before trying to calm him down, explaining that our initial collision, almost nonexistent, had likely caused no damage, while his subsequent reaction by driving along the wall had been what had mutilated his vehicle."

"One moment," interrupted Pons. "Describe this driver. I take it that he was alone?"

"Yes. He was a short fellow, about thirty years of age, with his dark hair pomaded liberally. He was wearing some sort of morning suit, which somehow didn't seem appropriate standing in that run-down street."

"Did you get his name?"

"I did. He insisted that we trade information. He kept referring to involving the authorities, and seeing justice done, and so on. Here is his card."

He fished out the worn pasteboard and handed it to Pons. The corner of my friend's mouth twitched, and he passed it to me. The name, Stephen Oliver, meant nothing to me. I glanced toward my friend's indexes on the shelf by the fireplace, and then saw that Pons had noticed my action with a glint of amusement in his eyes. He nodded for Leyton to continue.

"I thought that was the end of the matter. Oliver ranted about finding the police, but there were none there, and that suited me fine. He took our cards and said that his attorney would be in touch. Then he maneuvered his way back into the vehicle and drove away. We had walked around and seen that there was no damage to either the front of my vehicle or the rear of his, where they had actually touched, and that the contact with the wall had only affected Oliver's car in a cosmetic way, without hindering its ability to drive.

"I thought nothing more about the matter, really, except when it would fleetingly cross my mind over the next few days, wondering if we were going to hear from the fellow again. Then, this morning, I received a summons into my superior's office, in our suite of rooms off Regents Park.

"'Leyton,' said Mr. Felker, 'answer this!' And he threw down a folded sheet onto his desk.

"Reaching across, I unfolded it, discovering some sort of legal document, indicating that I was to be charged with recklessly operating a vehicle while in an impaired condition. 'There are two officers waiting in the other room,' said Mr. Felker. 'They presented themselves this morning in relation to an unreported automobile accident earlier this week.' He pushed across another sheet of paper. 'This statement is from Welter. He confirms your condition on Monday morning. I have no choice but to suspend you until this can be settled. Our negotiations are too delicate at this point to worry about the embarrassment that you might cause.'

"I picked up Welter's statement, and was astounded at what I read. He indicated that he believed me to have set out that morning in an impaired state, pointing out that my driving was reckless, and that I had already made a wrong turn and dangerous correction before we were involved in the accident. He described it as a 'violent collision', wherein I had argued vehemently with the other driver, even threatening physical abuse before the man was forced to flee!

"Nothing could be further from the truth, and I tried to defend myself to Mr. Felker, but my words were clumsy, and only seemed to make him judge me even more harshly. 'What about Hastings and MacDoig?' I asked. 'Surely they will verify what really happened!'

'MacDoig has returned to Scotland,' said Mr. Felker. 'His part of the project was complete after the meeting on Monday. And Hastings says that he was too upset to have an accurate memory, and in any case, he was in the back of the vehicle and didn't see what happened. He did confirm that you made a wrong turn and seemed quite nervous during the entire journey. In hindsight, he believes that it could have been because you had been drinking and were unsure about your abilities to drive that morning.'

"I didn't know what to say at that point. At no time have I ever driven or reported to work intoxicated, and I've never had any sort of problems related to alcohol. Mr. Felker rang through to his secretary, and the policemen came in, quietly explaining the situation, listening patiently as I denied the charges, and then they took me with them to a local station, where I was charged with a misdemeanor offense. Upon posting the small bail, I stepped outside to discover another total stranger, who forced a folded sheaf of papers into my hand and then scampered away. It was to notify me that I was being sued for damages to both Oliver's automobile, and also his physical person, as he had suffered 'grievous injuries' in what was described as a 'crash'."

"Most gratifying," murmured Pons. "Please continue."

"Well, I immediately wanted to return to work, but I was *persona non grata* there. Having nowhere else to go, I returned to the Langham, where I consumed endless cups of tea – I didn't feel that I should let anything stronger touch my lips in my situation! Then I went round and waited for Welter to return to his own lodgings, which he finally did, at about seven that night – last night.

"I ambushed him on the street outside his door, demanding to know how he could have made such a damaging and false statement. He wouldn't meet my gaze, trying to get around me from side to side. A passing constable noticed our interaction and took a step closer, asking if there was anything he could do, but obviously prepared to intervene if the situation turned violent. Realizing that I was doing nothing to help my situation, I stepped away and allowed Welter to pass. After a sleepless night, trying to understand how I could have so suddenly found myself apparently ruined and falsely accused, I resolved to get in touch with you, Mr. Pons. And here I am."

He sat back in the basket chair with a sigh, as if he had been holding a rope with a great weight at the other end, and had finally decided to turn it loose.

"This is really a most interesting little problem," said my friend. "Tell me more about Mr. Welter."

"Of course. As I said, he's been living over here for about three years, being sent here not long after he was hired by Atlantic Telephone. He's thirty, about ten years younger than myself, and unmarried. He has rooms near Gordon Square."

"And his duties within the company?"

"He is my opposite on this side of the Atlantic. Whereas I work with the engineers in America, picking the best locations for the new stations to be built to access the cables, as well as coordinating the installation of the cables themselves, Welter works with the British side of things."

"Do you have any ideas why he would have exaggerated the events, as described in his statement?"

"Exaggerated?" said Leyton, slightly raising his voice. "He lied completely. And no, I do not. Any effort to discredit me with Atlantic Telephone would not benefit him at all. Our positions are similar, but we are on completely different, though parallel, tracks. My removal will not help him advance one iota."

"What about MacDoig and Hastings? Have you attempted to reach them?"

"I did, but with no response. MacDoig has apparently already left Scotland for another project, and he's somewhere at sea. And Hastings simply wouldn't speak to me when I went to his home, instructing his landlady to turn me away."

"Do you have a copy of Welter's statement that was shown to you by Mr. Felker?"

"I do not. I was so flustered that I left without it. I sent a message to Mr. Felker yesterday, but he informed me that I am indefinitely suspended, pending the resolution of this matter. So here I sit, Mr. Pons, uncertain of my status. I am not even sure if Atlantic will continue to pay for my lodgings at the Langham. Should I return home? Would that be wise, with some sort of charges pending here? And if I were to leave without resolving it now, it might never be resolved. Also, to leave might be construed as some sort of admission of guilt, further ruining my chances of returning to my career. Do you think that you can help me?"

Pons stood in that sudden decisive motion of his. "I do, Mr. Leyton. It is a pretty little puzzle, and quite refreshing as compared to that of the sordid murderers that Parker and I exposed only yesterday. I believe that I have enough information to be going on with. We will be in touch."

And with that dismissal, Mr. Leyton was shown the door.

I was already stepping toward Pons's scrapbooks when he turned back toward me. "No need, Parker. Young Oliver is not in there, although perhaps he should be elevated to that status. He is well known to me, but he seems to be getting more active as he ages. This is the fourth time I've heard of him this year, and he's only twenty, and we're just barely into the month of June."

"Who is he, then?" I asked bluntly, returning to my chair by the fireplace while Pons paced back and forth, tugging his ear while answering me, but also obviously using a part of his brain to envision something else.

"Born in Spitalfields of German parents, who changed their names to Oliver after they arrived here a few years after the turn of the century. They ran a little restaurant there until they were killed in a fire, caused by an incendiary device dropped by a German blimp attack in May 1915. As you know, my activities during the War often kept me out of the country. But I was in London that night, and saw some of the damage first hand. Steven Oliver was taken in by a neighbor who, sadly, did not have the same moral fiber as the boy's parents.

"He first came to my attention in 1923, when he was identified as being on the periphery of the matter concerning Feral Daryl – I believe that you made some notes at the time. I attempted to talk to him then, like a Dutch Uncle, and recruit him into the Irregulars, but he would have none of it, and has continued to keep his toes on the wrong side of the law. When the Adam Brede gang tried to re-form last year, he was in the thick of it, but somehow escaped when the rest were bagged up. I feel badly for him, as he was cheated of so much by the loss of his parents. But he is stubborn, and heading for a fall."

"And what do you see as his involvement in this case?"

"It is somewhat obvious. He has been hired to provide the incident that will damage Mr. Leyton's career. I'm sure that after his performance with the automobile, and any subsequent participation necessary to get the arrest warrant and lawsuit in motion, he will be disengaged from the matter. The question about Mr. Leyton's reputation has been raised, and the damage done. As he's in a foreign country, it will be expected that he will flounder a bit before getting his legs back underneath him, and whatever reason that necessitated these actions will be firmly in place by then."

He seemed to come to a decision, heading for the door. "But they didn't count on Mr. Leyton's most intelligent reaction."

"By laying his problem before Solar Pons?" I said.

"Exactly." He reached for his deerstalker, but ignored the Inverness, as the night was quite warm. "I'll be in Rotherhithe," he said. "No need to join me."

"I hadn't planned to," I responded. "It has been a long day, and I fully expect another call at any moment."

With a wave he was gone, and I was proved right within the hour, as my patient requested my presence once again. However, in this case, it proved to be my final visit to him, as a lifetime of poor choices had finally been more than he could overcome.

It was long after midnight when I returned, and consequently I slept late the next morning. I went downstairs to ring for hot coffee and Mrs. Johnson's plain but excellent breakfast. According to our long-suffering landlady, Pons had been gone all night.

I was finishing with the morning newspapers when I heard the front door open and close, followed by Pons's energetic and characteristic dash up the steps – only altered on those occasions when he was returning in some disguise in an attempt to fool me, an event which happened far more than I should care to admit.

"Ah, Parker!" he cried, hanging his deerstalker and crossing the room. "Your patient?"

I shook my head. Pons immediately became more grave. "I am sorry, my friend. You did better with him than could have been expected."

"I suppose. The man could have lived another five years, if he'd only had the fortitude to give up his bad habits." I looked pointedly as Pons worked to light his pipe.

He smiled. "You and I both know another pipe smoker who will outlive us all," he said. "It's all a game of chance. Now, would you care to hear of my investigations?"

I nodded, and he began. "Last night, I made my way first to the offices of the Great Catherine shipping offices. As I expected, even though it was long after business hours, there were still a couple of men working. That sort of business never really sleeps, you know, and due to their recent contracts with Atlantic Telephone, they are burning the midnight oil to dot all the I's and cross the T's.

"I spoke with a Mr. Burke, a vice-president of something-or-other, who warily provided me with his opinion about the four men who were at Monday's meeting. He had been there himself, and said that they all spent a few minutes after arriving discussing the strange automobile accident outside in the street. Mr. Burke had gone out to examine the building and confirmed our client's story in that regard. His automobile appeared to be undamaged. He offered to show me the marks on the wall, but I had already examined them myself before knocking on their door.

"Mr. Burke also indicated that the gist of the discussion supported Mr. Leyton's version that Oliver had driven into the wall intentionally after the initial accident. The men theorized that Oliver had panicked in some way, accidentally accelerating the car and swerving into the building. Then, after gaining control, he had jumped out to confront Leyton, as some who are at fault will do in their embarrassment, attempting to shift the blame to someone else. Burke said that after five minutes or so, the novelty of the event had worn off, and they got down to the nuts-and-bolts of their meeting. He was much more cagey about that topic, but I didn't need to know about it anyway, and we parted as friends.

"Next I looked for Steven Oliver. That was more difficult, as he has worked his way west from his old haunts. He's living in a two-story walkup in a mews off of Rathbone Place. Needless to say, he was surprised to see me.

"I looked around his single room, clean but plain. Without letting him know why I was there, I spent a few moments inquiring after his well-being, while he became more and more nervous. Finally, he could stand it no longer, blurting out, 'If this is about that money that Breckinridge's in Covent Garden Market owes to the bookmakers, I wasn't even in town then. And anyways, Breckinridge wasn't hurt bad, and he said he isn't going to press charges.'

"I shook my head and smiled. 'Not that, Steven. Try again.'

"He appeared to be sincerely trying. 'The Liverpool Street Station snatch? No? That bit of green glass that the larks found at low tide near where the sewer empties at London Wharf?'

"'Not those either, Steven, although they certainly sound intriguing. No, I'd like to hear a bit more about that business in Butcher Row on Monday morning.'

"He seemed genuinely astonished that I'd be interested in that, when there were so many more interesting things to discuss. 'That? It was just a bit of playacting. Abel Bedford, he's the one who stood out on Cable Street and waved in the car, hired me and found me the clothes. I already knew how to work the car from the . . . well, let's just say that I knew how to run one. They knew how this gent would be arriving, although we didn't know just when. I was supposed to fix up some sort of accident, either by letting him hit me, or if not that, then whatever I could think of. Then, after I jumped out and picked a fight with him about it, I just had to drive away, and I was done.'

"'Did you meet with a policeman or attorney about swearing out a warrant for the man's arrest, or arranging a lawsuit against him.'

"Steven was puzzled. 'Not at all. I gave Abel the keys to the car, swapped back into my old clothes, and collected my five pounds. A nice morning's work.'

"'Where can I find Abel Bedford? He's normally across the river, isn't he?'

"'Not in a while. His wife died, and he made some new friends.'

"My trail then led back east, to Lowell Street, near the old iron works. Bedford had already settled in to drink himself to sleep, but he sobered up quickly when he understood what I was asking about.

"'It wasn't anything, Mr. Pons," he said. 'Just a little play-acting. It sounded like a joke, to be honest.'

"'In what way?'

141

"'No one was hurt. The fellow what hired me just wanted us to make this man driving the car angry.'

"'An expensive little joke. Who hired you?'

"'Fella named Welter.'"

I nodded. "It makes sense. For some reason he wanted to embarrass Leyton. Perhaps, in spite of Leyton's belief that they're on parallel tracks, Welter can advance his position within the company."

"A good theory, Parker, and if this were most companies, that might be the place to stop. But I'm afraid that a conversation with Mr. Welter made things a bit more complicated."

"How so?"

"You must remember who these men work for."

"Atlantic Telephone and Telegraph?"

"Exactly."

"I don't understand."

"Allow me to continue. By now it was well after midnight. I went around to the police station west of Regents Park, most likely to have been the one where Mr. Leyton was taken following his arrest and removal from the Atlantic offices. I spoke to the official on duty. You recall him, Parker – Sergeant Carlisle, from that Adjutant business."

I nodded, and Pons continued. "He let me read the official report. The officer to whom the official complaint had supposedly been made, in spite of Steven Oliver's insistence that he hadn't made any complaint to the police. I explained to Carlisle what had happened so far, and we both agreed that something fishy was going on. The officer in question was on a walking beat, and was summoned back to the station. Constable Elias Vander, twenty years on the force, none distinguishable.

"Taking the tack that we already knew the answers to our questions, we quickly had the man admitting to what was going on. He had taken a substantial bribe from Welter to file the report, with the understanding that the charges would be dropped within a few days, and the matter would be forgotten. He understood it was a matter relating to a business deal, and had made a point of learning no more than that. He obtained the assistance of another officer, innocent of the entire matter, and they had presented themselves the previous day to the Atlantic offices, taking Leyton into custody, and bringing him back to the station. Vander had questioned him without much effort and then released him, thinking that the matter was at an end.

"Vander was then held so that he could not communicate with Welter, and Carlisle knocked up our old friend Jamison, who accompanied me to Welter's flat off Gordon Square. It was well-appointed. Welter, who answered Jamison's authoritative pounding with a surly attitude, quickly became more cooperative as we made ourselves at home, picking dirty clothing from the furniture in order to find a place to sit.

"'Sorry,' said Welter. 'My housekeeper has been ill.'

"Jamison wasted no time. 'Vander has spilled the beans.'

"Welter half rose from his seat, his face turning ghastly white against the blue dressing gown he was wearing when he let us in. 'What . . . ?' he finally said weakly.

"Pressing our advantage, I said, 'Your only hope is a full and frank discussion of the facts. Who put you up to it?'

"Jamison glanced sharply at me – I believe that he still thought Welter was behind it all, but I could tell that this weak-minded man had risen to his position by more luck than skill, and that he hadn't conceived of the plan to discredit Leyton. 'It was Mr. Felker, wasn't it?' I asked.

"Welter nodded. 'He knew . . . he knows something about me . . . something that's a secret. He told me that it would stay a secret if I would help smear Leyton's reputation. It wouldn't be for long – just enough to keep Leyton from being involved with the Great Catherine part of the project.'

"'What's important about that?' I asked, but I was already beginning to understand.

"'Something to do with the Russians.'

"Jamison's eyes widened, and then he scowled.

"I shouldn't wonder," I said. For it had been just three weeks before that Russia had executed twenty British citizens for alleged espionage, following several tense weeks before that in which Britain had severed diplomatic relations with the Soviet Union due to revelations of espionage on *their* part, as well as their obvious agitation and encouragement of various revolutionary groups within England.

"'The Great Catherine Company,' I said to Jamison, 'has Russian ties. I think it's time to wake my brother.'

"This is becoming quite serious," I said. "All from Leyton being detoured onto a false automobile accident."

Pons nodded. "I think I would like a cup of tea before we go out. Are you free, Doctor?"

"Certainly. Armed?"

"Of course."

After resuming his seat, Pons continued. "Bancroft was, of course, not happy to see us. But he quickly put that aside in order to hear our story. I had purposely resisted questioning Welter further, but now did so, along with the occasional pointed question from Bancroft, and one or two surprisingly perceptive queries from Jamison as well.

"Welter was not privy to all of Felker's plans or motivations. However, a couple of weeks ago, he had been called into Felker's office, where he was told that Leyton was coming back to England to help set up the next phase of the latest trans-Atlantic cable project, and that he must be somehow pulled off the job. 'I can't accomplish it from within the company,' said Felker, 'as too many people on the New York side of things would see what I was doing. We have to work it so that Leyton disqualifies himself on this end. He'll be fine, but he can't be involved in this part of the job.'

"Welter stated that he felt some guilt, although he was reassured by Felker's statement that there would be no long-lasting consequences to Leyton's career. He pressed Felker for a reason why this had to take place. 'Because,' replied Felker, 'I need to be able to substitute in some specific men in the planning phases, and Leyton would want to know why. He's too conscientious, and too well behaved as well. That's why we'll have to fabricate something to sidetrack him.'

"Felker had then explained that he only had a general idea of what to do, but he would refine the plans once Leyton was in England. Felker then gave Welter a name, Abel Bedford, as a contact when the time came. 'Mr. Felker knows . . . something about me, you see. I had no choice but to help.

"'When Leyton arrived, and showed an interest in driving his own automobile, the plan to trap him with a faked accident began to take shape. There was an alternative plan to waylay him on the road over the weekend, but we didn't know exactly which route he had taken. We . . . we had a woman ready, if we could have found him, who was prepared to swear out charges against him, but he gave us the slip.'

"'Tell us about the Russians,' said Bancroft, clearly uninterested in the sordid mechanics of destroying Mr. Leyton's reputation.

"'I don't know much. I know that Mr. Felker has friends among them. He spent a lot of time there in his younger days, before moving back to New York and joining Atlantic. He's attended some Russian events here in London since he came over here.'

"Bancroft called Jamison and me over to the side, while a constable waited with Welter. 'It isn't common knowledge, even to you brother, that the Great Catherine Shipping Company has strong ties to the Soviets. The fact that such a company would be let in surreptitiously by this man Felker, involving them in the construction of the latest trans-Atlantic cable, is frankly terrifying. This cable is to be dedicated to the transfer of information relating to both government and financial matters. If the Soviets were somehow to be able to gain information in this way . . . .' Bancroft left the thought unfinished, but we knew what he meant. As the events of the last few weeks have shown, the Russians are never to be trusted, not the best of them."

At that point, Mrs. Johnson arrived with the tea that my friend had requested, as well as a tray of very tempting comestibles that he had not. However, to her annoyance, Pons simply poured a single cup, blowing on it until it was barely cool enough to drink, and then signaled to me that it was time to leave.

Gathering my gun, I reminded Pons that I had no idea where we were going. "The Atlantic offices off Regents Park, of course. Although it is the weekend, a false message from Welter has been sent to request Felker's presence there, in order to discuss important developments."

Outside, I was surprised to find an official car waiting for us. We headed east, a quick left on Edgware and a right onto Marylebone, both relatively deserted. At Baker Street, we turned north, and I glanced as always at 221 as we flew by, although Pons seemed oblivious as his thoughts focused on our upcoming encounter.

We pulled to a smooth stop in front of a tall gray building. Climbing out of the car ahead of us was Inspector Jamison and Pons's brother, Bancroft, still the same stout fellow that I had met back in '20, during the affair of Ricoletti. He nodded my way, and then gestured around him with his cane. "Fine neighborhood," he said. "Much better than our digs in Whitehall. I must see if I can work a change of venue for the department."

"If the next few minutes go as planned," said Pons with a smile, "you should have enough good will built up to ask for a wing of the palace."

"One step at a time, brother. Sufficient unto the day." Bancroft turned to Jamison. "It is all in place?"

"Felker arrived ten minutes ago, looking flustered. We listened when Welter called him earlier, and the lad put it over very well."

Pons smiled. "There will be some weeping amongst our Russian friends tonight."

"And possibly with your friend the Baron as well," added Bancroft. "He has been inexplicably working with the Russians of late. He's bound to know about this plot.'

"Indeed. I was unaware of that fact."

By this point we had entered the building, and the security guard, already briefed by the police, took us to the lift at the rear of the lobby. Waiting there in handcuffs was Welter, not exactly under arrest at this point, but prepared to be presented that way in order to shock a reaction from Felker.

The lift rose quickly, and soon we were stepping out into a well-appointed reception area, with entrances to three rooms. Leaving a constable on duty, both to guard against Felker's escape, and to inform the next batch of constables already on their way up of our direction, we followed Welter through a doorway on the left.

We entered a maze of hallways, and I was quickly lost as we cut this way and that before reaching a closed double door. "His office?" mouthed Jamison, and Welter nodded.

Without knocking, the inspector threw open the door, marching in with Welter's arm held in his powerful grip. Behind a desk across the room sat Felker, looking rumpled and confused. Then he spotted the handcuffs on Welter's wrists. He halfway rose, and then with a small noise of despair, he sank back into his tall leather chair.

"The game is up," said Pons, taking a step closer while Bancroft angled to the right and a wide red leather chair that sat in front of Felker's desk. "We know everything. Welter has told us of Abel Bedford. Even as we speak, the offices of the Good Catherine Shipping Company are being raided." He reached the edge of the desk. I swung wide, my hand holding my gun in my pocket. As I knew from a long time before meeting Solar Pons, a cornered man is more dangerous than a snake.

"It really won't do, Mr. Felker," drawled Bancroft. "After our citizens were executed by the Soviets on the ninth, we really are as angry as an overturned hive of hornets."

"I . . . I don't understand," said Felker feebly, trying to make a defense, but too late. "I don't know what you're talking about."

"Of course you do," replied Bancroft. "As soon as my brother alerted me to the problem, we were examining everything about you. We know about the payments, the meetings, and the other little jobs that you've pulled for your Soviet friends. We know about the hold you have over Mr. Welter here, and we know the manner in which you discovered it, which might surprise him. Your accounts are frozen, your position will soon be terminated, and you, sir, are under arrest."

Felker raised a shaking hand to cover his eyes, the other dropping behind the top of the desk in to his lap.

Pons observed it, even as I did. I tried to shift to one side, but Pons blocked my aim as he leapt across the desk.

Felker's other hand reappeared, now lifting a gun. Even as Pons reached out, Felker began to fit the barrel into his own mouth.

*"Better this way,"* I thought, *"than to kill someone else."* But before the man could carry out his last act, Pons pulled the gun loose. Felker still found a way to pull the trigger, but the bullet instead fired into the ceiling. Not, however, without wounding the man – with a cry, he whipped his head back, and I could see a bloody vertical furrow grooved along one cheek.

Pons knocked the gun away, and Felker stood. To our surprise, he dashed around the desk, past Bancroft – forcing me to hold my fire yet again – and in front of the astonished inspector and his prisoner Welter. He disappeared into the hallway, and I heard a yell from the constable on guard outside the door, along with erupting confusion in the room around me. I didn't stay to hear more as I made my own way out the door and onto the fugitive's trail.

I'm not sure why I took it upon myself to pursue him. Perhaps it was simply an instinct, the way a hound will jump to chase down startled and moving prey. I suppose I somehow realized that I was the only one in a position to immediately follow. Pons had been awkwardly draped across the desk, Jamison was holding tightly to Welter, seeming to forget that the man was handcuffed and wasn't technically in custody anyway, the constables in the hall were too surprised, and Bancroft – ah well, Bancroft would not be joining in any foot races.

I careened down the short hallway and quickly realized my dilemma. The intersecting rat's warren of corridors was well known to Felker, and a total mystery to me. I was nearly to the point in turning 'round in circles when I saw it: A small streak of blood along one wall, no more than a thread's width, stretching to my right. I had read the Holmes monograph on blood splatters, as well as Pons's own revisions, and knew what the varying widths, shapes, and direction of the blood drops could tell. The horizontal spot on the wall was like an elongated comma, with the tail indicating Felker's direction. I turned and ran.

I still didn't know where I was going, but other drops on the walls and floor were as obvious as breadcrumbs, and I needed no complex analysis of the direction of the dispersion of the droplets to know that I was on the man's trail. Yet I passed him by for just a second. It was the combination of the cessation of droplets, along with an unusual noise coming from a closed door to my right, that brought me to a stop. Heedless of the possibility that Felker had obtained another weapon, I kicked open the door to reveal the man standing beside a desk, holding a telephone to his ear.

I was suddenly aware that he was trying to notify his superiors that their plan had been discovered. I didn't know how this would affect Pons and Bancroft's plans, but I knew that was likely to be a bad thing. Raising my pistol, I aimed for his hand, hoping to knock the phone from his grip, and praying that I wouldn't miss and kill him entirely.

Just as I was about to pull the trigger, I realized that it wouldn't be necessary. He had glanced at me, but kept pushing a button the phone. He wasn't speaking, but was making whimpers of frustration, even as blood dripped from his chin and onto the desktop. Apparently he was unable to obtain an outside connection, probably because the office's switchboard was closed for the weekend. I stepped toward him, and this time he looked up without turning away. Letting the phone drop from his fingers, he sagged against the desk.

I heard footsteps thundering down the hall, and then sensed rather than saw a crowd of bodies filling in behind me. "Excellent, Parker," said Pons, his voice tight. "Was he able to get through to his Russian masters?"

I shook my head. "He didn't say a word. I believe the telephones are shut down until Monday."

Bancroft's voice, slightly out of breath, moved closer. "There is normally an outside connection left open for those who might be in on Saturday or Sunday. I had it pulled."

Handing my gun to Pons, I stepped closer to Felker. He made no acknowledgement as I took him by the chin and turned his face to better examine the injury. The bullet had grooved a path from the chin upward, taking out a notch from his right eyebrow. It would heal, but he would have a notable scar for the rest of his life. Worse was his right eye – clearly, the bullet itself had not touched it, but it must have passed so close, a less-than-paper-thin distance between the hot projectile to the surface of the cornea, that the exterior was clouded and seared, with evidence of blistering. Without doubt, he would be blind in that eye for the rest of his life.

Later, as we stood downstairs and watched Felker and Welter loaded into plain police vehicles, I asked what would happen to them.

"I'm not sure what the charge would be for Welter," said Jamison. "I suppose he's open to a civil suit for damages by Mr. Leyton. And as for Felker . . . ." He glanced toward Bancroft.

"Mr. Felker," said Pons's brother, speaking as the British Government, "is about to enter a very regulated lifestyle. On the surface, not much will change. From the time that Welter contacted him to meet us today, we've kept tight control on his movements. He has made no calls, left no messages or folded up pieces of paper beside the third pillar from the left at the Lyceum, or any other likely – or unlikely! – spots. His Soviet masters almost certainly have no idea that he has been compromised. And they, along with their agents at the Good Catherine Shipping Company – which is *not* being raided, despite statements to the contrary – will continue to think that their plan to somehow break in upon our trans-Atlantic communications has succeeded.

He added, "I look forward to the next couple of years, as we watch them base their military planning, as well as their investment commitments, on the various stratagems that my department can concoct. This will be the most fun we've had since 'Altamont', when the German cruisers were navigating the Solent according to the minefield plans which he furnished."

We laughed, and Bancroft signaled for his car to be brought closer. "I propose that we have a bit of lunch. My treat, and Dr. Parker's choice – he's the hero of the hour!"

I began to protest. I had done nothing but chase the man, only to find that there was no reason to do so, as the telephone he was attempting to use was turned off. I hadn't solved anything, I hadn't tracked down anyone, and I hadn't made any preparations, such as when Bancroft made sure the telephone was out of commission. However, the heavy-set man would not be denied.

"If for no other reason, I must bribe your silence in this matter," he said. "Should you follow in your own Illustrious Predecessor's footsteps someday, and start to publish my brother's exploits in a popular magazine, perhaps with the assistance of a literary agent – "

Pons, as he did upon occasion, muttered something that sounded like "*Teega mee bornie roosa.*" I knew it was a phrase he had learned in the Balkans during the War, during a series of events in Montenegro. Loosely translated, it meant, "*Over my dead body.*"

" – As I was saying," continued Bancroft, "Should you ever publish any accounts of my brother's investigations, I would ask that this one not be included – at least not for a very long time. Mr. Felker's usefulness will last us quite a while, and it wouldn't do to have the secret spoiled too soon."

"Agreed," I said, wondering how Bancroft could have known that the desire to publish some of Pons's adventures was steadily growing within me.

"Therefore," said Bancroft, "as I said, the choice of today's lunch is yours, Doctor. What shall it be? Simpsons? The Criterion?"

I surprised them all. "Fountains Abbey."

"A pub?" asked Bancroft, shocked.

Jamison laughed. "In Praed Street. The old favorites are always the best, eh, Doctor?"

"They are indeed."

Bancroft shrugged. "Well, I did indicate that it was your decision." He ambled toward the car.

Pons smiled. I knew what he was thinking. He, too, recalled that day in June 1919, when we first met at that fine old pub. I was there one afternoon, freshly back in England after the War, when my attention was directed toward a unique individual, wearing an Inverness and deerstalker. "Sherlock Holmes," the waiter whispered. "That's who he is. 'The Sherlock Holmes of Praed Street', is what the papers call him. His real name's Solar Pons. Ain't much choice between the two, eh?"

Within a few moments, the man identified to me as Solar Pons had finished his conversation with the barkeep and turned toward me.

We made wary conversation as he deduced a great deal about my background. I invited him to sit down. We talked of many things – his consulting practice, my studies at Heidelburg, and subsequently at the Columbia Medical School. I learned some of the details of his famous family, and in turn told him of my marriage to Louisa, our days in Sauk City, and how I had lost her on the *Titanic*. He told me a few stories of his adventures during the War, and I added a few of my own. By the end of the afternoon, and more ales than I can recall, we had formed the beginnings of a friendship. He explained that, following his separation from the government at the end of the conflict, he had resumed both his consulting practice and his lodgings at the Edgware Street end of Praed Street. He had been contemplating sharing the expenses, as his practice hadn't yet returned to levels of success he had enjoyed previously. Before long, I was walking with him down the street to No. 7, which would turn out to be my home and office for many years, before my second marriage moved me elsewhere.

Now our car drove past No. 7, and in just a moment pulled smoothly to the side of the street, where we exited and made our way inside Fountains Abbey. Bancroft was explaining to Jamison how having such a pub so close to a hospital, in this case St. Mary's right across the street, was so beneficial to both. Jamison disagreed for some reason or other, and Pons joined in, taking first one side and then the other. I was satisfied simply to listen, and to let the experiences of the recent days, deaths and successes alike, vanish like the dark ale in my pint glass.

# The Adventure of the Blood Doctor

That afternoon, Pons had been in no hurry as we dawdled over tea at the Holborn, but as the time for our appointment approached, he became good-naturedly impatient.

"If you are going to finish that last scone, Parker, have at it and be done! Doctor Dickinson is an impatient fellow, as you well recall."

Sadly, I *did* recall that trait from a number of years earlier, when I had briefly studied under the man. Impatient was only one way to describe that rather unusual fellow.

Glancing at the scone with an indecision that must have been amusing for my friend, considering his abrupt laugh, I did the right thing and quickly ate it. As I washed down the last of it with my tepid tea, Pons stood and moved toward the exit, throwing on his deerstalker, in spite of the warm spring temperatures.

Outside, we wound through the late afternoon streets. Some of our route I knew very well, while other segments were a revelation as Pons led me through various alleys, mews - both occupied and deserted - and finally around a corner into a street that was most familiar.

We passed through King Henry's Gate and into the courtyard of Barts. Bearing right, we came to that well-known obtruding door, jutting out at an odd angle into the court, and bearing the worn phrase on the lintel, *Whatsoever thy hand findeth to do, do it with thy might.* No matter how fleeting my trips were to this place, I always read those words as I passed through the doors. I saw Pons give them a glance as well.

Inside, we veered from the old medical library and instead began to ascend the bleak stone staircase. Several flights up, we came to the door of the laboratory where we were to meet Dr. Dickinson.

The chamber, as those who will have spent many formative hours there will recall, is high ceilinged, with two balconies running completely around the periphery. The lower was lined with shelves and displays, glass cabinets featuring most unusual preserved remains, while the upper, near the arched ceiling, was in shadow and used for storage.

On the main floor of the chamber, as one entered from the hallway, were rows of short tables, covered with the accoutrements of chemical research – bottles and test-tubes of all sizes, interconnected retorts and tubing. As with every chemical laboratory that I'd ever entered, there was the underlying stink of Sulphur, mixed with the suggestion of other delicate scents whose origins I would prefer not to imagine.

One thing that was apparently obvious was that the laboratory was completely empty. There was no sign of Dr. Dickinson, who was supposed to meet us here at this appointed hour. Pons called out, but with no response. "I'll see if he's upstairs in his office," he said, nodding to a closed door above us off the lower balcony, and walking back into the hallway, where the stairs continued to access the upper levels.

I glanced from side to side, as I often had when visiting this place, still wondering which table it was that had held Sherlock Holmes's interest on that New Year's Day, back in 1881. He had been working to find something better than the tired old Guiacum test, when my old friend and mentor, Dr. Watson, had been led into the room by Stamford, with the intention of introducing the two, as both had expressed interest on that same day towards finding someone to help share the expense of lodgings.

I still recalled reading of that first meeting as if it were yesterday:

> *This was a lofty chamber, lined and littered with countless bottles. Broad, low tables were scattered about, which bristled with retorts, test-tubes, and little Bunsen lamps, with their blue flickering flames. There was only one student in the room, who was bending over a distant table absorbed in his work. At the sound of our steps he glanced round and sprang to his feet with a cry of pleasure. "I've found it! I've found it!" he shouted to my companion, running towards us with a test-tube in his hand. "I have found a re-agent which is precipitated by hoemoglobin, and by nothing else." Had he discovered a gold mine, greater delight could not have shone upon his features.*
>
> *"Dr. Watson, Mr. Sherlock Holmes," said Stamford, introducing us.*
>
> *"How are you?" he said cordially, gripping my hand with a strength for which I should hardly have given him credit. "You have been in Afghanistan, I perceive."*

"*How on earth did you know that?*" I asked in astonishment.

"*Never mind,*" said he, chuckling to himself.

As with all my other visits, I was never able to determine where exactly this meeting had occurred. Some days I would decide it was *this* table because of the better light, and on others it must be *that* one, because of its easier access to the supply cabinet – although that cabinet could very well have moved in the forty-six years since the momentous encounter occurred.

My speculations were interrupted by Pons's short bark from the balcony behind me. I turned, and he was gesturing from the door, now open, leading to Dr. Dickinson's office.

"Immediately," he snapped, and turned back into the room.

Returning to the hallway outside the lab, I started upstairs. These steps were much steeper than those that had initially led up from the ground floor, narrower as well. They connected to the few offices tucked into the crannies at the top of that particular building, one of so many that together made up Barts Hospital. On each of the first and second levels accessed by these narrow steps were a couple of smaller offices, as well as the doors that allowed one to step out onto the balconies ringing the chemical laboratory. I was embarrassed to be slightly out of breath as I emerged onto the landing of the first balcony level, where Dr. Dickinson's office was located. I blamed it upon my sudden dash from the laboratory, as well as the strained tone in Pons's voice, and not upon the fact that I was solidly in my middle years, and had chosen to take that last scone, not a half-hour before.

I found Pons standing in the office, about fifteen feet square, staring at a crumpled figure across the room, lying on the floor in front of the fireplace. I could easily see that it was the unique figure of Dr. Dickinson, and I was fairly certain from the amount of blood and the unnatural sprawl of his limbs that the man was dead.

I stepped carefully toward the doctor. After nearly a decade of assisting my friend, I was aware of the importance of preserving any evidence that might present itself in the most minute of forms. I squatted down and touched the man's throat. He was already cooling, and there was no pulse. My earlier suspicion was confirmed. He was truly dead.

It would have been obvious, however, from the knife protruding from his chest that, if he was not already deceased, the end would not have been long in coming.

"Amazing," muttered Pons. "It's the same knife."

"What?"

"Later. Notice his hands, Parker," said Pons.

I lifted and turned one. It was heavy and fleshy, like the rest of the man. "Covered in chemical burns," I said. "Nothing unusual there."

"But no indication that he defended himself from the attack," added Pons. "Suggestive."

"Perhaps," I said, "but not conclusive. He may have been surprised. Every killer doesn't have a conversation with the victim, confronting him and explaining a list of grievances before doing the deed."

"Nevertheless," said my friend, tugging at the lobe of his ear.

While I examined the body, Pons quickly left the room. I heard him go up the additional flight of narrow steps to the upper rooms before quickly returning. "No one is up there."

As I stood, Pons began to prowl the office, muttering to himself and keeping up a running series of whistles and *hmm*'s, punctuated once by a softly exclaimed "Ha!"

"What is it?"

He gestured towards the desk. "Dr. Dickinson's appointment book. This may have been what precipitated his murder."

I glanced down. The volume was thrown open wide in the center of the desk, turned so that it would have been readable from the side upon which we stood, opposite the chair. Written in the space by five p.m. were the words: *Solar Pons. Bedford murder - finally proof!*

"The poor fool," I muttered. "He was ready to make an accusation. One of the suspects saw this, and then killed him."

"It is likely," agreed Pons. "The question of the murder has hung over these halls for twenty years. One can only imagine the tensions and suspicions that have poisoned the atmosphere here, with all of the likely suspects still employed in this building, one of them most likely the killer, always fearful of discovery while the rest suspected each other, and Dr. Dickinson continually reminding everyone that he had never forgotten, and one day would root out the truth."

I nodded my head and glanced back toward the dead man upon the floor. Solving the murder of his young protégé had become something of an *idée fixe* to Dr. Dickinson over the years, although one could not entirely hold it against him. He was a man given to *idées fixe*.

Like Pons, I was well aware of the facts of the case, such as they were. I had been living in America in 1907, working at Hanson's Hospital in Madison, Wisconsin, and only learned of the events many years later. Pons, on the other hand, had been in the process of establishing his own private consulting practice at the time, after having already served an apprenticeship of sorts.

Years later, after I had taken up lodgings with Pons in Praed Street, our casual conversations had revealed at some point that we were both acquainted with Dr. Dickinson of Barts. Pons happened to mention the Bedford murder, and when I expressed my ignorance of it, he had informed me of the details.

It had been in the summer, and he was finding to his chagrin that many of the visitors to his lodgings were thinking they were going to find Sherlock Holmes, rather than this not-quite-twenty-seven-year-old upstart. Still, his skills were more than enough to earn a few shekels. And he was steadily receiving enough referred work from that club in Pall Mall, where so much affecting the Empire was discreetly protected, to pay the rent.

Still, he had time to pursue various esoteric topics related to his profession, as well as other obscure interests, such as his researches into the Nan-Matal Ruins of Ponape, upon which he had published a monograph in 1905. He frequently visited the British Museum, took lessons from various fellows established in decidedly questionable professions, and even found time to look in occasionally at Barts, where he brushed up on his medical and chemical lessons.

Of course, one couldn't visit the chemical labs in those days without encountering Dr. Dickinson, who even then ruled the place as his own petty fiefdom. However, he was a benevolent ruler and was quite respected, if not beloved, for his fairness and knowledge. In his early forties then, the doctor was constantly attempting to balance his various responsibilities to the hospital with his own research, chiefly into matters relating to blood. The fellow was certainly eccentric, with his heavy dark-framed glasses and shaggy black hair, so obviously and pathetically dyed to give the illusion of youth.

He had a number of odd mannerisms, such as the way he held his hands tight to his hips when standing still, and losing track of a conversation in the middle when some rabbit-trail of a thought struck him, causing him to peer off into the distance while he pursued it to a conclusion that only he could see. But his smile was quick and easy and most friendly, and people forgave him of any of his other oddities because of it.

When recounting this case years later, Pons had told me that he was surprised on that day to get an urgent summons from the doctor. He had arrived at Barts to find a constable barring the door from the courtyard. However, when Pons identified himself, he was passed through and directed up to the chemical laboratory. More constables were in the hallway, and he negotiated his way past them to find Dr. Dickinson and a much younger Inspector Jamison standing over a body, lying on its chest, head turned to stare sightlessly toward the doorway, and surrounded by a sizeable pool of blood.

Stepping forward, Pons could see that it was young Joshua Bedford, a brilliant but disagreeable student of about twenty years. Sticking from his back was a knife.

"It went all the way through," explained Inspector Jamison, who had already been associated with Pons on several previous cases.

"Thus explaining the substantial amount of blood underneath the body," agreed Pons. "There is very little at the entrance wound on his back, as seen by these few stains on the white lab coat."

"This is terrible," said Dr. Dickinson in a subdued manner, standing stiffly upright with his hands pressed flat to his hips.

"From the location of the wound," continued Pons, "the knife must have penetrated the heart, or at least severed an artery or pierced the pericardial sac."

Pons bent to examine the body, noticing that the blood was not uniformly pooled as he had first thought. He nodded his head, indicating the streaks stretching a foot or two away from the door. "He was dragged just a bit."

"Perhaps he pulled himself," said the inspector.

Pons shook his head. "Witness the lab coat." He pointed toward the shoulder, which was pulled out of shape where the cloth was bunched into a wad. "This was where someone, almost undoubtedly the killer, grabbed the coat, deforming it there into a handle of sorts." He glanced up at Jamison. "How did you examine the body in order to observe that the blade had penetrated completely from back to front?"

"We lifted him from the side by his arm and rolled him up for just a moment, before then lowering back to the way he was found."

"Exactly. You would not have pulled the cloth at the shoulder in that manner to roll the body, and such a pattern in the shoulder would quickly settle out if a man were upright and wearing the lab coat in a normal manner."

The inspector turned suspiciously to Dr. Dickinson. "Did you pull him when you found him?"

The doctor returned to his senses with a shake of his head. "Me? Nonsense. I was simply making my way from my office upstairs into the lab. I entered and saw him as you do now. I called out as I rushed over, but he was already dead." He shook his head. "If only I'd had the door to the balcony beside my office open. I could have seen or heard something. Even so, I might not have found Bedford at all if I hadn't forgotten my display." He gestured toward a jar on a nearby table, containing some monstrosity preserved in formalin.

"Display?" asked the inspector.

"A tumor," explained the professor. "*Angiosarcoma.* I'm using it to illustrate a lecture I'm presenting this afternoon." He stopped abruptly. "I was already running late when I came in to get the jar. Now I've missed the lecture entirely."

"Did anyone know you were here?" interrupted Pons. "Was it common knowledge that you were going to be away this afternoon?"

"Certainly. I am diligent about posting my schedule. I've learned not to waste other people's time by forcing them to wait for me when I won't be here at all."

Pons pulled his lip and frowned. "Nothing unusual about the knife."

The inspector shook his head and tossed a thumb toward the doctor. "Dr. Dickinson says it's one that normally lies around the lab here, a useful tool for sometimes opening large containers."

"Any suspects?"

"Ah," replied Inspector Jamison. "I'm afraid so." Pons raised his eyebrows as the inspector continued. "Three of them. We've put them upstairs in the doctor's office."

As they climbed the narrow stairway, Pons was already certain that there was nothing about the body, the weapon, or the immediate location that would provide any clues. He felt certain he understood the reason that the body had been dragged, resulting in the misshapen cloth on the coat's shoulder. He also knew that it was unlikely that this explanation would help toward arriving at a solution. Perhaps the suspects would be able to provide some indications of how to proceed.

Arriving on the landing outside the small office, the same office in which Pons and I had discovered the Doctor Dickinson's body twenty years later, my friend looked through the small window in the closed and guarded door to see a constable looming over three seated individuals, each showing different reactions to their temporary detention. The first, as Pons had explained to me years later, turned out to be a brooding young man, also a student in his early twenties like the victim, named Isaac Kitchener. Then there was Carl Hobert, the janitor for this particular building, a sour looking fellow in his mid-forties. Finally, there was a slim blonde woman in her early thirties, Susan Nash, also a student of undetermined status. The daughter of a wealthy industrialist, she had appended herself to the department in some manner by way of donations made by her father, achieving permission to unofficially attend classes that interested her, and generally hanging about for so long that she become an accepted part of the landscape.

What had brought each of the three under scrutiny and suspicion, besides the fact that each had been involved recently with various disagreements with Bedford, was the fact that they all had what appeared to be some sort of bloodstains, to great or lesser degrees, upon their clothing.

"The fact that the doctor was able to discover the body so quickly," said the inspector in a quiet undertone, "helped us to lock everything up rather quickly. Obviously, the killer thought he had already departed for his lecture, and that there would be plenty of time before the discovery of the body. When he found the dead man, Dr. Dickinson went to the door and called for help. Luckily, two constables were downstairs, having been sent to obtain a package of unrelated research at the medical library. They heard the doctor's cries and bounded up the steps. One of them, Constable Kane here - " and the man touched a finger to his helmet - "stayed with the body, while Forsythe, who is in the office there, went outside to get additional help.

"We had men on the scene within minutes, and we rounded up everyone from nearby. This time of day, and during this season, the building is mostly deserted. The three of them there in the office were all found to have blood on them." He went on to name the three, as identified earlier. "Kitchener and Bedford were always rivals, and recently Bedford pointed out that some of Kitchener's research was suspect."

"We're giving him the benefit of the doubt, based on his youth and inexperience," interrupted the doctor, "but confidentially, it does seem as if he plagiarized, at best, some of the work of Jansky and Moss."

The inspector pursed his lips in irritation but continued. "Hobert has had a grudge against Bedford for several months. Bedford had some great mess of a complicated experiment set up, working toward the classification of blood - "

"My specialty as well, you know," added Dr. Dickinson.

" - and Hobert, while cleaning the lab, somehow contaminated it." He glanced in irritation at the doctor, perhaps wondering if every one of his statements would be elaborated upon. Pons motioned for him to continue. "It was a great bother of inconvenience and expense, but it could be rebuilt. However, Bedford claimed that there was something about the first experiment that made it unique, and he feared that he would be put off on the wrong track by trying to replicate it from scratch. He tried to have Hobert fired, and has kept trying, right up to the present."

"And Miss Nash?" said Pons, who had remembered seeing her around Barts in the past, knowing something of her dilettante-like arrangement.

"She freely admits that she had been pestered of late by Bedford, who seems to have become rather obsessed with her. She says that he has followed her home upon occasion, showed up in unlikely places to 'accidentally' cross her path, and has generally made himself something of an irritant."

Pons continued to observe the three suspects through the window – in fact, he had never stopped doing so during the inspector's informative recitation. "And the bloodstains?"

"I'll let them explain those for themselves, and see what you can make of it."

He reached to open the door, and the men entered the already crowded office, immediately making the place feel even more constrained and airless.

After introducing Pons, the inspector stepped back, allowing my friend to conduct the affair as he saw fit.

He introduced himself as a consulting detective who sometimes assisted the police, continuing, "I am somewhat aware of how each of you is acquainted with the deceased. Mr. Kitchener?"

He phrased it as a question, and the young man started in his seat. "Yes?" he said in a soft voice.

"I understand that Mr. Bedford recently brought the authorship of some of your work into question."

The young man's smooth face folded into a frown. "It's true that some of my research happens to be paralleling that of others, men who have been doing this for far longer than I, and thus are more well known. But we all must leave from the same station, so to speak, before our trains branch off in different directions. My own theories upon the classification of blood will revolutionize the field, but I haven't yet had the chance to set my own research down on paper – I've only managed to recount some of what has gone before. Bedford knew this, but before I could reach the point of recording my own original thoughts, he took it upon himself to slander me."

"And Mr. Hobert," continued Pons, turning to the man beside Kitchener. "I've heard that Mr. Bedford attempted to have you fired for ruining one of his experiments."

"He made it out to be much worse than it was," said the man in a surprisingly cultured voice. "He claimed that some of the cleaning fluid that I was using at the other end of the laboratory somehow made it into one of his beakers, contaminating the fluids. I never cleaned anywhere near his table. He simply couldn't make the experiment work to confirm his hypothesis, and he was looking for an excuse to explain why."

He sat up a bit straighter, and said, "One of the precepts of this sort of work is that the process and results have to be repeatable. If he couldn't do that, then isn't it likely that it *wasn't* repeatable? And that, in truth, it had never worked before."

"Hobert!" snapped Dr. Dickinson. "You forget your place!"

"You sound familiar with the process," said Pons, ignoring the doctor's rebuke as if he hadn't spoken.

Hobert lowered his head and nodded. "I studied here, once, but due to reversals in my family's fortunes, I was forced to take a more menial position."

Pons nodded, and then looked toward Miss Nash. "And your relations with the murdered man? I understand that he was pursuing you?"

She nodded with tight lips. Although from a slight distance she might appear attractive, there was a bitterness about her up close that was palpable. She seemed to be a fruit that had just started to wither on the vine. "I found it offensive. He wouldn't take no for an answer, and it quickly progressed from being a nuisance to almost threatening."

"Did he send you notes? Did he interrupt social engagements, or intrude upon you at your residence?"

"No, nothing like that. He would simply arrange 'encounters', as he called them, when I was going from here to there, or when we were alone here in the laboratory. But it was getting to the state that I almost felt endangered."

"And the blood on the cuff of your sleeve?" Pons asked, pivoting lightly to a new topic. Miss Nash jerked her head in a most unladylike way down to her folded hands. Then she raised her right hand, displaying a bandaged finger. "I cut myself earlier this morning while opening a letter. One must be careful doing so in this environment – we dabble with poisons a good deal here, you know."

"So I've heard. Did you obtain assistance with the wound?" asked Pons.

"Why, no. I cleaned and bandaged it myself."

"If I may?" my friend responded, walking forward.

Pons told me that she appeared to be choosing whether or not to be offended as this young man so obviously questioned her honesty. However, she proffered her hand, which he took and examined in a scientific manner, surprising her by looking at the sleeve first, before then proceeding to unwrap the bandage.

She gasped in outrage and tried to pull her hand away, but he held if firmly, revealing a clean but rather shallow cut across the ball of her thumb.

"Thank you," he said, releasing her hand. With her left, she awkwardly rewrapped the bandage while glaring upwards toward Pons. But he was ignoring her, now standing in front of Hobert.

"Those bloodstains on the front of your shirt, Mr. Hobert. How did you acquire those?"

"I assisted in cleaning one of the dissection labs this morning."

Pons glanced at Inspector Jamison, who nodded. "That's been verified."

"What was being dissected?"

"A sheep," came the surly reply.

"How did you come to get the blood across your chest?"

"It occurred when I leaned across a table without thinking to reach for a discarded piece of offal."

"Interesting. The pattern is more of a splatter, such as, for instance, what might have spurted from an arterial wound."

Hobert half-rose from his chair. "If you're trying to say that *I'm* the one – "

Pons made a calming gesture. "Peace, Mr. Hobert. Mr. Bedford was stabbed in the back, and there was very little bleeding from that direction. Any spurting, if there had been any, would have occurred at the exit wound. However," and Pons pointed towards the cuffs of Hobert's shirt, "you also have blood on your sleeves at the wrist. Who knows how that might have happened – blood can get in surprising places when one is around it."

"This is sheep's blood," said Hobert tightly.

"So you say," acknowledged Pons. "Mr. Kitchener?"

Instead of answering, Kitchener glanced down at the round stain upon his knee, about the diameter of a cricket ball. "My work involves blood," he said softly. "I often find unexpected splatters upon me."

"But that isn't a splatter. It's obviously a spot from where you have clearly kneeled in blood."

Kitchener shrugged. "Who can say? This may be days old. I don't pay attention."

Dr. Dickinson interrupted. "After a few hours, it's difficult to tell the age of a blood stain. Perhaps someday . . . ."

Pons stood, thinking intently. He told me later that he thought that he had an inkling of the guilty party, but was uncertain at that point how to proceed. The indicator might be conclusive, or there might be an innocent explanation, and he didn't want to reveal his hand too soon. While trying to figure how to proceed, he was interrupted by Dr. Dickinson.

"One of you killed that young man!" he cried. "His blood cries out for vengeance!"

It might have been comical, Pons told me, to see that heavy man declaiming in such a way, his dyed black hair atop his stiff frame, with his hands pressed closely to his torso. But he was clearly overwrought, and Pons only then realized the regard that the man must have felt for his student.

Unexpectedly, Dr. Dickinson smote his brow in frustration. "If only there was some way to determine the truth!" He turned to Pons. "We are still so far away from classifying blood. Someday, we might be able to sample the blood on these various pieces of clothing and not only tell its type, but whose blood it actually is! We would know which one of these people were lying!"

At that point, there was a general ruction that erupted from the three seated suspects, each protesting his or her innocence. Inspector Jamison calmed them down, rather forcefully, and in the case of Hobert, with the additional influence of Constable Forsythe's sizeable grip upon the janitor's shoulder. It was then that Dr. Dickinson demanded that he be given the three suspect's bloodstained clothing for further research.

This raised another clamor, but in the end, Dr. Dickinson received for his own use Miss Nash's blouse with its bloodstained sleeve, Mr. Hobert's shirt, and Mr. Kitchener's pants. And with these, he began researches that occupied him off and on, while carrying out his regular duties, for the next twenty years.

As for Pons – ? He was mortified. Although he had a favored suspect, he was unable to arrive at a conclusive solution. And he didn't just focus on that person – rather, he also turned his attention to the other two, with no better results.

"It was one of those cases of 'the perfect murder', Parker, when a person who has never killed before and may never kill again spontaneously commits the act, and then knows enough to stick with his or her story, and isn't panicked into finagling the details, trying to fix this or that loose end until they make a mistake. One of these people had committed a murder, and had then – *left it alone*! It was brilliant, and nothing I could do would shake things loose."

"And whom did you suspect?" I asked.

He smiled. "Ah, I'm still not ready to commit to an answer on that point. The case isn't closed you see, and it's possible that, someday, the killer will make a mistake.

"And so time has passed, Parker," he continued, as he related the details of the old case on that long-ago night in Praed Street, while we sat on either side of the fire after one of Mrs. Johnson's fine meals. "I knew that Bedford's murderer was still there at Barts. All of the suspects were, you see. Kitchener finished his studies and obtained a teaching position. He never quite fulfilled the promise of the researches that he was initially pursuing, as related to those documents he supposedly plagiarized. But he did produce enough acceptable original research on a different track, to use his metaphor, to be offered a place at the hospital. I was never able to establish any other links or animosity between him and the victim.

"Hobert continued as before, serving as a janitor in that place where he had once been a promising student. I've kept my eye on him over the years, but he's never stepped out of line. The same for Miss Nash, who never married, and has managed to parlay her constant presence and father's contributions into an administrative position at the hospital. She has other duties now, but still seems fascinated with the work that occurs in the chemical laboratory."

"And old Dr. Dickinson?" I asked. "I knew him when I was taking some classes there, and of course I've encountered him again over the years. Is he still obsessed with finding the killer of his young assistant, Bedford?"

"I'm not sure that 'obsessed' is the right phrase. I'm still interested in it as well, you see – it was one of my early failures, after all – and I revisit the matter on a regular basis, as does Dr. Dickinson. I know that he still has the items of clothing safely locked away, because we discussed it a few years ago when I ran into him. The desire to determine some conclusive fact from the bloodstains has spurred him to think along totally unexpected lines in terms of blood research. I believe that someday he will come up with something revolutionary, and if he does, it will mean that Bedford's death, the motivator for Dr. Dickinson's efforts, will not have been entirely in vain. But for now, the matter still remains unresolved."

That conversation had occurred in the autumn of 1919, not long after I had moved to 7B Praed Street, and when Pons and I were still relatively new friends. I was more interested then in hearing about this unknown aspect of Dr. Dickinson's past than pondering one of Pons's unsolved cases. But it had suddenly taken on more relevance earlier that day, in the spring of 1927, when Pons received a message from the doctor, explaining that he had made a breakthrough in his research, providing him with a solution to the mystery after all this time.

The doctor had called that afternoon, explaining that he had unexpectedly developed a new process for classifying blood that would conclusively determine the nature of the blood stains, and whether or not the suspects' stories were true. He refused to elaborate, explaining that he wished to meet with Pons first – with myself graciously included in the invitation – and he had arranged for the three suspects to be in attendance an hour later, where the matter would be explained to them.

Pons and I were expected to deliver some documents to a legal office in Lincoln's Inn Fields at three, so we agreed to a five p.m. appointment at Barts. Following our short conference with the solicitor, we had enjoyed tea in Holborn before proceeding east to Barts.

And now, standing in the doctor's office with his unfortunate corpse nearby, I felt certain that the killer, having somehow seen the appointment with Pons listed in the doctor's book, had killed the man with the hopes that his solution would die with him.

Pons nodded towards the doctor's appointment book. "The killer knew when we would be arriving and why, and killed the doctor beforehand. Any evidence he had will have been taken and likely destroyed already. But we have an advantage."

"And that would be?"

"The doctor didn't write in the appointment book that we would be meeting with the three suspects an hour later. Therefore, the killer, who knows about *that* appointment, doesn't know if *we* know about it. He or she won't know how to act – arrive innocently as invited? Don't show up, and pretend that there was no such appointment, even if the other two suspects do show up and state that there was? And the killer will be on pins and needles, waiting for us, even now, to summon the police after our discovery of the body."

"Which is what we should do," I replied.

165

"Not necessarily."

"Pons, it's expected when one finds a murder victim."

"Then we don't have to act as expected. The killer knew what time we would arrive, and will therefore be expecting a great hue and cry to erupt when the body is discovered. I propose that we take control of events and provide a different performance."

"In what way?"

"I suspect that the criminal will contrive to be around somewhere to see what happens. When nothing does, perhaps the unbalance created with result in a mistake. And there is a way to increase that likelihood."

"In what way?"

"By having Dr. Dickinson make an appearance."

"Pons – you're not suggesting . . . ."

But he was. While I waited on the stairs to make sure that the murdered didn't sneak back, trying to discover what was taking so long as related to finding the body, Pons used the doctor's telephone to reach Inspector Jamison at Scotland Yard. After explaining his plan, he received a reluctant agreement of official cooperation.

Thank goodness, at that point in his career, Pons had such respect from the Yard that he was able to get away with it. Otherwise, tampering with the body of a freshly discovered victim at a murder scene, before the police had been given the opportunity to examine it for themselves, would have certainly been punishable by a period in jail. But my friend was certain that he had observed all that already needed to be observed, so he set about hiding the body behind the doctor's desk. "Observe, Parker," he said, pulling the cloth at the shoulder of the doctor's labcoat into a handle as he dragged the poor man into concealment.

Then, taking a spare lab coat from the coat stand near the door, he put it on. In order to duplicate Dr. Dickinson's bulk, he set about stuffing a couple of pillows from a nearby chair strategically under the coat and buttoned it up. He stood upright and held his hands close to his body, in that peculiar way the doctor had always done. "What do you think?"

"You mimic him exactly," I said. "But only from the neck down. What about the rest of your appearance?"

"I've thought of that." He went to the desk, found a red pencil, and used his pocket knife to shave and pulverize some of the colored lead into powder, and thus onto a sheet of paper. Then, taking a bottle of calcium tablets from the desk, apparently kept there by the doctor for indigestion, he poured a couple onto the paper, mashing them up as well and then mixing the two powders. With his fingers, he then rubbed and spread it into various places upon his face, changing the planes and shadows, and skillfully making himself over with this homemade theatrical make-up in order to have the mottled skin that was so familiar upon the old doctor's visage.

I started to speak, but Pons, knowing my objection, raised a finger. Then he bent over, reaching around on the corpse, and then laid the doctor's heavy glasses on the desk. "But his hair?" I complained. "It is dyed black, and rather course and shaggy looking – nothing like yours, I'm afraid."

He reached down again, and then to my surprise laid another item on the desk. "Did you not realize that the man didn't dye his hair, Parker? Rather, he wore a wig. Now, while I put these on, make sure that you have that gun out that you always carry. It's nearly time."

I made my way downstairs to find a few constables waiting outside the laboratory door. They nodded as I passed into the lofty room. There, I found the three suspects, who had arrived while Pons and I were upstairs, all sitting in a tight cluster of chairs. Clearly, the killer had been afraid not to come.

I stepped over to where Inspector Jamison leaned against one of the low tables. He straightened and spoke in a low voice. "We haven't told them a thing. We were already on the scene when they started to arrive – Hobert first, then Miss Nash, and then Kitchener. Nothing was mentioned about finding a body. In fact, we haven't said a thing, except to seat them, even though they've all tried to ask once or twice what's going on. Hobert said he was asked to come here by Dr. Dickinson, and the other two piped in and agreed. Two of them must think they're here to learn more about the Bedford murder. But one of them *knows* that we've found the body by now, and has to be squirming inside, wondering why we haven't said anything about it."

"Pons has told me about the old case," I whispered. "He said it was a 'perfect crime', in that the killer knew not to fiddle with things, but rather to simply step back and let things take their course."

Jamison nodded. "That worked before. But he or she has to be wondering now if there wasn't some clue left this time, some indication upon Dickinson's body, which will reveal the truth when it wasn't revealed before." He glanced toward the three suspects. "Didn't he give any indication which one of them he suspects?"

I shook my head. "He told me the story years ago, and wouldn't share his suspicions with me then, either. It was the same upstairs." I glanced at my watch. Just a couple of minutes to go. "Perhaps, after all this time, his – and your – patience is about to pay off."

As we fell silent, I examined the three seated figures – now nothing like the figures from 1907 that I'd imagined. Kitchener was a man in his early forties, short and balding, with a noticeable collapse of physical stature from whatever he must have been in his younger days. There were deep grooves of disappointment running beside his mouth and between his brows, underneath wispy thinning hair. This was not a man who was happy with his overall lot.

Hobert was a big fellow in his sixties with a shiny bald head. He was perspiring copiously, frequently mopping his dome and neck with a large handkerchief. However, I couldn't necessarily attribute that to any guilt, as it was clear to me that he had some sort of medical condition related to his size. His clothing was worn but not shabby, and he sat up straight, as if he hadn't been broken by the burdens of his life in the way that Kitchener beside him appeared to be.

Miss Nash, a few years older than me, sat coiled, clutching a small and old-fashioned reticule. She was one of those sour prim women that cast evil looks upon playing children and write bitter letters to the editor complaining of nearly anything that might relate to the finer things of life that others enjoy, but have passed them by in a way that they could never comprehend. I knew from what Pons had said that she was a daughter of wealth, and that she had used her influence to obtain a position at the hospital. Many people would never have her opportunities, her security, or her good fortune at being able to find a position in an area that interested them. But somehow, there was something at her core that prevented her from ever blooming and finding true happiness. I was not being fanciful – it erupted from her in waves.

I saw that the door leading to the landing outside Doctor Dickinson's office, on the first balcony behind the seated suspects, was now open. Confirming that it was now time by my own watch, I cleared my throat and took a step forward.

My movement attracted the attention of Kitchener, Hobert, and Miss Nash. I didn't know if they understood who I was, but the killer was certainly aware that there had been an appointment with my friend scheduled for an hour before. Surely, running through one of their minds, was the question, *Where is Pons?*

Without bothering to introduce myself, I began. "Twenty years ago, in this room, Joshua Bedford was murdered." I didn't know where it had actually occurred, so I didn't direct their attention anywhere. However, it was unnecessary, as they all looked past me to a spot near Jamison. I knew they were seeing the dead man lying there, as he had two decades before. "At the time, all three of you were questioned, due to the fact that each of you had been known to have had disagreements with the dead man, and also because you had blood on your clothing."

Above them, in the shadows on the first balcony, I could see a deeper shadow as someone stepped out from the landing.

"As you know, the crime was never solved. The police have never closed the case, and they, along with Dr. Dickinson, have remained certain that one of you called here tonight, was the killer."

Kitchener made an outraged little cough, sitting himself up a bit straighter. I expected him to protest, but he held his tongue. Hobert simply wiped his neck, while Miss Nash's lips tightened even more, as if she had kissed a rotten lime.

The figure on the balcony had slid a few silent feet closer, still behind the view of the seated suspects.

"As you'll recall," I continued, "Dr. Dickinson took the bloody clothing that each of you was wearing that day. He has worked tirelessly to come up with a new process to identify the origin of the stains, thus allowing the police to know who told the truth and who lied."

Upstairs, now shifting just into the light, was a tall man in a lab coat, with dark-framed glasses and black hair, his hands held peculiarly to his hips.

"Today, Dr. Dickinson completed his research and is ready to reveal the killer."

Taking a few more steps forward, the image of the dead man became obvious to the peripheral vision of the three seated in the chairs. As one, they turned their heads to the right and looked up. Two of them appeared mildly surprised. The third, however, gasped and stood suddenly, causing the chair to slide violently backward.

"No! No!"

Pons slowly lifted his right hand from his hip and extended it, forefinger extended in accusation. By now, the two who had remained seated were glancing curiously at the standing figure, so obviously in distress.

"It can't be! *You're dead!*"

That was enough. We had forced the confession, although Pons had disdained his own idea upstairs as, he put it, "something of a cheap trick. My Illustrious Predecessor did something of the sort, although he made us of a pair of stilts," Pons had explained. "'As you came for me, I have come for you!' That sort of thing."

The killer had revealed knowledge of Dr. Dickinson's death. Now, all that was left was the arrest. But even as the constables and

Inspector Jamison started to move toward Miss Nash, she opened the small reticule that she carried and fumbled out a small pistol.

We were all too far away to do anything. She lined it up on Pons, who never flinched, continuing to point at her in a grim and terrible reproach. Dr. Dickinson - after so many years of seeking the truth - was unable to be here. But in a way he was, as Pons played the man's part to perfection.

Time seemed to slow as, with a shriek, Miss Nash pulled the trigger. But even as the rest of us seemed unable to move, Hobert shifted into motion with incredible speed. Granted, he didn't have very far to go, but he stood, throwing up an arm as he did so, and forcing Miss Nash's aim away from my friend and toward the great arched ceiling. The sound of the gunshot was almost simultaneous with the shattering of one of the glass windows above us. Shards fell around Pons, and still he did not move.

Then I was there, and with a twist, I had forced the gun from Miss Nash's fingers, her hand cold, with the fingers and wrist as thin as bird bones. She hissed and lurched forward as if she would have bitten me in the face, but two constables grabbed her by her narrow shoulders and pulled her back.

I glanced up at Pons, who had relinquished the dead doctor's identity and was pulling off the wig and glasses. He gave a wry smile and a nod. He did not seem to be shaken at all - he had enjoyed it. He should have been an actor.

In a few moments, he had joined us downstairs, walking in while pulling off Dickinson's spare lab coat. He stopped Hobert. "I owe you my thanks."

"You owe me nothing," the man rumbled, and turned to go.

"Wait," said Jamison. "Don't you want to hear the explanation?"

"No." And he departed without looking back.

Kitchener crossed his legs and said, "Well, I do." And he glanced with disdain at Miss Nash, now rocking slightly in her chair.

Jamison held up the small gun. "A derringer," he said. "For ladies' protection."

Pons shook his head. "It's doubtful that she could have even hit me with it from down here. Notoriously bad aim past a few feet."

"Still," I said, "it was a surprise."

"Indeed. But I should have thought of something like that. She has a history of impulsive decisions."

"Bad decisions," added Jamison.

Pons nodded. "Both the murders of Bedford and Dr. Dickinson were spontaneous." He looked over at the woman in the chair.

"Would you care to enlighten us, Miss Nash?" When she didn't respond, he added, "The murder of Mr. Bedford?"

She glanced up. "He rejected me," she said simply.

"But you said that *he* was pursuing *you*," interrupted Jamison.

"A lie to save her pride," said Pons. "Clearly that day, the murder was unpremeditated. Bedford must have turned away from her, probably after saying something that she didn't want to hear. She saw the knife, and without thought, plunged it into his back."

He turned fully to face Miss Nash. "You never thought about whether or not Dr. Dickinson was away at his lecture, did you? That wasn't a factor. You simply killed Joshua Bedford, and then – realizing what you had done – you reached down to drag the body away from the door in order to hide it behind something. That was the explanation for the bunching on the coat's shoulder. It never meant more than that, and could have pointed to any of the three suspects. But then you heard the doctor coming into the lab for the specimen that he'd forgotten."

She nodded, as if she were there reliving it. "I was only able to drag him a few feet when I heard the doctor coming down the stairs. I hid behind the screen where I'd intended to put the body. When the doctor found Joshua, he ran out for help. That gave me the chance to get out of the laboratory and down the hall."

"And the wound on your thumb?" I asked, starting to understand. "When you saw the blood on your sleeve, you knew it would implicate you. You couldn't know that two other suspects would also have bloody clothing. Did you inflict the wound as an explanation?"

She nodded. "I didn't have a spare dress. I had to explain away the stain."

I looked at Pons. "You knew it was her because of the wound, didn't you?"

He nodded, pleased at my insight. "Soon I won't need to bustle about and see things at all, Parker. You are becoming proficient enough at this sort of thing that you'll be able to serve as my eyes and ears, in the same way as that fellow that was hired last year by my cousin in New York."

I waved that away and indicated for him to continue. While I knew that the wound had provided him with the clue, I had no idea in what way.

"The wound was on her right thumb, and the stain was on her right sleeve as well," he continued. "I could tell from when I held and examined her hand, as well as from the observation of the musculature of both of her hands, that she was right-handed. This was confirmed when she awkwardly rebound the wound with her left hand after I'd examined it. However, she said that she had gotten the wound when opening a letter. You're right-handed, Parker. Imagine how you would do it."

I made the motion with my empty hands. Left hand holding the envelope, right hand with the blade – a letter opener, a knife, or perhaps a pair of scissors. Pulling the blade in my right hand along the sealed flap –

"The blade would have cut the ball of her *left* thumb, not her right."

"Exactly."

"But then," interrupted Jamison, "when she faked the wound, wouldn't she have also held the blade in her right hand and so cut her left thumb?"

"But you're forgetting the blood on her right sleeve. She felt that the wound *had* to be on the matching hand." Pons lowered his voice. "I recognized this fact all those years ago, but I knew that if I accused her, she could simply deny it, and there was nothing else that I could find that would shake loose the truth. Like Dr. Dickinson, I've been waiting all these years for some new factor to appear. Sadly, the doctor's discovery, whatever it was, turned out to be what was needed, but it resulted in his death."

Jamison shook his head and looked at Miss Nash. She neither confirmed nor denied, staring instead at the floor.

"So Dr. Dickinson is dead as well, then?" asked Kitchener, coldly. "She killed him too?"

"Earlier this afternoon," said Pons, his dislike for the small man evident. "She must have had business in his office and saw in his appointment book that he had written about solving the case, after all these years. She had gotten away with the perfect impulsive crime for so long, and now it seemed as if the truth were about to come out. Either Dr. Dickinson was out of the office when she saw his appointment book, returning to find her there, or they conversed beforehand, and somehow she maneuvered him to where he could be stabbed. Miss Nash?" But she ignored him.

Pons glanced at Jamison. "Am I correct in thinking that, after Bedford's murder, the knife was given back to Dr. Dickinson?"

Jamison nodded. "After a certain point, the case wasn't progressing, and he requested it, legitimately I might add, as part of his research."

Pons nodded. "You'll find that it was the same knife that was used to kill him as well. No doubt he had it out, probably lying on his desk as part of the evidence he intended to present tonight. She saw it and used it."

"Do you think that he really knew the answer?" I asked. "Or at least that his process would have led him to the killer?"

Pons shrugged. "Who knows? I had time to search his office before *resurrecting* him on the balcony, and there was nothing there, either naming the killer, or explaining the revolutionary new blood research. I fear that whatever process he discovered is now lost." He tried again, this time more firmly, to get Miss Nash's attention. She looked up at him, standing directly in front of her. "Did you destroy any of Dr. Dickinson's papers after you killed him?"

It took a moment for her to respond. One could almost see comprehension pass across her pinched face as Pons's words took meaning. Then she smiled, a terrible smile. "Of course I did," she said. "I saw that he knew, so I waited for him. Then, when he was dead, I scooped up what he had stacked on the desk, along with the old bloody clothes, and carried it back to my office across the courtyard. I burned it. I thought that I would be safe then."

Pons looked at me, a flash of anger in his eyes. Like him, I understood that, though the murderer was finally caught, whatever Dr. Dickinson had discovered was now lost, and might not be found again for many years, or even decades, to come – or maybe not at all.

Later, Pons and I had met the attendants as they carried the doctor's body down the stairs. Pons gravely refitted the wig and glasses back onto Dr. Dickinson. "The doctor would understand why I had to borrow them," Pons said softly, "but he should not be embarrassed by their absence any longer than necessary."

An odd sentiment for a dead man who was beyond caring, I thought, but then I remembered the odd yet dedicated doctor to whom he was referring. And what did it hurt, in the end, to make a small gesture of kindness to the fellow?

Outside, the sun was setting as we made our way out through King Henry's Gate and into the street. "Shall we find a cab?" I asked, already turning toward the south. I stopped after a step or two when I realized that Pons wasn't with me.

"I think I should prefer to walk, Parker, if you don't mind. At least part of the way. A twenty-year-old puzzle has been resolved, but strangely, I'm feeling unsettled."

I understood. "Would you care for some company along the way?"

He nodded. "Certainly."

And so, winding through some very curious byways indeed, we made our way west toward Praed Street. Along the way, Pons reminisced about other cases from his youth, including a couple that had also involved Dr. Dickinson, while I kept up, wondering what the morrow would bring.

# The Additional Heirs

### Part I

"Pons," I remarked one afternoon, looking down Praed Street from our sitting room window. "There is either a madman or a fool coming this way. I swear that he will need medical attention before another moment passes."

As I considered where I had most recently left my medical bag, Pons muttered with a distracted tone something about "Mad dogs and Englishmen...." and kept his attention focused on Countess Keller's blackmail letters, delivered into his hands not a quarter-hour before.

The man in the street, overweight and over-dressed, leaned against the lamppost directly across from my vantage point, his breath coming in lurching gasps. Even from one floor up, I could see that his suit, far too heavy for such weather, was soaked with perspiration, and that someone of his stout stature had no business walking about on such a hot August day. Yet, even as I prepared to move to his aid, he raised his hand to read a slip of paper, glanced across to our doorway, and then began to cross the street.

Letting my distracted friend know that he was likely to have a new client, I made my way downstairs and had the door open as our visitor arrived. "Mr. Pons?" he asked expectantly, his East London accent quite obvious, and at odds with the expensive nature of his clothing.

"I am Dr. Lyndon Parker. Mr. Pons is upstairs. May I help you inside?"

"Thank you, Doctor. I had no business trying to walk from the station."

I was mildly surprised but did not comment. Our rooms at No. 7 were no great distance from Paddington, just a matter of five or six short blocks, depending upon how one counted them, and usually just a few minutes' walk. As I pushed the front door shut, I examined our visitor more closely while he caught his breath. He looked to be about forty, with thinning hair and temples starting to show a few silver threads. In addition to his heavy-set frame, he had an unnatural color, a most greyish pallor, which conveyed to me some sort of heart problem. As mentioned, his suit was patchy with dampness, undoubtedly exacerbated by the unnaturally humid conditions outside, and his face was moist. "Mister – ?"

"Burnwell," he said, offering a hand. As expected, it was cool and clammy. "Adolph Burnwell."

"Sir, how long have you been ill?"

He smiled wearily and shook his head. "A while. But it's no worse now than it was five years ago. I just pushed myself today a little too hard, you see. I realized on the way here that I should have corresponded first, but I had made up my mind, and so I just came on, as is my way. And then, when I left Paddington, I thought that I could walk to this end of the street."

At that moment, our landlady poked her head from out of her rooms. "Doctor?" she inquired with uncertainty.

"A glass of water, please, Mrs. Johnson," I said. "And could Mr. Burnwell rest in your parlor for a few minutes? He's feeling a bit unwell."

"Certainly, certainly." She turned and disappeared toward the kitchen.

"I believe," interrupted Burnwell, "that you said Mr. Pons is upstairs?"

"I did."

"Then I must see him. That is, if he's available."

"He is, but you don't need to be climbing steps just now."

"No bother, Doctor. I know myself, and how far I can push. Please, take me to see Mr. Pons."

With a shrug and a shake of my head, I relented and led the man to the stairs. Before we were halfway up, we were rejoined by Mrs. Johnson, who handed me a tray with a pitcher of cold water and three glasses. I thanked her, especially as I realized that I was thirsty myself, and let Mr. Burnwell precede me slowly to the first floor landing. He stepped to the side, and I awkwardly opened the door while balancing the tray. "Pons – you have a visitor."

"Hmm?" He glanced up from the Countess' papers and past me to Burnwell, raised an eyebrow, and then laid them upon the small table by his chair. "Indeed," he said, rising, his tone showing his interest. "Come in, sir, come in! Take this chair! Not a good day to be traipsing the hot pavements, I fancy. Do you find it any cooler down Streatham way?"

I glanced at the man's waistcoat, where his return ticket protruded. Although I hadn't noticed it before, I had studied Pons's methods long enough to understand from whence he derived his deduction.

176

Pons noticed the direction of my gaze and smiled. "Not only the ticket, Doctor. Additionally, the soil upon his heels is quite distinctive."

Mr. Burnwell seemed impressed. Nodding, he wheezed, even as he settled into his chair. "Quite right, Mr. Pons. And not surprising that you would spot it. Your reputation for accurate and precise observations, leading to correct and inescapable conclusions, is well known, and that's why I've come to you – for just that kind of insight."

Pons sat back down, waving a hand. "That is nothing, Mr. – "

"Adolph Burnwell," I said, belatedly introducing him and pouring a couple of glasses of water. With a raised eyebrow, I asked if Pons would care for any, but he shook his head.

"Mr. Burnwell. Of greater interest is the story of how your fortunes have improved in recent months, but have recently, umm . . . shall we say, regressed. Does that have something to do with your visit today?"

Burnwell raised his eyebrows. "My fortunes? Is it that obvious, then?"

Pons gestured towards our guest. "Your hands, your manner of speaking, all indicate a background from the merchant class, while at the same time you've revealed just enough of a vocabulary to indicate a good education, and you were around well-spoken individuals – your parents? – while growing up. You've spent a great deal of your youth and adulthood in the vicinity of Stepney, based upon your accent, although there are also some hints of time upon the Continent in your childhood.

"However, in spite of the Stepney connection, your clothing is quite expensive and somewhat new, having been bought about nine months ago, give or take, back in the winter. The cuffs of your trousers have a turn that was briefly in fashion then, but has already trended toward something else. Additionally, these are tailor-made items of excellent quality, I believe from Tundell's in the Strand, and would have been made to fit. But now they are a bit tight, if you don't mind me mentioning it, indicating that – even though you were already somewhat stout when they were ordered – you have since put on some additional weight. It's likely that the same circumstances that afforded you the new clothing also gave you access to richer foods of higher quantity than you had eaten in the past. Thus, my statement that you have come into some good fortune within the last year. My only question is, why have you not also obtained summer-weight clothing of equivalent quality?"

I was about to chide Pons for his blunt observations, even if they were now obviously and certainly correct. However, Mr. Burnwell slapped a knee and laughed. "As I said – that's what I was looking for. I've heard of you, Mr. Pons. I knew that you could help me."

"Indeed. Then pray tell me your story – and why you haven't yet purchased a summer suit."

"I will, and that is related to the matter at hand. Briefly, let me provide a little information about my past, and how I ended up in a cushy berth, so that you might understand my problem."

I refilled his water glass, which he had emptied in the meantime, and with a nod he accepted it and took a sip. His coloring was already much better, and I was less worried about him than I had been just five minutes earlier.

"You have to understand my circumstances to comprehend what has happened. As you said, I was raised in Stepney, but I wasn't born there. I had a difficult childhood, for a number of reasons. Long ago, before my birth, my mother was the orphaned niece of a City banker. He had taken her in, and like a daughter to him she was, but there had been some trouble before I was born, and she left his home, breaking off all contact with him. She ran away with my father, who was a knight, if you can believe it, but his reputation had been destroyed by this same banker, my great-uncle, as part of what caused the rift with my mother. Dad lost everything and was hounded out of his former life. They fled to the Continent and there he married my mother. Theirs was a tempestuous romance to be sure, but they loved one another, and even though their past troubles sometimes caused them to quarrel viciously, they also helped pull them together.

"I didn't know it at the time, but my great-uncle had traced my mother to where we were living in Paris, and tried for a number of years to convince her to return to London. He had forgiven her, and still loved and missed her, you see, and regretted what had happened between them. But my mother understood that my father would never be truly forgiven or accepted by her uncle, so she ignored the pleas.

"You understand, I only found out about this years later. When I was twelve, my mother had the putrid throat and died. My father was devastated and became something of a broken man ever after. I was old enough then to realize that we had been living beyond our means, and without my mother's steadying hand, it all began to crumble down. Finally, my father seemed to sense what was happening, and we skipped out of Paris just ahead of his creditors, returning to London and settling in the East End.

"It must have been quite a shock for Dad, falling that low, and he soon took to drink. Well, that is to say that his drinking began to increase. However, while he fell into despair, I found that London was a whole new world to me, and I quickly made friends with a number of the lads and took to running the streets. I'm not proud of some of the things that we did, but I didn't know any better, and whenever there was something truly dodgy planned, I seemed to hear my mother whispering in my ear, keeping me out of it.

"Eventually, I grew old enough to find a job as an assistant in a small sundries shop in Colchester Street, off the Commercial Road, making myself useful to the point that, after a few years, I was allowed to work my way into a partnership. When the old man who had hired me died, I ended up owning the store outright, and was there ever since, until my amazing change in fortune.

"My poor father had continued along during all those years, barely making ends meet – sometimes honestly, and sometimes by gambling. Later, I was able to help him out a bit, and then more so as my circumstances bettered, but he never truly recovered from both the death of my mother, his one true love, and also the shame of his loss of position all those years earlier. He died eleven years ago.

"And now, having told you of those circumstances, I can steer toward the reason I came to seek your help, Mr. Pons. For years my life remained the same – working in the shop, going upstairs to my rooms at night. I've never married, and lived a solitary life in that regard, although I've made a number of friends in the East End. Then, late last year, I saw an advertisement in the newspaper.

"My great-uncle, then in his early nineties and getting quite frail, was seeking his heirs. I considered ignoring the situation, but not for too long I'll admit, and reached out to the solicitor mentioned in the advertisement, a Mr. Greaves. One thing led to another, and I was taken down to Streatham to meet the old man.

"It was quite moving, I assure you. He broke down, and told me much that I just told you, about what I didn't know of the old days. How his niece – my mother – while under the influence of my father, had taken some valuable object left in his care. It was only then that I realized what a scoundrel Dad must have been when he was younger. I heard how my great-uncle had tried for so long to convince my mother to return home, as how he'd always felt that she was like a daughter to him. He showed me her letters, where she had written to refuse him. It meant so much to him for me to be there, although it only filled half the hole in his heart.

"For it seems that years ago, during the events that had caused my mother to flee, the circumstances had played out so that my great-uncle had accused his own son of the crime that my mother and father had actually committed. After it was all over, this son had been so offended that he had moved himself off to America, never to return, and never sending a word of comfort, leaving the old man alone for all of those years. Finally, realizing that his time was short and that he had lost touch with whatever remained of his family, he had renewed his efforts to find his heirs, resorting to the advertisements in the hopes that he could somehow locate them.

"So there I was, with this unexpected offer of wealth and status. Although my life had been comfortable to that point, it was by no means luxurious. Can you blame me, gentlemen, that I gladly took him up on his request to move into Fairbank, his house in Streatham, and in fact to be his heir?

"We got along famously, and he set about making up for lost time. He arranged for me to be outfitted in new clothing, such as what you see here, and I'll admit to gaining a few stone living under his roof, as you've noticed. We were quite settled into our new arrangement when two things happened at once.

"First, my great-uncle took a spill, about three months ago, as he was climbing down from his carriage. He hit his head on the pavement and never regained consciousness, dying just a day later. Second, within a week or so of his death, his solicitor Greaves received a wire from America, indicating that the child of my great-uncle's son – his granddaughter – had finally seen his advertisement and was on her way to London.

"I must admit, I was of two minds – excited to see my long lost cousin, but wary at the same time. And then, my great-uncle's death had cast a pall over the whole reunion. When she arrived, she seemed grief-stricken that she had only just missed meeting him, but I felt that there was some sort of play-acting to the whole business."

"Was she the only grandchild on that side of the family, or does she have other siblings?"

"She said that she was the only one."

"I presume," interrupted Pons, "that all the legalities were verified."

Burnwell nodded. "The solicitor, Mr. Greaves, looked at the documents that she had brought with her, such as they were. Everything seemed to be in order – '*Okay*', as cousin Beryl says. That would be Beryl Holder, my great-uncle's granddaughter."

"And then, something else happened that complicated things?"

"Yes. The other heirs arrived."

"Indeed," said Pons with a twinkle in his eye. "*Other heirs?* Unknown heirs, I take it?"

"That's a fact. Mr. Greaves was satisfied with Beryl's papers, and he seemed anxious to move the estate toward probate – which was a good thing, because Greaves had frozen the assets until all the legal questions were settled, except for just enough to keep the house going. My allowance was cut off, and I must confess that I'd become accustomed to it. With no money to pay for them, I was unable to take possession of the summer suits I had ordered. Greaves couldn't be budged. And what little I'd made from selling my shop – well, let's just say that a few bad wagers on some ill-advised ponies soon relieved me of *that* burden. But what did I care? I was the heir to the Holder estate – or at least of a half-share. In any case, I was temporarily cut off.

"Then," he said with a deep sigh, "just a couple of weeks after Beryl's arrival, two more heirs, within days of one another, presented themselves at Greaves' office, each claiming to also be the sole grandchild of my great-uncle, and carrying their own sets of documents."

"Two of them?" I interrupted. "And you believe they are not legitimate?"

"How could they be?" Burnwell shook his head. "Beryl – the *first* Beryl, that is – professes that she has never heard of either of them, and likewise they claim to have never heard of her – or of each other! The second one that arrived, a small coarse woman, also calls herself Beryl, and then the last, a tall blonde, also goes by the name Beryl!" He took a sip of water. "At this point, Doctor, I question whether *any* of the three are legitimate."

"Fascinating," said Pons, his lean figure sitting a little straighter in his chair. "Three Beryls! And what evidence of their lineage has each presented?"

Burnwell gave a little groan. "All three of them are around thirty, about ten years younger than me. The first Beryl, who is a plump dark-haired woman with a laughing nature, had a faded certificate of birth and an old letter from my great-uncle to his son, begging for forgiveness. Both of the latter Beryl's produced their own copies of this same paperwork – *exact copies*, mind you, of what the first Beryl presented. They match perfectly." He settled a bit in his chair and frowned.

"But surely you can tell which are the originals?" I said. "The wear on the paper, for instance."

"Probably an expert could tell which were the originals," replied Burnwell. "But unfortunately, in the process of comparing the three sets, Mr. Greaves . . . well, he mixed them up. He cannot tell now which set of papers arrived with which heir."

Pons laughed, and a look of irritation crossed our visitor's face. "I had hoped," he huffed, "that I might have conveyed the seriousness of the situation."

"Don't mind him, Mr. Burnwell," I interceded. "This is exactly the kind of challenge that he lives for."

"My friend only speaks the truth," added Pons, composing himself. "I will be happy to look into the matter. I believe that the first step will be to visit Mr. Greaves. Might you give us the location of his office?"

Burnwell looked surprised that things had progressed so quickly, as if he had prepared to convince us for quite a while longer. "He and I have discussed that I would be consulting with you, although I'll confess he didn't see the necessity of it, and I believe that he will be expecting you." He rattled off an address near Lincoln's Inn Fields, along with how to find Fairbank in Streatham should the need arise, whereupon Pons stood, indicating that the interview was complete.

Burnwell pulled himself up with much less alacrity. "Please feel free to communicate if you recall anything pertinent that might aid in tracking the ladies' antecedents," said Pons. "I expect that, after establishing a few facts here in London, Doctor Parker and I shall venture down to Fairbank. We'll notify you beforehand. And now, good day!"

At the door, I ascertained that Burnwell felt capable enough of making his way back to Paddington Station without assistance. Shutting the door onto the landing and hearing the man's slow wheezing tread fade down the steps, I turned around to see that Pons was already examining his scrapbooks while making some sort of tuneless whistle. It was less than a minute before he exclaimed, "Ha!" and handed the book to me.

"I recalled clipping that advertisement when it appeared late last year, due to its unusual nature. That will be the one that Mr. Burnwell saw, leading to his return to the bosom of his family. You'll notice," he added, "that the advertisement is quite specific in referencing Mr. Burnwell's parents by name, asking that any possible heir to Alexander Holder get in touch with Solicitor Greaves."

"Why is that significant?" I asked. "It is the most likely way of addressing the situation."

"I have a little idea . . . ." He shook his head. "No, it is unwise to theorize in advance of one's data." He stepped toward the door. "It is still early in the day, Parker, and likely that Mr. Greaves can be found in his chambers. Would you care to join me?" He reached for the fore-and-aft cap that was so dear to him, summer or winter, city or country.

Balancing a sojourn in the humid August heat versus the tedium of remaining in our rooms, I chose the journey, and, putting on my own less noticeable hat, it wasn't long before Pons and I were making our way to Holborn and the solicitor's chambers.

## Part II

As the cab made its way east, Pons kept to himself for the most part. However, as we neared our destination, he roused himself. "These are dark waters, Parker," he said. "In its day, Holder and Stevenson, the firm founded by Alexander Holder, Mr. Burnwell's great-uncle, was the second largest private banking concern in the City. I believe that Holder made quite a tidy sum when he sold it, in addition to whatever fortune he already held. There are those who might be willing to dabble in quite a bit of trickery for a chance to grab that brass ring."

Our cab released us at the northeast corner of Lincoln's Inn Fields, and I looked toward the various austere chambers surrounding that open area, wondering which prosperous looking door was our destination. Pons cleared his throat to redirect my attention and nodded his head in the opposite direction, leading me instead down Gate Street and thence into the narrow lane by the Twyford Buildings. Pausing before a narrow opening in a mean little building, he glanced at the names painted upon the doorway to verify the tenancy of Mr. Greaves. Then he led me inside.

It was quite dark after the August glare, and it was a long moment that we waited for our eyes to adjust while being assaulted by the heavy smell of old books and a hint of damp, clearly emanating from the closed doors that gradually became visible on either side of us. Pons glanced around before settling on a heavy oak entrance on our right. He knocked, and then again with greater firmness when there was no response. He was raising his hand a third time when one of the doors on the opposite side of the passage was thrown open to reveal a most Dickensian figure, his ancient greenish suit wrapped tightly around his thin old form, hair wild in the dusty light shining from within.

"If you're seeking Greaves," he croaked, "he'll be around the corner in The Ships. Always is, this time of day." And with that and a dismissive grimace, he slammed the door, thereupon ending his sole intersection with this narrative.

Pons smiled and shrugged, and we repaired back outside, returning to Gate Street, and so on until we encountered the fine old tavern that has held down that corner since the 1500's. Pons and I knew it well, having once helped to reveal one of the several priest holes hidden throughout the place, some already known before he and I had become involved in the battle with the mad priest Joshua Carnaby and his misguided plans, and other chambers that were still likely to be hidden within the building to this very day.

The friendly barman remembered us and answered our question, and we found ourselves directed toward Mr. Greaves, seated in a nook along one of the walls, a tall stein of Old Peculier held in his right hand, and a barely begun plate of potatoes resting on the table before him.

He frowned when our shadows darkened his table, but then he seemed to recognize my friend, causing his mien to lighten. "Mr. Solar Pons," he said in a thin voice. Clearing it, he continued, "And you must be Dr. Parker. Adolph indicated that he would direct you my way. Please. Have a seat. May I order you something to drink or eat?"

Pons and I both accepted some liquid refreshment, he choosing a pint of dark porter, while I joined our new host in enjoying the Old Peculier. I took a sip, grateful for it after the August heat outside. After indicating that the old solicitor should continue to eat his lunch, Pons began from an unexpected direction. "Mr. Burnwell mentioned that his father was a knight. I take it, then, that the honor was not hereditary."

Greaves raised an eyebrow and smiled. "Surely you've heard of Sir George, Mr. Pons. No, our Mr. Burnwell's father was granted the title by the Queen for valor on the battlefield. He was at Rorke's Drift in '79, helping to rally against the Zulus, only to come home and find himself knighted for bravery. Sadly, his shining moment on the battlefield was not reflected by his character upon his return. He had some money from his grandfather, and he became known as a rakehell and a gambler."

"Did you know him?" I asked. "Mr. Burnwell's father?"

"I knew *of* him. I was an old friend of Alexander Holder, Mr. Burnwell's great-uncle. Alexander was the co-founder of the great bank Holder and Stevenson, which as you may know has now been rolled into Lloyds. I was on the Board for many years, and was consulted when Adolph's father, Sir George, seduced Alexander's niece, Mary, and coerced her into stealing an item of royal regalia that had been left as collateral with the bank. I advised Alexander against making the loan at the time, but he was too impressed by the man who wanted to make the arrangement." He glanced slyly at Pons. "I suspect that you're aware of the matter, and who it was that requested the loan."

Pons smiled. "I have some recollection of it."

"Then you know that in the end, after the stolen item was recovered in a damaged condition and the truth revealed, Mary – who was like a daughter to my friend Alexander – fled to the Continent with Sir George. It was expected by all concerned that he would quickly abandon her, leaving her a broken and ruined woman. Instead, they surprised us all and married, and in spite of living recklessly for a number of years, they appeared to be quite devoted to one another for the rest of her life. At least, that was the impression that was received here in London.

"Alexander, however, was left a broken man by the incident. At the time the item went missing – a minor crown that should never have been taken out of the Tower! – he had wrongly blamed his own son, Arthur, for the theft, and after the matter was resolved, Arthur took himself off to America, never to return."

"And the years passed," I said.

"They did indeed. You both would have been children when all of this took place. Alexander continued to run the bank, and quite successfully, I might add, but his heart wasn't in it any longer. Eventually, ten years ago at least, he sold his share – for quite a bit – and retired. I negotiated the transaction, and did quite well for him. I've managed his affairs ever since.

"I see what you're thinking," he added, nodding his head toward the door, and presumably past that, to his chambers a block or so away. "How can the estate be managed by someone in such shabby circumstances? No doubt you first went to my tumbledown little rooms, before being directed here by old Shively across the hall. But I wasn't always in such a modest location. I've simply moved there now in my old age in order to have a simple place to work, and to keep my hand in things, if just for a bit."

"Which brings us to the reason for our visit," said Pons.

"Yes. The additional heirs."

"That's correct. But before we discuss that . . . . How certain are you that Mr. Adolph Burnwell is in fact the man that *he* claims to be?"

"Quite certain." His lips pursed. "When he presented himself to my office, I was greatly surprised to learn that he has been living here in London, so close for so long, especially after I had been running advertisements, year in and year out, both here and in the United States, attempting to locate Alexander's relatives. After Adolph showed up, I hired an agent to establish his *bona fides*, and there was no doubt that he had returned here thirty years or so ago with his father. We verified that Sir George had subsequently died, and I even visited his neglected tomb in a shabby section of Highgate. No, there is no doubt that Adolph is Alexander's great-nephew.

"And the circumstances of Alexander Holder's death?" pressed Pons. "We were told that he collapsed while exiting a carriage and hit his head. Was there anything . . . suspicious about that?"

Greaves' eyes widened. "Certainly not! After all, the man was in his nineties! He had been out to a concert at the Royal Albert Hall, and had just arrived back at Fairbank when it happened."

"And Mr. Burnwell was where?"

"I see what you're asking," said the old solicitor. "But there was nothing suspicious about it. Adolph Burnwell was nowhere near London at the time. He had been in Dartmoor for the previous three days, lollying with a bunch of touts and trying to get a line on the next winner of the Wessex Cup. He hurried back as soon as he received the news." His mouth tightened. "I'm afraid that I cannot question either Adolph's fondness for his late uncle, or in turn my old friend's fondness for Adolph."

"But you would wish to question it?" I asked, catching a certain tone in the old man's voice.

"I recall the pain that my friend felt when he was betrayed many years ago, and I know what kind of man that Sir George Burnwell was. In spite of the fact that Adolph Burnwell seems to be of a somewhat different stripe, I cannot help but think that the apple - eventually - won't fall far from the tree. I suppose he mentioned that his allowance was cut off."

"He did," said Pons.

"He would. I haven't heard the end of it. It was only supposed to be temporary, of course, until certain estate matters were settled. Even when Beryl - the *first* Beryl - appeared, it would have been cleared up quite quickly. But then . . . the others began to arrive."

"To be fair," I said, "Mr. Burnwell only mentioned his short funds when Pons observed that the man was still wearing a winter suit. He didn't raise the issue on his own. Surely, if you were satisfied as to his identity, his own allowance could have been restored."

"There is certainly an argument for that, but with the confusion arising from the new claims upon the estate, I felt that things should absolutely be locked up tight for the present, so that no confusion can be generated with claims of malfeasance or unfair distribution of the estate funds. They would have all demanded an allowance, and when the false heirs were exposed, how would their portion be paid back? Besides," he added, "having seen how Adolph let his own allowance, as well as what he received from selling his shop, run through his fingers, it might be for the best that his access to the greater estate is limited – for his own good."

"These other heirs," said Pons. "We were told that each of them professes to have no knowledge of the others."

"That's true. First, it was Beryl – that is, the one that I believe to be the *true* Beryl – that showed up, just after Alexander passed, and just as I was prepared to accept her as Arthur Holder's daughter, in wandered the other two."

"And their paperwork duplicated that of the first heir?"

"'Duplicated' is the precise word. It's as if the documents were magically recreated thrice over." He scowled in apparent frustration. "The paper appears to be the same age and color. The writing is exactly the same on all of them. Why, even the faded spots and the ink smudges are exact."

"I'm sure that a detailed analysis can quickly reveal which was the original. It is unfortunate," Pons added quietly, "that the paperwork was mixed up, so that you are now uncertain as to which set goes with which woman."

The old man's mouth tightened. "Not my fault. I had the first set, from what I believe to be the correct Beryl, lying separately upon my desk from those of the other two. But the char who cleans my rooms will not listen to my standing instructions that my papers are not to be disturbed. She denies it, but she shuffled them all together to dust the edges of the desk. And now – ? Well, I'm fairly certain which is the first set, but I cannot be sure. I made the mistake of mentioning the fact that the papers have been confused, and the other two women were quick to grab at that thin straw as a way to keep this mess perpetuating. I was prepared to accept the first Beryl as Alexander's granddaughter – I still am, as a matter of fact, since there is something that rings false about the other two – but I cannot say now with any legal certainty."

"Perhaps, if I may examine the papers . . . ?"

Greaves waved a thin hand. "Certainly, certainly. We shall return to my chambers to retrieve them."

"Why," I asked, "do you seem more predisposed to accept the first Beryl as the true heir, rather than the others? Surely simply crossing the finish line first is not enough reason in this case to establish legitimacy."

"Good, Parker!" proclaimed Pons. "Exactly the question I was myself wondering."

Greaves pursed his lips. "Who can explain something like that? I suppose you'll meet them and see for yourself. She seems to have knowledge of her father, Arthur, that the others didn't initially reveal, although they have quickly parroted what she has said as if it's their own version. And she seems a decent sort, in spite of having been born and raised in a place curiously named 'Queens' in New York. Sadly, her parents died in a fire ten years ago, the same fire that destroyed most of her documents, and in the meantime, she has made a modest living as a spinster seamstress. All in all, she is much like one would have imagined and expected the daughter of Arthur Holder to be - honest and forthright. I cannot explain it exactly, except to say that there is a . . . coarseness about the other two."

"And yet," I stated, "Mr. Burnwell himself is rather coarse, and he has been established as the actual heir from that direction. Surely the path that shaped and defined a person, making them either polished or rough, cannot be held against them in a matter such as this."

The old man sighed. "True. I simply hope that my old friend's memory and legacy will be better represented by a sweet girl such as the first Beryl, rather than the others, who seem to be rather crude."

"Do the other two also claim to have previously lived in New York?" asked Pons.

"They do."

"Then surely," I said, "you only need to have an agent in the United States verify which Beryl lived in Queens."

"I always do my homework, gentlemen. I've contacted several agents in the intervening months, but so far they have proven unsuccessful."

"What information did you provide?"

Mr. Greaves frowned. "I must admit that Adolph initially took the lead in trying to obtain the evidence to disprove the girls - sadly, he has it in for all of them - and though I hate to say it, it's most likely because negating their claims as imposters would mean that he is in line for the whole inheritance. Adolph, who has many questionable friends, knows someone who is involved with a newspaper, and he arranged for this man to take a photograph of all three of the women.

There was some pretext about writing a story regarding the curious return of Alexander's heirs – not true, of course. There was never any article being written. Adolph simply arranged it with no previous explanation to them, so that they were unable to do otherwise but agree to participate, else it would look suspicious." He shook his head. "He got his photograph of the three of them, but his action offended Beryl – the *first* Beryl, that is. She is a sensitive girl, and was not expecting to land in this nest of chicanery. I hope that, when all is settled, the issue doesn't linger between the two of them as some sort of family breach. There has been too much of that already."

"After the photograph was made, what exactly did Mr. Burnwell do with it?" queried Pons.

"He gave several copies to me, with instructions to arrange for my agents in America to verify who is the *real* Beryl. Unfortunately, all their reports indicate that witnesses in Queens cannot verify one way or the other."

"Hmm. Might I borrow a copy of that photograph along with the documents?"

"Certainly. I would hope that you will get to the bottom of these two false Beryls."

"Again, you seem certain that the first Beryl is the actual granddaughter, while you mentioned that Mr. Burnwell is doubtful of all three," I said. "Are you that certain about the first woman?"

"I am," said Greaves, rather primly. "She is definitely of a different quality than the others." Then he slumped a bit. "I'm sorry, that sounded terribly snobbish."

He took the last swallow of his ale and wiped his mouth. "Shall we adjourn 'round the corner?"

Pons settled with the barkeep, paying for Mr. Greaves' lunch as well. Mr. Greaves half-heartedly offered to pay, but seemed willing enough to allow Pons to cover the charges. We three then reentered the humid heat that was engulfing the capital, and I immediately felt it sap my strength as we returned across the short distance to Greaves' chambers. Inside, there was no reappearance by the old man, Shively, across the hall, and soon we were in the somnambulant book-lined office of the old solicitor. I could hear the lazy buzzing of a fly as it slowly expired behind the drawn shade, and wondered how many of his relatives had found the same fate over the years in this place.

Greaves did not offer us seats, but rather moved directly to his desk, where he pulled out a small stack of papers. Handing them to Pons, he said, with a bitter twist to his lips, "I sometimes wish I'd never been involved in this mess. I only did it as a favor to my old friend.

Tracking and verifying heirs is a younger man's activity. Although I disagreed with Adolph about your involvement, I wish you good luck, Mr. Pons."

After verifying that he had received all of the papers and a photograph, and upon tucking them into an inner pocket, Pons replied, "I thank you, Mr. Greaves. We shall be in touch, should any other questions or revelations become apparent." And with that, we took our leave.

Back outside, Pons led me south and east, and so into the Strand. I was considering whether to ask that we hail a cab, but decided that the movement as we walked down the street was enough to give the illusion of a breeze. And when Pons informed me of his destination and the reason why, I realized that we did not have too far to go.

"I could certainly come to some determination about these papers on my own," he explained as we walked. The Strand became Fleet Street, and we passed the imposing Royal Courts of Justice. "But it is just as easy to ask our friend and professional associate to do it, freeing me up for other pursuits."

In a short while, our path took us turning right into Mitre Court, so long ago associated, under a cleverly disguised name, with a choking crowd of red-headed men. I glanced up in passing at the windows of the old first-floor rooms above the court, once shared by our associates Smith and Petrie, and wondered where in the world they could be right now. Pons, however, did not even turn his head that way, instead charging onwards through the narrow passage in the southern side of the court, and continuing down into King's Bench Walk.

At 5a, we learned that our friend Thorndyke, the medical juris-practitioner, was out on some investigation or other, but Pons handed the papers, *sans* photograph, into the care of Polton, his crinkly-faced laboratory technician, along with a detailed explanation of what he wished to learn. The man nodded and smiled, and without any extraneous chit-chat, shut the door, freeing us to return to Fleet Street. We paused at the edge of the walk to look at the photograph, still in Pons's hand.

As expected, it revealed three women, all of similar age and dress, beside one another on a settee. They appeared to have been arranged in order of their arrival: On the left was a sweet-faced plump girl with dark curly hair. In the middle was a small darkish-looking woman with a tight mouth and suspicious expression. And last was a tall blonde who, unlike the other two, was vacuously looking into the distance instead of facing the camera lens.

Pons replaced the photograph in his coat pocket and glanced at his watch. "The day is still young, Parker. I believe that I have time to do some additional research. I'll accomplish more alone at this point, if you don't mind."

I was not offended at Pons's abrupt decision to continue on his own. I knew that he would be moving fast and loose, and that his path might range from tedious excavations in neglected and dusty records offices to disguised observations of some person of unexpected interest. I let him know that I would return to Praed Street, and we parted – he heading toward the City, while I found a westbound cab.

Upon my return, I found that Mrs. Johnson had prepared a late lunch that, combined with my earlier consumption of Old Peculier and the warm afternoon, left me quite sleepy. I was napping in my chair several hours later when Pons returned. Pulling myself up, I noted that he was still dressed as before, and had not felt the need to resort to some disguise. He kept several hidey-holes throughout the city where he could quickly change his identity, depending on the need. Clearly, this day had not required him to assume the guise of a grimy automobile mechanic, a zealous non-conformist cleric, or a down-at-heels dock worker.

He confirmed what I suspected, that he had not taken time to eat, but he seemed content to wait until our evening repast. Settling into his chair, he began to recount the events since we had parted on Fleet Street.

"My first stop was the telegraph office, to send a number of wires to New York, requesting further information about Beryl Holder. You'll understand that I prefer verification from my own agents, rather than the second-hand points from Mr. Greaves."

I nodded, knowing whom he would have contacted, and then I smiled when I recalled that this person, with any number of cultivated eccentricities, would not have been pleased to know that I might presume to use the word "contact" as a verb. Pons regularly received reciprocal requests for data from this same man, an associate of Pons's from long before I had met my friend. Strangely, and for no reason that I have ever been able to establish. Pons has always been addressed in each message from New York by the sobriquet *Hitchcock* – no doubt related to some long-ago inside joke between the two of them.

Pons looked around. "No reply to my wire, I see?"

I shook my head. "Well," he continued, glancing at the clock on the mantel, "it is still just mid-day in Manhattan. I expect to hear something by morning." He continued. "After sending the wire, I went round to Sir Edward Soames' office, as he generally knows something about everything in terms of estate goings-ons. It turns out that there is no little curiosity in his circles about the appearance of the three Beryls, and also the move of Sir George Burnwell's son into the Holder family manse. Soames confirmed that the will, as written, divides Alexander Holder's estate equally between any proven children of either Holder's son, Arthur, or his niece, Mary."

"Why ask Soames?" I interrupted. "No doubt Mr. Greaves would have shown you the original will."

Pons smiled and continued. "I preferred to have some independent evaluation. The will continues by stating that if no heirs are found, the remainder of the estate is to be given to charity."

"Noble. But why, if Adolph Burnwell returned months ago, hadn't Alexander Holder revised the will to name him specifically."

"I asked that, and Soames believes it was because the old man hoped, right to the end, that any child of his son might also be located, and therefore he wanted to leave it open-ended. Unfortunately, he died before he learned of the appearance of the Beryls.

"Soames told me that it is understood to be a quite handsome estate. He was also able to recall that several years ago, Mr. Greaves did, as he stated, negotiate quite a sum for the sale of the private bank to Lloyds when Alexander Holder decided to retire. Upon hearing that, my next stop was to visit – "

But before he could finish that thought, our doorbell rang. Knowing that Mrs. Johnson was busy in the kitchen, Pons jumped up and went to answer it. Returning in a moment to his chair, he opened an oversize brown envelope, pulling out a sheaf of papers. I could see that they included the original documents from the three Beryls, along with a new letter. "From Thorndyke," he muttered, reading. Then, tossing the entire stack to me, he laughed.

The message was short, as was to be expected, and in the strong confident fist that I had observed before:

> *All three letters are written on identical English paper from the Sittingbourne Paper Mill, established 1769, still in business. Although the mill is old, the paper is new. Each sheet contains esparto grass imported from Southern Spain and Algeria, and also several modern fibers. The birth certificates are on specialized parchment, likely of German manufacture, although certainly trimmed from large sheets to avoid watermarks.*

*It's possible that these would have been used in the United States, but unlikely.*

*Various techniques were used to age the paper, including staining with coffee, baking, controlled use of mildew spotting in specific areas, and careful folding, rubbing, and wearing. You and I both know who is capable of creating this type of carefully crafted duplication. However, the paper is clearly of recent origin and artificially aged, which raises the question – as you will have seen yourself – why such a craftsman would carry out such an effort to give these documents the appearance of age, when a simple examination by an expert would easily reveal that they are on new paper. Said craftsman could have easily obtained paper of the correct age to add to the veracity of the deception.*

*Good hunting!*

*T*

I unfolded the letters and examined them for the first time. Each was in fact a duplicate of the others – three copies of a letter from Alexander Holder, written in July 1894, begging his son Arthur to return – and three formal looking certificates, topped with the name of a New York hospital, indicating that Beryl Holder, female, was born in September 1898 to Arthur and Grace Holder, residents of New York City. They each had the same folds, the same stains and tears, and the same feeling of worn use and age. I put them back in the envelope.

"Why *would* the forger use newer paper?" I asked.

"Clearly, it is a move to discredit the documents entirely, and therefore the bearers of the documents – *all* of them. These were easily proven to be recent forgeries, as was the intention of the man who commissioned them when he provided the originals to the forger."

"Why would there need to be an original at all?" I asked. "Surely the forger who could create these would have the skill to produce them from scratch without copying them."

"Oh, I know that there was an original." He reached into his coat and pulled out another set of documents. "I obtained these from the man who forged the other three sets." And he tossed those over too.

I opened them, thankful that the other three were separated and in the brown envelope – although I realized that an expert could easily tell them apart if I happened to get all of them – four sets now – mixed up. Indeed, these originals looked identical to the others, but I raised my eyes to Pons, who said, "Further analysis would certainly reveal that these, the true originals, are of different and older paper from that of the others."

"And where did you find them?"

"They were given to me by the man who made the forgeries."

"That was quick work, then. How did you locate him?"

"Even before we dropped the copies off in Kings Bench Walk, I could see that they were likely completely identical, and as such, all had to be forgeries. There are only three men who are skilled enough to make these. As Thorndyke mentioned, they are known to both of us.

"The first, Clayton Traynes, is serving a ten-year stretch in Dartmoor. You'll recall our last encounter which sent him there. The second, our old friend Dennis Golders, continues to be employed in His Majesty's Service, but I still took the time to verify that he didn't take on this additional work. That left Alan Dean, who lives in a rather unique warren in Spectacle Alley, coincidentally just a few hundred feet from Mr. Burnwell's old shop in Colchester Street, off the Commercial Road."

I raised an eyebrow, and Pons continued. "Yes, Parker, Dean and our client were neighbors in the East End. But don't anticipate my story, which is soon told. To be succinct: I entered Dean's den, reestablished our acquaintance – to his dismay I might add – and quickly had the story out of him, with a promise of leniency upon my part and testimony on his."

I sadly shook my head. "The apple, indeed, did not fall far from the tree, as Mr. Greaves predicted. Mr. Burnwell was behind this somehow, I'm assuming, calling upon one of his former East End friends to make the forgeries. Was it, as you said, to discredit all three women?"

"I believe so, and I hope some of my outstanding queries will fill in the rest of the picture. It would seem that Mr. Burnwell obtained the originals long enough to have copies made. He mentioned to Dean that he had entered Greaves' office while the man was out of town, apparently on a short holiday to the coast last month – and that he intended to replace the forgeries the same way when he was done. No doubt it was he and not the char woman who shuffled all three copies together.

"Burnwell insisted that the copies were to be made intentionally on relatively modern paper that could easily be proven false, and his subsequent insistence on hiring me was supposed to reveal that fact, thereby disqualifying all three of the heiresses – both the false women, and the one with the original papers. Clearly Mr. Burnwell wished for my involvement just so these forgeries could be discovered, but he probably never thought that I could lay my hands on the forger so easily, thereby establishing his involvement. In any case, I'm not sure that finding out what our dubious client was up to in this case advances our agenda one jot. It certainly shows that an attempt was made, in a clever but roundabout way, to discredit all three of the Beryls, but does it tell us which one is the true heiress – or if any of the women is truly legitimate?

"As I said, Burnwell had possession of these documents for a short while, whereupon he delivered them to Alan Dean, asking that he make three exact copies, and in a hurry. For Dean it was only the work of a day. When Burnwell returned to claim them, he asked Dean to give back the originals, but displaying his usual low-animal cunning, Dean retained them, the very same ones that you now hold, telling Burnwell that he had destroyed them, and pretending that it was his understanding that doing so was a part of his original instructions. At first, Burnwell was angry, but then he seemed to realize that it would fit with his plans."

"But," I realized, "if he used the first set of papers, the *authentic* papers – " and I waved the fourth set, " – to construct the other three, then the original Beryl that arrived just after Mr. Holder died must be the true Beryl after all."

"Not necessarily."

"But surely – "

"Nothing is sure yet. We must await further information from New York."

I frowned, continuing to follow my thought. "If . . . if Mr. Burnwell caused the additional sets to be made, then he must have given them to the two women who later showed up with them in their possession. He must therefore be involved somehow with the arrival of the second and third Beryls!"

"Good, Parker! My thoughts exactly. Which is why I considered how such involvement could occur. If Mr. Burnwell had already made use of one of his acquaintances, Dean the forger, then might he not make use of others? And who might he likely find to portray the additional Beryls?"

"Actresses!" I cried. "He hired actresses, with whom he was already acquainted, to show up with false papers and taint the claim of the first Beryl."

"So I thought."

A problem occurred to me. "But if he intends that the papers be so easily identified as false copies, then the actresses that he hired will quickly be exposed, and so will his involvement."

"True, and I haven't quite seen yet how he plans to get around that. The easiest solution is that he will have them vanish before the bogus papers have been revealed, so that they cannot be questioned."

"I assume that you've gone some way toward identifying these women."

"I have. After speaking with Dean, my next steps were to interview several actors and actresses of my acquaintance. It quickly became apparent that I was on the wrong track, however, so I backed up and went to see a few booking agents. Upon my third visit, I found success."

"He did hire actresses."

"Indeed. Solomon Britt is a long-time theatrical agent who was able to identify the second and third Beryls from the photograph. They are Letitia Foster, the small dark woman, who is an American, and Mildred Fosk, the tall blonde who can adequately portray one. Britt was able to confirm that both women have been off the circuit for a while – no doubt involved in Burnwell's job."

"But Mr. Britt was unable to identify the first Beryl."

"True. But we knew that she arrived from a different quarter, as Burnwell's whole scheme was concocted to discredit her."

I sighed. "It's so . . . clumsy. How did he think it would work?"

"Who knows? He has a certain low cunning, likely inherited from his father, but it is becoming obvious that he doesn't have the wherewithal to think through a greater plan. However," added Pons, "I believe that, with the information I hope to receive from New York, we shall have a clearer picture tomorrow of where we stand, and we shall certainly discuss my discoveries with Mr. Burnwell when we journey down to Streatham in the morning."

I made to ask another question, related to something that Pons had started to mention earlier after his visit to Sir Edward Soames, before being sidetracked by the arrival of Thorndyke's letter and the stunning revelations about Burnwell's amateurish plan. But at that moment I heard the tread of Mrs. Johnson on the stairs with our meal, and instead I rose, handing Pons back the papers and moving to open the door. Gradually, I forgot what I had meant to ask.

After we ate, Pons stood and moved to one of his bookshelves, where he selected a worn blue-bound periodical. I knew that it and the adjacent range of other similar volumes were some of his most treasured possessions, and something to which he often referred. Flipping to the desired page, he stepped over and handed it to me. "You might spend the evening profitably running your eyes over this, to review some of the events in the lives of Mr. Burnwell's parents and great-uncle from forty years ago." And then he said good night and went into his room.

"Of course," I said with a smile. "How could I have not seen it?" I was quite familiar with this recounting of the original case, having read about it in the early 1890's when I was around fourteen years of age, at the time when certain details were originally published. Like Pons, I had studied this account of the stolen crown numerous times during the intervening years, and with today's events fresh in my mind, I lost myself within it yet again, but now with new insight as to what happened after those long-ago final words had been written. Upon finishing it, I went upstairs to bed.

## Part III

It seemed that my head had barely touched the pillow when I heard Pons, leaning in from the landing, telling me to awaken. "It's murder, Parker. We must hurry. The game is afoot!" And with that tantalizing lure, he pulled the door shut.

I made ready and quickly joined him downstairs, where Pons was speaking in low tones to our landlady. Then we stepped outside where a cab was waiting to take us to the station. I was still getting my thoughts in order, and clearly Pons was not ready to provide any information. It was only when we were on the short ride to Streatham that my unspoken questions were answered.

"We had an urgent telegram from an Inspector Galyon. In the night, Burnwell became ill, and he died just a few hours ago. The police were called, and while opinion is still uncertain, as he was clearly in poor health, there has been an assertion that the man was poisoned."

I wanted to speculate – Pons had said that it was murder – but I knew that he would be turning things over in his own mind, evaluating possibilities, while at the same time being quite careful not to form theories before he had facts. Therefore, I remained silent, as anything that I might ask could distract him, or cause him to place too much emphasis upon some completely unsupported possibility.

He was silent the rest of the way, except for one instance. While passing through Brixton, he said softly, "This is a bad business, Parker. My case was nearly complete. Burnwell needn't have died."

After the quick railway journey, we alighted at the Streatham Hill Station on the High Road, and after conferring with an honest cab driver, learned that we could easily walk the distance to Fairbank, located at 18 Leigham Court Road, in about the same time as we could drive it. We set out, and I noted that the day was cooler than before, overcast and with a hint of possible afternoon rain. We walked to the southeast, arriving at the tragic house in just a few minutes.

It was a nicely-built square building, good-sized, and of white stone. It was set back from the road with a double-width drive and a pair of large iron gates, standing open. The grounds were a bit run down, no doubt reflecting Mr. Greaves' recent budgetary restrictions. The bushes and flowers were rather shaggy, but the color from the various flowers, primarily yellows and reds contrasting with the white walls, gave the place a rugged beauty. However, I could see that a number of the flowers, although pleasant, were actually weeds that had been allowed to run rampant. There was a path to the right and a small lane on the left. Several vehicles were parked in front, and a pair of constables stood by the main door.

We identified ourselves and were quickly passed inside. Two men were standing in the entry hall in low conversation, actually something of a disagreement: Mr. Greaves, looking as if he had thrown on his clothing in a hurry, and a harried fellow in his middle sixties who introduced himself as Inspector Galyon.

"Thank you for coming," said the official. "I understand that there have been some questions about the women who are staying in the house."

"As I've tried to explain, Inspector – " began Greaves, but Galyon held up a hand.

"Mr. Pons is known to me, if only by reputation. I would be glad to have his insight into this matter."

"Gladly," said Pons, while Greaves pursed his mouth in irritation. "But first we need to learn some specifics regarding what has happened. Dr. Parker and I only know that Mr. Burnwell has died, possibly from poisoning."

"That's right." The inspector glanced over his shoulder into an adjacent parlor, where I could see three women seated side-by-side, each showing different but obvious manifestations of tension. I recognized them from the photograph – these, then, were the three

Beryls. "Let's step outside for a moment," the inspector added softly. "I haven't let them know yet that it might be murder."

The four of us walked until we reached the gate and turned to face one another. The inspector nodded at the solicitor. "I received an urgent message around two this morning," began Greaves. "It was from Beryl - the *first* Beryl. Adolph had become ill, violently so. The cook had called a doctor, and the doctor called the police. Beryl, not knowing what to do, called me. I rushed down, but Adolph had died before I arrived. The local doctor was still with him, and what he described sounded very much as if Adolph had simply overindulged – no surprise, as he had notoriously poor eating habits. But this doctor, a man named Hatton, had become suspicious and had already notified the police. Of course, when they arrived and began speaking to the residents of the house, it came out that all three of them claimed to be Beryl Holder."

"And," interrupted Galyon, "with the question of a sizeable inheritance involved, I'd be a fool not to consider the possibility of murder."

"Nonsense," snapped Greaves. "One has nothing to do with the other."

"Doctor," said Galyon to me, ignoring the old man, "I'd appreciate if you could have a look at the body. The local doctor is still here, and you can confer – to see if your thoughts match his."

"Certainly," I said. "Glad to be of service."

The inspector held out a hand to point me back toward the house. Although not specifically invited, Pons followed, leaving Greaves standing angrily by the gate for just a moment before trotting to catch up with us. Inside and at the top of the stairs, Galyon whispered to a constable outside one of the bedroom doors, and the stout man stepped up and prevented Greaves from entering with the rest of us. The solicitor fumed as we shut the door in his face.

Burnwell's bedroom was at the back of the house and poorly lit. A thin man in his thirties was sitting in a straight chair by the window, and he stood as we entered. He introduced himself as Dr. Richard Hatton, and I found him to be a competent and knowledgeable fellow with a wry disposition. "Received the call about two a.m.," he began succinctly. "This fellow here was in a great deal of distress, with the usual issues devoted to a stomach illness. He couldn't tell me anything that helped – said he'd had dinner with the rest of the house, and then he drank wine until bedtime. An hour or so later, he began to suffer and called for help. The cook sent word to me." He gestured toward the obese shape on the bed. "As you can tell, he was a likely candidate for all sorts of problems, and I understand that he'd had difficulties with his heart."

I nodded and quickly explained my quick diagnosis the previous day.

Hatton continued. "A word with the ladies downstairs confirmed that he'd been drinking a lot last night. He seemed to favor some homemade wine that's kept in the cellar. He couldn't provide any useful information about what else he might have ingested, so I began to suspect that something had tainted it – possibly on purpose. I tried lavage and activated charcoal, but it must have been too late by then, and it was nearly three when he had the final seizure that finished him."

"Sounds straightforward enough," said Galyon. "Tell Dr. Parker what else made you suspicious."

"This." Hatton stepped toward the bed. "Doctor?"

He invited me toward our former client, now lying in death beneath a stained sheet. I pulled it back to reveal Burnwell, his features twisted in agony. Thankfully, his eyes had been closed.

I leaned forward, and Hatton positioned himself so that the light from the bedside lamp would illuminate the victim. He reached and turned Burnwell's head so that I could examine the inside of his mouth. It was quite obvious, and I would have been suspicious as well. "Did he report dizziness and confusion?" I asked, standing upright.

Hatton smiled. "He did, along with the expected breathing difficulties and final convulsions and paralysis." He reached to the table beside the bed for an empty wine bottle and a glass stained with dregs. "After he died, I fished this from the refuse bin. There in the glass is what I poured out of the bottle.

I took the glass from him and lifted it, turning it this way and that to catch the light. Then I reached in a finger and pushed around what was in the skim of wine.

"If he'd been in better health," added Dr. Hatton, "he might have recovered, in spite of the massive dose indicated by the burning inside his mouth and esophagus. As it was, the strain was simply too much for him."

"Poison, then?" asked Pons. "Something caustic?"

Gaylon growled.

"Indirectly," I said. "Of course, tests will need to be made, as there could also be a number of other factors, but I've seen something very much like this before, in the United States, and I gather that Dr. Hatton has too."

"In the Midlands. I saw a foolish child exhibit the exact same symptoms. But she recovered."

"Tell him," interrupted Galyon, somewhat exasperated.

I looked at Hatton, who nodded back to me. "Buttercups," I responded, holding up the glass.

Pons raised an eyebrow. "Indeed."

"Buttercups," Hatton repeated. "Innocent looking yellow flowers, and yet quite poisonous. You will have seen them growing in profusion right in front of this house – no doubt these came from there. Apparently someone picked a mass of them, mashed a substantial amount of both the petals and the stalks – the latter being the toxic part, actually – wrapped and tied them in a cheesecloth, and shoved it down into the wine bottle. The juices spread into the wine, and the poor man never noticed." He gestured to the bottle. "In his condition, it only took a few hours. The cheesecloth bundle is still in the bottle, but it looks to have come unfastened, and some of the petals have drifted out into the wine. Those in the bottom of the glass are what I found when I poured out a few drops."

Pons took the bottle and touched a finger to the rim, then moving the drop from there to his tongue. He grimaced and used his handkerchief to wipe away whatever remained.

"Not very wise," I warned him, but it wasn't the first time he had performed such a test.

"Curious," Pons muttered. "And so very original. Why not our old friend, arsenic, if someone wanted to remove Mr. Burnwell?"

"Possibly there is some of that as well," I said. "The buttercups might not have worked on their own, except for the man's poor physical condition."

"I've saved some of the victim's fluids for a work-up," added Hatton, "and I have no doubt that when the forensic chaps do a chemical analysis, a conclusion will be confirmed."

"So Dr. Parker – you confirm that it's murder then . . . ." muttered Galyon, still trying to get his mind around the fact that something so innocent and so often ignored could be deadly.

"Oh, yes," Hatton interrupted. "Someone sent him off quite painfully."

"With a method that they hoped was just unusual enough to pass unnoticed," I added.

"Well, this makes it worse," said Galyon with a scowl. "This is just wonderful. It's one of those *peculiar* murders, with three women downstairs who all claim to be the same person, and who will gain a fortune by this man's death. Why couldn't it just have been a blow with a candlestick to the fat man's head in the dining room? Death by buttercups, for Heaven's sake!" He snorted with disgust and looked at my friend, who had been standing back from the dead man's bed, a slight smile on his face while he tugged at his ear lobe. "Mr. Pons, I've heard about cases like this from the others at the Yard. I've had a career over four decades in length without a single one of these falling into my lap. Tell me: Can you sort it out?"

My friend nodded. "I believe so. Can you gather everyone in the parlor?"

Galyon sighed. "Certainly."

Greaves was waiting in the hallway, looking expectant, but if he thought that he'd be informed of our findings, he was mistaken. Galyon whispered to the same constable as before, and the old man was led toward the front of the house, grousing all the while. Then the inspector turned back to join us, where we stood with Hatton in the hallway.

"I spoke to the staff before the police arrived," said the doctor, "and they told me that the dead man has been steadily making his way through several cases of the homemade elderberry wine from the cellar. They were laid down long ago by Holder, the former owner of the house. The cook believes that it had already turned and was considered undrinkable, but for some reason the dead man liked it anyway. He drank it with old man Holder who died several months ago, and kept on doing so after he was gone. He couldn't get enough of the stuff. It's unlikely that he would have noticed any additional bitterness. The cook," he added, "Mrs. Mahaney, said that he was unusually boisterous last night, drinking even more than usual, and at a faster rate, only stopping when the bottle was empty."

Pons seemed to consider this, and then nodded and said, "I will join you in the parlor in a moment. I want to have a word with the cook."

The inspector followed Pons, while Hatton and I made our way to the front of the house, where we were met by the arrival of the police surgeon. Hatton excused himself and joined the man, pointing up the stairs. I made my way into the parlor, where the three women were still seated side-by-side, upright and tense, not speaking, and careful not to brush against one another. It was a curious thing, these three very different women sitting in a row upon the ornate sofa, its curving arms nestling all three Beryls as if they were jewels in some sort of oversized tiara.

Inspector Galyon came in and spoke with a pair of stolid constables by the door. In a heavy chair to the left of the women sat

Greaves, legs crossed and arms folded tightly around him, his elder head marred by a fierce scowl. Like the rest, his unfocused gaze was upon the center of the room, looking up only when Pons joined us, pulling the doors shut behind him. He then moved to the center of the room and stopped before the women, with his hands behind his back.

"Less than twenty-four hours ago," he began without any wasted time, "Dr. Parker and I were visited by Mr. Burnwell, who brought us an interesting little problem. He was the heir to at least half of his great-uncle's fortune, and three women had arrived within a short space of time of one another to claim the other half. However, each had the audacity to insist that she was the true Beryl Holder."

"Mr. Pons," interrupted Greaves, leaning forward, "I've explained that Beryl - " and he gestured toward the curly-haired woman on the left side of the sofa " - arrived first, before these other two, and that I believe her to be the true heir. There is no reason to include her with these imposters."

The second and third women, whom I now knew to be Letitia Foster, the small dark woman in the middle, and Mildred Fosk, the tall blonde on the right, both sat upright with angry expressions on their faces. "Here now," stated Letitia, in a flawless American accent that was no stretch for her, considering what I now knew of her American origins, while Mildred simply stared daggers at the old solicitor.

"You are correct, Mr. Greaves," said Pons. "These two women do have different stories entirely. In fact - "

Before he could continue, there was a knock on the door. The two women, sensing that Pons had been on the verge of revealing something to their detriment, each let out their breath. At the door, a constable leaned in, whispered to Inspector Galyon, who then nodded and said, "Bring her in."

The door widened, and I was amazed to see our own landlady, the indomitable Mrs. Johnson, rather wide-eyed as she looked around the crowded room. Her step never faltered, however, as she walked straight to Pons, handing him a thick fold of telegrams. "Ah, perfect timing!" He smiled. "You'll excuse me for a moment?" Then he stepped back, opened them, and nodded to himself as he read one sheet after the other. Finally, after refolding them and carelessly pushing them into a pocket of his coat, he said, "This will make all the difference, Mrs. Johnson. Thank you."

She nodded and turned to leave, but Pons added, almost as an afterthought, "Mrs. Johnson, would you care to stay? We shall be done soon, and can accompany you back to Praed Street."

Her eyes widened, clearly flattered and curious. I could see that she thought that she ought to go, but then she gave a quiet nod. I stood and ushered her to a chair beside my own, with our backs to the front window. She sat, remaining on the front of her chair, the bulky purse in her lap, clenched with both hands. Her eyes darted left and right, as if committing everything and every face to memory.

"Where was I?" resumed Pons. "Ah, yes. I was commenting on how the second and third Beryls have rather different stories than the first to arrive."

"As I expected," said Greaves, leaning back with a satisfied expression. "Have you already been able to identify them?"

"Indeed I have." Pons turned his gaze on the two women. Letitia Foster looked as if she were considering which way to bolt, while Mildred Fosk's lower lip protruded slightly. She already scented how the wind was turning and was about to weep.

"Ladies, there is no need to drag this out. We are dealing with a murder now, and you would do well to be completely forthright from here on out."

Both of their eyes widened in shock, as did the first Beryl beside them. Letitia opened her mouth to speak but caught herself. Pons continued. "You will recall the occasion when Mr. Burnwell obtained a photograph of you. He gave it to Mr. Greaves, asking that he verify information in New York regarding which of you women was the true Beryl Holder. In actuality, Mr. Burnwell only wanted to use it in the hopes of debunking the first Beryl, as he had no interest in using it to expose the pair of you. He already knew who you were, as he had personally selected you for this task. He certainly never intended, when he approached me, that I would use that same photograph to learn your true identities from Mr. Solomon Britt, the theatrical agent, in his Soho office."

The shocked expression on the faces of the two women was identical, and almost comical in its suddenness. Before they could react further, Pons continued. "I considered having Mr. Britt summoned down here as an aid to your unmasking, but what purpose would that serve? We know who you are: Miss Leticia Foster and Miss Mildred Fosk. We know how Mr. Burnwell hired you both to portray additional versions of his long-lost cousin, in order to discredit her. You may now consider yourselves to be in official custody, and formal verification of your identities will be obtained at leisure by the police. Thus, there was no need to roust Mr. Britt so early in the morning for something that can be established at any time." He paused, looking from one to the other, and then asked, "Do you have anything to say?"

At that point, Mildred Fosk did indeed begin to weep, silently, with great tears rolling down her cheeks. She made no move to wipe them away, and Pons reached for his handkerchief, before realizing that he had recently used it to wipe his tongue after tasting the tainted wine. I pulled out my own and handed it to her. Her eyes thanked me, but she remained silent. Letitia Foster, however, chose to speak.

"I told that fat fool it wouldn't work," she fumed. "He said it was only for a few weeks, and that all we had to do was repeat everything that *this one* said – " With that, she jerked a thumb toward the first Beryl, now sitting dumbfounded and aghast beside them, while making a not-so-subtle effort to curl in and scoot away as far as possible.

"You were hired by Mr. Burnwell to discredit Beryl Holder," clarified Pons.

"'*Discredit*,'" spat Letitia. "Yes, that's it. Somehow he'd gotten her papers and had copies made for us to use."

"What!" sputtered Greaves. "How could he – ?"

Pons held up a hand. "It was not your char that mixed up the papers, Mr. Greaves," he said. "Mr. Burnwell took the copies when you were on holiday and had *three* identical copies made, all designed to be easily identified as fakes, and he believed that the original set had then been destroyed, although I retrieved it. His clumsy plan was to make it easy to expose all three sets as forgeries, thereby implying that all three associated women were fake too. Before that happened, these two women would vanish into the night, leaving the third – you, Miss Holder – also represented by a set of obviously faked papers, instead of the true set from the United States. Ideally, the first claim would be discredited, along with the other two, leaving him with the entire fortune."

Pons then turned and gestured for Letitia Foster to continue. "He gave the copies to us," she related, "and swapped out *her* originals with another copy, as you said. He told us what to do, and that after a few weeks it would all come out, and that we could just slip away and disappear. No one would ever find us. In the meantime, the damage would have been done to *this one* – " and again she gestured toward the woman on her right, with great contempt, " – so that no one would believe her either." She looked down at her hands. "And then the great blooming idiot went and died before he could give us the word to leave."

"He didn't simply die," corrected Pons. "As I stated, he was murdered." Hearing the last word repeated yet again seemed to make them shrink in upon themselves. "But fear not, Misses Foster and Fosk," he added. "You weren't involved in that particular crime. For what would have been your motives?"

"What?" interrupted the old solicitor, sitting upright. "Their motives? There are any number of them. One or both of these two girls feared exposure, and killed the man who hired them. Or perhaps in their foolishness, one believed that she could truly be accepted as the real Beryl Holder."

"Ah, but Mr. Greaves, it won't do. Neither of those theories really holds up, and these women, while not entirely innocent, were simple pawns in Mr. Burnwell's twisted, naïve, and ultimately flawed attempt to keep the whole estate. Knowing him as you did, it shouldn't surprise you that he would try something so awkward."

"No, but I'm still not sure that you can so easily dismiss the involvement of these two women."

"Normally I wouldn't. But there are other factors to consider." He turned back to the women. "Misses Foster and Fosk. And also Miss Holder. What can you tell me about last night? Specifically, last night's dinner."

The two false Beryls simply looked at one another, but the first Beryl spoke. Her voice was thin and tense, and had the peculiar lilt that I'd heard from before when speaking to New York natives. "There was nothing unusual about it. We all ate together like every night, and it was unpleasant, as always. I *knew* that these two - " and she glared daggers at the other women beside her, " - were frauds, but Mr. Greaves had told me that we had to wait until things were cleared up properly."

"Quite right," muttered Greaves.

"That's not exactly what happened," said Miss Fosk, speaking for the first time. Her voice was surprisingly deep, with something quite Liverpudlian. I wondered how effective her New York accent had been. "Adolph was awfully happy about something yesterday. From the time he arrived home, he started drinking, even more than usual. And he kept talking all day long as if he knew a secret - dropping hints about something none of us understood. Saying phrases like 'the truth is going to come out now', and that things would 'start to happen quickly now', and that he'd been to see 'a famous detective'. It made me nervous, and finally, after dinner, I cornered him and he said that everything was working out as planned. He'd gotten impatient when that photograph hadn't accomplished anything, and he'd decided to hire a detective of his own. Any day now, that detective – you, I suppose – would figure out that the papers were false, but we would be gone by then. He said that Letitia and I would take a fade and be out of it. He was going to give us money to leave the country for a few months until everything settled down."

Pons nodded, and I knew that this went along with what he had already been thinking. "I confirmed with the cook, Mrs. Mahaney, that Mr. Burnwell was indeed quite jovial last night, much more than normal, and that he was drinking considerably more of the elderberry wine than usual."

Miss Foster nodded. "He was, and that's a fact."

"This is all well and good, Mr. Pons," said Inspector Galyon, who had stood patiently all this time near the doorway. "You've cleared up that Mr. Burnwell hired these women as part of some plot to get the entire fortune. But Burnwell is beyond our justice now. This does nothing to explain away his murder."

Greaves sputtered. "I still refuse to believe that there actually *was* a murder. The way he treated himself, Adolph was lucky to have lived as long as he did. You must be mistaken."

"There are still tests to be performed," said Galyon, "but two medical men have tentatively identified the substance used to kill Mr. Burnwell."

"Then . . . then surely it was one of these girls, as I said," growled the old man. "One of them was spooked when she heard that a detective had been hired."

Pons nodded. "When you put it that way, Mr. Greaves, I can see some sense in what you say."

The old man threw up his arms and settled back in a self-satisfied way. "There! At last. You see!"

"But Mr. Pons," said Galyon. "You disagreed when Mr. Greaves said the same thing just a few moments ago."

"Ah, but Inspector, he *didn't* say the same thing, did he? Before, he said something like '*One or both of these two girls feared exposure, and killed the man who hired them,*' referring specifically to our actress friends, while this time he said, '*It was surely one of these girls*' who '*was spooked when she heard that a detective had been hired*'. There is a world of difference."

"I'm afraid I don't see – " began Galyon, but then he stopped, noticing the grimace that crossed Greaves' face, along with as the amazing way that Beryl Holder - the *first* Beryl - suddenly went as white as a ghost.

"Nonsense," muttered Greaves. Then he cleared his throat and said in a firmer tone, "Nonsense!"

"Not at all," smiled Pons, ignoring the first Beryl entirely. To my surprise, he turned to me. "Parker. Do you recall yesterday evening when we were discussing the progress of my investigations?"

"I do."

"As we talked, I could follow the pattern of your thinking. At one point, you were about to ask me a question, but later it must have slipped your mind. Do you now recall what it was?"

I narrowed my eyes in thought. It was on the tip of my tongue, but I couldn't retrieve it. I cast farther back. Pons had visited Sir Edward Soames, and then -

"You had been to Sir Edward's office to ask about Alexander Holder's will, and you were going to tell me where you went next, when we were interrupted by the arrival of Thorndyke's report on the forged papers."

Greaves started to make some complaint, but he was ignored. "I knew," said Pons, "that you intended to remind me of that later, but then Mrs. Johnson - " and he smiled at our intently fascinated landlady " - brought our evening repast, and it slipped your mind. I let it remain that way, as I felt that it would be more amusing to reveal what I had learned later, in some substantially greater dramatic setting - *this* setting, as it tragically turns out. Would you care to guess where I went after seeing Sir Edward?"

I knew better than to waste my time. I nodded, and Pons stated, "I visited the home of Kenton Stevenson, the former partner of Alexander Holder."

Greaves' eyes, already narrowed from when he heard that Pons had been to see Sir Edward about the will, narrowed further, but he did not choose to speak.

"Mr. Stevenson was a veritable font of information. He confirmed that Alexander Holder did indeed receive a substantial fortune for his portion of the sale of Holder and Stevenson. That is to your credit, Mr. Greaves." The old man nodded, but retained his wary look. "But I'm afraid that he also balanced that credit for you against a substantial debit to your character. He indicated that he's never trusted you any farther than he could throw you, and that, as you will recall, he allowed you to have nothing whatsoever to do with the sale of *his* portion of the bank."

"Slanderous cur," muttered Greaves. "He would have been nothing without Alexander."

"Possibly. I cannot say. But he seems to have done quite well on his own since the days when his relations with Mr. Holder were severed upon that gentleman's retirement. Unlike you, Mr. Greaves. You see, Mr. Stevenson let me know about a number of the financial failures and outright peculations with which *you* have been associated in recent years. It is common knowledge, apparently, that you do *not* maintain chambers off Gate Lane simply to 'keep your hand in', as you told us yesterday. Rather, that is the best that you can afford, as was your luncheon yesterday of potatoes. In truth, not only do you keep your sparse office there, but you also reside there."

"This is outrageous!" hissed the solicitor.

"Mr. Stevenson further stated that it is his long-held belief that Mr. Holder's accounts should be examined – something he could never convince his old partner to do – and that, without having the income from the management of Alexander Holder's estate, you would have long since been in a state of bankruptcy . . . or prison."

"Why, I – this is monstrous! I'll file suit against him! And you too, Pons!"

"It will be an interesting case," said Pons. He reached into his pocket, retrieving the sheaf of telegrams that had been delivered by Mrs. Johnson. Without opening them again, he continued speaking. "Of course, Mr. Stevenson's comments gave me an entirely new direction to explore. Without having at that time the benefit of the completed analysis of the forged letter and birth certificate, but with the testimony of Mr. Burnwell's forger himself – who was easily found – I already understood the basics of Burnwell's plot. The second and third women that he had hired to discredit the first were explained.

"But now I needed to understand more about the *first* woman, in light of this new character assessment I'd received concerning the solicitor managing the estate. You see, this woman, one way or the other, had appeared in a most timely manner – sending a wire, seemingly out of the blue, announcing her existence within days of Alexander Holder's death. And most interesting, she was able to vouch for her identity with original documents that must have actually belonged at one time to Beryl Holder.

"So I sent a telegram – a lengthy one." He tapped the thick fold of sheets in his hand with a long forefinger. "The investigative work done by my New York associates was quick and thorough and very informative."

Pons smiled again at the solicitor, who had started upon hearing the words *New York*. "Yes, Mr. Greaves, like you, I also 'do my homework'. Not long after we left your office yesterday, I sent a message to my associate with a couple of specific tasks: Locate and verify any information whatsoever that was available regarding Miss Beryl Holder of Queens – thank you for that detail! – as soon as possible, and also examine any of the advertisements that were placed in the New York newspapers to locate Beryl Holder during the last ten years, with follow-up at the associated newspapers."

Pons took a few paces, and then turned to face us from a different perspective. "I see that last one struck a chord with our solicitor friend here, but the rest of you may be wondering why I would care about any past attempts to contact Beryl Holder, particularly with advertisements. It was because that I had caught Mr. Greaves in a lie. A small one, for sure, and something that he didn't realize might attract notice. But it did.

"Yesterday, he stated to Dr. Parker and myself that he had been running advertisements 'year in and year out', both here and in the United States, looking for Alexander Holder's heirs. I had one of these in my own files. I had clipped it due to its curious aspects, as I save interesting bits of ephemera like that, and it was this same advertisement that Adolph Burnwell saw late last year, leading him back to his family. But I'm a careful reader of the press, and particularly the advertisements and agony columns.

"Yesterday, I mentioned to Dr. Parker about the unusual fact that Burnwell's parents were specifically named. That was what had originally caused me to notice that specific advertisement in the first place, as I *recognized those names*. And I can say with certainty that no similar advertisements seeking these heirs were run 'year in and year out' here in London. I would have seen them. Why, then, would Mr. Greaves say that he was doing so? And how could he *not* advertise, while giving Mr. Holder the impression that he was doing so?

"I already knew, before Dr. Parker and I left Praed Street, that this advertisement had only run on one occasion. Mr. Greaves had lied, and from there on I knew that he would bear further examination. When I spoke to Mr. Stevenson, I knew to ask how it was that Mr. Holder never realized that there was no real search occurring for his heirs, and that no advertisements were being placed. The retired banker was able to answer that question for me. In his banking days, Mr. Holder could never bear to read a newspaper, preferring instead to relay on summaries of important events prepared by his staff. After his retirement, he simply continued ignoring the news, and when he was told that the advertisements were in the papers, 'year in and year out', he never doubted it, and never bothered to verify it – instead accepting the sad news 'year in and year out' that there had been no replies.

"Yet, I wanted to know more, and so I went to the London newspaper where that particular advertisement did appear late last year, the very one that winkled out Mr. Burnwell.

"Conversation with the advertising manager revealed that this notice was not placed by you at all, Mr. Greaves, but instead by Mr. Holder himself. After some digging, we found his name written on the copy in the receipt book. This was interesting, in that when he chose to place it himself, the advertisement actually *appeared* in the newspaper, while there was nothing at all during the 'years in and years out' when you said that you were doing so.

"I wonder how you reacted when that happened, Mr. Greaves? When he actually placed the advertisement? Did you hope that there would be no response? I suspect that if Mr. Holder had also continued to leave it to you, there would still have been no advertisements to this very day, and Mr. Burnwell would have continued to trundle on his worn path as an East End shopkeeper, fulfilling his days that way. Instead, because his great-uncle took the reins on that one occasion, Mr. Burnwell's fate was irrevocably altered, leading to him to his death bed upstairs, his alimentary canal blistered by poison."

The first Beryl gasped when she heard this and closed her eyes. Greaves turned to look at her, and then back to Pons, crossing his arms. "What does this have to do with anything?" he demanded. "I had explicit permission to manage the estate as I saw fit. Whether or not I ran advertisements is of no consequence."

"Ah, but it is," Pons countered. "For Mr. Stevenson, at my behest, is now taking a more active interest in examining what's left of the estate of Alexander Holder, even as we speak. The initial word that he gave to me indicates that Mr. Holder's collective assets are on the road to being gutted – all thanks to your sole manipulations, Mr. Greaves. There are still substantial funds left, of course, and a number of stocks that are available, along with the value of this house, but it's certainly not what it was.

"And now it can be demonstrated, through your lack of actually placing any advertisements, that you willfully tried to prevent the discovery of the true heirs, so that you could remain in control of the estate, even after Holder's death. Without heirs, the estate would, according to the will, theoretically be directed to charities – but at your discretion. And that," he added, "would never do. For one of the conditions of Alexander Holder's will was that, if no heirs were found, the administration of the estate for charity would be handled by *both* you, Mr. Greaves, *and Holder's former partner, Stevenson.* Allowing Mr. Holder's former partner to see the books would quickly reveal your finagling."

"Is that what's in the telegrams, Pons?" I asked, nodding toward the flimsy sheets in his hand. "In addition to information from New York? Stevenson's report on the situation?"

"No, Parker. Mr. Stevenson had already begun investigating the irregularities yesterday afternoon when I checked back with him before returning home. These – " and he waved the telegrams, "are solely from my New York associate. He has a very capable Man Friday who obtained a great deal of information in a short amount of time. These telegrams contain verifications regarding the similar complete lack of advertisements seeking Beryl Holder in New York – there have been none at all, over the last ten years – as well as filling in a completely different area of the painting."

He now turned his gaze back toward Beryl Holder.

"You understand, Miss, that you are about to be exposed." He held up the packet of telegrams. "It is conclusive, you see. *Miss Beryl Holder* died two years ago. So the time has come to tell the truth, *Miss Everston.*"

She rose, her mouth falling open in involuntary surprise. Then she sank back, her arms wrapping tightly around her as she began to slightly rock to and fro.

"Thank you for that little confirmation," said Pons. "I wasn't completely sure of your identity. However, with the help of my brother in the Foreign Office, I was able to exert some influence yesterday afternoon when attempting to verify where Beryl Holder had disembarked during the approximate dates when you entered the country. Interestingly, no Beryl Holder was shown on any records, meaning she didn't arrive here.

"However, based upon passport information recorded at the time, I did come up with a very short list of women of the approximate correct age who did. I sent these names in additional cables to my New York associate, and he was able to verify that one of those that had traveled to England at the correct time: Miss Carrie Everston, was from Staten Island, near enough to Queens. She has been away from her residence for coincidentally the same amount of time it would have taken you to depart and travel here.

"So the question now becomes, Miss Everston, how did you become involved in this sordid mess, and where did you obtain the original papers belonging to the actual Beryl Holder, who died two years ago, having taken a terrible fall one night from the Borden Avenue Bridge?"

Her eyes cut toward Greaves, who was fiercely scowling at my friend. She seemed as if she were about to speak, but the detective interrupted her. "There is no need to answer, Miss Everston. I believe that I can fill in some of the missing pieces.

"The original Beryl Hunter documents, now in my possession after retrieving them yesterday from the forger hired by Mr. Burnwell, either came into your possession by two ways – somehow you took them from Beryl Holder yourself, or they were given to you. But if you obtained them personally, one must question how you did so. Miss Holder's death was considered suspicious at the time. Though she was a lonely spinster, there was no apparent reason to kill herself, and no signs that she fell by accident. You, living in an adjacent borough, could have known her. In fact, you could have somehow learned of her rich grandfather, and plotted to kill her, taking on her identity – as you have in fact just attempted. But to do that, you would have somehow had to know that she *had* a rich grandfather. Did she tell you that? Did you hear it from her own lips?"

The girl shook her head, and Greaves growled, "How is that possible, Pons? You've already tried to point out that no advertisements were run in New York to find any heirs. How would the true Beryl have known about any inheritance?"

"Very good, Mr. Greaves," said Pons. "You're in a dark room, not knowing yet what faces you, but you're fighting anyway. As to your comment: It would be more accurate to say that *you* ran no advertisements, in spite of your representation to the contrary to Alexander Holder. And it does not go unnoticed that your attempt to ask a defensive question designed to deflect suspicion away from Miss Everston can only benefit you as well."

"What? I did no such thing. What are you babbling about?"

"Simply this: If Miss Everston didn't obtain those papers herself, as I said, then someone must have given them to her. In fact, someone must have obtained her services to pretend to *be* the real Beryl Holder, in an attempt to have her become the heir to the Holder Estate. Someone who had already obtained the papers himself, in order to give them to her for use when she came to England."

Greaves looked satisfied. "Then that lets me out. I see what you're implying. But how would I get those papers?"

"I spoke to a clerk at Lloyds yesterday afternoon," said Pons. "After they absorbed Holder and Stevenson, they still, to this day, continue to receive the occasional letter or inquiry. It is their official procedure to direct all Holder and Stevenson correspondence to Mr. Silas Greaves – you, sir. Now, suppose the real Beryl had finally decided to get in touch with her grandfather. Not knowing any other way, she might write to Holder and Stevenson. The letter would then be sent on to you as a matter of course. You, without feeling the need to notify your friend Alexander Holder, could then begin to correspond with her . . . ."

Then, Pons changed his tack and turned back to the girl. "Now is the time for truth, Miss Everston. If you don't want to be convicted for more than your own responsibility in this matter, you must reveal all. *Who hired you to portray Beryl Holder?*"

She seemed to take a firmer hold on herself, sitting up straight, dropping her arms, and gesturing toward the solicitor. "It was him," she said in her thin voice. "Greaves. He came to New York a year ago and hired me. I didn't know him from Adam, but he said he'd found out about me from . . . from a man that I know. This man said that I'd do a thing like this for money." She lowered her eyes. "And he was right. God help me, he was right."

"This is outrageous," muttered Greaves.

"And he did what, exactly?" pressed Pons.

"He gave me the papers – the letter and the birth certificate. He told me that he represented a large estate, and that the heirs were dead. If we kept it from going to charity, if I became this girl Beryl Holder, there would be a wonderful life in store for me. All I had to do was take the papers and come to England when I was called. He would take care of the rest. He said there was already another heir, but that would take care of itself."

"And so you waited? All this time?"

"I did. He sent money. He never put anything in writing, but I knew what it was for, and what to do when I received word from him. During his visit, he had told me a lot about this dead Beryl Holder, and I committed it to memory, so that I could *be* her when the time came."

"How did he explain having her papers?"

"He told me that he'd been in contact with her before she died, and that he'd been able to find out various details about her past that would make me seem like the real Beryl. As a lawyer, there wouldn't be any problems."

Pons turned back to Greaves. "What about that, Mr. Greaves? *Had* you been in contact with the true Beryl Holder?"

"I don't have to answer any of your insane suppositions."

"No matter. I'm certain that I understand how you obtained the original proofs. It was when you traveled to New York two years ago – " and he waved the telegrams " – as verified just a few hours ago by an employee of the U.S. government who owes my associate a favor – an employee who was able to show proof that you entered the United States through New York two days before the mysterious death of Beryl Holder in 1928 – and that you departed for England the day after."

Greaves focused his gaze like a lens, filled with hate, at my friend, who stood over him, unaffected. "But possibly I'm mistaken, and I'm maligning you without cause, Mr. Greaves. For our purpose here today, once all this brush has been cleared away, is actually to discover who killed poor Mr. Burnwell."

I realized that, with all of these other pell-mell revelations, I had forgotten about the dead man lying upstairs. I glanced at Mrs. Johnson, wondering how she fared with all this confusing talk of strangers and mysterious deaths, both here and on another continent. Unsurprisingly, her gaze was sharp, and she glanced intently from one of the seated individuals across the room to another, back-and-forth, as if attempting to see their secrets.

Returning his attention to Miss Everston, Pons said, "I believe that you can tell us. It might go a long way toward easing your own situation."

The girl frowned as she considered his words, and then she pointed toward the old man. "It was him!" she said. "He killed him, just like he killed that girl in New York!"

"For heaven's sake!" cried Greaves, standing up suddenly. At the door, both Galyon and the constables tensed, and I prepared myself to protect Mrs. Johnson, should the old man produce a weapon. But instead, he spun on his heel and faced the girl beside him.

"You liar!" he cried. "How dare you! Don't you see he's only manipulating you? All of us? He can't prove anything!"

"That's where you're wrong," said Pons. "These telegrams contain facts, placing you traveling to and from America on the dates in question. This is just the opening of the door. As we pull it wider, other pieces of the puzzle will be found. Your manipulations of the Holder estate are already being examined. Your communications with the real Beryl Holder – records of which may still be found in your chambers or with her personal effects – explaining just how the two of you became acquainted. Subsequent communications with Miss Everston."

"I can tell you about that!" cried the American girl. "How angry he was when the old man went out and found Burnwell on his own. And how he wired me when the old man died, to get over here as soon as I could."

"There you are, then, Mr. Greaves," said Pons. "We can tie all of it back to you, beginning to end, from the times you said you were trying to find the heirs but weren't, right up to Burnwell's poisoning. How long had that been planned? Clearly removing this other heir, in direct competition with your own game piece, would have to be accomplished at some point. You had already seen how he was draining the estate even faster than you could. Had you set the trap for him weeks ago, poisoning the wine bottle and waiting until he got around to drinking it, and only last night was it sprung? Or did something happen then that forced your hand?"

"Don't be a fool, Pons," said Greaves. "Of course it was this little snip that killed him. She panicked when Adolph was bragging about hiring a detective. She took me aside when I arrived here this morning and told me what she had done. The fool was proud of herself. She didn't realize how easily a poisoning can be spotted. She said that she'd had a sister that had died from buttercup poisoning, and that no one would ever suspect." He turned toward the girl and said dismissively, "You fool."

With a raw cry, Carrie Everston stood and charged at him, her fingers raked into claws. Before she was finished and the constables pulled her off of him, the old man had received terrible wounds across his cheeks and brow, and would suffer the loss of vision in his ruined left eye for the rest of his short life.

The room erupted into chaos, and I stepped around my friend, yelling, "Pons! See to Mrs. Johnson!" before giving what aid that I could to Greaves, now whipping and thrashing about on the floor. Somewhere during that time, I'm told that Letitia Foster and Mildred Fosk attempted to slip away, but they were stopped by none other than the cook, Mrs. Mahaney, waiting at the front door with a rolling pin.

A few minutes later, after the women and the wounded solicitor had been removed, Pons stepped across the room to Mrs. Johnson and me. "Thank you for bringing the telegrams when they arrived. It gave me the final proof of Greaves' trips to the United States, along with the information about the real Beryl Holder. I already had a basic understanding of what had happened, and it all fit together, but a good attorney could have argued against such a circumstantial case, and having proof in hand was enough to crack them. I needed to pivot back and forth between them, so that each was being accused, a little more each time, and yet each might see a way to save themselves by betraying the other – without having time to consider that in any event, they were both well and truly caught.

Mrs. Johnson simply beamed, while I considered with wonder how Pons already knew so much of the matter before he ever began his final play.

Later, after the house was left in the care of Mrs. Mahaney, Pons, Mrs. Johnson, and I waited out front while a constable obtained a cab, which we intended to take all the way back to Praed Street, avoiding further trips this morning on the local trains. It had been fine for the two of us to walk from the station an hour or so earlier, but it was not acceptable to have Mrs. Johnson do the same.

"So if Miss Everston hadn't panicked and poisoned Burnwell last night," I asked, "do you think that Greaves would have killed him later?"

"Probably, but not at first. However, he had to be worried about Burnwell's drain on the estate, and he could only cut off the man's allowance for so long. After the probate, Burnwell would have full control, and could have even chosen to cut Greaves out entirely from his managerial position."

"Would Miss Everston have been in danger as well?"

"Who knows? She knew the truth, and probably suspected that Greaves had killed the real Beryl Holder. That gave her power over him. Once he had realigned matters so that Stevenson would be cut out of any interference if the estate were to go to charity, it's likely that she would have met with some sort of accident too, leaving Greaves in a very pretty place indeed."

I had another thought. "Do you suppose that Greaves also had a hand in killing Alexander Holder? He could have slipped him something that caused him to fall and hit his head."

"It's possible. I mentioned something of the sort to Inspector Galyon as they were leaving. It is a question that can be explored during the interrogation. Or," he added, "the exhumation."

It is a matter of record that Silas Greaves did confess to drugging his old friend Alexander Holder, an act that led to the old man's death. His motivation was fear that Holder would, in fact, change his will in favor of Burnwell, possibly altering the circumstances to the point that Greaves would no longer have control of the funds, or that his fraud would be discovered.

"Poor Beryl," said Mrs. Johnson. "The real Beryl, I mean. That girl was only trying to find her family. That man killed her, then."

"He did," said Pons. "That would be when he took the papers from her rooms. I suspect that those – the birth certificate and the old letter – were all that there were. If there had been more documents, Greaves would have certainly taken and used them too. No doubt he kept them, and either gave them to Miss Everston when she arrived, or he simply reported that she had.

"Sadly, the real Beryl Holder was an unimportant girl, in the sense that her death was never even noted or reported here. When it came time for Greaves' hand-picked false heir to appear, he was the sole man responsible for checking to see whether the heir was legitimate, and no one else would have had any inkling of the dead girl in New York.

"But Alexander Holder complicated things when he finally decided to run his own advertisement, resulting in the appearance of his great-nephew, Burnwell, who had been living in London for years. Greaves was in no position to allow a true heir to take possession of the estate.

"And Burnwell was crafty in his own cunning way, and he came up with the plan to discredit the first Beryl. I suspect that he probably believed her to be legitimate – otherwise, why go to the trouble of making her seem false? But he didn't realize that Greaves was the man actually pulling the puppet strings, and when Burnwell took his photograph, hoping that it could be used to prove the first Beryl false, he never knew that giving it to Greaves would render it useless – that it wouldn't be sent to New York at all, but would rather sit on Greaves' desk until it was given to us to help disprove the two women hired by Burnside.

"Poor Burnwell," added Pons. "He was so full of his own cleverness. He never considered that someone might examine his story beyond the initial layer. And then, he bragged so much yesterday after he returned home that Carrie Everston was prompted to kill him."

"It makes my head spin," said Mrs. Johnson, "but I think that I understand it all. Still, it's too bad that no one is left from that old man's family."

"True." I shook my head. "There cannot always be a happy ending."

"Possibly not in the sense you mean," countered Pons. "But I should like to point out that there still is a substantial estate left, and the charity that was named, should no heirs be found, is an orphanage in Whitechapel which will benefit greatly from the money. I have it on good authority from Kenton Stevenson, both of us having already perceived how this was playing out, that the funds will be directed by Holder's former partner in the way that the old banker originally intended. I think that this is the best that could have been hoped for, and it is in fact not so unhappy a solution after all."

Mrs. Johnson and I agreed. While we waited for the cab, she turned to me and asked, "What will you call it?"

"I beg your pardon?"

"When you write this in your journals. What will you call it?"

"I haven't given it any thought. I suppose something like 'The Three Beryls' would be acceptable."

I saw that most subtle sign of dislike. "Mrs. Johnson," I continued. "I would be honored if you would pick the name."

She spoke without hesitation. "'The Adventure of the Additional Heirs'."

And so it is. The cab arrived, and both Pons and I helped her climb inside. We were soon headed back toward London and Praed Street, with our good lady describing the breakfast that she intended to prepare upon our arrival – a prospect that I highly anticipated.

# The Horror of
# St. Anne's Row

My friend, Solar Pons, patiently concluded his explanation to Inspector Jamison, who had summoned us that morning concerning the death of Peter Pendleton, one of his best men. As Jamison had explained, not an hour before, Pendleton had been sent out to cover Baron Ennesfred Kroll. Earlier in the week, he had broken off all communication with his superiors, before being found just that morning with a piece of paper clutched in his hand, printed with two green stars. The trail had led from where the body had been discovered in Culross Street, off Park Street in Mayfair, across Hyde Park and Kensington Gardens, and thus to Kensington Church Street, just west of Kensington Palace.

Typically, Pons had seemed to know exactly what was going on, identifying the murderer before Jamison and I even realized we were at the finish line. Now they were standing on the pavement in front of the killer's abode, discussing the finer points of evidence against the guilty party, while I looked around at the nearby houses. I myself had some sentimental attachment to this neighborhood, having lived just round the corner for a time as a boy. My father had been a civil engineer, often traveling in relation to his work, much of the time in the north. During one of our sojourns in London, my parents had happened upon a house in Vicarage Gate, and for several years, my brothers and I knew the area quite well – ranging those neighborhoods stretching between Hyde Park and Holland Park. Thankfully, we had been raised to be independent lads, and trusted to both stay out of trouble and not to cause it.

Seeing that Jamison was having difficulty in comprehending certain subtle aspects of Pons's reasoning, I caught their attention and nodded to the corner, indicating that I was going to walk away for a bit. Pons tipped his head and reiterated to Jamison the continued and frustrating reasons behind the difficulty in obtaining the necessary evidence against the Baron.

Turning into that confusing arrangement of nearby streets that are all known as Vicarage Gate, I walked until I located the one that had housed my family during those long-ago years. It was the southern spur, lined by only seven houses on the north side, and ending just behind St. Paul's Church. I stood in front of my own former home, which had figured peripherally so long ago in the destruction of the Heka Cult.

Then the church bells rang the noon hour, and I was reminded of the more peaceful days of my boyhood, when I had listened to those same dulcet tones.

I took a deep breath of the crisp air. London's skies had been washed clean, if only for a day or so, by a recent series of early spring storms. I toyed with the idea of knocking upon my old door, identifying myself as a former resident, and asking if I could look around. However, I quickly dismissed the notion. I had no real need to see inside, as it had only been one of a number of houses in which we'd lived while my brothers and I were growing up, and I was certain that whatever might seem familiar was not worth the bother to the current residents simply to satisfy my sentimentality.

As I was about to turn away, intending to retrace my steps and join Pons and Jamison, I noticed a curious fellow shambling my way from the direction of the church. As he was making directly toward me, with the obvious intent of speaking about something, I paused, allowing him to close the distance between us.

He came to a stop about five feet away, and I could see that he was in a bad way. Probably in his early sixties, his leathery skin gave the impression of even greater age. His eyes were naturally squinted, but with an unusual brownish-yellow color. He was clearly suffering from *sclera icterus*, but I saw no signs of excessive alcohol use which would help to explain his liver's failure to eliminate the body's bilirubin. Clearly, his condition was caused by something else.

I took a step toward him, and in doing so detected the sickly sweet odor of ketones. Again, this ketoacidosis might have been caused by alcoholism, but he didn't show any of the usual indicators. I suspected that the man's illness was preventing him from eating.

"Have you seen her?" he croaked, his voice almost a whisper. I looked left and right, but I hadn't recalled encountering a soul since walking away from Pons and Jamison. One of the lesser known facts to people unfamiliar with London is that, once one leaves the main thoroughfares, some of the side streets can often feel completely deserted.

I shook my head. "I haven't seen anyone. Whom do you seek?"

"My granddaughter," he said. "She is in my care now, and I've let her wander away. We had been to the church to pray, and as we walked out, she fell behind. When I looked back, she'd disappeared." He raised a hand in a gesture that encompassed the general area around us, showing a palm while he did so that was lined with the years and a number of scars as well. I had known Pons long enough to recognize that he was a craftsman of some sort.

"I haven't seen her," I repeated. "How old is she?"

"Six. And small for her age." He coughed and continued. "Her parents have disappeared, you see, and I came up to London from Walcott, in Norfolk, to take her back with me. I don't have long myself . . . ." With that, he drifted off for a moment before regaining his train of thought. He gave another little cough and looked this way and that. "You didn't see her then?"

I repeated again that I hadn't, realizing that he had fastened onto me, the only person in sight, as if I might be able to provide some sort of solution. I had seen this type of magical thinking before, when someone, at the end of his or her rope, seemed to cede responsibility for remedying a bad situation to another, in the same way that a child might declare with great faith that he or she is hungry with the sure knowledge that someone will step up and provide a meal. Sadly, I was unable to do more than sympathize with him. But, I thought, I did have friends who could offer assistance.

I hated to get too far from the church in case the little girl should wander into view, but I needed to involve Pons - and Jamison too, if he was willing - and I was afraid that if I left the man for even a moment, he too would be gone when I returned. Taking a step closer, I put a hand on his arm. It felt like a stick, and I realized that he had some sort of fever. He was more ill than I had observed, fitting with his statement about his time left. The thought crossed my mind that perhaps he was out of his head, and hallucinating the whole matter of the missing girl, but his eyes, while disconcerting in their discolored state, were not those of someone who has lost his faculties. Ill he might be, but he knew of what he spoke.

"I have friends in the next street," I said. "They can help us look. Come with me and explain what you've told me. We'll be back soon."

He considered for only a moment and then nodded. I turned to lead him back the way I had come and was gratified to note that he was following.

"What is your name?" I asked as we walked.

"Dorsey. Ned Dorsey."

"Don't worry, Mr. Dorsey, we'll find . . . . What is your granddaughter's name?"

"Sylvie."

Pons and Jamison were still in their discussion, but both stopped to observe our approach - Pons with his irrepressible curiosity, and

Jamison with the suspicion that is applied upon experienced policemen like layers of varnish, year after year.

Without waiting for my new companion to get to the matter in his own way, I quickly outlined what I knew - a six-year-old girl named Sylvie was missing after visiting the church, and the old man, her grandfather, had observed me nearby and asked if I'd seen her. Both Pons and Jamison perceived what was involved, and Pons excused himself to return to the church, while Jamison blew his whistle, bringing a couple of nearby constables in a hurry. They were quickly briefed and sent in different directions, leaving me and the old man alone on the corner. By unspoken agreement, he and I followed after Pons, back toward the church, although at a much slower pace.

Ahead of us, I could hear the policemen as they called from different directions, "Sylvie! Sylvie!" Jamison was marching with purpose toward the vicarage, and there was no sign of Pons - until he suddenly emerged from the alley between the church and the adjacent houses, leading to the next street. Sitting propped in his arms was a small girl with blonde - almost white - hair, a solemn look in her very blue eyes and her mouth stained a striking green by the flavored ice that she was methodically devouring from a paper cone.

I called to Jamison before he got too far away, and he turned. Seeing that the affair was settled, he whistled again for the constables, and they all gathered around us as Pons was transferring the girl back to her grandfather.

"Simple luck," declared Pons. "I heard the music from the ice vendor's cart in the next street and thought that it might have attracted the young lady's attention." He looked at the old man. "I hope that you don't mind that I bought her something, Mr. - ?"

"My apologies," I said. "This is Mr. Ned Dover. These men with the police are Inspector Jamison, and Constables Mecker and Phelps. And this is Mr. Solar Pons."

Dover's eyes widened. "Solar Pons? Well, that's a funny coincidence."

Pons turned his head slightly. "Indeed? And how so, Mr. Dover."

The old man gently lowered Sylvie to the ground. She stood close by, finishing her refreshment while hanging her other hand from the flap of her grandfather's coat pocket. "I had considered calling on you, before thinking that possibly I should let things lie and just return home."

"If I may be of any assistance . . . ." responded Pons, leaving the decision with Dover.

Our new acquaintance didn't take long to speak. "It's Fate, then," he said. "I'll lay it out for you, and then see what you think about it."

"Agreed." Pons turned to Jamison. "Is our business concluded?"

"It is, and with my thanks," responded the policeman. "I'll be by in the next day or so to clarify a few points, but I think I understand the gist of it. Once again, Mr. Pons: Well done!"

Our group splintered apart, the policemen returning toward the Gardens and the walk back to their vehicles in Mayfair, while Pons stepped out to the main intersection to snare a cab. Soon, Dover and his granddaughter were accompanying us to Praed Street.

Upon our arrival, Sylvie was given into the delighted care of Mrs. Johnson, who took her back toward the kitchen, promising a selection of treats that sadly didn't make their way very often up to our first floor sitting room. Meanwhile, Pons proceeded us up the stairs, and presently we were situated in front of the fire, which quickly rid us of the chill.

"Pray," said Pons, "share with us your story."

"It's told soon enough," said Dover. "I'm from Walcott, up above Norwich. I craft leather for the seafaring trade, and have a small shop on the Coast Road. My wife died long ago, and my only child, Carrie, married a sailor, Bill Patton, and moved here, to London."

He fished in his coat pocket and pulled out a leather fold of the sort to protect photographs. "Here they are, on their wedding day."

He handed it to Pons, who studied it for a moment before passing it to me. The photograph was the sort taken on wedding days, but the man and woman frozen at that moment in time hadn't exhibited the usual grim visages so often seen. Instead, they were laughing at something a few feet to their left. The woman was extraordinarily beautiful, with the same blonde hair as her daughter. The man was big and – even in the photograph – exuded both the confidence and capability that easily radiates from certain natural born leaders. A most handsome couple indeed.

As I returned the photograph to Mr. Dover, he continued. "I saw them sometimes when they'd journey my way, and once when I came up to London last year. My son-in-law is a good man. He's on the Liverpool, Dublin, and London Steam Packet Company. He takes good care of them. But now he and Carrie have disappeared." He fished into another pocket and pulled out a much-abused telegram form, apparently folded and refolded many times. "I received this two days ago."

Pons took and read it, and then sat for a moment before leaning to hand it to me. I read:

*Bill and Carrie gone. Sylvie at St. Dunstan's, Stepney. Come for her.*

There was no indication as to the sender. I could only imagine how the information might have been received by the stoic old man, and what effect it must have had on him. It was obvious to me, even without any complete examination, that he was in very bad shape from some consuming illness. News arriving that his daughter and son-in-law were missing and his granddaughter in the care of a church in one of the rougher parts of London could have been too much to bear.

"I was on the first train," Dover continued, "and here by yesterday morning. The whole time I wondered what had happened, but it was more important to get to Sylvie, instead of taking time to send telegrams and ask questions." He swallowed.

"Can I get you something to drink? A brandy, perhaps?" I asked, although I could see that Pons was anxious for him to continue his story.

"No, thank you. It doesn't agree with me." He coughed to clear his throat and continued. "Sylvie was at the church, just like the telegram said. The minister didn't know a thing. They'd found her asleep in one of the pews, on the same night that I got word to fetch her. She was wrapped in the same coat that she's wearing today. There was a note pinned to it, saying that her grandfather would come for her."

"Do you have that note?" asked Pons.

"Why, no. I left it with the minister."

"Did you recognize the handwriting?"

"I didn't. But to be honest, I have to puzzle out writing at the best of times, and knowing the difference between the ways different people write is beyond me."

Pons nodded. "What did you do then?"

"I gathered Sylvie up. She was groggy – they said she'd been that way since they found her, but she's gotten better since then. She recognized me quick enough, even though it's been over a year since I've seen her. I thanked the minister and took her around to Carrie's place. I thought that there might be some answers there – where they went, or who sent me a telegram, or who took Sylvie to the church. But when I got there, the landlady was angry and refused to tell me anything – at least at first. When I finally got her to listen, she seemed as puzzled as me. She knew Sylvie, of course, but she said that she'd never been friendly with Carrie or Bill. She said that they had moved away a week ago without letting her know – that's why she was angry. They'd left owing money, and somehow slipped out with everything they owned. She said that someone else was already living in their rooms now. She didn't know where they had gone, and no one had asked about them until I showed up."

"Curious," said Pons. "I assume you've used your time since then trying to ascertain what happened."

"I have," said the old man. "I tried to talk to the neighbors around Carrie's place, but they didn't tell me anything. Then I asked around at the dock, at the Liverpool and London boats where Bill works. It's been difficult, as I've had Sylvie with me. I didn't have anywhere to leave her, you see."

"What did they tell you at the boat office?"

"That a week ago, Bill just didn't show up one day."

Pons frowned and tapped a finger on the arm of his chair. Then, he stood. "Do you have somewhere to stay?"

"I do," said Dover. "We took a room in Drayson Mews, not too far from where Bill and Carrie lived. It's close to where we met this morning. We'd been over to walk in the Park, and I noticed the church. We stopped in to pray." He stood up then too. "Perhaps Sylvie getting lost and you bringing her back was an answer to my prayer."

"I don't know about that, but I hope to find some answers."

"I want to pay you for the ice. It was most generous of you. And about your fee . . . ." began Dover.

Pons waved a hand. "It would be wrong to charge money after being included in a divine intervention."

Dover frowned. "You mock me – " he began, but Pons cut him off.

"Not at all, sir, not at all. Not at all. Let us agree to discuss it later."

Dover stood up. "I need your help, Mr. Pons. However it works out, I need it."

As Dover turned to go, I stopped him. "Your health, Mr. Dover? I'm a doctor. Can I offer any assistance?"

He smiled wearily and shook his head. "No, thank you, sir. This has been coming on for a while, and I have a good doctor in Walcott who has already kept me going this long. With Sylvie to care for, he'll just have to keep me going a bit longer."

Pons was making his way toward his room when he called over his shoulder, "Mr. Dover, please leave the address of where you are staying with Dr. Parker, as well as that of your daughter's former lodgings. And if it were me," he added, "I would desist from asking any questions for a day or two."

Dover nodded. While he was providing the information, I could hear Pons rummaging about in the next room. The old man raised his eyes curiously, but I didn't offer any explanation, for the good reason that I didn't have one.

I shook hands with Dover and let him out onto the landing, so that he could go downstairs and retrieve his granddaughter. From below, I could hear the sound of six-year-old laughter, and I once again blessed the fates that had provided Pons and me with such a notably good-hearted landlady.

Shutting the door, I turned to find a shabby dockworker pulling down one of one of the scrapbooks on the shelf near the fireplace, a worn pea jacket covering a set of clothes much stained and patched. A jaunty but filthy cap was on Pons's head – for indeed it was Pons, having quickly assumed one of his most effective disguises.

He was muttering to himself, flipping the sheets back and forth with irritation. Then with a triumphant "Ha!" he pulled a little packet of papers free and snapped the book shut, returning it to its place.

He reviewed them for a moment, and then said, "This may be the lead for which I've been waiting." He paused to glance at the addresses provided by Mr. Dover, and then walked toward the door, handing me the folds of paper as he passed. "See if this sounds familiar." He paused with his hand on the doorknob. "I'm off to the docks, Parker. Should you need me, a wire to Frick will be forwarded on to wherever I might be."

I nodded, and he was gone.

I poured myself a small tot of whisky, as the day was a cool one, and settled into my chair, unfolding the little pack of newspaper clippings – for that is what they turned out to be. There were only three of them, the first written about a year before, in the spring. The second was from mid-summer, and the third related events from the previous fall. Each had a common theme – in fact, they were so similar that they might have been identical, if not for the fact that the people named in each were different.

The initial article, like all three, was a simple paragraph relating that a young husband and wife, Sidney and Enid Foy, had been reported missing from their usual haunts, but foul play was not suspected. The second couple, Thomas and Flora Billings, had also vanished, and like Sidney Foy, Thomas Billings had simply not shown up for work one day. The third couple, Edward and Violet Rainer, were reported missing like the others.

Pons always made a habit of cutting unusual items from the newspapers, and the first disappearance must have intrigued him. His gift for assimilating and classifying data had certainly caused him to notice the second article, resulting in his keeping it with the first. The same with the third. There must have been no other information, or surely Pons would have also docketed it and then pulled it from the scrapbook when retrieving these for my illumination.

What I found quite troubling was that apparently there was no follow-up information regarding these missing people. If there had been, Pons would have kept that as well. The absence of the missing couples was initially noticed and likely reported to the police. A newspaper reporter responsible for routinely making rounds through the police stations and gleaning bits from the daily reports would have cobbled together these little notices, but it was unlikely that the police had followed up if no real crime was indicated. Only Pons, with his feeling for patterns and *minutiae*, had seen a thread running through the various disappearances. I had to wonder how many others there might be that hadn't ever been reported.

I speculated upon what Pons might hope to find, and what he might be doing, but eventually gave it up as a fruitless venture. Instead, I pulled a volume from my shelves regarding liver illnesses, trying to recall some facts from my schooling and past patients, in the hopes that I might provide some suggestion to Mr. Dover. Of course I knew that what I was doing was as foolish in its own way as wasting time guessing at Pons's doings, especially as I hadn't been able to give the man any sort of proper examination. Yet, it helped to fill my day, both the rest of the morning, and that long afternoon following the tasty lunch brought up by Mrs. Johnson at the noon hour.

Evening had arrived, and from my chair, I could see that a most particular fog was rolling in. I stood and walked to the window to look down on Praed Street. The street beneath our window was just visible, but the buildings across the way had already vanished. If it was this bad here, several miles from the river, I could only imagine what Pons was facing at the docks.

I was starting to feel peckish and wondering what would be for dinner when the front bell rang. In a moment, I heard muttered conversation downstairs, and then light footsteps coming up to the sitting room. I wasn't surprised when there was a knock, followed by the entrance of Frick, Pons's agent in Limehouse, Whitechapel, and those other dangerous surrounding hamlets.

The man had done odd jobs for Pons since before the days when I had moved to Praed Street, and I knew that Pons trusted him implicitly. He was a sneaky little fellow, but quite loyal and most effective in his duties. I was aware that he had other activities besides what he did for Pons, but it was best not to think too much about those.

"He has need of you now, Doctor," Frick said. I nodded and started toward the door. "He wants you to bring his hat and coat. And," he added, "your gun."

"If I've learned anything during my years here," I responded, pulling on my coat, "it's that I don't go anywhere without being armed."

Frick smiled, probably understanding far better than I.

Down in the street, I was immediately assailed by the pungent odor from the thick rolling mist. The streetlights were isolated and oily looking orbs floating above us, and stepping away from the protection of one was like turning loose of a pier and setting out to swim through a dangerous current, hoping to navigate to the next handhold – in this case, the next streetlight.

I thought that if we had to walk through this all the way to our destination, we'd only be halfway there by morning. Luckily, we soon came upon a car near the intersection of the Edgware Road, its engine idling and its powerful headlights shining like a fixed lighthouse in the darkness. A police vehicle, I noticed.

"This will be slow," said Frick, echoing my thoughts and letting me climb in first, "but not as slow as walking."

"Agreed."

As I situated myself, I saw that the driver was a constable that I'd met before, Collins. Interesting, I thought to myself, considering just how unusual – or serious – this matter must be for Frick to be working this closely with the police. "The lion will lie down with the lamb . . . ." I muttered out loud.

"Eh, Doctor?" asked Frick as the auto set into motion.

"Nothing, Frick. Nothing at all."

We worked our way slowly but steadily across London. Our driver was quite skilled, and never once did he have to throw on his brakes when something loomed unexpectedly out of the white void. Nor did he ever waver from his chosen route, moving with confidence down side streets and across intersections with definite purpose and confidence.

Finally, we arrived at a little coffee shop, on some dark street that was completely unknown to me. At least, I believe that it was, as the billowing mists rendered everything completely new and menacing. The constable parked and shut off his headlights, but left the engine running. Frick led me inside, although the dim light there seemed nearly as dark as the outside. But it was dry and warm, and I was relieved that this appeared to be our destination, at least for a little while.

The only customers in the place were Pons, Inspector Jamison, and another old acquaintance, Superintendent Beauchamp, whom I had first met upon the occasion when his own wife had fallen under the spell of a spiritualist. It was only when she took to "donating" the family's silver and plate to the *faux* medium that the officer, too embarrassed to seek official help, had decided to visit 7B.

More recently, he had once again called upon Pons regarding a personal matter, the disappearance for a single day of his nearly twelve-year-old niece Claire, an orphan being raised by her other uncle, a noted archaeologist and the superintendent's brother. They had been on a trip to northern Scotland when she vanished, and Pons had found her quite handily. It was definitely a story for which the world is not yet prepared – and in any case, it's not my tale to tell.

I understood that the superintendent's presence elevated this matter to a much higher and more serious level.

Pons was now wearing completely normal clothing, having certainly changed from his dock-worker garb at one of his hidey-holes scattered throughout the city. He stood to accept his hat and coat with gratitude while waving to a girl standing nearby, indicating that she should bring two more cups of coffee.

When we had arranged ourselves around the table – Frick watching the policemen warily while they conspicuously ignored him – Pons began to speak.

"Prepare for grim doings, Parker. This could be one of the worst things that we have encountered – even more serious than that of the Burlstone Horror."

I groaned. "You have found them, then. Are they alive?"

"We don't yet know. This fog has delayed us, and I knew you'd want to be in at the finish. While the pieces of the trap are being set into place, we have a few more minutes, and we can catch you up." He shrugged gratefully deeper into his Inverness, for the room was cold, even if the fog was shut outside.

The girl brought fresh coffee for everyone, and then retreated out of earshot on the far side of the room. I glanced her way, and Pons read my thoughts. "She can be trusted."

I took a sip and began. "Where are we?" I asked.

"St. Anne's Street, in Limehouse. We were led here by the associate of the man who has been kidnapping likely couples from around London. He is in custody now, and was quite accommodating. Once we arrived here, where he told us to look, Frick helped us get the lay of the land."

"You've had a busy day," I said.

"You don't know the half of it," replied my friend. "And a lucky one."

"It was more than luck," grunted Superintendent Beauchamp. "You put together the pieces of something that was missed by the whole force for over a year – and maybe a lot longer than that."

Pons waved a hand and began to summarize the series of events that led us to this dim room. "After leaving Praed Street, I made my way to the East End, where I located Frick. Together, we visited the Liverpool and London Steamship offices, where Bill Patton had been employed, and quickly confirmed that he had stopped coming to work a week ago – very unlike him, we were told. Still, employees come and go rather frequently – even those who are conscientious and enjoy the level of responsibility held by Mr. Patton. The management of the company was disappointed, but not too surprised.

"However, questioning them revealed that there had been another man who stopped coming to work at the same time – the same day, as a matter of fact. This fellow had only worked there for about three weeks, and during that time, he seemed to have made a special effort to become friends with Bill Patton. Like our missing man, this fellow was a tall and outgoing fellow, exhibiting the same confidence, but with something subtly untrustworthy about him – 'A wrong 'un,' they said. While Mr. Patton's loss to the company was lamented, this other man, Caleb Tanner, was not missed.

"Frick and I questioned other likely individuals, but no more information was to be had, and this association with Mr. Tanner was nothing more than a point to be filed at that time. Leaving Frick at the docks to keep turning over stones, I hopped over to St. Dunstan's in Stepney to speak to the minister and see if he still had the note left with Sylvie. He did, but there was nothing telling about it whatsoever – plain cheap paper and ink, and obviously disguised writing. It was inscribed by a right-handed person, but that fact was singularly unhelpful, as most of the human race is thus inclined. The minister had nothing that would add to what Mr. Dover already told us.

"I then made my way to the room I keep in Holborn, where I changed to these clothes before going on to Kensington, and to the rooming house where the Pattons had lodged. There, I played the part of a law clerk attempting to serve some papers related to a fictitious lawsuit connected with Mr. Patton's job.

"The landlady, a Mrs. Kenton, was clearly uncomfortable speaking with me, but I have some skill at keeping a door open. I'm also practiced in getting facts from people when they don't know that they're revealing them. Mrs. Kenton confirmed for me which rooms the Pattons had rented, first floor front, while never realizing that she was telling me. In the meantime, she stuck to her story that the family had moved out the week before, completely in secret, while still owing rent. Clearly she was nervous, and more to the point, she was obviously lying.

"I let her shut the door and then walked around the corner, thinking. It had bothered me all along, since first listening to Mr. Dover's tale, that whoever had notified him to come for Sylvie had known where to send a message to find him. You'll recall that the telegram gave his specific address, when simply putting his name and Walcott, or Coast Road, would have been sufficient for delivery in such a small place.

"Now, we know nothing of the Pattons, and they could have countless close friends who might have this very knowledge of how to reach Mr. Dover in Walcott. But coupled with the landlady's nervous countenance, which left me suspicious, I decided that she might have known more than she was letting on.

"I realize that this was nothing more than a hunch, but I sensed that there was danger afoot for the Pattons, and too much time had passed already."

Pons looked toward the two policemen. "Cover your ears, gentleman." They smiled, and the superintendent took a long swallow of coffee.

"It was somewhat more difficult in daytime than darkness, but not too much more. I effected an entry into the lodging house, made my way upstairs, and so into the front rooms that I was told had belonged to the missing couple."

"Pons!" I said with a smile. "What if you had walked in on someone?"

"Fortunately – this time – I did not. The rooms were empty of persons, but still filled with possessions. A quick search verified that everything belonging to the Pattons was still there – including a letter carelessly tossed onto the dining table with Mr. Dover's address. Three things were obvious: This was where the address had been found to send him the message to retrieve Sylvie; the Pattons had not moved out and been replaced by someone else; and Mrs. Kenton was a liar.

"It was at that point that the official force was summoned. I slipped out unnoticed, sent a message to Jamison, and met him in the Kensington High Street within fifteen minutes. I explained the situation, and with his usual acumen, our friend here understood the connection to the other missing couples, and that the landlady likely had valuable information for us."

"And so I summoned the superintendent," said Jamison, clearly pleased to be included so favorably in Pons's summary.

"I was there soon," added Beauchamp. "We went in, and it didn't take long to get the story out of her – at least the part that she knows."

"And a terrible story it is, Parker," added Pons. "Before departing Scotland Yard, Superintendent Beauchamp brought the files that I'd requested concerning the previous missing couples. We gathered in the backroom of a nearby pub prior to our confronting the treacherous landlady and compared notes. I was surprised and disturbed to note that one of the previous couples, Sidney and Enid Foy, had actually lived in that same building as the Pattons. It was too much to be coincidence.

"We returned to the lodging house and quickly had an admission of guilt out of her. Apparently she had been on pins and needles following Mr. Dover's visit yesterday, and my questioning of her hadn't made things any better.

"She is in the employee of a man, a doctor, who is conducting . . . experiments. She wasn't sure as to their nature, but I'm certain that she suspected, and they can be inferred when it's pointed out that each of the couples taken are in their twenties and considered to be both healthy and handsome.

"She knows that there are several houses such as her own that attract young couples, offering amenities that suit young newlyweds. She had personally arranged for three couples, the Pattons, the Foys, and a husband and wife named Elgard, to be taken by this doctor for his foul purposes.

"The man who worked with her – in fact, he worked with the other houses as well – was this Caleb Tanner, as you may have already surmised. Mrs. Kenton would let the rooms, and then provide information about the likely tenants to Tanner. He would make friends with the husband while passing the information on to his master. That man would then decide whether he wanted the couple as subjects. Apparently he had specific requirements, and also only needed new fodder for his experiments at certain times, when the previous victims had served their purpose – whatever that might be."

"Pons," I whispered. "This is ghastly."

"Indeed," he responded. "When a doctor does go wrong he is the first of criminals." He took a sip of coffee and continued. "In the case of the Pattons, Mrs. Kenton had described her new tenants to Tanner as usual. But what made them different was the fact that they had a child. None of the others – either at her own home or the others, as far as she knew – had been blessed with children.

"Tanner passed on the information, and was soon back to report that his master was quite interested in both the husband and wife, and also the girl as well. Apparently that was the straw that broke the landlady's back, so to speak. She had willingly participated in the trapping of the previous childless couples, choosing to give little thought to what happened to them afterwards, but when the same was threatened toward six-year-old Sylvie, to whom she had taken a sentimental liking, she balked. Like always, she drugged the victims to make their removal easier. But before Tanner could retrieve them, she spirited a drugged Sylvie out to the church where she was later recovered, and she sent a message to the girl's grandfather.

"When Tanner came, she lied and said Sylvie had suspected something and run away. Tanner didn't seem concerned, although he did state that his employer would be disappointed. Then, he took the Pattons and departed."

"Good Lord, Pons," I said. "This is terrible. Do you have any idea of the scope of this madness?"

"Somewhat. We learned more from further questioning of Caleb Tanner."

"How did you trap him?"

"We finished our conversation with the most willing Mrs. Kenton by mid-afternoon, and concluded by having her send an urgent message to Tanner, indicating that she needed to speak to him as soon as possible. He obligingly showed up about an hour later and, except for a moment of physical resistance – almost as an experiment to see if escape was possible or if it was worth the bother – he became a most agreeable prisoner. Laughing about it, as if none of it were real. It wasn't long before he gave us more details than we could stomach. But among them were a few useful immediate facts, including where his employer, the doctor, can be found."

"Nearby, I take it."

"Indeed. Just around the corner, in the abandoned hospital in St. Anne's Row."

"I know the place. I served there for a short time as a young doctor." I didn't add that the memories were unpleasant. The plain building had been a fixture in the neighborhood for decades. One would have thought that any district would be considered lucky to have a hospital so accessible, but that wasn't the case. Located in the short block of St. Anne's Row, adjoining St. Anne's Street, and just south of where the larger road terminates at the Limehouse Cut, St. Anne's Hospital, as it was known, carried a grim reputation amongst those who were forced by necessity to go there. The death rate was high, and dark rumors surrounded it. I was glad to see the back of it when my path took me elsewhere, and had felt a sense of "Good riddance" when I heard years later that it had closed.

"And this madman?" I asked. "Who is he?"

At this, Pons seemed to hesitate, and I suspected that I would not like the answer.

Before Pons could name the man, Jamison spat, "Sir Bignell Crooks."

I was stunned, for I was acquainted with the man. Now in his sixties, he had built a respected career. I saw him on rare occasions at professional functions, or more likely in hospitals. In fact, he served at one of the hospitals where I had privileges. I considered his remarkable lifetime of honors and distinction.

Then I realized that I hadn't seen or heard of him in a while. I mentioned the fact.

"You are correct," answered Pons. "When we had his name, I sent Frick in a car to bring you, while we did some quick research. He has been largely absent from his usual haunts for the last year, at least. His research took a decidedly questionable slant, and the officials at the hospital were uncomfortable with his continued association."

"I remember now," I said. "Something about some articles he submitted to a medical journal."

"Yes. Related to that morally reprehensible movement gaining ground known as *Eugenics.*"

"My God," I whispered. "You said the couples were handsome. I remember his interests now. Based upon his papers, he must be conducting some kind of . . . *breeding experiment,* in the mistaken and evil belief that whatever he does can 'better' the human race."

"Breeding," muttered Jamison.

"Possibly. Or even worse."

"That's what we fear, Doctor," said Superintendent Beauchamp. "That's why it's gone beyond a police matter. If this was still under the control of the Yard, we would have stormed the building by now. But the government is involved now, with some quick assistance from Mr.

235

Pons's brother. Sir Bignell's presence made sure of that. We're waiting until they're ready to move."

With that statement, Pons pushed back his chair and stood. "And surely they're ready. Shall we step around the corner, gentlemen?"

Returning to the fog caused us all to take a collective shudder – no doubt augmented by knowledge of the terrible crimes that had been discovered. I knew that if we learned the full story, this would be more widespread and horrifying than we even imagined. And our imaginations were already feeding us visions of the horrors that we knew we would see in just a few moments. All of us – Pons, the policemen, Frick, and myself – had been witness to terrible things, both at home and far away. Some men developed a resistance to pain and suffering, the way alcoholics or drug addicts build up a tolerance to their chosen forms of destruction, requiring larger and larger dosages to achieve the same sorry results. But the five of us, while used to the vile things that were sometimes unavoidably presented, would never become accustomed or numb to it.

We were halfway down the block when a slim fellow in an overcoat and low hat stepped out of the shadows. "He's in there," he said in a soft voice.

Pons nodded. "Proceed."

The slim man turned away, gone in an instant as the fog seemed to swallow him. We continued in the direction in which we had started, while around us, seen but not heard, were sounds of quick-moving footsteps, converging somewhere in front of us.

I began to sense the shape of the place, squatting like some dark creature in our path, absorbing whatever of the little reflected light fell its way. A more fanciful man might have claimed to feel evil emanations from the place. I am not such a man. And yet, knowing in even the vaguest way what Sir Bignell was doing inside caused me to shudder.

A door opened, letting out a shaft of light into the night. We were closer than I had imagined. Several dark shapes flitted through the gap, and then the door was pulled shut, again plunging us back into darkness.

I wondered how long we would be required to wait, but nearly before I could complete the thought, three sharp tones from a constable's whistle sounded, apparently some sort of all-clear signal. My companions stepped forward, pulling open the door and leading me inside.

Pons moved with that easy confidence he always displayed, starting upstairs as if he had been in the building a dozen times before – although he would later confirm that this was his first visit. We rounded the landing at the top of first flight, and so on until we reached the highest floor – assuming that the termination of the stairs there so confirmed that fact. This part of the building was unfamiliar to me. It was the third floor, and we passed from the stairwell and into a hallway. At the end was a lighted double door. Loud voices were emanating from within, some barking urgent commands, and one shrill and desperate. They were becoming more understandable as we approached and I was certain that I heard the urgent and almost panicked call for a doctor. I markedly increased my pace.

How to describe the horrific scene that I confronted, while still staying within the boundaries of good taste – nay, of sanity itself? Even as Pons, Frick, and the policemen filled in behind me, I was attempting to understand exactly what I saw in front of me. Now, several decades after that terrible night, and with the full knowledge of the horrors that were carried out in the recent global war, I have no words to accurately describe what I beheld.

The space was wide and broad, and must have covered a quarter or even half of the square footage of that floor. The ceiling was high and dark. Before me was nothing less than a complete surgical operating room, in the sense that it held a metal table designed for such a purpose, banks of strong lights focused on the surgical field, and several carts and cabinets of instruments. All around the brightly lit center of the room was a void – that empty space around the center that stretched off into the darkness, impossible to accurately view while blinded by what was occurring in the middle.

And blinding it was, both because of the searing strength of the lights, and the horrible vision of what was revealed there.

A man in complete surgical garb, including cap and mask, was at the edge of the light. His arms were up in the air, and even as I watched, his right hand was violently shaking up and down, gripping an instrument of some sort, winking and flashing as it moved in the light. With one final and emphatic shake, his arm flew downwards, and the scalpel that he held – for now I understood it to be such an instrument – fell to the tiled floor and skittered in my direction. Only then did I perceive that the man in the surgical clothing hadn't made the motions on his own. Rather, a darkly garbed man was behind him, one arm firmly around the surgeon's neck, and the other gripping his right wrist. Their struggle only ended when the scalpel was thrown down and Sir Bignell Crooks – for that is who he was – realized that the battle was lost.

Pons had seemed as stunned as the rest of us, but he regained himself just a fraction faster than me. He stepped up to the table with its horrible occupant, careless of the blood pooling on the floor, and then quickly pivoted to me.

"Parker," he said quietly but with unmistakable urgency. "You are needed."

I joined him and understood. She was still alive.

I didn't have time to prepare, or to consider proper hygienic methods. This was equivalent to battlefield surgery. "Pons!" I snapped, throwing off my coat.

"Yes?"

"Push that tray of instruments this way. And for God's sake, hold her – I doubt that she has been properly sedated."

I was vaguely aware of the angry rants of Sir Bignell, demanding that I cease so that he could finish what had been started. Clearly he was mad – but that fact had already been established.

I saw at a glance that Jamison and the Superintendent were slowly circling at our periphery, stopping at a row of what seemed to be clear glass boxes on low tables, each individually lit by bulbs suspended above them. I heard the superintendent give a wretched cry before turning away, fighting not to be ill. But I didn't have time for that.

My own focus was the cavity in front of me, which the doctor had already laid open, no doubt with the scalpel that had been forced to the floor. He had begun his unholy incisions, but I was relieved that nothing yet had progressed to the state of permanent damage. However, the patient, Carrie Patton, whom I recognized from her wedding photo, was bleeding in a terrible way, and I was trying to operate in a race against her own heart as it continued to pump out her life's blood.

Pons sensed what I needed, and provided sponges to inhibit or block the flow so that I could see where I needed to suture. There was no time to be pretty, and if she survived the next ten minutes, then the poor woman would face further surgery in better surroundings. But for now, the only objective was to save her life.

And we did. By Heaven's Grace, we did.

As that fact became clear to me, I sensed the room around me once more. There were more lights – someone had turned on the overhead lamps, although in that island of bright surgical beams I hadn't been aware. I looked to where I had thought Sir Bignell was still standing, only to see a stranger. He was a big man, looking frantic to break loose from the constables holding him as he tried to approach the table. I vaguely realized that this was Bill Patton.

I nodded that the man should be released. He nearly stumbled, but then approached cautiously, almost fearfully, tears in his eyes.

"She will live," I said simply. He sobbed, just once, and took the woman's hand, while an ambulance crew entered from the hallway, ready to move her to the hospital.

Later, after I had cleaned up, I walked toward the doorway, where two constables still gripped Sir Bignell by each arm. Even though I knew it was useless, I wanted to ask him why. I wanted to understand. But hoping to receive such enlightenment from one such as he was a fool's venture.

He recognized me, saying, "Dr. Parker! Thanks heavens! Have them release me. Make them understand. Together we can finish what I've started. They know you – *they trust you!* If you can just explain to them . . . ."

I had to turn away, for fear of striking him. He was still calling my name when they dragged him from the room.

Pons was standing to one side, and I joined him. We walked around the doctor's laboratory. The surgical instruments were of the most modern and expensive sort, all cleaned to a blinding shine. The madman – for there was no doubt of his insanity – had clearly been working toward proving some of his demented ideas involving improvement of the species, and he had traveled quite an unforgiveable way down that road. There was clear evidence of just what he had needed – and taken – from each of his victims, both men and women, husbands and wives. Jamison and the Superintendent both looked quite pale, and I daresay that if I could have seen my own face, I would have matched them. Pons was tight-lipped, and I could tell that he was equally sickened and enraged.

A few minutes later, when Pons had to explain what we'd found to the man from the Home Office who wandered in, we all stepped away, unable to hear what was being described in such precise clinical detail. We didn't need to hear, as we had just seen it with our own eyes. In fact, I doubted that I would ever be able to forget those clear and well-lit glass boxes on low tables – incubators, as it turned out, usually built with the best of intentions to help the tiny infants who were born too small and weak to help themselves.

But Sir Bignell Crooks had violated that purpose, monstrously so. Now the incubators could only be destroyed – along with whatever it was that we had found growing within them – every one a nightmare and an abomination.

The next day, a bit of the horror had receded, and we were able to join Mr. Dover and Sylvie at the hospital, where she was reunited with her parents. Carrie Patton would recover completely, as we had stopped the mad doctor before he was able to complete his procedure. Bill Patton was unharmed as well. Apparently Sir Bignell required a few days to "prepare" his subjects, and our arrival had been just in time. To this day, I shudder to think of the results if we'd waited even a moment longer.

And as for the others, those eleven unfortunate couples (as determined from Dr. Crooks' painfully deciphered journals) who had been taken so early in their lives, with all hopes and promises before them? They hadn't survived, and it was decided – and blessedly and rightly so – by the highest authority that what remained of them in that dreadful laboratory, that which had been created by a perverted madman, must also not survive.

When the family was reunited, Mr. Dover broke down and wept, vowing that he would spend what time he had left with his family, rather than continue as he had, alone on the northeastern coast.

As we prepared to leave, we were thanked profusely by the little family. I took Mr. Dover aside and gave him a card with the name of a specialist that I believed might help him, based upon my research from the previous day. "Thank you," the old man murmured again. "Thank you both."

Bill Patton followed us into the hallway to thank us as well, as he had been unable to speak to us the previous night. He then related how easily he and his wife had been overcome by their landlady and Caleb Tanner, whom Patton had befriended at the docks, little realizing the man's dark intent.

He went on to explain that he and his wife had been drugged and taken to the building in St. Anne's Row. They had awakened to find themselves prisoners, locked in side-by-side cells. Their screams for help had gone unanswered, and they were only visited by Tanner and the fearful man in the white coat. He had watched them without conversation, making entries in a journal, 'preparing them,' he muttered, until the previous night, when Mrs. Patton had been rendered unconscious by way of a mist sprayed upon her while she cowered in her cell. As she passed out, Bill Patton had called to her and fought to reach her, suspecting what was planned as she was loaded onto a cart by the white-coated old man and wheeled into the adjoining room. When we had arrived, he had been unable to see what was happening, only hearing the screams and violence taking place beyond his vision, and it had nearly cost him his reason.

With a final thank you, he turned back to be with his family. As he reached them, little Sylvie turned toward us and shyly waved goodbye. I realized from Patton's story just how easily an ordered life can be ripped from its moorings, and thrown instantly into danger. I resolved to appreciate what I had, and to guard it.

We looked back one more time from the doorway. The four of them were clinging to one another.

Turning away, Pons whispered, "Well done, Parker. Well done."

"And you as well, my friend."

# The Adventure of the Failed Fellowship

Solar Pons looked around the cramped room with something like affection. "I spent a great deal of time here in my wayward youth, you know," he explained as we carried our various beverages to a quiet corner. As we settled at our table, I saw his eyes twinkle and followed his gaze to a small shelf, tacked high on the wall near the doorway, and holding a half-dozen volumes, the most obvious being a red-bound copy of *The Hound of the Baskervilles.*

Our host, Merivale Stagg, was sharing none of Pons's enjoyment at his return to The Eagle and Child, so long after my friend had attended University here in Oxford. As if reading my thoughts, Pons said, "It has been thirty-nine years, Parker, since I was a regular visitor here, although I've been back on a few occasions since. I matriculated from 1896 until 1899, wherein I took my degree and departed to the wider world, along the most interesting path that has led back here to this very table." As if now acknowledging the man who had summoned us from London, he turned his attention back to Stagg and asked, "How can we help you?"

"I'm afraid that someone is going to kill me!"

The plump man's eyes had held the same wild look that he'd displayed since he met us at the entry to the pub. In his telephone call, received by Pons that morning at 7B Praed Street, Stagg had identified himself as an Oxford banker, but he didn't want to meet at his place of business. He had been vague as to details and had suggested rendezvousing at Blackfriars, but Pons had countered with The Eagle and Child. Now I understood that he was feeling sentimental about the place. Stagg has stressed the urgency of the visit, but not the reason – a fact which Pons pointed out.

"I . . . one doesn't like to be melodramatic on the telephone," explained Stagg, glancing around, and then taking a deep swallow from his brandy. His appearance, especially the small broken veins across his cheeks and nose, testified that the liquid was an old friend.

Pons nodded, apparently deciding to take the comical man's fears seriously. "From where do you expect this danger to come?"

Stagg's eyes narrowed. "I have no doubts on that score. It is Samuel Magee!"

"And who is this man?"

"He used to be a friend!" spat Stagg. He glanced at the brandy beside his shaking hand, considered another drink, and then decided to pass for the moment. A small victory, to be sure, but his own.

"You seem quite certain. Perhaps you should begin at the beginning."

Stagg wiped his hands across his face, opened his mouth to speak, changed his mind long enough to give in and take the sip of the brandy he'd just decided to forego, and then spoke.

"You must understand that no one knows of this. I've kept the secret for over twenty years. I'm not sure now why Sam is trying to kill all of us – perhaps he's finally decided that he needs the money, after all these years!"

"Again, Mr. Stagg – from the beginning please."

Stagg nodded. With a sigh, he said, "As I said, it was twenty years ago – in the last days of the War. There were four of us from Sacker's Hollow, about fifteen miles north of here. Besides me, there was Sam Magee, Fred Sacker – his family has been there for ages! – and my cousin, Fawkes Tuck." Pons raised an eyebrow at this unusual name, and Stagg explained, "His mother was always fanciful. The same is true for all the Tucks.

"As I was saying, we were all just boys then, and we had joined up together, back in '15. We went away together and we stayed together, and saw some lively action here and there, quickly losing any idealism that might have motivated our initial enlistment.

"In the fall of 1917, we landed near Naples, part of the five divisions that were being assembled to participate in the Battle of the Piave River, far to the north. But we were destined to miss that entirely. You see, soon after arriving, we were seconded to help deliver medical supplies to a base hospital in a narrow valley some distance to the east. But not long after we departed, our vehicles were ambushed by a guerilla band, and we became separated. Fawkes and I ended up being rescued by a group of cavalrymen, while Sam and Fred were diverted to a camp several miles away. In the confusion, we lost touch with one another, and it was several long weeks before we were reunited.

"While waiting for the irregular transportation back to our base, I was able to tag along with the cavalry on a successful raid, while Fawkes made friends with some of the guards assigned to one of the local noblemen. You'll recall that Italy had been unified decades earlier, but so many of those counts and princes refused to completely give up their little fiefdoms and kingdoms. And that relates to what happened to Sam and Fred during our separation.

"We had no contact with them, although we had spread the word that we were looking for them. Finally, around the time that we were going to be forced to leave them behind and return to our units, word came that they had been found. They were being held prisoner by the very guerillas who had attacked our convoy. Word came to us through one of these local noblemen of whom I spoke – arrogant, thought of himself as a king. Some of his men had been captured as well, and he had arranged for a swap of prisoners. Fawkes and I were welcome to go along if we wished. Of course we said yes.

"The nobleman, who called his band the *Aquilas*, had arranged to make the exchange at a neutral location, although it turned out that he viewed it more as a rescue. Their prisoners and ours walked across a no man's land in between the two forces, and we could see our friends amongst those approaching from the other side. They and the other captured *Aquilas* had made it back when suddenly the nobleman uncovered a hidden machine gun, and the guerillas were mowed down to a man, both the captors and the returning prisoners. It was brutal, but it was war. We were simply glad to have our friends back.

"Later, as we were traveling back to our unit, Sam and Fred quietly explained what had happened to them. It was so much more than simply being captured. They hadn't been prisoners the whole time. During the initial attack, Fred had received a wound, stabbed a glancing blow by a bayonet along his side. It wasn't serious, but Sam had stuck with him, seeking medical help. When they were loaded and taken to one of our field hospitals, it was in the opposite direction from where Fawkes and I had headed, explaining how we lost track of them. Sam felt a certain responsibility for Fred, both because all four us had grown up together, but also because, before the War, Sam had worked for Fred's family, Fred's uncle being something of the squire from Sacker's Hollow, our little forgotten part of Oxfordshire.

"Soon Fred he was up and about. At around that time, the two of them met some sneaky little Italian named Grimaldi who was an orderly at the hospital. The long and short of it was that he told them a story of a treasure, located in a villa a number of miles to the east. Grimaldi had overheard a conversation several days before, from a rich man who owned the property and had been forced to abandon it during the shifting of the fighting. He was discussing with his son about where he had hidden a chest of jewels and gold before he departed to safer territory. The little Italian Grimaldi was too afraid to go for the treasure himself, and had inexplicably decided to enlist the aid of my companions, not trusting his own people.

"Of course, Fred and Sam didn't trust him either, but Fred felt strong enough, and both heard the call of the treasure, so they stole a truck and set off, with no thoughts as to the rights and wrongs of it. They skirted Mount Vesuvius and found the villa just where Grimaldi had indicated it would be, on the slopes of the old volcano. It was empty, but in reasonably good shape, and the little Italian led them to a cistern. As Grimaldi was too scared to enter, and Fred still wounded, Sam was lowered by a rope, and soon he found the chest, tucked along one of the walls amidst the spider webs.

"They decided that it would be too risky to try and get it back with them just then, so they agreed to hide it somewhere nearby, a site mutually picked that would be agreeable to all three of them. Locating a copse with four tall trees forming a '*W*', visible from across the countryside, they centered the chest and buried it, and then returned to the villa to see what else they could find. Just as they got there, they were captured by the guerillas, who had arrived to forage for food.

"Apparently Grimaldi tried to fight back, and he was shot and killed outright. Because of their British uniforms, Sam and Fred were taken prisoners and removed to a nearby encampment, where they remained until the prisoner exchange with the *Aquilas*."

"Fascinating," said Pons. "I spent some time in Italy myself during the War, and I can vouch for the vicious nature of the guerilla fighters."

Stagg nodded. "I thought that the two of you had the look, and of course you're both of the right age. What unit?"

"Intelligence," said Pons simply.

"I was in Egypt," I stated.

Stagg waited for a moment, but when there was no further elaboration, he continued.

"We learned all of this from Sam and Fred as we made our way back to Naples, to catch up with our unit. I suppose that they both felt the need to talk about it. We'd been through so much together before then, and it had bonded us, for better or worse, for the rest of our lives. Sam said that he and Fred had talked it over between them, and that they wanted us to have a share of the treasure. After the war, we could return to Italy in secret, get the lay of the land, and then dig it up, returning to England as rich men."

"Didn't it trouble you," I asked, rather wryly, "that the treasure belonged to someone else?"

Stagg looked rather shameful. "It did. A little. But the fortunes of war, and all that. We were risking our lives, so it seemed as if Fate had somehow rewarded us by putting our feet on this road."

"Actually, Sam Magee and Fred Sacker's feet," said Pons. "I'm still not sure why, even if you'd been together through so much, that you would be included for a share."

"It made some sort of sense then, Mr. Pons. After all those years, we were more than just boys from the same village. We were brothers-in-arms. We had seen things, done things, that linked us forever. It seemed the most natural thing in the world. Who would know that being tied together like this for the rest of our lives like that would end up being such a burden?"

"Ah," said my friend. "The board is set. We come to it at last - your belief that Mr. Magee is trying to kill you."

"And he will, unless he's stopped."

"It relates to this treasure?"

"It does. Even as we traveled away from the scenes of our adventures and heard of this treasure, Fawkes and I were understandably full of questions. Fred was quiet about it all, possibly because he was still recovering from his wound - but then, he's always been a quiet one. Sam looked around to make sure that no one was watching, and then said, 'Show them, Fred.'

"From deep within a pocket of his uniform, Fred pulled out a ring. It was thick and gold. It had no jewel, but there was no doubt that it was precious metal. He let us look at it, but he kept hold of it, protectively. It was covered with some sort of markings, like letters, but nothing that I recognized. Then, just as quickly, he put it away. And that was all that we ever saw of this treasure."

"Really? You've never seen it, in all the years since? Then where is the motivation to kill you?"

"There was none, really, for years and years. We finished with the War, came back home, and resumed our lives. I went to work in the bank, advancing to a senior position. I married, but my wife died young, and I've been alone ever since. Fred's uncle died soon after the War, and Fred took up his position as squire, spending his time living on his uncle's money, reading and collecting books, and writing the occasional letter to *The Times*. My cousin Fawkes, well . . . ." His voice drifted off and he shook his head sadly, but at Pons's prodding, he continued. "He has always been something of a wastrel, you see, and after the War, he was just . . . broken inside, somehow. He had a little money from his father, and he's proceeded to ruin himself over the years."

"And Mr. Magee?" I asked.

"He resumed his position, working on Fred's land as something of a tenant farmer. He's never seemed to have much luck. He married and had a couple of children, now gone. He's always seemed to be scrabbling just to stay even."

"The treasure?" I asked. "I take it, then, that it was never retrieved."

"But it was!"

"Yet, you said that the ring was all that was ever seen of it," I pointed out.

"We haven't seen the treasure, that's true. At least, Fawkes and I haven't. But sometime in the early twenties, unknown to my cousin and me, Sam and Fred slipped away, back to Italy, and dug it up. They brought it back with them, you see."

"And yet, you say that you haven't seen it," I said. "They retrieved it, but you've indicated that Mr. Magee's fortunes have not improved."

"Right enough. After they returned, Sam and Fred asked for Fawkes and me to pay a visit at Fred's manor house in Sacker's Hollow. It was there that they revealed to us that they'd returned to Italy and recovered the chest, right from where they buried it, where it still rested under the '*W*' of trees. But instead of letting us see it, Sam explained that he and Fred had hidden it *again*, this time somewhere on Fred's estate, and they were going to keep the location a secret, even from Fawkes and me. He then said that he had a proposal. An agreement where it would be winner take all. Last man standing, and all of that. The final member of our group left alive would receive a document, to be kept by Sam, telling where the treasure was buried."

"A tontine," said Pons dryly.

Stagg nodded. "Yes. A tontine."

Pons rolled his eyes in disgust. "Was there ever such a contrivance that has caused more mischief and misery?"

Stagg shook his head fervently. "You only speak the truth, Mr. Pons. At the time, it seemed something of a lark, although I must admit that I felt a bit of resentment when we weren't allowed to see the treasure, or divide it up right then. It seemed important to Sam that we maintain our ties with one another, and this was a way to do it. It made no sense, really, although I suppose it's a mercy that Fawkes didn't get hold of his share – it would have destroyed him even faster! – and I didn't really need it any longer. But Sam certainly needed the money, and really, he and Fred could have split it between them and never even told Fawkes and me about it. We would have never known any different. I guess it was the idea that they *had* told us that left me feeling a bit grateful to have been included at all, even if it meant waiting a lifetime to collect, once my three companions had died.

"Of course, as time passed, we couldn't really say that we were friends any longer. Rather, we were simply people who had shared a terrible experience long ago, and were all now just keeping an eye on each other to see when our own percentages of success would increase by a quarter, then a third, and then half, until we won." He shook his head in disgust and sipped the brandy.

"Now let me jump to the present," said Pons. "Someone within your group has died, and you suspect that another of this fellowship has decided to advance the timetable when he can take possession of the entire treasure."

"Yes," said Stagg. "My cousin Fawkes passed suspiciously last night."

"Indeed. What were the circumstances?"

"As I told you, his dissolute lifestyle had dogged him since the War, and he was less and less successful at escaping it through the passing years. Finally, he was hospitalized a week ago, and last night, I received word that he had died. I was his only relative."

"But surely," I said, "that is not unexpected, nor suspicious. It's been twenty years since your return from the War. If someone had wanted to kill for a better chance at the treasure, why wait until now? And in any case, people die in hospitals every day. After all, he was there for a reason."

"Nevertheless, I have a feeling that something is happening, after all these years. First, Fred left England a month ago – quite strangely, I might add – and now Fawkes dying. I'm certain that Sam is behind it. He was always the wise one."

"Mr. Sacker has left?" said Pons. "You didn't mention that. Pray elaborate."

Stagg took another sip from the brandy, which was getting dangerously low – from his perspective – and continued.

"As I said, it was last month. He didn't say goodbye to anyone, but instead just left a note. Fred had never quite recovered from that bayonet wound he received during the guerilla attack all those years ago, but he'd suffered in silence. Once, about ten years ago, it began to pain him much worse, and there was some indication that he'd need specialized surgery, as the internal scarring was apparently intruding upon his organs. I'm afraid I never learned anything more specific – the very idea has always upset me.

"In any case, he couldn't find any doctors here that inspired him with confidence, but he learned of a specialist at the Mayo Clinic in

Minnesota, in the United States. He traveled there, and whatever surgery they accomplished relieved his complaint. However, just in the last year, the problem seems to have resurfaced. No one knew that he'd planned a return trip to the American hospital until he'd already left. I admit that none of us are as close as we were, but the first I heard of it was when Sam stopped by the bank one day to let me know that Fred had gone into the west, and that he'd learned of it by way of the note left for him, indicating that he, Sam, had authority to continue to maintain the property as a steward until the return of the squire.

"I examined the note, and while it wasn't exactly a legal document, it did appear to be in Fred's handwriting, and, well, you see, we're a small village, so I've allowed Sam access to what funds are needed to reasonably keep the place running. And yet, something has seemed suspicious to me from the beginning, as Sam also claimed that he had no knowledge of Fred's trip until he received the note, after Fred had departed, apparently in secret. I've wondered about it for weeks, and now Fawkes has died. I spent a sleepless night asking myself . . . *what if Sam killed Fred, and has now killed Fawkes as well?*"

"But how would that benefit him?" I had to ask. "Your cousin Fawkes is certifiably deceased. Yet, in Sacker's case, there is no *corpus delecti*. With nothing to prove him either dead or alive, there would be no way to say for sure, and thus the treasure couldn't be dispersed to the single remaining survivor."

"Only four know of it," said Pons. "No legalities of this arrangement, or the allocating of secret shares, need be revealed."

Stagg pondered this before speaking. "And yet," he said, pulling a sheet from his pocket, "my suspicions still appear to have some validity." Passing it to Pons, he continued. "I sent a wire to the Mayo Clinic. They indicate that Fred, though truly scheduled for surgery nearly a month ago, *never arrived!*"

Pons looked at the telegram and then handed it to me. I confirmed what Stagg had just related. "What do you think happened to set this in motion after two decades?" I asked.

"I think that it was Fred that caused it," explained Stagg. "As I said, he's always been bookish. During the last couple of years, he got the notion that he wanted to be a writer. He's been getting more and more vocal about what's going on over in Germany, and writing more and more letters to the newspapers. One thing led to another, and he began to support the legitimacy of his opinions by mentioning in the letters his own service during the War. It escalated, and then he began to mention to whomever would listen that he should write a book, telling about war from the enlisted man's perspective, instead of that from a brittle old general who never saw anything closer than twenty miles behind the front. He kept going on with the idea that one should write about what one knows, and he finally began recording a history of *our* adventures in the War. He told us all about it, and showed us the big red journal where he was making his notes.

"There was quite a bit that the four of us got into during the War besides that one treasure story that I related, so he certainly had plenty to write about. At first, it just amused us, and it even got some local attention, which made him happy. In fact, since last year he's even been talking quite a bit about it with a professor here in Oxford. This fellow had been over there as well, and was slowly helping Fred shape his stories, as well as coaxing others out of him. But I know from occasional conversations with Sam that he was starting to get worried that Fred would keep going until he finally revealed the truth about finding the treasure, and how they both went and brought it back, and our subsequent arrangement."

"So then you believe, with this as supporting evidence," Pons said, tapping a long finger on the note, "that Sam Magee murdered Fred Sacker, both to prevent him from eventually revealing the story of the treasure, and also to increase his chances toward owning it outright in the end."

"I do. And when he saw how well that worked, he decided to murder Fawkes, as my poor cousin was nearly dead anyway, and an easy target. And now . . . *now*," he cried, suddenly breaking. I noticed that the brandy was gone. "*There's only me between him and the fortune!*"

"But Mr. Stagg," I said, trying to calm him. "He's known where it was for twenty years. He helped to hide it. He's known ever since he and Fred Sacker retrieved it and buried it together. You never saw any of it – except for the gold ring that was shown to you. He could have recovered it at any time, or at least removed some of it as needed. You would never have known the difference."

"But *Fred* would have known. If it was opened up some day and some was missing, Fred would realize it. That's another reason that he killed him!"

"But theoretically," I countered, "it would only be opened when only one of you has finally survived. If Mr. Sacker was the last, he would know that Sam had stolen some or all of it years earlier, but there would be nothing that he could do about it. You and your cousin wouldn't know the difference. And if Sam, that is, Mr. Magee, was the last survivor, he would already know that *he'd* taken it." I turned over a hand reasonably. "That isn't a motivation."

"And really, all he would have to do is kill Fred Sacker to eliminate any other knowledge of where the treasure is located," added Pons. "And you must not assume that Mr. Sacker is dead as a fact quite yet." He took a sip of his beer. "Doctor Parker mentioned the gold ring. Have you ever seen it again? Since that one time during the War?"

"I have. We all have. After we returned, and when things settled back to normal, Sam began to fancy getting married. Fred was never interested, and he seemed to lose his fascination with the ring at some point, so he gave it to Sam for use as his wife's wedding ring. She still wears it, although it's quite an awkward looking thing."

"Oh? How so?"

"Well, for one thing, it's too big for her. It's a man's ring, really. And Sam's wife is not . . . shall we say the most *elegant* of creatures – the ring seems extravagant on her. But in spite of her flaws, Sam was taken with her from the start, nonetheless. In fact, it was right here, in The Eagle and Child, where he first saw her. It wasn't long after we got back, and we were here, sharing a pint and reliving our adventures. Sam wasn't quite so . . . imposing in those days, and he had his eye on this girl, you see. Eventually, he got up the courage to talk to her, and when it was time to propose, he showed her the ring, a gift by then from Fred for just that purpose. It won her over, and she still wears it, a constant reminder through the years to the rest of us of that hidden treasure from whence it came."

Pons was silent for a moment before rising to his feet. "I believe that there is reason enough to investigate this matter a bit further, if only because of the telegram from Minnesota. Is your cousin's body still at the hospital?"

"It is. When I suspected foul play, I asked them to hold it until I could consult with you. I fear that they are amused by me, but I insisted. I do have some influence in this community."

"That may be useful. Let us proceed there immediately."

Stagg and I rose as well and, as we made to put on our coats, we observed the arrival of a group of three or four men, obviously Oxford dons, approaching our table, each carrying drinks from the bar. "Forgive us," said one, a gangling, balding fellow in his mid-forties. "Are you finished with the table?"

"Quite," said Pons, while I noticed that Staggs observed the fellow with wariness.

"Excellent," responded the stranger. "This is where we fellows meet to have our discussions. It appears that we timed things just right."

We let them pass and made our way out to St. Giles Street. "That's him," hissed Stagg. "That's the professor that was working with Fred last year about his book. Perhaps he learned something. Perhaps he is involved!"

"What would be his motive?" I asked. "If he learned of the treasure, he would just go dig it up. Why kill anyone? And even if this professor did kill Mr. Sacker, so that his own involvement in the matter would remain unknown, there would be no reason to kill your cousin as well."

Pons smiled. "And we have no indication as yet that either Mr. Sacker or your cousin has been killed. And in any case, I'm certain that the man we just met is harmless. Although he apparently doesn't remember me, encountering us out of context in this way, he consulted me several years ago in my capacity as a cryptographer regarding some ancient texts that he had discovered on the Cornish coast, back before the War. He had also visited my Illustrious Predecessor in Sussex, who gave him some advice, and then referred him to me. I was able to set him straight on a few basic code-breaking techniques, and I believe, from random communications that I received from him until they stopped altogether, that he is on the trail of a story that might rock the world.

"But that is neither here nor there. Let us be off to the hospital."

The banker led us down the street to where an automobile was parked. I was surprised that the man drove himself, and a bit trepidacious, considering how much brandy Stagg had consumed. However, he had apparently learned long ago to compensate for his steady imbibing, and we reached our destination without incident.

This was not the first time that I had visited that particular facility, nor would it be the last. I was always impressed by the professionalism, and today was no different. Stagg introduced us to the doctor in charge, a man named Randolph. Tall and imposing with a long white beard, he was known far and wide for his sense of humor, as well as his dogged tenaciousness when fighting disease, and many of his unique methods with the figurative Staff of Asclepius had given him the local reputation of being something of a medical wizard.

He led us to the morgue, and - while Stagg waited outside - we made our examination of the unfortunate Fawkes Tuck. Pons and I, between observations of various points of interest, explained vaguely that Stagg feared that his cousin had been murdered. Dr. Randolph allowed that he had heard as much from his staff and, while he could not understand why someone would want to snuff out the spark of the wrecked individual upon the table before us, he did know from long experience that stranger things were possible.

Pons and I finished our examination. With unspoken agreement, I called over the old doctor while Pons adjusted the bright lamp closer. Pulling back the dead man's lips, I showed him what we had found, and he understood immediately. "Are the man's bed linens still available?" Pons asked.

Randolph nodded to a laundry bag alongside one wall. "They are. I haven't had time myself to make the examination, you understand, but when I heard that there was a question, and that you would be up today, I ordered that they be retained."

It was but the work of a moment to find what we expected on Fawkes Tuck's pillow. Returning to our client, we shared the grim news.

"It was murder," said Pons shortly. "He was smothered with his own pillow. There were traces of saliva and teeth marks on the pillow case, and there was marked cyanosis about the face, with paleness around the nostrils and lips. Additionally, there was bruising and laceration within the mouth and along the gums and tongue."

"Oh, my God. Who could have done this?" asked Randolph, sadly shaking his head.

"Who was working last night?" countered Pons.

"Nurse Farmore. She's here now. I'll have her summoned."

Within moments, a bright blonde young woman presented herself. Randolph took her hand and said, "Eleanor, what can you tell us about Mr. Tuck's passing?"

She cocked her head, knowing that only something unusual would prompt such a question. "It was peaceful. He died in his sleep. I noted at eight p.m. that he was still unconscious, and that his functions seemed to be decreasing as expected. When I returned half-an-hour later, he was gone. Possibly a bit sooner than we would have thought, but one never knows." She looked with sympathy toward Stagg. "It was expected," she said again.

"Eleanor," said the bearded old man, "I'm afraid that I have to tell you that he was murdered. Smothered. Did you see anything last night, any*one*, that could have done this thing?"

The woman was clearly shocked, and would have been more upset if she was less of a professional. "Oh, no, sir. It was quite routine." Then her eyes were cast to the left as she recalled something. "Though there was the fat doctor."

"Yes?" said Pons, drawing her attention to him and away from Randolph. "Pray elaborate."

She frowned, as if wondering who this man holding a fore-and-aft cap might be. "It was sometime after eight, when the night girls depart, that I happened to notice a fat man, a doctor, walking down the hallway toward the exit. I didn't recognize him, and as I was involved in making notations on the patients' charts at the time, it slipped my mind until just now."

"How did you decide that he was a doctor?"

"He was dressed like one. You know, the white coat."

"And you say that he was heavy?"

"He was. Quite a bit, as a matter of fact."

"Is it possible that he could have gone into Mr. Tuck's room?"

"Certainly. The ward is closed to visitors by that point, and the staff has reduced in number as well."

"Sam is fat," murmured Stagg. Randolph and the nurse looked at him with interest, and Pons frowned.

When it was obvious that no other useful information was forthcoming, Pons arranged with Dr. Randolph and Nurse Farmore to keep the facts related to the murder to themselves – "We will notify the authorities," he assured them – and for the body to be stored properly until a further official autopsy could be done. Outside, we stopped on the walk to converse.

"I knew it was murder!" hissed Stagg. "And Sam did it! You heard her. It was a fat man pretending to be a doctor!"

"Or it could have really been a doctor, here for another reason, and someone simply unknown to the nurse," I said. "That kind of thing can happen all the time. We must not be distracted onto a false path if this man actually was a physician, visiting here on a completely innocent errand."

"I agree," said Pons. "There is still no motive for having killed your cousin – clearly, from our examination, it was apparent that he would die within days in any case. Why rush the process?"

"But he *was* murdered! You said so yourself!"

"Yes."

"Then what shall we do? Shall I swear out a warrant?"

"No, Mr. Stagg, that would be unwise at this point. Instead, I believe that we need to visit Mr. Magee."

Suddenly, Stagg seemed hesitant. "I'm not . . . that is, I believe that I'd prefer not to see him right now."

"Come now, Mr. Stagg," I said. "We'll be with you. And it's the most natural thing in the world for you to visit him, when your common brother-in-arms has passed."

He nodded reluctantly. "I suppose that you're right."

Returning to Stagg's automobile, we were soon barreling northwards toward the village of Sacker's Hollow, a ways outside of Oxford proper, where Sam Magee lived on a portion of Fred Sacker's estate. "Fred's family has been around here since Norman times," explained Stagg. "Of course, that's why the village, such as it has, has the family name. They had fallen into hard times, but a generation ago, Fred's uncle traveled east with a group of merchants to the orient. He was gone for a couple of years, so long that they thought he had died, as a matter of fact. He returned, having made his fortune, and restored the manor. Ever since he died, Fred's been living on his inheritance."

Passing onto the Sacker property, we first came to the manor house itself, apparently closed up now, and set back against a low hill, almost as if it were a part of it. Moving on, we gradually dropped down to an earthy little house near a stream – our apparent destination.

We exited the vehicle and walked through the gate, past a weedy little garden, and up to the doorway. The place had a feeling of weary neglect, and I couldn't imagine that a man responsible for maintaining the estate could let his own home get into such poor shape. Then, the door opened, and I understood.

Sam Magee – for it could only be he – answered his own door. He was a great behemoth of a man, nearing twenty-eight stone if he was an ounce. He stood in the doorway wheezing, as if the simple journey to answer our knock had thoroughly exhausted him. He was barefoot, his great hairy feet turned awkwardly to support his weight, the arches long since collapsed. His stomach lapped over his belt, forcing him to throw his own shoulders back to maintain some kind of balance. When he saw Stagg, his eyes lit in what seemed to be a genuine smile, but then he looked past him to Pons and me, and his happiness ran away like chalk being washed off a sidewalk by the rain. "Bad news, then?" he panted.

Stagg nodded, and the massive man shifted sideways to allow us to enter. Leaving Magee to shut the door, Stagg led us deeper into the house, where we heard a harsh voice ahead of us. "Who is it? What do they want?"

We rounded a doorway into a parlor, where a low fire burned in a fireplace that had likely been cheery at some distant point in the past. Standing by a chair, from which she had clearly just risen, was the speaker. If ever a woman matched her husband, it was Mrs. Magee.

She had reddish-blonde hair, tied into a long girlish plait that hung down and around her thick neck. It only served to emphasize the grotesquery of the rest of her, as she leaned forward, peering through the dim light toward us. She was quite heavy, although the weight she carried was even more disproportionate than that of her husband. Her head and body each had the same matching flaws, narrow at the top of the crown and shoulders respectively, but widening dramatically as the heavy fleshy weights were dragged down, pulling and spreading by gravity. She had the appearance of a giant potato that had started to rot and was slowly collapsing upon itself, liquefying and pooling upon the floor. And upon her left hand, glinting orange in the fire light, was the treasure ring, her wedding ring, which had been described to us.

"Who are you?" she rasped, varying her earlier questions so as to expend as little effort as possible. "What do you want?"

"It's about Fawkes," said Stagg.

"We heard," said Magee, laying a great hand on our client's shoulder. Stagg flinched and then stood still. "We're sorry."

"He was murdered!" blurted the banker into a suddenly silent room, except for the crackles from the fireplace.

Then, softly, Magee said, "Murdered? Whatever can you mean?"

"We've just come from the hospital. He was smothered in his bed!"

"Who are these men?" asked Mrs. McGee. "Policemen?"

"I am Solar Pons," said my friend, "and this is my associate, Dr. Parker. We've come up from London to investigate the matter."

Clearly our identities meant nothing to her. "London?" asked the shrewish woman. "What for? He couldn't have been murdered."

"But he was," said Stagg, finally throwing off Magee's great ham-hand. "For the treasure!"

"What?" rumbled the giant man, only to dissolve in a painful coughing fit. He stumbled over to a chair near the fire, clearly his own, and collapsed into it with a groan, matched only by a similar sound from the chair itself.

"It is Mr. Stagg's fear – his belief, actually – " said Pons, "that the treasure that you brought back from Italy after the War may have been a motivation for this crime."

Magee looks at Stagg in shock. "*You told them?* About the treasure? It was supposed to be a secret!"

"They didn't need to know!" shrilled Mrs. Magee. "It was a secret!" she repeated, thus revealing that it hadn't been a secret from her.

"Nevertheless, there is some concern that the four of you who were part of the arrangement to recover and then conceal this treasure for so long are now in danger. Mr. Tuck, who was likely to pass at any time, was hurried on his way, and the fear is that the same fate has befallen Mr. Sacker as well."

"Fred?" said Magee. "Nonsense. He's gone off to the west, to get treatment for his lingering wound."

"He never arrived!" said Stagg, almost triumphantly, as if now he could find satisfaction in revealing that he had begun to see through the plot. "I had word from the Mayo Clinic that he never arrived!"

"Mr. Stagg, please," said Pons. Turning back to Magee, he continued, "That much is true. We have a wire indicating that he didn't show up for his appointment a month ago. I understand that he told you that he was going, and he left you in charge of the estate."

"Well, not exactly. He'd been talking about going for quite a while, as his pain grew worse, but the first that I knew of it was when I found a note from him in the box one morning, saying that he was going and for me to watch over things, and pay the bills as needed. I arranged it with you, didn't I, Merivale?"

Stagg nodded, but didn't speak.

"If you have no objections," said Pons, "I would like to make an examination of the manor house, in order to see if there any indication where Mr. Sacker traveled, instead of making his way to Minnesota."

"Certainly, certainly. The key is hanging by the door. You'll understand," said the man with a cough, "that I won't accompany you." He wiggled a bare foot. "Too much trouble, you see."

Stagg and I turned to accompany Pons, but my friend put up a hand. "If you don't mind, Mr. Stagg, please stay behind and keep an eye on things here. I'm sure that you can all find something to talk about." Pons leaned closer, and I could hear him say something softly about keeping an eye on the Magees, and making sure they didn't get up to something, or - ludicrously - try to escape.

I could see that Stagg wanted to accompany us, but he reluctantly agreed to carry out his mission. Pons retrieved the key, and we stepped outside. The wind had picked up, and the day was becoming dark with approaching rain clouds. Pulling our coats closer, we made our way over several hills back to the manor house.

We were fortunate in our arrival, as the rains began just as we gained entry. Shutting the door behind us eliminated the rising sounds of the wind, and I was struck by the heavy quiet inside. That, and an odor that was all too familiar.

"Dear Lord," I whispered, for the atmosphere didn't encourage normal conversation. "He didn't go to America."

"No. He never left the house. Let us locate him."

It didn't take long at all. The place must have been closed up for a month. We followed the smell as it became stronger, finally leading us into a study at the rear of the building. At first, there was no sign of our goal. However, Pons pulled aside a heavy drape to reveal the decomposing corpse, lying between it and the wall at the base of a darkly glassed mullioned window.

Little can be gained by describing what we found, except to note that the poor man's head had been crushed by a heavy candlestick – Pons located the weapon immediately on a nearby table, still covered with dried gore – and that there was no doubt the victim was Fred Sacker, based upon the old bayonet scar that we located upon his thin torso.

After our examination, Pons made to roll the body back where it had been found, behind the drape. I expressed surprise. "Much of this matter still puzzles me, Parker," he said. "As we've examined the situation from every angle, there is simply no need for Mr. Magee to kill these people – he could take the treasure at any time – and obviously he has not, as shown by the condition of his surroundings. Fawkes Tuck was going to die anyway. And Fred Sacker here, he was going to be leaving." His eyes narrowed, and then he gave a slight nod. "Unless . . . .

"No," he continued after another moment, "there are still questions to be answered. I don't believe that it's yet time to 'officially' discover Mr. Sacker."

"But surely Magee will know that we've found him!" I cried. "It's been a month. He would realize that the decomposition of the body in this closed house would be obvious."

"Perhaps, although one shouldn't rush to judgement. We cannot say for certain that Magee did this crime."

"But the fat doctor at the hospital?"

"As you pointed out, that fellow could have been there for an entirely different reason. In any case, it's certainly apparent that no one has made any effort to visit the house in the last month, since the murder occurred, Magee or otherwise. It certainly hasn't been cleaned. In addition to the odor, there is quite a bit of dust upon all the surfaces. Surely, if one wanted to hide the body, there would have been a chance to return in darkness and do so in during the month that has passed. No, this poor man was left here for a reason."

Pons spent a few more minutes investigating the room and the rest of the house, although his examination upstairs was cursory at best. He seemed satisfied with what he had already seen, especially on the floor near the body, and he led me back outside.

Locking the door behind us, we returned to the fresh air, and I was grateful – at least for a while – for the cleansing rain that fell upon us. While not unfamiliar with death in all of its varied guises, I still took in great draughts of the cool damp air in order to rid myself of that terrible smell and the creeping taste that accompanied it.

Back at the Magee house, we let ourselves in to discover a raging row – at least, as much of one as there could be. Apparently in our absence, Stagg had given way to venting his accusations against Magee. The fat man himself appeared to be saddened that his old friend could believe such a thing about him, but his wife was on her feet, nearly spitting with her wheezy vehement rebuttals. Pons stepped between them and attempted to quiet the raging storm.

"We found nothing to help us," said Pons, while I watched Magee's face. He gave no indication that anything was amiss. "I believe that we will need to return to London and research this question from the other end. Perhaps there is some way to trace where Mr. Sacker's journey went awry. In the meantime, please let me ask that none of this be discussed in public."

"And the treasure?" snapped Mrs. Magee. "Now that you know of it, I suppose you'll be rooting around trying to find it yourself!"

"Nonsense," said Sam Magee, looking at her with a frown. "These men are the police. They wouldn't do such a thing." He lowered his voice and looked toward Stagg. "But I do wish that you hadn't told anyone, Merivale."

"We'll keep your secret," said Pons, "and as I mentioned before, we are not policemen, but rather consultants. I hope to have news for you in a few days."

With that, he turned and led us toward the door, indicating to the Magees that we would let ourselves out, a fact that seemed to suit them. As soon as the door closed behind us, Pons whispered urgently, "I have no time to explain, Mr. Stagg. Go back inside. Tell them that, until this matter is settled, you are going up to London with us until further notice. The first thing tomorrow morning! No, don't ask questions! Make them believe it. Tell them how upset this has made you. Use all of the business skills that you've acquired to convince them. Now, go!"

And our client, with only a split's second of bewildered peering, spun on his heel and re-entered the little house. "Pray he can pull it off!" muttered Pons.

In just a moment, a nervous Stagg rejoined us, indicating that he had done as Pons asked. "And you made sure that they know that you're leaving in the morning?"

"Well, tomorrow at any rate. That's what you told me." He looked back and forth between us, wanting more information. "And now what?" he finally asked.

"You, in fact, will go to London. But tonight instead of in the morning."

Stagg drove us to his own home not far away, where he packed a bag. He sent word to his bank, and we then went with him to the Oxford station, where we put him on the local to London, with instructions to put himself up at the Northumberland Hotel. There, he should await instructions, which Pons hoped would arrive speedily. Then, when our client had gone, Pons wired his brother Bancroft, asking him to have his men make certain that Staggs went where he was supposed to go, and that he stayed there.

"Now, Parker, we must hurry, in order to be back and well hidden in Staggs' house before nightfall. And there is much to arrange."

What followed is soon told, and there wasn't as much to arrange as Pons had implied. At the house, Pons picked the lock and we let ourselves in. It didn't take long to familiarize ourselves with the modest layout, and to arrange things so that only one door could be easily entered from the outside – in fact, it would remain unlocked to provide easy access. Drapes were shut, except for one key window, which would allow someone on the outside to see into the study, once the sun went down and the sole lamp was lit. I argued that Pons, who would be seated in the dim room disguised as Merivale Stagg, would be making himself an unnecessary target – after all, why come inside, as our trap was constructed to encourage, if one could simply shoot him through the window? However, he would not be swayed, indicating that the killer was not the shooting type, and in the end, his understanding of the psychology involved proved to be the correct one.

It was only an hour or two after sunset, but darkness had fallen long before that as the rain clouds thickened, providing an ever-increasing downpour throughout the afternoon and evening. Early on,

Pons had placed himself, wearing Stagg's well-padded clothing, in the banker's study chair, slumped in despair. I knew that Pons could wait like that for hours, with the patience of a jungle hunter slung along a branch, poised motionless above a game trail before pouncing on the unsuspecting prey below. I, however, was not so patient, and from my position in a side room down the hall, along the path that the killer would be forced to take, I frequently shifted from side to side, as well as passing my gun from hand to hand, striving to stay alert. Thankfully, things were resolved sooner rather than later.

Pons had scattered some gravels outside the unlocked door, and the killer's footsteps upon them were quite obvious. The door opened, and it was soon clear that an attempt was being made to control the wheezing coming down the hallway and past where I stood, hidden. Then, the door to the study was pushed open, allowing a wash of light to run my way, silhouetting the killer's massive body in the entryway. There was no mistaking the fireplace poker gripped in the right hand.

Beyond, I could see Pons, still slumped in the chair, looking remarkably like Stagg in the dim light. He sat there, unmoving, even as the killer approached, raising the poker. I couldn't have done it, to sit there like that as if completely unaware. I was preparing to fling myself forward, or to shoot the iron rod out of the killer's hand, when Pons glanced around, speaking in an even tone.

"Good evening, Mrs. Magee. A terrible night for visiting, don't you think?"

With a bellow, she raised the poker, even as Pons spun out of the chair, putting the desk between himself and the crazed woman. I tried to wrap my mind around the fact that the assassin was the wife and not the husband. The fact was driven home as I saw the great wedding ring, too big for even her swollen fingers, glinting upon her left hand in the lamplight.

She cried and whipped the poker down, once, twice, three times, missing him comfortably, but irreparably damaging the desk. It was only when she felt the cold metal of my gun barrel on the back of her rolled neck, to the side of the ridiculous reddish-blonde plait, that she sagged in defeat. And yet, even then, I did not believe it for a moment – and a good thing, too, for she suddenly swung the poker around in a deadly lateral arc toward me. It just missed me, but I fell backwards, my gun going off and firing a bullet uselessly into the ceiling. Even as I dropped, I saw her step forward, raising the weapon for another go. It was only when Pons shattered a massive vase across the base of her skull that she settled unconscious in defeat.

"Good Lord, Pons," I gasped, staggering to my feet. "You've killed her."

"Unlikely, Parker. Her kind doesn't die easily."

He was right, of course. She didn't regain consciousness until the police arrived. As she was being led out to the waiting van, she uttered a string of vile and violent epithets that made me fear for her sanity. I said so, and Pons replied, "I suspect that you are right. She will likely end her days in Broadmoor. Her plan was a complete mess from the beginning." How typical that he would judge her sanity on the ability, or lack thereof, to accomplish her mission.

"Elaborate upon that thought," I suggested, but Pons refused, indicating that we would discuss it in the morning, when the other principals could participate.

A little after ten a.m. on the following day, we met back at Magee's house – Pons and I, Stagg, a local inspector named Burton, and the prisoner, in the custody of a trio of burly constables. By her side was a reedy little solicitor named Gates, questioning the nature of this proceeding and urging Mrs. Magee to remain silent. It quickly became apparent that she would do no such thing, and that Gates might as well have stayed home.

"Why, Rosie?" asked Magee. He clearly hadn't slept at all the previous night, understandably. "Why?"

"I was tired of waiting!" she snapped. Gates tried again to make her be quiet, but she literally growled at him, and, having performed his due diligence, he subsided into the background.

"For what?" asked her bewildered husband.

"For the treasure, you fat fool!"

Magee looked stunned, and Stagg didn't appear to be much different. "The treasure?" Magee finally muttered weakly. "This is because of the treasure?"

"Of course it is! I've waited since we married to get our share of it. I finally got tired of waiting. I thought that Mr. Fred would die ten years ago, but he didn't. That place in America healed him. And then he got sick again, and he was going to back there and get better and outlive us all! He stopped by that morning, when you weren't here, and he told me all about it. It was just like him to make sudden decisions that way. I saw him getting away from us. Getting better. And I knew what I had to do. I told him that I'd let you know, and then when he went back home, I followed him and took care of it."

"Rosie . . . ."

"I waited to see if anyone would catch on, but they didn't. Day after day, week after week. He always was a strange little cove, and him going away didn't surprise anybody. Later, I told you that I was going to clean over in the manor, so that you wouldn't go, but I never went back."

"What was your plan?" asked Pons. "With the body? Surely at some point he would be found, and it would be obvious that he was murdered. And you couldn't just hide him away forever."

"I would make it look like an accident."

"Surely not. He was hit from behind by a candle stick."

"I'd make it look like an accident," she reaffirmed, and Pons looked at her with great curiosity, as if she were insisting that the sky were green or two plus two equaled five. When he realized that she would provide no better explanation - in fact, could not - he waved for her to continue. "So you then decided to kill Mr. Tuck as well."

"As time went by," she explained, "I got the itch again - to make it happen faster."

"So you dressed as a doctor two nights ago," continued Pons, "snuck into the hospital, and smothered Mr. Tuck."

"I did."

"That took a great deal of confidence."

"I worked there years ago. During the War."

"And your husband? Did he not notice that you had gone?"

She snorted - there is no other way to describe it. "Him? He never did. Anyway, I put a little something in his dinner to make sure that he dropped off."

"But not enough to kill him, certainly. He was your ticket to the treasure."

She gave him a flashing glare filled with hate, but then it faded and she became quite conversational. "Yes," she said agreeably. I understood then that she was quite mad.

"And so you smothered Mr. Tuck."

"Yes."

"Why, if he was going to die soon anyway?"

"How could I know that? People get better all the time!" She looked crafty then. "How did you find out it was me?"

"Your footprints, in the manor house. On the floor near where you hid the body. They overlay everything else, and they had approximately one month's dust covering them." he said. "You have a distinctive splayed foot. Your husband's is spread in much the same way, but to a greater extent, and he obviously wears a different sort of shoe. The rest fit together easily enough. Knowing that you were killing the men in the Tontine - "

"The what?"

"Tontine. The arrangement that the four men had made to split the treasure. You had obviously killed Sacker before he could get out of your reach. I suspected that you finished Mr. Tuck along the same lines that you've described. Knowing that you were in the process of eliminating these men, I came up with the idea of luring you into killing Mr. Stagg as well, before he could leave the area and also get out of your reach. Granted, you would have only had to be patient until he gave up and returned, but I sense that you've acquired the taste for murder, and the thought of it has been on your mind ever since"

"It is, I suppose. But you're wrong. That isn't it."

"What isn't?"

"The taste. There is no taste. It's just something I see in my head. And I just didn't want to lose my chance at the treasure."

"*Your* chance?"

"Of course. The last man standing gets it. And just look at *him*!" She jerked a thumb at Sam Magee, collapsed in his defeated chair, a look of despair melting his face. "Do you think someone like that is going to be the last man? Even if Fawkes Took drank himself to death early, the other two would have outlasted this one by decades. He promised me that treasure, he did. He *promised* it! Why else would I have married him? And ever since then, he's done nothing but eat himself to death, digging his own grave with his spoon and fork."

"Oh, Rosie," moaned Magee, covering his eyes with a shaking hand.

"Do you have something relevant to add, Mr. Magee?" asked Pons.

The man shook his head, and then reconsidered. He looked over at his wife, his expression suddenly turning angry. "You call me a fat fool. Well, *you're* the fool, Rosie Magee. You've killed these men. You've thrown away our happiness. Our golden years. For nothing. For nothing! *For there never was any treasure!*"

The silence was absolute – that is, until Mr. Gates, forgotten over by the wall, gave a nervous giggle. Then, Pons said, "I suspected as much. It was always just the ring, wasn't it, Mr. Magee? Nothing more."

The fat man shook his head. "No, there was a treasure. Fred and me found it, just like we said. That part was true. I'm guessing that Merivale has told you the story. But we didn't actually bury it under a grove of '*W*'-shaped trees, and we certainly never went back to get it after the War."

"Sam . . . ." said Merivale Stagg.

"No, we found it all right, but before we could hide it, we were captured, early on, with it still in our possession. The guerillas took it, and we never saw it again. Fred had managed to hide the one ring in his clothes, but that's all we ever had."

"But you told us," interrupted Stagg. "You said that you'd found it. That you'd share it."

"It started out as a lark, I suppose. Something to make for an interesting tale. But then, we came back and you all got on with your lives, and my life wasn't moving at all. I still saw Mr. Fred, of course, but you and Fawkes were drifting away. So I came up with this idea - to tell you that we had gone back and found the treasure and brought it home. I thought that that would tie us all up again like brothers, the way that we had been before, after we had been through so much, to the end of our days. Mr. Fred went along with it - he was always dreaming of other things, his stories and such, I suppose, so he didn't much care one way or the other.

"As the years went by, we still drifted apart. I guess there was no stopping it. But when we would see each other, it was there. Something that still connected us. And it lasted all the way, right until now, here at the end of all things."

Throughout this explanation, I had watched Rosie Magee as her face went from shock to outright disbelief to rage. Finally, she could be silent no longer.

"No treasure? *No treasure*? You promised me a *treasure*! Why else would I have married you? Every year, day in and day out, we talked about what we'd do when you got your share, and every year that went by, nothing happened, and we rotted here! And you mean to tell me that it was all a *lie*!"

"Rosie," said Magee. "You wouldn't . . . you wouldn't have married me if I hadn't told you that I had a treasure."

She looked with naked hatred at her husband. Then, she began to twist and wrench her shackled hands, crying and sobbing, until she had them turned in such a way that she could tug on the gold ring, circling the fourth finger of her left hand. With a grunt, she pulled it loose, lifted both hands above her head - joined as they were at the wrists - and brought them down sharply, flinging the ring toward Magee as true as a bullet.

It winked in the light as it turned, and seemed to take forever, although it was surely less than a second, the distance being no greater than it was. As I'd somehow known that it would, it hit Magee squarely upon his forehead, apparently upon one of its edges, for I later saw that it had nicked out a small chunk of meat. Then, it ricocheted between the man and his wife and landed in the fire, disappearing neatly into the coals. No one made any move to retrieve it, even as Mrs. Magee's voice rose in a shrill ululation of meaningless rage, the last thread to her frayed sanity snapped.

As the inspector, who had yet to say a word, led out his entourage of prisoner, constables, and solicitor, I moved to treat the wound on Magee's forehead, now bleeding freely. He just sat there without moving, tears flowing silently down his unhealthy cheeks. I glanced over and saw, running out of the coals along the blackened brick flooring of the fireplace, a thin thread of melted gold, all that remained of the so-called treasure that had bound this fellowship together for far longer than it ever should have been.

Later, I stood outside with Pons and Stagg, who held a bottle of cheap brandy in his shaking hands, filched from the Magee kitchen. He hadn't bothered to steal a glass, drinking directly from the bottle's lip.

"I don't know what to say," said the banker. "Poor Sam. Poor Fred and Fawkes."

Pons nodded. "So much misery from a wartime tall tale."

"You knew that it was her when we left the manor yesterday," I said, changing the subject. "Why didn't you simply force a confession then? She would have certainly cracked if you had confronted her with the evidence. I've seen you do the same thing hundreds of times before."

He smiled but didn't answer. "You wanted to force her into trying to kill you," I theorized.

He nodded. "It's all about how one plays The Game. When we returned from the manor yesterday, as you said, I knew that she had been the killer from the footprint evidence, as well as how it all tied together. And I realized that she would be suspicious of what we had found during our search. I observed that you were watching her husband when we announced that we had found nothing. But I was also watching *Mrs. Magee* to see how *she* reacted, since she was the one who knew that there *was* something to find. The expression on her face had a unique and primitive animal cunning about it – she was wondering why we didn't reveal what we had discovered, or if we had discovered anything at all – and I decided then and there to see if we could lure her into conclusively acting, thus revealing not only what she had already done, but possibly the truth about the treasure as well."

"Ah, the treasure," moaned Stagg, taking another drink. "Was there ever such a foolish game?"

"Don't blame your old friend too much," said Pons with surprising compassion. "He did the best that he could with his limited resources, and this idea of keeping his old friends, and even securing a wife, with a fictional trove, was clever in its own way. Who can say how many other devices, literally and figuratively, have been used to forge ties between groups and bind them?"

The matter was greatly forgotten when something of an epilogue occurred, six or eight months later. We had a visit in our Praed Street rooms from the Oxford professor who had initially befriended Fred Sacker, encouraging his writing. The professor had decided to work on his own version of some sort of story related to the events of the wartime fellowship and the treasure that turned out to be nothing more than a seemingly cursed ring. He had a note from Merivale Stagg giving full permission for Pons to relate various details of the case.

I listened for a bit while matters pertained to the events that I had witnessed. It became more interesting when Pons pulled out his monograph from six or seven years earlier, *An Examination of the Cthulhu Cult and Others*, making some point – over my head, I'm afraid – about its relevance to the story of the four friends. However, when the conversation began to devolve into matters of ancient history, particularly related to the ancient documents that the professor had discovered long ago in Cornwall and had subsequently brought to Pons's attention for help decoding, I excused myself and stepped down Praed Street to Fountains Abbey, where I enjoyed a pint and read the reality of the day's newspapers – much more interesting than the doings of mythical treasures and lost civilizations and their fantastical doings.

# The Adventure of the Obrisset Snuffbox

When I first met Solar Pons, I was still becoming re-accustomed to life in England. Those first weeks were filled with the day-to-day tasks of arranging our possessions in ways that suited us. Pons, having spent his time during the conflict in a variety of locales connected with his duties, hadn't been back in England much longer than I, and he was quite accommodating in deference to his new fellow lodger. Gradually, we began to settle into a routine.

Over the next few months, as I came to learn more about this unique individual, I began to make notes – first simple entries in my notebooks, and then more ambitious sketches of the different cases that earned Pons his bread and cheese. Sometimes I recorded those involved and convoluted matters that began with a client's visit or a summons to the scene of a crime, while on other occasions I simply jotted down scraps of conversations, occurring on those quiet evenings when no one claimed my friend's attention.

The topics of these talks might range from Bohr's model of the atom to recidivism to the recently unveiled cenotaph in Whitehall. I was occasionally given glimpses of his early cases, and through these, as well as more direct comments and examples, I learned much about Pons's beliefs and systemic way of thinking.

I have a brief note of one such conversation in my notebooks from this period, wherein Pons and I were discussing coincidence.

"One cannot ignore it," he maintained, "for in an existence of this complexity, with so many independently acting factors, all possibilities are bound to occur at some point."

"I have read something of the sort," I replied, warming to the subject. "There is a theory that, given an infinite amount of time, a monkey, pecking at a typewriter and hitting random keys, will eventually produce a combination of letters that, when examined, would be an exact duplicate of the works of Shakespeare – his, of course, being painstakingly created by his own definite decisions and labor, while the monkey's work would be happenstance."

"Yes. I believe that theory was initially postulated by the French mathematician Borel several years ago. I read something of it during the War – we were attempting to create a non-specific and random-based code, and the use of theories related to these completely unsystematic mathematical possibilities was of some interest, before we eventually abandoned it."

"Unworkable?"

"Not at all – except that we would need a calculating engine of such magnitude that it would be impractical – as impractical, I might add, as finding a monkey of infinite lifespan that would be able to generate the works of The Bard."

"Of course, if such a thing were possible," I added, "the probability is just as likely that the *first* thing the monkey randomly typed would be *Hamlet* – the element of chance making that just as possible as if it were in a version produced ten-thousand or ten-million years from now."

"I see your point," agreed Pons, "and that returns us to my initial statement that one cannot ignore coincidence, as it might crop up at any point. And yet, it's a messy thing for an investigator to manage and take into account, and it should never be accepted until all other possibilities are ruled out."

"You reluctantly accept coincidence, then," I said. "What about the idea of *Fate*?"

"There is a subtle difference. Coincidence is the random chance of something occurring, while Fate implies a pre-ordained path or a controlling hand."

"So you don't believe in Fate?"

He made a small shrug with his head. "During the course of my career, I have seen things that could make one wonder. Let us say I don't discount it either."

Perhaps it was coincidence or fate that led me to find the scrap of this conversation just now, while cleaning my desk just a week after the conclusion of the events which I now propose to recount. But was it coincidence or fate that led to a boy's impulse, resulting in – but I'm telling my tale out of order. Best to begin at the beginning.

I find recorded in my notes that it was on Thursday, 20 September, 1923, that Pons and I were drawn into the curious matter of the Obrisset Snuffbox. It was a cool and overcast morning, and we were both sitting in our armchairs, discussing the events of the previous night, when our long vigil had prevented the suicide of Lady Lois Grefnell, forced to such straits by the lies of her fiancé, the American confidence man Calvin Treathaway. I was raising a question or two about Pons's deductions when a frantic ringing of our front doorbell shattered our weary reflections.

Pons rose, and I was making a move to join him, my joints aching following the fisticuffs of just a few hours before, when we both heard the sound of scampering footsteps approaching our first floor rooms. Mrs. Johnson called from below, but her tone wasn't urgent or angry – there was more concern than anything else. Pons looked my way knowingly. "Peake, I expect."

When our sitting room door slammed open, coming to an abrupt stop when the knob hit the plaster of the wall behind it, I understood Mrs. Johnson's tolerance. This was no angry invader – a former foe perhaps, here to seek revenge against Pons, and me as well, as his friend and associate. No, this lad was known to us.

Alfred Peake was the leader of Pons's own Praed Street Irregulars, that band of boys – and a few girls – that served as his unofficial eyes and ears in various parts of the city. Working on the assumption that they could go anywhere and see anything while being ignored, he often made use of them when gathering information or having someone watched or followed when other means were not available. When I first met Pons, the basic structure of this little organization was well established, and young Alfred, certainly not the oldest of the group, had already earned his position at the head of the battalion by way of his wit, intelligence, bravery, and boldness. I had encountered him on countless occasions, but this was the first time that I observed him to be frightened.

"You've got to help, Mr. Pons," he said breathlessly. "He didn't do it!"

Pons laid a calming hand on the boy's shoulder and shepherded him into a chair before the fire, while glancing toward Mrs. Johnson, who stood concerned in the doorway. "Some tea would not be unwelcome," he said, and she nodded before retreating, pulling the door shut behind her.

"Now, Peake," said Pons, resuming his own chair, as I did mine. "Who did not do what?"

"Karl Drayton," he replied. "He didn't do it!"

"So you said. At least we now know *who*, if not *how* or *why* or *what*. Karl is in trouble, then?"

I knew of whom they spoke. The Irregulars were an ever-changing bunch – some moved away, some outgrew their association, and others simply drifted. There was always a core group of a dozen or so, however, whose faces and names were familiar. Over the last year or so, I had become aware of a boy that seemed to be present more often than not when Pons was giving instructions to his rag-tag army. This boy, Karl Drayton, was taller than the others, and always very quiet and watchful. I couldn't tell if he was pondering deep thoughts, or unwittingly following the Proverb that a fool is thought wise if he keeps silent, and discerning if he holds his tongue. In any case, he had become one of the regular Irregulars, so to speak, and appeared to have earned Pons's trust, and therefore my own as well.

"He didn't hurt that man," said Alfred, catching his breath.

"Ah, we progress," said Pons in a calming voice. "From the beginning, Peake."

Alfred straightened in his seat, remembering how he had been trained to report. "It was not a half-hour ago. Over on Weymouth Street, at the corner of Upper Wimpole. We - that is, Karl and me - were standing around, after we'd delivered a package from Mr. Delgado."

Pons nodded. Delgado owned a small what-not store near Paddington, and had developed a reputation for providing his clientele with out-of-the-way sundries, shipped to him from various obscure spots. In my own case, he kept his eyes open for a particular brand of tobacco that I favored. His reputation for success gained his little shop a steady trade throughout the capital. I was aware that Peake and some of the other Irregulars, who certainly were not employed by Pons on anything approaching a steady basis, often accepted commissions from various merchants such as Delgado.

"While we stood by a lamppost," continued Alfred, "we saw a man, all hunched over he was, ring the bell of the corner house opposite. When the servant answered the door, the crooked man handed him something and scooted off, down the step and toward Marylebone High Street. We thought nothing of it, but in just a minute, the door of the house flew open, and a different man - not the servant - came rushing out, looking up and down the street. He looked scared, he did! He had something gripped in his hand, and he'd look at it, and then back at the street.

"That was when it happened. He started down the step, and his feet went out from under him. It was still wet from the rain last night. He fell and hit his head. I started over, but Karl took off running! He was there in a flash, bent over and trying to help the man.

"As I got closer, I could see that there was already a lot of blood. It had puddled and out and onto the walk. Just then, when I was just halfway there, the front door opened again, and the servant came back out. He looked down and saw Karl leaning over the man, and without even asking, he began to yell for a constable! Just our luck, there was one close by, and he blew his whistle and started toward us. I knew that all we had to do was explain, but Karl bolted, running the other way. I didn't know what else to do, so I followed him.

"I didn't catch him until I saw him turn into Paddington Street Gardens. I knew where he'd go – there's a certain corner where the bushes seem thick, but if you know just where, you can crawl inside to something like a little room. He was in there, sitting on the ground, all curled into a ball. You know Karl – he's bigger than most of us, but in some ways younger. He's awfully quiet, and he wouldn't hurt a fly. When he heard the constable yelling at him, he panicked, I expect. He scares easy – ever since what happened to his parents."

A few months earlier, Alfred had shared what he knew of Karl's past. The boy's father was German, and his mother English. They had both been killed by an explosion in Alsace-Lorraine late in the War, and young Karl had been kept safe by a friend of the family. Later, the boy's aunt had somehow managed to arrange his transport to England, as nothing was known of his father's people. Sadly, just a few months after his arrival in England, the aunt, a charwoman who had previously been alone in the world, was struck and killed by an omnibus in Shaftesbury Avenue. Karl had found himself adrift, and had fallen into the welcome company of the Irregulars.

"A couple of the fellows," Alfred continued, "Michael and Clark, had seen us running through the park and followed. While they sat with Karl, I went back to Upper Wimpole Street to see what I could see. There were police all around. I asked a refuse man nearby what was happening, and he said that the master of that house, a Mr. Lemuel, had been attacked in the street by a boy and was now near death's door! The police are looking for the boy, and it's just a matter of time before they find him.

"The refuse man gave me a suspicious look, and I went back to the park, where several more of us were with Karl. He wouldn't talk, just sat there rocking. I don't know if it was seeing the man bleeding or if it was the constable chasing after him, but he can't think straight.

"While I was trying to get some sense into him, I noticed something in Michael's hand. I asked him what it was, and he said that Karl had been holding it tight. He handed it to me, and I thought that it might be what the man had when he ran out of the house. I don't know where else Karl could have found it." And with that, he reached into his pocket and pulled out the object, handing it to Pons.

From my seat, I could see that it was of a dull color, metallic looking and oval-shaped, about three inches at its longer length, flat, and approximately half-an-inch thick. The top surface had some sort of design shaped into it. Even as I watched, Pons fiddled and popped it open. The engraved segment was hinged to the bottom, and it swung back, revealing a small cavity, apparently empty.

"Some sort of pill box?" I asked.

Pons shook his head, raised the object to his nose, and sniffed. Then, clicking it shut, he tossed it across to me. I caught it, thankful that I was able to give our visitor the impression that I maintained that level of grace at all times. Later, when I gained a sense of what the little box was worth, I was quite glad that I hadn't fumbled it across the room, smashing it into a wall or batting it into the fire.

Peering at it, I could see that the item wasn't metallic at all, but instead was of some ivory-like material, discolored with age. The design on top was a shallow engraving of a middle-aged woman, rather plump, and facing to my left. Her hair was done up, her clothing quite of another age, and her expression rather unhappy.

"Queen Victoria?" I asked.

"Rather before her time, I fancy," replied Pons. "I do not recognize this lady."

Recalling Pons's actions, I prized open the lid with a thumbnail and raised it to my nose. "Snuff," I said, identifying that odor which never failed to remind me of my grandfather.

"Indeed," said Pons. "A snuffbox fashioned by a known genius of the form."

"Really?" I said, clicking it shut. It really wasn't that attractive. "And who would that be?"

"John Obrisset. That box in your hand is a masterpiece, created over two centuries ago, and likely worth a great deal."

Turning it this way and that, I asked, "Is this ivory? Scrimshaw?"

"Not at all. It is horn from some animal. Made from the same material, *keratin*, as your fingernails."

I looked at the details of the woman's features. Suddenly, understanding what the artist had achieved with such a material increased my appreciation.

"And you say that this Obrisset was well known for this sort of thing?"

"He was."

"How are you aware of him?"

"During those years when I was learning my craft, I sought to have an understanding of all sorts of objects that might be considered valuable – even snuffboxes. One never knows what will end up being stolen. Obrisset's work is well known in certain circles."

"Well, not mine," I muttered, raising halfway from my chair to hand the snuffbox – and *not* to toss it – back into Pons's care.

"Assuming that this was the object in the man's hand when he raced out of his house, and not something that Karl had already picked up elsewhere, or even brought with him from the Continent – what significance could it have, causing such a reaction from the man, and leading to such a tragedy?"

Pons stood in that abrupt way of his. "That is the question, isn't it? Peake?" he said, looking down at the boy. "Is Karl somewhere safe?"

Alfred nodded, saying, "We took him to my house. My mother is taking care of him." Pons nodded. We were both long acquainted with Sally Peake, née Wiggins. Karl would be in good hands. At that moment, Mrs. Johnson entered with a tea tray. I noticed that, in addition to the pot and cups, there was a plate of cakes. Even though she was occasionally vexed by the Irregulars and their unruly entrances, she was a soft-hearted woman, and she worried about them more than she would ever let on.

Pons had clearly risen to set forth on this new investigation. However, seeing Mrs. Johnson's effort, which he had specifically requested, he glanced my way with a rueful smile and instead moved to help her place the tray on our dining table, thanking her graciously. She beamed and set about pouring three cups of steaming tea. Pons brought a cup and the plate of sweets to Alfred, who tucked in without comment as only growing boys can. He then carried over a cup for himself and me.

After our landlady departed, Pons set his cup down untouched. "Parker," he said, "you and I shall go 'round to Upper Wimpole Street and see what we shall see. There's more to this than meets the eye, and we can't have poor Karl under any sort of suspicion. In any event, I must find out exactly how this little snuffbox is involved. When you're finished . . . ." he left the thought hanging and looked pointedly at my cup, held in my hand undrunk as I waited for it to cool. I nodded and blew on it with vigor.

Soon enough, Pons and I were preparing to depart, with instructions for Alfred to return to his home, but to get word to Mrs. Johnson should any new developments arise. Then, as it was a cool day, we donned our coats and hats, with Pons placing the Obrisset snuffbox in an inner pocket, and we set off for Upper Wimpole Street.

Eschewing a cab for the relatively short journey, we walked east, almost immediately crossing the Edgware Road, and so on into Homer and Crawford Streets. The blocks ticked away – Upper Montague Street, Gloucester Place, Baker Street – until we reached the Marylebone High Street. A quick right and left brought us into Weymouth Street and, not far down, we reached the north turning into Upper Wimpole. Our destination was easily identified. A police car was still standing in front of No. 2, just back from the corner, and more importantly, a constable stood stolidly against the front door, confirming for certain the address of the incident described by Alfred.

It was a typical whitewashed building for the area, four floors, with a wide black doorway was on the left, reached by just a couple of low steps. It was bracketed by the typical spiked black iron railings that framed the entry and then turned to line the areaways all the way up the street. The neighborhood consisted of private residences and ground floor businesses, and any given year, a building that had been one might change to the other, or back again.

As we stepped forward, the constable shook himself into motion, his mouth opening to warn us off. Then, he seemed to recognize my friend's deerstalker and Inverness, for he stood a little straighter and said, "Mr. Pons! Dr. Parker! I wasn't told that you'd been summoned."

"Because we weren't," answered Pons with a smile. He gestured toward where the drying blood stains were still spread across the stone work and seeping into the cracks. "Who is in charge?"

"Inspector Jamison is inside," answered the constable. "Normally it wouldn't be a Yard matter, you understand, but the injured man is somebody of importance – rather, his wife is."

"Injured?" I asked. "So he is still alive then, Constable – Ferrers, isn't it?"

"Yes, sir." He touched his helmet in a quick salute. "He's still amongst the living – last I've heard, anyway," he rumbled. Then he seemed to remember that we weren't there to gossip with him. Turning, he said, "Let me notify the inspector that you're here."

"Very good," replied Pons.

After the constable disappeared inside, Pons bent to examine the drying blood and prod the dead leaves and bits of accumulated trash that had blown against the step. In the meantime, I looked up and down the street. There was nothing to be learned. A number of people were standing at a reasonable distance – residents of the neighborhood, no doubt – huddled together and looking our way, discussing what could possibly have necessitated a visit from the police. No doubt Pons's presence, in his distinctive hat and coat, would only add fuel to the fire.

It seemed as if Constable Ferrers had only been gone for a moment before the door opened to reveal our old friend, Inspector

Seymour Jamison. Always a friend and ally, some might have had the impression that he was lacking in abilities, but I can testify that he had a long and successful career with the Yard. It only seemed, on certain occasions when a case required Pons's special abilities, that Jamison might have been wanting for imagination. This was certainly not the case this day, as he seemed to bristle with intuited knowledge.

"That boy!" he exploded as he stepped onto the porch. "One of your Irregulars, no doubt. It makes sense. That's why you're here!"

Pons nodded. "Very good, Jamison." I noticed that Constable Ferrers, resuming his place nearby and facing the street, had still contrived to turn so that he could overhear our conversation.

"I suppose then that you'll tell me he's innocent. That he didn't attack Mr. Lemuel when the man opened the door and stepped outside."

"That is exactly what I assert."

Jamison sighed and rubbed a hand across his face. In a softer town, he said, "To be honest, I didn't think that he had done it either, although heaven knows I've seen such things through the years. Still, Wilson, the butler, swears that it was the boy that hit him."

"He is wrong," I interjected. "Apparently the man came rushing out, anxious to see who had just rung the bell, and slipped on the damp pavement, injuring his head. The boy only rushed over to help him."

"Then what of the trinket, then?" asked Jamison, his face becoming suspicious once again. "Perhaps he didn't hit him, but he certainly took time to rob him."

"Did he?" asked Pons, pulling the snuffbox from his pocket. "Were the man's pockets rifled? I suspect that this was simply picked up on impulse, and held tight without thinking when the constable arrived, causing him to flee."

"You suspect? Did he not tell you it was so when he came to you and gave you the object?"

"It's not that simple," I said. "The boy is somewhat traumatized. It was one of his friends that brought the snuffbox to us and asked for help."

"Oh, ho," said Jamison knowingly. "One of his friends. That scamp Alfred Peake, I'll be bound. And so you're here to make sure this mysterious other boy stays out of trouble."

"To make sure that he isn't unfairly accused," corrected Pons, "although it sounds as if you had already discerned the truth." He raised the Obrisset snuffbox and turned it this way and that. "This is a valuable little item. I find it curious that a stranger would pass it to the butler and then leave, and that it would then cause such a reaction from the man who received it."

Jamison nodded. "That's the butler's story, now confirmed by this mysterious Irregular of yours. A rough looking man rang the doorbell, and asked that an envelope be taken into Mr. Lemuel. It must have contained the – the snuffbox, you say?"

"Yes. The man asked for Lemuel by name?"

"He did. The butler, Wilson, said that Lemuel took the envelope, opened it and looked inside, and took something out. He went white as a ghost, and ran for the door, nearly falling on his way through the house. He threw open the door and went outside. Wilson, following along from behind, came through a minute later and peeked through the window to see his master flat on his back, a puddle of blood around his head, and a big lad kneeling over him. What was he to think, but that Lemuel had been attacked? He called for the police, and the boy ran away." Jamison nodded. "And he reported that another boy appeared from nowhere, out in the street, and ran away with the first. Peak, I'm sure."

Pons smiled, but declined by his silence to confirm or deny.

"What is Lemuel's condition?" I asked.

"He is upstairs with a concussion. He bled quite a bit, but that's typical of head wounds, as he received a great gash when his scalp split on the paving stone as he fell. The doctor says there's the possibility of an '*epidural hema . . . hema -* '"

"*Epidural haemorrhage*," I finished. "A build-up of blood between the skull and the brain."

"That's right," agreed the inspector. "

"Still unconscious, I assume," said Pons.

Jamison nodded. "Otherwise, we'd have had a statement from him by now. Although," said Jamison, "I don't suppose it matters now, for what is the crime? He ran outside, fell, and hit his head. An accident. I'm only here because the butler thought the man had been attacked, which he wasn't, and because Ferrers here, who answered the call, is aware of who Lemuel's wife is, and decided the Yard should be involved."

"And who is the wife?" I asked, turning to the constable.

He cleared his throat. "She's the daughter of an important banker. Sir Chase Sanderford."

"And you know this how . . . ?" asked Pons.

"This is my beat," he said simply. "It helps to know who lives here, and word had come down that this was a house of importance."

"Hilda Lemuel, *née* Sanderford," said Pons. "I'm acquainted with her father, Sir Chase." Turning to Jamison, he asked, "Has anyone notified him?"

"Word has been sent to his bank."

"As I recall, her mother is dead, and she is the only child. Are there any other family members?"

Ferrers frowned, and Jamison said he didn't know.

"May we speak to her?" asked Pons. "In order to return the snuffbox?"

Jamison frowned but nodded and turned abruptly to open the door. It caught for a moment, and the reason was revealed when the inspector tried a second time, pushing it open to reveal a man in livery, soon identified as the butler, Wilson, backing away from where he had obviously been standing in the darkened hallway, attempting to listen to our conversation.

"You're a sneaky one," growled Jamison. "Go and tell your mistress that I need to speak to her one more time." Jamison glanced at us and muttered, "Wilson. The butler."

He was an old pale fellow in his sixties with wisps of white feathery hair combed across his pink scalp. He nodded and attempted to efface himself while turning away from us.

"Wait," said Pons. "First, a question."

The fellow stopped and took a step in our direction. "The man who brought the item for your master," asked Pons. "Describe him."

Wilson frowned, and then said, in a surprisingly deep voice, "There isn't much to tell, sirs. He was wearing a worn plaid overcoat, buttoned up, and a wide-brimmed hat pulled down over his eyes. I never saw his face."

"His voice," I asked. "British, or foreign?"

"British I would say. But he talked quite softly, and his voice was rough, as if he hadn't spoken in a while."

"What did he say?" asked Pons.

"He simply handed me an envelope and told me to take it to Mr. Lemuel."

"And he named him specifically?"

"He did."

"Can you think of any other feature of interest?"

Wilson's eyes widened. "I believe that I can, sir. When he handed me the envelope, I saw that the back of his hand – his right hand. It had a long scar across it, running from side to side. I only saw it for a second, but it looked old – not fresh, you understand."

"Thank you," said Pons, dismissing him. "And now, if you could ask if your mistress can see us?"

The fellow nodded and backed away, facing us until he turned on his heel at the bottom of the stairs. For his age, he moved quickly, and soon he was out of sight.

"Sneaky," muttered Jamison again.

"The envelope," countered Pons. "Where is it?"

Jamison pulled it from his coat. "It was on the dining room table, where Lemuel had dropped it before dashing out."

He handed it to Pons, who looked it over, inside and out, front and back. Then, with a frown, he handed it back, stating, "Nothing. Simply a plain envelope, no doubt purchased for this purpose."

As Jamison replaced the envelope in his inner pocket, a thought struck him. "There was no attack, as the butler thought, but the man who brought the snuffbox still sounds dodgy. There might be something to all of this after all. Do you think the snuffbox had some sort of message in it? A threat?"

"A distinct possibility," replied Pons. He appeared to be willing to continue, but at that moment, the butler reappeared, coming down the steps with a light step that belied his age.

"Mrs. Lemuel will see you now," he said. "May I take your coats?"

We handed them to him, along with our hats, and he turned to place them in a side room. Then, he led us upstairs.

On the first floor, we turned left down a short hallway and were led into a drawing room looking out over the street. From the impression that I'd gathered, the house was well furnished and recently remodeled. Still, I was puzzled that the daughter of such a noted financial advisor would live here, rather than in more posh surroundings.

The butler introduced us and backed out, pulling the door shut behind him. I was tempted to throw it open again and catch him with his ear to the keyhole, but restrained myself.

The lady of the house rose to greet us. She was quite petite, not even five feet tall, and looked rather like a large doll. She had very large neotenic eyes, now quite red from weeping. She clutched a handkerchief, and frequently touched it to her face during our interview.

Jamison introduced us, and then Pons said, "We are sorry to disturb you, Mrs. Lemuel. How is your husband?"

"The doctor told me that he has some sort of concussion. I haven't heard anything else since he discussed it with me a few minutes ago and went back into the bedroom."

I raised an eyebrow. "Your husband wasn't removed to hospital, then?"

She shook her head. "It was felt at this point that nothing would be accomplished, and that it might actually be dangerous to do so."

I didn't know the facts, but I was not certain that I agreed with that statement. "If I can offer any assistance . . . ." I began, but she shook her head.

"No, thank you, Doctor. Our family physician, Dr. Cates, will be sufficient.

I nodded, some of my uncertainty resolved. Cates was sought after amongst the upper classes, for excellent reasons. He had a good bedside manner, and his medical knowledge was certain.

Pons pulled the snuffbox from his pocket, he held it out to the small woman. "We believe this is the object that was delivered to your husband, just before he ran outside and was injured. Do you recognize it?"

Clearly she did, for she reached and took it as if in a trance. She looked at it in wonder for a moment, and then her tiny hand closed around it. I noticed that the knuckles were white.

"It cannot be . . . ." she whispered.

"What, madam?" asked Pons gently.

She closed her eyes, and when they reopened, she was now focused on us again, rather than whatever she had just seen in her imagination. "This snuffbox," she said, and then she swallowed. Beginning again, she answered, "This snuffbox belonged to my husband's great-grandfather. During the Regency. But it was lost."

"Lost?"

"Yes. During the War."

"Obviously," I prompted, "it has provoked a strong memory."

"It does. I . . . I never thought to see it again. You see, it was carried by my fiancé. That is, the man to whom I was engaged . . . before he died."

"I'm sorry that this matter has caused you pain," said Pons. "Can you tell us more about it, and about the man who delivered it to your husband this morning?"

She nodded, and I stepped across the room to take her elbow, helping her resume the seat that she had obviously vacated upon our entry. Her arm was as thin as a rope, and trembling. She glanced up at me with gratitude, and I nodded before turning to take a seat near Pons and Jamison.

"I really don't know anything," she said. "Just what Wilson told me. My husband and I were downstairs in the breakfast room when the doorbell rang. In a moment, Wilson brought in an envelope and handed it to Kenneth. He opened it, and I couldn't see what was inside, but he gave a cry and dashed from the room. I rose but didn't know whether to follow. Then, I heard Wilson yelling, and I made my way outside to find my husband bleeding on the pavement." She paused to touch her eyes with the handkerchief. "Wilson said that he had been attacked by a boy in the street."

Jamison cleared his throat. "We've since established that the boy is innocent. Your husband simply slipped on the wet step."

Mrs. Lemuel closed her eyes. Seemingly without thinking, she raised the hand still curled around the snuffbox and pressed it to her cheek.

"Mrs. Lemuel," said Pons in a low tone. "What about the snuffbox could have caused your husband's reaction?"

Her eyes opened, with something of a flash of fire. This, then was the daughter of Sir Chase Sanderford, not quite so helpless after all. "Why do you wish to know?" she asked.

"Why, to locate the man who delivered it."

"And what would that accomplish?" Her tone had remarkably sharpened.

"I have some sense, based upon the testimony of someone that saw your husband in the street, that he was quite agitated. Perhaps the snuffbox represented a threat. It would be good to either verify that, or rule it out."

"It could not be a threat, Mr. Pons. That would be impossible. The man who owned this snuffbox died six years ago."

"Your fiancé," said Pons. "Are you sure that he died?"

She seemed taken aback. "Of course I am. He was killed in Brazil."

"But suppose that he wasn't," I interjected.

"You do not know all the facts," she said, frowning.

"This is true."

"Charles would never threaten his own brother."

"His brother?"

"Kenneth. My husband. He and Charles, my first fiancé, were brothers."

Pons sat back, his gaze turning inward as he idly reached to tug at the lobe of his ear. Then, he asked, "What were the circumstances of his death?"

"He and my husband were in Brazil, along with their youngest brother, Clifford, meeting with banking interests."

Calculating the likely ages of the three brothers, I said delicately, "They were not in the armed services, then?"

She frowned. "They served their country in other ways, Doctor. The financial aspects of the War were a nightmare. All three of them acted as agents for my father."

"And what happened in Brazil?" asked Pons.

"It was in April of 1917. Brazil was still neutral then, but the Germans had torpedoed a Brazilian ship. There were riots in the street. A fire. Charles somehow became caught up in it and was . . . was killed."

"Was his body returned to England for burial?" asked Pons.

The lady shook her head. "It could not be found." Pons made as if to ask another question, but Mrs. Lemuel continued, "My husband, Kenneth, was injured in the same fire, trying to rescue his brother. Clifford brought him back home . . . ." She drifted to a stop.

"And the snuffbox?" said Pons, interrupting her reverie. "You say it belonged to Charles Lemuel?"

She looked up and nodded. "It did. He was the oldest."

"And so he had it with him. When his body was left behind, so was the *objet*."

"I suppose so."

Pons stood and began to pace, while the petite woman's unnaturally large eyes followed his progress. "Madame," he said, "it must be considered that your brother-in-law, the man to whom you were first betrothed, may in truth be alive."

"I refuse to believe it," she said softly.

"It *is* possible," I added.

"I see where you're headed," offered Jamison. "But why does it have to be the brother that brought the snuffbox today? Perhaps someone else delivered it – a person who was there at the time of the fire in Brazil. Perhaps he had obtained it somehow and has taken it upon himself to return it."

"That could be true, Pons," I agreed. "Stranger things have happened. Kenneth Lemuel's reaction upon seeing the box after all this time, and considering the circumstances in which it was lost, would be natural enough, even if it were delivered by a stranger."

"Yes," said Pons, almost to himself. "But I wonder . . . ." He stopped his pacing and turned to our host. "Thank you for allowing us to take some of your time. My best wishes for your husband's speedy recovery."

The lady stood with a puzzled frown at Pons's abrupt conclusion of the interview, but nodded graciously. As we stepped into the hall and pulled the door shut behind us, I looked back and saw her staring intently at the snuffbox, cupped in her tiny palm.

In the hallway, Wilson was surprisingly nowhere to be seen. However, coming toward us was Dr. Eldridge Cates, a frown on his face. He noticed us with no little surprise but, recognizing Jamison, he followed us as directed back downstairs.

We stood in a small circle in the entry hall, introducing ourselves and quietly discussing the patient's condition. "A bad concussion," he said. He glanced at me, adding, "I know what you're thinking, Doctor, and normally I would agree with you. But in this case, I believe that moving him would pose an even greater danger than simply letting him recover in his own bed. There are a couple of nurses with him upstairs, and I've sent for Sir John Boyer."

This was serious, I thought. Sir John could rarely be enticed from his own researches.

"The prognosis is grim, then?" asked Pons.

"Too soon to tell. He doesn't show some of the classic signs, such as a dilated pupil, but there are other indications that a crisis may be approaching."

"Whom have you told?"

Cates raised a bushy white eyebrow. "No one, as yet. I was on the way to let his wife know when you diverted me downstairs."

Pons smiled, a grim smile that often boded ill for someone. "Might you keep your negative diagnosis to yourself for a bit longer – twenty-four hours, perhaps? After all, it could not hurt to be a bit more encouraging in your estimation of the patient's condition."

"But she is the man's wife – !" hissed Cates.

"If it is bad news, a little delay won't matter – she may already be expecting the worst. And if he does improve . . . well, it will be good news."

"May I ask why you require this course of action?"

"I believe that the patient's condition may provoke a reaction from the man who caused this to happen in the first place.

The doctor looked at him, realizing that this was really no answer at all. Then, he closed his eyes and shook his head. "You wouldn't know it," he said, "but my sister was Agatha Wheland, whom you were good enough to rescue from that bounder, Brooks, four years ago." He stuck out his hand. "I trust you, Mr. Pons. I can be cryptic for twenty-four hours."

"Excellent." He returned the doctor's grip. "And might I add, do not just keep the knowledge from Mrs. Lemuel. Spare illuminating Wilson the butler as well."

Cates smiled and gestured to the right or left. "That shifty fellow could be hiding behind one of us right now for all I know, and might have already overheard our conversation. But I will do as you ask and give him a suitable report as well. Might I assume that one day you'll tell me why this is necessary?"

"You may, but give me a day. I promise that your questions will be answered."

"That is good enough for me, then," said Cates.

"Thank you," replied my friend simply.

The doctor returned upstairs, and as we were retrieving our coats and hats from the side room, Wilson joined us from somewhere on the ground floor, apparently surprised that we had made it that far without his involvement. With curt thanks, Pons, Jamison, and I returned to the street, past Constable Ferrers, still on duty, seemingly oblivious to the various watchers up and down the street.

Pons glanced around with a sharp eye. "Come with me around the corner, where we can discuss this without being watched so closely."

Jamison looked surprised, and turned his head to look along Upper Wimpole Street and the knots of people clustered there. Then he grunted in agreement, and we followed Pons into a small teashop on the next block.

We were seated and sipping tea when we learned that Jamison was impatient. "There has been no crime here," he said, "so I believe that I'll withdraw the constable and be off. Although," he mused, his tone softening, "I'll admit that this is interesting, and that the return of the snuffbox is some indication that brother Charles may have survived the fire in Brazil. However, I'm more inclined to think it likely that a stranger brought the box home to Kenneth Lemuel."

"I agree, Pons," I said. "That would explain why the man didn't wait, but instead simply gave the box into Wilson's keeping and walked away."

"I might have had thought that, too," said Pons, "if not for one other factor that you haven't known to consider."

"What's that?" demanded Jamison.

"The message that was in the snuffbox." And so saying, he reached into an inner pocket and retrieved a tiny square of folded blue paper, not more than an inch each way. Spreading it open, he held it up so we could see it:

"'*Mondego*'" read Jamison, puzzled.

"Where was it?" I asked. "It wasn't in the snuffbox when we examined it in Praed Street."

"I found it by the front step, near the blood stains."

I recalled how he had looked around while we waited for the constable to fetch Jamison. "But how do you know it came from the snuffbox?" I asked.

"Smell it."

I did, and the aroma of snuff, the same smell that I'd encountered just an hour or so before, served again to remind me of my grandfather. "I believe that this slip of paper was in the snuffbox when Kenneth Lemuel opened it in the dining room. His wife wasn't paying attention, or else she wasn't in a position to see. The inherent meaning of the message was enough to send him racing to the street. When he came out on the step and his feet slipped, it must have been in his hand, and it fell away when he lost consciousness."

"This Mondego," interrupted Jamison. "Is he the man who delivered the snuffbox?"

"No. But the presence of this note elevates the matter to a level of greater concern than might have been previously indicated."

Jamison growled. "As usual, you know more than I do. Whatever this note means, you were already aware of it when we spoke to Mrs. Lemuel, and also when you warned the doctor to be cagy when describing his condition." He lowered is voice. "Is he in danger still?"

"He *is* – and not necessarily from his concussion. Certainly his condition leaves him in a helpless state, as I'm sure you see."

Jamison's expression turned from irritation to concern. "If someone is going to try and get at him, I'll double his protection. He isn't going to be left as some tethered goat to trap a killer."

"I agree," said Pons, "although catching someone in the act is certainly worth more in court than simply the discovery of an implied threat."

Jamison nodded. "I see your point, If we're too obvious about guarding the injured man, this Mondego will be warned off for now, and who's to say that he won't go away, only to return in a month, or a year, or even longer."

"An extra man in the house, along with the constable by the doorway, should be sufficient. And one other thing . . . ."

"Yes?"

"It wouldn't hurt to have whoever is on duty at the door, Ferrers or his relief, pass on to whomever questions them that you're still searching for the boy who attacked Kenneth Lemuel – and that the man is expected to make a full recovery."

Jamison smiled. "I understand. And what will you be doing in the meantime?"

"I'll initiate another line or two of inquiry."

"No doubt using those lads of yours."

"That is a distinct possibility."

"You can tell me now – how are they involved?"

Between us, Pons and I shared the events leading to our arrival at the Lemuel house, along with what we knew of Karl Drayton's unfortunate history. Jamison seemed moved by it.

"Poor lad," he muttered.

Pons stood, and we joined him. "We must be about our business," he said. "We'll see you soon, back at the Lemuel house."

"Playing it close, aren't you?" grimaced Jamison, but it was in a good-natured way, and I knew that he was pleased that Pons had taken charge of whatever was happening, since it was unlikely – nay, impossible – that Jamison would have recognized the situation on his own, and that a tragedy might have occurred but for Pons's unforeseen involvement.

We parted then, Jamison to arrange for a second man to keep watch at the Lemuel house, while Pons and I walked east. In Portland Place, nearly to New Cavendish Street, Pons's searching glances were rewarded upon finding one Trey Billings, third son of a coal-man, and a some-time Praed Street Irregular. The transfer of a coin sent the boy into motion, and in less than thirty minutes, Alfred Peake presented himself to us on the same corner.

"How is Karl?" was Pons's first question. Alfred replied that he was somewhat better, and that the shock of seeing the blood – for that is what he believed had precipitated the boy's condition – seemed to have abated with the consumption of a hot meal, as prepared by Alfred's mother.

Pons nodded and explained that he needed a number of the lads to position themselves around Upper Wimpole Street. "I believe that the man you saw this morning, who knocked on the door, will return, either openly to inquire about the injured man's condition, or possibly in a more surreptitious manner."

Alfred frowned at this word, but Pons never mitigated his vocabulary for him, and I knew that Alfred would puzzle out what he meant. In the meantime, Pons continued. "If this man should return and then depart, follow him. If he should try to get in, notify the constable at the door. Any questions?"

The leader of the Irregulars shook his head and dashed off. Pons and I then made our way back to the Lemuel residence. We found Jamison standing out front, with Constables Ferrers and Tracy. Pons directed them a few dozen feet away, and I knew he wanted to prevent anything being overheard by the curious Wilson.

Jamison had already briefed them, but he reiterated that the man who delivered the snuffbox earlier in the day might return to check on the condition of the injured man. "Don't look, but he may even be amongst the people watching from up the street right now." He added that, should the man approach Ferrell or his relief on the front steps, he should only be told that Kenneth Lemuel's condition was guardedly optimistic.

"And me, Mr. Pons?" asked Constable Tracy. "What shall I do?"

"You will find a comfortable chair and keep watch in the hallway outside the injured man's door. All night long, or until Jamison arranges for you to be relieved."

"In case this fellow gets inside?"

Pons nodded, and dismissed the men to their duties. Then he turned to Jamison. "Any luck in reaching Sir Chase?"

Jamison shook his head. "His bank informs me that he's in Monte Carlo on urgent business. I've sent a wire."

"In the meantime, Parker and I will track down the third Lemuel brother, Clifford."

"That's a good idea," agreed Jamison. "He was in Brazil when this whole business started. He might be able to give us some insight, or to tell us something about 'Mondego'."

"One more thing," added Pons. And he whispered a word or two to Constable Tracy, whose eyes widened as he nodded. Returning to us, he said to Jamison, "Word sent to Praed Street will reach us." And we parted.

We found a cab, and Pons gave an address in The City. Traffic was light, and in no time we were entering a staid and ponderous building, tucked between more sizeable structures on Bartholomew Lane. This, then, was Sir Chase's bank.

Pons identified himself and asked to speak to a certain officer of the institution who must remain nameless. The victim of a particularly seamy blackmail scheme, he had been rescued, almost collaterally, when Pons arranged the downfall of the blackmailer. Since then, the man had been quite grateful, although in our subsequent encounters, I had always seen a shiftiness and resentful shame in his eyes, as he recalled what we had learned about his private life. Pons had made use of him on two occasions since the man had been salvaged, and each of those encounters, in a pub in a different part of town, had been awkward at best. Now, here we were, sitting in the man's office. He was understandably nervous.

Learning our purpose – specifically, to locate Clifford Lemuel – did nothing to lessen the man's unease. However, he quickly confirmed that Lemuel was an employee of the bank – "of sorts" he sniffed in disdain – explaining that the young man carried out various chores for Sir Chase.

"I understand that Sir Chase is currently in Monte Carlo," said Pons.

"He is. As you may know, it's almost certain that Germany is going to default on their reparations. The financial leaders are working on a plan."

Pons was not interested. "When will Sir Chase return?"

"The end of the week, I expect."

"We will need both Clifford Lemuel's address, and a way to reach Sir Chase."

The fellow complied without comment, and in a moment, we had the information, written on a sheet of bank stationery. "Thank you, then. We shall be in touch."

The man frowned, and I realized with a bit of chagrin that, in being freed from the blackmailer, the fellow had simply been passed to a different master, although Pons, who would only press the fellow for information when necessary, was certainly not the same sort of quicksand in which the man had previously been trapped.

In a cab, Pons called out Clifford Lemuel's address in Piccadilly, nearly to Park Lane, just across from the Green Park. We were both lost in thought, and I was surprised at how quickly the cabbie announced, "No. 112, guv'."

The building was a noted residential hotel, offering luxurious apartments to the wealthy, many of them younger sons of the nobility. We made our way upstairs unhindered and so on to Clifford Lemuel's rooms. I started to knock, but Pons plucked at my sleeve. "A moment, Parker." And he indicated the doorframe, where a thin thread of light indicated that the door was not quite shut. He gave it a push, and it opened slowly. I coughed – the widening of the opening had allowed the smell trapped inside to waft out – a smell of death.

There is little to tell. The man, later verified to be Clifford Lemuel, was stretched flat on his back in the center of the foyer, his eyes opened in wide surprise as he pondered the molded ceiling. A hole, surrounded by scorched cloth, was centered over his heart. There was no bleeding to speak of.

Pons waved me back while he began to examine the scene. He pulled a pocket tape measure from his pocket, measuring distances on the expensive carpet. He used a thin metal probe to prod the area of the wound, obviously a bullet wound fired from a gun pressed against the man's chest. As there was no blood on the carpet, I assumed (correctly, as it was later determined) that the gun was of a small caliber, resulting in the bullet remaining in the body. The gun's size, along with its proximity to the body at the time of the shot, helped to explain where there was likely very little noise to attract anyone's attention when the man died – and that must have been instantaneous.

Finally, Pons stood up, nodding. "I have identified the man's footprints and his height, based on his stride. The most interesting fact is this." And he nodded toward a blue square of paper on the floor, resting beside the dead man's right hand. I had seen it from the beginning, but its meaning was no more clear to me than the other, which had been delivered with the Obrisset snuffbox just a few hours earlier:

An hour later, Jamison had joined us, along with a number of constables and Scotland Yard scientists. He didn't quite know what reaction to take – amazement that another incident had occurred, this one clearly murder, and obviously connected with the first, or shock at the news he brought with him.

"Sir Chase is dead," he said. "I just received word, right before your message arrived."

"Murdered as well?" I asked, stunned at how quickly the rapidity of the events had escalated.

"No, it seems as if it is an accident. He was being driven last night along one of the corniche roads that run along the cliffs from Nice to Monte Carlo, and the brakes failed on his automobile. Both he and the driver died in the accident. Word just reached us."

"If you wouldn't mind," said Pons, "would you send word to the local police to see if one of these notes was found with Sir Chase? In his pockets, or the vehicle? Or perhaps with the papers in his rooms?"

"Another note?" asked Jamison. "Do you think that it wasn't an accident after all?"

"I don't want to grant the possibility of coincidence until all other possibilities have been examined. Have them look for a blue piece of paper. Possibly, although I shouldn't stick my neck out quite this far yet, it will have written upon it the word '*Danglars*'".

Jamison's eyes widened, and he started to ask a question before stopping himself. He simply turned away and made a call on the room's telephone, passing on Pons's request. In a few moments, he returned. "They'll let us know," he said. "Now what?"

"We'll continue to be on the lookout for our mystery man, but in the meantime, we wait. I believe that he will reveal himself through his curiosity about the situation in Upper Wimpole Street, and the Irregulars will track him. I'm not sure what his plan was, but Kenneth Lemuel falling and injuring himself was definitely not what he expected, or how he intended to accomplish his task."

"Murder, you mean," I said. "He meant to kill Kenneth Lemuel as well, but not simply by having him fall and hit his head."

"Exactly. If he asks about Lemuel's condition, he will be told that the prognosis is good, and he'll know that he has to stay and complete his work."

"He," said Jamison. "Then this man must be the oldest brother, Charles."

"I believe it's likely. Only he can tell us his story, but he's now decided to return to this part of the world in a quest for vengeance."

"Two down, one to go," said Jamison. "Or are there others?"

"There may be one or two others, but based on the names he has written on the papers, I believe that, with the death of his brother Kenneth, his work will be complete."

"The names!" exploded Jamison. "You obviously recognize them! What do they mean?"

"Ah, not yet, Inspector," smiled Pons. "It will add nothing to your efforts, and in the meantime, you can wrack your memory now, or curse your lack of education later."

"And now?" I asked.

"And now," he repeated, "we wait. You can reach us in Praed Street, Inspector."

With his pieces in place, and a notification that we should be notified if anything of importance occurred, we returned to our rooms.

Sometime in the middle of the afternoon, I roused myself and checked the scrapbooks that Pons maintained, consisting of countless annotated clippings and jottings that served as the physical annex to his great mind. He watched with amusement as I pulled out the spectacularly fat "*M*" volume – one of his finest, he maintained. There was no listing for *Mondego*, and likewise, there was nothing in "*C*" for *Caderousse* or "*D*" for *Danglars*. I was bound that I would not ask if he chose to preserve the significance of the names in order to effect one of his dramatic revelations at the end of the case.

"You're looking in the wrong book," he said cryptically and with a smile, but instead of responding, I simply returned the scrapbooks to their places and settled back in my chair. Later, when Pons had gone out for a few minutes to send a few telegrams, I glanced over at the different bookshelves scattered about, hoping to see which specific book that he actually meant, but I observed nothing that would seem to provide the information that I sought.

The afternoon passed, with the monotony only broken twice – once when Pons received a telegram, and a second time when young Trey Billings presented himself, just a moment later, proudly but succinctly stating a certain address in Hackney.

"Excellent," said Pons, rising to his feet and scribbling a reply to the wire. "I've asked Jamison to join us." We gathered our coats and hats and went out to the street, pausing only when Pons handed a telegram form to Mrs. Johnson, asking that it be sent immediately. Soon, we were in a cab, speeding to the northeast.

Pons handed me the telegram, which was from Jamison. I read: *Blue note with the word "Danglars" found in Sir Chase's papers.* I folded the telegram and put it in my pocket, intending to discuss it with Pons more thoroughly, but he had already turned his attention to questioning the boy.

"The man you're looking for came up to the constable, not a half-hour after you left. Alfred recognized him, but the constable gave us the sign as well that the man was asking about the sick fellow inside. After that, he started walking, north and east. He was easy to follow. He moves slow, like he's hurt."

Pons nodded, and asked a few other questions about the building where the man had gone to ground. "A rooming house in Fenn Street," answered Trey. "Alfred and the others have it watched from all sides."

"Very good." He looked at me. "You have your revolver, Parker?"

I nodded, having learned long ago never to leave Praed Street without it.

There was no more conversation until our cab came to a halt in front of Sutton House in Homerton High Street, where we found Jamison and a number of policemen already present. "It was lucky that I received your wire," said the inspector. "I was just going back to Upper Wimpole Street to question Mrs. Lemuel."

"Whatever for?" asked Pons with surprise.

"To see if she might be in collusion with this former fiancé of hers. If so, then her husband would be in that much more danger, with her right there in the house."

"Although I think putting her on her guard would have been a mistake," said Pons, "I agree with your thinking. That's why I had a word with Constable Tracy, telling him to take extra care whenever Mrs. Lemuel was spending time with her husband."

Jamison shook his head with a smile. "Always two steps ahead!"

Pons sent young Trey scampering off, and in a moment he returned with Alfred Peake and, surprisingly, Karl Drayton as well. They approached rather skittishly, as if expecting a policeman to lunge for them. Instead, Jamison cleared his throat and questioned them about the layout of the house. "He has the back room on the second floor," said Alfred. "We saw him open the curtains after he went in."

"Very good," replied the inspector before deploying his men. Then, warning the boys to stay a safe distance away, we maneuvered down the block and into Fenn Street. With his men surrounding the house, we entered quietly and made our way upstairs.

Our quarry was taken unawares, literally caught napping. As he awoke and realized what was happening, he fought like a tiger, throwing himself from side to side, but he was no match for the two burly constables that held him, and it was soon apparent that he was unwell, and had not the strength to maintain a prolonged resistance. After he stopped fighting, and following Jamison's declaration that he was under arrest and his words might be used against him, he seemed to adopt an almost friendly tone.

As Jamison scribbled in a small brown notebook, Charles Lemuel said, "What does it matter? My work is done."

"Is it?" said Pons. "Your brother Kenneth may recover."

"Even if he does, he'll know that I survived what he did to me. He'll never have a moment's peace."

"And what exactly *did* he do?" I asked, as we all stood around the captive, who sat manacled between the two constables.

"He thought that he had killed me, so that he could marry my fiancé, Hilda."

"How?" asked Pons.

"We were in Rio de Janerio, my brothers and I, arranging for credits from the bank, should Brazil enter the War. While we were there, the Germans torpedoed a Brazilian ship, and riots broke out. We knew enough to stay out of the way, and we were supposed to leave in a couple of days. But one night, the mobs began making their way down the street where our rooms were located. Our brother Clifford was out, and Kenneth and I watched from our window as the people approached, breaking windows, and even tossing torches into buildings. I was still looking from the window when they passed us by. I turned to comment about our lucky escape when I saw Kenneth standing behind me with the fireplace poker.

"He was smiling, saying that this opportunity was too good to pass up. He swung, and I blocked him with my hand." He held it up, showing the scar across the back, a wormy red weal that looked as if it had never healed properly. "I tried to reason with him, asking him why he was doing this thing. He said that he had always wanted Hilda, but that I had prevented him from having her. He said the same was true at the bank - I had used my position as elder brother to block him from advancement.

"Still believing then that he could be calmed, I tried to promise him that we could work something out, but I could see that he was set. He began to laugh, saying that Sir Chase, and even our brother Clifford, would welcome my death, as it would solve so many problems for them. Later, after my survival, I saw how Kenneth had been rewarded with the hand of the woman who should have been mine, and how Clifford's position had advanced as well, and I knew that what he said must be true - even if Kenneth was the one who tried to kill me, the others were not sorry.

"He continued to advance with the poker, and I tried to back away across the room. He followed, swinging again, this time catching me across the shoulder. I felt something break, and I fell. In doing so, the carpet underneath my feet was pushed into the fire.

"Kenneth approached and hit me again and again. Once, a blow landed on my head, and I lost consciousness. Perhaps it was then that he believed me finally dead, for he stopped hitting me. As I watched through slitted eyes, hoping that he would think me finished so that he would let me alone, he laughed and began to build up the fire. He took the lamps and poured the oil on the furniture and walls, and across the floor. He did what he could to spread the flames, and when it was burning uncontrollably, he left. I heard the front door slam, leaving me alone in a burning building.

"I should have died then. I lost consciousness, and only awakened days later, in the care of a man who had ventured into the burning building - one might like to credit him with heroism, but I believe that he was in truth a looter. Although our building had been burned by my brother's arson, it was only one of many that went up in flames on that street due to the angry mobs, and therefore there was no suspicion about the cause of that particular fire.

"For the longest time, I had no memory of who I was, or what had happened – a result, no doubt, of the blows to my head. I gradually came to learn that some past act on my part – a kind word in the street, possibly, although I don't know the specifics – had caused my rescuer to pull me from the flames. He and his family cared for me, and as I had no memories of my past, I was quite happy to stay there. But nothing lasts, and my simple peace began to be disturbed by flashes of memory. Gradually, these separate scenes stitched themselves together, and I understood who I was, what had been taken from me, and who had taken it.

"It took quite a while, but I was finally able to make my way back to England. I could have obtained passage in an instant by contacting our Embassy, or by reaching out to any of a dozen people. But I wanted to return in secret.

"You can guess the rest. I arrived a week or so ago, and set about following my enemies – my brothers, and Sir Chase. It nearly killed me when I saw my Hilda from a distance, and it only served to firm my resolve. First, I sent a note to my former employer, and the man who would have been my father-in-law, hoping that he would understand."

"With the name '*Danglars*'," interrupted Pons. "Because he was the banker."

An odd look came across Charles Lemuel's face, but it softened into a smile. "*You* understand. *You* must be the fellow that led the police here, then. I should have just killed them. But I've always had a poetic streak."

Pons nodded for him to continue. "I found out that he was going to Monte Carlo. I should have waited until he returned, but I wanted him to be the first. I made my way over there two days ago and tinkered with the brakes on his car. It might or might not get him. If not, I could try again."

"It worked," said Jamison. "His car went over the cliff, killing him, along with his innocent chauffeur."

"Innocent!" the man shouted, instantly inflamed into rage. "None of them are innocent! I know what we were doing in the War, and how the money was supposed to be used. And from all of that suffering, they – Sir Chase and others like him – amassed fortunes! Anyone in his pay, including this chauffeur, are *evil!*"

His breathing had grown ragged, and he hunched over, as if he was in pain, but gradually he calmed himself, and his red face smoothed into a sardonic smile. "And then there was Clifford."

"*Caderousse*," said Pons.

Charles Lemuel nodded. "Yes. The greedy one. I wasn't sure if he was guilty – at least, in terms of what happened to me, although he was certainly willing to take Sir Chase's ill-gotten money. Late last night, I slipped into his hotel and confronted him."

"And killed him," added Pons.

"Well, yes, of course. He had to pay, you see. And then it was Kenneth's turn."

"So you went there this morning, not to kill him outright, but to make him suffer first."

"You do understand."

"*Mondego*," said Pons. "The betrayer."

"Yes, yes. For love. Because he wanted the woman."

"Wait!" cried Jamison, raising his eyes from his notebook. "Enough! Before we go any further, explain these names!"

"Certainly," said Pons. "You really should read more, Jamison. They come from *The Count of Monte Cristo*."

I felt like slapping my forehead. "Of course! The villains who betrayed Edmond Dantes."

"Exactly. During the years that Dantes is falsely imprisoned, Danglars makes a fortune and becomes a banker." He glanced at Charles Lemuel. "Close enough to Sir Chase, I imagine?"

The captive nodded and smiled. Pons continued. "Caderousse was incredibly jealous of Dantes."

He glanced at Lemuel, who said, "And Clifford was jealous of me as well. No doubt, in spite of his denials, that's why he allowed me to be killed without question."

Pons resumed. "Finally, Fernand Mondego was the man who initially betrayed Dantes in order to have Mercedes, Dantes' true love. Hence, the tenuous link with brother Kenneth."

"Yes. Kenneth always wanted Hilda, and this was his way of having her. And you managed to get on my trail because I left the name for him in the snuffbox," mused Charles Lemuel. "That was a mistake."

"Indeed."

Jamison finished scratching the last of his notes while the rest of us reposed in silence. Then, closing the notebook and placing it in his pocket, he stood, motioning the constables to remove the prisoner.

Downstairs, Pons knocked on the landlady's door. She opened it to see Lemuel being shuffled out the door by a brace of constables. Her surprise was manifest. Pons had one question for her: "Might I know the name of the fellow that's being arrested?"

She swallowed, nodded, and then spoke timidly. "That's Mr. Dantes. He . . . he said he was in town on business."

Pons smiled and thanked her, and we stepped outside.

Seeing that the matter was settled, a group of boys began to appear from all directions of the compass. As they approached, they formed up behind Alfred Peak and Karl Drayton.

Pons thanked them for their service, and indicated that he would settle up with Alfred later. They grinned and began to disperse. "Hold on," interrupted Jamison. "You two. Wait just a minute."

Alfred looked worried, while Karl simply turned his gaze toward the ground. I worried that the gruff voice of the policeman would make him bolt again. But then, Jamison surprised me with a tone that contrasted sharply with his previous words.

"Lad," he said softly to the tall boy. "Where do you live?"

Karl shook his head, as if a fly was buzzing around his ears.ABgently, Jamison repeated the question. Karl raised his eyes then, and they had a most lonely look. "Around," he said.

"We all take care of him," interrupted Alfred. "He's one of us."

"That's what I thought," said Jamison. He took a deep breath. "We, that is, the missus and me, have several of our own. Children, that is. And . . . well, what I mean is, that . . . I suppose one more . . . that is . . . I don't think it would be a problem if you were to stay with us. It would be a good thing, I think."

Karl had watched Jamison's face during this somewhat awkward invitation. Short as it was, there was time for a gamut of emotions to pass through Karl's eyes as they widened. After Jamison finished speaking, leaving the offer hanging, the silence grew to the point of nearly being embarrassing. Then, with a sharp prod from Alfred's elbow, Karl swallowed and nodded. There was almost a smile on his face – but not quite yet. Soon . . . .

As Jamison put an arm around the boy and walked him to one side, Alfred beamed and back and forth from Pons to me. Then, standing straighter, he said, "I'll come by in the morning."

"See that you do, Peake," said Pons with a smile.

Later that evening, as we each smoked a pipe in front of our sitting room fire. "Dr. Cates sent word that Kenneth Lemuel is improving."

Pons frowned. "I'm not sure that the physical improvement will offset the decline in his fortunes once his brother's story becomes known. His benefactor, Sir Chase, is dead, as well as his brother, and his wife will now know the truth of what he did to her initial fiancé. No, I don't believe that Kenneth Lemuel's situation has improved at all."

"At least," I said, "things are looking up for Karl Drayton. Who could have known that events would play out in this fashion?"

"More than you realize, Parker."

"How so?"

He thought for a moment, and then said, "You and I have discussed coincidence and fate before. I did not believe it to be a coincidence that Clifford Lemuel should be killed just as his brother received a message that caused him such distress. Likewise, that Sir Chase should die from an unfortunate car accident along a cliff when these other events took place was quite unlikely. That dismissal of coincidence led me to ask whether a blue note was found in Sir Chase's effects."

"I see your point."

"No, for I haven't made it yet. I have dismissed coincidence, but one cannot ignore the Hand of Fate in this matter."

"Really, Pons? Espousing Fate? You?"

"I cannot ignore it. In the great scheme of things, the players were on the board in such a way that Alfred and Karl were across the street from the Lemuel house when brother Charles arrived. That in itself is not necessarily fate – simply one of the millions of random interactions that occur throughout any given day. But one small action, just one, led to the discovery of a crime that might have otherwise passed unnoticed. I refer to the instant when Karl's hand closed on the Obrisset snuffbox, just as he was being challenged by Constable Ferrers.

"For if he hadn't picked it up – if he'd left it there on the street – nothing would have been discovered. Alfred would have still come to us with his tale, but we would have likely just sent word to the officials that they were looking in the wrong direction, as Kenneth Lemuel had slipped and hit his head. We probably wouldn't have gone to Upper Wimpole Street, the *Mondego* message would have remained undiscovered in the leaves by the doorway, the death of Sir Chase would have been filed as an accident, and the death of Clifford Lemuel in the hotel in Piccadilly, even with its mysterious note, would have probably been classified as an unsolved crime, as that note would seem to have had no connection with anything else."

"Still," I argued, "the very oddity of Clifford Lemuel's murder, with the curious blue note and the word *Caderousse*, might have come to your attention."

"True, but things would have played out very differently. Without the corresponding note at Upper Wimpole Street, I might have been tempted to put down the death of one brother and the accidental hitting of his head following the receipt of a snuffbox – with the note inside still undiscovered – as that coincidence which I so despise. Even learning of Sir Chase's death, should it have come to my attention at all, might not have led to a solution. Things worked out that Charles Lemuel was caught because we had enough time to set the Irregulars in place if he came back asking questions.

"No, it appears to me that, if Karl hadn't brought the snuffbox away with him, events might have taken a very different path. So I put it to you, Parker, that this was a matter involving Fate."

He was silent after that, continuing to ponder the convoluted and alternative possibilities, even after his pipe went out. He was still there when I said goodnight and made my way upstairs to sleep.

# The Folio Matter

"Mr. Pons! You must come with me at once!"

From his seat at the breakfast table, Solar Pons looked toward the door with amusement. "General York! What a surprise! Will you join us?"

I could see our landlady, Mrs. Johnson, as an expression of frustration crossed her face. Clearly she had tried to stop our visitor from barging in during the morning meal, but General Eustace York had never been a man to take no for an answer, as he had demonstrated at the Battle of Megiddo, nearly eleven years earlier. His skills at maneuvering the use of aeroplanes, artillery, infantry, and cavalry had led to a decisive breakthrough, allowing the Allies to quickly take Damascus and Aleppo. Even now, in the early days of his eighth decade, he was a force with which to reckon.

The general looked impatient. "There is no time. You must come with me now. I'll explain on the way!"

Pons stood and tossed his napkin down upon the table beside his barely begun breakfast. With a snort of disgust, Mrs. Johnson turned and, pulling the door shut behind her, started back downstairs.

I looked at my half-finished meal, thankful that I had reached the table somewhat before Pons and had been able to consume at least some of my bacon and eggs. Taking a long drink of coffee and then pushing a piece of toast into my mouth, I stood and joined Pons as we retrieved our coats and hats.

Outside, the March air was damp, and I shrugged my coat collar closer to my neck before climbing into the general's car. His chauffeur slammed the door behind us, climbed in, and set off down Praed Street to nearby Edgware Road before turning south.

I knew that Pons would not have dropped everything and simply departed without an explanation for just anyone. But he held the general in high regard, based upon work that they had done together during the War. Since that time, they had stayed in touch, and I had gotten to know the old warrior as well, often trading reminiscences about our past days in Egypt over glasses of whisky.

"Is this in reference to the recent theft of your papers?" asked Pons. "I would have been around sooner to offer my assistance, but I've only finished up that nasty business of the Seven Fingered Necklace."

The general waved impatiently. "So I understood from Bancroft."

I interrupted. "I'm sorry, but I haven't seen any news in a week. What papers?"

"My research," said the old man. "Into the true authorship, you know."

I understood immediately, and noted a twinkle in Pons's eye. It had long been a bee in the general's bonnet, shared by a good many others as well, that William Shakespeare was not the true author of those works attributed to him. The general's personal candidate for the actual bard was Edward de Vere, 17th Earl of Oxford. In fact, our friend had contributed significantly to a work earlier in the decade outlining that very theory.

"What did they get?" asked Pons.

"Some notes copied from manuscripts during my trip abroad. A rough draft of my latest treatise. But most importantly, the folio edition that I bought late last year in Rome." He lowered his voice. "It was rumored to come from the Vatican Libraries!"

"Tut, tut," chided Pons. "Dealing in stolen properties, General? Just knowing about it places Parker and myself in danger of being scooped up as accessories."

The old man snorted. "It wasn't stated as such, just implied. And there has never been any announcement from the Vatican that anything of the sort was stolen. In any case, it needed to go to someone like me, who could appreciate what it revealed, rather than simply into some anonymous collector's case."

"What were the circumstances of the theft?"

The general braced himself as the car swung smoothly around the Marble Arch and continued south. "It was last Tuesday evening, a few hours after dinner. I was working in my study, and Eloise was up in her parlor. The housekeeper and her girls were downstairs. I heard a knock at the front door and went to answer it."

It was a peculiarity of the general and his wife that they lived quite frugally – that is, as much as one can when inhabiting a fine home in Mayfair. Always contrary, the General had long eschewed the use of a full stable of servants. Instead, his wife insisted on a housekeeper-cook and few couple of maids, and the general made do with his old batman, now ensconced as the establishment's butler, but there were no other regular servants on the premises. In keeping with his democratic attitudes, the general took on a number of duties himself, including answering the door if he was nearby. Just such a thing had happened on the night of the robbery.

"I opened the door to find a figure huddled against my doorframe. He was painfully thin, and dressed in robes, obviously some sort of Lascar. Before I could demand what he wanted, he pulled himself upright and forced his way into the house.

"I yelled for Bettelman to come help, and of course that drew Eloise's attention. I was attempting to stop the man from pushing further into the hall, and I was doing a good job at holding him there when everyone came piling in behind me. Between us, Bettelman and I got the fellow by the arms, whereupon he gave up. It was at that point that the policemen showed up."

"Very timely," said Pons wryly.

"Indeed. They said that they had been passing by and heard the commotion. It was a sergeant and two constables. In the dim light of the hall, I ended up paying too much attention to the prisoner, and not enough to the official force – at least not at first.

"They took charge of the man, and then told us that we would all be required to come with them to the police station to make a statement. This seemed outrageous to me, as there was no need to involve my wife and the servants in such a tactic. Even as I started to argue against it, for it was quite a raw night, and my wife and the other women certainly couldn't add anything to our testimony, I happened to notice the shabby state of one of the constables. His buttons were mismatched, and his boots were not the regular heavy issues of the official force. I began to suspect a rat."

Pons laughed. "Ha! A man after our own hearts, Parker. Please continue, General. This is unique in my experience."

The general nodded. We had by this time turned into that warren of streets to the west of Berkeley Square, specifically Hill Street. We pulled up before the general's handsome but unobtrusive quarters, but he made no move to disembark from the vehicle.

"After I made it clear that we would certainly not be going to the police station, the sergeant shook his head. 'That's too bad,' he said. 'We'll have to do it the hard way, then.' And he pulled a gun, even as the two constables released the Lascar, who stood up beside them."

"A ploy," said Pons. "Intended to get all of you out of the house."

"Indeed. We all ended up herded into the front parlor, guarded by the two false constables and the Lascar. In the meantime, the man pretending to be a sergeant made himself at home in my study across the hall, picking out the items that I've mentioned to carry away.

"When he was finished, he impertinently thanked me, and they all hustled out and disappeared. I immediately rushed out to give the alarm, but it was no use. They were already gone."

"I'll do everything that I can to help," said Pons, "and I'm sorry that I wasn't available sooner, but I'm not sure what has caused the urgency this morning."

"There's more to the story," snapped the irascible officer. Pons motioned for him to continue.

"When it became apparent that the police were not going to offer any help, I decided to take matters into my own hands."

"I don't like the sound of this," said Pons, but with a small smile. The general saw it and returned a frank grin. "I gave a few interviews to the newspapers, lamenting about the robbery, and making sure to mention that the thieves had missed the best and most important parts of the papers."

"Surely not!" I said. "You were setting yourself up for another attack."

"Exactly."

"And did they return?"

"Yes, last night. There was another knock at the door, same as before, and when I opened it, they came charging in. But we'd been prepared, Bettelman and I. Upon each night since the story had appeared in the newspapers, the women had stayed away, in the home of my sister. Bettelman had brought in his nephews, two cousins from Bushey. For my part, I had secured both gas masks from the armory, as well as several spray bottles containing chloroform from a chemist friend of mine. We were waiting for them when they burst in, wearing our masks, and before they knew what had hit them, we'd sprayed all four in the face! Down they went!"

He laughed and slapped his knee, and Pons and I joined in at the picture of the intruders' complete and surprising defeat.

When we stopped laughing, Pons asked, "And what did the police learn from interviewing them?"

"I didn't call the police."

"What?"

"No, I still have them."

"In your house? Prisoners?"

"That's right. The police were no help before. We tied them up last night and stood guard. They wouldn't talk to me, so I hot-footed it over to Praed Street this morning as soon as it was decent. It would have been rude to knock you up any earlier."

Pons and I looked at one another for a moment, and then burst out laughing once more. "General," said my friend, "you truly represent all that is the best of us. Lead on!"

Inside, we were greeted by Bettelman, the batman-turned-butler. He nodded to us, and then gestured with the pistol in his hand toward the front parlor, overlooking the street. "No trouble, General," he advised.

We followed our host into the room, lit by a couple of table lamps. The front curtains were drawn. In the shadows by the doorway were two large and similar men, no doubt the batman's nephews. Their resemblance to Bettelman confirmed their family connection.

With the general's permission, Pons opened the drapes, and then turned to look at the four men tied on the floor. The Lascar was obvious, as were the two constables, both in their early twenties, and looking resentful. Pons gave quick but discerning glances at the first three, but reserved most of his attention for the sergeant, looking back at him with a rueful grin.

"This is a fine mess, Deavers," said the detective to the prisoner.

"That's the truth, Mr. Pons," replied the man with a low rumble. "As you might expect, it wasn't quite supposed to work out like this."

"I expect not."

One of the faux constables hissed at Deavers, only to receive a rebuke. "Hush, Hammond. We was caught fair an' proper." Turning back to Pons, he added, "That's my son. I've done a poor job of parenting, as I suspect you'll agree."

"It's true that you might have made different choices," agreed Pons. "And the other two?"

"Him on the end, the Lascar, is Alim. And then there's Long Lester, as we call him." He lowered his voice, while glancing at the second constable. "He isn't quite right."

Pons turned toward the general and me. "I've known Deavers for years. He was a prize-fighter, essentially harmless." Then, over his shoulder, "Isn't that right, Deavers?"

"Right as rain, Mr. Pons. We just needed the money. Our guns weren't even loaded."

"That was even more foolhardy, considering whose home you invaded. Don't you know who this is?"

"General York, I was told."

"That's right. York of Megiddo."

Deavers looked blank for a moment, and then recognition flooded his face as he realized the chance that he had inadvertently taken. He squirmed a bit, straightening out as best he could on the floor. "My apologies, General. I didn't know. I was at Aleppo."

The general cleared his throat, clearly in an awkward spot, accepting respect from a twice-intruder who had been his prisoner for the last twelve hours. He cleared his throat again.

"General," interjected Pons, "I understand that the sanctity of your home has been repeatedly violated, although your defense was brilliant. However, I believe that a little leniency might go a long way toward finding out who is behind this – "

"I'll tell you anyway, Mr. Pons," interrupted Deavers. Pons glanced toward the prisoners, while the shadow of a grin tightened the general's lips.

"Hush," said Pons, "I'm negotiating." Turning back to the septuagenarian, he added, "That is, if you're willing."

The general gave the appearance of grave thought, but it was clear that his mind was already made up. "Turn them loose," he finally growled. "Can't be cluttering up the jails and the courts, and I've always found that a little mercy goes a long way." A wave of his hand toward the cousins from Bushey set them into motion, untying ropes and helping the four men, no now longer prisoners, to their feet.

"Now," said the general, placing himself in front of Deavers and looking up into the big man's face, "about that name."

"Yes, sir." Deavers pulled himself taller, arms to his sides. "It was Webster Archer, general. He hired us, and told us exactly what to get. He said he'd been here before, and told me right where to look."

"And he came up with this unique plan to get the general and his people out of the house," added Pons.

"Exactly."

The general was looking at the floor, and clearly fit to be tied. "Webster Archer!" he roared, his head snapping up. "That traitor! The man has been a guest in my home! And now, to do something like this . . . ."

"Archer, who has disagreed with you in the past?" I asked.

"The same. Friendly disagreements about the plays actually being written by de Vere. He favors Christopher Marlow – what nonsense! He couldn't stand it when I brought back the folio from Rome. He's had it stolen to destroy it!"

"Possibly not," replied Pons. "He obtained the folio last Tuesday. If destroying it was his only objective, the mission is complete. But instead, you lured him into sending his agents back with the promise of additional and better materials. Clearly, he is interested in studying the papers as well, and not simply doing away with them."

The general was always quick, and he nodded, seeing the sense in Pons's argument. "What shall we do? Go to him now?"

"Rather, Parker and I will go. With any luck, we can lay it out that his involvement is known, and we'll have everything back within the day."

And so it was agreed. Pons and I, along with Deavers and his son, Long Lester, and the Lascar Alim, quickly found ourselves on the pavement in front of the general's house, while inside calls were being made to let the women-folk know that it was safe to return. Deavers held out his hand. "Thank you, Mr. Pons. Times have been hard, but that's no excuse. I never should have gotten myself into this mess. Or these other fellows. It won't happen again."

Pons returned his handshake. "I'm sure of it." Then, taking out one of his cards, he wrote something on the back. "Contact this man. He owes me a favor or two. I suspect that, if you mention my name, he will be able to find something a little more rewarding for all of you than poorly impersonating officers of the law."

Deavers glanced at the card, and then looked again with greater intensity. "This is a mighty powerful favor indeed, Mr. Pons. Are you sure that you want to waste it on the likes of us?"

"Not a waste at all, Mr. Deavers," said Pons. "Not at all." Turning to me, he said, "Shall we, Parker?" Then he gestured toward the general's car, which had been placed at our disposal. Within moments, we were on our way to Greyshade, the home of Webster Archer.

We wound our way to Piccadilly, down St. James and through Pall Mall, and so on to Trafalgar Square and then into Whitehall. Pons was silent throughout the trip, and I left him to think, confident that he would have a scheme in mind when we reached our destination.

The sun was feebly trying to peek through as we passed between the Palace of Westminster and the Abbey. Abingdon to Millbank, thence into Church Street – our driver, clearly a former military man like his master, handled the vehicle with an easy competence, never finding the need to accelerate or suddenly stop, but rather to always fit smoothly and exactly as required into the conditions around him.

We pulled gently to the north side of Smith Square, within the shadows of Parliament, before a dark brick house, exuding quiet confidence and solidity. This was in keeping with all that I knew of Webster Archer. Scholar, Financier, Benefactor. I was having great difficulty believing that this man was involved in something so shabby.

Big Ben was just tolling in the clock tower as we climbed out of the car, Pons having anticipated our driver's efforts to open the door for us. He led the way up the low step and was ringing the doorbell by the time that I joined him. We waited patiently, and Pons was just pulling the bell a second time when the door opened, revealing a wizened fellow with a pained expression upon his face. "May I help you?"

Pons snapped his card into the man's outstretched hand. "Mr. Pons and Dr. Parker to see Mr. Archer. You might mention that it concerns General York."

At the time, I thought it might have been my imagination that the man's eyes narrowed. I was later to learn that I had been right, as this loyal servant knew why we were there. He asked us to step inside, and then bade us to wait by the door while he carried Pons's message deeper into the house.

"These are dark waters, Parker," said Pons softly, eyeing the fine pieces of furniture in the entry way.

"Why would someone as respected as Webster Archer let himself get tied up in an affair of this sort," I asked, "using agents that could so easily reveal his involvement?"

Before Pons could answer, the old man returned, indicating that we should follow him. We passed through several darkened corridors, and I could not help but feel that some sort of shadow was hanging over this household. I knew that Archer was long a widower with no children, and that he was in his twilight days. And yet, this home had always had a reputation as one of London's brighter lights. What could have altered it so much?

We were taken to a small room, quite warm from the fireplace, located underneath the marble mantelpiece across from the hallway door. Huddled in front of it, wrapped in a shawl against the damp of the day, was Webster Archer.

I had seen him before, in passing. Assisting Pons as I did, it would have been impossible not to have crossed paths with Archer at some point in the past. Although I'd never been introduced, I had long been impressed with his energy and intelligence. How could that man have been reduced to this sad figure now before us?

He waved a hand, gesturing for us to approach. "So I have been undone," he said with a weary chuckle. "I didn't handle it very well, did I? I suppose that my exposure was inevitable. I have betrayed my friend and wasted my character, and now I must end my days in ignominy."

"I don't think it has come to that quite yet," said Pons cryptically. He took another step closer. "How did he pressure you to do it?"

Archer raised his eyebrows. "How did you know – ? Ah, but that isn't important, is it?" He passed a shaking hand across his eyes. "My son," he finally replied.

I suppose that I expressed some sort of audible surprise, as Archer glanced up. "Don't be shocked, Doctor, to learn that I have an offspring. I was young once, you know, although it was long before *your* time." He smiled. "Forgive me. Won't you both have a seat?"

We made ourselves comfortable, and he continued. "My son is a good man. He knows that I am his father, and that he is my heir when the time comes. But he also understands why it cannot be acknowledged publicly – not yet. None of that is relevant, except that you must understand that our relationship is not common knowledge – it cannot be – and that is my Achilles Heel. It has long been a carefully guarded secret, but it was discovered, nonetheless. Not only did they threaten exposure. They used the threat to harm him as a way to blackmail my collection from me. I could have accepted that – I am old, and I have only been its caretaker, never its owner. But then, they insisted that I help them get the Crown Jewel from my old friend York's collection as well."

"Why?" I asked, dimly beginning to understand. "Why not just steal it? What would be accomplished by all of this rigmarole of blackmail, and using you, Mr. Archer, as a surrogate thief?"

"Destabilization," replied Pons, and Archer nodded. "It is not simply the intent here to steal the objects. They are just a component of the overall plan, whose aim is a very weakening of the British foundation."

I glanced with some puzzlement toward Pons, who had clearly divined more than I. More likely, he already had his finger on some thread related to this matter. "I was approached," interrupted Archer, "and given suggestions about how to carry out the theft. But I was to handle it myself, making all the arrangements. I was used as a tool."

It became somewhat clearer. "So not only were items stolen, but those involved are destabilized, as you said, Pons. Trust is broken, and the seeds of uncertainty sewn among former allies. I assume, then, that we are talking about our old acquaintance in Limehouse."

Pons nodded. "He is clearly ramping up for something, and this is only the latest instance. Your papers, Mr. Archer, and the general's folio, are just a few of a number of items that have been finagled away from their owners in recent months."

"I had no idea," said Archer.

"Neither did I," was my response. "What other items have been taken?"

"I first became aware of this matter several months ago," Pons answered, "when it was reported that a number of Boswell's original diaries had been tricked from their current owners, in schemes similar in nature to that aimed at the general. At the time, it seemed as if it was theft for theft's sake, and the usual routines were followed to see when the items went up for sale among that shadowy network of collectors and dealers trafficking in such stolen goods. However, no word surfaced. I had been consulted by one of the owners, and I advised at that point that all one could do would be to wait and see.

"But then I received a visitor – back when you were in Madrid, Parker. It was Lord Felman, of the British Library. He had a curious item to show me. It was one of the stolen Boswell diaries, but it had been altered, cleverly so and with great subtlety, to indicate that Samuel Johnson was a wretch of the worst sort. Pages had been completely replaced and the book resewn so that the substitution was nearly indistinguishable. The handwriting matched the original sheets around it, as did the ink itself. It was a thing of beauty, if one can step back and admire the craftsmanship of such deviltry. Lord Felman had no false pride in telling me that he doubted that there was anyone else but him that could have ferreted out the minute clues that revealed the substitution.

"Since then, other similar items have been appearing as well, each relating to diaries or documents or letters that were earlier reported stolen. Altered diaries by former P.M's such as Salisbury and Gladstone have appeared, casting doubts on both their actions and their characters. A journal belonging to Queen Victoria was stolen, only to reappear weeks later, now containing shockingly lurid details about Abdul Karim, the *Munshi*, and before him, John Brown. And just last month, following Lillie Langtry's death, her diary surfaced, listing countless names in a web that could shatter families and international alliances. Expert examination revealed that parts were forged, mixed in with the true sheets. But to a gossiping shop girl or men jawing in a pub, which is more interesting? The idea that parts may be false because someone is spreading a rumor, or graphic and lurid details repeated again and again over a round of drinks."

"I had no idea of the scale of this," said Mr. Archer.

Pons nodded. "The thefts have been orchestrated to sow discord between allies. Documents connected to Tennyson, Jane Austen, Sir Walter Scott – a dozen others – have been appearing, each with brilliantly made changes in the original, casting doubt on the integrity and behavior of the original authors. Although each item has been recovered and returned to its original owner, the forgeries are unfortunately and irretrievably a part of them now. And the rumors are starting to spread. A clerk at the auction house that received Victoria's diary, for instance, has renewed the whispers from several generations back about the inappropriate nature of the Queen's relations, now seemingly confirmed by this journal.

"More recently, documents related to King George himself, playing up the man's German ancestry, have been floating around, along with rumors of some sort of coming financial crisis. The implication seems to be that, when the crisis comes, possibly in the form of a great worldwide depression, the King will throw in his lot with his German cousins, who themselves have been in dire straits for the last decade following the War. This alliance, subjugating the British under German rule, will be swift and absolute. The appearance of the King's forged letters – or to be more accurate, the portions of forged letters mixed in with the real segments – have been seen by enough people that the story is spreading, and growing with the telling. It is almost to the point to be considered a crisis of national security.

"I've been staying peripherally involved, by way of my brother Bancroft, as this is now perceived to be an attack of sorts on some of Britain's institutions. It was through my contacts that I was able to track a brilliantly skilled Chinese forger of whom I'd long been aware. He himself had gone missing, but his family was still living in their rooms in Limehouse, and they were able to provide the connection that told me whom he was working for.

"Hence, that devil doctor," I muttered.

Pons nodded. "Correct. He has been quiet for some months, and after conferring with Smith, who has recently resigned from the Yard to go on special assignment in Bancroft's department, it appears as if this is definitely the doctor's work."

"I had no clue that it was so wide-spread," said Archer. "When my role in the matter was explained to me, it was mentioned that a similar scheme had been carried out against Sir Aiden Grimes, who has some early Dickens correspondence. It makes sense now, as I recall that these letters related to the old charges against Dickens, implying that he stole the ideas for the first chapters of *The Pickwick Papers* from the original illustrator, Robert Seymour."

"I recall that," I interrupted. "Seymour was to draw a series of plates showing various sporting scenes, and Dickens, merely a reporter at the time, was hired to write short humorous scenes to describe the plates. Instead, his story quickly overwhelmed the project, and Seymour was forced to draw his pictures to fit Dickens' narrative. After two installments, Seymour committed suicide."

Pons nodded. "By altering these Dickens letters, another foundational reputation would be ruined, slowly and steadily eroded by whispers and declarations from the ignorant who are certain that they are 'in the know'. Apparently, this scheme with the Shakespeare papers, proposing that either de Vere or Marlow was the true author, is to be carried out toward the same purpose."

Archer's eyes narrowed when it was implied that his own personal bee-in-his-bonnet, the Marlow authorship, was being played up as part of a spurious plan. But he swallowed and said, "Then you must know that another plan is also in place, with my help, I'm ashamed to say, to obtain the papers of Sir George Newnes."

"The founder of *The Strand?*" I asked.

"The same. After his death in 1910, his papers passed to his son Frank. From there, they have apparently dispersed throughout the family, with some coming to rest with my cousin, Gerald Alderbury. It was explained to me that I should conceive and arrange a theft similar to that carried out against my friend General York, only this time to obtain letters and documents between Newnes, Watson, and Doyle."

Pons raised an eyebrow. "To what purpose?"

"I gather that it was to alter these papers to indicate that Doyle was the actual author, rather than simply the Literary Agent."

Pons smiled. "Then, friend Parker, we have become involved at just the right time. Neither the Good Doctor nor Sir Arthur would appreciate that sort of literary hoax."

"And your Illustrious Predecessor – ?"

" – Could probably not care less." Pons stood up. "Thank you very much, Mr. Archer, for helping to lock the final pieces into place. It seems as if the time is now right to put a stop to this."

The old man ran a hand across his eyes. "Thank heavens that your path led to my door, and that you were able to discern my involvement."

"I can take no credit so far. It was General York who fought back, capturing the false policemen. He asked for my help, but the intruders willingly gave you up. I fear that, as a criminal spider sitting in the middle of a vast web, you are severely inexperienced, and do not invoke the terror in your minions that is required to successfully carry out such an operation. Parker and I have done nothing so far except follow a trail. But now that we're involved, I rather think that we're more than qualified to carry it to the next level."

With our thanks, we left Archer in front of the blazing fire, seemingly less careworn than when we had arrived. As we were being let outside, Archer's man seemed to give us a look of subdued gratitude. Outside, I turned to Pons. "I appreciate the sentiment that I shall be able to help, and you know that I shall accompany you to settle this when you like and where you like, but I must admit to some confusion."

"Certainly all is clear, Parker."

"Not entirely. You took him at his word a little too quickly, if you ask me. I can't see someone as powerful as the doctor dealing directly with Webster Archer, identifying himself and even explaining his plan to him. It appears that intermediaries and agents could have dealt with Archer, and the need to reveal who was behind the plot would have been completely unnecessary. Let alone telling Archer about specific details and reasons about the plot to ruin Dickens' and Watson's reputations."

"Ah, but you forget the twisted thinking of our enemy. First, a man like Archer wouldn't have succumbed to threats and blackmail from strangers, even to protect his son. He has resources still, and he would have fought back, at least at first. Only the knowledge of whom he was actually facing would convince him to roll over and act with submission. Additionally, it is actually in the interest of the doctor's plan to let aspects of the forgeries be known. After all, he cannot be unaware that the government and scholars at the British Museum and Library are onto him by now. It will help his plan to have learned men pooh-poohing these fraudulent revelations. It will only serve to fan the fires of the rumor-spreaders who love a good conspiracy, and view any attempts to explain it away as simply more evidence that it must be true. It becomes a matter of more smoke, indicating that there must be an even bigger fire."

Pons adjusted his fore-and-aft hat and pointed at a house just down the square from where we still stood at the top of Archer's step. "Although I've been following this particular matter for some time, and have been – with Bancroft's help – laying my plans accordingly, it is only a fortuitous accident that we are involved this morning, and that we'll be able to put a stop to this sooner rather than later. Rather like the accidental encounter that took place over there, back in '86. Do you know of it?"

I shook my head, looking at the brick building, not unlike the one where we stood. Its black door and high windows revealed nothing. "Not likely," I said wryly. "I was only eight years old at that time."

"And I was a bit younger then too, but I think that you'll recall it if I tell you that, back in those days, the building across from us was the home of Eduardo Lucas, amateur tenor, ladies' man, and spy."

I closed my eyes a moment, and then had it. "That's the house where he was killed, then? Where the stolen treaty was hidden under one of the wooden floor squares?"

"Where it was hidden, and then taken elsewhere. It was only by a fortuitous accident that my mentor was able to understand and pursue the connection between Lucas and the person who had retrieved the treaty at the time of his murder. If Inspector Lestrade, nearly half-a-century ago, hadn't realized that the curiosity of the misplaced second stain on the rug would be of interest to the *outré*-craving Sherlock Holmes, then the path might never have been discerned, and the pieces never connected. Or more likely, they would have been, but possibly too late, and under a completely different set of circumstances.

"This case is like that, as I'm reminded by seeing Lucas's old home across the way. If General York hadn't called us in this morning, the matter would still have progressed further along its path. Although it would have eventually been taken care of one way or another, who knows what additional damage might have occurred? But we are now involved, sooner than we might have been, and I intend that we will put a stop to it this very day. Shall we?" And so saying, he led me down the steps to the general's automobile. Just a few moments of driving brought us back up to Whitehall and the Foreign Office, where we were quickly shown into the lair of Bancroft Pons.

I looked around the office, without any extraneous decoration or distraction. From year to year it did not change, and seemingly, neither did Bancroft Pons, except for a possibly greater strain upon the buttons of his waistcoat.

Solar Pons quickly explained what had occurred to bring matters to a head. With a sigh somewhere between satisfaction and weariness, Bancroft lifted his telephone and spoke a few quiet and, from where I sat, unintelligible words. Within moments, a smart-looking uniformed lad carried in a sheaf of papers. "As we planned," said Bancroft, knocking them against the desktop once or twice to straighten them. "Awaiting the right time to use them."

He carefully handed them to Pons, who flipped through them, and then folded them in half. Bancroft winced while his brother shoved them into an inner pocket of his Inverness. "I'll take your word for it," he said. "I don't read that language."

"The Doctor does. He will be convinced."

"Let us hope so. Are you ready, Parker?"

I started to point out that I had no idea how to answer that question, but instead I simply stood, nodding toward Bancroft Pons. I was not sure why we had come here, but now I wished that we might stay longer, as I had the impression that events were swiftly hurtling toward some unpleasant encounter.

Back outside, I was surprised to find that the general's car had been replaced by a government limousine. "We had no business involving the chauffeur in this expedition," explained Pons. "Herbert, here – " and he gestured toward an old soldier holding the door, " – an acquaintance from the War, I might add, understands the risks. Isn't that right, Herbert?"

"As rain, Mr. Pons," he said, touching a finger to his brow, and then closing the door behind us when we had found our seats. He took control of the vehicle and drove with confidence into East London.

"Right into the lion's den," I said.

"Where else would one expect to most easily find the lion?"

"At least we might have passed by Praed Street in order for me to retrieve more ammunition."

"Parker, you've met the Doctor before. Do you really think that would accomplish anything? He will listen to what we have to say."

"We're betting heavily upon that."

"Oh, absolutely. With our lives. But," he smiled, "you can be confident that, should something go wrong, we will be avenged."

"What a comfort, then, that the already long list of charges against our Limehouse friend will become that much more absolute."

"Indeed." And with that, Pons fell silent.

We made our way around Aldgate and entered the Commercial Road at a confident and steady speed, and so into Whitechapel. Continuing, we neared Dockland, through the northern edge of Shadwell, and then right onto the Stepney Causeway. A left on Brook Street, right into Cranford, and finally a sharp left into a narrow dead-end alley labeled Bere Street. On our left was a tall building, four stories, with an odd arched window at its top. At the base of this building was a recessed doorway, apparently our destination.

As we stepped from the car, I could feel a multitude of eyes upon us. "Wait here, Herbert," said my friend, before turning and walking to the door. "I don't expect any trouble."

We walked at a steady pace toward the doorway. "This has been identified as the latest hide-out of our friend," added Pons softly. "It has been used by other groups over the years, and will no doubt find that purpose with others in the future. As you might suspect, there is a great deal more going on below ground than above." With that, we reached our goal and he knocked smartly.

The door opened immediately, revealing a veritable mountain of a man in clothing unusually foreign to England, loose colorful robes and shoes better made for storing tobacco than walking. He was almost certainly Chinese as based upon his association with the fellow we were seeking. Pons held out his card. "I believe that the Doctor will see us now," he said.

The fellow looked at the tiny rectangle of paper in his massive hand, and his lips moved through the reading of it two or three times before he glanced back, his eyes cutting up under his heavy brow. Then, he guided us inside and shut the door.

I was immediately overwhelmed by the smell of sandalwood incense, much as I had been over four years earlier, when Pons and I had found our way into another of the Doctor's underground lairs during the search for Lionel Ruthel's murderer. Upon that occasion, we had blundered into the tunnels uninvited before being overwhelmed, garroted into unconsciousness, and then waking in an opulent chamber. I hoped that today's meeting would be a bit more civilized.

The giant led us down a series of steps, and Pons muttered something about the same old *modus operandi*. At the bottom, we entered a hallway. A gesture told us to wait, and I was happy to comply, although I kept my hand near my collar to prevent a strangling loop of leather from dropping and tightening around my neck. Thankfully, it never came, and in a moment, our guide was back, gesturing us toward a nearby and very prosaic doorway.

Inside, we found that every effort had been made to slather luxury into this underground room, which had quite likely been formerly used as some sort of office. Expensive silks or bright colors were draped about the walls, and a thick Asian carpet covered the floor. There were a number of electric lights, for which I was glad, as smoke from torches would have suffocated us. Still, the sandalwood was almost chokingly strong here, and I could not keep from coughing until I adjusted to it.

"I apologize, Dr. Parker, if my attempt to beat back the damp smell of the Thames is too much for you," hissed a voice that I recognized, seemingly coming from everywhere and nowhere at once.

The Doctor had used such anonymous methods of communication before – the last time had been with some sort of speaking tube. I looked around, and then realized that a series of amplification devices, such as might be used in a theatre or hall, were spaced unobtrusively around the room. Pons did not seem to have been fooled. Instead, he was looking straight at an elaborate hanging curtain across the far side of the room, moving slightly from the influence of something concealed behind it.

"How may we address you this time?" he asked. "We don't know your actual name, just your title, your sobriquet, as it were. Previously, you went by 'Simon Fance', before later explaining that names meant nothing."

"As is still the case," said the voice. There was no doubt that we had achieved the first of our objectives – to find this fiend. Now to achieve the second, which I would have to take on faith, since I had not been given any information about it. "I confess that I had expected to see you at some point, Mr. Pons, although perhaps not quite so soon," said the voice. Taking Pons's cue, I faced the curtain, and the man secreted there. "I understand that you play chess. Is this perhaps a precipitous move, coming here so early in the game?"

Pons glanced around. "Possibly, although you were right to expect us," he said, including me graciously – or perhaps not. "We have been aware of your latest activities for quite a while."

"As you were meant to be. It did not hinder my objectives in the least for you to know. In fact, I benefited by not wasting my resources upon concealment. I was not aware, however – " and the voice became a bit sharper " – that you knew of how to find me at this particular location."

"As I was explaining to Parker when we arrived, this . . . facility has been used for similar purposes at various times in the past. The Professor was known to operate from here, as did one of the Egyptian factions attempting to recover the Eye of Heka back in '88. A gang of Russian nihilists at the turn of the century, and later their displaced royalist brothers during the War. The old wheel turns, as I was taught so long ago. This place is never vacant for very long."

"I do wonder, then, who will move in when I leave," hissed our host, if he might be called that. When we had stumbled into his previous lair, he had offered us some excellent Scotch before gassing us into unconsciousness. I saw no evidence of any bottles this time.

"I admit that it was fortunate that we found where you were staying, sooner rather than later. I hesitate to explain that it was not too difficult, as your minions make no sincere attempts to moderate their dress with an eye toward fitting in." And he glanced at the giant, still lurking behind us.

"Enough of these pleasantries," said the voice. "You walked up to my front door, gentlemen. You must have something to tell me."

"Of course. If I may show you some papers?"

A pause. And then – "Yes." The last "s" hissed away like a dying gasp.

Pons carefully reached into the Inverness, pulling out the fold of documents that he had obtained from Bancroft. "I'll admit," he said, holding them up, "that I cannot read these, although I'm aware of what they say. I was, in fact, consulted upon their content before they were actually written. These, of course, are copies, for your benefit. The originals have been placed with a myriad of individuals, men and women who have no love for you, who are spread out in various strategic locations throughout your sphere of influence." He waved the bundle. "Shall I bring them to you behind the curtain, or would you rather that . . . Sancho Panza here deliver them?"

Dare I say that there was a trace of amusement in the reply? "Hand them to Peng." Then, he said something else in that sibilant tongue, causing the mountainous man behind us to lurch into motion. He took the papers from Pons, stepped to the curtain, and passed them behind it, never once taking his eyes from us. For one second only, a hand was visible as it reached to accept the papers. Its thin white fingers, each tipped with long filed and lacquered nails, accepted the sheets almost delicately, further adding to my feeling of revulsion and horror at the reptilian motion. Then – it was gone.

We heard, by way of the amplification devices, the sound of sheets being turned, one after another, slowly at first, and then with greater speed and urgency. Finally, with a crumpling sound, the voice snarled, "You lie."

"I'm afraid not, Doctor." Pons took a single step forward toward the curtain, stopping before Peng could do more than tense his shoulders. "Copies of these letters have been placed throughout the provinces in the Orient, held by Chinese – some who are under the control of our agents, others who are willing participants. At any given time, the letters – and there could be dozens of them – can be sent to both your enemies *and* your patrons. Granted, with communications being as slow as they are, it may take days or weeks to set the entire process in motion, but that works to our advantage, as it lends credibility to the scheme by having it come out in dribs and drabs, rather than all at once. Little does it matter that the tale they tell is a fabrication. Will anyone doubt your duplicitous nature? Your enemies will seize upon this information, fanning the flames. Your allies will abandon you. Once the message to activate the plan leaves London, it will be unstoppable. Even if a second message were to be sent to countermand the initial instructions, it would take just as long to reach China."

"You lie," the voice repeated, but now more as if to convince itself. "How can this benefit you? It would be no more than mutually assured destruction. You must know that I would retaliate, with my back to the wall and nothing left to lose." Then, a thought must have suggested itself. "Such a method is nothing more than an attempt to control me . . . for now. To coerce me into some direction that you desire." The voice, which had assumed a pondering aspect for just a moment, firmed. "Why, if you knew where I was located, did you not instead simply attempt to destroy me? It does not make sense!"

"Ah, but it does, Doctor. Because, you see, for now it suits us *not* to destroy you."

Silence for a long moment. Then: "I see. You are uncertain as to who . . . or *what* would fill the void if I were to be removed."

"Not so uncertain, I'm afraid. Right now you are a thorn in our side, but a known thorn. And, as you say, you fill the void, holding back opposing forces against others that you know."

"Baron Kroll," added the voice.

"Yes. Among others. There are also members of your own coterie, as you surely realize, that would take the opportunity of your removal from the board to advance their own game."

"Better the devil that you know, Mr. Pons?"

"Um, yes."

There was a long silence before the voice continued. "Then what would you have from me?"

"For now? Stasis. Knowing that the day-to-day aspects of your operation will exist no matter who is in charge is unfortunate but inevitable. The usual cat-and-mouse between the police and your low-level agents will continue as it always has. Our visit today has a deeper purpose. More specifically, the malicious destruction of both the physical documents and the reputations of our historical figures – politicians and artists – as well as the damage to the bonds of trust between the leaders of our society, must stop. Surely you, as a student of history, must feel some revulsion at what you have done, both to the original artifacts and the facts themselves."

"Feel, Mr. Pons? You play the short game. It is demeaning for one of your intellect to refer to feelings, or to use such a blunt instrument as blackmail."

"We use the tools at hand, Doctor. Am I to take it that we have an understanding?"

"For now."

"And the stolen documents? Both those that have been altered and not yet released, and the others more recently taken? They must be returned immediately."

"They will be at your lodgings within the hour. 7B Praed Street, I believe. Owned by a Mrs. Johnson."

"Of course."

"As you see, I know where to find you as well, my friend. But I can assure you that next time, you will have to search a bit harder to locate me. Within the hour I shall have vacated these premises."

"I would have expected no less," said Pons. "However, it might be well to leave some line of communication in place, should we need to speak in the future. After all, loathe as I am to admit it, there may be times, as there were during the War, when our interests run along the same track."

"Parallel tracks, surely, Mr. Pons. You refer, of course, to those others that you spoke of before, who would be happy to fill my shoes."

"I do."

"The enemy of my enemy."

"Indeed."

"You'll forgive me, however, if I hope that we do not meet again."

"If you can call this a meeting, I understand."

"Then our business is concluded."

With that, I tensed, looking from side to side. The voice gave a dry chuckle. "Do not fear, Dr. Parker. There is no need to render you unconscious as before, in order to convey you to your lodgings. As I said, we will soon be gone to a location already prepared for just such an eventuality as this, and in any case, I wouldn't want to cause any distress for your government driver waiting outside." He then sibilated a short phrase, and the vast Peng gestured toward the door.

"Farewell, Doctor," said Pons with a nod toward the curtain before leading me out.

We were quickly returned to the outer door where, without a gesture or sound, Peng let us out. The door closed behind us with a firm thud, and I could only imagine the frenzied activity that was already being carried out beneath us as the Doctor's hive, its true extent unknown to us, exploded into motion.

"If he's smart," said Pons in a low tone as we approached our car, "he'll move deeper into the tunnels and catacombs underneath this block instead of going to the trouble of completely moving, and simply seal up this entrance to give the appearance that it's been deserted."

"I take it that you know of what you speak."

"I do. I was given a tour of the place during my apprenticeship, back during a time between occupants. But better now to take him at his word and assume that he's moving. There are ways – secret ways – back in from another direction that I can use later to penetrate these underground byways and determine if he has really gone. But as for now, I really feel that we have done a good day's work."

I was unsurprised to find that, after we had leisurely made our way across London, that the documents from the Doctor had already been delivered. "He wastes no time," said Pons, "and his resources really are impressive."

I laughed. "Pons, it almost sounds as if you admire the man."

"In a strange way, I do. I disagree with his aims and motives, of course, but his organization and will are formidable and impressive. Would that we had been able to recruit him to our side, back in those long-ago days when he was still pliable. But that's another story entirely."

I wanted to ask more, but Pons had, at this time, already focused deeply upon the papers and documents. He spent the evening in his chair before the fire, pipe clenched between his strong teeth, moving through the pile and separating it into smaller stacks. He spoke only once, to ask whether I would be available on the morrow to help return various items to their proper owners, spending some extra time at certain locations, explaining why this or that item had been ruined, but that the threat that had led to their theft had now been neutralized.

I went through one of the piles that had already been examined and located the Newnes papers, thankfully not yet ruined. Wishing Pons a good night, I climbed to my room, to read through the yellowed correspondence between my old friend Watson, his Literary Agent, and his publisher. As I expected, it was full of surprises, and it was quite a while before I fell asleep.

# The Affair of
# The Distasteful Society

"Here will be fine, Reynolds," said my friend, Solar Pons, indicating a poorly-lit corner just ahead of us. The building that I took to be our destination loomed out, crowding the sidewalk, and looking even darker than the surrounding structures. Reynolds, a cabbie who owed his very freedom to Pons, gave an affirmative grunt and slowed, coasting to a smooth stop.

We stepped out, and Pons made to hand a few coins to the fellow. "No charge, Mr. Pons," he said. The cab returned to motion, leaving us with Reynolds's final, "You gentlemen have a good night," as he disappeared into the gloom and finally vanished.

"Are you sure this is the correct spot?" I asked, looking around at the deserted and shadowed block. "Perhaps we misunderstood the time. There does not seem to be any activity here." It was not yet seven o'clock, and at this time of summer, in mid-July, it should have been much brighter. However, a London fog was rolling in from the south, advancing the fall of night by several hours as the sunlight was cut off.

"You saw the invitation, Parker. This is the right location. Although I must say, as I did when we were first invited to this gathering, that the location is something of a puzzle. It would have seemed fitting to pick a more public place, or even the home of the organizer, rather than this lonely little church."

I agreed with him. The old structure, in the heart of Bloomsbury, had seen better days. In harsh daylight, I'm sure it would have appeared worse. The foggy gloom at least gave it an air of sinister and romantic mystery, which, I realized, was not exactly how a church likely wished to present itself.

Pons looked up and down the street. There were no automobiles parked there, and neither were there any horse-drawn vehicles, still occasionally seen in London. He turned back to me, his Inverness spinning slowly to follow. "Shall we go in?" And he gestured toward the large double wooden doors, probably older than some countries.

Pons and I had been fairly busy for the last few weeks, and had most recently been involved in a matter designated in my notes as that of "The Haunted Library." When the invitation to this event had arrived, it had seemed like something of a lark after several of our recent affairs. Now, at this grim old building, it did not promise to be as enjoyable as I had initially believed.

The doors were unlocked, and inside we immediately felt the cool air from the old stone building wash over us, unaffected by the dying day's heat outside. I gave a small shiver, while Pons looked here and there before walking toward a faintly lit door at the back of the chancel.

I glanced to the left and right, towards the leaded-glass windows that rose above us on each side before meeting the groined ceiling. The figures immortalized in stained glass were dark now, simply grim outlines looming over one another, or pointing accusatory fingers. I only had a quick moment to study them as I walked from the back of the room toward the lighted door, but I could perceive no sign of forgiveness or absolution in the illustrated scenes.

Stepping through the door and out of the nave, I found myself in a much more prosaic hallway, with rooms set up as offices on either side. Here was where the day-to-day operations of the church were carried out. Somehow, however, it felt less like an office area and more like the backstage of a theater. It was better-lit than where we had just been, with the glow coming from a pair of open double doors about halfway down the hall. I could hear murmurs of conversation there, and it seemed to be our logical destination.

We entered the room to find something like an unadorned banquet hall. This was apparently where members of the church could gather for less-formal occasions, such as receptions, meetings to discuss church business, and so on. It was well lit by a number of electric lamps around the wall, although there was evidence of old gas fixtures here and there. At the front and end-on to the door was a long table, facing rows of portable chairs stretching to the other end of the room. There were a great number of these chairs, but only half-a-dozen people or so, five of whom – four men and a woman – were clustered at the front table. A sixth was at a smaller table behind the first, apparently some sort of servant, fussing with liquid refreshments.

The last and seventh person, who seemed to be of significant age, was in a chair at the end of one of the empty rows of chairs filling the greater part of the room, about halfway back. He was facing the long table and apparently slumped in sleep.

"Ah, Mr. Pons," said the man seated in the middle. "I'm glad you could join us." His words were gracious, but his tone less so. He seemed perturbed at best, and as he stood, he bumped the servant who had approached him from behind and was leaning in with a dark goblet. The servant reacted quickly, but not before a splash of some dark amber liquid sloshed onto some of the papers on the table in front of the man who had spoken.

"Idiot," the man muttered, taking an unexpected step backwards and away from his place at the table, which caused him to intrude into the space of a well-dressed and small-boned man immediately to his right. This fellow in turn half stood, crowding a fat man to *his* right. The woman seated nearest us, to the right of the fat man, had stood as well, throwing out her arms and leaning toward the table as if to protect her territory, and certainly the glass in front of her.

They soon sorted themselves out and settled back to their places. The first man who had spoken, located at the center of the table, and whom I now recognized as Sir Amory Clarke, realized that he had nearly intruded into the perimeter of the slight man beside him, and he muttered an apology.

The fat man, whom I could now see was quite fat indeed and rather oily-looking, gave a sour grunt of a laugh. I knew him as well. It was Leonard Rath, the banker who had been so effective during the War, but then had *not* received an expected knighthood following the conclusion of the hostilities. Rumors and speculations ranged from profiteering to collaboration with the enemy, but nothing definite was ever confirmed, at least not for the general public. Whatever the reason for Rath's absence from the Birthday Honors list, he had continued as the leader of his financial institution, although he was reputed to be a more bitter man than he had been seven years earlier, at the start of the conflict.

Sir Amory turned to the small-boned man on his right, seated between him and Leonard Rath. "Dry those off, Carstairs," he said, gesturing toward the dampened papers before him.

"Right away, Sir Amory," said the fellow with a lazy drawl, pulling a handkerchief from his pocket. It seemed to me that Carstairs was some sort of secretary. I soon learned that my assumption was correct.

As mentioned, the room's sole woman was seated at the end of the table closest to the door, to Rath's right. The banker was turned to face the other men at the table, leaving his back to her. She did not appear to mind in the least. She looked to be in her mid-forties, wearing a clean but rather threadbare coat buttoned right up to her neck. She had a little ashtray-of-a-hat pinned to her steel-gray hair, not a one of which was out of place, and she possessively clutched a large and scuffed leather bag on her lap, as if she feared that someone would try to take it away.

"Welcome," said Sir Amory, recovering his composure and resuming his possession of the center of the table. "Sorry for the little confusion, Mr. Pons. And this must be Dr. Parker. We are glad to have you both here. Especially," he said, his tone turning angry as he resumed his seat once again, "since it is likely that no one else is going to attend."

He lifted some of the damp papers in front of him, now presumably dried by Carstairs. "Sir James Saunders wrote that he has another engagement. Sir James Damery pleads the same thing. Superintendent Hopkins at the Yard declined. Sir Percy Phelps? Lady Hilda Trelawney Hope? Both turned us down, indicating that they didn't feel it would be the correct thing to do. Sir Henry Baskerville used stronger language than that. Inspector Lestrade's refusal was quite definite, in spite of my offer to let him be the keynote speaker. Of course, that was only after Mr. Holmes and Dr. Watson didn't even bother to respond to the invitations at all. Quite frankly, gentlemen, I'm surprised that the two of you are here."

"May I read my paper now?" said the last man seated at the table, by himself and off to Sir Amory's left, farthest from the door. "It is getting late, you know, and I simply must catch my train." The end of the table where he sat was in a pocket of shadow, and before this time, I confess that I had mostly ignored the fellow while watching Sir Amory's little dance away from his seat as his drink was spilled. Now I made an effort to see this unidentified man more closely. Though he was seated, I could tell that he was thin, and in his early- to mid-thirties. Most important, however, was the fact that he was clearly a Catholic priest.

"Gentlemen," said Sir Amory, "may I present Father Ronald Pounds, from Ware, in Hertfordshire." Turning to the priest, he said, "Surely it will be too late for you to return home tonight. I had expected to put you up as my guest. I'm staying in town right now myself."

"No, no, I must be getting back. I told them that I would. Would it be possible to begin?" He pulled out a watch. "We are already ten minutes overdue. That time should have been used for whatever introductions and speeches you had planned to mark this auspicious occasion, and so on. But now time is up and I must begin, if I hope to finish in time to catch my train. That was our agreement, you know."

Sir Amory turned back toward us. "Father Pounds here is - "

"You may refer to me as 'Father Ronald'" said the man. "I find that it makes me more accessible to my flock."

"Um, well, certainly then, Father Ronald. As I was saying, Father Ronald wrote a paper nearly ten years ago, when he was up at Trinity

College in Oxford, applying a kind of higher criticism to the subject of our gathering tonight. First of its kind, really."

"It was really something of a jest, you know," said Father Ronald. "I doubt if it shall ever be published, but somehow Sir Amory heard of it, apparently from a friend of a friend, and he decided to invite me here tonight."

"I felt that if we are to form a society dedicated to the study and acclimation of the methods of Mr. Sherlock Holmes, we should set the proper tone at the very start with a scholarly paper." He lowered his voice somewhat. "It turns out that there was only *one* scholarly paper to be found, and as the good Father says, it hasn't even been published yet."

"Where would one go for peer review?" asked Father Ronald.

"Hear, hear," said Leonard Rath, raising his glass, dark and heavy like the rest of those along the table. He then drained it, before gesturing toward the nearby servant, at the small table on along the back wall. The servant grabbed a wide and dark bottle and moved to Rath's side, where he proceeded to refill the fat man's glass. The woman watched Rath with intense distaste.

Pons looked at those present. "And who might you be, madam?" he asked the sole lady, to our far left as we faced the table..

"*Miss* Gertrude Thrush," she said, with clear emphasis on her unattached marital status. "I am a member of this church, and I char here as well. I saw on the posted schedule that this gathering was planned for tonight in order to organize some sort of Sherlock Holmes Society, and I thought that it was open to the public. I've always admired Mr. Holmes, ever since he proved that my father was not involved in some shady goings-on over near Aldgate when I was a young lady. I did not realize until after I was here that this fete was by invitation only. Sir Amory was kind enough to let me stay." And she glared at Leonard Rath beside her. He seemed to toast her with a gesture of his glass, and took a long swallow, forcing him to close his eyes for a moment.

"Well, yes, Miss Thrush, we are certainly happy to have you," said Sir Amory. He glanced at the stack of refusals to attend on the table in front of him. "It is good to have *someone* here whose situation has been personally improved by the actions of Mr. Holmes during one of his investigations. I personally have always taken a keen interest in the tales of Dr. Watson, and have made an effort to collect them all, as well as to seek out and speak with many of the individuals involved in the original investigations. Often, I've had to play a bit of the detective myself, you know, finding out the *real* name of a person whose identity was obfuscated by Watson when the stories were first published in *The Strand.*

"I also like to collect actual artifacts from the investigations. For instance, I recently acquired Grimesby Roylott's safe and milk saucer, and I have my eye on locating the man's dog whip as well, which I believe is still in the possession of the current owner of the house in Stoke Moran.

"As I said, Father Ronald was asked to attend tonight for our initial meeting due to his scholarly paper from nearly a decade ago, in 1912, and I'm told that it is apparently still as witty and fresh as the day it was written. You, Mr. Pons, and Dr. Parker, have been invited because of your obvious connection to Mr. Holmes, as well as your own experiences as 'The Sherlock Holmes of Praed Street.'"

Sir Amory paused and looked past us, at the sleeping man halfway back. He lowered his voice somewhat. "I must confess that I do not know that gentleman, or anything of his connection or interest in the cases of Mr. Holmes. He wandered in soon after the rest of us had arrived, found that seat, and promptly dropped off to sleep."

"Ah," said Pons, "I must confess that I myself took the liberty of inviting him. Although when I did so, I believed at the time that there would be more people here, and that his presence wouldn't be quite so obvious. That is Sir Wilmer Dougal, a long-time acquaintance of Mr. Holmes. I felt that he would especially enjoy seeing and hearing the discussion tonight."

"That explains it, then," said Sir Amory. "He is welcome as well, although I fear that he will miss whatever we have to discuss, since he appears to be dead to the world. At least," continued the man, his tone tinged with slight anger, "we can say that we had eight people at our first meeting, rather than seven. That sounds so much better, doesn't it?"

Rath waved languidly toward the servant at the drinks table. "You've forgotten Jeffrey again," he said. "Surely his presence counts? I understand that he has always been a factor. With him here, we are nine, not eight."

Sir Amory glared at Rath, and then said shortly, "Fine. Nine, then."

"Congratulations, Jeffrey. You have joined our exalted company. Now refill my drink with some of the excellent Rhenish that was brought by your master."

Jeffery, the servant, quickly moved to refill Rath's glass. Then he said, "More water, Miss Thrush?"

She placed a hand over the glass before her on the table. "No, thank you."

Rath laughed. "Miss Thrush, surely you will join us. This is an auspicious night to give up being a teetotaler."

"*No, thank you*, I said!" she exclaimed, nearly shrieking, and making it plain with those three words how she judged both the use of alcohol and Leonard Rath.

Pons gestured towards the sheets on the table in front of Sir Amory. "I gather that you sent out an extensive list of invitations, and that you were overwhelmingly turned down."

"That is correct. One would almost think that there was some conspiracy afoot to make sure this event failed. I had especially hoped that Mr. Holmes might journey up from Sussex, or that Dr. Watson, who still lives right here in London, would have attended. They would have been greatly honored, I can assure you. But as I said, neither even felt the need or courtesy to make a reply."

"Perhaps the idea of such a society, devoted to the study of their exploits, is distasteful to them," said Pons.

"Nonsense," said Sir Amory. He glanced behind him. "Shut the doors, Jeffrey. I don't believe that anyone else is coming."

Jeffrey walked across the room with the Rhenish still in hand and pushed the double doors to the hallway closed. As he made his way back to his station with the bottle, Rath stood. "Let me see those rejections," he said. "I'm curious as to just who was invited." He moved around Carstairs and leaned over Sir Amory's shoulder. Sir Amory clearly found the man's presence unpleasant, but he politely began to show the different rejection letters, comparing them with an invitation list, and making small quiet comments about each.

"I see that you invited Thorndyke, and that little Belgian over on Farraway Street," said Rath.

"And Sexton Blake as well," replied Sir Amory.

"Sexton Blake is a fictional character, Sir Amory," said Pons with a smile.

"Ah, quite, quite. Then that would explain at least one of the non-replies to my invitations."

"I really would like to read my paper now," said Father Ronald, apparently to no one. "It is entitled 'Studies in the Literature of Sherlock Holmes'." He pointedly rattled a sheaf of papers in his hand and began, raising his voice in a most-querulous manner. "'*If there is anything pleasant in life,*' " he read, "'*it is doing what we aren't meant to do. If there is anything pleasant in criticism, it is finding out what we aren't meant to find out.*' "

Sir Amory turned an annoyed look toward Father Ronald, but a question from Rath drew his attention back to the replies. Pons faced toward Miss Thrush and said in a louder voice, "You indicated that you are a member of this church, as well as providing cleaning services here. Is that correct?"

"Yes, it is," she said.

Father Ronald raised his voice. "*'It is the method by which we treat as significant what the author did not mean to be significant, by which we single out as essential what the author regarded as incidental . . . .'*"

Carstairs smiled as Father Ronald continued, and raised his glass to his lips, taking a sip and making a face.

Pons continued, "I would welcome, at your convenience, of course, the opportunity to question you further about the church's beliefs. I understand that the original church was founded by men returning home from the Crusades, and that it combines a rather strict interpretation of the Gospel, as influenced by some of the more harsh aspects of the Middle Eastern religions, as brought back by the returning soldiers."

"I'm not sure about that," said Miss Thrush, "but I'll be happy to answer any questions that you might have."

"Excellent," said Pons. "What about sometime tomorrow morning? I happen to be in the process of gathering my thoughts toward writing a monograph on the influences of religious dogma as a motivation toward crime, and I am certain – "

"I think – " said Carstairs. Then, with a grunting sound that did not even seem possible from a human throat, he jerked, his body twisting with a great spasm. He rolled toward his right, coming to rest for a moment on Rath's empty chair. Miss Thrush went rigid with surprise, clutching the leather bag on her lap. Then Carstairs appeared to be pulled backwards, his face tightening in a rictus of agony as he arched on his chair. He froze and looked directly into Miss Thrush's eyes, and she stared back, apparently unable to look away.

Carstairs broke the contact for her, lurching out of his seat and ending up on the floor behind his own chair. I rushed around to him, kneeling down in the shadows behind the table. As I tried to find a pulse, I already knew the truth. The man was dead.

As a physician, I have always felt that death was an enemy. It is never pretty, but even so, there are sometimes what we call "good deaths". A life well lived, with loving family members gathered nearby, and all the necessary goodbyes made. When it is time, the dying man or woman simply slips peacefully away. I have seen miracles that have saved lives, and I have seen them at the time of death as well.

Carstairs's death was not a "good death". He had died quickly, true enough, and had not suffered for very long, but it was quite clear that he had indeed suffered intensely during his final moments. And who can say how long, to him, that those final moments had seemed? Might they have been like an eternity? Or even as he felt the agony that was apparent to all of us, did he still wish for it to continue, because when it stopped it would all be over?

I became aware of Pons standing above me. He came around and settled beside me, leaning in to sniff the dead man's lips.

"A fast-acting alkaloid?" he murmured.

"Incredibly fast," I said.

Pons glanced up toward the table, and the glass still standing in front of Carstairs's chair.

"I doubt that he could have been saved," I added, "even if he had drunk it while standing in the middle of a hospital."

"In the drink?" Pons asked.

"I believe so."

"As do I."

Pons stood, and I followed. "Is he . . . is he dead?" asked Miss Thrush in a hushed voice.

"Yes, Miss Thrush. Murdered." She gasped and put a hand to her mouth.

"Jeffrey," said Sir Amory, standing up as well, and pushing back against Rath, who had still been leaning over him while he watched the enfolding drama on the floor behind him. "Summon the police."

"Wait," said Pons, moving to intercept the quick-acting Jeffrey. "We need to answer a few questions first, while the scene is still fresh. Then we can alert the authorities."

Father Ronald sighed ruefully and dropped the papers in his hand to the table. "I believe that I am going to miss my train." He stood. "I suppose that I should perform the last rights . . . ."

Pons said, "If you could wait just a bit, Father, I believe that Mr. Carstairs will be more at peace if we do what we can to find his killer first." He moved to where Carstairs had been seated and reached for the half-full glass on the table. Lifting it gently, he smelled the contents, and then involuntarily jerked his head back. He caught my eye and nodded. It was poisoned.

"Jeffrey," he said, "what was Carstairs drinking?"

"The double-blend from Scotland," he answered. He gestured toward the small table filled with a variety of uniquely shaped bottles, along with several rows of the dark goblets. "Sir Amory had me bring a good selection with us tonight. Among them is the whisky, which Mr. Carstairs drank, the Rhenish favored by Sir Amory, and two fine bottles of wine from the cellars, a red and a white. No one wanted either of those, so they remain unopened."

"And what did the others drink? Mr. Rath, for instance?"

"He had a . . . a great deal of the Rhenish as well. He . . . he commented that it was better than what he could get at home."

"And you only speak the truth, Jeffrey," said Rath, reaching for his glass.

"Do not touch that!" said Pons, commandingly. Rath jerked his hand back. "No one touch any of the glasses until we ascertain that the others have not been poisoned as well. Now Jeffrey, you were telling me about what everyone drank."

"Right. Miss Thrush and Father Ronald only wanted water. And that man," he said, nodding toward Sir Wilmer, still slumped in his chair across the room, "did not stay awake long enough to ask for anything at all."

Pons stepped to the table and reached for Rath's glass. Raising it to the light and looking over the rim, he observed the contents, and then he smelled it. With his other hand, he took Sir Amory's glass as well and compared the two.

"These glasses both contain the Rhenish," he said. "However, Carstair's glass does *not* seem to have a double-blended whisky. In spite of the obvious presence of the poison, I perceive that it contains some sort of cheap spirit with a high raw alcohol content. This is obvious from the smell alone, even without any more elaborate analysis."

Pons replaced the two glasses of Rhenish on the table. "Sir Amory, did Carstairs show any signs of suicidal behavior?"

"Certainly not! The man had everything to live for."

"Then our assumption that he was murdered is likely correct. In any case, why would he choose this location to kill himself, it that were his intent? Since it looks certain that he was murdered, the real question is, was he the intended victim?" Turning his gaze to Rath, he asked, "Did you have any reasons to wish for Mr. Carstairs's death?"

"What?" said Rath with a forced laugh. "Certainly not!"

"Do you carry a flask, Mr. Rath?" asked Pons. "You strike me as the sort of man that would."

"I do," replied the fat man, reaching into his coat. He pulled out the silver item and proceeded to unscrew the cap. "Do you think that I might be carrying poison with me, and tipped it into Carstair's glass when he wasn't looking? I'll put paid to that notion, then." And he tipped up the flask and began to drink, pulling long and greedy swallows.

"Wait!" cried Pons. Rath lowered the flask, and then wiped his mouth with his sleeve. "You'd best save some of that, if you want to prove that you had nothing to do with Carstairs's death. In spite of your demonstration, it may still need to be analyzed, to prove that it contains pure spirits, and is not some poisoned drink to which you have already ingested the antidote. May I?" And he reached for the flask. Receiving it without hesitation, he smelled the opening. "Brandy," he said.

"Cognac," replied Rath. "The finest."

"No doubt," said Pons, replacing the cap and placing the flask on the table.

"Why are you here, Mr. Rath?" asked Pons. "I doubt that you have any interest in the subject matter. Was he an invited guest, Sir Amory?"

"Certainly not. I can tell you that I was greatly surprised when he walked in."

"As was I when I entered and saw him here," replied Pons. "It has been well-reported in the press that you are one of Mr. Rath's greatest critics, Sir Amory. One might even go so far as to say that you are his nemesis. Would I be correct in pointing out that it was mainly due to your efforts that Mr. Rath's knighthood was denied following the War?"

"Yes," said Sir Amory, "yes, that would be a fair statement."

"Then I repeat, Mr. Rath, why are you here?"

"Because of this," said the unpleasant fat man, reaching into a pocket and tossing a folded piece of paper on the table. Pons retrieved it, and I examined it over his shoulder. It was a cheap, octavo-sized sheet, with a single sentence printed on it: "If you would have justice done, be at the Sherlock Holmes meeting tonight at 7. Richard's Church off Tottenham Ct Rd."

Pons glanced toward me. "Cheap paper," I said, "watery blue ink, worn pen nib. Possibly written in the lobby of a bank, hotel, or post office."

"Excellent, Parker," he said. "Anything else?"

"The writing appears to be that of a poorly-educated person, ill-formed and awkward. However, the use of an apostrophe in 'Richard's' indicates that the person is perhaps more educated than they would have us believe."

"Correct. I believe that the person has tried the double-reversal trick of first writing a version of this message normally, and then turning that paper upside down. Then, the writer copied the upside-down letters, probably using the left, non-dominant hand. I have used this trick myself upon occasion."

Turning back to the banker, Pons said, "Mr. Rath, how was this note delivered?"

"Just as you see it, folded without an envelope, and placed on my doorstep where my man found it this morning."

"And what justice did you expect to find when you decided to keep the appointment?"

"I wasn't entirely sure. I asked around and discovered that this meeting was being hosted by Sir Amory. I thought perhaps he wanted to have me here to discuss some of our past differences, and – "

"Past differences?" cried Sir Amory. "How can we have *differences*? The facts speak for themselves! You're a profiteer, sir! You have a long history of – "

"Sir Amory, please," said Pons. "You were saying, Mr. Rath?"

"After I arrived tonight, I could see that Sir Amory was completely surprised by my appearance, and obviously did not want me here at all. I decided to stay and see what the game was all about. When he pulled out his list of invitees, I wanted a look to see if some name on that list might suggest itself to me, in order to determine who had sent the invitation."

While Rath had been speaking, a look of horror had crossed Sir Amory's face. He turned to the small table and said, "Oh, no, Jeffrey. Surely *you* didn't . . . ."

"No, no, of course not," replied Jeffrey, a trace of panic in his voice. "Amory, you know that I didn't! I wouldn't!"

"Would you care to explain, Sir Amory?" said Pons.

Sir Amory appeared to collect himself for a minute, and then he reached for his glass. "Tut, Sir Amory," said Pons, interrupting his movement. "We have established that your glass contains the genuine Rhenish, but for now we must all remain thirsty. Nothing else shall be consumed here tonight until it has all been officially examined."

"Of course, of course." Sir Amory looked back toward Jeffrey, and then said, "You must understand that Jeffrey is my . . . well, he is my brother. My half-brother, really. We have different mothers, you see. But he has always been raised as part of my family. After his mother died when I was but a boy, Father took Jeffrey in, and we grew up together. He is my confidante in many matters. He knows much, if not all, of my business. And he was aware of my . . . difficulties with

Mr. Rath here. In fact, Mr. Rath's efforts to push back against the case that I have been helping to build against him have somewhat . . . pinched me a little tightly of late. I have . . . I may have said, upon occasion, that my life would be . . . simplified if . . . if Mr. Rath would . . . go away." He looked back at Jeffrey. "But surely he . . . surely you wouldn't *poison* him, Jeffrey!"

"I didn't, Amory! I swear it!"

"Jeffrey," said Pons. "Tell us about the last serving of drinks."

"Certainly. Mr. Carstairs, well, we had made sure to bring the whisky that he favors. I refilled his glass quite a while before he . . . before he died. He was a gulper. Sir Amory's glass was recharged at the same time. Miss Thrush and Father Ronald asked for water early on, before you and Dr. Parker arrived, and they haven't needed to be refilled." He frowned. "Mr. Rath has requested a number of refills since his arrival. When he learned that we had the Rhenish, he made some comment about Sir Amory's hospitality. The last time that I topped off his glass was just before Sir Amory told me to shut the door."

"And you have no cheap whisky, such as that which contains the poison in Carstairs's glass? Did he ever drink anything like that?"

"Not at all. He liked his usual, and that is what we kept for him."

"Sir Amory," asked Pons, "why did you pick this location, of all possible sites available to you, as the spot to hold the inaugural meeting of your new society?"

"Um, well, no particular reason. Nothing that means anything, anyway. I've read about the place, with its unique history and rather stern and forbidding exterior, and I thought it might have a fitting atmosphere somehow. And I suppose it seemed more . . . democratic, somehow, and that people from all walks, such as former clients of Mr. Holmes, or police inspectors for instance, might be more likely to attend, as compared to having the meeting in my house here in town."

"Just so. And Miss Thrush, how do you feel when you hear Sir Amory describe your church as 'forbidding'? Do you find that offensive in any way?"

"Of course not, Mr. Pons. We wish for our church to reflect our beliefs. Life is hard, and God expects us to struggle, in order to test and strengthen our souls. There are no promises of beauty or ease on this side of the veil."

"Quite." He thought for a moment, pulling on his ear. Then, in a more conversational tone, he stated, "I must admit that I am still quite curious about your beliefs, Miss Thrush. I'm not sure that I can wait until tomorrow morning for our planned discussion. Tell me, what do you think about capital punishment? Is it a sin?"

"Certainly not, Mr. Pons," she answered. "It is all explained in the Bible. Leviticus 24:17: '*And he that killeth any man shall surely be put to death.*'"

"I see," he said. "Food for thought."

Turning abruptly to Sir Amory, Pons asked, "I believe that Mr. Carstairs was right-handed. Is that not so?"

"Why, yes, he was," said Sir Amory, somewhat puzzled at this non sequitur. "Did you observe it from some sort of musculature clues as you examined the body? Is his right hand more developed than the left?"

"I did not conduct a thorough examination of the corpse. I simply recall seeing him drink with his right hand. And you are left-handed, is that correct, Mr. Rath?"

"It is."

"So when you set your glass upon the table, you would ordinarily place it at your left side, while Mr. Carstairs, being right-handed, would place his upon his right. And since your left hand was adjacent to his right hand, so to speak, your glasses would rest near each other on the table."

"I suppose so. Yes, that's right."

"So the question is: Who was meant to die? Carstairs? Or Rath?" Turning back to Miss Thrush, Pons asked sharply, "Does your church consider it a sin to lie?"

"Of course. We are not heathens, Mr. Pons. We are good Christians."

"Indeed. And if I asked you a simple yes or no question, would you be compelled by your beliefs, here within your own church, to tell the truth?"

She narrowed her eyes and returned his gaze. "Certainly."

Pons nodded, but did not say anything. He glanced over his shoulder toward Sir Wilmer, still in repose. Pons then placed his hands behind his back and paced slowly around for a moment or two before ending up immediately beside Miss Thrush. She appeared to be puzzled as she watched him, and her patient reserve seemed to fractionally erode. Finally, when Pons made no move to step away, she twisted so that she could look up at him from a better angle.

"Did you have a question, Mr. Pons?" she said.

"Oh, yes," he said, as if suddenly recalled to himself. "I was simply wondering if you are carrying any sort of flask or similar container in that bag of yours?"

Her mouth popped open, but she made no sound. Her fingers gripped the bag tighter, as if to prevent someone from taking it away from her. Pons turned slightly toward the rest of us, his tone conversational.

"It is a curious thing," he said, "this curse of mine to *see* things. Sadly, I didn't notice when the poisoned drink was placed before Carstairs. Or perhaps I should correctly say, placed before both Carstairs *and* Rath. For their glasses were together, due to their adjacent left- and right-handedness, and indistinguishable from one another, as are all the rest. That made things more difficult. I assume the switch was made during the occasion just after Parker and I arrived, when the drink was spilled, although that event certainly couldn't have been foreseen. I'm sure, however, that if *that particular opportunity* hadn't presented itself, then another surely would have come along before the night was over. This was definitely planned and carried out on a minute-to-minute basis.

"As I said, I didn't see when the glasses were switched, and the cheap poisoned whisky was set down and the good whisky taken away. But I have noticed something else."

Turning back to face Miss Thrush, he said, "Jeffrey stated that you received a glass of water when you first arrived, and you have had no refills since that time. Yet I myself have seen you, on a number of occasions since I arrived, lift that glass in front of you to your lips. However, I can tell from here that the level of the water in the glass never seems to decrease – it is as full now as when we arrived. Why is that, Miss Thrush? Why do you not actually *drink* any of the contents of that glass?"

"Good heavens, Pons," I said. "The contents of *her* glass are poisoned as well, and she knows it!"

"Not quite, Parker, although they do say that one man's meat is another man's poison. Or perhaps more accurately in this case, one *woman's water*. The contents of Miss Thrush's glass are completely safe for any of *us* to drink. Isn't that right, Miss Thrush? She simply chooses *not* to actually take a sip from it for a completely different reason." He moved a step closer to her. "Perhaps it is a *moral conviction* against the consumption of alcohol that prevents you from taking a drink?" He reached forward with his hand. "Miss Thrush, may I see that glass?"

Her hand darted forward then, sweeping and pushing the glass toward the edge of the table. But Pons's hand was quicker, and he caught it as it started its parabolic descent toward the hard floor. A splash or two swirled out and away, but the majority of the liquid remained within the container. Miss Thrush made a hiss and half-rose from her chair, making a grab for the glass in Pons's hand, but he took a quick step back and out of her reach. She sank back and glared at him, her mouth in a tight, white horizontal line.

Pons sniffed the glass, nodded, and handed it to me. I brought it to my nose, and smelled the rich peaty aroma of a true double-blended whisky.

"Then *this* was Carstairs glass," I said.

"Precisely. When Miss Thrush hurriedly switched her glass – into which she had previously placed the poison – with this one during the incident of the spill, she did not realize that she had taken away that of *Carstairs*, instead of the one containing Rath's Rhenish, which was her true aim.

"That is whom you meant to kill, isn't it?" She didn't answer. "No matter," continued Pons. "I could see how shocked you looked when Carstairs was the man who died, for he was not your prey."

"But . . . why would a char woman wish to kill Rath?" asked Sir Amory.

"I believe, if we ask the correct questions, that Miss Thrush will have no choice but to tell us. Isn't that correct, Miss Thrush? Since, as you confirmed earlier, it is *a sin to lie!*"

Her glare did not alter, and Pons asked once again, "Are you carrying any sort of flask or similar container in that bag? If so, I would be much obliged if you would let me examine it. If not now, then you will certainly be compelled to do so when the police arrive."

The woman sat like a wooden carving for a long moment, and then seemed to bend, but just a little, as if she were a brittle stick. She lowered her gaze from wherever far-off place it had been and opened her bag, from which she withdrew a small bottle, mostly empty except for a small amount of some brownish liquid at the bottom.

Pons took it and examined it against the light. Then, opening it, he smelled the contents quickly before passing it to me. It has the same smell of cheap whisky, along with a vapor of something much more dangerous, as had been in the glass last used by Carstairs.

"You finished your water early on, and then surreptitiously poured the contents of this bottle into your empty glass, awaiting an opportunity?" Pons asked. When she didn't answer, he said. "It doesn't matter now. You failed to execute Mr. Rath," said Pons to the guilty woman. Behind him, Rath made a strangled sound. "Can you tell us why you felt such an action was justified?"

She reached again for her bag, and Pons tensed. But she withdrew a set of folded papers, yellowed with age. "My father was ruined by Rath, back when I was a young woman. Mr. Holmes was able to keep Father from going to jail, but his reputation was still destroyed. And it was all because of this man!" She glared at Rath.

"But surely you didn't need to kill him," I said, "effectively throwing away your own life, if not your soul, in the bargain?"

"My soul would have been fine," she said. "Did I not say that the Bible allows for a man to be put to death if he has taken the life of another man? Mr. Rath here took my father's life. Only my poor father didn't actually die. He had to live another twenty years in sorrow and shame, a broken man."

She tapped the papers. "He spent all those years gathering evidence to clear his name, but he was always too frightened to use it, believing that Mr. Rath would somehow move against him or his family."

Pons reached out gently, and she placed the papers in his hand. He glanced at them quickly, and then looked up, his face hawk-like and intent. "There is more than enough here to indict Mr. Rath, despite the passage of time and any statute of limitations. Some of these documents are only a few years old. Apparently your father was able to keep tabs on the man up until the time that he died. Why did *you* not go to the authorities when they came into your possession? Or better yet, you could have brought these papers to me, or to Sherlock Holmes himself."

"I had never heard of you, Mr. Pons, although you certainly resemble Mr. Holmes in many ways. And as I said before, I've always *admired* Mr. Holmes for what he did, but I never said that I trusted him."

"Then what made you decide to act now?"

"I saw where Sir Amory had scheduled this event here at the church. I knew from the newspapers that he and Mr. Rath had had their differences, so I thought of a way to trick Mr. Rath into attending tonight. It might be the only time that I would ever be able to get near him. His reputation as a drinker is well known, so I prepared a mixture of whisky and some mashed-up berries that grow outside my house."

"How did you know what berries to use?"

"I read a lot of mysteries," she replied, simply.

Pons looked over his shoulder at me. "That fact has probably caused more mischief than half the wars," he said. Turning back to Miss Thrush, he said, "Did you not find it difficult to purchase the whisky? Is that not against your beliefs?"

"I keep a little bottle of it, for medicinal purposes only."

"I see." Pons took a step back. "Your ignorance in matters of spirits prevented you from realizing that there is a reason some whiskies are expensive, while others are cheap. You thought that your own supply could be swapped unnoticed.

"When you decided to execute Mr. Rath, didn't it bother you to take the law into your own hands? What about a trial by jury?"

"What did I need with a jury? I read in the newspaper at the time that Sir Amory called Mr. Rath 'the greatest villain yet unhanged'. That was good enough for me."

I glanced at Sir Amory. He had a look of horror struggling to force its way past his normally stoic face.

"You do realize," said Pons, his tone softer, but every word clear, nonetheless, "do you not, that what you intended initially as an execution is now, in fact, a murder?"

Miss Thrush nodded. "I do," she said, lowering her head. "God help me, I do." And then, though her body was still stiff and tense, she began to quietly weep.

For several moments, the only sound was that of the guilty woman weeping. Then Pons spoke softly to Jeffrey, indicating that he was now free to leave the room and seek a constable.

Later, the change in the room was palpable, as if it had turned from night to day. Sir Amory and Jeffrey were gathered with Father Ronald, talking with great animation. Initially, Inspector Jamison had wanted to know how Pons was able to focus his attention so quickly on Miss Thrush. "After all," he said, "the switching of the glasses could have been interpreted several different ways. She could have been trying to kill Carstairs, for instance, or Rath could have, or Jeffery could have been the one to poison the drinks."

"Jeffrey would have had to be a fool to wait until this very public occasion to try and kill Rath, in the place where he would be the most likely suspect. The same could be said for the others. Miss Thrush was the only one who might not get another chance to make the attempt. And as I explained, when I saw that, over and over again, she was pretending to sip water from her glass without actually consuming any, my suspicions toward her were intensified enough to question her further. I quickly knew that I was on the right track."

Inspector Jamison turned to speak with Sir Amory, discussing the packet of papers provided by Miss Thrush, while Leonard Rath sat alone, a man defeated. He was not under arrest - yet - but according to Sir Amory, he soon would be, once the entire scope of the Thrush papers was examined.

The body of the unfortunate Mr. Carstairs had been taken away, as had Miss Thrush, but not before Pons had spoken to her once again, confirming that he still had an appointment to speak with her on the following morning, as already arranged, to discuss matters of her religion. She agreed, rather enthusiastically I thought, considering her circumstances, adding that her schedule was now at the discretion of her captors. Currently, Pons was on the far side of the room, speaking in a low voice with Sir Wilmer Dougal, now standing beside my friend, wide awake and blinking near-sightedly across his tangled whiskers.

In a few moments, Pons left Sir Wilmer to rejoin us, and Sir Amory spoke up excitedly. "That was a most amazing demonstration, Mr. Pons," he said. "Far better than simply reading about it in a book, you know. Don't you agree, Father Ronald?"

"Not really," replied the priest. "I would much prefer staying away from this sort of thing. I would rather read of it in the comfort of my own study, and take it on faith that such men as you, Mr. Pons, and Mr. Holmes as well, are out there, instead of forcing me to encounter it in real life. It is all somewhat seamy when viewed up close, you understand."

Sir Amory frowned "Well, I disagree. Perhaps we should form a society dedicated to the study of *your* exploits, Mr. Pons. Might we count on your participation?"

Pons smiled tightly, his lips barely parting. "In the immortal and extremely useful words of Bartleby, the Scrivener, '*I would prefer not to.*'"

Inspector Jamison stepped over, looking slightly exasperated. "Have any of you gentlemen seen Sir Wilmer Dougal? I would like to get his statement."

"I took it upon myself to parole Sir Wilmer and gave him permission to depart," said Pons. "After all, he slept through the entire affair, never approached the table or the poisoned glass at all, and was cleared of any suspicion before he even woke up. I'm sure that you'll agree that a man of Sir Wilmer's position and status can be spared such an inconvenience."

"Well, I suppose so," said Jamison, "but I would at least like to know how to reach him in the future, should he be needed for anything. What if he woke up for just an instant and saw Miss Thrush switching the glasses?"

"What is the need for any possible corroboration that he might provide?" asked Pons. "She has, after all, confessed."

"Well, I would like to speak to him as well," said Sir Amory, slightly puzzled. "In all my life, I've never even *heard* of Sir Wilmer Dougal."

Within a few minutes, Pons made our excuses, and we both departed from the church. As we reached the outdoors, Pons said, "I do believe that a Sherlock Holmes Society is something for which the world is not yet prepared."

"Or, perhaps, a Solar Pons Club?" I murmured.

He smiled but did not reply, and looked back and forth along the street. The fog that had been rolling in earlier had vanished, and the lightened sky of a July night vaulted over us. We decided to walk back to Praed Street.

We had left Bloomsbury and crossed Regent Street, winding this-way-and-that along the smaller, quiet streets. We passed through Queen Anne Street, and I looked up to see that our friend Watson's windows were dark.

"I almost wish that he and Holmes had joined us tonight," I said. "It would have done Watson good to get out. He has been somewhat despondent since his wife passed earlier this year, in spite of his and Holmes's recent return from America."

"I discussed it with him the other day, and he did not wish to attend. There was no budging him on that point. My Illustrious Predecessor, now – Well, that is another story indeed. He wouldn't have missed it for the world."

"Well, he *did* miss it. He – " I looked at Pons, who was looking back with a grin on his face and a twinkle in his eyes. Then we moved out from under the streetlamp, and all I could see were his teeth, with the rest of his face in shadow underneath his fore-and-aft cap.

"Sir Wilmer Dougal!" I cried. "Holmes *was* there!"

"Of course he was. Why do you think I made sure that he managed to escape before he could be questioned? Good luck to Jamison and the rest in trying to track down 'Sir Wilmer'. Try as they might, he won't be found anywhere in Burke's Peerage!"

"And of course he wasn't asleep. Not Holmes! Knowing him, he was watching everything that was happening like a hawk." A thought struck me. "Then he no doubt saw – "

"Yes, he saw Miss Thrush set down her glass and take up another, not realizing that she was taking advantage of the drink spill to reach across and intentionally switch the glasses. It was a bold move on her part, and luckily I was able to determine what had happened without resorting to questioning or involving my 'surprise' witness."

"What an odd little affair," I said. "I cannot wait until I next see Watson to tell him about it."

"Well, I suppose you'll see him in about twenty minutes. Holmes was going to stop and get him, and then meet us back at Praed Street without giving Watson a chance to say no. But I'm fairly certain that he will have already given the good doctor a full account of the matter by now."

And when we reached 7B Praed Street, we found that to be exactly the case.

*A Sherlock Holmes Adventure*
*In Re: Solar Pons's Origins*

# The Adventure of the Other Brother

*From the Journals of
Dr. John H. Watson*

*In 2008, I was laid off from an engineering job – The Great Recession wasn't a good time for civil engineers. Each morning I would do those things that one does when looking for a job, and then . . . .*

*One explanation of what happened during that time was that I, like Conan Doyle when he had nothing to do, decided to write about Sherlock Holmes. After all, I've been reading and collecting Holmes pastiches since I was ten years old in the mid-1970's, and have literally thousands of them, so why not contribute to The Great Holmes Tapestry? (The Pons adventures are a very important subset of this larger whole.)*

*Another possibility of what I did during that period, as I explain in the introduction to* The Papers of Sherlock Holmes, *was* to find one of Dr. Watson's lost notebooks.

*That year I "edited" nine of Watson's writings about previously unknown Holmes adventures. The most important one, the longest and last of the set, was called "The Adventure of the Other Brother", revealing many details about Holmes's background. I say "revealing", but perhaps I should instead write "confirming", as this tale seemed to elaborate upon the work of famed Holmes biographer, William S. Baring-Gould.*

*At about the same time I discovered Holmes, even before I'd read all of The Canon, my parents gave me a copy of Baring-Gould's incredibly influential biography,* Sherlock Holmes of Baker Street. *I don't agree with quite everything in it, but mostly I do. It makes a great jumping-off place, and so much of it has influenced the way that I now enjoy the world of Mr. Holmes – and a lot of other people as well!*

*Baring-Gould revealed details of Holmes's family, including other members besides the mysterious Mycroft. He also refined and established some of the previous thinking that had been written in the 1950's and 1960's about the origins of Nero Wolfe of West 35$^{th}$ Street, my second favorite "book friend" (as my son used to call them) after Holmes. But much of what appeared in "The Other Brother" went beyond anything that Baring-Gould had suggested.*

*I had long asked myself, "Who exactly is Solar Pons?" and furthermore, what was his true connection to Sherlock Holmes? It was a question that I continued to ask myself a lot over the years. When I was in college, I managed to get my own copy of De Waal's* The World Bibliography of Sherlock Holmes and Dr. Watson, *and I began to track down various pastiches in greater earnest. In the Solar Pons section of the great reference book, I found an entry referring* to an essay by Bruce Dettman, "In the Master's Footsteps", (De Waal 5699), published in the December 1967 issue of The Pontine Dossier (Vol.I, No.2). The World Bibliography *listing for this work says this about Dettman's essay:*

> "After the Master had gone to his bee keeping in Sussex, William Pons [Billy the page boy], having long before decided on a career modeled after Holmes . . . set off to make his own name as a consulting detective."

*It was many years before I obtained my own copies of the* Pontine Dossier *and was able to read Dettman's essay for myself, but I had long ago decided that Billy the Page Boy was definitely not* Solar Pons. *Who, then, could Pons be?*

*I pondered this conundrum off-and-on for years. For a short time, I theorized that Pons might actually be young Lord Saltire from* "The Priory School", *who, after being rescued from his half-brother's plot, might have interested himself in learning the methods of his rescuer. Fortunately, I quickly left that idea behind. Pons and Lord Saltire's ages don't match up. Also, even though I disagree with a great deal of Philip Jose Farmer's* Wold Newton *family tree, I do agree with his correct identification of who Lord Saltire really is, as well the true identities of his illustrious cousin and half-nephew. But I digress . . . .*

*In the end, I returned to that great work by William S. Baring-Gould,* Sherlock Holmes of Baker Street, *and it was obvious.*

*In 2008, when I was laid off from an engineering job and had time to "edit" some of Watson's papers, the tale of Pons's origins was the one that I most wanted to explore, but I realized that it was too big to approach initially. That's why I "edited" the other eight stories that were in my first book,* The Papers of Sherlock Holmes, *in order to prepare for "The Other Brother".*

*After polishing those nine stories in 2008, I did nothing with them for a few years. Finally, in 2011 I had the urge to see them in print, and they were published later that year by The Battered Silicon Dispatch Box, and then reprinted (and divided into two volumes) by MX Publishing in 2013. Since then, they've been released as an audio book, published in Russia, and re-released again in a combined hardcover edition. Additionally, I've converted two of the tales into scripts that were recorded and broadcast nationally on the Imagination Theatre radio network, and those two scripts have been reprinted in the* Sherlock Holmes Mystery Magazine. *I've certainly gotten a lot of mileage from those initial efforts back in 2008, not to mention how that experience helped to spring me into the wider world of Sherlockian writing and editing.*

*It has always been my hope that "The Other Brother" would serve to answer some questions about Pons's background – a subject, I assure you, that took a lot of pondering on my part over several years. I've also hoped that, along with this volume, the story would serve to awaken – or reawaken – interest in Solar Pons, the Sherlock Holmes of Praed Street. He's an amazing fellow, and he deserves to be much better known.*

# The Adventure of the Other Brother

*From the Journals of
Dr. John H. Watson*

*With many thanks to Sir Arthur Conan Doyle,
August Derleth, and Rex Stout (the Literary Agents),
and William S. Baring-Gould (a Perceptive Biographer)*

Part I: The Other Brother

In late October 1896, I had been involved in a series of personal matters that caused me no little distress, as well as the inconvenient requirement that I temporarily move out of our Baker Street lodgings for nearly a week. During that time, I had seen Mr. Sherlock Holmes on a daily basis, as I stopped in to get fresh clothing and linens, as well as to retrieve my mail. As my presence was not always required elsewhere during the daytime hours, I had also accompanied Holmes on several investigations during that time.

On the last day of the month, I had returned to Baker Street for good, my business completed. Although the specific details of the matter have no relation to the present narrative, they did contribute to my mood that day. I was quite grim following a long week of struggles with a patient whose identity must remain anonymous. It was in such a dark attitude that I dropped into my chair in front of the sitting room fire.

Holmes was moving around in his bedroom. I could hear his occasional murmurs as he opened and closed drawers in the bedroom behind me. Soon he came in, and as if noticing the darkness of the room for the first time that afternoon, he stepped to the windows and threw back the drapes.

The weak additional light barely improved the condition of the dark room. Holmes sat in his chair across from me and glanced at my bag standing near the landing door. "It is finished, then?" he asked.

I nodded. "For better or worse."

"I, too, have received word today of some business relating to a painful matter from the past." He tossed me a telegram that had been hidden in his dressing gown pocket.

As I scanned the message, the events of the previous summer came flooding back to me, temporarily pushing aside my despondency over the day's conclusion.

"So he has escaped," I said softly.

"And apparently with no great difficulty. He must have been biding his time. The local constabulary waited far too long before notifying any other authorities. By the time Mycroft became aware of the matter, and was able to bring more skilled forces to bear, it had become apparent that the fugitive had fled across the German sea. . . ."

We were silent for a moment. "Do you think we shall meet him again?" I finally asked.

Holmes reached for his pipe. He did not answer as he went through the process of packing it with the dry shag tobacco from the Persian slipper. Finally, he replied, "Yes, Watson. I do not know how or when, but I very much fear that we shall meet him again."

As we continued to sit in the growing darkness, I recalled the events of half-a-year earlier. I had been amazed at the time, as well as angry with Holmes for his infernal habit of keeping secrets from me. However, at the conclusion of the case, I had believed that a great wrong had been righted. Now I knew that we would always be waiting to learn when this evil would reappear.

It was on a morning in early June of that same year that we became involved in the affair that I have always called "The Other Brother." I had been in the process of writing up several matters relating to Holmes's activities, including some incidents that took place during his travels for the Foreign Office from 1891-94, when everyone but his brother Mycroft believed him to be dead. Unfortunately, except for certain members of Her Majesty's government, the exact details of these events must remain secret until late into the next century.

Holmes had been involved for several days in a number of cases, including most recently the singularly unrewarding matter of Mr. Josiah Uppenham's tedious financial miscalculations. He was sitting at our dining table, surrounded by numerous stacks of documents, each threatening to slide and spill into its neighbor. At times Holmes would mutter, and lean forward with his head on his hand, squinting at the minuscule purple entries and jottings. Sometimes he would make a note, and other times he would lean back, sigh, and reshuffle and stack the papers a different way, occasionally making a note on a document as some sort of cross-referencing.

I did not know how long this would go on, but I suspected that Holmes would stop soon, if only to relieve the pain he must be feeling in his stooped back. It was into this setting that Mrs. Hudson arrived with a telegram.

Holmes stood, sighed, and stretched with an audible crack from his back. "Watson, I am tempted to let Mr. Uppenham suffer the consequences of his foolishness," he said, opening the wire. "He needs a team of sharp solicitors, not a lone consulting detective with a leery respect at best for mathematics. Luckily I am being generously compensated, in this instance for my reputation, I believe, more than my skills. . . ."

His voice trailed off as he read the telegram. The fatigue seemed to slough from him as he stood taller. He finished reading, looked toward the door for a short moment, and then moved toward his bedroom. Over his shoulder, he stated, "Can you come to Yorkshire today, Watson? Are you available for several days?"

I turned in my desk chair. "Of course," I replied.

He returned to the door, carrying some folded clothing. "Bring your service revolver."

I stood up as he turned back into the bedroom. "What is it, Holmes?"

He called from the other room, "My brother has been arrested for murder."

"What?" I cried. "Mycroft arrested? In Yorkshire?"

"Not Mycroft," he said, reappearing around the doorway. "My older brother, Sherrinford."

Later, as we sat in our compartment on the northbound train, I caught Holmes's eye and asked the obvious question. "You have another brother?"

He looked at me for another moment, and then out the window at the landscape, which began to pass more quickly as we left the sprawl surrounding London.

Earlier, I had grabbed my bag and gun, meeting Holmes on the landing within minutes of his request for my company on the trip. I am an old campaigner, and after years attending Holmes on his investigations, I had learned to always keep a bag ready for immediate departure. We had been silent in the hansom ride to King's Cross, and I could tell that Holmes was in deep thought and would not appreciate being disturbed.

He had, however, at one point silently handed me the telegram that had precipitated this journey. It simply said, "*Sherrinford arrested* for murder. Compartment booked for you on special train, King's Cross. Information to follow upon your arrival. Mycroft."

Now, in the train, I wanted answers, and knew that we had several hours for Holmes to provide them. "Perhaps," he said, "I should give you a little background information about my family, so that you will know something about them when we arrive." I nodded, and he continued.

"In the fall of 1888," he began, "I believe you were surprised to learn that I had an older brother, Mycroft."

"Surprised is hardly the word," I replied. I still remembered that evening vividly. Holmes and I had been sitting before our fireplace, long periods of companionable silence mixed with random conversation.

Holmes had begun to explain that he believed traits and abilities often ran in families. He had sought to prove this point by saying that his older brother Mycroft possessed even greater deductive skills than did Holmes himself. My amazement at learning of a brother, after having known Holmes for over seven years, had led to our visiting Mycroft at the Diogenes Club, that odd gathering place for the most unclubbable men in London. Before the evening was over we were involved in the strange matter of Mr. Melas, the Greek Interpreter.

"At the time, I had come to believe that you had as little family in England as I," I said.

"I had kept Mycroft's existence a secret for several reasons, not the least of which is my own natural tendency towards a certain reluctance for sharing information unnecessarily. It was not that I did not trust you, Watson. I simply had felt no need up to that point in time to mention Mycroft.

"As I said at the time, Mycroft was employed within the British government. I recall mentioning to you last year, during the matter of the stolen submarine plans, that on occasion Mycroft *is* the British government. Again, I did not distrust you by not mentioning this sooner. It was simply not relevant in 1888 to let you know how important Mycroft's position was and continues to be.

"In 1868, Mycroft graduated from Oxford and obtained a government position through the influence of a family friend. He moved to London, and found lodgings in Montague Street near the British Museum. The building was owned by a distant family relation, and it would in fact be these rooms in which I would reside when I came down to London several years later.

"Of course, given Mycroft's incredible skills at sorting information and perceiving various relationships between facts unnoticed by others, he was soon being consulted by all sorts of departments within the government. It was a natural progression that he would find himself offering opinions on the mysterious activities and motivations of foreign countries and their leaders. During that time, Mycroft was not nearly as sedate as he would later become, and on several occasions he traveled abroad on a number of secret missions, the nature of which he has never revealed, not even to me.

"During this time, I was a young fellow, spending my time alternately between my family's home in Yorkshire and several schools in different parts of England. My family consisted of my father Siger, my mother Violet, my older brother Sherrinford, and his growing family.

"My father was the second son of a country squire, and had spent time serving as an officer in the military in India before being invalided home due to an injury. His older brother lived in Yorkshire as the squire of the estate. During the time my father was traveling home, his older brother had died, and my father arrived on Portsmouth jetty to learn that he had inherited the estate.

"Not long after taking up his position as a country squire, my father met and married my mother, Violet Sherrinford, the daughter of Sir Edward Sherrinford, a not too distant neighbor. My brother Sherrinford was born about a year later, in 1845. Mycroft followed in 1847. I was born in 1854.

"My father was a great bear of a man, loud and with a full black beard. He was strong-willed and highly opinionated, and he knew exactly what he wanted for each of his three sons. Sherrinford, the oldest, was to be educated and then take over the family estate, continuing the line of country squires that had run the place for ages. Mycroft was to attend university as well and then obtain a position within the government.

"Each of my brothers followed my father's plan and ended up where they were supposed to be. For myself, my father had decided that I was to be an engineer. It was with this in mind that he hired a mathematics tutor to get me ready during the summer of 1872. As I have related before, Watson, this tutor was none other than Professor James Moriarty.

"The Professor and I did not get along at all during that time, but I had no idea then how our differences would grow. In later years, as I became aware of a criminal network forming in England, I still had difficulty believing for sure that my former mathematics tutor had become the leader of the vast underworld machine that he himself created. During that long summer before I went away to university, the house was filled with tension as I fought with Moriarty over the need to learn mathematical theorems, which I felt to be irrelevant, and I questioned my father endlessly about whether I really had to become an engineer.

"The only enjoyment that I had during that summer was playing with my young nephew, William, who had been born the previous year. He is a fine lad, much like his father Sherrinford, and even at that young age his intelligence seemed remarkable. He has also always been a wonderfully even-tempered boy, considering that for a portion of his early years he grew up in the same house as my tempestuous father.

"I credit William's wonderful nature to his mother, Roberta, formerly Roberta MacIvor, who had married Sherrinford in 1868. She became like a second mother to me, especially as my own mother was already in failing health at that time.

"In the fall of 1872, I left Yorkshire to attend Oxford. I was not at home during early 1873 when Sherrinford's second son, Bancroft, was born. I did try to stay in contact with the family as often as I could. On several occasions, however, I accepted invitations to visit other homes with friends I had made while away at school. It was during one of these trips with Victor Trevor to Norfolk in the summer of 1874 that I finally realized my future lay not in the field of engineering, but rather in defining and creating the profession of consulting detective." I recalled the matter of which he spoke. I had learned of it in early 1888, following the death of my first wife. I had moved back to Baker Street, and Holmes had begun to tell me some about his past and a few earlier cases as a way to help me forget my grief. I had later chronicled the matter under the title "The *Gloria Scott.*"

"As you might expect, my father was not pleased when I informed him of my decision," Holmes continued, "and he quickly wrote to me, explaining that he would continue to provide funding for me, but that he never wanted to see me again. Thus released from my duties as a student engineer, I traveled to London, moved into the rooms in Montague Street, and promptly enrolled in Cambridge for the fall, feeling that its scientific emphasis might be better suited in order to prepare me for my new calling.

"For several years I alternated between classes at Cambridge and the Montague Street rooms, learning what I could in the classroom, and more practical lessons on the streets of London at other times. During this period, I found what cases that I could, always trying to use each as a way to extrapolate knowledge for my future profession.

"Over the next few years, I attended classes less and less and worked much more often. I began to build a fairly steady practice, and started to believe that I could make a true profession out of my work. I had also managed to arrange an uneasy truce with my father, and I was able to visit my family as frequently as I could get away, which sadly, was not very often. In 1880, as you know, I traveled with a Shakespearean acting company for a good part of the year to various parts of the United States, and so had no contact with them at all for several months.

"It was during this time that Sherrinford's youngest and last son was born. Coincidentally, Watson, he arrived on the twenty-seventh of July, 1880, the same day that you were fighting for your life at Maiwand. After my return to England in August, I traveled briefly to Yorkshire, where I met this nephew for the first time.

"I must say that of Sherrinford's three children, it is this fellow to whom I feel closest. His name is Siger, after his grandfather, and physically he is very much like me. Although all of my brothers and nephews are quite adept in the art of deduction, which does seem to run in the family as I have previously stated, Siger seems to approach the matter more like me than the others. Interestingly, my oldest nephew, William, is much like Sherrinford, warm and intelligent and suited for country life, while the middle son, Bancroft, is in many ways like his uncle Mycroft. He and Mycroft both have that coldly analytical trait that works so well for those involved in government intrigues.

"In fact, Bancroft has been working for several years in Mycroft's department in London, although in a rather strange way. When he completed his studies at university in 1892, Bancroft expressed a desire to follow in Mycroft's footsteps. However, he wanted it made very clear that anything that he accomplished would be on his own merits, and not due to the influence of his uncle Mycroft or the Holmes name. Therefore, when he went to work, he fashioned a different last name for himself, and has used it ever since, preferring that no one there know that he and Mycroft are related.

"Bancroft based his name on a variation of his father's name, Sherrinford, which comes from the old name for a local spot in a stream used for shearing sheep. The area was known as the *shearing ford,* which was later simply pronounced *sherrinford.* Likewise, the name *Mycroft* comes from a similar local derivation, based on an ancestor exclaiming *'My croft!'* Thankfully, I am not aware of any local words or phrases that have been derived or corrupted into *Sherlock.*

"Since his father's name was based on a ford across a stream, Bancroft decided that he would figuratively build a bridge across that stream, instead of using the ford. He initially took the last name *Bridge*, but he decided that he did not like the alliteration of *Bancroft Bridge*, and subsequently changed his pseudonym to the Latin for bridge, *Pons*. Bancroft's choice to change his last name and the way he created it are typical of the crafty and, if I may say it, rather twisted way that his and my brother Mycroft's minds work. No doubt this is why they get along so well together, and also the reason for the great success of the department that Mycroft has created.

"As I said, Bancroft went to work in Mycroft's department in 1892, and he was soon placed in charge of managing my activities as I traveled throughout Asia and the Middle East, as well as various locations in Europe and the United States. It was good practice for him, as I understand that he is now fairly in charge of most of Mycroft's field agents, as a good part of Mycroft's time is still spent collecting and arranging data from all departments of the government, not just for the Foreign Office, as well as dealing with politicians and military leaders."

By now, we were quite a distance from London, and the train was moving at a good pace. I could not believe how much information about his past that Holmes had just related to me. I had understood for years that he had no family, and had been amazed years before when I learned about Mycroft. To learn that there were others, parents, a brother and sister-in-law, and three nephews who each strangely mimicked the three older Holmes brothers, was almost too amazing. I did my best not to interrupt, as I did not want Holmes to realize just how much he was revealing and suddenly decide to stop. However, I had to ask one question.

"I still do not understand," I said, "why these people had to remain a secret."

"Ah," said Holmes. "Normally they would not. However, there was an incident which threatened them, and it was felt that a certain . . . separation between the Yorkshire family and their wayward London relations was necessary.

"As I said, Mycroft began to be noticed by the government early on, and his position advanced at a very quick rate. Soon he was helping to evaluate and decide policy for many departments. It was also not long before agents of foreign governments began to hear of this wonderful man whose brain was being used as some sort of human calculating machine.

"To this day, I do not know all the details of what happened. Likewise, Sherrinford's family does not know exactly what threat faced them, only that they were in danger, and Mycroft will not disclose what happened, or what action was taken against the aggressors. All I do know is that in September 1880, just a month after I visited my new nephew Siger, something happened to threaten the family at the Yorkshire home, and it was clearly related somehow to Mycroft's position with the government. Even then, Mycroft's incredible value to the Crown was recognized, and it was decided at the highest levels to prevent anything like that from happening again, so that nothing of the sort could be used against him or to bring pressure on him.

"Members of the village around the family estate were contacted by agents of Her Majesty's government and asked to help give the impression that the Holmes family of North Riding had nothing to do with Mycroft, and me as well. I suppose that even then, I had been of some use on a few matters, and Mycroft included me in the plan, as he knew I would be staying in London and continuing to get into all sorts of trouble with the more questionable elements of society.

"After making sure that the local individuals understood what was required and were willing to cooperate, references to Mycroft, myself, and various other family members were quietly removed from the official records. That is why you will not find a record of me at Oxford, or Cambridge, or at Barts Hospital. And none of that branch of the Holmes family will be recorded in the local Parish book near our family home.

"It was not a perfect plan, but it was hoped that it would be enough to confuse or stop the actions of an enemy agent trying to use threats against Sherrinford's family to coerce Mycroft or myself. Over the years, neighbors have reported occasional attempts to find out something about our family, sometimes by reporters, at other times by mysterious individuals whom we can only assume have been agents of criminal or foreign organizations.

"Our biggest fear was always some sort of threat from Professor Moriarty or his organization. The man had actually stayed in our house for most of a summer, and he certainly knew where and who we were. However, he never made a move against my family, and I can only assume he had some sort of odd code of honor that prevented him from doing so. Perhaps he felt a sense of obligation due to the fact that he was well treated while he was there. Possibly he thought that I knew something about his own family as well, and he mistakenly believed that I would make a move against them in retaliation. Perhaps I would have. Luckily, he appears to have kept all information about us and the summer that he stayed there to himself, because there has never been any indication that the subsequent individuals who tried to resurrect his criminal web have any clue of our existence."

We pondered these thoughts in silence for a moment, before I said, "You have described your family in Yorkshire as Sherrinford's family. Does this imply that your parents are no longer living?"

"My mother passed away in April 1888. I did not mention the fact to you then, although you were living in Baker Street. In retrospect, the event left me far more shaken than I acknowledged at the time. My father had died much earlier, in the summer of 1877, before he ever had a chance to see that I had managed to make a real success of the career that I had chosen, and that he had ridiculed."

I recalled that spring of 1888. Holmes had never given any indication to me at the time of the death of his mother. Perhaps the only sign of a problem at all was a stumble during a few of his cases, most noticeably the investigation into the mysterious tenant living in the house adjacent to Mr. Grant Munro. It will be recalled that Holmes had theorized a completely incorrect and rather grim solution, and upon learning that the truth was far more pleasant, he had asked me to whisper "Norbury" in his ear if he ever again seemed to be becoming over-confident in his powers, or not taking the proper amount of interest or care in a case.

The train sped on, and we sat in silence for a number of miles, each lost in our own memories. I understood how Holmes felt. My father had died of alcohol poisoning following a wasted life that had spiraled down from success, solidity, and respectability to unbeatable failure. The death of my mother, which occurred much sooner than it should have due to anguish over my father's abandonment, had left me unsettled and grief-stricken. When I was older, after becoming a doctor, I had traveled for a number of years, as well as spent time in the army, coming to grips with the bitter feelings I had retained following my parents' deaths.

I gradually became aware of the train compartment, and Holmes watching me from his seat on the other side. Clearing my throat, I asked, "So now who resides at the family home?"

"Sherrinford and Roberta, their oldest son William, who has not yet married, and Siger, who is about to turn sixteen. I confess I am looking forward to seeing Siger again. It has been a year or so since I visited. The last time was just prior to my return to London in April '94, a day or so after I arrived back on English soil. When I saw him then he was already using the methods of ratiocination in a way far more advanced of my skills when I was at that age."

I laughed. Most people would have commented that the boy was taller than expected, or some such observation. Only Holmes would think in terms of deductive skills. "You still thought that you were going to be an engineer at that age," I said. "An engineer, indeed."

He laughed as well, but just for a moment before the seriousness returned to his expression.

"Do you know anything of Sherrinford's arrest?" I asked.

He shook his head. "Nothing more than what is in that telegram. I assume we will be able to begin our investigation as soon as we arrive. No doubt Mycroft will manage to reach us with any information that he believes we will need."

We continued on northward, each lost in our private thoughts. As for myself, I was still thinking of the wealth of information that I had just received regarding Holmes's background and family life. Holmes's frowning face was pinched in concentration, his pipe — which had long since gone out — clamped in his teeth. Although he made it a practice never to theorize in advance of data, I did not see how he would be able to refrain from some sort of speculation regarding his brother Sherrinford's dilemma. However, I knew he would be unwilling to discuss the matter, and I left him to his thoughts.

## Part II: Home

We changed trains in York for the line to Thirsk. After arriving in that picturesque town, we found seats on a smaller branch line, and I must have slept at some point. When I awoke we were pulling into a tiny village station. Following Holmes's lead, I began to gather my things for departure. We had no sooner stepped onto the platform than a neatly dressed man stepped forward to intercept us.

"Mr. Holmes," he said. "Dr. Watson? I am Inspector Tenley. I have been briefed on the matter, and I will be accompanying you to your family home."

In actuality, Tenley did not say "your family home." Rather, he named the community which was our destination. However, in spite of the passage of years since these events took place, I will not name or identify the location any more specifically than I have already done so. Even though this narrative will be placed in my tin dispatch box following its completion, where it is intended to remain for at least seventy-five years after my death, I am not willing to compromise the security of the Holmes family, or to negate the incredible efforts already made over the years by the British government to shield and protect them.

Tenley led us to a connecting train for the remaining journey to the village in question. The trip was tedious, as we were in a compartment with a stranger, requiring that we make no discussion of the case to pass the time.

Arriving at the village station, Tenley gestured toward the adjacent roadway. "This way, gentlemen," he said. "I have transportation waiting."

Outside, a rugged four-wheeler stood, pulled by a stout and patient horse. Holding the reins was a small, wiry man who looked once at us, then faced forward again without comment. As we found our seats, Tenley said, "This is Griffin. He can be trusted."

Griffin softly snapped the reins and the four-wheeler lurched into motion. "I believe we have time to discuss the details of the case now, Mr. Holmes, if you prefer."

"That will be fine," Holmes said. "We know virtually nothing, as we left London immediately after being notified of the arrest. The charge is murder, then?"

"Yes, sir. No possibility of an accidental death or suicide. Your brother has been very cooperative, but professes to have total ignorance on the matter."

"Pray give me the facts," said Holmes, shifting in his seat toward Tenley.

Tenley watched for a moment as Holmes closed his eyes, so that he might better concentrate on the narrative. "Yesterday morning," Tenley began, "your nephew William arrived at the local police station, quite agitated, requesting that the constable accompany him back to the Holmes farm, where the body of a middle-aged man had just been discovered, brutally murdered.

"The officer, Constable Worth, quickly joined William, who drove them in a carriage the five miles or so out to the house. Upon entering the estate, they bypassed the house and adjacent farm buildings, driving out into a pasture several hundred feet away. The area is rock-bound, and has many low and hidden areas created by the steeply rolling hills."

"The north pasture," Holmes said, without opening his eyes. "Go on."

"The entire area has been used for sheep grazing, as I'm sure you know," continued Tenley. "William drove the carriage around a number of rocky areas until they reached a low spot, surrounded by several farm hands and your brother Sherrinford.

"Upon reaching their destination, Worth jumped down and advanced through the ring of silent men, all staring at something below them. The location is a natural pit in the earth, an inverted cone some eight or ten feet deep, and whatever is in it would be quite hidden below the view of anyone on the surrounding pasture. I was told that during times of heavy rain, the pit fills with water before it gradually seeps away into the ground. We have had no rain, however, for several weeks, and at the time of the murder, it was dry. Although," he said, glancing at the sky, "I suspect we are due for some rain shortly."

"I know of the place you speak," said Holmes. "I used to camp there as a small boy."

Tenley nodded, unnoticed by Holmes. "At the bottom of the pit was the body of the victim, a fellow in his early fifties. He was lying on his back, and had apparently only been there a few hours, as there was no sign of disturbance of the corpse by birds or animals.

"Constable Worth questioned your brother, Sherrinford, who told him that William discovered the body that morning. While walking toward a distant field, he had happened to glance into the pit as he skirted its edge. Upon seeing the body, he rushed down and ascertained that the man was dead. He then returned to the house, where he informed his father. By that time, a number of farmhands had gathered around them. Sherrinford sent William for the police, saying that he and the hands would guard the body until William returned. Sherrinford then walked to the body's location with the other men. He made sure that no one approached the body while they awaited the constable's arrival. He stated that he was aware, Mr. Holmes, of the need to preserve the area around the body.

"Constable Worth is a capable man, a typical rural official and quite observant in his own way. He made a cursory examination of the area. He did not see any signs of footprints or disturbances around the body, although as I have said, we have had no rain for several weeks, and it is unlikely that anything would show on the ground. Worth was unable to even see any of William's footprints at the immediate site, or any of his own, for that matter.

"The body had a great torn cut on the throat, but strangely there was very little blood around that wound or on the collar of the man's suit. There was more blood on the man's back that had soaked through the coat, but a quick examination by Worth did not reveal the nature of that wound. Also, Worth reported that there was very little blood on the ground below the body. I have since verified this, as well as Worth's conclusion that no footprints were detectable in the hollow. Based upon the evidence of the blood, the fellow was murdered elsewhere and the body was placed there after the fact.

"Worth immediately recognized the murdered man, and asked Sherrinford if he knew who it was, as well. 'Of course,' replied Sherrinford. 'We all know him. It is Davison Wilkies. I have given him and his people permission to camp on my land. They have been here for a week or so.'

"This agreed with Worth's knowledge of the situation. Wilkies was the leader of a group of a dozen or so odd folk, apparently part of some self-styled religious cult. They had arrived in the area about ten days ago, like a band of gypsies, all traveling in six or eight large wagons pulled by heavy teams of horses. Your brother had given them permission to stay on the Holmes land, although he directed them to the southern side, where the fields are much flatter and more hospitable, and there is access to water from the stream.

"It was common knowledge that Sherrinford had visited with Wilkies at the campsite on a number of occasions, usually in the evening. Your brother stated that he was curious about the group's beliefs, and that he was simply going to see Wilkies in order to ask questions. We learned this from both Sherrinford, as well as from Wilkies's daughter, Sophia.

"Sophia indicated that on the night of the murder, Wednesday night, your brother visited Wilkies's wagon, as usual. She states that while she did not hear the exact conversation, the tone between the two men became tense, and then somewhat hostile. They appeared to be arguing regarding the nature and validity of Wilkies's beliefs. Sophia indicated that Sherrinford appeared to be of the opinion that Wilkies had turned away from the 'true path,' whatever that means. Sherrinford denies that this conversation ever took place, and states that his visit that night was cordial, and no different than those of other nights. He also does not even know what was meant by the phrase 'true path,' since he was only a curious and casual visitor with little knowledge of Wilkies's beliefs.

"No one else in the campsite can be found to verify or disprove either of their statements. However, Sophia said that she doubted if anyone else would have overhead the conversation. Although she says that the two men were disagreeing quite strongly, they were quiet about it, and even though Sophia overheard some of the conversation from her location immediately outside the wagon, she does not believe the voices would have carried any farther.

"Sophia initially related this information to Constable Worth, when he questioned her yesterday morning following the notification of her father's death. When asked who might have had a reason to kill her father, she could think of no one, with the exception of your brother, whom she stated had argued with her father the night before. She indicated that the group did not know anyone else in the area, and that no one within her group would have had any reason for murdering her father.

"She also did not know how her father's body could have come to be located so far away from the campsite. Wilkies's party is quite a distance to the south of the house, while the rocky area where he was discovered is to the north. Constable Worth's investigations did not show any signs of blood in the campsite, indicating that he was not murdered there, and my subsequent examination confirmed this.

"Based on Sophia's statement, Worth returned to the Holmes farm, where he made a surreptitious examination of the grounds and outbuildings. In one of the barns, he thought that he found something of interest, a bundle of old clothing, consisting of an old shirt, the sleeves covered in blood and gore. However, subsequent investigation revealed this to be simply an old shirt belonging to one of the farm workers, used in the past during butchering time. However, based on the evidence of Sophia's story, Worth felt that he had no choice but to arrest Sherrinford.

"It is Worth's belief that Wilkies and Sherrinford must have known each other at some time in the past, although Sherrinford denies it. Worth feels that Wilkies did not just come to this area by chance, and that he was actually invited here by Sherrinford, who let him stay on the Holmes property because of their past relation. They must have both been members of the same religious belief at some point in the past, but Wilkies has changed or modified his beliefs. Sherrinford was dismayed upon learning that Wilkies no longer followed the 'true path,' and this turned to anger, which led to Wilkies's murder.

"Worth believes that Sherrinford lured Wilkies to some spot Wednesday night, where he killed him, before concealing the body in the hollow. He intended to return and bury it the next night, but it was discovered by William before he was able do so. He then had to play along. Worth has not yet found where Wilkies was killed, but he is still looking. Obviously, wherever the murder took place, a great deal of blood will have been spilled, and there is no sign of this in any of the farm buildings or on locations immediately near them. It is Worth's contention that Sherrinford hid his own bloody clothing and knife, having changed following the murder. He meant to bury them with the body, but he never got the chance. He hid the body in the dark following the murder, not realizing that it would be visible when that area was in daylight.

"As I said, Mr. Holmes, this is Constable Worth's contention. He did investigate the likelihood of any other possibility all yesterday, but by late evening he had no choice but to arrest your brother. As of right now, we have found no evidence to the contrary, so I have allowed Worth's arrest of your brother to stand. However, I am interested in finding all the facts in order to get at the truth.

"Following Sherrinford's arrest, his family, of course, wasted no time in contacting London. Within hours, I was assigned to the case. I came out with Worth this morning, and we reexamined the hollow where the body was found, and spoke with both your brother and Sophia. I reported directly to your brother, Mycroft, in London. He informed me that you would be arriving soon to investigate as well."

Holmes opened his eyes. "Is Sherrinford being held in the village, or in the facilities of some larger town?"

"In the village," Tenley replied. "Worth is rather ambitious, and he seemed to want to keep the matter within his own sphere of influence. He had made no effort on his own to call for any assistance, believing that he was handling the case sufficiently by himself. He was in fact somewhat resentful when your family arranged for my participation."

Tenley added, "As I said, Mr. Holmes, Worth is quite competent and observant, but also ambitious. I will be watching to make sure that his ambition does not cloud his judgment."

"Quite," replied Holmes. "And the body? Is it also still in the village?"

"Yes," replied Tenley. "Worth requested an autopsy this morning, but I stopped it until you could be here to examine the body first."

"Excellent," said Holmes. "Who will be doing the autopsy?"

"Dr. Dalton," said Tenley.

Holmes smiled tightly. "As I supposed."

"Do you wish to see the body first, or go on to the site of its discovery?" Tenley asked.

Holmes glanced at the low clouds. The wind had picked up somewhat since we had left the train station, and the air was noticeably cooler. I agreed with Tenley's earlier observation about the imminent arrival of rain.

"I suppose we should see the hollow first," said Holmes, "although I am sure that you are correct and that very little will be discovered."

Tenley instructed Griffin to continue on to the farm. We rode in silence, Tenley and Holmes both wrapped in their own thoughts, while I looked from side to side at the surrounding fields and copses, examining with interest that area from which Holmes had sprung. I tried to imagine him as a boy, with his great and curious intellect, roaming and exploring this countryside. It was difficult, to say the least. Holmes had always been comfortable and competent in all situations, but I generally thought of him as a man of the city. However, I also knew that he had showed a familiarity with country life, including knowledgeable experience with horses, and that living once in a rude stone hut on the wilds of Dartmoor had not seemed to cause him any serious distress. Obviously, he had gathered these and other skills here, as a boy.

We topped a low rise, and spread out before us was a tidy manor house, surrounded by a cluster of barns and smaller farm buildings. The house was unostentatious but well kept. On several sides were fenced paddocks, and the fence rails were brightly whitewashed. The ground around the buildings was flat and trim, and stretched away smoothly to the south. Behind the house, beyond the trees obviously planted as windbreaks, the land changed, turning rocky and rippled toward the north. I knew that this was the area where the body was found. "What is in that direction?" I asked, gesturing toward the rocky piles.

"Nothing," said Holmes. "Eventually one would run into the German Sea. The ground stays jumbled that way for a number of miles before flattening out on a high, rough tableland. There are a few shepherd cottages scattered out there. I suppose that is where William was going yesterday morning when he discovered the body."

"That is correct, Mr. Holmes," said Tenley. "He was going to take a message to one of the men out there, asking him to drive the sheep back toward the main house. Your brother says he wanted to examine them to make sure there were no signs of any infectious disease in the flock. There had been reports of something going through farms in nearby towns."

As we approached the house, the front door opened, and two men and a woman stepped out. Two or three farmhands also moved into the darkening daylight from a nearby barn. They stayed there, in the doorway, while the people from the house moved closer to us. The four-wheeler stopped, and the woman walked to the side.

"Sherlock," she said. "Thank you for coming." Holmes stepped down, and the woman reached and drew him into a hug. Holmes looked mildly uncomfortable for a moment, and then relented to the woman, hugging her back.

I looked at the woman, assuming that this was Roberta, whom Holmes had said was like a second mother to him. She was short, not much over five feet in height, with thick brown hair pulled back into a loose bun. The hair was somewhat shot with gray, but it only added to her commanding and confident presence. "Why have you waited so long to visit?" she asked. "It shouldn't have taken something like this to get you up here."

She turned to me. "And you must be Dr. Watson," she said, shaking my hand with a firm and warm two-handed grip. There was no pretense of delicate lady-like behavior here. She was a woman of the country, strong and not uncomfortable about showing it. "I am Roberta Holmes. I'm so happy to finally meet you, and sorry that it has taken this long to do so," she said, glancing at Holmes with scolding eyes. "You have no idea how many times I have told Sherlock to invite you. It has been nearly impossible, however, to even get *him* to visit . . . . "

While she had been speaking, the older of the two young men behind her stepped forward, his hand outstretched toward Holmes. "Uncle," he said. "I'm very glad that you're here."

Holmes returned his handshake. "William," he said. "It has been too long."

William was a tall, solid fellow in his mid-twenties. He was more heavily built than Holmes had been at that age, although not nearly as portly as his uncle Mycroft. His face clearly showed the Holmes family features, including a high hairline, aquiline nose, and piercing gray eyes. He was dressed in work clothes, and when he turned and shook my hand, I could feel the rough calluses on his palms.

Holmes turned to face the second young man, a thin fellow who was the spitting image of a young Sherlock Holmes. Tall, perhaps an inch taller even than Holmes, with Holmes's same sharp gaze and precise movements. I knew that he was nearly sixteen, but he seemed much older. He was not dressed for farm work. Rather, he was in more casual clothing, as if our arrival had interrupted his studies. He stuck out his hand, which Holmes grasped and shook.

"Siger," he cried. "Your mother wrote that you had grown, but I did not realize how much so. How have you been?"

"Tolerable," Siger replied. "I will be better when I can get down to London."

"Siger," his mother interrupted, with a warning tone. "This is not the time to start that, with our visitors just setting foot on the place."

She turned to us. "You'll hear all about it before you go, but life on the farm is not going to satisfy Siger, here. He has heard too much of London from his brother Bancroft, as well as what he has gleaned over the years from you, Sherlock, and Mycroft, and your writings, Dr. Watson."

Siger turned in my direction. "Ah, Dr. Watson, we finally meet." He shook my hand, and then said, "You have been in Thirsk, I perceive."

Then he laughed in a peculiar silent way. I had only ever heard one other person laugh that way: Sherlock Holmes.

I smiled, recognizing the source of Siger's joke, but Roberta said, sternly, "None of that smart tongue of yours, Siger." Turning to me, she apologized. "He reads too much, I think, doctor."

"Not at all, mother," said Siger. "Of course he's been in Thirsk. They just arrived here on the train. But I didn't just assume it and accept it. I *verified* it." He pointed to my shoes, which had a grayish mud clinging to the instep. "That mud is only at one location around here. It is from the side yard at the Thirsk station, where the coal dust and crushed clinker mixes with the local soil to form this distinctive gray material. There has been no rain for several days, so obviously the doctor walked through a damp spot of that particular mud while getting to their vehicle. There is some of it on the floor of the four-wheeler there, where the doctor was sitting. It has obviously fallen off of his shoes.

"It isn't enough to assume that they came from Thirsk simply because we knew their approximate arrival time and also that Thirsk has the closest major train station. I was able to verify it by observing the mud and relating it to the assumption. Isn't that the correct way to do it, Uncle?" Siger concluded, turning to Holmes.

"Exactly right," answered Holmes. "You are learning. Keep it up. There will be a place for you in London if you do."

"Don't go filling his head full of *that*," said Roberta. "He's going to university in a year or so, and that's that."

"Be careful of whom you hire as a math tutor," Holmes muttered softly, so that only I could hear.

Roberta turned toward the house. "Now come inside and have something to eat or drink, and let's talk about why you're here. I'm sure you'll want to examine things, and I know Sherrinford is looking forward to speaking with you."

"I'm afraid we cannot join you inside just yet," said Holmes. "We must get out to the pit where the body was found before the rains come."

All eyes glanced skyward. The wind was picking up, and sighing through the nearby windbreak. Hanging from one of the eaves of the house was a set of wind chimes, tolling anxiously.

"Of course," said Roberta. "We will be here when you return."

"May I go with them, mother?" asked Siger eagerly, seeing that William had moved to join us.

Roberta smiled with tolerant affection. "Yes, but try to leave something for your uncle to solve, won't you?"

As she returned to the house, we climbed back into the four-wheeler with Griffin, who turned the horse and drove us out of the yard. Passing several of the outbuildings, we were observed by the farmhands who had come out to watch our arrival. They nodded in our direction, and then returned inside to their tasks.

As we passed the trees, the wind hit us full on, carrying with it a strong indication of impending rain. Siger shifted in his seat to face me.

"When will you be publishing some more narratives of my uncle's cases, Dr. Watson?" he asked.

I glanced at Holmes, whose mouth tightened in irritation, although conversely his eyes crinkled in suppressed humor. "I am currently . . . prohibited from making public any of the records of Holmes's investigations."

"And it shall remain that way," added Holmes. "Perhaps someday, when I am retired, I will write an extended monograph detailing my methods and how they were applied in specific instances. However, they will be published in a single volume encompassing the whole art of detection, and not as romanticized segments in a throw-away magazine."

Inspector Tenley caught my eye with an amused smile. I shrugged.

Siger, however, did not appear to notice, as he was looking at his uncle with some shock. "I am sure that I cannot wait until you have retired to hear more of your adventures," he said. "I have attempted to make use of Dr. Watson's narratives as something of a guide for my own studies, and frankly I need more information. Two dozen narratives do not provide enough data for well-rounded instruction. And besides," he added, with a grin, "I don't even know the real story of why you allowed us to believe you were dead for three years, what you were doing while you were gone, and how you managed to come back. When I have asked Bancroft, he simply informs me that I am too young. Typical Bancroft bluster."

"Most people do not know the story of Holmes's journey and subsequent return," I said. "He has refused to allow me to publish it. In the meantime, his practice has increased substantially over what it was before his hiatus, and many of the clients indicate that it is because they became aware of Holmes through my writings."

"And how many of them express surprise that I am a real person, and not some fictional creation in a storyteller's tale?" asked Holmes acidly.

"You cannot blame me for that," I said. "It was your brother, Mycroft, who managed to spread the word during your supposed 'death' that you were a fictional character, no doubt in order to aid some scheme of his while you carried out his tasks during your disappearance."

Siger leaned forward intently, and I realized that I might possibly be on the verge of revealing too much of Holmes's activities during his travels. Holmes, seeing that I needed a way to escape from this path of the conversation, said, "Siger, if you are serious about following in my footsteps, take my advice. Do not let the facts of your cases be placed into narrative form, giving the majority of the public the impression that you were created by a doctor with too much time on his hands." Seeing the somewhat hurt expression on my face, he added, "However, if you are able to find a doctor who is of invaluable assistance both in your work and as a friend, I highly recommend it."

Feeling somewhat mollified, I looked around me as the four-wheeler slowed to a halt. We were near a rocky outcropping, sprawled around a hollow in the ground before it. We climbed down and walked to it. Only when we were at the edge were we able to see into the bottom of the pit.

It was about fifteen feet across and eight feet deep, with steeply sloping sides. The bottom was irregular, pierced in several areas by boulders sticking up out of the ground. At the top, there was a path running along the front side, opposite the rocky outcropping. It lay quite close to the edge of the pit, so that someone walking on it would have no trouble seeing what lay at the bottom. Even from a few feet further away, however, the contents of the pit would be hidden.

"Where was the body?" asked Holmes, looking about on the path.

"On the front side of the pit," said Tenley, "directly below the trail. Still, it might have remained unseen if William here hadn't looked in while he was walking by."

"It is a regular thing when I pass this way, to make sure that no sheep have fallen in," added William.

Holmes moved several feet up and down the trail. "Nothing left here," he said. "Too many people have passed this way, beginning with William, and then Sherrinford and the farm hands standing here to guard the body." He moved along the edge of the pit, back to where the rocky outcropping behind it began to rise. Then he climbed down, choosing that spot to enter so that he would not disturb where the body had rested.

William watched the darkening clouds, while Siger followed his uncle's actions with a hawk-like intensity. He stepped to the rim of the pit, but away from where the body would have been placed, somehow instinctively knowing where he should stand so as not to impede his uncle's investigation.

In the hole, Holmes moved back and forth across the bottom, bent nearly double so that his eyes were close to the ground. In a moment he called, "How did the body lie?"

Tenley replied, "He was sitting up with his back against the wall of the pit, right under the trail side so that he wouldn't be seen unless you were standing right on the edge, looking down. The arms were tucked in around him. He was obviously placed in that way intentionally after he was rolled in."

Holmes's examination of the bottom only lasted a further few minutes. As he climbed back out, the first drops of heavy rain began to fall around us. "You were correct, Inspector. There is no blood here. The man was killed elsewhere and brought later." He looked up at the sky, they pulled his cap tighter. "We can learn nothing else here. We'd better get back to the house."

We climbed into the four-wheeler, which Griffin immediately set into motion, moving at a faster pace than when we had traveled out to the pit.

The rain began to fall harder, and we huddled into our coats. Siger had not brought a coat or hat, and was somewhat more miserable than the rest of us. Looking at Holmes's fore-and-aft cap, he stated, "That hat would surely be useful right about now. I'm going to get one of those."

Holmes smiled. "I can tell you, it is a fine item for the country, but I often get odd looks in the city." He gestured over his shoulder. "It is not much further to the house." Soon, we arrived, and the lights of the building and smell of wood smoke made the place seem very inviting indeed.

Inside, the house was warm and pleasant, with the lingering smell of a baked dessert. Roberta asked if we wanted a full meal, but we declined. Roberta insisted that we partake of something. Soon we were seated around a large table as she cut a large iced cake, which had been made that morning. "You seem to be holding up very well," said Holmes, his voice cutting across the muted conversations, "considering the fact that a little over a day ago, a murdered man was found nearby, and your husband arrested."

The people in the room fell silent, and Roberta paused for an almost unnoticed second before she resumed cutting the cake. Passing a filled plate around the table, she answered, "Of course I'm calm. This is all a terrible mistake, and it will soon be sorted out."

We ate for a moment, although none of the conversation resumed.

Suddenly, a knock at the front door made us all look at one another. We heard the front door open, followed by quiet conversation. Then an elderly woman, a member of the household staff, stepped into the room.

"Mr. Augustus Morland is here, ma'am," she said.

Before Roberta could reply, a man appeared in the doorway behind the old woman, who looked back and forth between him and her mistress in a flustered way. The man handed his rain-soaked outer garment to the woman, who took it automatically. "That's all right, Hilda," said Roberta, moving across the room and patting the woman on the shoulder. "Go on back to the kitchen." Turning to the man, her voice grew flat and less friendly, as she said, "What can we do for you, Mr. Morland?"

The man was in his late forties or early fifties, well dressed, and with somewhat long hair combed down beside his thin face. He stood there with a posed arrogance, examining each of us quickly but dismissively. When he looked at me, I could see that his eyes were an odd light brown, and the whites around the pupils were discolored and bloodshot, giving the impression that each entire eyeball was one solid muddy marble. His nose was large and red, covered with tiny broken capillaries that extended out onto his lined red cheeks. In a few seconds, his expressionless gaze at me moved on, but in that short space of time, I felt that he had judged me and found me to be useless.

"I'm sorry to disturb you," he said, his voice strangely high-pitched and staccato. "I simply wanted to stop by and see if there was any help that I could provide."

"Thank you, no," replied Roberta. "We appreciate the gesture. I would offer you some cake, but as you can see, we are having a family meeting with Inspector Tenley here," she said, gesturing toward the inspector, who nodded, "and our discussions are confidential."

"Of course, of course," Morland said. "But before I go, I would like to take a moment to introduce myself to Mr. Holmes." He turned to Holmes. "I was speaking to Constable Worth earlier, and he told me that you were expected in today to look into the matter." He stepped forward, his hand outstretched. "Augustus Morland. Pleased to meet you."

Holmes rose and returned the handshake. Nodding toward me, he said, "This is my associate, Dr. John Watson."

I rose as well, extending my hand, but Morland barely glanced my way. "Yes, of course. I assumed he would be here as well." He moved back toward the door. "Well, I will be going, but as I said, if there is anything that I can do to help during this time, do not hesitate to let me know."

With that, he stepped out of the room, followed by Roberta, who led him to the front door. As she shut it behind him, Tenley said, "Well, what do you suppose was the purpose of that?"

"Not actually an offer to help, I'll wager," said William.

Roberta returned to the room, scowling. "That man!" She said. "You can bet that he is probably enjoying this."

"How do you mean?" asked Holmes.

"Because he's been pressuring father to sell the place," said Siger, sitting forward on his chair.

"Now, Siger," began his mother, but he interrupted her.

"It's true. Just because you haven't chosen to tell me about it, doesn't mean that I didn't know. He's some rich man from Manchester who moved here last year, bought up several of the old farms, and keeps trying to acquire more. He has talked to father several times about buying this place, but father has always turned him down." Roberta shook her head and sat down. "I can see that you've been eavesdropping when we thought you were studying, young man."

"That's not all," continued Siger, without any sign of contrition. "Like William said, he didn't come here to offer help. He wanted to let us know that he knew about our affairs, and that he was receiving information from Constable Worth. I'll bet that Uncle Sherlock's arrival this morning and involvement in the investigation was supposed to remain confidential, was it not, Inspector Tenley?"

Tenley nodded. "It was. You can be certain that I will be speaking to Worth about this."

Holmes spoke to Roberta. "Tell me more about Morland's offers for the property."

"As Siger said," she replied, "the man moved here late last year. His agents had already purchased a couple of adjacent farms before his arrival, and he moved into the larger of the farmhouses when he got here. He is supposedly very wealthy, and there's talk that he may be knighted soon. Within weeks of his arrival, he had purchased several additional holdings, some that had been in families for countless generations, by making huge offers that they couldn't refuse. He's bought one or two more since then, but he has slowed down somewhat. His time has been taken up with other activities, as he has begun building a huge house, a mile or so from the one where he currently resides.

"Not long after arriving here, he visited Sherrinford one day, arriving in the late afternoon. He introduced himself out in the yard, by the big barn, and declined an offer to come inside. Instead, he jumped right to the point, saying he had decided to buy this farm. Sherrinford said that Morland put it as if the place had already been for sale and he was doing us some kind of favor by taking it off our hands. He then named a ridiculously high sum and asked when the matter could be settled legally.

"Sherrinford simply laughed, and explained that the place wasn't for sale. Sherrinford told me that Morland looked at him for a minute, in that curious way you just saw, and then said, 'Everything is for sale. If money doesn't interest you, perhaps you can be persuaded another way.'

"He turned and left that day, but he has been back several times since, increasing his original offer, and becoming more and more frustrated when we kept turning him down."

"And you say he's from Manchester?" Holmes asked Siger.

Siger nodded. "I haven't been able to determine yet how he made his money."

"'Determine yet'?" his mother said. "Have you been investigating the man?"

"Of course," replied Siger. "As much as I could, anyway. I've asked around the village, and in Thirsk as well, when I've gone there. He has had a number of visitors at his home, all passing through the village. None have Manchester accents. He also receives a lot of telegrams from Manchester and London."

"And how do you know that?" asked Roberta.

"I questioned people," Siger replied. "I considered contacting Bancroft in London, but I decided that he would simply have turned around and let you and father know what I was doing. I would have been able to find out more," he added, "if I had access to better sources of information, and if I was not trapped out here in the middle of nowhere."

William laughed at this statement, and Holmes looked proudly at his young nephew. Roberta threw up her hands in mock despair, before laughing herself, although rather ruefully.

Part III: Gathering Information

After another twenty minutes or so, I could see that Holmes was getting restless. Finally he announced that it was time to return to the village, where the autopsy was being delayed until Holmes could examine the body. "Dr. Dalton will not appreciate it if we wait any longer."

We stood and went to the front door, where we began to put on our damp coats. Only after a moment did I realize that Siger had prepared for departure as well. I caught his mother's eye. She smiled and turned her head, as if to accept what she could not change.

Outside, the rain had slackened, and Griffin drove out of the barn, where he had been watching for us.

The drive back into the village passed without conversation. We were soon at a tidy stone house, well kept, with a small sign informing us that we were at Dr. Dalton's surgery. We were arriving well past consulting hours, but in this case it did not matter.

A knock on the door was followed by footsteps echoing across the floorboards inside, and in a moment the door flew open to reveal a man in his early forties, lit from behind by several bright lanterns. He was in his shirtsleeves and waistcoat, and his hair was somewhat long and curly, dancing in the light.

"Come in, come in," he said, moving aside and gesturing for us to enter. "I saw you go by hours ago, thought you might stop then, certainly expected you back before now."

We entered the waiting room, which had apparently once been the front parlor of the house, and removed our coats and hats, which our host set about hanging up. I was able to observe him better, and I could see that he was well built and over six feet in height. He had a weathered face, most notably marked by a strong square chin. There were lines around his eyes, but they seemed more likely to have been formed by years of squinting in the outdoor sunshine rather than from laughter. He shook Tenley's hand, and then mine after Tenley's mumbled introduction. He nodded at Siger and William, and then turned to Holmes.

"Well, well," he said. "The prodigal returns."

Holmes returned his gaze for a silent moment, before remarking, "Wesley. It has been too long."

"Yes, it has. Long enough for you to have died, and then returned."

He gave a short bark of a laugh and stuck out his hand. "Welcome back, Sherlock."

They shook hands, and the tension which I had felt since we entered the home seemed to change somewhat, although it did not entirely abate.

Dalton stepped back, and his face took on a peevish air. "I have really delayed my duties long enough. Are you here to make your examination of the body so that I may proceed with the official one?"

"Certainly," said Holmes. "Please lead the way."

Dr. Dalton took us back through a short hallway, into an examining room. Over his shoulder, he remarked to me, "I live upstairs, and the housekeeper has the run of the kitchen at the back of the house. The rest of the ground floor is given over to my practice. We are going to my laboratory, which is set up along one side of the building."

As he finished speaking, we entered a small room, obviously at some time in the past designed to be a ground floor bedroom. Now its walls were covered with shelves containing books, chemicals, and scientific apparatus. In the center of the room was an examination table, upon which lay the body of the dead man, unclothed except for a sheet draped across it.

"As the local coroner," Dalton said, "I am occasionally called upon to conduct autopsies on unfortunate individuals."

Holmes ignored him, stepping closer to the body. I followed, while Siger moved along the other side of the table, showing no signs whatsoever of squeamishness or timidity in the presence of violent death.

The victim was a heavy-set man in his fifties, his head covered in a still-thick toss of grey hair. His face was covered with a thick beard and mustache, both quite unkempt, with the untrimmed beard climbing his cheeks halfway to his eyes. His nose was broad, and appeared to have been broken at some point in the distant past. His eyebrows were a tangled thicket, jutting up from the broad shelf of his forehead like a hedge across his face, running unbroken from side to side.

All of this, however, was secondary to the most noticeable characteristic of the man; namely, a wide puckered gash running across his throat.

"You say that there was very little bleeding from the throat wound?" asked Holmes.

"That is right," said Tenley. "The man's collar and clothing were hardly stained. The wound must have occurred after death."

"The killer was right-handed," interrupted Siger, leaning closely over the gaping opening.

"Correct," said Holmes. "And his throat was cut by someone standing in front of him."

I leaned in and confirmed their conclusions, noticing where the initial tear on the right side of the man's throat was hesitant and somewhat ripped before becoming a clean slice that moved slightly upward toward his left.

"How can you tell that it wasn't caused by a left-handed man standing behind him and reaching across before drawing the weapon back?" asked William.

"The direction of the slash, upward as the blade moved from Wilkies's right to his left, indicates that the killer was moving his arm in that direction while standing in front of him, and that it would have been in the killer's right hand. A man cutting from behind would have most likely pulled the blade in a downward path. Here," said Holmes, moving behind Dalton, "let me show you."

He stepped behind the doctor, and then placed his left arm around the doctor's chest, so that his left hand rested on Dalton's right shoulder.

"Now," he said, "the blade makes initial contact with the throat on the victim's right side, causing a rip before the actual clean slice begins."

He began to pull his hand slowly from his right to left, across Dalton's upper chest. "As you can see, my hand, which would have been holding the blade, drops as it moves across your throat. It would be awkward to pull the blade in an upward direction as it crosses."

"And," said Siger, stepping up to Dalton from the front, "if I were to slash you from the front," he said, crossing his arm so that his right hand was over Dalton's right shoulder, "my hand makes the initial cut in the same place, but as my knife hand, the right hand, moves across your throat, it tends to swing up, as so." And he proceeded to demonstrate, to Dalton's discomfort.

"Yes, yes, thank you very much," he said, pulling himself loose from Holmes and out from underneath Siger's imaginary knife. "However, I'm not sure what difference it makes. Most people are right-handed, you know."

"Yes, but if we encounter a left-handed suspect, it will be something else to weigh in the balance while we consider him," replied Holmes. "Or her." He turned, and resumed his examination of the body. He muttered to himself as he turned the sheet down, peering at the corpse through his lens. Then, with the help of Siger and myself, he rolled the body, and examined the massive wound in the fellow's back.

"Most of the blood on his clothing was from the back wound, you say?" Holmes asked.

"That's right," Dalton confirmed.

"May I see the clothing?"

"Certainly, although I examined it myself. There is nothing in the pockets to give any indication of the murderer's identity. In fact, the pockets were completely empty."

"Nevertheless," said Holmes, taking the bloody bundle from Dalton.

In spite of Dalton's statement, Holmes proceeded to examine the clothing carefully, beginning first with a minute examination of the pockets. As expected, there was nothing in them, not even any lint.

Finally, Holmes shook out the clothes and laid them across the body. Turning them this way and that, he finally said, "Hello, what's this?"

"What?" asked Dalton, although Holmes ignored him.

"Siger," said Holmes, "see if you notice anything."

Siger examined the clothing for less than a minute before announcing, "Wilkies was not wearing these clothes when he was killed."

"*What!*" exclaimed Dalton. Tenley and I were silent. Tenley was watching intently, and I had been around Holmes for too long to be surprised. Holmes nodded for Siger to continue.

"It is obvious that the throat wound was committed sometime after death, due to the lack of bleeding from that site, and that death would have been immediate from the large stab wound in the back, correct?"

"Correct," said Dalton. "The back wound went straight through the heart, and in fact it appears that the knife was rotated and twisted within the body, as if to cause the maximum amount of immediate damage."

"This would appear to be confirmed by the vast amounts of blood on the back of the man's shirt and coat?" continued Siger.

"Yes," said Dalton, with a wary tone. "A wound of that sort would produce copious amounts of blood."

"Then we must ask ourselves," said Siger, warming to his speech, "why the man's shirt and coat, which are both soaked in blood, have no rip or tear in them whatsoever which would have allowed passage of the knife through them and into Wilkies's back?"

"Let me see that!" Dalton said, stepping forward. He leaned in, and then began lifting the clothing to the light. It was obvious that the shirt and coat were whole, and even though the backs of both garments were crusted with blood, there were no holes in the fabrics.

"What does it mean?" asked Dalton.

"Simply that, for reasons unknown to us at this time, Wilkies was killed by a vicious blow to the back. He was either wearing something else at the time, or perhaps entirely unclothed, although this seems less likely to me. Soon after death, the clothes were changed. The wound was still fresh, and so large that a great deal of blood continued to spill from it, staining the clothing. Sometime later, after the bleeding had completely stopped, the throat was cut, possibly after Wilkies was propped at the side of the pit."

"But doesn't that invalidate all your evidence about a right-handed man standing in front of him?" asked Dalton.

"Exactly the opposite," replied Holmes. "If the body was propped up and then the killer slashed it, probably to add further evidence of violence, or to complete some ritual, the cut would travel up and to Wilkies's left, as I have theorized. If the killer then stood in the pit, held Wilkies's head back by the hair, and slashed up and to the right, it would be exactly as I have surmised."

Dalton looked irritated. Refolding the clothing, he said, "I would have noticed the lack of cuts in the garments myself, eventually." Placing them on a shelf, he turned back to us. "After all, I have been prevented from carrying out the full autopsy as I have been waiting for your arrival."

Holmes smiled. "Then by all means, Wesley, let us not delay you for another moment. Please let me know of any other information you discover." Then he turned to go. Tenley and I stayed to shake hands with Dalton, although Siger had already departed with his uncle.

Outside in the four-wheeler, Holmes shook his head. "I had forgotten how sensitive and proud Wesley can sometimes be," he stated. "He and I were always competitors as boys. I think that he was rather gratified when he learned that I did not finish my degrees at either Oxford or Cambridge, while he went on to become a doctor. Upon the completion of his medical degree, he returned here and has become an important man in the area. It cannot sit well for him to have me return and intrude on what he thinks of as his own personal bailiwick."

Tenley asked where Holmes wished to go next. "To visit my brother, Sherrinford," replied Holmes.

Part IV: The Prisoner

It was only a matter of minutes to wind through the village to an odd building, standing alone from its neighbors and quite tall for the area, reaching three stories above the ground. On the top floor I could see barred windows.

"This is new," said Holmes, looking at the building.

"Yes sir," said Tenley. "It was constructed a year or so ago. A man in York, Sir Clive Owenby, put up the money. He made some talk about providing proper facilities for the local law enforcement authorities. I believe that he is a close acquaintance of your brother Mycroft."

We entered the building and began to divest ourselves of our wet outer garments. From a side office emerged a short, powerfully built man in a spotless uniform. I was not surprised when he introduced himself as Constable Worth.

"It is a pleasure to meet you, gentlemen," he said, shaking our hands. "Unpleasant business all around, I'm afraid."

"Have you learned anything further since we last spoke?" asked Tenley, cutting through the introductions.

"Not a thing, sir. The prisoner has not made any further statements."

"I meant from anyone else, such as members of Wilkies's campsite."

"No, sir. Haven't been back out there."

Tenley gestured to us. "These men will be going up to visit Mr. Holmes. May I have the key to the cell?"

Worth looked surprised. "Sir, these cells are my responsibility . . . ."

"The keys, Constable," said Tenley, holding out his hand. Worth reluctantly produced the keys, laying them in Tenley's palm.

Tenley immediately handed them to Holmes. "Top of the stairs, sir," he said. "I will stay down here with Constable Worth and discuss today's visit by Mr. Morland."

"But sir," said Worth. "The prisoner . . . These men are not authorized to just go up and open the door. They are members of his family, sir . . . ."

Tenley waved his hand. "These people are entirely trustworthy, and I vouch for them completely. Mr. Holmes and Dr. Watson have performed countless services for the government of this country. And young Siger, here, is training as well to continue his uncle's work."

Siger widened his eyes and pulled himself straighter, adding to the already existing impression of great height and leanness. Holmes caught my eye, his lips turned up in a minuscule smile. As one, we turned from Tenley and Worth.

We started upstairs, leaving Worth looking uncomfortable in the feeble light of the entrance hall. We reached a landing on the stairs, and then climbed to the first floor, which seemed to consist of a series of closed rooms all opening from the small landing by the stairs. Only a single gaslight burned on that floor to illuminate our progress. We turned toward the next set of stairs, moving past the final landing before reaching the top floor. I arrived first, and waited for my friends, all of whom were more out of breath than I.

Holmes stepped in front of me to a closed door. Turning the knob revealed a short hallway, with metal-barred cells on each side. The room was lit by a single lamp hanging in the hall from the ceiling between the cells. Siger stepped through the door and stopped at the first cell on the left. Taking the keys from Holmes, he opened the door.

A man was sitting in the shadows at the back of the cell. He stirred, rose, and stepped forward into the light. He was several inches over six feet, and looked much like his brothers, but mostly like his son William.

He thrust his arms out when he saw Sherlock Holmes and smiled. The expression lit his face with kindness and good-hearted joy, and in spite of the grimness of the location, with the rain pounding on the roof above us, I grinned myself.

Sherrinford Holmes hugged his younger brother and laughed. I glanced at Siger and William and saw that they were smiling as well. I knew immediately that Sherrinford was a good man, and could not be in any way responsible for that of which he was accused. There was an air of kindness about him that I was unable to define, but it existed nonetheless. It was as if someone had managed to combine Sherlock Holmes and Father Christmas.

I missed whatever Sherrinford mumbled to Holmes. Then he released his brother and reached for his sons, who also received great hugs. Then he turned to me. I feared that I would be clasped to the big man, but instead he thrust out a great paw of a hand and grasped mine, shaking it and introducing himself.

"I am so sorry it has taken us so long to meet, Dr. Watson," he cried. "It is as much my fault as my brother's, I'm afraid. I'll wager he never even told you that he had people up here in Yorkshire, did he?" Without waiting for an answer, he continued. "It has always been his way. However, I have not made my way down to London to see him, either. Not in all the years that he has been down there. Unforgivable, doctor, simply unforgivable on my part."

He stepped back, and looked at Holmes in mock sternness. "I understand that Dr. Watson was wounded in Afghanistan, Sherlock, shortly before the two of you met." Holmes nodded, and Sherrinford continued. "I now perceive that the wound was in his leg. Tell me, why on earth did you make him take the room upstairs from your sitting room at your lodgings? Shouldn't you have offered to let the wounded war veteran have the more easily accessible bedroom on the first floor near the sitting room, while you took the one upstairs on the second?"

He moved back into the cell, gesturing for us to enter. I had known Sherlock Holmes at that time for over fifteen years, counting the years when he had disappeared. I had seen his brother, Mycroft, on numerous occasions since meeting him in the fall of 1888. By now I should have been used to the deductions of the Holmes brothers, and if I could not immediately follow their logic to understand how their conclusions were reached, I should have at least learned to keep my mouth shut. However, as was usually the case, I had to know.

"How did you know that my bedroom is upstairs and your brother's bedroom on the first floor?" I asked.

Sherrinford smiled. "Siger?" he asked, "will you explain it to the doctor?"

Siger stepped forward, his hands clasped in front of him, as if he were reciting his multiplication tables at school. "Was it Dr. Watson's breathing?" he asked.

Sherrinford nodded. "Exactly. Go ahead."

Holmes moved into the cell, leaning against one of the walls. Sherrinford gestured toward his cot, offering me a place to sit. I shook my head, and Sherrinford seated himself in the middle of the rickety structure.

Siger took a deep breath. "When we reached this floor, Dr. Watson arrived first, while Uncle Sherlock, William, and I arrived seconds later. No doubt you had been expecting us, and you were listening for our footsteps. You heard Dr. Watson first, during the several seconds he was alone at the top of the steps, and you realized from his limp who he was. You also could tell that he was not out of breath. Then you heard the rest of us arrive, and we paused to catch our wind for a few seconds, before entering the cells.

"You already knew about Dr. Watson's war service from his narrative, *A Study In Scarlet*, as well as other published accounts. You were able to determine that his wound was in the leg, both from the limp, and also from the fact that he is quite comfortable with it at this point, sixteen years later, so much so that he was able to climb the steps better than his companions.

"The evenness of the doctor's breathing indicated that he is used to climbing to the second floor on a regular basis, while Uncle Sherlock is not. Obviously both men are conditioned to climb to the first floor, where their sitting room is located, but since Uncle Sherlock has not had to get used to climbing any higher on a regular basis, his bedroom is obviously on the same floor as the sitting room at their lodgings, while the doctor's room is one floor higher."

"Absolutely right," said Sherrinford. "And of course, Siger, as active as you are, there are not many steps for you to climb at our house, either, so you were as out of breath as your uncle."

"But why couldn't I be used to climbing to the second story somewhere else," I asked. "Why do you assume I have only conditioned myself to climb that many steps to my rooms at our lodgings? Couldn't I have done so at my practice, or at a hospital?"

"I knew from Sherlock's letters that you had sold your practice and had placed yourself back in harness with my brother," stated Sherrinford. "It seemed logical that the only place you were regularly climbing that many stairs would be at your home." He looked at Holmes. "However, Sherlock, you didn't answer my question. Why did you make Dr. Watson take the higher room all those years ago when he was a recently invalided soldier?"

Holmes looked slightly uncomfortable, and even, perhaps, guilty. "When I found the rooms in Baker Street, I knew that I could not afford them by myself. When I mentioned the need to find a fellow lodger to my friend Stamford, at Bart's, I did not seriously believe that anything would come of it, and I never really thought that I would be able to obtain the rooms. When Stamford introduced me to Watson, I immediately saw that he had been wounded in Afghanistan, but in all honesty, it simply never occurred to me to offer him the bedroom adjacent to the sitting room on the first floor.

"I suppose that I rationalized that since I had been the one to find the rooms I should take the more accessible one. Also, to be honest, I was not certain that Watson would be residing there for any length of time"

He smiled in my direction. "I believed that a combination of my increased professional success, allowing me to afford the rooms by myself, as well as my generally poor attractiveness as a fellow lodger, would soon encourage you to move on to something better. And I must admit, that until now, I have selfishly never thought of the added discomfort climbing those extra steps must have caused you, my dear Watson."

Holmes lifted his hand. "It is far too late to ask, but would you like to trade rooms?"

I laughed, and everyone joined in. "Of course not," I said. "Climbing up and down those steps was probably excellent therapy for me. Besides," I added, "I was so lazy in those early days that climbing to my room every time you needed the sitting room to meet with one of your clients was the only exercise I took."

Sherrinford nodded. "Excellent job of reasoning, Siger," he said to his son.

Siger looked surprised. "But I was just explaining what *you* had determined," he said.

Sherrinford waved this away, and turned to Holmes. "I don't have to reason anything out to determine why you are here," he said. "Roberta must have contacted you."

"Actually, she contacted Mycroft, who in turn enlisted the efforts of Inspector Tenley, followed by Watson and myself."

Sherrinford nodded. "What do you need to ask me?"

"Simply begin at the beginning, and I will ask questions as needed."

"Well," said Sherrinford, rubbing his hands together and settling on the cot, "about two weeks ago, in the morning, a group of wagons arrived at the farm. The lead wagon pulled a little closer to the house, and a man hopped down. I was in the barn and went out to meet him.

"Of course, it was Wilkies. He introduced himself, and pointed to his daughter, who had remained on the seat of the wagon. He said that he and his group were heading into the north for the summer, and they wondered if they could stop on our land for a week or so before moving on. They seemed respectable enough, and I agreed. I directed them to the southern fields, where I knew the conditions would be pleasant, with shade trees, and there would be plenty of water from the stream.

"That night, after they had set up camp, I walked over to see how they were doing. Wilkies invited me into his tent, a large, spacious affair that was obviously military surplus. There were nearly a dozen other tents, spread around a central area, and each with its own campfire. A rope paddock had been set up somewhat downstream for the livestock.

"Wilkies instructed his daughter to prepare tea. She did so without comment, moving silently about the tent, and, if I may speculate, somewhat resentfully of my presence. While she worked, I questioned Wilkies about the nature of his group. His description led me to believe that they are some sort of offshoot of Druidism, with an eccentric mixture of Christianity, Egyptian pantheism, and some Germanic mythology as well. He had apparently been a Church of England theology student in his early twenties, before developing his own unique beliefs. He published some tracts ten or fifteen years ago explaining his theology, and at one point had started his own church, where he attracted a few loyal followers. At some time, he was forced to leave his church building, and he and his congregation took to the road, traveling throughout the countryside, much like gypsies from north to south, and back again.

"I visited his tent every two or three days, questioning him about his beliefs. In the second week, I was becoming somewhat curious as to when he intended to depart, as his people had shown no signs of preparing to leave. However, I never came right out and asked him, and he never volunteered the information on his own.

"The night of the murder was simply another visit, and there was no anger between us. In fact, there was not much conversation at all. He and I sat on camp stools in front of his tent, facing the fire, in companionable silence. I saw no signs of his daughter, Sophia, although it is possible she may have been in the tent. As to what she claims to have heard, I can only say that if she believes that conversation to have taken place between me and her father, she is completely mistaken. Perhaps she heard him arguing later, with someone else. I do not know what the phrase 'the true path,' which was attributed to me, refers to."

"Did you ever have any conversations with any of the other followers, either at the camp or elsewhere?" Holmes asked.

"Never," replied his brother. "As far as I know, none of them ever ventured away from camp, and they kept to themselves when I was there. For that matter, Sophia never spoke to me either. She would simply meet my eyes with a somewhat reserved expression before looking away, or gesturing me toward the tent where her father and I would talk."

Holmes was silent for several minutes, before asking, "What can you tell me of Augustus Morland?"

Sherrinford cleared his throat and looked at Siger. "Have you been telling Sherlock of your suspicions of Morland?"

"He came to the house today," said Siger. "He claimed that he wanted to offer his help, after he had been told of your arrest by Constable Worth." Then he added, "How did you know of my suspicions about him?"

Sherrinford waved a hand. "Fathers know everything, son." He turned back to his brother. "I have met Morland half-a-dozen times or so in the last few months. He has been trying to buy up all the land in this area, including ours." He went on to relate the same narrative of events that had earlier been provided to us by Roberta. "He appears to be trying to create an unbroken estate stretching from here all the way to the sea. And he seems to have the money and resources to do so, eventually. If he doesn't get our land, he will simply buy some around it until he gets the contiguous layout that he desires."

Holmes shifted away from the wall. "Have you conferred with legal counsel?"

"Not yet," replied Sherrinford. "I believe that Worth has forgotten about it. Tenley and I talked earlier today, and we both felt that at this point it was not necessary. I am willing to wait here for a little while longer while the investigation progresses. Hopefully, this will lull the real murderer into a false sense of security, if he believes that his plan to frame me has been completely accepted." Sherrinford stood. "Can I tell you anything else?"

"I think that I have heard enough for tonight," he said. "Is there anything we can do for you? Can we bring you anything?"

"No, no, I am quite all right," Sherrinford replied. "Worth is basically a good fellow, for all his pretensions. I am quite sure that you will have me out of here in a day or so."

"I am confident of that as well," said Holmes. "I begin to see where to pull the red thread running through this tangled skein."

Sherrinford stepped forward, and Holmes shook his hand. Then Sherrinford shook mine as well, before drawing his sons into another hug. "Give my love to your mother," he said.

"We will," replied Siger, quietly. We left the cell, and Siger solemnly relocked the door.

Downstairs, he handed the keys to Tenley, who was standing near the front door. In a side room we could see Worth, sitting at his desk, looking chastened and somewhat embarrassed. I nodded to the man, and we left the building. Tenley followed in a moment, after returning the keys to Worth.

In the four-wheeler, Tenley said, "What next, gentlemen?"

"I need to send some wires, and then back to the farm for the night, I suppose," replied Holmes. The ever-patient Griffin turned the horse, and then drove the four-wheeler for a few short minutes to the office where Holmes jumped down, going in to send his telegrams. Siger, William, Tenley, and I waited in the four-wheeler, grateful that the rain had stopped, although a cold damp wind still blew.

Holmes returned in a minute, climbed in, and we set off for the Holmes farm. It was not long before we arrived. Tenley asked, "What do you have planned for tomorrow, Mr. Holmes?"

"If you and Griffin could be back here by about nine o'clock, I believe that we will interview Miss Sophia at the campsite."

"Very good," said Tenley, as we climbed down. "See you in the morning, then."

As they drove away, the door opened, spilling light into the damp yard. We went inside to find that Roberta had prepared something of a feast. Siger passed on the good wishes of his father, and we sat down to eat. Over the years I had often thought of Sherlock Holmes as a lonely man, buried in his studies and thoughts. That night, I was able to see a new side of him, as part of a family that treasured and cherished him. As Holmes's friend, I was given some of that affection as well. The entire evening was somewhat muted, due to the absence of Sherrinford and the awful events that had led to his arrest. However, in spite of that, there was an optimism that the incarceration was only temporary, and the warm feelings of that house could not be quelled.

As we climbed the stairs to our rooms later that night, I told Holmes, "I am honored to meet your family. They are fine people, indeed."

"Yes, they are," he replied. "I must never take them for granted. Perhaps I should try to visit here more often."

"I agree, Holmes. I heartily agree." We reached the door of my room.

"Good night, Holmes."

He continued down the hallway. Over his shoulder, he said "And good night to you as well, Watson."

Part V: The Camp

We arose early next morning to find that Roberta had prepared a large farm breakfast, which I greeted with enthusiasm. I was unsurprised to see that Holmes picked at his food, and seemed content to consume several cups of strong black coffee. William kept pace with my appetite, but Siger seemed to eat even less than his uncle. He looked tired, and acted rather nervous, glancing at Holmes often before directing his eyes elsewhere around the room.

After William and I had eaten as much as we could, William pushed back from the table and stood, announcing that he wished us good luck, and that he would like to accompany us but someone must continue to direct the daily activities of the farm. With a wave he departed. Siger, who had grown more and more nervous, finally blurted out,

"Uncle, may I have a word with you and Dr. Watson? Outside," he added, cutting his eyes toward his mother. Roberta smiled, but did not say anything. Thanking her for a wonderful meal, we stepped out of the house and into the yard. Siger was carrying a worn knapsack, which he had kept beside him throughout breakfast.

Holmes pulled out his watch. "Tenley should be here in ten minutes or so. What is it, Siger?"

His nephew appeared uncertain, now that he had his uncle's attention. After a few awkward seconds of silence, he said, "I have discovered something important, uncle, but in doing so I may have jeopardized your case."

Holmes indicated that he should continue. "Last night," said Siger, "I could not sleep. Without taking time to explain all my reasoning and the various dead ends I let my mind travel, I finally came to the conclusion that Mr. Morland must somehow be involved in this matter. So I arose and slipped out of the house. I then made my way over the fields to Morland's."

Holmes looked quickly at me, and then back to his nephew. A glint had caught fire in Holmes's hooded eyes. "And what did you find?" he asked.

"What I expected to find," Siger said, opening the knapsack. "And more that I did not expect." He reached in, and pulled out a rolled bundle of white bloodstained cloth. Glancing toward the house to make sure he was unobserved, Siger dropped the knapsack and began to unroll his discovery. His hands revealed some sort of religious robe, almost completely soaked in dried blood. As the bundle was nearly unrolled, he stopped and carefully extricated two items which had been tucked in the center.

The first was a dagger, its thin narrow blade about six inches long. It seemed quite old, and the handle appeared to be made of iron, with blunt and clumsy runes engraved in it. The blade was covered with dried blood. The second item from the bundle was something far more sinister.

I had seen a thing like it once before, years earlier, although I never expected to see one again, and surely not in the heart of beautiful Yorkshire. It was a Hand of Glory, the foul device used by witches' covens while practicing their hated black magic. In the early eighties, Holmes and I had been involved in the destruction of a nest of the evil practitioners. At the time, I had been shocked to my core by the evil to which the human heart was capable of sinking, in spite of my experiences on many continents and the horrors I had seen in war.

I must have gasped, because both Holmes and Siger looked away from the bundle and toward me. I swallowed and said, "Holmes, what can it mean?"

He did not reply. Instead, he reached for the white robe. Taking it from Siger, he finished unfolding it. He searched for a moment with his long thin fingers before finding what he sought. On the back of the robe, centered in the place equivalent to where Wilkies's fatal wound had been on his body, was a long ragged slit. This part of the robe was the most blood-soaked portion of the whole garment.

"This is what Wilkies was wearing when he was murdered," said Holmes, pushing his finger through the hole. "It is some sort of ceremonial robe. For some reason, he was changed into conventional clothing after death." He rotated the robe to examine the clean neck line. "And his throat was not slit while he was wearing this. As we believed, it took place post-mortem."

He then held up the knife, turning it from side to side in the morning sunlight. "I think it is safe to say that this is the murder weapon," he said. "The width of the blade corresponds to some of the marks on the body." Turning to Siger, he asked, "Where did you find this?"

"It was in one of Morland's stable buildings, an unused one, in an empty stall under some straw."

"How did you know to look there?"

"It wasn't the first place that I looked," replied Siger. "Of course, I couldn't get in the house, but I did think that I would be able to search most of the out-buildings."

"Weren't you afraid of being caught?" I asked.

Siger replied, with a look that must have made his uncle proud, "When I search, I do not get caught."

"Why did you decide to search Morland's premises?" asked Holmes.

"I simply reasoned that he, of all the people currently around here, would have the most reason to frame my father, simply because

Father will not sell him our farm. If someone in the religious camp wanted to murder Wilkies, they would have done so without involving my father."

"That is not necessarily so," said Holmes, "but no matter, right now. Did you expect to find this?" he asked, holding up the robe and the items that had been hidden within it.

"Not exactly," said Siger. "I knew that Wilkies had not been murdered in the clothing in which he was found. I decided to look for the actual murder clothing, which must have been taken away by the murderer. If my assumption was correct, and Morland was involved, then logically he would have taken the clothing.

"Of course, there was every reason to think that it could have been already destroyed, or hidden somewhere in the fields, or even buried or burned. However, if I spent the night exploring Mr. Morland's barns, all I could lose would be a night's sleep, and look what I found." He gestured at the robe, and added, "Of course, I did not expect to find this, exactly. I thought I would possibly just discover another suit similar to the one that Wilkies was wearing when his body was found."

Holmes was silent for a moment, and then he began to re-roll the bundle, making sure that the dagger and the Hand of Glory were concealed within. "It is very important," he said, "when gathering information in a criminal case, to protect the chain of evidence. By that, I mean that one must be able to demonstrate in a court of law that the evidence has been untainted and unaltered before it is discovered by a legitimate and verifiable source." He pushed the bundle into Siger's knapsack. "I realize that you took this in order to show it to me, and also to make sure that it was not removed and destroyed in the meantime. However, the authenticity of the evidence is now somewhat compromised."

Siger lowered his head. "I am sorry, uncle."

"I agree with you that somehow, Morland is involved in this matter. I had decided that yesterday, before your important discovery. However, if the matter came to court as it stands now, Morland's attorneys could argue that he was an innocent victim of a plot, or that one of his own employees had hidden the items without his knowledge. In fact, they could even argue that you, Siger, had been involved in the murder yourself and that you had pretended to find the items at Morland's farm in order to frame *him*."

Siger looked up with an apprehensive expression. "Inspector Tenley would tell you the same thing," continued Holmes. "By removing this evidence, its effectiveness is decreased or eliminated altogether." Holmes handed the knapsack to Siger, who widened his eyes in surprise. "Inspector Tenley would tell you that, I suppose, if he knew about it."

Holmes turned and glanced down the lane, toward the approaching four-wheeler containing Tenley and Griffin. "We are going to Morland's house later this morning," said Holmes. "Would you be so kind, Siger, to slip away from us at some point so that you can replace the items in question where you found them? Without being observed, of course. We are taking a chance that they will not be destroyed in the meantime, until we are ready to find them legitimately. Also, we can only hope that their absence has not already been discovered, causing the murderer to move before we are ready to outflank him."

Holmes continued to stare at the approaching vehicle, while Siger shouldered the knapsack. He turned to me with a relieved smile on his face. I reached out and gripped his shoulder.

The four-wheeler had barely stopped before Tenley jumped down, reaching us in a few steps. "These arrived this morning, Mr. Holmes, from Mycroft," he said, holding a stack of telegrams out in front of him.

"They were addressed to both of us, so I've already read them. I think you will find them interesting."

Holmes took the forms and quickly studied them, one after another, before passing them to me. As I finished them, I handed them on to Siger.

"Will we be going to Mr. Morland's, then?" asked Tenley.

"Not yet," replied Holmes. "First I want to go to Wilkies's camp, and to meet his daughter."

In the four-wheeler, I pondered the astounding information I had read in the long telegraph forms. Obviously Mycroft, working for the government, had no hesitation at sending extensively long wires when the mood suited him.

The telegram forms consisted of one long message, relating the curious and sinister history of Augustus Morland. It seemed that Morland had moved to Yorkshire from Manchester, as we had already heard. However, his background was slightly more convoluted than the story of his origin in Manchester had led us to believe. He had graduated from university nearly twenty-five years earlier, and had immediately left on a year-long tour of the continent. While this was not unusual, the subsequent events were. Soon after his arrival in one of the smaller German spa towns, he had disappeared. The local police were unable to find him, and for over a year there was no sign of him whatsoever. During that time, his mother in Manchester had sickened with despair and died.

At that time, in the early 1870's, Germany had still been a patchwork of small kingdoms, duchies, and petty fiefdoms, with little cooperation or communication between them. It had proved nearly impossible to discover anything about the disappearance and whereabouts of young Morland. Then, over a year after he had gone missing, Morland had resurfaced, claiming that he had been kidnapped by anarchists who had argued amongst themselves the entire time about whether to kill him outright or request a ransom. Finally he had managed to escape and make his way to safety. However, he had refused to return home to England, instead stating that he preferred to remain in Germany.

His father had begged him to come home, sending urgent letters and telegrams, but young Morland refused. The father, already sickened by the death of his wife and the extended mystery of his missing son, was too weak to travel to Germany in order to try in person to convince the young man that he should return to England. The father soon died, and Morland inherited the estates.

Morland remained ensconced in Germany for nearly a quarter of a century, maintaining his business interests from there, and increasing his wealth many times over. It was only in the last year or so that he had returned to his family home in Manchester, where he had lived for a few months before moving again, this time to Yorkshire, where he began his bullying acquisitions of the surrounding farm lands.

The final sheets of the telegram revealed that Mycroft Holmes, as well as his nephew Bancroft, had become interested in Morland several months earlier. A closer investigation was made into the man's past, and Mycroft's agents had recently determined that the man was not actually Morland at all, but rather an imposter who had been set in place years earlier, following the original abduction and murder of the actual young man.

"I knew it!" stated Siger, as we discussed the matter in the rocking four-wheeler. "I knew that there was something wrong about the man."

"Is the telegraph agent who took this information completely reliable?" Holmes asked Tenley. "Can he keep the information confidential?"

"He is one of my men," Tenley replied. "He can be trusted."

Holmes eyed Tenley speculatively. "You do not seem surprised by what is in these messages," he said.

"Your brother, Mycroft, keeps a pretty close eye on things," he said. "Especially around here. Apparently, when Morland started buying up vast amounts of land, it came to Mycroft's attention pretty quickly."

"I would wager that you knew about it as well," said Holmes. "Probably for quite a while before this murder actually took place." He shifted in his seat. "Why wasn't I told about this aspect of the case to begin with?"

"Your brother felt that you would benefit by beginning your investigation with an open mind. He was not necessarily convinced that Morland's background and activities were directly related to the murder. Mycroft decided to reveal Morland's background to you after you had gotten the initial lay of the land. At that point, you could determine Morland's relevance to the investigation. However, your wires to London last night indicated that you had already decided that Morland is somehow involved."

Holmes asked, "Are you actually an inspector with the Yard, or do your responsibilities require you to pursue different activities?"

Tenley smiled. "They know me at the Yard. However, much of my work is carried out more in your brother's purview."

"I thought as much," Holmes said, nodding. "You are one of my brother's agents." Holmes folded the telegraph forms and put them in his pocket. "Were you assigned to this area as part of your responsibilities to my brother's department?"

Tenley nodded. "Keeping an eye on Morland is just part of my job up here."

Holmes gestured around him. "Just how much land has this German agent actually bought?"

"Enough," Tenley replied. "Too much. We think that he hopes to obtain even more, so that he can create some sort of vast staging area, with buffer zones on either side so that no one will be able to notice or tell."

"Tell what?" asked Siger. "That there are German soldiers surreptitiously landing in England?"

"Soldiers?" I asked. "Is it to be war, then?"

"Eventually," said Tenley, without emotion. "Not this year, maybe not through the rest of this century, or even into the first part of the next, but it is coming. The Kaiser is interested in creating his own global empire, and he is too resentful of the British Empire, as well as the restraining influence of his grandmother, Queen Victoria. Eventually the Germans will lash out."

"Mycroft and I have been predicting as much for years," said Holmes. "However, as respected as Mycroft is, he has had the devil of a time convincing his superiors of the obvious facts."

"'A prophet hath no honor in his own country.' Eh, Mr. Holmes?" asked Tenley with a smile.

"John 4:44," replied both Holmes and Siger at the same time. They looked at each other with surprise, and then they began to laugh. Tenley and I joined in. Griffin, as emotionless as ever, continued to guide the horses. We were soon within sight of Wilkies's camp.

As we had been told the day before, the campsite consisted of a loose grouping of tents. These were clustered underneath the trees that grew beside the stream watering the south side of the Holmes land. From my military days, I was able to quickly confirm that the tents were military castoffs of a style that had gone out of date at least twenty years before.

Each of the tents was a dull brown color, the original dyes having long been faded and replaced by weathering and mildew of too many years of use. Each tent's ugly hue, however, was tempered somewhat by the canvas patches of varying shades that were randomly sewn along their sides, giving them something of a gypsy air.

Tenley led us to the larger and more central tent, in front of which sat a young woman on a camp stool. Before her were the smoking remains of a fire, apparently left to die following the completion of her breakfast preparations. As we approached, the woman stood to face us, dropping her arms and holding her fisted hands at her sides.

"Sophia," said Tenley, "these are the men from London who are here to investigate your father's death. This is Mr. Sherlock Holmes, and Dr. Watson. And this young man is Siger Holmes, the son of Sherrinford Holmes."

"The son of a murderer, you mean!" she hissed, turning quickly in Siger's direction. He was surprised, and took a startled step backward before remembering himself and holding his ground.

Sophie Wilkies was a sallow young woman in her early twenties, not much over five feet in height. Her hair was loose, with shading somewhere between black and dark brown. Her hair was actually her most attractive feature, and it shone in the morning sunlight, obviously freshly brushed. She was somewhat unfortunate in her facial features, as she had bushy eyebrows similar to her late father's, on a prominent ridge shading her dark eyes. Also, her lower lip was heavy and pendulous, and tended to sag toward her rather weak chin, revealing white but quite crooked lower teeth. When she spoke, her lip would tighten, giving her whole face a look of determination, As she completed her thought, however, her face would relax and her lip would droop back down, again revealing her unfortunate and rather distracting mouth.

"Miss Wilkies," said Holmes, "I was wondering whether you could repeat for us the conversation that you said that you heard the night your father was murdered."

"I didn't *say* I heard it. I *did* hear it! That man had come around here again, that *murderer*, and started in browbeating my father about how he had abandoned 'the true path,' whatever that means. They had discussed it every single night that the man visited, but the night when he killed my father, he was much more angry about it. He even threatened my father. He said that anyone who turned away from the 'true path' would not have long in this world to reconsider his mistake."

"You say he threatened your father?" asked Tenley. "You did not mention that when we spoke of this matter before."

"I just remembered it," said the girl, crossing her arms defiantly.

"What is the 'true path'?" asked Holmes.

"I do not know," said the girl. "My father has been the shepherd of this flock since before I was born. When I was a little girl, we had a church building, but my father decided that his calling was to lead the faithful to sojourn at the holy sites of Britain, reawakening the lost beliefs. In the last few years, we have occasionally traveled to the continent as well, visiting holy sites in France, Germany, and even Sackerium."

"How does your congregation finance itself?" asked Holmes. I had wondered the same thing myself. The condition of the campsite did not indicate that funds were immediately available for pilgrimages across the Channel.

"My father inherited some money as a young man," Sophia answered. "And members of our congregation have funds of their own that they provide for us all when they join our group. They contribute as needed. As you can see, our wants are simple." She gestured toward the other tents, where several members of the group were going about their own business, mending clothing, or tending to pots suspended over small fires.

"Who will lead your group, now that your father is gone?" I asked.

"I will," the girl said simply. "My father would have wanted it that way."

"Did your father have any enemies?" asked Holmes.

"I see what you are doing!" cried the girl. "You want me to say that maybe someone else could have killed my father. Well, no one else did. It was this boy's father who did it! I will swear to it!"

Holmes and Tenley continued to ask questions for a few more minutes, but the girl provided no additional information, and could not be swayed in her single-minded belief that the murderer of her father was Sherrinford Holmes. Her dogmatic assertions tended to reveal her somewhat limited intellectual gifts. Siger stood to the side, watching uncomfortably as the girl's story remained unshaken. His knuckles, gripping the straps of his knapsack, were white.

Finally we thanked the girl and left. She flounced into her tent and pulled the flap down, shutting herself inside. We started to walk toward the four-wheeler, where patient Griffin sat hunched in the warming morning sunshine. We were thirty or forty feet from the girl's tent when an old man, sitting on a stool in front of a much smaller tent, hailed us.

"Her father never talked any about 'the true path' with anyone," he said. "The only people who ever discussed that around here was Sophia herself, and that rich man who has been coming around here to see her."

We crowded closer, keeping our voices low so that no one would overhear us. "What rich man?" Holmes asked.

"That Morland fellow," the old man replied. "He has been here several times since we made camp. He and Sophia huddle and whisper to each other, usually near my tent. They don't pay me any attention, and they don't seem to mind talking in front of me."

"What have they said?" asked Tenley.

"Sophia talks about how she is the one that's going to lead everyone back to the 'true path,' and that what her father has always believed is simply a weak and watered-down reflection of the truth. Morland whispers to her, telling her how right she is, dear, and they will lead the people together, dear. It right makes me sick."

"What is the 'true path,' then?" asked Holmes.

"I don't really know," said the old man. "From what I could hear, Sophia believes that her father was right to visit the old places, the great stones and ruins and such, but that when we were there, he was wasting his time trying to get in touch with the wrong kind of spirits. It sounds to me as if the spirits Sophia wants to reach are quite a bit more grim than what her father believed in."

"And what exactly did her father believe in?"

"Well, I don't know exactly," said the old man.

"What?" I said, reflecting the astonishment of my friends.

"Well, I don't. I don't believe in all this stuff. Don't pay any attention to it, really. My wife did, though, and when she wanted to travel with these people, I didn't really object to it. I had roamed some in my younger days, and always found it agreeable. When my wife wanted to go a-traveling I didn't mind at all, even though it meant going about with these folks, but I never was really a part of this group. I just enjoyed the journey, you see, and got to visit some places I might not have seen otherwise.

"I had inherited a little money, and once long ago I had a store that I later sold for enough of a profit to pay for my daily bread, so I can afford to play at this game with these people. They all seem nice enough, and harmless, too, I suppose. All except for Sophia. After my wife died a year or so ago, I decided to just keep going about with them. No one has said anything against it, and I guess I've been a part of the group for so long that no one questions it anymore, even though my wife was the real believer."

"How often has Mr. Morland been here?" asked Holmes.

"Usually every day, since we started camping here a couple of weeks ago. At first he spoke to both Wilkies and Sophia, but later he just came by to see Sophia by herself. I don't even know if her father realized it, because he was usually in his tent at the time, praying, or taking a nap."

The old man shifted in his seat and leaned forward, lowering his voice somewhat. "Morland hasn't been back here since Wilkies was murdered, though." He glanced at Sophia's tent. "I'll tell you something else, as well. This wasn't the first time we had met this Mr. Morland. He first showed up a couple of years ago, when we were traveling through Germany. He looked a lot different then, wasn't dressed nearly so fine, but it was him.

"Depending on where we camp, we sometimes get visitors from the nearby towns who are curious about whatever it is that Wilkies was teaching. In some German town, I forget which, Morland showed up one day with a group of those people. It wasn't long before he and Sophia met each other. Even then, the two of them would find time to walk apart from everyone else and whisper to one another. I first thought it was something romantic, but all Sophia seems to be interested in is reforming her father's religion, and Morland seems happy to encourage it."

"You said he looked different," asked Holmes. "In what way?"

"He looked more . . . German when we met him in Germany," replied the old man. "His beard and mustache were cut in a different way, and he walked stiffer, somehow. He didn't wear fancy clothes like he does now, but what he did wear still seemed . . . expensive, if you know what I mean. And of course he spoke German. Sophia speaks some German too, you know, although they've been speaking in English whenever Morland visits this camp. I heard that Sophia's mother was originally from Germany. Maybe that's how she learned it."

Despite further questioning, the old man could provide no additional information, and he assured us that he would not be telling anyone else about our conversation, especially Sophia. We thanked him, and Holmes stated that he appreciated the old man's observations. "That's *my* religion," the fellow replied. "Watching people. There isn't any better entertainment than to sit back, smoke a pipe or two, and watch folks going about their daily business. Sometimes it gets a little tedious, I will admit, but generally after a while someone will do something worth watching."

We stepped away from him, to the center of the camp, and Holmes thought for a moment. Then he led us closer to Sophia's tent, while telling me, "Watson, I need you to feign an illness. Just for a moment or two, that's a good chap."

Without giving me time to protest or prepare myself, he signaled that I was to begin. I froze for just a moment, before letting out a feeble moan. Holmes's brows contracted in irritation, and I could tell that he expected a better effort from me. With a sigh, I began to stagger while braying like some farm animal that has gotten into fermented feed. As I began to sag, lowering myself to a less dusty part of the clearing, I could see that Holmes was running to Sophia's tent, calling her forth for help.

In a moment, Sophia was kneeling beside me as I groaned and attempted to keep her attention. Over her shoulder, I could see other members of the community gathering around us while Holmes slipped unseen into Sophia's tent. Sophia kept asking me where it was hurting and what the matter was, but I pretended not to understand her, repeating this process until I saw Holmes exiting the tent and walking toward us.

Holmes nodded, and my illness miraculously healed itself. Within moments I was able to rise to my feet, thanking Sophia for her help, and assuring her that I had simply had an attack related to a fever picked up during my war service overseas, and that there was no need to be concerned. She seemed puzzled, but then with a gesture that she was washing her hands of me, she turned and went back into her tent.

As we walked to four-wheeler, Holmes said, "Excellent, Watson. I almost believed it myself."

"I hope you got what you came for," I whispered with irritation.

"What were you looking for?" asked Siger as our four-wheeler rolled away from the camp.

"This," replied Holmes, fishing a pair of folded notes from his waistcoat pocket. "Finding them was a long shot, but it will save us some trouble, I think."

He handed the papers to Siger, who unfolded them and spread them on his knee, where Tenley and I could see them. The first was simply a scrap of paper with a supply list scribbled on it. It was on poor quality paper, and the handwriting was poorly formed and uneducated. "That is a sample of Sophia's handwriting," said Holmes. "I thought it might come in handy later for a little idea that I have."

The second sheet of paper was about five inches square, and of exceptional thickness and good quality. The top edge was somewhat ragged, as if it had been torn, while the sides and bottom were straight and clean.

"It is a sheet of expensive stationery," said Holmes. "It was originally an inch or two longer."

"The portion with the monogram at the top has been torn off," said Siger, "in order to disguise the identity of the sender."

"It isn't disguised very well," said Tenley. "This paper is still somewhat unique. I'll bet we won't have to look too hard to find a matching sheet."

"Indeed," said Holmes. "That reminds me. Griffin, would you take us to Mr. Morland's house next, please?"

Griffin did not respond, but nudged his horses into a slightly faster gait.

"What do you make of the message?" asked Holmes.

It was handwritten, and quite short. In bold pen strokes, someone had written:

*Nyy vf jryy. Frr lbh fbba. Z*

"It is code," I said, causing everyone's eyes to raise and look toward me. Holmes's expression seemed somewhat irritated, while Siger and Tenley looked amused. I hastened to add, "Written by a man with a good quality pen and expensive black ink."

"Much better, Watson," said Holmes. "Does anyone want to take a try at decoding it?"

Tenley and I looked at one another, and then by tacit agreement, deferred to Siger, who was bent over the paper, his brows bunched in concentration.

"The letter *e* is the most common letter, and is likely to occur in double letters," he said softly. "However, there are several sets of double letters in this message, any of which could be *e*. If this were a simple substitution code . . . ."

He fell silent for a few moments, but his concentration never abated. The four-wheeler rocked down the road, and I glanced over at Holmes, who was looking fondly at his nephew. He turned his head to me, saw that I was watching him, and nodded in reply.

After a few moments, Siger's expression cleared, and he looked up with a joyous expression. "That wasn't so difficult," he said.

"It would have to be a simple code, so that Sophia could remember it," replied Holmes.

Tenley and I looked at one another, before I stated, "But what does it say?"

"Oh, that," said Siger. "It simply says '*All is well. See you soon. M.*'"

"M.," I said. "Morland!"

"Of course," said Holmes.

"Tell us about the code, Siger," said Tenley.

"Luckily, it was not too difficult," replied the young man. "The letter *e* is the most common letter used in the English language and can present itself as a double letter, such as in the word *seek*. This short message, however, had three sets of double letters, *yy*, which was used twice, *rr*, and *bb*. The simplest code is a substitution code, where one letter of the alphabet is substituted for another. If one wanted to make this code even simpler, the letters are not substituted at random, but are simply shifted, so that *a* can equal *b*, *b* equals *c*, and so on.

"Sometimes the coded alphabet will be reversed, so that *a* equals *z*, and *b* equals *y*. I quickly ran through a few of these combinations in my head, but none seemed to make sense. Then I thought that perhaps the coded alphabet had shifted more than just a letter or two. I started trying the message as if each double letter combination was *ee*. None of them worked until I tried *rr* as *ee*.

"This combination did produce an actual message, and I was able to see that the code simply shifted the alphabet so that *a* equaled *n*, *m* equaled *z*, and *n* equaled *a*. By shifting the alphabet exactly halfway, by thirteen of the twenty-six letters, perception of the more obvious substitutions would be avoided, but there was no need to have a key for the code lying around, which would have been the case if the letters were random substitutions.

"Excellent, Siger," said Tenley. "You have quite a gift for cryptography."

Siger looked somewhat bashful. "I simply read my Uncle Sherlock's monograph on the subject," he said, causing a momentary flash of pride to pass through Holmes's eyes. I was certain that he had already decoded the message before he ever revealed it to us. However, he had allowed his nephew the pleasure of solving the small mystery. I knew Sherlock Holmes was a wise man, but he continued to surprise me by revealing that wisdom in new and unexpected ways.

Griffin chose that moment to gesture ahead of us, muttering in his gruff and efficient manner, "Morland's."

It was time for the next act of our drama to begin.

## Part VI: Setting the Trap

We had been told by Roberta the day before that Augustus Morland was constructing a new, large home a few miles from where he currently lived. It seemed rather foolish to me, considering that the old manor house where he was currently living was very large on its own. I asked myself what use a single man could have for occupying such a large house while building an even bigger one. Then I remembered Tenley's description of a staging area, with hidden German troops quartered in secret until they could be turned loose on an unsuspecting nation.

Suddenly, the idea of huge houses standing throughout the largely empty Yorkshire countryside, each filled with smuggled arms and men over a long period of time and waiting until needed, made more sense.

We stopped at the front door and climbed down to the ground. There were several outbuildings scattered in the distance, but there did not seem to be any people working or carrying out the day-to-day tasks of running an estate. I wondered which of the buildings had been the location of Siger's grisly discovery.

As if reading my mind, Holmes said, "Siger, I would like for you to make a small reconnaissance of the outbuildings. See how many people are about. Afterwards, join us in the house, but as soon as it is convenient, try to wander off and obtain a sheet or two of Mr. Morland's stationery. You will know the type I mean. Some of it was used to write that coded message to Sophia."

Siger nodded and slipped away, as the rest of us turned to the front door, upon which Holmes knocked with authority. Tenley watched Siger disappear around the corner of the house in a speculative manner. In a moment, the door opened to reveal an old man, wearing ill-fitting and faded clothing. Holmes presented his card to the man. We were ushered in and asked to wait in the drawing room while the old fellow checked to see if Morland was available.

While Tenley perched himself in a chair, Holmes and I wandered about the room, looking at the artworks hanging from the walls and resting on table-tops. The items were obviously quite expensive, and showed good taste, but they were layered with accumulated dust. "These came with the house," said Holmes. "Morland cannot take credit for originally acquiring them."

Our inspection was interrupted by the arrival of Augustus Morland, who strode into the room looking somewhat peeved. However, he made an effort to sound gracious, welcoming us and offering us refreshments, which we refused. He motioned for us to be seated, then lowered himself into a chair with the window at his back, haloing his figure against the morning sun.

"What can I do for you gentlemen today?" he asked. I tried to perceive any hint of his hidden German ancestry, but he revealed no sign whatsoever, from his appearance to his perfect Manchester accent.

"We are simply speaking to some of the people in the area, and wanted to see if you had any relevant information to add to our investigation," said Holmes.

"Such as?" asked Morland, in his odd high-pitched voice.

"Oh, the usual type of thing. Are you aware of any problems Wilkies had with the neighbors? Have you heard of anyone speaking out against him, or possibly resenting that he and his congregation have been staying in the area?"

"No, no, nothing like that. In fact, I'm afraid the only stories I've heard about anyone having ill feelings toward Wilkies came from the testimony of his daughter, Sophia." He shook his head with a smile. "Such as it is."

Holmes raised an eyebrow. "What do you mean?"

"Oh, nothing, I suppose. From the few times I have seen her, she seems somewhat . . . limited in her thought processes. You may have met her yourself?" We nodded. "Then I think you must agree that she did not inherit her father's intellect."

"I had not heard it established that her father was an intellectual," said Holmes. "Am I to understand that you met him?"

"I visited their camp a few times, to introduce myself, and to see what type of people your brother was allowing to stay in our area."

"You were making rather free with Sherrinford Holmes's borders, weren't you, Mr. Morland?" asked Tenley. "After all, they were camped on his land. Wouldn't your visits be something of a trespass?"

"I, um, I didn't see it as a problem," said Morland. "We are all quite friendly here in the country. I meant no harm, I assure you. In any event, the important fact is that I was able to meet both Wilkies and his daughter, and it allowed me to form my opinions of Sophia, with which I'm sure you must agree. I would think that her limited intellectual powers would actually tend to support the veracity of her claim that your brother, Mr. Holmes, had serious words with Wilkies. Someone like Sophia, someone who is rather simple like that, would not be distracted by uncertainties. If she heard your brother arguing with Wilkies, and saying the things that he said to Wilkies, it would be definite."

"As you might imagine," replied Holmes, "my efforts are directed toward discovering a somewhat different interpretation of events."

"And Inspector Tenley here?" asked Morland. "Is he with you because he agrees that there is a different interpretation, or is it simply professional courtesy that causes him to accompany you? Do you believe, Inspector, that you have gotten the correct man in your cells?"

"I believe that based on the evidence initially presented, Constable Worth was correct in placing Mr. Sherrinford Holmes in custody," replied Tenley. "However, Mr. Sherlock Holmes here has a lot of clout, especially with my superiors, and it does not do any harm for me to accompany him during his further explorations of the case."

Morland nodded, then looked over us toward the entrance to the room. I turned to see Siger standing there, his knapsack held in front of him, looking much emptier than when we had arrived. I had not heard him come in. He nodded at his uncle, and then at Morland.

"Sorry, sir," he said, "I was just admiring your house a little bit."

Morland waved his hand. "Ah, boys must be boys. The temptation to explore is great, no doubt." He stood, as if indicating the interview was at an end. "But temptation must always be tempered with good manners, as well. Remember that, my boy."

Ringing for the servant, Morland said, "I'm sorry that I cannot help you in your quest to save your brother, Mr. Holmes. Even to me, it seems that the case against your brother is too strong to tear apart.

As a famed criminologist, you must confess that the evidence is only open to one interpretation."

"I have found," said Holmes, "that interpretations can change with just a slight shift of perspective. An illusion, painstakingly created, can be revealed to be nothing more than canvas and wires if one simply walks a little to one side or the other and sees exactly how the construct is propped up. Good day to you, sir."

We followed the old man to the door. Outside, we climbed into the four-wheeler, where Holmes asked Siger, "Was your mission successful?"

"In all aspects, sir," he replied. "Even better than expected, if I may say so."

"Excellent."

"Did you get some of Morland's stationery?" asked Tenley, unaware that part of Siger's tasks included returning the bloody items to the empty outbuilding.

"Not only that," said Siger, glancing to make sure that we were far enough from Morland's house, "I found this on his desk."

He opened the knapsack, pulling out several sheets of new stationery and a soiled plain piece of cheap paper, containing a short written message. The stationery was the same as the torn and coded square that Holmes had found in Sophia's tent. The plain piece of paper, matching Sophia's supply list taken from the tent, had another similar coded message on it:

*Jura pna V frr lbh? F*

"'*When can I see you? S.*'" said Holmes, almost instantly.

Siger nodded. "'*S* for Sophia. She even capitalized the *V* for the word *I*. To make the code less clear, they should probably only use lower-case letters, and run the words together. However, that might be a little too complicated for Sophia to manage."

"Where was this?" asked Holmes, holding up the coded sheet.

"On Morland's desk, upstairs. It was lying in a pile of other papers, bills and receipts. He had made no effort to hide it, but it wasn't lying out in an obvious way, either. I think he had simply tossed it there, and I don't think he will miss it."

"Were you seen?" asked Tenley.

"Not at all," said Siger. "Not anywhere that I went," he added, for Holmes and my benefit, I was sure, in order to let us know that he had not been observed while replacing the items in the empty outbuilding.

"The place is nearly deserted. After looking around the outbuildings, I came in through the garden. No one was around, so I went up the back stairs and searched until I located Mr. Morland's office. Finding the stationery was simple, and the message from Sophia was easily seen. After that, I came back downstairs."

Holmes held up the papers. "This is really excellent, Siger. This makes my little plan even easier to accomplish than I had originally imagined it to be."

"And what plan would that be, Mr. Holmes?" Tenley asked.

"If you would have Griffin take us back to the family home, I will give my nephew a little lesson in forgery. In the meantime, let me explain what I have in mind."

And he did. It would be something of a gamble, but it also seemed the simplest shortcut to bring this whole business to a close. I sighed, imagining yet another night, like so many before, squatting outdoors in the darkness waiting for a criminal to fall into one of Holmes's traps. At least, I thought, this time there will be no Hell Hound to deal with.

Back at the Holmes farm, Tenley asked what time he should return.

"Around ten, I expect," replied Holmes. "That will be after dark, but will still give us a couple of hours to get into position."

"I'll have my men watching earlier than that," said Tenley. "The outbuildings, you say?"

"Yes," replied Holmes. "To see if Morland visits any of them."

Tenley turned to Siger with a wry smile. "Any particular outbuilding, Siger?" he asked.

Siger looked startled. Tenley reached out and tapped the limp knapsack hanging from Siger's hand. "I won't ask what was in here," he said. "I'm not sure that I want to know at this point, and I trust Mr. Holmes. If I was really a Scotland Yard Inspector I might worry a little more about what is going on, but I'm not.

"Whatever was in this bag is not there now, and it disappeared sometime while you were searching around Morland's property. Now, you may have hidden it in the house, but since Mr. Holmes wants me to have the outbuildings watched, I'm betting it's hidden in one of them. So I ask again, just so we won't take a chance on missing it, is there any particular outbuilding that we should watch?"

Siger looked at his uncle, who appeared both pleased and amused.

Holmes nodded, and Siger replied, "The empty stable, to the west of the house." He looked down at the knapsack, and back to

Tenley. "Your men should be especially aware if they see Morland go there, and then leave the building carrying something. Perhaps a white bundle, for example."

"Very good," said Tenley, with a smile.

"Tenley," said Holmes.

"Yes, sir?"

"Do not let my brother waste your talents," said Holmes.

"Oh, he doesn't, sir. I can assure you of that. He never has." He touched the brim of his hat and turned to go.

After Tenley and Griffin departed, Holmes, Siger, and I looked at one another with expressions of amusement and relief. Then Holmes and I moved to return to the house. Siger stopped us with a question.

"What exactly was that . . . that mummified and pickled hand that was wrapped in the murdered man's robes?" he asked.

Holmes glanced at me, as if to ask how much to tell the boy. My look must have indicated to be perfectly frank, because Holmes answered with complete candor. "It is called a 'Hand of Glory.' It is an item used in the practice of black magic."

"I suspected as much," said Siger. "I knew that something like that must be used for an evil purpose. But why is such a thing in the heart of Yorkshire? What can these people believe such a thing is for?"

"No doubt it is used in dark rituals, probably the 'true path' that seems to interest Sophia so much. I suspect that it was used in the murder, giving it some sort of ceremonial flavor. Somehow, Wilkies was convinced to wear his robe and was taken to some obscure place we may not find. There, he was murdered by both Sophia and Morland, although I do not yet know if anyone else was involved, although I doubt it. Then he was placed in the pit.

"After Wilkies died and his clothing was changed to hide the ritual nature of the murder, the body was propped up in the pit, and a ceremonial slash was made across his throat, resulting in very little blood on the man's regular collar, as he was already dead at the time, and had bled out through the great wound in his back."

Siger was silent for a moment, before asking, "Where does such an item as the dead hand come from? I don't imagine one could buy something like that at just any shop in London."

Holmes replied, "These items are usually made from the dried and preserved hand of a man who has been executed, most often for murder. Usually the left, or *sinister*, hand is taken, although sometimes, if the hand is removed from a murderer, the . . . believers will try to obtain the hand that actually committed the murder.

"Occasionally the hand will be used to hold a candle, with the belief being that only the user can see the light. More extreme practitioners of the dark arts may try to make the candle from actual fat rendered from the dead man who supplied the hand. It is also believed that the possessor of such a talisman can unlock any door.

"Watson and I stumbled across a group of practitioners making use of a Hand of Glory back in the early eighties."

"What happened?" asked Siger, with wide eyes.

"They were convinced to stop using it," said Holmes, with characteristic understatement. He managed to give no indication of the danger we had both faced, and the terror and pain that we had managed to bring to an end by the violent destruction of the Black Coven. I would never forget the escape we both made though the burning house, which stood over the entrance to the coven's underground catacombs, and how we had nearly lost our lives, as well as that of the small child that I had carried up from the smoke-filled tunnels.

"That Hand of Glory is now in a museum in Walsall," Holmes added, turning toward the door. With a pat on Siger's shoulder, I followed Holmes into the house.

Inside, Holmes announced to Roberta that we would have need of the dining room for a little while. She acquiesced with a silent smile, and Holmes sent Siger off to search the house for whatever types of inks and pens he could find.

When Siger returned, he laid all the items on the table before Holmes, who had taken off his coat and rolled up his sleeves. Siger observed but did not comment on the various scars and acid marks dotting his uncle's forearms. Holmes laid out the coded messages, samples of handwriting, and blank stationery. Then, he searched among the pens and ink until he found those that most suited his purpose.

"Forgery," he said, "is an art, not a science. I can, and probably will at some point, teach you the specifics of ink types, paper qualities and manufacture, pen nibs, and so on. However, at the end of the day, the only real way to produce a forged document is to have practiced interminably beforehand, so that one knows exactly what task one's hand will be expected to perform. But also, you will need to have some sort of inborn skill, and that can never be taught, simply refined and improved. I have no doubts that you can learn the intellectual basics of the forger's business, Siger. It remains to be seen whether you have the artistic ability.

"However," he added, "we are descended from Vernet, both you and I, and that must count for something."

"Art in the blood," I muttered. Holmes thought for a moment, and then, with a sure hand, began to write a coded message on some of Morland's blank stationery. He did not write it out beforehand in order to check that he had used the correct substituted letters. Rather, he produced the final message with surety and confidence. As the letters appeared on the paper, I glanced at Morland's original message to Sophia. The writing between the two was indistinguishable.

"'Must see you, midnight tonight, Great Rock at edge of valley forest. Urgent. M.' " Siger read, translating over his uncle's shoulder. "Do you think she will know where that is?" he asked.

"Probably," said Holmes. "It is one of the landmarks of the area, and not too far from either the campsite or Morland's house. If she does not know, she has time to find out." He blotted the paper carefully, and then said to Siger, "Can you find me a sheet of cheap paper, such as Sophia uses, so that I can construct a similar message for Mr. Morland?"

"Certainly," said Siger, dashing from the room with the enthusiasm that only a sixteen year old can produce.

I smiled at Holmes. "You are going to teach him to be a forger?" I asked. Holmes raised an eyebrow, and I said, "His mother will never forgive you."

Siger returned with several sheets of cheap paper, nearly identical to that used by Sophia. Holmes took one, thought for a moment, and then composed a similar message to Morland, signed S. After blotting it, he reached for the forged message to Morland and began to tear off the monogram at the top. Then, he stopped for a moment and handed one of the duplicate cheap sheets to Siger. "See what you can do," he said.

Siger's face took on a frown of concentration, but he showed no hesitation. He picked up the pen previously used by Holmes, pulled over the correct ink bottle, and thought for a moment, observing both the sheets with Sophia's original handwriting, and Holmes's more recent forgery. His hand moved over the blank sheet, but he did not write, not yet, as his fingers made practice swoops and lines, over and over.

Finally, he dipped his pen into the ink, lowered his hand to the paper, and wrote the coded message with confidence.

After he was done, he pushed it back, and then remembered to blot it. Then he handed it to his uncle.

Holmes examined it critically for a moment before stating, "Not bad. Not bad at all. You have captured her vowels correctly, and the narrowness of her capitals, and the down-slope of her line. However, there is too much confidence in the k's and h's, and the loops of your t's are too narrow." He dropped in onto the table. "Try again."

Siger took another blank sheet of paper, and this time, with only a moment of thought, again wrote quickly and without seeming hesitation. Blotting the message, he handed it to Holmes, who studied it intently before looking up at his anxiously watching nephew.

"Very good," he declared. "We shall send yours to Mr. Morland."

Siger nodded, and did not show much expression, but I could not miss the excitement and pride which flared just for a moment like twin lanterns deep within his gray eyes. His enthusiasm was interrupted, however, when Holmes said to him, "Go get into your oldest clothes."

"Why?" Siger asked.

"Because," said Holmes, "after a suitable amount of disguise, you are going to deliver these messages to Mr. Morland and Sophia."

As Siger bounded out of the room, I shook my head, considering what Roberta's reaction would be if she discovered what Holmes had in mind for her youngest son. I decided that I would not be the one to tell her. Siger returned within moments, wearing a set of very old and tattered clothes, somewhat too small for him, with the bottom hem of his pants legs showing several inches of shin above old boots, with noticeable holes worn in the sides. Holmes stood and led Siger outside, where he proceeded to brush the lad's face and hair with dirt from the yard.

Arranging Siger's hair down over his eyes, he instructed him in the proper way to carry himself with a different posture, taking several inches off his height, and how to maintain a subservient attitude that would cause him to be ignored by most of the people that he would encounter.

"It is important," said Holmes, "for Morland to think that you have come from Wilkies's camp, while Sophia must think that you are one of Morland's stable boys. Both have met you, so it will be a challenge to make them see you as someone else. Perhaps, although I am loathe to suggest it, you might smear a little horse manure on your boots or your cuffs. That way they will be anxious for you to depart, and will pay even less attention to you."

Without hesitation, Siger stepped out, away from the house, to a mound of horse manure, in which he proceeded to muck about for a moment or two. With a grin, he returned to us, noting our involuntary expressions of distaste.

"Exactly," said Holmes. "Now let us see you walk."

Siger settled into a slouch and began to make his way back and forth across the yard. The transformation was incredible. He appeared to be nothing like the young man who had sat across from us at the dining table just a few minutes earlier. Instead, he looked like any one of the anonymous stable lads one sees and ignores everyday throughout the length of the countryside. Clearly, this boy had inherited more than just his family's deductive abilities and resemblance to his uncle. He had inborn acting talent, as well.

"Excellent," said Holmes. "Remember to seem somewhat more . . . penitent when you visit Mr. Morland. After all, you are supposed to be religious. And appear more horsey when you are at Sophia's camp. Report to us when you get back."

With that, Holmes turned and went back in. Siger, amazed that he was being trusted to do something so important with no further warnings or instructions, stood for just a moment before turning toward Morland's house.

Siger had only been gone for a few moments when a man on horseback rode up to the house. "I work with Inspector Tenley," he said. "Another cable has arrived for you, sir." Handing them to Holmes, he touched his fingers to his brow, wheeled the horse, and without a further word, turned back toward the village.

Opening the flimsy sheet, Holmes read it and then passed it to me. It simply contained more about Augustus Morland's true German background, and the name of his actual identity. "I can't see that this adds anything to helping us solve our immediate problem," I said.

"All information is useful," said Holmes.

As we walked toward the house, I said, "Didn't you once tell me that the brain is like a lumber room with limited space, and one must be careful what one takes in, so that it remains organized and does not become littered with unnecessary items, in order that something new does not crowd out something older and more useful?"

He waved his hand languidly. "I was younger then. Times and beliefs change. One must adapt or die."

Inside, Holmes seemed indisposed to talk, indicating that he wished to be alone for a while, to smoke and order his thoughts. I settled myself in a chair in the sitting room, intending to rest and think about the case. I had no sooner arranged myself, however, than I stood again, walking across the room to examine several photographs that I had not previously noticed, perched on a cabinet near the window.

They were obviously old, done in the antique style used during the middle of the century. I observed one stiffly posed formal shot of a gruff man of early middle age, with a wild black beard, and the petite blonde woman beside him. Presumably these were Holmes's parents. Beside it was a small oval-shaped frame, containing a photograph of three boys.

Certainly this was of Holmes and his two older brothers. Holmes was no doubt the small fellow, only around one year of age, dressed in some sort of gown. Beside him was an already pudgy boy with extremely intelligent eyes, around eight years of age. Mycroft, I was sure. And at the right of the picture was Sherrinford, slightly older and taller, but already looking like the man he would grow to become.

There were a few other photographs of more recent origin scattered along the cabinet, all of Sherrinford, Roberta, and their three sons. I was interested to see Bancroft, the nephew that I had not yet met, and had never heard of until yesterday. He was posed in an academic gown, looking extremely intelligent, but rather haughty and proud, and already somewhat heavyset. I could see a strong resemblance to his uncle Mycroft, for whom he worked in London. "So this is the young man," I thought, "who wants to make his future without relying on the Holmes name. Bancroft Pons, indeed."

I returned to my chair, wondering when I might find something for lunch, and intending to think about the day's events and what was planned for that night. It was not long, however, before I fell asleep, that heavy afternoon sleep when the dream world and the waking world appear to merge. When the front door slammed several hours later, announcing Siger's return, I had a difficult time separating its actuality from dreamlike fantasy as I struggled to awaken.

As I rose from my chair, I heard Holmes meet Siger in the entrance hall. "How did it go?" he asked.

"Without any problems whatsoever," said Siger, with barely suppressed excitement. "They took the notes without even glancing at me, and when I mumbled about a reply, they both dismissed me. Morland either decoded his message immediately, or decided to wait until later, because he dropped the hand holding the message almost as soon as he looked at it. Sophia was hunched over when I left, puzzling through it."

"And there seemed to be no suspicion about the paper or the writing? Or about the method of delivery?"

"None at all," replied Siger. "This must have been similar to how they communicated in the past." Siger began to remove his dusty jacket.

"What do we do now?"

"We wait," said Holmes. "And hope that they simply plan to meet each other at the Great Rock tonight, without sending each other additional clarifying messages, leading to the unfortunate unraveling of our scheme."

"There is one thing that you can do, Siger," I added. Siger turned to me with an inquiring glance.

"You can take off those manure-covered boots outside before your mother sees you tracking them further into the house."

Part VII: At the Great Rock

At a little before ten o'clock, Tenley and Griffin arrived, pulling up to the front of the house in Griffin's four-wheeler. I realized that I had never seen the man when he wasn't sitting on the driver's bench, his hands loosely holding the reins. We stepped outside and met Tenley, who had hopped down from his seat.

With us was Siger, who had informed his mother in no uncertain terms that he was coming too. We were all armed, and I could see the protests forming on Roberta's lips. However, she had held her tongue, although right before we stepped outside, she had made Siger and William promise to be careful, all the while looking at Holmes as if to make him understand that he was responsible for her sons' safety.

"Are your men in place?" Holmes asked.

Tenley nodded. "I sent some people that I trust, all with no love for Morland. They were in place soon after dark. They reported that he never went near that outbuilding. They did see him ride away for a time this afternoon, but they had no orders to follow him, so we do not know where he went." Tenley coughed, looked at the ground, and then looked back up at Holmes. "I took it upon myself to sneak into the empty stable after dark. You'll never guess what I found, Mr. Holmes. Why, it was the murdered man's robes, with the murder weapon, and something far more sinister."

"Really," said Holmes. "Well, it is fortunate indeed that it was discovered by a representative of the law, so that it can be properly taken into evidence."

"No curiosity about what else I found wrapped in the robes, Mr. Holmes?" Tenley asked with a smile.

Holmes gestured with his hand. "Time is wasting, Tenley. Perhaps we should start making our way to the Great Rock," he said, "so that we can be well concealed before our visitors arrive." We began to stroll away from the light spilling into the yard from the house windows, and into the darkened fields.

"Finding that dead hand," said Tenley, abandoning the pretense that we didn't know what he had found wrapped in the bloody robe, "puts this whole matter into a different light. It's not just a murder now, but rather some sort of diabolical execution."

"I'm sure that was how Sophia perceived it," said Holmes. "She sincerely believes that her father's form of religion was too tame, and needs to be replaced with something more evil. As for Mr. Morland, I'm not so sure. I believe that he simply used Sophia, convincing her to murder her father as a means of implicating Sherrinford so that his land grab could continue. If he hadn't found Sophia to manipulate, he would have arranged for something else to remove Sherrinford from the board."

Tenley nodded. "When he met her in Germany, back before his move to England and when he took on the Morland identity, he must have learned from her then that she disagreed with her father's teachings. At that time, he might have just spoken with her, or possibly even encouraged her, with no idea that she would be useful in the future."

"Exactly," said Holmes. "Later, when Morland was here, he decided that he needed to get rid of Sherrinford, who was an important holdout in his land purchases. Murdering him outright would cause too many problems, so he decided to have Sherrinford framed for murder instead. Having stayed in touch with Sophia, he realized that he could use her. He sent her a message and no doubt suggested that she arrange for Wilkies's group to camp here. There are certainly no old ruins or ancient sites here that would have attracted them otherwise.

"After they arrived, Morland no doubt began convincing Sophia that her father would need to be killed as a sacrifice to the 'true path,' and that Sherrinford would be the perfect man to take the blame. Sophia is obviously easily influenced, and Morland is certainly a master of manipulation. Morland has probably told Sophia that he believes the same things that she does. Possibly, he has even romanced the poor deluded girl, and she believes that he will marry her. Who knows?"

By this point, we were well away from the house, and our eyes had adjusted to the bright starlight. The fields flowed gently over rolling hillsides, and in the distance I could just make out a darkness crawling along the bottom of a low spot. This must be the valley forest, in which we planned to hide. Standing some feet out from it, shining bright in the reflected light, was a tall thin stone, fifteen to twenty feet in height. This, I was certain, was the Great Rock.

"In any event," continued Holmes, "Wilkies was ritually murdered. The weak link, of course, is Sophia, although her dogmatic stubbornness may actually keep her quiet about what was done. However, I have no doubt that at some point in the future, Morland plans to have Sophia eliminated, so that the only person who can tell the truth about what they did will be gone."

As we approached the stone, I glanced at William and Siger. William, who had been briefed by his brother earlier in the afternoon, walked forward and looked straight ahead, seemingly intent on his task. His brother, Siger, was much more alert, and his eyes darted between his forward path and Holmes. The boy listened intently to everything his uncle said, almost physically leaning toward Holmes as he walked.

"This is it," said Holmes, stopping before the tall stone. "The Great Rock. Perhaps it is not one of the old places that Wilkies traveled about to visit, but it is the closest thing that we have to it around here. Possibly Sophia will feel some sort of energy here that will make her feel like talking." Holmes glanced about. "We already have enough information on Morland to have him arrested as a spy. Now we need to get him and Sophia talking in order to have them discuss what was done to Wilkies, and so clear Sherrinford."

"Aren't you taking something of a chance with Sophia's life," I asked Holmes. "As you said, at some point Morland would probably need to eliminate her, as she is the weak link in his plan."

"I am, Watson, but I have to make that gamble. I must confess, I do not like the idea that Morland rode away this afternoon and no one knows where he went."

A figure stepped out of the nearby trees. "Everyone is hidden, sir," said Constable Worth to Tenley. "As you ordered."

"Very good," said Tenley. "I suggest that we get ourselves under cover as well." He pulled out his watch. "Ten-thirty," he said. "We must be well hidden before they arrive, especially if anyone makes an early appearance to see if the place is safely deserted."

We entered the darkness of the trees, and each settled to wait in his own way. Holmes and I sat with our backs to a large tree trunk, patient as the old hunters that we were, while Siger crouched easily several feet away. William spread his coat and sat upon it cross-legged, and Tenley moved off to confer with his men.

The time passed more swiftly than it sometimes did when Holmes and I had waited in the past. The night temperature was not uncomfortable, and it was too early in the season for insects to be a problem. I could see where this low-lying growth of forest might be somewhat damp at other times of the year. A few night birds called, from one part of the forest and then another. A breeze rustled the leaves overhead, but did not make enough noise to impede our attempts to hear anyone that might be approaching.

Siger occasionally shifted from side to side, but never lost the hawk-like focus that had settled on his face from the very beginning of our vigil. William, on the other hand, appeared introspective, always looking alert, but generally watching his hands, folded on the rifle lying across his knees.

As midnight approached, we all became more alert, expecting the momentary arrival of our targets. I knew that Holmes hoped that Morland and Sophia would say something incriminating to one another, especially when they realized that each had not written and sent the coded messages to the other. Hopefully, in their momentary confusion, they would make admissions that could be used against them, in order to open them up during interrogation.

I looked at my watch as midnight came, and checked it many times again over the next quarter hour, when there was no sign of any approaching visitors. Beside me, I could sense Holmes's frustration and disappointment that his stratagem had apparently failed. Finally, he signaled Tenley to draw closer, and in a whispered conference, they conceded that Morland and Sophia probably weren't coming. Siger, William, and Constable Worth joined us. After listening for a few minutes to Holmes and Tenley discuss possible options, Worth interrupted. "I think that you've been mistaken about Mr. Morland all along."

Holmes turned to him with raised eyebrows. "I concede that you have known him longer than we have," Holmes said. "What makes you think that he is not involved in this crime?"

"What would he have to gain?" asked Worth. "An important man like that, with big plans for this whole area, would not involve himself in the murder of some itinerant preacher."

"What big plans are you talking about?" asked Holmes.

"Why, the man means to bring prosperity to this corner of England," said Worth. He added, somewhat proudly, "He has discussed it with me on several occasions. It is only a matter of time until he owns all the land, creating a vast estate that he can develop into an industrial area to rival the Midlands."

"And does he have a place for you in all this?"

"Well, of course he has mentioned something of it," replied Worth. "He recognizes real talent when he sees it, and he knows the value of using a local man to police a local area."

Something in Worth's tone must have alerted Holmes. With a sharp change in his voice, Holmes asked, "How many pieces of silver did it take for you to betray us to Morland? When did you tell him that tonight was a trap?"

Worth seemed to be puzzled for a moment, as if he did not understand the question. Then he took a step back, shaking his head. "No, Mr. Holmes, you've got it all wrong. I didn't take any money."

"So you just told him as a favor between a friend to a friend?"

"No, it wasn't like that. We're not friends. He's too important to be friends with a man like me. But he respects me, and he's got important plans for this whole area. He visited me this afternoon, and he asked me how the investigation was going. I know the Inspector told me not to discuss it with Mr. Morland, so I just let him know that you and the Inspector were on the wrong track. He asked me if you were involved in a message to lure him out to the Great Rock tonight. I told him I didn't know anything about a message, but there was something being planned tonight, and that he need not inconvenience himself by coming out here at midnight."

Holmes looked at Tenley. "Inspector?"

Tenley looked into the darkness. "Holder! Jacobs! Come here!"

Two burly men appeared beside us. I hadn't heard them coming, and never saw them until they were standing there. Tenley gestured toward Worth. "Take him into custody." As the men grabbed Worth, he gave one sob and momentarily sagged toward the ground, before scrabbling his feet and trying to stand again. Tenley turned toward Holmes. "Holder and Jacobs are men that I can trust." He pulled Holmes and me aside. Siger and William followed.

"What do we do now, Mr. Holmes?" Tenley asked. "Morland is bound to be onto us."

Holmes turned back to Worth. "Constable!" he said sharply. "When you told Mr. Morland about tonight's trap, did he ask any other questions about the message used to lure him here?"

Worth ignored him, and Holmes stepped closer, raising his voice and asking the question again. One of the big men holding Worth shook him, and he finally seemed to comprehend what was being asked. "No, no he didn't. But he . . . He just said something about how the girl must have sold him out."

Holmes turned back to us. "We must get to Morland's house as quickly as possible. Tenley, how many men do you have here tonight?"

"Ten," said Tenley. "Holder and Jacobs, and eight more still out there in the dark."

"Can you trust them all?"

"Yes. I recruited them myself. They have nothing to do with Worth."

"Good. William," he said, turning to his oldest nephew. "Take four men and go to Wilkies's camp. Take Sophia into custody. Keep her there, but allow no one in to speak to her, either members of the camp, or anyone from the outside. Wait until we arrive."

William nodded, and Tenley called for the additional men still hiding in the trees to come forth. Picking four of them, William turned without a word and headed for the campsite.

Holmes said, "Holder and Jacobs. Constable Worth is under arrest. Please accompany him to the village, where he should be locked into a cell. Do not let him speak to anyone along the way. And," he added, "tell my brother that he will soon be free."

"Right, sir," said the taller of the two big men.

"Wait," said Tenley. He stepped to Worth and fished in the man's pockets, coming up with the keys to the cells. "Use these to lock up Worth, and to release Mr. Sherrinford Holmes." The big men nodded, and with little effort on their part, they began to walk the little constable between them across the fields, back toward the village.

"Right, then," said Holmes. "The rest of us, on to Morland's."

We set out at a quick pace, the eight of us, and made good time across the fields until we reached the road, where we began to increase our speed even more. There was no conversation between us, each concentrating on keeping up with Holmes, who had set a fast pace with himself out in front. Siger's long legs matched his uncle's strides. The countryside was fairly well lit by stars, in that way that is possible only in the country, where the light from the cities does not occlude the sky's visibility. Eventually, however, I began to notice a glow bleeding from behind a distant hillside. This would be Morland's house, well-lit, although it was now quite past midnight.

Reaching the house, Tenley dispersed his four men to various sides of the building, setting them in place to watch all the exits. Then we remaining four approached the front door, whereupon Holmes tried the knob, only to reveal that the door had been unlocked all along. Glancing at Tenley, who nodded to go ahead, Holmes opened the door, and we silently advanced inside.

We quickly moved from room to room, finding the ground floor abandoned. Meeting at the base of the stairs, Holmes whispered, "Siger, where is Morland's office?"

"Just upstairs, to the right," the young man replied.

"Lead on, then."

We climbed the stairs, and it did not go unnoticed by me that as we ascended, Tenley placed himself in front, taking the lead from Siger. I do not think that Siger realized what Tenley had done, so intent was he on glancing from left to right and back again, his sharp eyes missing nothing.

At the top of the stairs, Siger gestured toward a nearby doorway, lit from within and spilling light into the dark hallway. Holmes nodded and stepped to the door. I reached him as he said, "Going somewhere, Mr. Morland?"

Inside, a single desk lamp burned, revealing the thin man packing papers into a dispatch case. He looked up, more with irritation than surprise or guilt. "As a matter of fact, I have been called back to Manchester. I must leave immediately. Family business, you know."

"I don't think so," said Holmes. "You see, Sophia Wilkies has told us everything."

Siger glanced at his uncle, but showed no surprise in his face, and nothing to give away his uncle's lie. "Everything?" Morland asked. "Everything about what?"

"About the murder of her father. About how you planned it, and helped her to do it. About how you both lured him to some obscure spot in his robes, telling him it was some sort of ceremony relating to his own beliefs, and then ritually executed him. About how you changed him back to his regular clothing, propped him up in the pit, and then cut his throat."

"'Ritually executed him'?" repeated Morland. "Are you quite mad? I have no doubt that the girl is insane, but anything she has said that involves me is untrue. I shall have her prosecuted for slander. And you as well, I believe."

"She didn't tell us everything, of course," continued Holmes. "Not quite everything. Yet. For example, we do not know yet whether the Hand of Glory belonged to her, or if it was originally yours."

Hearing about the evil talisman used during the murder seemed to shake Morland. He did not realize that we had found it, and as far as he knew, it was still wrapped in his empty stable.

"Hand of Glory?" he said. "Don't know what you mean." He reached back toward the desk for more papers. Holmes and Siger both raised their guns higher. Seeing that, I raised mine also. "You need to step back from the desk," said Holmes. "Now," in a stronger, more commanding tone.

With a smile, Morland raised his hands and took a step backward.

"Watson?" asked Holmes. I stepped forward, taking care to stay out of my friends' line of fire, and pulled open the desk drawer for which Morland had been reaching. Inside, lying on a stack of papers, was a small, but deadly and efficient, pistol. It was obviously freshly cleaned, as gun oil had soaked and spread through the papers on which it rested.

Picking it up, I placed it in my pocket and stepped back.

"Did you wonder about the coded message from Sophia?" asked Holmes. "Would she have written it and helped to lure you into a trap if she hadn't already revealed everything to us?" he bluffed.

"Message?" asked Morland. "Do you mean that scrap of gibberish that was brought to me this afternoon by that filthy gypsy boy? Are you saying that it was a coded message from Sophia, luring me into a trap? This is quite ridiculous, Mr. Holmes. Surely if I could have understood that message, I would have gone to this meeting, thus confirming your suspicions. But since I didn't go to see her, obviously it was because I could not understand the code, which therefore confirms my innocence."

"You didn't go because Constable Worth warned you," said Holmes, noting the narrowing of Morland's eyes. "We have Worth's testimony as well. You really are caught, you know," he added. "We have even retrieved the dead man's robes and what was contained within them from where you hid them in your stalls." Morland said nothing for a moment. He did not even allow any expression to pass across his face. Finally, he said, with just a possibility of tentativeness in his voice, "Robes? In my stalls? I don't know what you're talking about. If you found anything in my out-buildings, it must have been placed there by someone else. Possibly this mad Sophia put it there, or one of her people. Maybe that filthy boy that delivered the message did it."

"This is the 'filthy boy,' " said Tenley, nodding his head toward Siger. "He brought the message to you. You're not as smart as you think. You didn't even take a good look at who he was."

"You are the one who is not very smart, Inspector," said Morland. "You have burst into my house, held me at gunpoint, and detained me from my lawful activities, based on the ridiculous story of some crazy girl who apparently murdered her father, and has since tried to mask her own guilt by spreading it around onto her betters! I'm soon to be a peer of the realm. I cannot be treated this way!"

"Peer of the realm?" said Holmes. "It won't do, *Mr.* Morland. It really won't. Or perhaps I should address you as *Baron Ennesfred Kroll!*" Morland stepped back, and seemed to sag for just a moment before pulling himself back up. His eyes widened, and he moved his mouth as if to speak, but nothing came forth.

"We really do know it all, Baron Kroll," said Holmes. "We know about your true identity, and how you assumed that of the real Morland more than twenty years ago, following his death in Germany. We know how you took over the family fortune, estates, and title following the death of Morland's father, and how you ran the Morland business from Germany.

"We know about how you met Sophia when she was in Germany, and learned of her fascination with the Satanic religions, something her father never would have tolerated. We know how you finally returned to this country, and began buying lands to create a vast unobserved area on the northeast coast of England, which could be used at some point in the future as a sort of secret German colony, for troops and supplies to be assembled and organized under cover, should an invasion ever occur.

"Finally, we know how my brother was a hold-out to your plan, refusing to sell his large and centrally located estate. It wasn't supposed to happen that way, was it, Baron Kroll? All of the land owners were supposed to be easily swayed by your offers and your seeming infinite financial resources, backed by the very German treasury itself. We know how you manipulated Sophia into convincing her father to come to this area, and finally how you helped her to murder him, using the iron dagger, with its oddly Germanic markings, and the hideous dead man's Hand of Glory.

"As you can see, Baron Kroll, we know it all. And we have known it for quite a while. There is an old saying about giving a man enough rope to hang himself. Do you have such a saying in Germany? Well, you were being given rope, and far earlier than was expected, you hung yourself by becoming involved in a murder."

The sound of footsteps came up the stairs and then down the short hallway. William stepped into the room, breathing hard. I knew that he was supposed to stay with Sophia, and wondered what could have happened to make him come here instead.

"Well?" asked Holmes.

"She was dead," replied William. "In her tent. Throat cut. None of those people heard or saw anything. Or so they say."

Holmes cursed and met my eyes. We both knew where Morland had gone this afternoon when no one followed him. I was aware that Holmes would hold himself responsible for allowing the girl's death to occur. Morland, or Baron Kroll, as I would have to think of him now, smiled and said, "I believe that without a witness, any attempt to link me to this murder will be doomed to failure." He stepped forward. "Now, as I said, Inspector, I must be leaving on family business. I do not know what this foolishness is about me being a German citizen, but I can assure you that if you do not stand aside, I will make sure that you yourself are brought up on charges. Do I make myself clear?"

Tenley smiled. "You don't seriously think I'm going to let you walk out of here, do you, Baron Kroll? Because I – "

Before he could finish, Kroll had pivoted and dropped, reaching for a lower drawer on his desk. Pulling it open, he rose in one fluid movement, holding another pistol, and swinging it up. From my position, I could not tell where he intended to aim it, and I could not see whether his finger was tightening as he prepared to fire. In any case, I considered the man to be as dangerous as a mad dog, and I had no hesitation whatsoever.

I fired twice. The first bullet passed through Kroll's upraised wrist, causing the gun to spin and sag on his forefinger before dropping to the floor. The sound of it hitting the wood was unheard as it was drowned out by my second shot, the bullet flying true into Baron Kroll's knee. As he turned to me in shock, and started to sag to the ground, I stepped forward, kicking him to one side as I knocked his fallen gun to the other.

"Well done, Dr. Watson!" cried Siger. "Oh, well done!"

I cleared my throat. "Holmes usually prefers to avoid this type of conclusion to his cases," I said. "However, I suspect that if I had allowed this madman to shoot either of her children, or even her brother-in-law, Roberta Holmes would have shot me as well, and I did not travel all the way to Yorkshire in order to make such fine new friends, only to have to turn around and bury some of them."

## Part VIII: A Family Reunited

When we arrived at the village cells, Holmes paused for a moment in front, staring up at the tall structure. "You say this oversized building was financed and built by Sir Clive Owenby?" he asked.

Tenley regarded him with a smile. "Yes," he replied. "Sir Clive lives in York."

"I believe that you stated that he is a crony of my brother Mycroft's," said Holmes.

"They are somewhat acquainted," confirmed Tenley. "Is it important?"

"I theorize," said Holmes, "that the idea behind this building's construction lies along the same lines of thinking as Baron Kroll's attempts to create a pocket German fiefdom here in Yorkshire. This building is intended to remain here, looking simply like the location of an oversize village constabulary, until such time as it might be needed. Sir Clive, at my brother's urging, has financed this inconspicuous fortress. No doubt there are some interesting secrets inside, possibly an unknown cellar, or cellars. And perhaps some of the Queen's weapons stored in them as well, in case the citizens might someday need to be armed at short notice against German invaders?"

Tenley looked to make sure that Kroll was a considerable distance away. "I won't confirm anything specific, Mr. Holmes, but I will say that whatever secrets that building does contain, they are well hidden and there is no way Constable Worth of any of his ilk ever suspected anything, and certainly no way that the Germans could know about it."

Upstairs, we found Sherrinford talking with Holder and Jacobs, while Constable Worth sat on the cot in his locked cell, his head resting in his hands. Outside in the hall, Baron Kroll was surrounded by all of Tenley's remaining men and Dr. Dalton, who had been summoned to treat Kroll's wounds. Kroll was nearly completely hidden within the cluster of angry Yorkshiremen and one grim doctor. Sherrinford stepped forward, embracing his two sons, and then grabbing Holmes in a bear hug, before releasing him and shaking his hand. Then he turned toward me. I stepped forward, my hand outstretched, but he bypassed it, hugging me as well. After releasing me, he turned back to Tenley. "Worth hasn't said a word since he got here," he said. "Holder and Jacobs let me know what he did. What has happened since they brought him here?"

We related to Sherrinford the confrontation at the Morland house, and William's subsequent revelation that Sophia had been murdered. Worth moaned to himself. Upon hearing of the girl's violent death, Sherrinford leaned to one side, looking into the hall as if to get a glimpse of Kroll. He was unable to see him, however, due to the fact that the German was blocked by the big country men surrounding him.

"I think that we shall have to release Worth on his own recognizance," said Holmes, to our surprise.

"Why, Mr. Holmes?" asked Tenley. "If we leave them together, we might overhear some incriminating conversation."

"True," replied Holmes. "However, Baron Kroll is going to be a very different kind of prisoner, and we would do well to keep him entirely separated from Worth. The murders of Wilkies and his daughter are simply a small part of the bigger picture. This man is a German agent. Mycroft may or may not decide that it is more effective for Kroll to disappear into a prison somewhere, leaving the Germans in disarray and confusion regarding their land-grab plan and the disappearance of their man. Or it may be decided to try Kroll as Augustus Morland for the murders, but limit information from the trial that is released to the public. In any case, we need to keep Kroll separate from everyone that we can from this moment on.

"I'm sure," he added, glancing at Worth, "that this man can be released without any risk of flight. After all, only a few of us here know about his involvement. He is a ruined and broken man, and I'm certain that he knows what's good for him. He will not be the type to talk about these events, which put him in such a bad light. I'm certain that we can count on his discretion."

Worth, who had apparently been listening despite his attitude of despair, jumped up. "Oh, I promise, sirs!" he cried. "I won't say anything. I have learned my lesson."

"Of course," Holmes went on, conversationally, "you have resigned your position as constable, effective immediately, and you will be observed closely for a long time to come." Worth stared at him, seeing that his freedom was not going to come without some cost, after all. He swallowed once or twice, and then said, in a much quieter and emotionless voice, "Yes, sir. Of course. I understand."

Worth's cell was soon unlocked, and he was led by one of his big guards — I never did know which was Holder and which was Jacobs — out past the group of men in the hall, making sure that he was allowed no contact whatsoever with Kroll. After he had gone, Kroll was placed in a center cell. Holmes remained behind for a moment, staring wordlessly at the prisoner, who returned his gaze with venomous hate.

Then Holmes joined us in the hall, leaving the German under guard by several of our night's companions. Downstairs, Tenley emphasized to the remaining men the need to keep the entire affair secret, no matter what version of events that they might hear in the next few days. The men, all good British citizens, agreed and departed.

"I will cable London and your brother with the details," said Tenley. "You get Mr. Sherrinford Holmes here back to his family."

He shook hands with all of us, and went back inside. I looked around, and saw, sitting off to the side of the building, Griffin. He was on the driver's seat, as usual, with no indication that he wanted to be anywhere else, in spite of the fact that it was after three in the morning. Stepping over to him, I asked whether he could take us back to the Holmes farm. Without a word, he nodded. In a moment, the five of us were on board and the short trip began.

Roberta was still up when we arrived. Her joy at seeing the safe return of her husband and two sons was palpable. She would not rest until she heard the whole story. We had to repeatedly decline her offer to make a full meal right then instead of waiting for breakfast. Finally, as the sky began to lighten with the coming dawn, we made our way to bed in order to catch a few hours of sleep. All of us, that is, except Holmes and Siger.

If Siger was like his uncle, he did not need much sleep in any case, so I doubt if staying up the rest of the night seriously tired either of them. To this day, I do not know what they talked about, although I am fairly certain that the discussion probably included an examination of the minute details of the recent events. I also believe that they discussed Siger's chosen future.

I do know that later that year, Siger entered Oxford at the young age of sixteen. His intellect was a deciding factor, but possibly the influence of his uncles helped as well. A few years later, in 1899, Siger graduated and immediately approached his uncle, asking Holmes to allow Siger to become something of an apprentice, learning the varied skills needed by a consulting detective. At that time, I was still living in Baker Street, and I had been prohibited by Holmes from publishing any more of his cases. Holmes knew that I still kept extensive notes on his investigations, however, and he instructed me that I was never to mention Siger in any of them, most likely because he wanted to spare Siger from gaining a reputation based upon appearances in a popular publication.

In October 1903, Holmes was faced with an unexpected crisis in the form of the sudden death of Irene Adler. I have never mentioned in any published accounts the regard Holmes had always felt for Irene, who had been widowed by Godfrey Norton in late 1890. The following year she had given birth to Godfrey's daughter, and had resumed her career on the operatic stage. Holmes had become reacquainted with her soon after his supposed disappearance at the Reichenbach Falls. In 1892, she gave birth to a son, Scott. After Holmes's return to England in 1894, we had infrequent contact with her. Her fortunes went into decline, and in the late 1890's she married a wealthy man who subsequently died.

Several more meetings between Irene, Holmes, and myself took place over the next few years. Eventually Irene moved with her family to Montenegro, a location that seemed to hold some sentimental attachment for her. In 1901, she married her third husband, a man named Vukcic, which loosely translates to "little wolf." Vukcic had a son of his own. Irene remained in Montenegro until her untimely death.

I had initially believed Irene Adler was something of an adventuress, based upon the original description of her by the King of Bohemia, but as I came to know her in later years, I realized that she was a lady of high morals who had been much maligned by the king. As this document which I am preparing will be placed with my other records at the Cox and Company Bank for at least seventy-five years after my death, I feel that I can elaborate on what happened after Irene's death, and how those events relate to Siger, without bringing any negative reflection on the lady.

I will never forget that October 1903, when I received Holmes's request to visit his rooms in Baker Street. I had remarried by then, and was living several streets away in Queen Anne Street, where I had resumed my private medical practice. I found Holmes smoking in his chair before his fire. Littering the floor of the sitting room were several packing boxes. "Going somewhere?" I asked Holmes.

"I have decided to retire."

Before I could process this odd and unexpected statement, for Holmes was only forty-nine years old at the time, Holmes handed me the telegram, containing the details of Irene's death in a railway accident. The implications washed over me. Some were obvious, and some I was not supposed to know but had figured out for myself.

"What about her son and daughter?" I asked.

"They are all right," said Holmes. "Her daughter wishes to remain in Montenegro. Her son . . . . He will be here in a few days."

He paused for a second, and said, "Watson, there is something that I must tell you about the boy." He shifted in his seat, looking uncomfortable, one of the few times I have ever seen him so. The time he had apologized to me after making me believe that he had been poisoned by Culverton Smith. The time that he had returned from a three-year absence, leaving me to believe that he was dead, while only his brother Mycroft had known the truth. A few others as well. I saw no reason to extend his discomfort.

"I already know, Holmes." He didn't look up. "I know that he is your son."

We were silent for a moment, and he did not ask how that I knew. We never discussed it again, and to this day I do not know the details. Nor do I want to. After a moment, he began to speak. He told me how he had been spending more and more time of late working on matters for his brother Mycroft, especially relating to Britain's relations with the rest of the world, and specifically Germany. For a year or more, Mycroft had been pressuring him to become something of a full-time agent for the shadowy secret department that Mycroft controlled, as the certainty of war with Germany loomed ever closer. The arrival of the boy would allow Holmes to do as Mycroft wished, in a limited way.

He intended to announce his retirement immediately, and depart to live near Beachy Head in Sussex, in a small coastal cottage that he had acquired several years earlier, during the course of an investigation. He intended to maintain the Baker Street rooms, however, as a retreat while in London. Mrs. Hudson had agreed to move to Sussex with him, to help care for the boy. And he was going to keep bees.

In order to complete the illusion of Holmes's retirement, I would begin to publish accounts of his cases once again in *The Strand* magazine, which had been approached by the government and was more than willing to help, considering the financial windfall they would be reaping. My old friend and literary agent, Conan Doyle, had already been briefed and was willing to help. The first published case would be *The Empty House,* relating Holmes's return to life in 1894. And I must specifically include a statement that Holmes had retired, and that it was only due to that reason that I was allowed to resume publication of the stories.

And so, within a day or so, Holmes had ensconced himself in Sussex. Soon after that, Scott Adler Holmes arrived at his father's new home.

I was there when the precocious eleven-year-old greeted his father.

They had met several times over the years, but I never knew if Scott realized before his mother's death and the subsequent reading of her will that Holmes was his father. Mrs. Hudson bustled around and made the boy feel at home, and I did my best to welcome him as well. However, I do not think that anyone comforted him more during that time than did his cousin, Siger Holmes.

At that time, Siger had trained with Holmes for several years, one of several apprentices that Holmes had taken on during the early years of the century. Siger's activities had transitioned gradually from those of a consulting detective to that of an agent, working for his uncle Mycroft and brother Bancroft, now himself quite a rising figure within the British government. Siger had been on hand during Holmes's move to Sussex.

At that time, he was twenty-three years of age, tall and lean, and looked almost exactly like his uncle Sherlock. He still retained much of his boyish enthusiasm, however, and I believe that was what bonded him to Scott Holmes.

The young boy adapted well. He met Mycroft and Bancroft a few days after his arrival, and I went with them all to Yorkshire in November, where Scott was welcomed by the rest of his new family. It warmed my heart to see how Roberta mothered the boy, immediately surrounding him with the unconditional love with which she had filled her home and had raised three fine sons. In later years, while Holmes was off continuing his investigations, Scott would spend a great deal of time in Yorkshire, and Roberta would become like a second mother to him, as she had been to his father as well.

That November was the last time that the Holmes family, with myself included as a sort of adopted uncle and brother, would all be together in one place. In later years, with the War approaching, the family would be scattered, and there was never a chance to assemble the entire group again.

As Scott grew, his friendship with Siger grew as well. Siger nicknamed the boy "Caesar" due to Scott's assured bearing and attitude.

By this point, Scott was showing the same deductive skills as evidenced by the rest of his family. In 1907, Siger opened his own practice as a consulting detective, finding increasing success over the course of several years. However, he was dismayed that many people came to him expecting the services of his uncle Sherlock, based upon the name Holmes. He began to see why his brother Bancroft had taken a different last name.

In 1911, Scott inadvertently became involved in a series of events that resulted in the defeat of a group that would have prevented the crowning of King George V. By that time, the nineteen-year-old young man had eschewed college, preferring to educate himself, learning more that way than he probably could have by attending any university. As a result of Scott's service to the Crown, he was officially recruited into Mycroft Holmes's organization, where he and Siger became a team that was unparalleled for its masterful successes in discovering information to aid the British government as the threat of war rolled ever closer.

Working together, the two young men criss-crossed Europe. Siger often used the name "Mr. Bridges," an Anglicization of his brother's assumed last name, *Pons*. Scott would usually go by his nickname, Caesar, or other names of Roman leaders, combined with variants of the word *wolf* as a surname. Their exploits and antics during this time became something of a legend, and although they frequently vexed Mycroft Holmes and Bancroft Pons to no end, no one could argue with their results.

This continued, of course, until the Great War began. I was staying with Holmes in Sussex in late August of that year, 1914, when Siger came to see his uncle. Both realized that their conversation might be the last quiet visit they would have for some time. Holmes had recently returned from a two-and-a-half-year absence, traveling the United States and Great Britain as "Altamont," the renegade Irishman and German agent. His masterful impersonation had ended only a few weeks before, with the arrest of the sinister von Bork.

Siger stated that after the War, he wished to resume his private practice, but he would like to make his own name, and not rest on his uncle's reputation, as had been the earlier problem. He seemed to be asking for some sort of permission from Holmes to step away from the family name. Holmes suggested that Siger use an alias, based on Siger's previous preference for "Mr. Bridges" and also his brother Bancroft's changed surname at the Foreign Office. They experimented with several variations before Holmes suggested something appealing, recalling a comment made by Holmes at the end of the Yorkshire investigation in June 1896. Siger decided that he would adopt the name suggested to him by Sherlock Holmes: *Solar Pons*.

Of course, that was years in the future. Little did Holmes and Siger know, during that early morning conversation in Yorkshire while the rest of the family slept, what was ahead of all of us on our long road. The successes and tragedies were all hidden from us then, as well as the fact that Baron Ennesfred Kroll would escape from British custody in October of that same year, only to resume his true identity and vex Siger in later years, much as Professor Moriarty had plagued Holmes.

I arose late that morning, and was dismayed and embarrassed to see my watch indicating that the morning was nearly gone. I dressed hurriedly and went downstairs, where Roberta did her best to make me feel as if my long slumber was the most natural thing in the world. She and Sherrinford, along with William, had been up since daybreak, taking care of the daily work, while Holmes and Siger had gone back to the village to check on the prisoner.

Later that morning, I was just finishing my belated breakfast when a commotion arose out in the yard. Roberta leaned in and said, "You'd better come out, Dr. Watson."

Stepping into the sunshine, I saw several men descending from Griffin's sturdy four-wheeler. As my eyes adjusted to the light, I saw Holmes and Siger, followed by the heavier and more awkward figures of Mycroft Holmes and a similar looking younger fellow who could only be Bancroft.

Sherrinford and Roberta greeted their prodigal son, while William and Siger grinned. Mycroft nodded in my direction, and when Bancroft was free, he stepped over and introduced himself.

"Bancroft Pons, doctor. A pleasure to meet you."

"The pleasure is all mine," I said, shaking his hand.

"Bancroft *Holmes*," said his mother. "You are home now. That other silly name can remain in London."

"As you like," replied Bancroft.

We went inside, where Roberta bustled about, serving refreshments. I was not very hungry, having just eaten, but I did manage to put away at least one serving of a delicious yellow cake. As I was eating, discussions moved quickly around the table, as everyone was caught up on the events of the last few days. Mycroft and Bancroft explained that they had arranged a special train to leave London as soon as they had received Tenley's wire, explaining the details of Baron Kroll's arrest.

"I understand you were quite helpful, brother," said Bancroft to Siger.

"He was truly a bridge of sunlight throughout the whole affair," said Holmes, causing his youngest nephew to puff up in a most comical way with pride.

Bancroft snorted. "A bridge of sunlight, indeed! If only you could approach your studies with the same solar intensity that you have shown relating to your desire to become a detective."

"By the way, Watson," Holmes said, changing the subject, "Baron Kroll tried to kill himself last night."

I raised my eyebrows. "Really? How?"

"His guards thought he was asleep, and he tried to fashion a noose from a bed sheet. He was caught, however, and his attempt was prevented."

"Just as well, I suppose," said Mycroft. "We will have to let him go, eventually, but not before we get all the use out of him that we can."

Baron Kroll ended up staying in the village lock-up for several months, during which time he was closely interrogated by Tenley and other individuals sent up from London. He was not moved to a larger prison in order to preserve the security of his arrest. Before he could be officially sent back to Germany, he escaped.

Mycroft shifted his big frame in the small chair. "Baron Kroll does seem to have conceived an intense dislike for the Holmes name."

"And the Pons name, as well," added Bancroft. "After we identified ourselves, I could see him committing it to memory with the same hatred that he was showing towards you, uncle."

"Pons, Pons," cried Roberta. "I wish you'd never decided to use that name."

"Actually, the boy comes by it honestly," said Sherrinford, speaking for the first time. He had been looking with quiet fondness from one member of his family to another since we had come inside.

"How do you mean?" asked Siger.

"He is not the first to use that alias," replied Sherrinford. "I myself used it, a few years back."

Roberta and Mycroft both looked at him suddenly, their glances filled with similar warnings. Sherrinford continued as if he did not notice.

"William probably remembers some of this, and I know Bancroft is aware of the details, but you have never heard this story, Siger. Back in 1880, just before you were born, I did a little favor for your uncle Mycroft."

Siger sat up straight, eyes alert. I glanced at Holmes, and could tell that he had never heard this tale, either. "Without getting into many specifics," Sherrinford continued, "I was asked to travel to Prague, where I carried out a mission for Her Majesty's government, delivering a message to the Bohemian royal family. In order to hide my activities, I traveled with my family. William was only nine, and Bancroft was about seven. And your mother was very much burdened with you at that point Siger, since this was right before the time of your birth."

"A mad time to make me travel," muttered Roberta. "Although I will admit that Prague was a lovely city . . . ."

"In any case," said Sherrinford, "I carried out my mission, although I must say that sort of intrigue is not to my liking. I am happy to leave it to those who enjoy it. While we were there in Prague, Siger, you were born."

"I did not know that," said Siger softly.

"Neither did I," said Holmes. "As I recall, I visited Yorkshire a month or so after Siger's birth, and you were all here at home as if you had never left, and no one mentioned a thing to me at all about a trip to Prague."

"I'm sure you understand the nature of security, Sherlock," interrupted Mycroft, "As do you, Sherrinford. I think that this discussion should be concluded."

"Strange," continued Holmes, ignoring Mycroft, "when I met the King of Bohemia, he never mentioned having previously met my brother."

"He didn't know me as your brother, you see," replied Sherrinford. "Hence my previous use of the name *Pons*. When I traveled there, I went under the identity of Asenath Pons, a visiting consular official. Years later, when Bancroft went to work for Mycroft, he must have read the file and taken the name Pons as well, for his own reasons."

"And I always thought you came up with it on your own," said Siger to his brother, who did not comment.

"As did I, said Holmes. "I understand the derivation of the name Pons from your name, Sherrinford, but I wonder if mad old cousin Asenath would appreciate that you appropriated *his* name for your role?

"He will never hear about it," grinned Sherrinford. "Security, you know."

Mycroft interrupted at that point, urging that all discussion of the matter be dropped. Siger and Bancroft joined in as well, with Holmes and Sherrinford offering their opinions, and in a moment, even William was participating. I watched them, two generations of Holmes brothers, the air in the room nearly popping with the electricity being generated by their combined personalities and intellects. I became aware of Roberta, sitting beside me and watching them as well, her lovely face beaming with pride.

"They are something wonderful, are they not, doctor?" she said, very softly.

"Indeed," I replied. "And you have made a wonderful home for them here."

"Thank you," she said. Then turning slightly toward me, she said, "You must consider this your home, and yourself a part of this family, as well."

Her earnest gaze stopped any polite refusal that might have initially risen to my lips. I glanced back at the group of men, all arguing and teasing each other in a good-natured way. I realized that I would be very happy, indeed, to be included in such a group.

"Thank you," I said to her. "It pleases me very much to be a part of your family."

She patted my arm and turned back to look at the men surrounding the table. I realized that I was hungrier than I thought, and reached to cut another piece of cake.

# Appendices

# Basil Rathbone's Solar Pons Films

Author's Note: *The following is a version of an essay that I wrote which was originally published in* The Baker Street Journal *(Vol.63, No.4, Winter 2013). More recently it was reprinted in my occasional online blog* A Seventeen Step Program:

*http://17stepprogram.blogspot.com/*

*Over the past few years, whenever I've seen discussion about the "modern" (at that time) settings of the Basil Rathbone films produced by Universal Studios in the 1940's, I've referenced this essay, and then sent PDF's of it to those who showed an interest. Here is my chance to present it in connection with this new set of Pons stories.*

As two Sherlock Holmes (in name only) television shows have competed in recent years on either side of the Atlantic to determine which one presents the more successful modern version of our heroes, many traditional Sherlockians watch with enthusiastic interest, hoping for nods toward the original stories. Other viewers, however, grind their teeth at the painfully shocking way in which an updated Holmes and Watson are being treated. These current television shows are not the first occasions in which our heroes have been moved from their correct time period and shown instead in present-day settings. The most famous examples are the final twelve Basil Rathbone films, produced by Universal Studios in the 1940's. However, it's time to reveal that three of these Rathbone films aren't even Holmes tales at all. They are about someone else.

When I read the original Holmes stories, as well as any traditional pastiche that I can get my hands on, I play *The Game*, thinking about how the events in the narrative relate to both The Canon and historical events. Several years ago, while re-watching the newly-restored Rathbone films on DVD, I found myself – as I often do with many pastiches – being forced to rationalize away various incorrect or anachronistic elements as something that had been grafted onto Watson's original notes by an editor or film maker with his or her own agenda. In the last nine Universal films, the modernizing aspects are fairly benign and can generally be ignored. The actual events of these stories could just as easily have taken place in the years before, during, or following the First World War, instead of during World War II. Occasional updated comments and modern devices were dropped into the films by script writers in order to make the films seem as if they're actually taking place in the 1940's.

But the first three Universal films, *Sherlock Holmes and the Voice of Terror* (1942), *Sherlock Holmes and the Secret Weapon* (1943), and *Sherlock Holmes in Washington* (1943), all have such modernized specifics incorporated into the narratives - airplanes, radio signals, complex equipment for dropping bombs - that there is no way that these could be any of Holmes's World War I investigations, reworked and updated with just a few added modern details inserted here and there for 1940's audiences. Clearly, these cases actually did take place in World War II, and were being investigated by a different sleuth entirely.

Consider another heroic detective, so much like Holmes that he must have apprenticed to him, and who would have been involved in the events of World War II, fighting Nazis, listening to radio broadcasts, traveling to Washington and searching for secret microfilms. Who else could it be but *Solar Pons*, with the assistance of his friend and Boswell, *Dr. Lyndon Parker*?

As a long-time devotee of Solar Pons, I've realized that the first three Rathbone Universal films are not Holmes adventures at all. Rather, they are Solar Pons narratives, with *Pons* and *Parker's* names changed to *Holmes* and *Watson* for easier familiarity to the 1940's movie-going public.

In the early 1940's, with U.S. film studios' efforts turning toward war-related topics, film producers decided - in their ignorance - to make movies showing Holmes fighting Nazis. After all, who better to pick than England's most shining knight? The studios' research quickly revealed that Watson had been dead for over ten years, and Holmes was in his late eighties. However, there was a successor to Holmes, named Solar Pons, who had a close family relationship to Holmes and who had no doubt rejoined British Intelligence in the summer of 1939, soon after the conclusion of the chronologically-last Pons story, "The Adventure of the Golden Bracelet", occurring just before Britain was pulled into World War II. After all, Pons was just fifty-nine years old at that time, and he would have certainly helped in the British war effort.

Therefore, the first three Rathbone films from Universal, *The Voice of Terror*, *The Secret Weapon*, and *Sherlock Holmes in Washington*, were actually Solar Pons cases, relating Pons's efforts against the Nazis. In fact, these are the only films ever made that show Solar Pons in action, albeit under Holmes's name. The public probably wouldn't have been as enthused by *Solar Pons and the Voice of Terror* or *Solar Pons in Washington*. Nigel Bruce didn't accurately portray Dr. Parker any better than he did Dr. Watson, but there was something comforting about his avuncular presence that served a valuable purpose for war-time audiences.

After realizing how three of Pons's wartime adventures had obviously been taken and updated by film makers, I realized that several of Pons's other post-World War II cases had also been altered in the same way by later editors of Dr. Parker's notes, and pulled into more modern times. For example, the book *Sherlock Holmes in Dallas* (1980) edited by Edmund Aubrey, has "Holmes and Watson" traveling to the United States in order to investigate the Kennedy Assassination. It's an interesting idea, but obviously Holmes and Watson weren't around to do that. However, *Pons and Parker* certainly would have been. Later, when the narrative was published, the editor decided to change Pons and Parker's names to Holmes and Watson so that modern readers, who might not buy *Solar Pons in Dallas*, would recognize the more familiar names. Several other pastiches and collections, such as *Sherlock Holmes in Modern Times* (1980), edited by Ira Bernard Dworkin, also benefit from this same kind of updating and provide additional Pons stories when they don't work either logically or chronologically as Holmes stories.

Having concluded that some of these "modernized" Holmes cases are actually those of Solar Pons, I'm still at a loss to know just who is actually being portrayed in either the BBC's *Sherlock* or CBS Television's *Elementary*. It certainly isn't Holmes, Watson, Pons, or Parker. However, I am glad to finally be able to completely enjoy the first three "modernized" Rathbone Universal films, knowing that they're actually about Pons. It's time that Solar Pons had some more recogn

# NOTE

* As related in "The Adventure of the Other Brother", in this volume and in *The Papers of Sherlock Holmes – Volume II* (2011, 2013)

# Chronologist's Notes

For those Chronologists who are interested in such things, these are the dates (some approximate) when the narratives contained in this volume took place.

I am very much a Chronologicist, having spent over twenty years compiling a huge *Whole Art of Detection* of the lives of Sherlock Holmes and Dr. Watson. It has spiraled out to include other related figures in their world, such as Solar Pons, Nero Wolfe, Ellery Queen, and Hercule Poirot.

Now at over six-hundred dense pages, my Chronology includes events from The Sherlockian Canon, those pitifully few original sixty stories, as well as any everything that I can find in other stories from other Literary Agents that relates the *true* and *correct* versions of cases involving Our Heroes.

My Holmes Chronology covers the literal thousands of traditional Holmes adventures in my collection, consisting of novels and short stories, radio and television episodes, movies and scripts, comics and fan fiction, and unpublished manuscripts. It takes these cases and breaks them down by book, chapter, page, paragraph, panel, or scene, and fits them with other adventures that have been arranged the same way into one large volume chronicling the *entire* lives of Holmes and Watson, presented by year, month, day, and even hour.

It's a very satisfying way to study Holmes and Watson, and gives a unique understanding to The Great Holmes Tapestry.

As Pons and Parker begin to be relevant within the later years of the Holmes Chronology, their adventures are chronologicized as well. Related to that, I've also constructed an extensive and complete Pons Chronology, separate and more in depth, to arrange the facts in Pons and Parker's lives.

The stories in this volume, *The Papers of Solar Pons*, fit into that chronology upon these dates:

**1921**
Mid-July:            "The Affair of the Distasteful Society"

**1923**
Mid-May: "The Park Lane Solution" *(Just after "The Amateur Philologist")*
August: "The Additional Heirs"
September 20: "The Adventure of the Obrisset Snuffbox"

**1927**
Mid-April: "The Adventure of the Blood Doctor" *(With portions in late July 1907 and early September 1919)*
Early June: "The Plight of the American Driver" *(Just after "The Sussex Archers")*

**1929**
Late March: "The Folio Matter"

**1930**
Early March: "The Horror of St. Anne's Row"
Early May: "The Adventure of the Doctor's Box"
Mid-October: "The Singular Affair of the Blue Girl"

**1933**
Late Dec: "The Poe Problem" *(Part I)*

**1934**
January 20: "The Poe Problem" *(Part II)*

**1938**
Early April: The Adventure of the Failed Fellowship

# The Solar Pons Stories

### *By August Derleth*

"In Re: Sherlock Holmes" (The Adventures of Solar Pons) (1945)
- *A Word From Dr. Lyndon Parker*
- The Adventure of the Frightened Baronet
- The Adventure of the Late Mr. Faversham
- The Adventure of the Black Narcissus
- The Adventure of the Norcross Riddle
- The Adventure of the Retired Novelist
- The Adventure of the Three Red Dwarfs
- The Adventure of the Sotheby Salesman
- The Adventure of the Purloined Periapt
- The Adventure of the Limping Man
- The Adventure of the Seven Passengers
- The Adventure of the Lost Holiday
- The Adventure of the Man With a Broken Face

The Memoirs of Solar Pons (1951)
- The Adventure of the Circular Room
- The Adventure of the Perfect Husband
- The Adventure of the Broken Chessman
- The Adventure of the Dog in the Manger
- The Adventure of the Proper Comma
- The Adventure of Ricoletti of the Club Foot
- The Adventure of the Six Silver Spiders
- The Adventure of the Lost Locomotive
- The Adventure of the Tottenham Werewolf
- The Adventure of the Five Royal Coachmen
- The Adventure of the Paralytic Mendicant

The Return of Solar Pons (1958)
- The Adventure of the Lost Dutchman
- The Adventure of the Devil's Footprints
- The Adventure of the Dorrington Inheritance
- The Adventure of the "Triple Kent"
- The Adventure of the Rydberg Numbers
- The Adventure of the Grice-Paterson Curse
- The Adventure of the Stone of Scone
- The Adventure of the Remarkable Worm
- The Adventure of the Penny Magenta

- The Adventure of the Trained Cormorant
- The Adventure of the Camberwell Beauty
- The Adventure of the Little Hangman
- The Adventure of the Swedenborg Signatures

**The Reminiscences of Solar Pons** (1961)
- The Adventure of the Mazarine Blue
- The Adventure of the Hats of M. Dulac
- The Adventure of the Mosaic Cylinders
- The Adventure of the Praed Street Irregulars
- The Adventure of the Cloverdale Kennels
- The Adventure of the Black Cardinal
- The Adventure of the Troubled Magistrate
- The Adventure of the Blind Clairaudient

**The Casebook of Solar Pons** (1965)
- The Adventure of the Sussex Archers
- The Adventure of the Haunted Library
- The Adventure of the Fatal Glance
- The Adventure of the Intarsia Box
- The Adventure of the Spurious Tamerlaine
- The Adventure of the China Cottage
- The Adventure of the Ascot Scandal
- The Adventure of the Crouching Dog
- The Adventure of the Missing Huntsman
- The Adventure of the Amateur Philologist
- The Adventure of the Whispering Knights
- The Adventure of the Innkeeper's Clerk

**A Praed Street Dossier** (1968 – *Associational Volume*)
- From the Notebooks of Dr. Lyndon Parker
- The Adventure of the Bookseller's Clerk
- The Adventure of the Snitch in Time (*with Mack Reynolds*)
- The Adventure of the Ball of Nostradamus (*with Mack Reynolds*)

**Mr. Fairlie's Final Journey** (1968 – *Novel*)

**The Chronicles of Solar Pons** (1973)
- The Adventure of the Red Leech
- The Adventure of the Orient Express
- The Adventure of the Golden Bracelet
- The Adventure of the Shaplow Millions

- The Adventure of the Benin Bronze
- The Adventure of the Missing Tenants
- The Adventure of the Aluminum Crutch
- The Adventure of the Seven Sisters
- The Adventure of the Bishop's Companion
- The Adventure of the Unique Dickensians

**The Final Adventures of Solar Pons** (1998)
- Terror Over London (*Novel*)
- The Adventures of Gresham Old Place
- The Adventure of the Burlstone Horror
- The Adventure of the Viennese Musician
- The Adventure of the Muttering Man
- The Adventure of the Nosferatu (*with Mack Reynolds*)
- The Adventure of the Extra-Terrestrial (*with Mack Reynolds*)
- More from Dr. Parker's Notebooks

**The Unpublished Solar Pons** (1994)
- The Adventure of the Viennese Musician
- The Adventure of the Muttering Man
- The Adventure of the Sinister House (*An early version of "The Burlstone Horror"*)
- The Adventure of the Green Stars (*Fragment*)

**The Dragnet Solar Pons** *et al.* (2011 - *Original pulp magazine and manuscript versions*)
- The Adventure of the Black Narcissus
- The Adventure of the Missing Tenants
- The Adventure of the Broken Chessman
- The Adventure of the Late Mr. Faversham
- The Adventure of the Limping Man
- Two Black Buttons
- The Adventure of the Red Dwarfs
- The Adventure of Gresham Marshes (*An early version of* "Gresham Old Place")
- The Adventure of the Black Cardinal
- The Adventure of the Norcross Riddle
- The Adventure of the Yarpool Horror (*An early version of* "The Burlstone Horror")
- The Adventure of the Muttering Man

**The Solar Pons Omnibus** (1982)

The Original Text Solar Pons Omnibus Edition (2000)

## *By Basil Copper*

### The Dossier of Solar Pons (1979)
- The Adventure of the Perplexed Photographer
- The Adventure of the Sealed Spire
- The Adventure of the Six Gold Doubloons
- The Adventure of the Ipi Idol
- The Adventure of Buffington Old Grange
- The Adventure of the Hammer of Hate.

### The Further Adventures of Solar Pons (1979)
- The Adventure of the Shaft of Death
- The Adventure of the Defeated Doctor
- The Adventure of the Surrey Sadist
- The Adventure of the Missing Student

### The Secret Files of Solar Pons (1979)
- The Adventure of the Crawling Horror
- The Adventure of the Anguished Actor
- The Adventure of the Ignored Idols
- The Adventure of the Horrified Heiress
- 

### The Uncollected Cases of Solar Pons (1979)
- The Adventure of the Haunted Rectory
- The Adventure of the Singular Sandwich
- Murder at the Zoo
- The Adventure of the Frightened Governess

### The Exploits of Solar Pons (1993)
- The Adventure of the Callous Colonel
- The Adventure of the Phantom Face
- The Adventure of the Verger's Thumb
- Death at the Metropole

### The Recollections of Solar Pons (1995)
- The Adventure of the Cursed Curator
- The Adventure of the Hound of Hell
- The Adventure of the Mad Millionaire
- The Adventure of the Singular Sandwich (*Revised Version*)

### Solar Pons versus The Devil's Claw (2004 – *Novel*)

Solar Pons: The Final Cases (2005)
- The Adventures of The Haunted Rectory (*Revised Version*)
- The Ignored Idols (*Revised Version*)
- The Adventure of the Horrified Heiress (*Revised Version*)
- The Adventure of the Baffled Baron (*Revised Version*)
- The Adventure of the Anguished Actor (*Revised Version*)
- The Adventure of the Persecuted Painter (*A Sherlock Holmes story*)

The Complete Solar Pons (2017 – The Complete Basil Copper Stories)

## *By David Marcum*

The Papers of Sherlock Holmes (2017)
- *A Word from Dr. Lyndon Parker*
- The Adventure of the Doctor's Box
- The Park Lane Solution
- The Poe Problem
- The Singular Affair of the Blue Girl
- The Plight of the American Driver
- The Adventure of the Blood Doctor
- The Additional Heirs
- The Horror of St. Anne's Row
- The Adventure of the Failed Fellowship
- The Adventure of the Obrisset Snuffbox
- The Folio Matter
- The Affair of the Distasteful Society
- The Adventure of the Other Brother (*A Sherlock Holmes/Solar Pons story*)

## *Solar Pons will return . . . .*

# About the Author

**David Marcum, PSI** plays The Game with deadly seriousness. He first discovered Sherlock Holmes in 1975, at the age of ten, while trading with a friend to obtain Hardy Boys books, he received an abridged version of *The Adventures of Sherlock Holmes*, thrown in as a last-minute and little-welcomed addition. Soon after, he saw the Holmes film *A Study in Terror* (1965) on television, found and read that copy of *The Adventures*, and began to search out other Holmes stories, both Canon and pastiche.

    He borrowed far ahead on his allowance and bought a copy of the Doubleday edition of *The Complete Sherlock Holmes* and started to discover the rest of The Canon that night. His parents gave him Baring-Gould's *Sherlock Holmes of Baker Street* for Christmas and his fate was sealed.

    Since that time, David has collected literally thousands of traditional Holmes pastiches in the form of novels, short stories, radio and television episodes, movies and scripts, comics, fan-fiction, and unpublished manuscripts. After reading so many Holmes adventures, he decided to contribute to The Great Holmes Tapestry, and is the author of *The Papers of Sherlock Holmes Vol.'s I* and *II* (2011, 2013), *Sherlock Holmes and A Quantity of Debt* (2013, 2016) and

*Sherlock Holmes – Tangled Skeins* (2015, 2017), and *The Papers of Solar Pons* (2017).

Additionally, he is the editor of the three-volume set *Sherlock Holmes in Montague Street* (2014, recasting Arthur Morrison's Martin Hewitt stories as early Holmes adventures,), the two-volume collection of Great Hiatus stories, *Holmes Away From Home* (2016), *Sherlock Holmes: Before Baker Street* (2017), *Imagination Theatre's Sherlock Holmes* (2017 – Forthcoming), and most recently the ongoing collection, *The MX Book of New Sherlock Holmes Stories* (2015-   ), now at eight volumes, with two more in preparation as of this writing.

He has contributed stories, essays, and scripts to *The Baker Street Journal*, *The Watsonian*, *Beyond Watson*, *Sherlock Holmes Mystery Magazine*, *About Sixty*, *About Being a Sherlockian* (Forthcoming), *The Solar Pons Gazette*, Imagination Theater, *The Proceedings of the Pondicherry Lodge*, and *The Gazette*, the journal of the Nero Wolfe *Wolfe Pack*.

He began his adult work life as a Federal Investigator for an obscure U.S. Government agency, before the organization was eliminated. He returned to school for a second degree, and is now a licensed Civil Engineer, living in Tennessee with his wife and son. He is a member of *The Sherlock Holmes Society of London*, *The Occupants of the Full House* and *The Diogenes Club of Washington, D.C.* (both Scions of *The Baker Street Irregulars*), *The John H. Watson Society* ("Marker"), *The Praed Street Irregulars* ("The Obrisset Snuff Box"), *The Solar Pons Society of London*, and *The Diogenes Club West (East Tennessee Annex)*, a curious and unofficial Scion of one.

Since the age of nineteen, he has worn a deerstalker as his regular-and-only hat from autumn to spring. In 2013, he and his deerstalker were finally able make his first trip-of-a-lifetime Holmes (and Pons) Pilgrimage to England, with return pilgrimages in 2015 and 2016, where you may have spotted him. If you ever run into him and his deerstalker out and about, feel free to say hello!

# David Marcum can be reached at:
*thepapersofsherlockholmes@gmail.com*

Author photo by Dan Marcum

*The Author at No. 7 Praed Street, London –
which looks quite a bit different than
when it was tenanted by
Solar Pons and Dr. Parker*

# ALSO BY DAVID MARCUM

*As author....*

The Papers of Sherlock Holmes (*Vol's I and II*)
Sherlock Holmes and A Quantity of Debt
Sherlock Holmes – Tangled Skeins
The Papers of Solar Pons

*As editor....*

Sherlock Holmes in Montague Street
The MX Book of New Sherlock Holmes Stories
(*Vol's I-VIII... and counting!*)
Holmes Away From Home (*Vol's I and II*)
Sherlock Holmes: Before Baker Street

## *A note about the typeface . . . .*

This volume is appropriately set in *Baskerville Old Face*, a variation of the original serif typeface created by John Baskerville (1706-1775) of Birmingham, England.

It is still unestablished how he was related to Sir Hugh Baskerville of Dartmoor, who died under such grim circumstances a more than half-a-century before John Baskerville was born.

Belanger Books

Printed in Great Britain
by Amazon